READER'S DIGEST
CONDENSED BOOKS

www.readersdigest.co.uk

The Reader's Digest Association
Limited 11 Westferry Circus
Canary Wharf London E14 4HE

For information as to ownership of
copyright in the material of this
book, and acknowledgments, see
last page.

Printed in France
ISBN 0 276 42824 5

READER'S DIGEST
CONDENSED BOOKS

Selected and edited
by Reader's Digest

CONDENSED BOOKS DIVISION

THE READER'S DIGEST ASSOCIATION LIMITED, LONDON

CONTENTS

Paul Janson has put his career as a covert operative behind him, but he is forced out of retirement when Peter Novak, the billionaire diplomat who once saved his life, is kidnapped by terrorists. Janson assembles a crack rescue team, but when the operation goes horribly wrong he finds himself a marked man. His only hope is to uncover the truth about what has happened, a truth that threatens the very course of world history.

PUBLISHED BY ORION

When Sheriff Townsend comes across a man standing in the middle of the road with a knife in each hand and a dead body at his feet, it seems he has an open and shut case. But the mysterious suspect refuses to answer questions and there is no forensic evidence to link him to the murder. So the sheriff calls in his old friend, private eye Alex Rourke, to help him solve the crime. A powerful and atmospheric mystery about a ruthless killer with a chilling agenda.

PUBLISHED BY MICHAEL JOSEPH

THE HOUSE SITTER

Peter Lovesey

It's a busy week for Detective Hen Mallin of the Sussex police force. A criminal psychologist has been found strangled on Hen's patch and, for all her efforts, she's getting nowhere with the case. Reluctantly she calls in Peter Diamond of Bath CID, a man who gets results but can be unorthodox and difficult. The partnership might just work, so long as Diamond realises exactly who is boss. A lively, thoroughly British crime story.

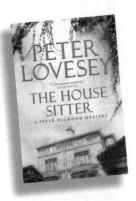

PUBLISHED BY LITTLE BROWN

I'M NOT SCARED

Niccolò Ammaniti

One hot summer's day, nine-year-old Michele and his friends are innocently playing in the scorched countryside around their remote Italian village when they come across an abandoned farmhouse. While exploring, Michele stumbles on a shocking secret with terrible implications. Even as he copes with a stark new perspective on the adult world, he knows he must summon all his reserves of courage in order to do the right thing.

PUBLISHED BY CANONGATE

ROBERT LUDLUM
THE JANSON DIRECTIVE

When Hungarian philanthropist and billionaire Peter Novak is kidnapped by terrorist extremists, the only man who can save him is legendary former secret service agent Paul Janson.

But the night-time rescue operation in the heart of tropical Anura doesn't go to plan. And before long, Janson himself is on the run . . .

PROLOGUE

Northwestern Anura, 250 miles east of Sri Lanka. The night was oppressive, the air at body temperature and almost motionless. Earlier in the evening there had been light, cooling rains, but now everything seemed to radiate heat, even the silvery half-moon, its countenance brushed with wisps of cloud. The jungle itself seemed to exhale the hot, moist breath of a predator lying in wait.

Shyam shifted restlessly in his canvas chair. It was, he knew, a fairly ordinary night on the island of Anura for this time of year: early in the monsoon season, the air was always heavy with a sense of foreboding. At half past one in the morning, Shyam reckoned he had been on checkpoint duty for four and a half hours. In that time, precisely seven motorists had come their way. The checkpoint consisted of two parallel lines of barbed-wire frames—'knife rests'—eighty feet apart on the road. Shyam and Arjun were the two sentries on forward duty. A pair of back-ups was supposedly on duty on the other side of the hill, but the hours of silence from them suggested that they were dozing, along with the men in the makeshift barracks a few hundred feet down the road.

Now, drifting in with the breeze, as faint as a distant insect drone, came the sound of a gunned motor. Shyam slowly got to his feet.

'*Arjun*,' he called out in a singsong tone. 'Car coming.'

Arjun rubbed his eyes. 'At this hour?'

In the dark of the semiforested terrain, Shyam could see the headlights. Over a revved-up motor, whoops of delight could be heard.

'Dirty farm kids,' Arjun grumbled.

Shyam, for his part, was grateful for anything that interrupted the tedium. He had spent the past seven days on the night shift at the vehicle checkpoint, and it felt like a hardship post. Naturally, their stone-faced superior had emphasised how important the assignment was. The checkpoint was just up the road from the Stone Palace, where the government was holding some sort of hush-hush gathering. This was the only road that connected the palace to the rebel-held region to the north. The guerrillas of the Kagama Liberation Front knew about the checkpoints, however, and kept away.

The truck came into view; two shirtless young men were in the cab. The roof was down. One of boys was standing up, pouring a sudsy can of beer over his chest and cheering. The truck—probably loaded with some poor farmer's root crops—was rounding the bend at upward of eighty miles per hour, as fast as the groaning engine would go. American rock music blared.

Shyam stepped into the road with his rifle. The truck kept barrelling forward, and he stepped back. A beer can was lobbed into the air, hitting the ground with a thunk. From the sound, it was full.

The truck veered round the first knife rest, then the second, and kept going.

'Let Shiva tear them limb from limb,' Arjun said. 'No need to radio the backstop. You can hear these kids for miles.' He flicked a thumb at the can on the road and grinned. 'Sounds like that's still got beer in it. Pukka refreshment, my friend.'

WHEN THE TRUCK was half a mile past the roadblock, the driver eased up on the accelerator, and the young man riding shotgun sat down, wiping himself off with a towel before putting on a black T-shirt and strapping himself in. Both guerrillas looked grave.

An older man was seated on the flat bench behind them. The KLF officer had been prone and invisible when the truck crashed the checkpoint. Now he flicked the COMMUNICATE button on his walkie-talkie and grunted some instructions.

With a metallic groan, the rear door of the truck's trailer was cracked open so that the armed men inside could get some air.

ORDINARILY, THE LEADER of the KLF, the man they called the Caliph, would never be exposed to the unpredictability of an armed engagement. But history was being written this night. How could the Caliph *not* be present? Besides, he knew that his decision to join his men on the terrain of battle had increased their morale immeasurably. The stout-hearted Kagama wanted him to be a witness to their heroism—or their martyrdom. They looked at the planes of his face, his fine ebony features, his strong jaw, and saw not merely a man anointed by the Prophet to lead them to freedom but a man who would inscribe their deeds in the book of life, for all posterity.

And so the Caliph kept vigil with his special detail, on a carefully chosen mountainous perch. The ground was hard and wet beneath his thin-soled boots, but the Stone Palace glowed before him. The east wall was a vast expanse of limestone, its weathered stones and wide, freshly painted gate bathed in lights that were sunk into the ground every few feet. It shimmered. It beckoned.

The chief radio operator whispered in the Caliph's ear. The Kaffra base of the Anuran tyrants had been destroyed, its communications infrastructure dismantled. Even if they managed to get word out, the guards at the Stone Palace had no hope for back-up. Thirty seconds later, the radio operator had another message to convey: confirmation that a second army base had been reclaimed by the people. The Caliph felt his spine tingle. Within hours, the entire province of Kenna would be wrested from a despotic death grip. National liberation would glimmer over the horizon with the sun.

Nothing, however, was more important than taking the Stone Palace. *Nothing*. The Go-Between had been emphatic about it, and so far the Go-Between had been right about everything, starting with the value of his own contributions. He had been generous to the point of profligacy with his armaments and intelligence. He had not disappointed the Caliph, and the Caliph would not disappoint him. But his debt to the Go-Between would remain a matter between him and Allah. Many would die in the next few hours but there was one person in the Stone Palace who would not be killed—not yet. He was a special man, a man who had come to the island in an attempt to broker a peace. He was revered by millions but he was an agent of neocolonialism nevertheless. He would not be shot. For him the proper niceties would be observed.

And then he would be beheaded as the criminal he was.

'IT'S STILL COLD!' Arjun cried out with delight as he picked up the beer can. The outside of the can was actually frosty.

'And it's really full?' Shyam said doubtfully.

'Unopened,' Arjun said. 'Heavy with the health drink!' And it *was* heavy, unexpectedly so. Arjun's thick fingers scrabbled for the pull tab, then gave it a firm yank.

The muffled pop of the detonator came milliseconds before the twelve ounces of plastique exploded. The blast was a shattering moment of light and sound that instantly expanded into an immense, fiery oval of destruction. The shock waves destroyed the two knife rests and the wooden roadside booth, as well as the barracks and those who slept there. The pair of guards who were supposed to have been on duty as backstop at the other end of the roadblock died before they awoke.

Fifteen minutes later, when a convoy of canvas-topped personnel carriers made its way through what remained of the checkpoint, no subterfuge would be necessary.

CHAPTER ONE

Two uniformed women were standing behind a counter as Paul Janson entered the Platinum Club lounge of Pacifica Airlines. The uniforms and the counter were both the same blue-grey hue. The women's jackets featured the sort of epaulettes to which the major airlines were so devoted. In another place and time, Janson reflected, they would have rewarded extensive battlefield experience.

'Your boarding card, please,' one of the women said. She had brassy hair and a powdery tan that ended below her chin.

Janson flashed his ticket and the plastic card with which Pacifica rewarded its extremely frequent fliers.

'Welcome to the Pacifica Platinum Club, Mr Janson,' the other attendant said. 'We'll let you know when your plane is about to board.' She gestured towards the entrance to the lounge area. 'Meantime, enjoy our hospitality facilities.'

Janson settled heavily into one of the cloth-upholstered armchairs. His fellow passengers took little interest in him. For Janson, it was a point of pride that he seldom got a second look. Though he was athletic and solidly built, his appearance was unremarkable, utterly nondescript. With his creased forehead and short-cropped steel-grey hair, he looked his five decades. Whether on Wall Street or the Bourse, he knew how to make himself all but invisible. Even his expensively tailored grey suit was perfect camouflage, as appropriate to the corporate jungle as the green and black face paint he once wore in Vietnam was to the real jungle. One would have to be a trained observer to detect that it was the man's shoulders, not shoulder pads, that filled out the suit. And one would have to have spent some time with him to notice the way his slate eyes took everything in.

In his highly specialised work as a corporate security consultant he had established a reputation for being unusually effective and discreet, and demand for his services exceeded both his time and his interest. But his personal life was less successful. He was lonely, that was the truth of it, and his loneliness was never more acute than in the interstices of his overscheduled life—the time spent waiting before takeoff or in overdesigned reception areas. At the end of his next flight, nobody was anticipating his arrival except another visored limo driver who would have misspelt his name on a white cardboard sign, and then another corporate client, an anxious division head of a Los Angeles-based light industrial firm.

'Paging Richard Alexander,' a nasal voice called through the public announcement system. 'Passenger Richard Alexander. Please report to any Pacifica counter.'

It was the background noise of any airport, but it jolted Janson out of his reverie. Richard Alexander was an operational alias he had often used in bygone days. A coincidence, he thought, and then realised that his cellphone was purring, deep in his breast pocket.

He inserted the earphone. 'Yes?'

'Mr Janson? Or should I say, Mr Alexander?' A woman's voice.

'Who is this?' Janson spoke quietly.

'Please, Mr Janson. It's urgent that we meet *at once*.' The vowels and consonants had a precision that was peculiar to those who were both foreign-born and well educated. And the background noise was even more suggestive: the caller was obviously in close proximity.

'Say more.'

There was a pause. 'When we meet.'

Janson hung up. His eyes darted from person to person as he tried to figure out who would seek him out this way.

Was it a trap, set by an old, unforgiving adversary? There were many who would feel avenged by his death. And yet the prospect seemed unlikely. He was not in the field. He was in O'Hare Airport, for God's sake. Which may have been why this rendezvous was chosen. People tended to feel safe at an airport, moated by metal detectors and uniformed security guards. It would be a cunning act to take advantage of that illusion of security.

Possibilities were considered and swiftly discarded. By the thick plate glass overlooking the tarmac, a blonde woman was apparently studying a spreadsheet on her laptop; her cellphone was at her side. Another woman, closer to the entrance, was engaged in spirited conversation with a man whose wedding ring was visible only as a band of pale skin on an otherwise bronzed hand.

Janson's eyes kept roaming until he saw her. Sitting in a dim corner of the lounge was an elegant, middle-aged woman holding a cellphone to her ear. Her hair was white, worn up, and she was attired in a navy Chanel suit with discreet mother-of-pearl buttons. Yes, she was the one: he was certain. Was she an assassin, or part of a kidnapping team? These were among a hundred possibilities that, however remote, he had to rule out. Standard tactical protocol, ingrained from years in the field, demanded it.

Janson sprang to his feet. He had to change his location: that rule was basic. *It's urgent that we meet at once*, the caller had said. If so, they would meet on his terms. He made his way out of the VIP lounge, grabbing a paper cup from a water cooler he passed. He approached the greeting counter with the paper cup held in front of him, as if it were full. Then he yawned, squeezing his eyes shut, and walked straight into a heavyset FAA inspector.

'I am so sorry,' Janson blurted, looking mortified. 'I didn't *spill* anything on you, did I?' Janson's hands moved rapidly over the man's blazer. 'Did I get you wet? I'm really sorry.'

'No harm done,' the inspector replied with a trace of impatience. 'Just, you know, watch where you're going, OK?'

As Janson made his way down the corridor that led towards Concourse B, his cellphone buzzed again, as he had known it would.

'I don't think you understand the urgency,' the caller began.

'That's correct,' Janson snapped. 'I don't. Why don't you let me know what this is about?' In an angled stretch of the corridor, he saw a recessed area, about three feet deep, and then a door. UNAUTHORISED PERSONNEL KEEP OUT was emblazoned on a plaque above it.

'I can't,' the caller said after a beat. 'Not over the phone, I'm afraid. But I'm in the airport and could meet you—'

'In that case, call me back in one minute,' Janson interjected, ending the conversation. He hit the door's horizontal push bar and made his way inside. It turned out to be a room that was lined with electrical panels. Three airline employees in navy-blue twill uniforms were seated round a small Formica table, drinking coffee.

'What do you think you're doing?' one of them yelled at Janson as the door banged shut behind him. 'You can't *be* here.'

Janson smiled without warmth. 'You're going to hate me, boys. But guess what?' He pulled out an FAA badge, the item he had lifted from the heavyset man in the lounge. 'Another drug-abatement initiative. Random testing for a drug-free air-transport work force—to quote the administrator's latest memorandum on the subject.'

'This is *bullshit!*' another one yowled in disgust.

'Haul ass, guys,' Janson barked. 'We're following a whole new procedure this time. My team's assembled over at gate two in Concourse A. Don't make them wait. When they get impatient, sometimes they make mistakes with the samples, if you get my drift.'

All three men hastened out of the room. It would take them a good ten minutes before they reached Concourse A, Janson knew. He glanced at his watch and counted the few remaining seconds until his cellphone buzzed; the caller had waited one minute exactly.

'There's a food court near the ticketing pavilion,' Janson said. 'I'll meet you there.' He waited in the recessed area and thirty seconds later, he saw the white-haired woman walking past.

'Hey, honey!' he called out as, in one continuous movement, he reached an arm around her waist, clamped a hand over her mouth, and hustled her into the now-abandoned service room. There was nobody around to see the three-second manoeuvre; if there had been, Janson's actions would have been taken for a romantic embrace.

The woman was rigid with fear but did not scream, displaying a professional composure that Janson did not find reassuring.

Once the door had closed behind them, Janson brusquely gestured the woman to take a seat at the Formica table.

She sat down on one of the chairs. Janson remained standing.

'I'm not going to list the infractions of protocol here,' he said. 'But by the time we're finished here, I'd better know everything I want to know.' Even if she were legitimately seeking his services, the public nature of the contact was completely inappropriate. And the use of a field legend of his, albeit a long-disused one, was a cardinal violation.

'We have very little time, Mr Janson,' she said.

'I have all the time in the world.'

'Peter Novak doesn't.'

Peter Novak. A legendary Hungarian financier and philanthropist,

Novak had received a Nobel Peace Prize the previous year for his role in conflict resolution around the world. He was the founder and director of the Liberty Foundation, which was devoted to 'directed democracy'—Novak's great passion—and had offices throughout Eastern Europe and other parts of the less developed world. But Janson had reasons of his own to remember Peter Novak. He owed the man an immense debt.

'Who are you?' Janson demanded.

'My name is Márta Lang, and I work for Peter Novak. I'm the deputy director of the Foundation. Peter Novak needs help. As you once did. In Baaqlina.'

Márta Lang pronounced the name of that dusty town as if it were a sentence, a paragraph, a chapter. For Janson, it was.

'I haven't forgotten,' he said quietly.

'Our jet is on the runway, cleared for immediate departure.' She stood. 'We must go now.'

'Where to?'

'That, Mr Janson, will be our question to you.'

AS JANSON FOLLOWED HER up the aluminium steps to Novak's Gulfstream V, his eye was caught by a legend that was painted on its side: *Sok kicsi sokra megy*. Hungarian, and meaningless to him.

Four men and women, evidently members of Márta Lang's staff, were seated in the back of the plane. Márta gestured for him to take the seat opposite her, in the front of the cabin, then picked up an internal phone and murmured a few words. Faintly Janson could detect the whine of the engine revving up as the plane began to taxi.

'That inscription on the fuselage—what does it mean?'

'It means "Many small things can add up to a big one." A Hungarian folk saying and a favourite motto of Peter Novak's. I'm sure you can appreciate why.'

'You can't say he's forgotten where he came from.'

'For better or worse, Hungary made him who he is. And Peter is not one to forget his debts.' A meaningful look.

'Nor am I.'

'I'm aware of that. It's why we know we can rely upon you.'

'If he has an assignment for me, I'd like to hear about it sooner rather than later. And from him rather than someone else.'

'You will have to make do with me. I'm his deputy.'

'So why am I here?' Janson asked. 'And where's Peter Novak?'

Márta Lang took a deep breath. 'He's a captive of the Kagama rebels. We need you to set him free. An "exfiltration" is what I gather you people call it. Otherwise, he will die where he is, in Anura.'

Anura. A captive of the Kagama Liberation Front. One more reason—the main reason, no doubt—that they wanted him for the job. Anura. A place he thought about nearly every day and had for the past five years. His own private hell.

'A few days ago, Peter Novak arrived on the island, trying to broker a peace between the rebels and the government. The KLF said they regarded Peter Novak as an honest broker, and a meeting place in the Kenna province was agreed upon. A lasting accord in Anura—an end to the terror—would be a very great thing. I think you understand that as well as anyone.'

Janson said nothing, but his heart began to pound.

THEIR HOME, furnished by the embassy, was in Cinnamon Gardens, in the capital city of Caligo. In the morning breeze, leaves rustled and birds cawed. What roused him from sleep, though, was a soft coughing noise from the bathroom, then the sound of running water. Helene came back from the bathroom, brushing her teeth. 'Maybe you should stay home from work today,' he'd said drowsily. Helene shook her head. 'It's called morning sickness for a reason, my darling,' she told him with a smile. 'It vanishes like the dew.' She started dressing for work at the embassy. 'Take the day off,' he'd told her, and she'd said, 'Better not, my darling. Either they'll miss me or they won't, and either way that's not good.' She kissed him on the forehead as she left. If only she had stayed with him. If only.

Anura, an island in the Indian Ocean, had a population of twelve million, and was blessed with rare natural beauty. Janson had been posted there for eighteen months, charged with assessing the island's volatile political situation. For during the past decade and a half, Paradise had been disrupted by one of the deadliest terror organisations in the world, the Kagama Liberation Front. Thousands of young men, in thrall to the man they called the Caliph, wore leather pendants with a cyanide capsule at the end; it symbolised their readiness to give their lives for the cause. The Caliph had a particular fondness for suicide bombings. One of his proudest moments was a truck bombing in downtown Caligo that had delivered death to a dozen staff members in the US embassy in Anura.

Among those dozen was Helene.

IN THE JET, Márta placed a hand on Janson's wrist. 'I'm sorry, Mr Janson. I appreciate the anguish this must bring back.'

'Of course you do,' Janson said. 'It's part of why you chose me.'

Márta did not avert her gaze. 'Peter Novak is about to die. The conference in the province of Kenna was a trap.'

'It was insanity to begin with,' Janson snapped. 'The KLF believes in the inherent nobility of revolutionary violence. How do you negotiate with such fanatics?' He sighed. 'Just give them what they want.'

'The don't want anything,' Lang said softly. 'We've invited them to name their price, as long as Peter is released alive. We keep getting the same answer: Peter Novak has been sentenced to death for crimes against the colonised, and the execution decree is "irrevocable". Are you familiar with the traditional Sunni holy day of Id ul-Kabir?'

'It commemorates the sacrifice of Abraham.'

Lang nodded. 'This year it will be celebrated by the sacrifice of Peter Novak. He will be beheaded on Id ul-Kabir. That's *this* Friday.'

'Why? For God's sakes, why?'

'*Because,*' Lang said. 'Because he's a sinister agent of neocolonialism—that's what the KLF says. Because doing so will put the KLF on the map, gain them greater notoriety than they've achieved in fifteen years of bombings. Who the hell knows why?'

'But if he's trying to aggrandise himself this way, why hasn't the Caliph publicised it yet? Why hasn't the media got hold of it?'

'He's canny. By waiting until the deed is done to publicise it, he staves off any international pressure to intervene. Meanwhile, he knows we don't dare publicise it, because it would eliminate even the possibility of a negotiated solution, however remote.'

'Why are you talking to me? Why not turn to Washington to help?'

'It's the first thing we did. They believe that any US-identified intervention would endanger the lives of dozens of American citizens who are now in rebel-occupied territory. And then there's the matter of Donna Hedderman.'

Janson nodded. 'A Columbia grad student in anthropology. Doing field work in northeast Anura. Captured by the Kagama rebels, who accused her of being a CIA agent.'

'She's been held by them for two months, incommunicado. Lip service aside, the United States hasn't done a damn thing. Didn't want to "complicate an already complicated situation".'

'I'm getting the picture. If the United States refuses to intervene on behalf of an American national—'

'—how will it look if it turns around and sends a rescue team for the Hungarian billionaire? Yes. They didn't put it so bluntly, but that's the point they made. And then—'

'Let me guess,' Janson said. 'My name came up.'

'Repeatedly. State and Central Intelligence strongly recommended you. You're not part of the government any more. You're a free agent with international connections to others in what used to be your line of work. According to your former colleagues at Consular Operations, Paul Janson is "the best there is at what he does".'

'The present tense is misleading. They told you I retired. I wonder whether they told you why.'

DISENGAGING FROM CONSULAR Operations had involved a dozen exit interviews. The one he remembered best was with Undersecretary Derek Collins. On paper, he was the director of the State Department's Bureau of Intelligence and Research; in reality, he was the director of its covert branch, Consular Operations. Even now, Janson could see Collins wearily removing his black-framed glasses and massaging the bridge of his nose.

'I think I pity you, Janson,' Collins had said. 'You were the guy with a slab of granite where your heart's supposed to be. Now you say you're repulsed by the thing you're best at.'

'I don't expect you to understand, Collins,' he had replied. 'Let's just say I've had a change of heart.'

A short, bark-like laugh. 'I know people, Janson. You tell me you're sickened by the killing. I'm telling you what you'll discover one day for yourself: that's the only way you'll ever feel alive.'

Janson shook his head. The implication made him shudder and reminded him why he had to leave, why he should have done so long before. 'What kind of man has to *kill* to feel *alive?*'

Collins's gaze seemed to burrow through his flesh. 'I guess I'd ask you the same thing, Janson.'

'YES, MR JANSON,' said Márta Lang. 'Your former employers explained that you had unfinished business with the Kagama.

'Is that the phrase they used? "Unfinished business"?'

She nodded.

'So be it,' Janson said after a pause. 'These aren't men with poetry in their souls.'

'Come.' Lang stood up. 'I'm going to introduce you to my team.

Any information you need, they'll have, or know how to find out. We have dossiers filled with signals-intelligence intercepts, and all the relevant information we could gather in what little time we had. It's all at your disposal.'

Janson spent the next hour going through the dossiers and listening to presentations by Márta Lang's four associates. Much of the material was familiar; some of the analyses even reflected his own reports from Caligo, submitted more than five years ago. Two nights earlier, the rebels had taken over army bases, surged through checkpoints and seized control of the province of Kenna.

There were a few new details. Ahmad Tabari, the man they called the Caliph, had gained in popular support during the past few years. Some of his food programmes, it emerged, had won him sympathisers even among Hindu peasants. They had nicknamed him the Exterminator—not because of his propensity to murder civilians but because of a pest-eradication campaign he had launched. In the areas controlled by the KLF, aggressive measures were taken against the bandicoot rat, an indigenous species of vermin destructive to poultry and grain. In fact, Tabari's campaign was motivated by an ancient superstition. In Tabari's clan the bandicoot rat represented death.

Janson scrutinised maps, grainy satellite imagery and old blueprints of the building on Adam's Hill where Novak was being held. It had once been a colonial governor-general's compound and, before that, a fortress—known by the Dutch as the Steenpaleis, the Stone Palace. One conclusion was inescapable: any exfiltration operation had an extremely remote probability of success.

Lang's associates knew it. He could see it in their faces: they were asking him to conduct a mission that was doomed from the start. But Peter Novak *was* a great man. Many owed their lives to him. And Janson knew he was among them.

Abruptly, Janson sat up straight. There *was* a way—perhaps.

'We'll need aircraft, boats, and most of all, the right operatives.'

Márta Lang looked at the others expectantly; for the moment, anyway, the look of grim resignation had lifted.

'I'm talking about a crack team of specialists. There's no time for training exercises—it's going to have to be people who have worked together before, people *I've* worked with and can trust.' A succession of faces flashed in his mind like so many file photos, and he mentally culled the list until four remained. Each was someone he felt he could trust with his life; indeed, each was someone who owed him his life, and who would respect a debt of honour. He gave Lang the list.

Next Janson started to go over a list of military equipment with one of Lang's associates, a man who served as a de facto logistics officer. To each request the man responded not with a yes or no but with a time interval—the number of hours that would be necessary to locate and ship the equipment to the rendezvous point Janson had determined, in the Nicobar archipelago.

Through the windows, the setting sun was a golden orb, cushioned by white, fluffy-looking clouds. When Lang's eyes lowered to her watch, he knew she was looking at more than simply the time of day. She was looking at the number of hours Peter Novak had left.

She met his gaze. 'Whatever happens,' she said, 'I want to thank you for what you've given us.'

'I've given you nothing,' Janson protested.

'You've given us hope,' she said.

Janson started to say something about the realities, the long odds, the abundant downside scenarios, but he stopped himself. At this stage of a mission, false hope was better than none at all.

CHAPTER TWO

The memories were thirty years old, but they could have been yesterday's. They unspooled in his dreams at night—always the night before an operation, fuelled by repressed anxiety—and though they started and ended at different points, it was as though they were from the same continuous loop of tape.

In the jungle was a base. In the base was an office. In the office was a desk. On the desk was a sheet of paper.

It was the list for that date's Harassment & Interdiction fire.

A pile of slips on Lieutenant Commander Alan Demarest's desk was filled with similar reports sent by the Military Assistance Command, Vietnam—MACV. The reports came from double agents, from Viet Cong sympathisers, from paid informants, and sometimes from villagers who had scores to settle and had figured out an easy way to get someone else to destroy a rival's paddy dike.

'These are supposed to be the basis for our Harassment and Interdiction fire,' Demarest had said to Janson and Maguire. 'But they're bullshit. Some four-eyed Charlie in Hanoi wrote these for our sake, and piped them through the pencil dicks at MACV. These, gentlemen, are a waste of artillery. Know how I know?' He held up a filmy slip, fluttering it like a flag. 'There's no blood on this paper.'

A twelfth-century choral work played through the speakers of a tape system, one of Demarest's small enthusiasms. 'You get me a goddamn VC courier,' he went on, scowling. 'No, get me a dozen. If they've got paper on them, bring it back—certified with VC blood.'

That evening, six of them had rolled over the gunwales of the SEAL tactical assault boat, and into the bath-warm shallow water of Ham Luong. They paddled through an eighth of a mile of riverine silt and landed on the pear-shaped island. 'Come back with prisoners, or don't come back,' their CO had told them. With luck, they would do so: the island was known to be controlled by Viet Cong. But luck had lately been in scarce supply.

The six men wore black pyjamas, like their foe. No dog tags, no signs of rank or unit, of the fact that they were a SEAL team, of the even more pertinent fact that they were Demarest's Devils.

Janson was on point, paired with Hardaway, when the crack of a rifle told them the enemy had learned of their presence. Blood erupted from Hardaway's neck. He collapsed to the ground.

As Maguire began to fire his machine gun over their heads, Janson scrambled over to Hardaway. He cradled his friend's head, applying pressure with both hands to the pulsing wound on his neck, from which bright arterial blood was gouting.

In a sudden display of strength, Hardaway wrenched Janson's hands from his neck. 'Leave me, Janson.' He crawled away a few feet, then used his arms to raise himself, his head swivelling as he tried to make out the shapes of his assailants around the tree line.

Immediately, a blast hit his midriff, slamming him to the ground. His abdomen had been torn apart, Janson saw. Recovery was out of the question. One man down. How many more?

The VC had been lying in wait for them. There was no way the fire could be this heavy and well targeted unless Charlie had received advance word of the infiltration.

'Get us the fuck out of here!' Janson radioed back to base. 'We need back-up now! Send a Mike boat. Do it *now*!'

Janson heard the voice of his commanding officer coming on the line: 'You holding up OK, son?' Demarest asked.

'Sir, they were expecting us!' Janson said.

After a pause, Demarest's voice crackled on the radio headphones. 'Of course they were.'

'But *how*, sir?'

'Just consider it a test, son. A test that will show which of my men have what it takes.' Janson heard choral music in the background.

'But Hardaway—'

Demarest cut him off. 'He was weak. He failed the test.'

JANSON OPENED HIS EYES with a shudder as the plane touched down.

Katchall had for years been declared a no-entry location by India's navy, part of a security zone that included most of the Nicobar Islands. Once it was rezoned, it became a trading post. Mangoes, papaya, durian, PRC-101s, and C-130s all made their way to and from the sun-scorched oval of land. It was, Janson knew, one of the few places where nobody would blink at the sudden arrival of military transport and munitions.

A Jeep took him directly from the plane to the compound along the western shore. His team would already be assembling in the olive-drab Quonset hut. A small prefab warehouse adjoined it. The Liberty Foundation had a regional office in Rangoon, and so was able to ensure that the rendezvous sites were in order.

Theo Katsaris had already arrived when Janson pulled up, and the two men embraced warmly. Katsaris, a Greek national, was probably the most skilled operative Janson had ever worked with. His very presence would raise morale; he had the sunny aura of a man to whom nothing bad would ever happen.

Manuel Honwana had been in the nearby hangar but made his way back when he learned of Janson's arrival. He was a former colonel in the Mozambican air force, Russian-trained and unequalled at ground-hugging flight over hilly tropical terrain. And there was Finn Andressen, a Norwegian and a former officer in his country's armed forces, who had degrees in geology and a well-honed instinct for terrain assessment. He arrived within the hour, followed in short order by Sean Hennessy, an unflappable Irish airman. The team members greeted one another with hearty shoulder clasps or quiet handshakes, depending on their temperament.

Janson led them through the plan of attack, starting with the broad outlines and descending to details and alternative options. Then they set about fine-tuning the plan. Honwana, Andressen and Hennessy reviewed maps of wind and ocean currents. Janson and

Katsaris studied a Plasticine mock-up of the Stone Palace.

Janson now turned from the model to the highly detailed blue-prints. Those blueprints, he knew, represented an enormous effort. They had been prepared in the past forty hours by a task force of architects and engineers assembled by the Liberty Foundation. The experts had been provided with extensive verbal descriptions from visitors, a profusion of historical photographs, and satellite imagery. Colonial archives in the Netherlands had been consulted as well.

'As long as we can hold off until around four hundred hours,' Andressen said, 'we'll be almost guaranteed a heavy cloud cover. That's obviously advisable for the purposes of stealth.'

'You're talking about a high-altitude jump through heavy cloud cover?' Hennessy asked. 'Jumping blind?'

'A leap of faith,' said the Norseman. 'Like religion.'

'I thought this was a commando operation, not a kamikaze one,' Hennessy put in. 'Tell me, Paul, what bloody fool is going to be making this jump?'

Janson looked at Katsaris. 'You,' he told the Greek. 'And me.'

Katsaris stared at him for a few moments. 'I can live with that.'

THE PREMISE of a team was that anybody would accept personal risk to reduce a risk borne by another. An ethos of equality was crucial; any sense of favouritism was destructive to it. When they met as a group, Janson therefore dealt with the men in a tone that was at once brusque and friendly. But even within elites, there were elites—and even within the innermost circles of excellence, there is the chosen one, the golden boy.

Janson had once been that person, almost three decades earlier. Just a few weeks after he'd arrived at the SEAL training camp at Little Creek, Alan Demarest had picked him out from the trainees, had him transferred to ever more elite combat teams, ever more gruelling regimens of combat drills. The training groups got smaller and smaller—more and more of his peers dropped out, defeated by the punishing schedule of exercises—until, by the end, Demarest isolated him for intensive sessions of one-on-one training.

And thus did one legendary warrior create another. When Janson had first met Theo Katsaris, years back, he *knew*—he simply knew, the way Demarest must have known about him.

Yet even if Katsaris had not been so extraordinarily gifted, opera-tional equality could not supplant the bonds of loyalty forged over time, and Janson's friendship with him went far beyond the context of the commando mission. It was a thing compounded of shared memories and mutual indebtedness.

The two made their way to the end of the warehouse, where Foundation-supplied weaponry had been stowed earlier that day.

'You know why I'm doing this,' Janson said.

'Two reasons,' Katsaris said. 'Arguably the two reasons you shouldn't be doing this.'

'And in my position?'

'I'd do exactly the same,' Katsaris said. 'The military wing of the Harakat al-Muqawama al-Islamiya never had a good reputation for returning stolen property.'

Stolen property: hostages, especially those suspected of being assets of American intelligence. Seven years ago, in Baaqlina, Lebanon, Janson had been captured by the extremist group; his captors initially thought they had taken an American businessman, accepting his legend at face value, but the flurry of high-level reactions fuelled other suspicions. Negotiations quickly went off the rails, foundering on power struggles within the faction. Only the timely intervention of a third party—the Liberty Foundation, as it later emerged—caused them to alter their plans. After twelve days of captivity, Janson walked free.

'For all we know, Novak wasn't even involved, didn't have any knowledge of the situation,' Katsaris went on. 'But it's his foundation. Ergo, you owe the man your life. So this lady comes up to you and says, Baaqlina has come due. You've got to say yes.'

Janson smiled. 'I always feel like an open book around you.'

'Tell me something. How often do you think about Helene?'

'Every day.'

Katsaris reached over, placed a hand on Janson's shoulder. 'You once told me something, Paul. Years ago. Now I'm going to tell it to you. *There is no revenge*. Not on this earth. That's storybook stuff. In our world, there are strikes and reprisals and more reprisals. But that neat, slate-cleaning fantasy of revenge—it doesn't exist.'

'I know.'

'Helene's dead, Paul.'

'Oh. That must be why she hasn't been answering my phone calls.' His deadpan was masking a world of pain, and not very well.

Katsaris's gaze did not waver, but he squeezed Janson's shoulder harder. 'There is nothing—*nothing*—that can ever bring her back.

Do what you want to the Kagama fanatics, but know this.'

Janson exhaled heavily. 'You're afraid I'm going to go berserk and visit the wrath of God upon the terrorists who killed my wife.'

'No,' Katsaris said. 'I'm afraid that on some gut level, you think that the way to wipe the slate clean, the way to honour Helene, is to get yourself killed by them, too.'

Janson shook his head violently, though he wondered whether there could be any truth to what Katsaris said. 'Nobody's going to die tonight,' he said. It was a ritual of self-assurance, they both knew, rather than a statement of probabilities.

THE NORTH COASTLINE of Anura nipped in like a deeply grooved valentine's heart. The eastern lobe was mostly jungle, sparsely inhabited. Honwana flew the BA609 tiltrotor aircraft low to the ground through the Nikala jungle. Once over the sea, the plane angled upwards, banking nearly forty degrees.

Andressen and Hennessy were up front with Honwana, part of the crew, providing essential navigational support. Separated by a bulkhead, the two paratroopers were in the rear of the aircraft.

'So tell me, Theo,' Janson said, 'how's the beautiful Marina.'

Katsaris laughed. 'Right now she's positively radiant.' He pronounced the last word with special emphasis.

'Wait a minute,' Janson said. 'You don't mean she's . . .'

'Early days, still. Touch of morning sickness. Otherwise, she's doing great.'

'Then you're going to be a father,' Janson said. The rush of warmth he had felt on hearing the news quickly cooled.

'You don't sound overjoyed,' Katsaris said.

'You should have told me.'

'Why?' he returned lightly. 'Marina's the one who's pregnant.'

'You know why.'

'We were going to tell you soon. In fact, we were hoping you'd agree to be the godfather.'

Janson's tone was truculent. 'You should have told me before.'

Theo shrugged. 'I'm going to be a father, and that makes me very, very happy. But it isn't going to change the way I lead my life. That's not who I am. Marina knows that. You know it, too. Besides, if this operation is too risky for me, how can you in good conscience ask another person to take my place?'

Janson just shook his head.

'You need me,' Katsaris said.

'I could have gotten somebody else.'

'Not somebody as good.' His brown eyes were unwavering. 'I'm not going to let you down,' he said quietly.

'Tell me something I don't know,' Janson said.

AS THEY APPROACHED the drop zone, Katsaris and Janson put on full black-nylon combat garb and face paint. To have done so too far in advance would have been to risk overheating.

Now came the first great improbability. He and Katsaris had 3,000 jumps between them. But what would be required tonight was beyond anything they had experienced.

Janson had been pleased with himself when he had the insight that the compound's sole point of vulnerability was directly overhead—that the one possibility of an undetected arrival would be from the night sky to the centre of the courtyard. But whether there was a serious chance of accomplishing this remained conjectural.

To arrive undetected, they would have to fall through the starless, moonless night that the monsoon season would provide. The satellite weather maps confirmed that at four o'clock in the morning the cloud cover would be total. To succeed, they would have to land with extraordinary precision. To make things worse, the same weather system that provided cloud cover also provided unpredictable winds—an enemy of precision.

Honwana opened the hatch at 20,000 feet. At that altitude, the air would be frigid, perhaps 30 below zero. But exposure to those temperatures would be relatively brief. Goggles, gloves and the tight-fitting swimming-cap-like helmets they wore would help, as would their nylon flight suits.

They wanted to release off the water, more than a lateral mile from the Stone Palace. As they descended, they would be able to discard items like the ripcord handle and their gloves, with the assurance that these items would not come raining down over their target like so many warning leaflets. The high-altitude release would also give them time to manoeuvre into position.

'OK,' Janson said, standing before the open hatch. 'Time to play follow-the-leader.'

'Not fair,' Katsaris said. 'You always get to go first.'

'Age before beauty,' Janson grunted, making his way down the aluminium ramp. Then he leapt out into the inky skies.

FACE DOWN, Janson arched hard, spreading out his arms and legs to slow the descent. Freezing winds whipped at his rig, equipment and clothing. He moved his right wrist slowly towards his face and peered through his goggles at the large, luminous displays of the altimeter and the GPS unit. He had forty seconds to make it to the drop zone.

He had to move into track position. Tracking meant turning one's body into an aerofoil, with the humped profile of an aeroplane's wing, so that one acquired some lift. For several seconds, Janson accelerated, with his head down and his limbs spread out slightly. He bent his arms and waist a little and rolled his shoulders forward, as if preparing to kowtow. Finally, he pulled his head back as he put his legs together, pointing his toes like a ballet dancer.

It took ten seconds before he experienced a sense of lift and his dive began to flatten. In a maximum track, it should be possible to move as rapidly horizontally as vertically—so that every yard downwards took one almost a yard forwards. In theory.

In reality, he was an equipment-laden commando who, beneath his flight suit, had forty pounds of gear hooked to his combat vest. In reality, he was a forty-nine-year-old man whose joints were stiffening in the subzero air that blasted its way through his flight suit. A max track required him to maintain perfect form, and it was not clear how long his skeletal muscles would permit him to do so.

A vibration at his wrist. The altimeter alarm. A warning that he was reaching the height below which the only sure thing was death on impact. The manuals put it less dramatically: they referred to the 'minimum altitude for parachute deployment'.

He arched himself into a vertical position, reached for the ripcord handle and tugged. There was a brief flutter as the chute spread itself in the air and the lines stretched out. He felt the familiar jolt, the sense of being gripped at his shoulders and seat.

He tossed the ripcord handle away and peered up to make sure the black nylon canopy was properly flared. He had difficulty making out its outlines in the night sky, just fifteen feet above him.

He felt himself pushed sideways by a gusting crosscurrent and his GPS indicator showed that he had drifted off course.

He pulled his right steering line down. The effect of the pull was almost instantaneous: he found himself swinging out from under the canopy, arcing wildly. And the altimeter told him that his speed of descent had just increased considerably. Not good. He was closer to the ground than he should be. He raised the steering lines again, allowing the canopy to yawn to its full 250 square feet and maximise its vertical drag. Finally, he found he was able to make gentle S-turns astride the wind line. The process required complete concentration.

His pulse quickened. Like the mast of a ghost ship, battlements were becoming visible through the fog, the white limestone reflecting the faintest light seeping through the cloud cover. Quickly, he cast off his gloves and flight cap.

He prayed that no sudden turn would be necessary to position himself over the centre of the courtyard, for a fast turn would dangerously hasten his descent. There was no margin for error; the compound's high walls made a low approach impossible.

He was suddenly aware how hot and moist the air was—it was as if he had moved from a meat locker into a steam bath. He glided towards the centre of the courtyard. As soon as his hands were free, he deactivated his instruments, lest their glow give his presence away.

His boots were now fifteen feet above the ground. He brought both toggles down to shoulder level, and then pulled them down between his thighs, stopping his forward motion. As he sank down the remaining few feet, he tensed his leg muscles and rotated his body in the direction of the fall, bending his knees slightly.

Keeping his leg muscles flexed, he sank to the ground on the soft rubber soles of his boots. Soundlessly, he bounced on the balls of his feet, preparing to fall. But he did not.

He was standing. In the courtyard. He had made it.

He looked around him, and in the starless night could just make out the contours of a vast deserted courtyard. A large white structure—the old fountain, as the blueprints had specified—loomed several yards away. He was almost exactly in the centre of an area the size of half a football field. It was eerily quiet. There was no sign of movement—no sign that his arrival had been observed.

He unhooked his rig, removed his flight suit and gathered the canopy from the cobblestoned courtyard.

A faint rustle—the sound of the cells of a nylon canopy gently collapsing overhead. Janson looked up. It was Katsaris, floating down slowly. He flared his chute and landed with a noiseless roll. Then he scrambled to his feet and came towards Janson.

Now there were two of them. Two highly experienced, highly skilled operatives.

Two of them—against an entire battalion of armed guerrillas.

Still, it was a start.

CHAPTER THREE

Janson activated the communication system and *tsked* into the filament microphone near his mouth. Military protocol.

Katsaris followed his lead: he silently removed his flight suit, then gathered the canopy into a tight bundle.

The two of them packed the canopies and suits into the basin of the stone fountain in the centre of the courtyard.

Janson unhooked his night-vision glasses from his combat vest and raised them to his eyes; the courtyard was suddenly bathed in a soft green glow. He and Katsaris stood back-to-back, each conducting an NV sweep of the opposite quadrants.

On the north side of the courtyard were three orange phosphorescent blobs, two leaning towards each other—a sudden white flare emerging between their spectral forms. Janson depowered the scope before lowering it to view the scene with his naked eyes. Even from twenty yards away, he could clearly see the flickering flame. A match had been struck and two of the guards were lighting cigarettes.

Katsaris whispered into his filament microphone, his voice amplified in Janson's earpiece: 'One sentry. Southeast corner. Seated.'

Janson replied in a subwhisper: 'Three sentries. North verandah.'

The blueprints made it clear the dungeon was located beneath the northern face of the courtyard. Janson moved to his left, along the wall, and then beneath the overhang of the western verandah, walking half-crouched beneath the parapet.

He was now fifteen feet from the nearest sentry, and could see the men's faces: broad peasant faces, young, unwary and unsophisticated. *Amateurs*, he mused, but it was not a wholly reassuring thought. The KLF was too well-organised to have entrusted so valuable a treasure to the protection of such men. They were a first line of defence only.

And where was Katsaris? Janson peered across the courtyard, across sixty feet of darkness, and could make out nothing.

He made a quiet *tsk* into the filament mike, trying to modify the sound to echo the insect and avian noises of the night. He heard an answering *tsk* in his earpiece. Katsaris was in place, ready.

Was it safe to take out these men? Were the men themselves decoys—birds on a wire? *Was* there a wire?

Janson looked through the NV scope, angling it towards the iron grille behind the smoking peasants. Nothing.

No, *something*. An orange spot, too small to correspond to a body. In all likelihood, it was a hand belonging to a body concealed behind a stone wall.

From a thigh pocket, Janson withdrew a blackened aluminium tube, thirteen inches in length, four in diameter. Inside it was lined with a snug steel mesh, which prevented the living creature within from making any noise. An atmosphere of 90 per cent pure oxygen prevented asphyxiation during the operation. The time had come for noise, for distraction. He unscrewed one sealed end.

By its long tail, he removed the rodent and flung it towards the verandah in a high parabola. It landed as if, in its nocturnal travels, it had lost its purchase and dropped off the terracotta-tiled roof.

Its glossy black pelt was now standing on end, and the creature made its telltale piglike grunts. The sentries had a visitor, and within seconds they knew it. The short head, wide muzzle, scaly, hairless tail. One foot long, two and a half pounds. A bandicoot rat. Quite literally, Ahmad Tabari's *bête noire*.

The Kagama guards broke out into hushed, frantic exchanges. When the animal scurried towards an entryway, they tried to stop it. If the Beloved One, asleep in the governor's suite, were to come across this harbinger of death in his living quarters, there was no telling how he would react.

The consternation had, as Janson had hoped, brought out the others—the second team. How many? Three—no, four.

Janson withdrew a second bandicoot rat. A low, underhand toss. Its small, sharp claws grabbing at thin air, the rat landed on the head of one of the peasant sentries—who let out a piercing scream.

Janson watched the confusion that swept through the northern verandah. His destination was the space beneath that verandah, and there was no covered route to it, for the stone walkways that projected from the long east and west walls of the compound stopped fifteen feet before they reached the wall opposite.

Thirty feet away and six feet up, an older man appeared on the verandah, enjoining silence. As Janson focused on the older man, his unease grew. The man spoke of silence, but his face told Janson that it was not his sole, or even primary, concern. Only a larger sense of suspicion could explain the squinted, searching gaze, which moved quickly from the panicked sentries to the shadowy courtyard beyond.

The older man was the one to take out first. But had enough time passed? By now, word of the commotion would have spread among those on duty. It was crucial that an explanation for it—the appearance of the accursed bandicoot—had spread as well. Because there would be other noises. That was inevitable. Noises that had an explanation were innocuous. Noises that lacked an explanation would prompt further investigation, and could be deadly.

Janson withdrew the Blo-Jector, a twenty-inch pipe of anodised aluminium, from a pouch on his black fatigues. He whispered into his lip mike. He would take the older man and the guard to his right; Katsaris should aim for the others. Janson now raised the blowpipe to his lips, sighting over the end of the tube. The dart was a fine-gauge needle and bolus housed within a replica of a wasp. He puffed hard into the mouthpiece, then quickly inserted another dart, and discharged it. He returned to his crouching position.

The older man grabbed at his neck, pulled out the dart, and peered at it in the dim light. Had he removed it before it had injected its bolus? The object had visual resemblances to a large stinging insect. But its weight would be wrong, particularly if it still contained the incapacitant fluid, one millilitre of carfentanil citrate. The man stared at it furiously, and then looked directly at Janson. Focusing intently, he had evidently made out his form in the shadowed corner.

The soldier's hand reached for a revolver, holstered on his side—and then he toppled forward off the verandah. Janson could hear the thud of his body hitting the cobblestones six feet below him. Two other sentries slid to the ground, losing consciousness.

A jabbering exchange broke out between the remaining guards, to his far left. They knew something was wrong. Then, one after another, as the darts took effect, they woozily collapsed.

Janson and Katsaris dashed for the darkness beneath the north verandah, sliding between the stout piers that supported it at three-foot intervals. According to the blueprints, the circular stone lid to the dungeon was at the midpoint of the northern wall. Blindly, Janson felt along the ground, his hands moving along the rubble-work foundations where ground and building met.

'I *found* it,' Theo whispered, from a few feet away.

Janson turned on a small infrared flashlight and strapped on his night-vision scope, adjusting it from starlight mode to IR mode.

Theo was crouching before a large stone disk. The grotto under their feet had been used for any number of purposes over the years.

The storage of prisoners was a principal one. Beneath the heavy circular masonry was a vertical passageway that served as a chute.

The lid was fashioned with handholds on either side. Janson and Theo crouched over it and lifted in one coordinated movement. The lid was eight inches thick and meant to be moved by four strong men, not two. But it could be done. Using all their strength, they eased it up and placed it gently on the ground to one side.

Janson peered down into the hole they had uncovered. Just under the lid there was a grate. And through it, he heard a welter of voices drifting up from the subterranean space.

The chute, they knew, descended through several feet of stone, angled at 45 degrees for most of the way, then bending and funnelling down more shallowly.

Katsaris handed Janson the fibre-optic camera kit. Its cord was the thickness of a phone wire and had a tip hardly bigger than a match head. Within the cable ran a double-layered glass strand that would transmit images to a three-by-five-inch screen at the other end.

Janson kept an eye on the display as he fed the cord down the grate. The screen was suffused with grey hues, which grew lighter and lighter. Abruptly, it filled with a bird's-eye view of a dimly lit room. Janson pulled the cord up so that it was a fraction of an inch from the end of the chute, unlikely to be detected. After five seconds, the device's automatic focusing program brought the visual field into maximal sharpness and brightness.

'How many?' Katsaris asked.

Janson fingered a button that rotated the camera tip before he replied. 'Seventeen guards. Armed to the teeth. But who's counting?'

'How about we drop a frag grenade down right now?'

'All you need is a single survivor, and the prisoner's dead,' Janson said. Through a blue haze of cigarette smoke, he saw that the men were sitting round two tables, playing cards. Manipulating the fibre-optic cuff, he shifted the field of vision to the worn staircase at the end of the room. 'Stairway,' he said. 'Landing. Ductwork. Ledge.' Projecting from the midlevel landing was a shelf of poured concrete.

'Can't get there without being spotted.'

'Not necessarily. The period of exposure—going from landing to concrete shelf—would be brief, the room is filled with cigarette smoke, and they're all playing a pretty engrossing game of cards.'

'And what guarantee is there that there won't be a guard hived off, stationed in the dungeon with the prison?'

'Any close contact with Peter Novak would be dangerous. The KLF knows that—they'll guard him, but they'll keep him isolated from any of the Kagama rebels.'

'What are they afraid of—that he'll stab a guard with a cuff link?'

'His *words* are what they're afraid of, Theo. In a poor country, the words of a plutocrat are dangerous things—implements of escape more formidable than any hacksaw. If you're a Kagama rebel, and he's telling you he could make you and your family rich beyond the dreams of avarice, you're going to think about it—it's human nature. So they guard him, but they isolate him, too. It's the only safe way.'

Removing the grate required them both, and the effort needed was doubled by the imperative that it be removed noiselessly. By the time Janson left Katsaris there, his joints and muscles were protesting furiously. A humbling thought crossed his mind: maybe *he* could have stayed by the chute, and let Katsaris do the next part.

Janson clambered up the rubblework wall towards the narrow rectangular gap that would lead to the inside edge of the verandah. The rectangular space, one of several along the roof line, served to prevent water from pooling on the ground floor during the downpours of monsoon season. He wriggled through the eighteen-inch-wide drainage port and made his way down a service corridor adjoining the stateroom of the north wing. He flashed on the blueprints: down the corridor to the left, twenty feet. The door to the dungeon would be at the end of the hallway. Discreet. Wood-clad stone. Two chairs to either side were empty. The men, who had been summoned by the earlier commotion, would be still unconscious at the foot of the verandah. The same was true of the back-up pair of guards, who would have had a clear view of the hallway.

Janson's pulse quickened as he stood before the door. He produced a small tension wrench a little larger than a matchstick. He placed the bent end of the wrench in the keyway, pushing on its far end, so as to maximise both the torque and his tactile sensitivity. One by one, he pulled each tumbler away from the shear line. After ten seconds, the tumblers had been picked. Now he inserted a second tool, a carbide steel pick, thin yet inflexible, and applied clockwise torque.

Holding his breath, he kept both instruments in the keyway as he heard the tongue withdraw and pulled the door a few inches towards him. The door swung easily on well-oiled hinges. Those hinges *had* to be well oiled: as it opened, he saw that the door was fully eighteen inches thick.

Janson verified that the immediate passageway was clear. He walked through the door and, using electrical tape, secured the brass tongue to the door so it would not relock. Then he made his way down the stone stairs. A few more steps down the landing led to a hinged grate of steel bars.

The portcullis-like grate succumbed to his slim tools without difficulty; unlike the door above, however, it was far from soundless. It opened with a distinct scraping noise, of metal against stone—one that the assembled guards could not have failed to hear.

Astonishingly, they did not react. Why?

Then Janson caught the word *Theyilai!* Even with only his guidebook Anuran, he knew that word: *tea*. The guards were expecting somebody—somebody coming with a samovar of tea for them.

Everything now was a question of timing. Janson knew Katsaris was awaiting his command, a silent thermite grenade in hand. Both men had a modified MP5K, a submachine gun with a short barrel and a sound suppressor.

Janson took six steps down, then swung himself soundlessly onto the four-foot-deep concrete ledge. So far, so good. The soldiers were studying their cards; no one was scanning the ceiling.

Now he flattened himself against the wall and inched along the ledge; soldiers at one end of the larger table would be able to see him if they looked up and into the shadowed ledge.

'*Veda theyilai?*' A young soldier spoke the words in a tone of slight annoyance, and rolled his eyes. Had anything registered?

After a beat, the soldier lifted his eyes again, peering into the gloom of the overhead shelf. His hands moved towards his cradled gun.

Janson's scalp was crawling. *He had been made.*

'*Now!*' Janson whispered into his lip mike and slid to a prone position on the furthest recess of the concrete ledge as he put on his polarised goggles. He flipped his weapon's safety down.

The young man stood up suddenly, shouting in Kagama. He fired his gun towards the area where he had seen Janson, and the bullet took a bite out of the concrete just an inch from his head.

Suddenly, the dimly lit room filled with a flare of eye-searing brightness. The slow-burning thermite grenade had arrived: a small, indoor sun, blinding even those who tried to look away.

Through his nearly black goggles, Janson saw the soldiers in disarray and confusion, some shielding their eyes with forearms and hands, others firing blindly towards the ceiling. He returned fire, depleting one thirty-round magazine and snapping in another.

Now Katsaris appeared, bounding down the stairway with polarised goggles and a softly buzzing MP5K, directing bullets at the guerrillas from another angle. In seconds it was over.

As gloom and shadows returned, Janson and Katsaris removed their goggles. The naked, forty-watt overhead bulb, Janson noticed, was still intact. The guards were not so lucky.

The grotto was an abattoir, filled with the stench of blood. Janson felt something hot and acidic in the back of his throat. Had he lost it?

He wanted to throw up. He also knew he would not. Not in front of Theo, his beloved protégé. Not in the middle of a mission.

A coolly remonstrating voice in his head took over: their victims were soldiers. They belonged to a terrorist movement that had taken a man of international renown and sworn to execute him. In guarding a civilian unjustly held captive, they had placed themselves in the line of fire. For Ahmad Tabari, el Caliph, they had pledged to give their lives. Janson had merely taken them up on the offer.

'Let's go,' Janson called to Katsaris. The excuses were not without validity, yet they could not make the slaughter any more tolerable.

His own sense of repugnance was the only thing that gave solace. To contemplate such violence with equanimity was the province of the terrorist, the extremist, the fanatic—a breed he had spent a lifetime combating, a breed he had feared he was, in his own way, becoming. Whatever his actions, the fact that he could not contemplate them without horror indicated that he was not yet a monster.

Now he moved swiftly down from the concrete ledge and joined Katsaris at the iron-plated gate to the dungeon.

'I'll do the honours,' Katsaris said. He was holding a big, antique-looking hoop of keys, taken from one of the slain guards.

Three keys. Three dead bolts. The door swung open, and the two stepped into a narrow, dark space. It was difficult to make anything out. Katsaris toggled his flashlight from infrared to optical light. Its powerful beam cut through the murk.

In silence, they listened.

The sound of breathing was audible somewhere in the gloom.

A narrow passageway broadened out, and they saw that the dungeon consisted of a row of impossibly thick iron bars set only four feet away from the stone walls. Every eight feet, a stone partition segmented the long row of cells. There were no windows, no illumination from the few kerosene lanterns that were set in the bulkheads.

The area behind the grate was shrouded in darkness. Katsaris swept his flashlight along the corner of the cages until they saw him.

A man. A man who did not look glad to see them.

He had flattened himself against the cell wall, trembling with fright. As the beam of light illuminated him, he dropped to the ground, crouching in the corner, hoping to make himself disappear.

'Peter Novak?' Janson asked softly.

The man buried his face in his arms.

Katsaris's flashlight settled on the cowering man, and Janson could make out the incongruously elegant broadcloth shirt, stiff not with a French launderer's starch but with grime and dried blood.

Janson spoke words he had once merely fantasised he would be able to say. 'Mr Novak, my name is Paul Janson. You saved my life once. I'm here to return the favour.'

For seconds, the man remained motionless. Then he raised his face; Katsaris quickly redirected the beam, so as not to dazzle him.

It was Janson who was dazzled.

A few feet from him was the countenance that had adorned countless magazines and newspapers. The thick shock of floppy hair, still more black than grey. The high, nearly Asiatic cheekbones. Peter Novak. A humanitarian like none the world had ever known.

The very familiarity of his visage made Novak's condition all the more shocking. The hollows beneath his eyes were dark; a once-resolute gaze was now filled with terror. As the man shakily brought himself to his feet, small tremors convulsed his body.

Janson was familiar with this look: it was the look of a man who had given up hope. He was familiar with this look because it had once been his. *Baaqlina*. A dusty town in Lebanon. It was destined to be his place of death—he had never been so convinced of anything. In the end, of course, he walked free after the Liberty Foundation intervened.

'We've come for you,' Janson told Novak as Katsaris matched a key from the ring to the grate of the cell. The grate swung open. 'We have to leave now.'

'No—there's someone else!' Peter Novak whispered. 'Another prisoner.' He gestured to the cell at the end of the passageway. 'An American. I won't leave without her.'

'That's impossible!' Katsaris interjected.

'If you leave her behind, they'll kill her at once!' The humanitarian's eyes were imploring, and then commanding. 'I cannot have that on my conscience.' His English was manicured, precise, with just a faint Hungarian inflection. 'It need not be on yours.'

Janson studied Novak's unwavering gaze. 'And if we can't . . .?'

'Then you'll have to leave me behind.'

Janson stared at him in disbelief.

A twitch played out on Novak's face, and then he spoke again. 'I doubt your rescue plans provide for an unwilling hostage.'

It was clear that his mind was still blazingly fast. He had played the tactical card immediately, impressing on Janson that no further discussion would be possible.

A minute later, Katsaris fiddled with the lock of another iron gate as Novak and Janson looked on. The gate opened with a groan.

The flashlight played off matted hair that had once been blonde.

'Please don't hurt me,' the woman whimpered, cowering in her cell.

'We're just going to take you home,' Theo said, angling the beam so that they could assess her physical condition.

It was Donna Hedderman, the anthropology student; Janson recognised her face from photos in newspaper articles.

'Who do you work for?' she asked in a quavering voice.

'We work for Mr Novak,' Janson said. A sidelong glance.

Novak nodded. 'Yes,' he said. 'They are our friends.'

Hedderman got to her feet and made her way towards the open gate. Oedema had swollen her ankles, making her stride unsteady.

Now Janson conferred quietly with Katsaris. 'Kerosene lanterns.' Janson gestured towards them. 'Before the place was electrified, it would have been the primary source of illumination. The blueprint has a tank positioned approximately two hundred metres in from the northwest retaining wall. It's obvious now what it was for.'

They led Peter Novak and Donna Hedderman along the dank subterranean corridor that led to the old kerosene tank. Hedderman held on to Janson's arm as she walked.

The tank, obviously long neglected, had an iron door with lead flanges to maintain a tight seal.

'The hinges are already rusting off,' Janson said. 'They just need help.' He made a run at the door, throwing up a foot as he reached it. The door gave way, collapsing in a cloud of dust and oxidised metal.

Janson coughed. 'Get out your Semtex,' he said.

The copper-lined chamber was still suffused with an oily smell.

Katsaris packed the ivory-coloured putty, about the size of a wad of bubble gum, around the rusting iron bunghole. Into it he pressed twin silvery wires, attached to a small, round lithium battery.

Janson primed his own wad of Semtex, then took a few moments to determine the optimal position of the second blast. So far, they had been protected by the isolation of the dungeon—the layers of stone insulating it from the rest of the north wing. Mayhem had occurred, but no sound would have been audible to those who were not its victims. There was no way to make a soundless exit, however.

Now Janson pressed his ounce of Semtex to the corner of the far wall where it met the curving top of the copper-lined tank, three feet above Katsaris's ounce.

Theo and Janson exited the tank. Once the two rejoined the hostages, around a bend in the corridor, they depressed in unison the radio frequency controllers that activated the batteries.

The explosion was deafening. The shock waves caused their eyes to vibrate. White smoke billowed inwards, bringing with it the familiar scent of plastique—and something else, too: the salty tang of the sea breeze. They had a route to the compound's exterior.

A portion of the stone wall had crumbled under the blast, and Theo's penlight confirmed what the moist sea breeze had promised. The opening was wide enough to enable them to clamber out.

Seconds later, the four of them were on the outside. The night sky was brighter than it had been; the cloud cover was beginning to break up. Stars were visible, and so was a patch of moon.

Janson stood against the limestone wall with the others. The area beneath the wall of the compound was safer, in certain respects, than the area further out. The seaside battlements, he saw, were filled with armed men, some manning heavy artillery. The further out they were, the more exposed they would be.

'Can you run?' Janson asked Novak.

'I'll do my damnedest,' the billionaire replied.

Janson put a hand on Donna Hedderman's arm and pointed to the rocky outcropping, fifty yards away, where the promontory dropped off in a sheer cliff. 'That's where we're going.'

Katsaris and Novak sprinted to the rocky outcropping; Janson, slowed by the wheezing American woman, followed.

'Find anchor!' Janson called to Katsaris.

Katsaris wrapped two loops of rope round a horn of rock, and secured them with an overhand knot. If one strand were cut—by friction against a sharp crag, or a stray bullet—the other would hold.

Janson trussed Novak into a climbing harness. This would not be a controlled rappel; the work would be done by the equipment not the man. A figure-eight descender would serve as the rappel brake. It was a piece of polished steel with two rings on either end of a centre stem, one big, the other small.

Katsaris passed a bight of the rappel rope through the big ring and looped it round the stem. He clipped the small ring onto Peter Novak's harness with a locking carabiner.

From a corner tower above the battlements, a guard aimed a long burst of gunfire in their direction.

They had been spotted.

Janson tossed the rope coil over the cliff.

'Now what?' asked Novak. 'I'm no rock climber.'

'Jump,' Katsaris urged. '*Now!*'

'You're *mad!*' Novak cried out, aghast.

Katsaris abruptly lifted the great man and, taking care not to lose his own footing, pitched him off the side of the cliff.

Janson heard the controlled slither of the rope as it fed through the figure-eight brake, confirming that the cord would bear Novak to the water-plashed rocks below at a regulated speed of descent.

As Theo made a double cord loop around another rock horn, another burst of gunfire kicked up a painful spray of rock.

'Rig yourself,' Janson ordered Katsaris. Meanwhile, Janson belayed the woman with what was to have been his own harness. A less-than-gentle push, and she was on her way down.

That left Janson with neither a harness nor a rappelling device. Facing the anchor Katsaris had rigged, he straddled the rope, looping it in an *S* round his upper body. Clasping the rope palm up, he could move it off his back to increase speed, and winch it round his hip to slow down.

Several buzz-saw-like bursts of gunfire pelted the cliff like a hailstorm of lead. The rock at their feet exploded, only inches away; fragments stung Janson's face.

Janson and Katsaris eased off the overhang. Bending at the waist, the two men kept their legs perpendicular to the sheer surface, 'walking down' where it was possible. For Janson, the descent was excruciating as the cord bit into his flesh. The only way to lessen the pressure was to increase the demands on his already aching muscles. He had to keep reminding himself that, at the base of the cliff, the other team members would be waiting for them, in the ultralightweight rigid inflatable boat that had been stowed on the BA609.

Just when his muscles had reached the point of total depletion,

Janson felt hands reaching up to grab him. As he took his seat in the flat-bottomed watercraft, he looked around. There were six of them. Novak. Hedderman. Katsaris. Andressen. Honwana. Hennessy would be piloting the BA609, taking second shift.

The motor whined as the rigid inflatable boat shot off from the rocks, hugging the shore for half a mile as it moved south, and then out into the mist-shrouded waters. The poor visibility would make it difficult to sight the RIB, and they had chosen a course that would take them out of the way of the rebels' fixed artillery.

'All accounted for,' Andressen said into his communicator, alerting Hennessy in the BA609. 'Plus one guest.'

A few bullets pocked the waters some distance from them. Only when they were half a mile out could they no longer hear the sounds of the rebel forces.

Peter Novak faced the direction in which they were travelling. From the set of his jaw, Janson could see that he was beginning to regain a sense of his identity, a sense of his selfhood.

The six in the RIB could hear the *whomp-whomp* of the rotors before they could see the craft. Now the aircraft came into view. It was resting on a flotational helipad of self-inflating black rubber. The downwash from the rotors caused the sea to bowl around it.

Dawn was breaking, into what was now an almost clear sky.

Hennessy opened his window. 'Mary, Mother of God, Janson. This extraction was for *one*. We can't take another hundred pounds of cargo without running out of fuel before we reach the landing zone. That's how fine the tolerances are.'

'I understand.'

'You should. It was your plan. So give me an alternative LZ.'

Janson shook his head. 'There's no place nearer that's safe.'

'And what does your plan call for now?' the Irishman demanded.

'I'll stay behind,' Janson said. 'There's enough fuel in the RIB to get me to Sri Lanka.' Hennessy looked incredulous, and Janson added, 'Using reduced speed, and taking advantage of the currents.'

'Sri Lanka's not safe. You said so yourself.'

'Not safe for Novak is what I said. I'll make do. I've prepared contingency plans, in case something like this came up.' He was only half bluffing. The plan he had specified would work, but it was not an eventuality he had foreseen.

'Mr Janson?' The Hungarian's voice was reedy and clear. 'You're a very brave man. You humble me, and I'm not easily humbled.'

41

ROBERT LUDLUM

He clasped Janson's upper arm. 'I won't forget this.'

Janson bowed his head.

Katsaris helped Novak and Donna Hedderman into the aircraft and then faced Janson. 'I stay. You go. You're needed. Mission control, yes? In case things go wrong.'

'Nothing can go wrong at this point,' Janson said.

'A hundred miles on the open sea in an inflatable boat—that's no joke,' Katsaris said stonily.

'My call, my screw-up, my foul. No member of my team takes a risk that should be mine.' It was a point of pride—of what passed for manhood or honour in the shadowy world of secret ops.

Katsaris swallowed hard, and did as he was instructed.

Janson downshifted the RIB's motor: fuel efficiency would be increased at a more moderate speed. Next he verified his direction with the compass on his watch face.

It would take him three or four hours to reach Sri Lanka. There, he had a contact who could put him on a lorry to Colombo Airport.

He watched the small turquoise aircraft rise into the air, and was filled with a sense of growing calm and relief.

And then—no!— he saw the flash, the fiery blast and plume of a midair explosion. A pulse of white bleached the early-morning sky, followed by a vast secondary flare, the yellow-white of combusted fuel. Small pieces of fuselage began to drift towards the sea.

For several long seconds, Janson felt perfectly numb. He closed his eyes and reopened them. Had he imagined it?

A detached propeller twirled lazily before it crashed into the sea. *Oh, dear God.*

An incredible triumph had turned into a nightmare.

CHAPTER FOUR

'THE PRIME DIRECTIVE here is secrecy,' the man from the Defense Intelligence Agency said to the others in the room. With his thick, dark eyebrows, broad shoulders and brawny forearms, he had the look of someone who worked with his hands; in fact, Douglas Albright was an intensely cerebral man, given to brooding and deliberation.

The venue for this hastily convened interdepartmental meeting was

42

a blandly handsome building just a mile from the White House.

Sitting opposite the DIA man, the deputy director of the National Security Agency had a high forehead and small, pinched features. 'Secrecy, yes—the nature of the directive is clear,' he said. 'The nature of our subject is not.'

'Paul Elie Janson,' said the State Department undersecretary, who was, on paper, the director of that department's Bureau of Intelligence and Research. A smooth-faced, athletic man with tousled, straw-coloured hair, he was lent gravitas by heavy black-framed glasses. 'Janson was one of ours, as you know.'

'One of your damn killing machines, Derek, that's what he is,' said Albright, glowering at the undersecretary. Despite Albright's high rank, he had spent a career in analysis, and had an ingrained mistrust of his counterparts in operations. 'You create these soulless pieces of machinery, loose them on the world, and then leave someone else to clean up the mess. I just don't understand what kind of game he's playing.'

The man from State flushed angrily. 'Have you considered the possibility that someone is running a game on *him?*' A hard stare: 'Jumping to conclusions could be dangerous. I'm not willing to stipulate that Janson is a renegade.'

'The point is, we can't be certain,' the NSA man, Sanford Hildreth, said. He turned to the man seated next to him, a computer scientist who had earned a reputation as a Wunderkind when he almost single-handedly redesigned the primary intelligence database for the CIA. 'Is there some data set we're overlooking, Kaz?'

Kazuo Onishi shook his head. 'I can tell you we've had anomalous activities, potential breaches of security firewalls. What I can't do is identify the perpetrator. Not yet, anyway.'

'Say you're correct, Derek,' Hildreth went on. 'Then my heart goes out to him. But nothing can compromise the programme. It doesn't matter what he thought he was doing. All we can say is that this fellow Janson doesn't know what he's blundered into. And he's never *going* to know.' The words were more declaration than observation.

'That much I'll accept,' the man from State said. 'Has Charlotte been briefed?' Charlotte Ainsley was the president's National Security Adviser and the principal White House liaison.

'Later today,' said the NSA man.

'It'll go easier if he doesn't struggle,' the DIA analyst said.

'But he will, if I know my man,' said Derek Collins. 'Mightily.'

'Then extreme measures are going to have to be taken,' Albright said. 'If the programme gets exposed, it destroys everything anybody here cares about. The past twenty years of history gets rolled back, and that's a best-case scenario. The likelier outcome looks a lot more like another world war.'

JANSON HAD TAKEN a direct flight from Bombay to Athens, arriving at Hellenikon International Airport. He felt a deadness within; he was a besuited zombie going about his business. *You were the guy with a slab of granite where your heart's supposed to be.* If only it were so.

He had called Márta Lang repeatedly, to no avail. The number she had given him would reach her wherever she was, she had told him: it would go directly to her desk, on her private line, and if she did not pick up after three rings, it would bounce to her cell number. And yet all it ever yielded was the electronic purr of an unanswered line. He had dialled various regional headquarters of the Liberty Foundation, in New York, Amsterdam, Bucharest. *Ms Lang is unavailable*, subalterns with talcum-smooth voices informed him. Janson was insistent. It was an emergency. It concerned Peter Novak himself. He had tried every approach and made no headway.

A message will be conveyed, he was told each time. But they could not convey the real message, the words of a dreadful truth. For what could Janson tell them? That Peter Novak was dead? Those he spoke to at the Foundation gave no indication that they were aware of it, and Janson knew better than to provide the information.

Had she been killed, too? Or was she herself part of a plot? Had Novak been killed by a member or members of his own organisation? Yet why kill a man who was under a death sentence?

Janson settled into the airport taxi that would bear him to the Mets neighbourhood of Athens. He had to tell Marina Katsaris what had happened, had to tell her face to face.

Katsaris's house was on a narrow street half a dozen blocks from the Olympic Stadium. Janson sent the driver on his way with 2,500 drachmas, and rang the doorbell.

The door opened, and there stood Marina. Janson took in her high cheekbones, honeyed complexion, steady brown eyes, her straight and silky black hair. The swelling of her belly was barely detectable, another voluptuous curve that was merely hinted at beneath her loose, raw-silk frock.

'Paul!' she exclaimed, delighted. The delight evaporated as she read his expression; the colour drained from her face. *'No,'* she breathed. She began to tremble visibly, her face contorted by grief, then rage.

He followed her inside, where she turned and struck him on the face. She did so again, lashing out in broad, flailing strokes, as if to beat back a truth that would destroy her world.

Finally, Janson grabbed her wrists. 'Marina,' he said, his own voice thick with grief. '*Please*, I don't have words to say how sorry I am.'

She stared at him. 'I blame myself. I let him *go*, didn't I? If I insisted, he would have stayed. But I didn't insist. Because even if he stayed home this time, there'd be another call, and another, and another. And not to go, not *ever* to go—that, too, would have killed him. Theo was great at what he did. I know that, Paul. It's what made him proudest of himself. How could I take that from him?'

A dam within her suddenly broke. Her sobs were animal-like, wild and unrestrained; over the next few minutes, they wracked her.

Janson wrapped his arms around her, holding her tight.

When she looked at him next, it was through a lens of tears. 'Tell me what happened,' she said.

He told her what had happened. He was the only one who knew just how Theo had died. Marina *needed* to know, and he would tell her. Yet, even as he spoke, he became aware of how much he didn't know. So many questions to which he had no answers. All he knew was that he would find those answers, or die trying.

'YOUR ROOM will be ready in five minutes,' the man at the front desk of the Hotel Spyrios told him carefully. 'Have a seat in the lobby and we'll be right with you.'

The five minutes, being metered out in Athenian time, were more like ten, but eventually Janson was given his key card, and made his way to his room. He inserted the narrow card in the slot, waited for the green diode to blink, and pushed the heavy door inwards.

The curtains were drawn, at an hour when they would normally have been left open. Only when his eyes adjusted to the light did he see the man who was seated in an upholstered chair.

Janson started, reaching for a gun he didn't have.

'It's been a long time between drinks, Paul,' the seated man said.

Janson recognised the man's silky, unctuous tones, the cultivated English with just a slight Greek accent. Nikos Andros.

He was flooded with memories, few of them fond. Andros belonged to another era in Janson's life, to a temporal compartment he had sealed off when he left Consular Operations.

'I don't care how you got in here—my only question to you is how you prefer to leave,' said Janson.

'Is that any way to talk to a friend?' Andros wore his dark hair severely short. His clothing was, as always, expensive, neatly pressed, fastidious: the black blazer was cashmere, the midnight-blue shirt was silk, his shoes a soft, burnished calfskin.

'A friend? We did *business* together, Nikos. But that's in the past.'

'I'm in the charity business today. I'm not here to sell information. I'm here to give you information. Absolutely gratis.'

Andros's connoisseurship and erudition in classical archaeology made him a sought-after guest in the drawing rooms of the rich and powerful throughout Europe. Janson knew that Andros's hard-won social prominence was crucial to his sub rosa career as an information broker during the Cold War. It was a time when Athens sector was a centre for networks run by the CIA and by the KGB alike.

'If you have something to say,' Janson said, 'say it and get out.'

Andros sighed. 'Your former employers want you to *come in*.'

Come in—report to headquarters, submit to interrogation, or whatever form of debriefing was deemed appropriate.

'If Cons Op wanted me to come in, they wouldn't give the message to a pampered sociopath like you.'

'In this case, the message belongs to the one who can locate its recipient. Thousands of carrier pigeons were sent out—this one happened to arrive. It seems that by the time your old colleagues got word you'd arrived in this country, they'd lost your scent. They needed me, with my network of connections. I put word out, I got word back. If I were you, I'd fret less about the singer and more about the song. You see, they're especially anxious about talking to you because they need you to *explain* certain matters.'

'What matters?'

'Questions have arisen concerning your recent activities.'

'There's something you're not saying,' Janson prodded.

'I've told you what I was instructed to tell you,' Andros replied.

'You've told me what you've told me. Now tell me what you haven't.'

Andros shrugged. 'I hear things.'

'What things?'

He shook his head. 'I don't work for you. No pay, no play.'

'You son of a bitch. Tell me what you know or—'

'Or what? What are you going to do—shoot me? Leave your hotel room stained with the blood of an American asset in good standing? That'll clear the air, all right.'

'I'd never shoot you, Nikos. But an agent of your new employers just might. After they learn about your connection to 17 Noemvri.'

His reference to Greece's 17 November group, terrorists long sought by American intelligence, provoked an immediate reaction.

'There's no such connection!' Andros snapped. 'That's slander.'

'Yes.' Something like a smile played around Janson's lips.

'Well.' Andros fidgeted. 'They wouldn't believe you, anyway.'

'Don't you think I can still play the system? I've spent years in counterintelligence—I know just how to plant information so that it can never be traced back to me and so that it gains credibility with each remove from its source.'

Andros clenched and unclenched his jaw for a few moments; a vein visibly throbbed on his forehead. 'The word is,' he said, 'they want to know why you have sixteen million dollars in your Cayman Islands account. The Bank of Mont Verde. Sixteen million dollars that was not there only a few days ago.'

'More of your lies!' Janson roared.

'No!' Andros pleaded, and the fear in his eyes was real enough. 'True or false, it's what they *believe*. And that is no lie.'

Janson took a few deep breaths. 'Get out of here,' he said.

Without another word, Andros rushed out of Janson's hotel.

Alone in his room, Janson found his thoughts tumbling. It made no sense. Andros was a professional liar, but this message—the implication that he had some secret fortune stowed away—was a falsehood of another order. More disturbing still was the reference to the Cayman Islands account; Janson did have such an account, but he had always kept its existence hidden. There was no official record of it—no evidence of it anywhere. What could explain a reference to an account that only he should have known about?

Janson turned on his tri-band wireless PDA and inserted the numbers that would give him an Internet connection to his bank in the Caymans. The signals would be two-way encoded, using a random string that would never be used again. No message interception would be possible. The process was slow, but within ten minutes, Janson had downloaded his latest account-activity records.

The account, when he last checked it, had contained $700,000.

Now it contained $16.7 million.

Yet how was that possible? The account was safeguarded against unauthorised deposits, as it was against unauthorised withdrawals.

Over the next thirty minutes, Janson combed through a series of transfers that involved his own unique digital signature, a nonreplicable set of numbers entrusted only to him—a digital 'private key' that even the bank had no access to. *It was impossible*. And yet the electronic record was irrefutable: Janson had himself authorised the receipt of $16 million. The money had arrived in two instalments of $8 million each. Eight million had arrived four days ago. Eight million had arrived yesterday, at 7.21pm Eastern Standard Time.

Approximately a quarter of an hour after Peter Novak's death.

JANSON SOUGHT OUT the cooler, clearer air of the National Gardens. He nodded at a white-haired man on a park bench who seemed to be looking in his direction. The man averted his gaze just a little too quickly, it seemed, given the affability of most Greeks.

Now Janson walked down Stadíou. What first caught his attention was not a familiar face but a face that turned too quickly when he approached. A man had been squinting at a street sign when Janson rounded the corner, then abruptly turned his gaze to a shop.

A block later, he noticed the woman across the street peering into the jewellery shop. The sun slanted fiercely at the plate glass, making it a better mirror than a window. If she were, in fact, trying to make out the display in the window, she would have had to stand at the opposite angle, with her back to the sun, creating a shadow through which the window would be restored to transparency.

Janson's field instincts began signalling. He was being watched.

He strode into the Omónia meat market. To his left, several stalls over: a customer, poking at one of the pork bellies—the same man who had averted his gaze in the National Gardens. Janson moved swiftly to the other side of a curtain of mutton. From between two carcasses, he saw the white-haired customer quickly lose interest in the pig. The man walked along the row of hanging sheep, straining for a view of the other side. Janson pulled back one of the larger specimens, grabbing its rear hoofs, and then, as the white-haired man was walking past, swung the carcass towards him, sending him sprawling into a quivering bed of calves' tripe.

Vociferous exclamations in Greek erupted, and Janson swiftly dodged the commotion, striking out towards the other end of the meat market and onto the street again. Now he made his way to a nearby department store, Lambropouli Bros.

He paused in front of the store, peering into the glass until he noticed a man in a yellow windcheater hovering near a leather-goods store opposite. Then Janson entered and headed towards the men's clothing area. He looked at suits, glancing at the small ceiling-mounted mirrors strategically placed to deter theft. Five minutes elapsed. Even if every entrance was guarded, no member of a sur-veillance team allows his subject to disappear for five minutes.

Sure enough, the man in the yellow windcheater made his way into Lambropouli Bros, crossing the aisles until he spotted Janson. Then he stationed himself near the glass-and-chrome fragrance display.

Janson took a suit and a shirt to the changing rooms, and waited. The store was short-staffed, and the salesman had more customers than he could deal with. He would not miss Janson.

But the watcher would. As the minutes ticked by, he would wonder if Janson had escaped. He would have no choice but to enter the changing rooms himself and investigate.

Three minutes later, the man in the yellow windcheater did precisely that. From the crack of the changing-room door, Janson saw him wander through the alcove with a pair of trousers draped over an arm. Just as he passed the door, Janson swung it open with explosive force. He sprang out and dragged the stunned watcher back to the end of the alcove and through a door that led to an employees-only area.

'One word and you die,' Janson told the dazed man softly, holding a small knife to his right carotid artery.

Even in the gloom of the storage facility, Janson could see the man's earpiece, a wire disappearing into his clothing. He tore open the man's shirt and removed the wire, which ran to a radio communicator in his trouser pocket. Then he took a second look at a plastic bracelet on the man's wrist; it was, in fact, a positional transponder, signalling his location to whoever was directing the team.

This was not an elaborate system; the whole surveillance effort had been hasty and ad hoc, with instrumentation to match. Indeed, the same went for the human capital deployed. He took the measure of the man before him: the weathered face, the soft hands. He knew the type—a marine who'd been on desk duty too long, summoned with little notice, an auxiliary reassigned to meet an unexpected need.

'Why were you following me?' Janson asked.

'I don't know,' the man said, wide-eyed. 'They didn't say why. The instructions were to watch, not interfere.'

'Who's *they*?'

'Like you don't know.'

'Security chief at the consulate,' Janson said, sizing up his prisoner. 'You're part of the marine detail.'

The man nodded.

'How many of you?'

'Just me.'

'Now you're pissing me off.' With stiffened fingers, Janson jabbed at the man's hypoglossal nerve, just inside the lower edge of his jaw. He knew the pain would be breathtaking, and he simultaneously clamped a hand over the man's mouth. 'How *many*?' he demanded. After a moment, he removed his hand, permitting the man to speak.

'Six,' the watcher gasped, rigid with pain and fear.

Tearing strips from the man's shirt, Janson bound his wrists and ankles, and fashioned a makeshift gag. He took the transponder bracelet, put on the man's yellow windcheater and grey cap and made his way out of the department store's side entrance at a trot.

The watcher had been approximately his height and build; from a distance, Janson would be indistinguishable from him.

What had Nikos Andros told them?

A small feral cat bounded down the sidewalk. Janson was nearing Athens's feline capital, the National Gardens. Now he raced to catch up with the animal. A few bystanders looked at him oddly.

'Greta!' he cried, scooping up the cat. 'You've lost your collar!'

He snapped the transponder round the animal's neck. It was a snug but not uncomfortable fit. As he approached the gardens, he freed the squirming animal, which bounded into the thickets, in search of field mice. Then Janson stepped into the park's rest rooms and shoved the cap and yellow windcheater in a waste canister.

Within minutes, he was on the number 1 trolley bus, no surveillance in evidence. The team members would soon be converging on the feline-infested centre of the gardens. If he knew the Athens sector, their real ingenuity would go into face-saving reports later.

Athens sector. He'd spent time there in the late Seventies. He racked his mind to remember someone he might know who could explain what was going on—explain it from the inside. Plenty of people owed him favours; it was time to collect.

The face came to him a moment before the name: a middle-aged desk jockey from the CIA who worked in the US embassy.

Nelson Agger—thin, balding, gangly—was an oddly likable soul. It was hard to explain why Janson got along with him so well. Part of it was because Agger was a cynic. But Janson had to admit that another reason was the simple fact that Agger liked and looked up to him. He never bothered to hide his admiration. Or his gratitude.

In years past, Janson had occasionally seen to it that Agger was the first person to receive a particular piece of intelligence. In a few instances, Agger was able to tailor his reports to make them seem prescient by the time the intelligence cables reached their channels.

Agger was precisely the sort of person who could help him.

Now Janson sat in the back of a café opposite the American embassy, sipping a mug of the strong, sweet coffee Athenians favoured, and phoned the station switchboard on his Ericsson.

'Trade protocols,' the voice answered.

'Agger, please.'

Three clicks could be heard; the call would be taped and logged.

'May I say who's calling?'

'Alexander,' Janson said. 'Richard Alexander.'

A few seconds. Then Agger's voice came on the line. 'It's been a long time since I've heard that name,' he said.

'Fancy a glass of retsina?' Deliberately casual. 'Can you get away now? There's the *tavernos* on Lakhitos . . .'

'I have a better idea,' Agger said. 'The café on Papadhima. Kaladza. You remember it. A little farther, but the food's excellent.'

Janson felt a stab of adrenaline. They both knew the food at Kaladza was terrible; it had been a subject of their conversation when they last spoke, four years ago. 'The worst in town,' Agger had said, taking a mouthful of doubtful calamari and looking green.

Agger was telling him they would have to take precautions.

'Sounds great,' Janson said heartily, for the sake of anyone else who was or would be listening. 'Take your cellphone. If I get held up, I'll let you know.'

'Good idea,' Agger said. '*Good* idea.'

From the café, Janson observed Agger leaving from a side door and making his way down the street towards Kaladza.

Then he saw, in Agger's wake, a woman and a man emerge from the grey-brick office building adjoining the embassy and set off in his direction. He was being tailed.

Whoever had been listening in on their phone conversation had recognised the legend name and responded immediately. Janson's relationship with Agger had doubtless been taken account of, the possibility of his making contact with the analyst anticipated.

Janson slipped a wad of drachmas beneath his coffee mug and set off. The Lykavittós was the tallest hill in Athens, and the high ground would make it hard for a surveillance team to take up position undetected—especially if he staked it out first. At the moment, he was armed with only a small pair of binoculars. Was he being paranoid to worry that this would not suffice?

Janson rode the railway up the hill. The summit was ringed with observation decks and cafés.

He telephoned Agger on his cellphone. 'Change of plans, old bean.'

'They say change is good,' Agger said.

Janson paused. Should he tell him about the tail? It would be best not to. Being aware of them might spook Agger. Better to give him an itinerary that gave him a shot at shaking his pursuers willy-nilly.

'Listen carefully, my friend. I want you to take this series of street trams.' Janson detailed a complex sequence of transfers.

'A pretty roundabout route,' Agger commented.

'Trust me on this,' Janson said. What would hold back a watcher wasn't the physical task of keeping up with him; it was the diminishing odds of doing so without being noticed.

'Right,' Agger said with the voice of someone who knew he was in over his head. 'Of course.'

'Now, when you finally get off the cable car to Lykavittós, we'll meet in front of the fountain of Elijah.'

'You'll have to give me, what, an hour?'

'See you then.'

Now Janson stationed himself within a dense copse of Aleppo pine and took an inventory of others in the area. On sweltering days, many Athenians sought refuge here from the heat and smog.

As five minutes stretched into ten and then fifteen, people came and went in a seemingly random procession. Yet not everything was random. Thirty yards to his left, a man in a caftanlike shirt was sketching the landscape; his hand moved in large, looping gestures. Janson focused his binoculars, zooming in on his strong, powerful hands. One hand loosely gripped a stick of charcoal and was filling the pad with random squiggles. Whatever he was interested in, it wasn't the landscape in front of him. Janson zoomed in on his face and felt a pang. This man was not like the Americans he had encountered earlier. The powerful neck straining at his collar, the dead eyes—this man was a professional killer, a gun for hire.

Diagonally opposite, another man was reading the newspaper. He was dressed like a businessman in a suit. Janson zoomed in: his lips were moving. Nor was he reading out loud, for when his eyes darted off, he continued speaking. He was communicating—the microphone could have been in his tie or lapel—to a confederate.

The two figures he'd identified, the businessman and the artist, were clearly Greek, not American; that was plain from their physiognomy, attire, even posture. Conclusion: an inexpert American tag team had been replaced with local talent, people who knew the terrain and could react quickly. But why the dragnet? The simple existence of incriminating evidence did not explain the willingness to accept its import. Janson had been an agent of one of America's most secret intelligence branches for twenty-five years. If he were after a big score, he could have arranged one long ago in a hundred different ways. Yet now, it seemed, the worst had been assumed of him, no alternative interpretation of the evidence entertained.

What had changed—something he'd done or was believed to have done? Was it something he knew? One of those things made him a threat to the planners in Washington.

At four o'clock, a worried-looking Agger came into view, his navy jacket flung over a shoulder, his blue shirt dappled with sweat. He sat down on the long marble bench by the fountain, breathing heavily, looking around for his old drinking companion.

Janson lowered himself to the ground and crawled through the untamed arbour, staying close to a long retaining wall made of piled shale. Two minutes later, he raised his head above the berm line, verifying that he was within a few feet of the man with the sketch pad.

That man was standing now. His back was to him, and Janson could see how powerfully built the young 'artist' was. The man's gaze was resolutely on Agger, on the marble bench before the fountain. Then Janson saw him reach for something under his caftanlike shirt.

Janson lifted a large piece of shale from the rock terrace, hoisted it above his head and flung it with all his strength, aiming for the back of the Greek's neck. The shale struck the man and he staggered to the ground. Janson stepped over the low wall and seized the man by his hair, clamping his forearm against his mouth. He flipped him over the wall and onto his back.

He yanked a Walther from the man's trouser band and ran his fingers along the man's collar, feeling for the microphone. He flipped over the fabric, exposing a blue-black plastic disk with a copper wire running out from it.

'Tell your friend it's an emergency!' he said, knowing that the task would not have been outsourced to people who did not speak English and might misunderstand orders.

'*Den omilo tin Aggliki*,' the man said.

Janson pushed his knee against the man's throat. 'Don't speak English? Then I guess there's no reason for me not to kill you.'

The man's eyes widened. 'No! *Please*, I do what you say.'

'And remember. I understand Greek.' A half-truth, anyway.

The Greek spoke into his microphone, the urgency made more intense as Janson gouged his Walther into his temple.

Once the message was relayed, he slammed the Greek assassin to the shale wall. The man's cranium absorbed most of the impact; he would be unconscious for an hour, probably two.

Through his binoculars, Janson saw the businessman stride towards the arbour. Something about the way he carried the folded newspaper made it clear it was serving to conceal something.

Quickly, Janson positioned himself at the end of the arbourway. As the man emerged, Janson swung the Walther into his face, shattering teeth and bone. Blood spewed from the man's mouth as he collapsed; the paper dropped and the silenced weapon it concealed clattered to the ground. Janson turned over the man's lapel, exposing a blue-black disk, identical to the one worn by the other Greek.

Janson returned the Walther to his waistband. An inner bleakness was creeping upon him. In the past few days, he had fallen back into everything he had once prayed he'd left behind him—the violence, the lethal subterfuge, a career's worth of ingrained habits. Still, this was no time to gaze into the abyss. He strode over to Agger.

'Paul,' Agger said. 'I'm so glad you called. I've been worried about you. You cannot believe the garbage they're talking about you.'

Janson laughed, mostly for Agger's sake. 'I guess I first got wind something was up this morning. I walk down Stadíou, and it's like a class reunion of the embassy security detail.'

'It's crazy,' Agger said. 'But they're saying that you took a job, Paul. A job you shouldn't have taken.'

'And?'

'Everybody wants to know who you did the job for. A lot of people want to know why you took it. Some people think there are sixteen million answers to that one.'

'How could anybody think that? I'm a known quantity.'

Agger's gaze was searching. 'You don't have to tell me that.'

Almost bashfully, he added, 'So . . . it's true you took the job?'

'Yes, I took the job—for Peter Novak. His people contacted me. I owed him one, big-time. Anyway, I was a referral. From State.'

'See, the thing is, State denies it. The Agency, too. It doesn't even know what went on in Anura. Reports are sketchy. But the word is you were paid to make sure Peter Novak never left the island.'

'That's insane.'

'Interesting you should use that word. We've been told that you may have gone insane, though the actual words are a lot fancier. Dissociative disorder. Post-traumatic abreaction . . .'

'Do I seem crazy to *you*, Agger?'

'Of course not,' Agger said quickly. An awkward pause followed. 'But look, we all know what you've been through. All those months of VC torture. I mean, that's got to mess with your head . . .'

A chill ran down Janson's spine. 'Nelson, what are you telling me?'

'Just that there are a lot of worried people, and they're way up the intelligence food chain.'

Did they think he was insane? If so, they couldn't afford to let him wander free, not with everything the former Cons Op agent had in his head—the extensive knowledge of procedures, informants, networks that remained in operation. A security breach could destroy years of work and would simply not be countenanced. Janson knew the chain of official reasoning in a case like that.

'I have no explanation for the money,' Janson said. 'Maybe the Liberty Foundation has an eccentric way of rendering payment. Compensation was referred to. Look, that wasn't a principal motivation on my part. It was a debt of honour. You know why.'

'Paul, my friend, I want to get all this straightened out, and I'll do whatever I can. But you've got to help me out, give me some facts. When did Novak's people make their first approach to you?'

'Monday. Forty-eight hours after Novak's abduction.'

'The first eight million was deposited *before* you say these people approached you. *Before* they knew you'd say yes. Before they knew an extraction might be necessary. It doesn't make sense.'

'Did anybody ask Novak's people about it?'

'Paul, they don't know who you are. They don't know about the abduction. They don't even know the boss is dead.'

'How did they react when you told them?'

'We didn't.'

'Why not?'

'Orders from the top. We're in the information-collecting business, not the information-dissemination business. And speaking of collection, that's why people are so determined that you come in. It's the only way. If you don't, assumptions are going to be made. And acted upon. OK? Do I have to say more?'

Janson couldn't fail to notice the way the analyst had grown less deferential in the course of the conversation. 'I'll think about it.'

'That means no,' Agger said blandly. 'And that's not good enough.' He reached over to his lapel, and fingered the buttonhole, in an overly casual gesture.

Janson reached over and turned up Agger's lapel. On the reverse side was the familiar blue-black disk. All at once, he felt numb.

The Greeks weren't tails. *They were his back-up*.

Standing so as to hide his actions from bystanders, Janson pulled out the Walther. 'What were the orders if I refused to report in?' He pressed the revolver hard against Agger's sternum.

'*Stop!*' Agger called out. 'You're hurting me.' He spoke loudly, as if panicked, but Agger, though scarcely a field agent, was no amateur, and however anxious he was not given to hysterics. The shout was not meant for him; it was meant to notify others, others within earshot.

'Sorry. I should have mentioned earlier, your Greek friends were unavoidably detained. They'll send their regrets. As soon as they regain consciousness.'

Agger's eyes narrowed. 'Christ, it's true. *You're out of control!*'

CHAPTER FIVE

A lorry swung off the M11 onto Queen's Road, Cambridge. There it pulled up beside several parked trucks bearing construction equipment for a major renovation project.

After the driver pulled in, the man he'd given a ride to stepped out onto the gravel. Instead of going to work, though, the man, who wore a taupe work suit, ducked inside one of the cabins near the building site. When he emerged, he was wearing a grey herringbone jacket of Harris tweed. It was a uniform of another sort, one that would render him inconspicuous as he strolled along the 'Backs', the swath of green that ran along the oldest of the Cambridge colleges.

Janson had spoken so many lies, in so many accents, over the past twenty-four hours that his head ached. But soon he would meet someone who could sweep all the mystification away. His lifeline would be at Trinity College: a brilliant don named Angus Fielding.

Janson had studied with him as a Marshall Fellow back in the early Seventies, and the gentle scholar had taken him on for a series of tutorials in economic history. Something about Fielding's sinuous mind had captivated Janson, and there was something about Janson, in turn, that the savant found engaging.

Janson hated to involve Fielding in his hazardous investigation, but there was no other choice. His old academic mentor, an expert in the global financial system, had been a member of a brains trust that Peter Novak had put together to guide the Liberty Foundation. He was also a member of the Tuesday Club, a group of intellectuals and analysts who had connections with British intelligence. And he was now the master of Trinity College.

Janson walked to the master's lodge and rang the bell.

A servant cracked open a window. 'Bit early, aren't you? Never mind, dear. Why don't you come round the front and I'll let you in?' Obviously, she had taken him for someone who had an appointment.

Inside the master's lodge, the broad stairs led past a portrait gallery of Trinity luminaries from centuries past. At the top was a large drawing room in which Janson found himself staring, rapt, at portraits of long-departed kings and counsellors. He started when he heard the sound of a man clearing his throat.

'My heavens, it *is* you!' Angus Fielding trumpeted. 'Forgive me— I've been looking at you looking at the portraits and *wondering* whether it was possible. Something about the shoulders, the gait. Dear boy, it's been far too long. But, really, this is the most *delightful* surprise. Gilly told me that my ten o'clock was here, so I was preparing to talk to one of my graduate students about Condorcet.'

Janson's old academic mentor was now in his late sixties. His face was etched with age, his white hair thinner than Janson had remembered; yet he was still lean and rangy, and his pale blue eyes retained the brightness of someone who was in on some nameless cosmic joke.

'Come along, dear boy,' Fielding said. He led Janson down a short hallway and into his spacious office, where shelves were filled with books and journals and offprints of his articles.

'Angus,' Janson began. 'I'm here to talk about Peter Novak.'

'You bring news from him?'

'About him,' Janson said. 'Angus, he's dead.'

The master of Trinity blanched, and took a seat on a harp-backed wooden chair in front of his desk. 'There have been false rumours of his demise in the past,' he said feebly.

Janson took the seat next to him. 'I saw him die.'

'It's not possible,' Angus Fielding murmured. 'It can't be.'

Janson told Fielding what had happened in Anura. Fielding listened, nodding gently, as if listening to a pupil during a tutorial.

Janson had once been one of those pupils. When he arrived at Trinity, Janson had been a physical wreck, sallow and skeletal, still trying to heal his emaciated body and devastated spirit from his eighteen-month ordeal as a POW, and all the brutalities that had preceded it. The year was 1974, and he was trying to pick up where he had left off, pursuing the study of economic history he had begun as an undergraduate at the University of Michigan.

Janson's assignment to Fielding was not accidental. Fielding had friends in Washington who had been impressed with the young man's unusual profile and capabilities; they had wanted the don to keep an eye out for him. Even now, Janson was hard put to say whether Fielding had recruited him to Consular Operations or whether he had merely gestured vaguely in that direction and allowed Janson to make the decision that felt right to him.

Now Fielding dabbed his eyes with a handkerchief. 'He was a great man, Paul. I've never known anybody like him. My God, the vision, the brilliance, the compassion—there was something extraordinary about Peter Novak. I always felt I was blessed to know him.'

'I owed him everything,' Janson said, remembering Baaqlina.

'As does the world,' Fielding said. 'That's why I said it cannot be. My reference was not to fact but to consequence. He must not die. Too much depends upon him. Too many delicate efforts towards peace and stability, all sponsored by him, guided by him, inspired by him. If he perishes, many will perish with him. Bad things will happen. *They* will have won.'

'Yet he has perished,' Janson said quietly.

For a while Fielding said nothing at all. Then he opened his light blue eyes wide. 'What's so odd is that none of this has been reported anywhere—neither his abduction nor his murder. So very odd. You have told me the facts, but not the explanation.'

'I guess I was hoping you'd be able to help me there,' Janson said. 'The question is, who would want Peter Novak dead?'

The don slowly shook his head. 'The question is, who *wouldn't*? Outsized benevolence always attracts outsized malevolence.'

'Walk me through this, OK? Just now you spoke of "they"—you said "they" will have won. What did you mean?'

'Do you know much about Novak's origins?'

'Very little. A child of war-torn Hungary.'

'His origins were at once extremely privileged and extremely *not*. He was one of the few survivors of a village that was liquidated in a battle between Hitler's soldiers and Stalin's. Novak's father was a Magyar nobleman who served in Miklós Kállay's government in the Forties before he defected, and it's said that he feared, obsessively, for the safety of his only child. He had made enemies who, he was convinced, would try to avenge themselves against his scion.'

'That's more than half a century ago. Who could possibly care, all these decades later, what his dad was up to in the Forties?'

'You obviously haven't spent much time in Hungary,' Fielding said. 'It's in Hungary, still, that you'll find his greatest admirers, and most impassioned foes. But you ask who would like to see him dead, and I must tell you it's a long list of malefactors. There's China: the old men of that gerontocracy fear, above all else, the "directed democracy" to which Novak's organisation has been dedicated. They know he considers China the next frontier of democratisation, and they are powerful enemies. In Eastern Europe, there's a whole cabal of moguls—former Communist officials who seized the plunder of "privatised" industries. The anticorruption campaigns spearheaded by the Liberty Foundation in their own back yards are their most direct threat, and they've sworn to take action. One cannot perform good deeds without a few people feeling threatened by them. You asked what I meant by "they", and that's as good a specification as any.'

'You were part of his brains trust,' said Janson. 'How did it work?'

Fielding shrugged. 'He'd solicit my opinions from time to time. Perhaps once a month, we'd talk on the phone. Perhaps once a year, we'd meet face to face.'

'The Foundation has raised the drawbridge as far as I'm concerned—I can't speak to anybody in a position to know. I need to reach those people who worked closely with Novak. Maybe someone who used to be in the inner circle and fell out of it. I can't rule it out that Novak was done in by a person or persons close to him.'

Fielding raised an eyebrow. 'You might direct that same curiosity towards those who are, or were, close to *you*.'

'What are you suggesting?'

'You were asking me about Peter Novak's enemies, and I said they were widely dispersed. Are you so confident about your own government? Is it even possible that your own former colleagues in Consular Operations have had some involvement here?'

Janson winced. The don's speculations had struck a nerve; the question, though seemingly far-fetched, had haunted him since Athens. 'But why?' he demanded.

'Peter Novak had become more powerful than many sovereign nations. Might an American strategist have deemed him too powerful, too much of a threat, simply as an independent actor on the stage of world politics?'

Fielding's speculations were all too cogent for comfort. Márta Lang had met with high-powered people in the State Department and elsewhere. They had urged her to employ Janson. Who were these officials? Consular Operations, presumably. And then the inculpating transfers to his Cayman Islands account; Janson had believed that his former employers remained ignorant of it, but he also knew that the American government could apply subtle pressure to offshore banking institutions when the activities of US citizens were at issue. Who would have been better placed to interfere with his financial records than high-level members of the American intelligence services? Janson had not forgotten the rancour and ill will that surrounded his departure. His knowledge of networks and procedures meant that he was, in principle, a potential threat.

Was it simply that a golden opportunity had presented itself to quick-thinking tacticians? Two birds with one stone: kill the meddlesome mogul, blame the noncompliant ex-agent?

Yet why not leave the Kagama extremists to carry out their plan?

There was the muted sound of an old-fashioned brass bell: somebody was at the rear door, which led to a waiting area outside.

Fielding stood up. 'Excuse me for a minute—I'll be right back.'

The flow chart branched out. In one branch, the United States does nothing, and Novak is killed. Yet there were risks in inaction— the risks of political embarrassment. Peter Novak was a widely loved man. If he were killed, ordinary people would wonder why the United States had refused to help a secular saint in his hour of need. The Liberty Foundation might denounce the US for refusing to provide assistance. It would be easy to imagine the ensuing deluge of congressional hearings, TV reports, newspaper editorials. What looked like the path of caution was in fact strewn with broken glass.

But what if there was *another* explanation?

The Liberty Foundation, typical of its go-it-alone ways, assembles its own international commando team in a reckless attempt to spirit away the captive. Who can they blame but themselves if things go badly? Midlevel employees at the State Department would 'leak' the word to the press: *Novak's people rejected our offers of help. They were afraid it would compromise his aura of independence.*

Fielding's minute stretched to three, and when he reappeared, closing the door behind him, there was something different about him.

'The aforementioned grad student,' Fielding assured him, in a slightly piping voice. 'Hopeless Hal, I think of him. Trying to unknot an argument in Condorcet. I can't get him to see that in Condorcet the knots themselves are what's interesting.'

Janson's spine prickled. Something in the master's demeanour had altered—his tone was brittle, as it had never been, and wasn't there a slight tremor in his hands? Janson saw that something had upset his old teacher, and profoundly.

The don made his way to a rostrum where a fat dictionary reposed. 'Just want to look up one thing,' he said. But Janson heard the stress beneath the pleasantries. Not the stress of bereavement or loss, but of another emotion. Alarm. Suspicion.

There was something else about his manner. What?

Angus Fielding was no longer making eye contact: that was it. Some people almost never did, but Fielding was not one of them. When he spoke to you, his eyes swept back to yours regularly. Almost involuntarily, Janson felt one of his own hands reaching behind him.

He stared, mesmerised, as Fielding, with his back to him, opened the tome, and—*it couldn't be.*

The master of Trinity College spun around to face Janson, brandishing a small pistol in a shaking hand. Just behind Fielding, Janson saw the hollowed-out section carved into the dictionary's pages, where the side arm had been secreted.

'Why have you really come here?' Fielding asked.

At last his eyes met Janson's, and what Janson saw in them took his breath away: murderous rage.

'Novak was a good man,' Fielding said in a tremulous voice. 'Possibly a great one. *I've just learned that you killed him.*'

The ageing don lowered his gaze momentarily and gasped. For Janson, too, was holding a gun in his hand—the gun he had, in a

61

fluid motion, grasped from his rear holster as his subconscious mind registered what his conscious mind had difficulty accepting.

Janson thumbed the safety up of his snub-nosed weapon. For a few seconds, the two men stood facing each other in silence.

Whoever Fielding's visitor had been, it was no graduate student in economic history. 'Why don't you put that antique in your hand aside?' Janson said. 'It doesn't suit you.'

The economist snorted. 'So you can kill me, too?'

'Oh, for Christ's sake, Angus!' Janson erupted. 'Use that magnificent brain of yours. All I wanted to learn was—'

'The location of Peter's colleagues—in order to hunt them too!' the professor said hotly. 'The "inner circle", as you referred to it.'

'You just met with someone—tell me who?' Janson's eyes darted back to the college master's weapon, a .22 Webley pistol, the smallest and most easily concealed of those in use by British intelligence agents during the early Sixties.

'So you can add another name to your bloodstained list?'

Janson looked intently at the ageing scholar's face; he saw a man who feared he was confronting a treacherous opponent. But he also saw a glimmering of doubt—saw a man who was not absolutely certain of his judgment. *Everything you know must be continually reassessed, critically reviewed. Abandoned if necessary.*

'I find it striking that your source persuaded you to direct a deadly weapon towards someone you have known for years.' Janson felt, and sounded, oddly calm. 'I don't know exactly what's going on, but I do know that somebody lied to you. And knowing that, I'm having a hard time staying mad at you.' He shook his head sadly. 'You want to squeeze that trigger? Then you'd better be surer than sure that you're doing the right thing. Are you, Angus? I don't believe you are.'

Without breaking eye contact, Janson extended his gun hand, unfurled his fingers and held out his hand, palm up, the weapon lying on it not as a threat but as an offering. 'If you're going to shoot me, use mine. That flintlock of yours is liable to backfire.'

The tremor in Fielding's hand grew.

'*Take it,*' Janson said in a tone of reprimand.

The master of Trinity was ashen, torn between the humanitarian he had come to revere and a former pupil to whom he had once been devoted. 'May God have mercy on your soul,' he said at last, lowering his side arm. The words were something between a benediction and a curse.

THE NATIONAL SECURITY Adviser was an immaculately attired, round-faced black woman with large, probing eyes. It was the first meeting Charlotte Ainsley had attended since the crisis began, but the deputy director of the NSA, Sanford Hildreth, had kept her up-to-date. 'Maybe we're missing something—let's review your man's records again,' she said to Derek Collins, undersecretary of state and the director of Consular Operations. 'Just the high points.'

'Paul Elie Janson,' Collins said. 'Grew up in Norfolk, Connecticut. His mother was an émigré from what was then Czechoslovakia. Alec Janson was an insurance executive. In 1969, Paul leaves U-Michigan and joins the navy. Turns out he's got this gift for tactics and combat, gets himself transferred to the Navy SEALs, the youngest person ever to have received SEAL training. Assigned to a counterintelligence division. We're talking about a learning curve like a rocket. Guy serves one tour after another, continuous combat exposure, no breaks. Then captured in the spring of 1971 by the Viet Cong. Held as a POW for eighteen months, in abysmal conditions.'

'Care to specify?' Charlotte Ainsley asked.

'Tortured. Starved. Kept part of the time in a cage—six feet high, maybe four feet round. When we found him, he weighed eighty-three pounds. He grew so skeletal that the manacles slid off his feet one day. Made about three escape attempts. The last one succeeded.'

'Was treatment like that typical?'

'No,' the undersecretary said. 'But trying so relentlessly and resourcefully to escape wasn't typical, either. They knew he was part of a counterintelligence division, so they tried pumping him pretty hard. He was lucky he survived.'

'Not lucky he got captured,' the National Security Adviser said.

'Well, that's where things get complicated, of course. Janson believed that he'd been set up. That the VC had been given information about him and he'd been deliberately led into an ambush.'

'Set up? By whom?' Ainsley's voice was sharp.

'His commanding officer. It seems Janson had threatened to report him to the high command. Crimes of war.'

'The warrior Wunderkind had a psychotic break?'

'No. Janson's suspicions were correct. And once he'd returned stateside, he made a stink about it—within channels, of course. He wanted to see his commanding officer court-martialled.'

'And was he?'

The undersecretary stared. 'You mean you really don't know?'

'Let's cut the drumroll. You've got something to say, say it.'

'You don't know who Janson's commanding officer was?'

She shook her head, her eyes intent, penetrating.

'A man named Alan Demarest,' the undersecretary replied. 'Or maybe I should say Lieutenant Commander Demarest.'

'"I see," said the blind man.' Her largely suppressed Southern accent broke through, as it did at times of stress.

'When next we see our man Janson, it's graduate studies at Cambridge University on a government fellowship. Winds up back on board, in Consular Operations.'

'Under you,' Charlotte Ainsley said.

'Yes. In a manner of speaking.' Collins's tone implied that Janson was not the most subordinate of subordinates.

'Granted, there's a great deal we don't know,' Charlotte Ainsley said. 'But it comes down to this: is he working for us or against us? Well, here's one thing we do know. He's not working for us.'

'This guy is a variable we can't control,' said the DIA's deputy director, Douglas Albright, resting his hamlike forearms on the table. 'Outcome optimisation means we've got to erase that variable.'

'A "variable" who happens to have given three decades of his life to his country,' Collins shot back. 'A funny thing about our business—the loftier the language, the lower the deed.'

'Come off it, Derek. Nobody's hands are dirtier than yours. Except your boy Janson. One of your goddamn killing machines.' The DIA man glared at the undersecretary. 'Needs a taste of his own medicine. My English plain enough?'

The undersecretary returned the analyst's unfriendly look. Still, it was clear enough which way the wind was blowing. He glanced at Clayton Ackerley, the man from the CIA's Directorate of Operations. 'Why don't you let your cowboys have another go?'

'Derek, you know the rules,' Ainsley said. 'Everybody cleans up his own litter box. I don't want another Athens. Nobody knows his methods like the cadre that trained him. Come on, your senior operations managers must already have filed a contingency plan.'

'Well, sure,' said Collins. 'Plans call for the dispatch of a special team of highly trained snipers.'

'Terminate orders in effect?'

'Current orders are locate, watch and wait.'

'Activate,' she said. 'This is a collective decision. Mr Janson is beyond salvage. Green-light the sanction. *Now*.'

ATTIRED IN A navy suit and a polka-dot tie, Janson strode down Pall Mall. He did not stop at his destination, however, but instead walked past it, his darting eyes alert to any signs of irregularity.

His mind kept returning to Trinity College: he must have stumbled on a trip wire there. It was more likely that his old mentor had been under surveillance than that he had been followed. Even so, both the size of the net and the rapidity of the response were formidable. He could no longer take anything for granted.

Still, his instincts told him that he could enter the Athenaeum Club unobserved. It was not a meeting place he himself would have selected. For his purposes, though, it would be helpful to meet Grigori Berman on his own terms. Besides, at an old-fashioned gentleman's club it would be difficult to station an unfamiliar face. Janson would be there as the guest of a member. He doubted whether members of a surveillance team could gain similar access.

Inside the club, he identified himself and the member he was awaiting to a uniformed guard. Then he proceeded to the foyer.

Grigori Berman was someone who, if he had developed a nodding acquaintance with morality, preferred to keep the relationship at arm's length. Trained as an accountant in the former Soviet Union, he had made his fortune working for the Russian *mafiya*, specialising in the complex architecture of money laundering. Several years earlier, Janson had deliberately let him slip through a dragnet that Consular Operations had run. Dozens of international criminals had been apprehended, but Janson let their financial whiz kid go free.

In fact, the decision represented reason, not whim. It meant that Berman would be in Janson's debt: the Russian could be converted from adversary to asset. And having someone who understood the intricacies of international money laundering represented a very significant asset indeed.

There was something else, too. Janson had come to know the principals of the scheme. Many were cold-blooded, thuggish figures. Berman, for his part, deliberately insulated himself from the details; he was cheerfully amoral, but he wasn't *unkind*. He was perfectly happy to cheat people out of their funds but could be quite generous with his own. And, somewhere along the line, Janson acquired a trace of sympathy for the high-living rogue.

'Paulie!' the bearlike man boomed, opening his arms wide.

Janson allowed himself to be enveloped in the Russian's embrace.

'I hug you and I kiss you,' Berman told Janson, pressing his lips to both his cheeks. The fabric of Berman's pinstripe bespoke suit was a feltlike cashmere, and he smelt faintly of extract of limes.

'You're looking . . . sleek and well fed, Grigori,' Janson said.

Grigori patted his generous midriff. 'Inside I'm wasting away. Come, we'll eat. Chop-chop.' He squired Janson to the dining room, with an arm round his shoulder.

Inside, waiters beamed and bobbed their heads as the ebullient Russian appeared, ushering him immediately to a table.

Settling into his cushioned seat, Berman summoned a wine steward with a glance. 'That Puligny-Montrachet we had yesterday? Could we have bottle of that, Freddy?' He turned to Paul. 'It's the greatest. You'll see.'

'I have to say I'm surprised to find you here, ensconced at the heart of the British establishment.'

'A rogue like me, you mean—how could they ever let me in?' Berman roared with laughter. 'It's a great story.'

'You'll have to tell me about it another time,' Janson said pointedly. 'I come to you with an interesting problem, Grigori. One that will, I think, intrigue you.'

The Russian looked at him, brightly expectant. 'Grigori is all ears.'

Janson sketched out what had happened: the $16 million that had been deposited in a Cayman Islands account without the account holder's knowledge, yet validated by electronic signatures that should have been accessible to him alone. A clever strike. Yet could it also be a *clue*? Was there a chance that, in the cascade of transfer digits, someone had left digital fingerprints?

As Janson spoke, Berman appeared to be wholly occupied by his food, but Janson could see his mind whirring.

Finally the moneyman put down his fork. 'You know, last week I was in Canary Wharf Tower, visiting Russian friend, Ludmilla. And we're forty floors up and I'm looking out window, bee-yoo-tiful view of this city, and suddenly guess what I see floating through air.'

'A bank note?'

'Butterfly.' Berman said it with grand finality. 'Why butterfly? What butterfly *doing* forty storeys high, middle of city? No flowers forty storeys high. Nothing for butterfly to do, up here in sky. All the same: butterfly.' He raised a finger for emphasis.

'Thank you, Grigori. I knew I could count on you to make everything clear.'

'Must always look for butterfly. In the middle of nothing, thing that does not belong. In cascade of digital transfer codes, you ask: is there butterfly? Yes. Always butterfly. So. You must know how to look.'

'I see,' Janson replied. 'And will you help me look?'

'All right. I bring you to my 'umble abode, *da?* Have fancy IBM machine there. RS/6000 supercomputer. And we look for butterfly.'

'We *find* butterfly,' Janson said.

CHAPTER SIX

Berthwick House—what the Russian had described as his humble abode—was in fact a Georgian mansion abutting Regent's Park.

Berman took Janson downstairs, to a carpeted basement room that contained several computer workstations. A butler, dressed in a black four-button long coat and a stiff pique shirt, arrived with tea and scones, arrayed on Bristol delft plates. He laid them out on a small corner table, along with small ceramic pots filled with clotted cream and jam. Then he glided off.

Glancing longingly at the scones, Berman sat down at a keyboard and activated a series of firewall-penetration programs. He turned to Janson. 'Tell Grigori what you get me into.'

Janson disclosed the essential elements of his predicament. Grigori listened, then typed the values of an algebraic matrix into the program he was running.

'We let these programs run, then maybe get results in time.'

'How much time?'

'Run machine twenty-four hours, coordinate with global parallel-processing network of computers, then maybe . . .' Berman looked off. 'Eight months? No, I think nine months. Like make baby.'

'You're kidding.'

'You want Grigori to do what others can't do? Must supply Grigori with *numbers* others don't have. You have public-key sequence to account, *da?* We use this, we have special advantage. Otherwise, back to making baby—nine months.'

Reluctantly, Janson supplied him with the public-key sequence for his bank account. Ten seconds after he typed in the sequence, Berman's screen filled with jumbled digits, scrolling down his monitor like the closing credits of a film.

'Numbers meaningless,' he said. 'Now we must do pattern recognition. Look for butterfly.'

'*Find* butterfly,' Janson stressed.

'Pah!' Berman said. But for the next five minutes, he studied sequences of confirmation codes with an intensity that shut out everything else. At last, he read a series of digits out loud. 'Butterfly *here*—5467-001-0087. That is butterfly.'

'The numbers mean nothing to me.'

'Same numbers mean everything to me,' said Berman. 'Numbers say beautiful blonde women and filthy canals and brown café where you smoke hashish.'

'You're saying you're looking at a transfer code from Amsterdam.'

'*Da!* Amsterdam transfer code cycles through too many times to be accident. Your fairy godmother uses an Amsterdam bank.'

'Can you tell which one?'

'Impossible to get specific account unless . . . *Nyet*, impossible.'

'Unless what?'

'Private key?' Berman cringed as if he expected to be slapped for saying those words. Moving funds in or out of the account required a private key, an authorising sequence of digits known only to the account holder; the key would not appear in any transmission. This ultrasecure digital pathway protected both the customer and the bank.

Janson was silent for a while. To provide Berman with the private key would present him with a tremendous temptation: he could siphon off its contents with a few keystrokes. Yet at what cost? Berman loved his life here; he knew that to make an enemy of Janson would jeopardise everything he had, and was. No threats were necessary to underscore the risks.

Janson recited the fifteen-digit string and watched Berman type the sequence. Within moments, the Russian had established connections to dozens of financial institutions, burrowing from within the Bank of Mont Verde mainframe to retrieve the digital signatures that uniquely identified the counterparty to every transaction.

Several minutes elapsed, the silence disturbed only by the soft clicking of keys. Then Berman stood up. '*Da!*' he said. 'ING. Which stands for International Netherlands Group Bank.'

'If you can identify the bank, can't you narrow it even further?'

'Very difficult,' said Grigori, biting into a scone.

'"Difficult" doesn't mean impossible. Or is there somebody else you'd recommend for the job?'

His host looked injured. 'Nothing impossible for Grigori.' With a hangdog expression, he padded back to the workstation.

Fifteen minutes later, Berman, sweating with concentration, suddenly looked up and turned round. 'Is great joke,' he said, smiling.

'How do you mean?' Janson demanded.

'I traced the originating account. Very difficult. Required non-reusable back-door codes. Reversed asymmetric algorithm. Data-mining software go on hunt for pattern, search out signal buried in noise. Very difficult . . .'

'Grigori, my friend, I don't need the *War and Peace* version.'

Berman shrugged, slightly miffed. 'Powerful computer program does digital equivalent of triathlon, Olympic level, no East German steroids to help, but still identified originating account.'

Janson's pulse began to race. 'You *are* a wizard.'

'And all a great joke,' Berman repeated.

'What are you saying?'

Berman's smile grew wider. 'Man who pay you to kill Peter Novak? Is Peter Novak.'

'How the hell can you know such a thing?'

'Account in name of Peter Novak.'

'You're telling me that at a time when Peter Novak was locked away in a dungeon in Anura, he authorised a transfer of sixteen million dollars into a blind account I controlled?'

'Could be preauthorisation.'

'Could somebody else have laid their hands on the Novak account, got control of it somehow?'

The Russian shrugged. 'Origination code just tell me ownership of account. Could be many specifications as to access. This I cannot tell you from here. This information not flow from modem to modem. Legal certification held by institution of origination. Bank in Amsterdam follows instructions established by owner. Account suffix says it's linked to Foundation.'

What now seemed irrefutable was that whoever had betrayed Novak was in a position to have earned his trust. But to what end?

'You come with me,' Berman said. 'I show you house.' He put an arm round Janson's shoulder and propelled him up the stairs, through the magnificent hall, and into the kitchen.

Berman stepped towards the glittering stainless-steel sink, where the casement windows looked onto a beautiful rose garden. Beyond it stretched Regent's Park. 'Twenty-four hundred acres in the middle of

London, like my back yard.' He pulled out the sink spray nozzle and held it to his mouth like microphone. 'Someone left the scones out in the rain,' he sang in a thick Russian basso. 'I don't think that I can take it . . .' He pulled Janson closer, trying to form a duet. He raised an expressive hand high in the air, like an opera singer on the stage.

There was a tinkle of glass, and Berman broke off with a sharp expulsion of breath. A moment later, he slumped to the floor.

A small red hole was just visible on the front of his hand. On the upper left quadrant of his shirt front was another puncture wound, just slightly rimmed with red.

'Jesus Christ!' Janson shouted. He looked out of the window. Outside, there was no sign of disturbance whatever.

He heard the approaching footsteps of the butler, roused by his exclamation. The butler pulled Berman's body out of range of the window, sliding it along the floor. He, too, scanned the view from the window, holding a pistol in one hand as he did so. He had seen what Janson had seen; an exchange of glances revealed his bafflement. Just a few seconds elapsed before the two retreated to the hallway, safely away from the window. From the floor, Berman made rasping, wet noises, as breath forced its way through his injured airway, and his fingers began to scrabble at his chest wound.

The fingers of his intact right hand trembled with exertion, as the Russian probed his wound with remarkable single-mindedness. He was fishing for the bullet. Gasping for breath, he yanked a crumpled mass of brass and lead from his chest.

'Look,' Janson said to the butler. 'I know this has to be a shock to you, but I'm going to need you to stay calm, Mr . . .'

'Thwaite. And I've had fifteen years in the SAS. This isn't a perimeter breach; we both know we're looking at something else.'

'SAS, huh?'

'Mr Berman may be crazy, but he's not a fool. A man like that's got enemies. We've prepared for the usual exigencies. But that shot came out of the clear blue. I can't explain it.'

Janson's mind filled with elliptic curves and right angles. He connected the point of penetration of Berman's upstretched arm to the upper-left-quadrant chest wound. An elevation of approximately thirty-five degrees from the horizontal. Yet there was nothing visible in the vicinity at that angle.

Ergo the bullet had not been fired from the immediate vicinity.

The mass that Berman had pulled out was confirmation. It had to have been a long-distance shot, towards the end of its trajectory. Had it been fired within a hundred yards, it would have penetrated Berman's body and punched an exit wound. But penetration had been only two inches. Janson estimated that the distance traversed would have been around 1,200 yards, or two-thirds of a mile.

His mind filled with the skyline of the area, the Palladian roofs of Hanover Terrace, the round dome of the Central London Mosque . . . and the minaret, the tower with the small balcony, used by the muezzin to summon the faithful to prayer. It was probably unguarded; a professional would have had no problem gaining entry. If Janson's calculations were correct, one had.

But how many men were capable of such a shot? A couple of Russians. The Norwegian who came first in a worldwide competition last year. A couple of Israelis. A handful of Americans.

And who was the target?

He recalled Berman's arm round his shoulder, drawing him close. The bullet that hit the Russian was fifteen inches from Janson's head.

Fifteen inches. An uncontrollable variance at two-thirds of a mile. The sensible assumption was that Janson was the target. He was the only new element in the situation.

He could hear the siren of the ambulance Thwaite had summoned. And now he felt a tug on his trouser leg—Berman.

'Janson,' he said, speaking as if through a mouthful of water. 'Get son of whore who did this. *Da?*'

'*Da,*' Janson said huskily.

THWAITE TOOK JANSON aside and spoke to him in a low voice. 'Whoever you are, Mr Berman must have trusted you, or he wouldn't have invited you here. But I've got to ask you to make tracks.'

Janson raced out through a rear exit. A few minutes later, he had vaulted over the wrought-iron fence into Regent's Park, and was jogging towards the boating lake. As he approached a great willow tree, the thick trunk suddenly revealed a rude patch of white. A soft, tapping noise: lead hitting puckered bark.

A shot that had missed him, again, by a matter of inches.

He craned his neck round as he ran, but could see nothing. The only sound he had heard was that of the projectile slamming into the tree: there was no sound of the detonation within a rifle chamber. Sound-suppression gear was possibly in use. But even with a silenced rifle, a supersonic round produced a noise as it emerged from the

71

muzzle—not necessarily a conspicuous one, but a noise all the same, like the crack of a whip. The fact that he had not heard it suggested that it was another long-distance shot. Conclusion: an extremely skilled marksman was in pursuit. Or a *team* of them.

Where were they? The shot came from the southwest, where he could see nothing but, a few hundred yards away, a stand of oaks.

Standing on a stone path nearby, a stocky woman in a denim skirt was handing a pair of binoculars to her little girl.

'See the one with the blue on its wing? That means it's a bluetit.'

There was a safety factor just now: a breeze was passing through, ruffling the leaves of the trees. A distance shooter would be vigilant about evidence of irregular wind, knowing how much it could disturb the shot's trajectory. If they had any choice, and they did, the snipers would wait until it subsided.

Janson approached the woman and girl. Though conscious of his lethal halo, he had to trust to the professional self-regard of the marksmen: snipers of that order prided themselves on their precision; hitting bystanders would look like unacceptable amateurism. And the breeze was still gusting.

'Excuse me, madam,' he said to the woman. 'But I wonder if I might borrow your binoculars.' He winked at the little girl.

'*No*, Mummy!' the girl cried. 'They're mine, mine, *mine!*'

'Don't cry, my poppet,' the mother said. She turned to Janson. 'Can't you see you've upset her? Please leave us alone.'

'Would it matter if I said it was a matter of life and death?' Janson flashed what he hoped was a winning smile.

'My *gawd*,' the mother said, 'you Yanks, you think you own the bloody *world*. Take no for an answer, would you?'

Too many seconds had elapsed. The breeze had subsided. Janson dropped to the ground, adopting a sitting position by the crying girl. 'Hey,' he said to her. 'It's going to be all right.' He gently took her binoculars, and quickly set off.

'What the *hell* do you think you're doing?' the mother bellowed.

Janson dashed towards the bandstand, 200 yards away.

Thwack. A bullet struck the wood of the bandstand and Janson rolled on the ground until he was under it.

Now he looked through the binoculars at the trees. Oak, beech, chestnut, ash. Which was the tallest, and the densest? A rough eyeballing of the arboreal clusters suggested a couple of candidates. Now Janson focused the binoculars and scrutinised just those trees.

Leaves. Twigs. Branches. And—

Movement. The hairs on his neck rose.

A breeze was scurrying through the trees: of course there was movement. Yet the branch that moved was too thick to have been affected by the passing gust. It moved—why?

Because it was not a branch at all. The reason that the branch seemed unnaturally straight was that it was a rifle. The twigs were attached with furred twist-wires. The tiny area of darkness at the end was not a tar-healed tree wound, but the rifle's bore hole.

I'm coming for you, Janson thought to himself.

A team of soccer players were making their way along the side of the boating lake towards the playing fields, and he joined them, knowing that, from a distance, he would be hard to pick out among the crowd. The lake thinned into a stream, and, as the men crossed the wooden bridge, he rolled off into the water.

He expelled all the air from his lungs and swam through the murky water, staying near the bottom. If his misdirection succeeded, the sniper scopes would still be trained on the crowd of athletes. High-powered scopes inevitably had a narrow field of vision; it would be impossible to keep an eye on the rest of the terrain and follow the crowd. But how much longer before they realised he was not in it?

He crossed the water to the south bank, pulled himself up the concrete basin wall, and dashed over to a copse of beech trees.

He sprinted towards one tree, waited, then rushed towards another.

If his instincts were correct, he was directly below the tree where at least one of the snipers had positioned himself.

Marksmanship was an activity of intense concentration. It required shutting out peripheral stimuli. Tunnel vision was a matter not merely of the narrowness of field through the scope but of the intensity of mental focus. Now he had to take advantage of that tunnel vision. The snipers would have radiophones to keep them in touch with their coordinator. These would further reduce their sensitivity to ambient sounds.

He heaved himself up the trunk, as quietly as he could. When he reached ten feet, he saw that the entire apron of branches on which the sniper reposed was fake. It was incredibly lifelike, but up close he could see it was an artificial construction attached to the trunk by means of metal rigging, an arrangement of steel-wire rope, rings, and bolts, all spray-painted an olive drab.

He reached for the rigging and, with a yank, released the central eyebolt. The steel cable slithered free, and the sniper's nest was suddenly unanchored.

He heard a muffled curse, and the whole nest dropped through the tree, breaking branches as it tumbled to the ground.

Finally, Janson could make out the green-clad body of the sniper beneath him. He was a slender young man, momentarily stunned by the fall. Janson lowered himself and stood over him.

Now he wrenched the rifle, a modified M40A1, from the marksman's hands.

'Damn!' the curse was light in timbre, the voice of a youth.

Janson reached down and knotted the sniper's collar around his neck, ripping off the radio communicator. Janson noticed his short, spiky brown hair, his slender legs and arms: not a formidable specimen of manhood at first glance. He started to pat the sniper down, removing a Beretta from his waistband.

'Get your stinking hands off me,' the sniper hissed, rolling over.

'Christ,' Janson said, involuntarily. 'You're—'

'What?' A defiant glare.

Janson just shook his head. The sniper reared up and Janson responded with force, shoving the sniper back down to the ground.

The sniper was lithe, agile, surprisingly strong—and a woman.

She lunged at him again, trying to retrieve her rifle. Janson stepped back and pulled back the slide lock with his thumb.

'You're overmatched, Janson,' she said. 'No embassy lardasses this time. This time they cared enough to send the best.' Her voice had the twang of the Appalachian backcountry.

He smiled. 'Now, here's a proposition. You deal, or I kill you.'

She snorted. 'Think you're lookin' at number forty-seven? In your dreams, old man.'

'What are you talking about?'

'You've done forty-six people, right? I'm talking sanctioned, infield killings.'

Janson's face went cold. The number—never a source of pride and increasingly a source of anguish—was accurate. But it was also a count that few people knew.

'First things first,' Janson said. 'Who are you?'

'What do you think?' the sniper replied.

'No games.' Janson pressed the muzzle of her M40A1 hard into her diaphragm.

She coughed. 'Same as you—same as you *were*.'

'Cons Op,' Janson ventured.

'You got it.'

'Then you're a member of its Sniper Lambda Team.'

The woman nodded. 'And Lambda always gets its man.'

She was telling the truth. And it meant one thing: a beyond-salvage order had gone out. Consular Operations had sent a directive to an elite squad of specialists: a directive to kill.

'OK, sport,' Janson said. 'I need to know the location of the others. And don't bullshit me.' He stripped the M40A1 of its magazine, then levelled the Beretta at her head.

She glared at him for a few long moments. He returned her look with complete impassivity: he would kill her, without compunction. Only luck had prevented her from killing him.

'There's one other guy,' she started.

With his gun hand, Janson cuffed her hard on the side of the head.

'Let's not begin this relationship with lies, sweetheart,' he said. 'I admire your discretion. But if you're no use to me alive, I really can't afford to keep you around.' He cocked the Beretta, his forefinger curling around the trigger.

'OK, OK,' she blurted. 'I'll deal.'

'My game, my rules. You give me the location of the nearest sniper. We approach. If you're wrong, you die. If you give me away, you die. Remember, I know the systems, the protocols and the procedures. I probably wrote half of them.'

She stood up shakily. 'All right, man. Take my range finder. You don't trust me, you can see for yourself. Marksman B is three hundred yards northwest.' It was a low brick structure that housed telecom equipment. 'He's on top. There are men on foot on Baker Street, Gloucester Place and York Terrace Way. Strollers with Glocks. Two sharpshooters have a complete review of Regent's Canal. And there's a man on the roof of Regent's College.'

Keeping the gun securely in one hand, Janson looked through her range-finder scope. The concrete bunker she'd mentioned was the sort of structure that dotted the urban landscape, that people saw without seeing. A good position. He dialled up the magnification until he saw—something. A glove? Part of a boot? Impossible to say.

'You're coming with me.' Janson grabbed the sniper's wrist.

'I get it,' she said. 'It's just like at the Hamas encampment in Syria, near Qael-Gita. You took one of the sentries hostage, forced him to divulge the location of another one, repeated the process, had the perimeter defences peeled off in less than twenty minutes.'

'Who the hell have you been talking to?' Janson said. Those details were not widely known, even within the organisation.

'Oh, you'd be surprised the things I know about you,' she said.

He strode down the greenway, dragging her along with him.

They approached the concrete bunker, and Janson placed a finger on his lips. The Beretta remained loosely gripped in his hand.

He stooped, signalling her to do the same. Atop the low brick structure, the marksman was, he could now see, in prone position.

'Victor!' the woman called out suddenly.

The gunman swivelled his rifle round and squeezed off a shot, wildly. Janson leapt to one side. Then he somersaulted towards the bunker and jerked the gun out of the marksman's grasp. As the man reached for his side arm, Janson swung the rifle, connecting with the man's head. He slumped forward, unconscious.

The woman propelled herself towards Janson, seized his jacket and hammered her knee towards his groin. As he torqued his pelvis back defensively, she flexed her wrist into a slap block, and sent the Beretta flying through the air.

Both took a few steps back.

The woman assumed the classic military stance: her left arm was out and perpendicular to her body, a barrier to a rush. Her right arm was extended straight down, and held a small knife; it had been boot-holstered, and he had not even seen her draw it. She was good, faster and more agile than he was.

The fact that she was well trained was her weakness. He knew what she would do because he knew what she had been taught. He had taught enough people those very manoeuvres.

Suddenly, he fell forward, grabbing her extended arm; she raised her knife hand, as he had predicted, and he delivered a crushing blow to its wrist. The median nerve was vulnerable about an inch from the heel of her hand; his precisely directed blow caused her knife hand to open involuntarily. He grabbed the weapon she had released and swept his foot towards her right knee, destabilising her footing. She toppled backwards, but his own leg sweep wrongfooted him, and he ended up falling on top of her.

He could feel the heat of her body beneath him, feel her muscles tense as she squirmed and thrashed. With his thighs, he pinned her legs down. He hammered his elbows outwards and pinned her arms to the ground, relying on his greater weight and brute strength.

He saw the muscles of her neck flex, saw she intended to break his nose by butting with her forehead, and pressed his forehead to her own, immobilising it. Her breath was warm against his face.

'You really want to kill me, don't you,' Janson said.

'Shit, no,' she said with heavy sarcasm. 'This is just foreplay as far as I'm concerned.' Struggling mightily, she thrashed beneath him, and he only barely maintained his position.

'So what did they tell you? About me?'

'You're somebody who murdered for money,' she said.

'Bullshit.'

'Bullshit's what you are. Double-crossed everything and everybody you could. Sold out the agency, sold out your country.'

'That right?' he said. 'A sharp cookie like you—you belicve everything they tell you?' He grunted. 'No shame in it. I did once.'

Her eyes narrowed to slits. 'You got another story? I'm listening. Can't *do* anything else.'

'I was set up. I served in Consular Operations for over two decades. Look, you seem to know a lot about me. Ask yourself if what they've told you really fits the picture.' He inhaled deeply, his chest expanding next to hers. He felt her relax beneath him.

'OK,' she said. 'Get offa me. I ain't gonna rear, ain't gonna run—I know you'd get to the rifle first.'

He made sure her body was completely slack and then rolled off her in a quick movement. He had a destination in mind: the Beretta. He grabbed it and stowed it in his waistband.

Looking wobbly and uncertain, the woman rose to her feet. 'Why? Why would they set you up?'

'You think I haven't been asking myself that?'

'You were a legend in Cons Op. You've no idea, Janson. No idea how demoralising it was when they told us you'd turned traitor. They'd never do that on a whim. If somebody's scapegoating you, they've got to have a good reason.'

'What they *believe* is a good reason. A good reason that might strike others as an administrative convenience.'

She looked confused. 'OK, take a peek through the range finder again. Marksman C you'll find in the really tall tree near North Gate.'

He lifted the scope to his eyes. As he parsed the foliage, a crushing blow landed on the side of his head. He reeled back, stunned.

It was the woman. A ridged steel rod in her hand, the kind used in reinforced concrete. One end was wet with his blood. She had wrenched it from the stack of construction materials behind the bunker a few feet away.

Sprawled on the ground, he could hear the blood pounding in his head, like a steam engine. Groggily, he reached for the Beretta, but it was too late. She was racing away from him at top speed.

The impact of the steel rod had caused a mild concussion at the least; it would take him a few minutes to struggle back to his feet.

He felt a wave of nausea welling from his gut. He glanced at his watch, tried to rise, and blacked out.

HE FORCED his eyes open, looked at his watch again. Two minutes had elapsed. The retention of consciousness would be a supreme effort, yet one at which he must not fail.

The collapse of the sniper formation must already have been detected, simply by the absence of radio signals. Others would proceed into the area. Vision swimming, head ringing with pulsing, pounding agony, he crashed through an obstacle course of cone-shaped yews until he had made his way to Hanover Gate.

A black cab was letting out an elderly couple as he staggered to the kerb. He waited for them to pay then slid inside the vehicle.

'Where you bound, guv?' the driver asked. Then he looked at Janson through the rearview mirror and winced. 'Got yourself a nasty gash there. You better not get any claret on my upholstery.'

Janson pushed a fifty-pound note through the glass partition. 'Just floor it,' he said, hunching down in his seat.

CHAPTER SEVEN

'No, don't bring them in,' the lieutenant commander had told Janson. 'I'll come out there.' Faintly, even in the weather-befouled headphones, he could hear choral music. 'Tell you what, take them to Candle Bog.'

Candle Bog was what the Americans had named a clearing with a couple of huts in the jungle four clicks north of their camp.

Demarest was waiting for them when they arrived. He was in a Jeep, with his executive officer, Tom Bewick, behind the wheel. He turned to his XO. 'Tom,' he said. 'Could you . . . do the honours?'

Bewick's tawny face looked as if it were carved of wood, with crude gashes for eyes and mouth. His movements were swift and efficient, but jerky rather than fluid. It added to Janson's sense that Bewick had become a mannequin of Demarest's.

Bewick strode over to the two prisoners, withdrew a knife and sawed through the restraints that kept their arms to their sides. He fashioned a sling of cord, knotted it round the prisoners' wrists and ankles, then snaked it round the central beams of each hut. They were splayed, spread-eagled, their limbs extended by the rope.

Demarest approached the prisoner nearest him. 'Do you speak English? It doesn't matter if you do, because I speak Vietnamese.'

The first one spoke, at last. 'Yes.' His voice was tight.

Demarest rewarded him with a smile. 'You're farmers, right?'

'We farm.'

'You're not VC at all, are you? Just honest fishermen, right?'

'*Déng.*' Right.

'Or did you say you were farmers?'

The two looked confused. 'No VC,' the first man said.

'You people have suffered a lot, haven't you?'

'Much suffering.'

'Like our saviour, Jesus Christ. Do you know that he died for our sins? Do you want to know *how* he died? Let me tell you. No, better idea: let me show you.' Demarest turned to Bewick. 'Bewick, it's downright uncivil to leave these poor young men on the ground.'

Bewick grinned. Then, rotating a wooden stick twice, he winched the rope tighter. The tension of the rope lifted the prisoners off the ground; the weight of their bodies was supported by their wrists and ankles. Each emitted a loud, panicked gasp.

They were in agony, their limbs hyperextended, their arms straining at their sockets. Their position made breathing difficult, and exertion only increased the torque on their extremities.

Janson flushed. 'Sir,' he said sharply. 'You're torturing them.'

'You think that's torture?' Demarest shook his head disgustedly. 'Lieutenant Bewick, Lieutenant Janson is upset. For his own protection, I need you to restrain him.'

Bewick levelled his combat pistol at Janson's head.

Demarest walked over to the Jeep and pressed the PLAY button on his portable tape cassette. Choral music spilled from tinny speakers. 'Hildegard von Bingen,' he said. 'Spent most of her life in a convent, in the twelfth century. She became the greatest composer of her age.

Each time she sat down to create, it was always after she had suffered the most excruciating pain—what she called the scourge of God. For only when the pain brought her to the point of hallucination did her work pour from her—the antiphons and plainsongs.' He pulled a small knife from a waist holster and made a small slice in the second prisoner's belly. The skin and the fascia beneath immediately sheared, pulled apart by the tension of the ropes. 'Pain will make you sing, too.'

The man screamed.

'Now, *that's* torture,' Demarest called to Janson. He returned to the screaming man beneath him. 'Do you think you'll be a hero to your people by resisting me? Not a chance. You see, I am a very bad man. You think Americans are soft. You think you can wait us out. But you think these things because you've never come across Alan Demarest. Of all Satan's tricks, the greatest was persuading man he did not exist. Look into my eyes, my fisherman friend, because I exist. A fisherman like you. A fisherman of men's souls.'

Alan Demarest was mad. No: worse than that, he was all too sane, too in control of his actions and their controllable consequences. At the same time, he was wholly devoid of conscience.

'Look into my eyes,' Demarest intoned, and leaned closer to the man's face, which was already stretched in agony. 'Who's your ARVN contact? Which South Vietnamese do you deal with?'

'I farm!' the man whimpered. 'No Viet Cong!'

Demarest pulled down the man's pyjama trousers, exposing his genitals. 'Prevarication will be punished,' he said in a bored tone. 'Time for the jumper cables.'

Janson heaved a few times and a hot flow of vomit surged up the back of his throat and splattered on the ground before him.

'Nothing to be ashamed of, my son. It's like surgery,' Demarest said, soothingly. 'The first time you see it done, it's a little rocky. But you'll get the hang of it in no time. We'll give him every chance to talk. And if he doesn't, he'll die the most painful death we can contrive.' Demarest looked at Janson's stricken face. 'But don't worry,' he continued. 'His companion will be kept alive. You see, it's important to leave somebody to spread the news among the VC: this is what you get when you fuck with Americans.'

And, horrifyingly, he winked at Janson, as if to invite him to join the debauchery. An old refrain echoed in the dim recesses of Janson's mind. *Where are you going? Crazy—want to come along?*

Want to come along?

PRINSENGRACHT, perhaps the most gracious of the canal streets of Amsterdam, was built in the early seventeenth century. The street-front façades had, at first glance, the regularity of accordion-folded paper dolls, but when one looked more closely, one saw all the ways each house had been painstakingly differentiated from its neighbours.

Janson strode down the street, attired in a light jacket and sturdy brogues, like so many of his fellow pedestrians. He kept his hands in his pockets, and his eyes regularly scanned his surroundings.

A few blocks along, he encountered a cluster of houseboats on the canal. He scrutinised each in turn. Finally, he saw the familiar blue-painted cabin with an abandoned look. The flowerpots were mainly empty; the windows were small and sooty. Many years had passed since he had last been there. Had it changed hands? As Janson approached, he detected the distinctive scent of cannabis, and knew it had not. He stepped on board and then walked through the door of the cabin; as he expected, it was unlocked.

In one corner of the sun-dappled space, a man with long, dirty-grey hair was crouched over a large square of vellum. He had pastels in both hands, which veered towards the paper in alternation. A smouldering marijuana cigarette lay next to a red pastel.

'Freeze,' Janson said softly.

Barry Cooper turned round slowly, giggling at some private joke. When he identified his visitor, he sobered up a little: 'Hey, we're cool, right? You and me, we're cool, right?'

'Yeah, Barry, we're cool.'

His relief was visible. He held his arms open wide. 'Show me some love, baby. How long has it been? *Jeepers.*'

'Too long,' Janson said. 'Or not long enough. What do you think?' The history they shared was complex; neither man fully understood the other, but both understood enough for a working relationship.

'I can make you some coffee,' Cooper said.

'Fine.' Janson sat down on a lumpy brown sofa and looked around.

Little had changed. It was the same old Barry Cooper, a little scary and somewhat crazy, but mostly neither. In his youth, the ratios had been different. In the early Seventies, he had drifted from college radicalism to the real thing and, by incremental steps, ended up a member of the Weather Underground. Small pranks, designed to nettle law enforcement, led to more extreme acts.

One day, in New York, he found himself in a Greenwich Village house when a bomb one of the members was concocting went off prematurely. He had been taking a shower and, singed and sooty, walked around in a daze for a while before he was arrested. When out on bail, he fled the country, ending up in Europe.

Exaggerated reports about him circulated by American law enforcement were swallowed whole by the radical groups of Europe's revolutionary left. They welcomed him into their circles, asking him for advice. Barry Cooper was pleased by the adulation, but while he knew a great deal about varieties of marijuana he had little interest in the practical affairs of revolution. When he was among the revolutionaries, he kept this to himself, hiding behind gnomic responses. His lack of interest in their activities rattled them: clearly the American terrorist didn't take them seriously as revolutionaries. They responded by revealing to him their most ambitious plans, trying to impress him by disclosing the extent of their human and material assets.

As time passed, Barry Cooper grew uncomfortable, and not simply with the masquerade; he had no stomach for the acts of violence they vividly described.

Janson paid him a visit. In the attempt to gain entrée to the shadowy world of these terrorist organisations, Janson searched for people whose fealty to civilisation had not completely eroded—people who were not yet dead to so-called bourgeois morality. Barry Cooper's association with those organisations always struck him as odd. He knew Cooper's file, and what he saw was someone who was essentially a clown rather than a killer.

Cooper was already living in Amsterdam, in the same houseboat, making a living selling sketches of the old town to tourists. The two men did not bond right away: it was hard to imagine two souls less alike. Still, Cooper finally appreciated that his visitor from the US government tried neither to ingratiate himself nor to make threats. He played it straight. Rather than jeering at his politics, Janson was happy to concede that there was much to criticise in the Western democracies—but then rejected the dehumanising simplifications of the terrorists in hard-hitting language: *Our society betrays humanity whenever it doesn't live up to its own expressed ideals. And the world your friends wish to create? It betrays humanity whenever it does live up to its expressed ideals.* Was the choice so hard?

That's deep, Barry Cooper had said, sincerely. And his information proved to be the undoing of dozens of violent cells.

In return, the State Department quietly desisted in its attempts to seek extradition.

Now Janson sipped hot coffee from a mug that still bore smudges of acrylic paint.

'I know you're here just to hang,' Cooper said. 'I know you don't, like, *want* something from me.'

'Hey,' Janson said. 'OK if I crash here for a while?'

'*Mi casa es su casa, amigo,*' Cooper replied.

Janson surveyed the balled-up papers on the floor near the pastels. 'Got a newspaper?'

Cooper padded over to the corner and triumphantly returned with a copy of the latest *De Volksrant*.

Janson scanned the headlines, getting the gist of most. He turned the page, and a small article caught his eye. 'Here,' he said, tapping it with a forefinger. 'Could you translate this one for me?'

'No sweat, man.' Cooper began to read the article, laboriously translating the Dutch into English for Janson's benefit. It was not, on the face of it, a remarkable story. The Czech foreign minister was visiting Amsterdam. He would be meeting leading figures of its financial community, to discuss Dutch–Czech cooperative ventures. An inconsequential trip. But it might solve a problem for Janson.

'Let's go shopping,' Janson said, standing up.

Cooper was not taken aback by the sudden change of topic; his cannabis haze made the world as aleatory as a roll of the dice. 'Cool,' he said. 'Munchies?'

'Clothes shopping. Fancy stuff. Top of the line.'

A SMALL MOTORCADE of three black Mercedes-Benzes made its stately way down Stadhouderskade and onto Leidsestraat, stopping at the Liberty Foundation headquarters. A uniformed driver of the stretch limo walked round to the rear and held open the door. A dark-suited man with horn-rimmed glasses and a felt-brimmed hat came out. Then the uniformed man—the minister's personal factotum, it appeared—pressed the buzzer beside the deeply carved front door. Ten seconds later, the door was opened.

The uniformed man spoke to the woman at the door. 'Madame, the foreign minister of the Czech Republic, Jan Kubelik.'

The foreign minister spoke a few words of Czech to his factotum and made a gesture of dismissal. The uniformed man turned and stepped back towards the limousine.

'You almost look as if you were not expecting me,' the man in the elegant navy suit told the red-haired receptionist.

Her eyes widened. 'Of *course* not, Minister Kubelik. We are most pleased by your arrival.'

A small panic had swept through the Foundation's support staff when they received the phone call, thirty minutes earlier, telling them that the recently appointed foreign minister would be keeping his appointment with the executive director. A series of flustered underlings compared notes, for the appointment had gone unrecorded. One of the secretaries maintained that the error was probably on the side of the Czech bureaucrats. Yet it would be impossible, a hopeless breach of protocol, to tell them so.

Now the receptionist led the minister to a fancy antechamber. 'Our executive director will be with you shortly,' she said.

'You're very kind,' the Czech diplomat said, removing his hat. 'This is a beautiful property. Do you mind if I look around?'

'Sir, we would be honoured,' she replied as if by rote.

SO FAR, SO GOOD, Janson thought to himself. Cooper had cleaned up remarkably well, and, once attired in that silly uniform, conducted himself in a manner that did not quite slide into parody. His movements were stiff and official, his expressions imbued with a servile pomposity, every inch the dedicated assistant of a very important official. Janson himself was relying on the assumption that nobody would have any idea what the Czech foreign minister looked like. The man had been in the job for a mere two weeks, after all.

No disguise was the best disguise: a bit of grease in his hair, a pair of spectacles in a style fashionable in Eastern Europe, the sort of suiting common to diplomats all over the Continent . . . and a manner that was by turns amiable and imperious. The fact that Janson's mother was Czech was helpful, of course, though chiefly in imbuing his English with a persuasive Czech accent. A Czech diplomat would be expected to speak English in a country like Holland.

Janson peered at the receptionist over his round horn-rimmed glasses. 'And Peter Novak? He is here as well?'

The woman smiled dreamily. 'Oh no, sir. He spends most of his time on the road. Sometimes we don't see him for weeks.'

When Janson had arrived, he did not know whether a pall of grief would be hanging over the Foundation. But clearly they still had no idea that anything had befallen their revered founder.

'But his wife is in today, sir. Susanna Novak. She helps run the NGO development programme.'

Janson nodded. 'And what's over here?' He pointed towards another room, to the left of the main hallways.

'Peter Novak's office,' she said. 'Where you would surely be meeting Mr Novak if he were in town—he'd insist on it.' She opened the door and pointed to the portrait of a nobleman on the wall opposite. 'That painting is by Van Dyck. Remarkable, don't you think?'

Janson strode towards the canvas. 'Extraordinary,' he said. 'One of my favourite artists, you know.' He reached into his pocket and, fingering the buttons of his cellphone, dialled a preprogrammed number. This number went to the receptionist's direct line.

'Would you excuse me,' she said, hearing her phone ring.

'Certainly,' Janson said. As she hastened to her telephone, he scanned the papers that lay neatly stacked on Novak's desk. One item of correspondence caused a memory to clang distantly, hazily. Not the brief, innocuous message, but the letterhead. UNITECH LTD. The company name meant something to him—but did it mean something to Paul Janson, corporate security consultant, or Paul Janson, quondam Consular Operations agent? He wasn't sure.

'Minister Kubelik?' A woman's voice.

'Yes?' Janson looked up to see a tall blonde woman smiling at him.

'I'm Peter Novak's wife. I'd like to welcome you here on his behalf. Our executive director is still in a meeting. He won't be long.' She spoke with a neutral American accent.

The woman's frosted, wet-looking lipstick seemed less than businesslike, but it suited her, as did the chartreuse suit that hugged her contours a little more snugly than was strictly necessary.

This was not a woman in mourning. She could not have known. She did not know. Yet how could that be?

Janson strode up to her and bowed slightly. Would a Czech diplomat kiss her hand? He decided that a handshake would suffice. But he could not take his eyes off her. Something about her was familiar. Hauntingly so. The blue-green eyes, those long, elegant fingers . . .

Had he seen her before? He racked his brain. Where?

Her gaze was almost playful—verging on the flirtatious.

'Come,' she said. 'I'll take you upstairs to the conference room.'

The conference room faced the canal, and the sun slanted through a multipaned picture window, casting golden parallelograms on the polished teak table. As Janson entered, he was greeted by a man of less than average height with neatly combed grey hair.

'I'm Dr Tilsen,' the man said. 'My title is executive director for

Europe. A bit misleading, no?' He laughed a tidy, dry laugh. 'Our Europe *programme* would be more accurate.'

'You'll be safe with Dr Tilsen,' Susanna Novak said. 'A lot safer with him than with me,' she added.

Janson sat down opposite the administrator. What to discuss?

'I expect you know why I wanted to contact you,' he began.

'Well, I think so,' Dr Tilsen said. 'Over the years, the Czech government has been very supportive of some of our efforts, and less so of others. We understand that our objectives will not always mesh with those of any particular government.'

'Quite so,' Janson said. 'Quite so. But I have begun to wonder whether my predecessors have been too hasty in their judgments. Perhaps a more harmonious relationship might be possible.'

'That would be most pleasing to contemplate,' Dr Tilsen said.

'Of course, if you provide me with a *tour d'horizon* of your projects in our country, I would be able to make the case more effectively with my colleagues and associates. Really, I'm here to listen.'

For the next thirty minutes, Tilsen described a battery of initiatives and programmes and projects. Janson's eyes began to glaze.

A knock at the door. The redhead from downstairs.

'I'm sorry, Dr Tilsen. A call from the prime minister's office.'

'Ah,' Dr Tilsen said. 'You will kindly excuse me.'

'But of course,' said Janson. Left to himself, he walked over to the window and looked at the busy canal below. A feeling of cold ran down his spine, as if it had been stroked with a shard of ice. Why? Something in his field of vision—an anomaly he responded to instinctively before he could rationally analyse or describe it.

What?

Behind the gable of the house opposite, was that the shadow of a man crouched upon the tiles? Or was it his overheated imagination? The bruise on the side of his head throbbed painfully.

Then one of the small panes exploded, and he heard the harsh splitting of wood as a bullet buried itself in the parquet. He sank to the floor, and began to roll towards the door as another pane exploded.

Gunshots without shots: they had come from a silenced rifle.

Then a loud gun blast came from outdoors, an odd counterpoint to the silenced firing. Other sounds ensued: the screeching of tyres, a car door opening and closing. And from inside the mansion, screams.

The throbbing of his temple had grown so forceful that it required a conscious exertion simply to focus his eyes.

Think! He had to think! What made sense of the assault, the contrast in weaponry and approach?

Two teams were attacking. Two teams that were not coordinated.

Mrs Novak must have reported him. She had been onto him the whole time, playing along. She was one of Them.

He phoned Barry on his Ericsson.

Cooper was uncharacteristically flustered. '*Jeepers*, Paul! What the hell's going on? It's like the Battle of Midway out here.'

'Can you make visual on anyone?'

'Um, you mean, can I see 'em? A glimpse, once in a while. There's a couple of them in military drab. They look mean. The arms-are-for-hugging message hasn't reached these guys, Paul.'

'Listen, Barry, we specified that the limo have bulletproof windows. You'll be safest there. But be ready to haul ass at my signal.'

Janson bolted for the door and raced down the stairs to the ground floor. When he reached the hallway, he saw the security guard unholster his weapon and approach the front window. Then the gun clattered to the floor and the guard toppled.

Janson crawled over and retrieved the man's gun, a Glock, then dragged the body towards the foyer, knowing he would be shielded by the brick wall beneath the window. He draped his jacket on the man and jammed his hat on the corpse's head.

He could have Cooper pull up in the armoured limo, but just the few feet of exposure could prove deadly.

Janson heaved the corpse upwards in a vaulting movement across the main front room, and studied the reaction.

An unsilenced blast shattered what remained of the window, followed by a cluster of spits, shots that were sound-suppressed but no less deadly. How many guns were trained on this house? At least five.

An all-out assault on Peter Novak's headquarters was in progress. Had he brought this about by his presence? It strained belief, but then little made sense any longer.

All he was certain of was that he had to get out of the house and that he could not use the doors. He charged up four flights of stairs, then clambered up a ladder that led to the loft. A moment later, he arrived stumbling on the roof. It was steeper than he expected, and he clung to the nearby chimney. He scanned the adjoining rooftops.

Perched on a higher rooftop, diagonally opposite to his right, he could make out the deadly brunette from Regent's Park. There she had narrowly missed him from an enormous distance. Now she was a hundred feet away. She could not fail to hit her target.

He turned his head and saw, to his dismay, that there was another rifleman on the adjoining roof, just thirty feet to his left.

The rifleman was now swivelling his weapon towards him.

Alerted by the drab-suited rifleman, the deadly brunette raised her scope to roof level. His bruised temple flared once again, with almost incapacitating pain.

He saw the woman squinting through her scope, saw the utter blackness of the rifle's bore hole. It was a shot she could not miss. He forced himself to focus on the countenance of his executioner: he would look death in the face.

What he saw was a play of confusion on her face as she swivelled her rifle a few degrees to the left and squeezed off a shot.

The rifleman on the next roof over tumbled off the roof.

What the hell was going on?

The noisy chatter of a nearby automatic weapon immediately followed—aimed not at him but at *her*. A piece of the ornate cornice behind which she was stationed broke off.

He tried to puzzle out the complex geometry. Two teams, as he supposed. One using American-issue sniper equipment, the sniper team from Consular Operations. And the other? An odd assortment of weaponry. Irregulars. Hirelings. To judge from the fabric and hardware, Eastern Europeans. In whose employ?

The enemy of my enemy is my friend. Was it true?

The man with the automatic, a Russian-made AKS-74, stood above the parapet, trying to get a better angle on the woman sniper.

'Hey,' Janson called out to him.

The man—Janson was near enough to see his coarse features, close-set eyes, and two days' growth of beard—grinned at Janson, and turned towards him. With his gun set at full fire.

As a blast hit the roof, Janson dived into a roll, hurtling down the tiled incline. Finally, his body slammed against the balustrade.

What had just happened? The woman had him within her sights. *She had him.* Why hadn't she taken the shot?

And the other team—who were they? He was their target. But so was the team from Consular Operations. How could that be?

There was no time. He poked his pistol between the ornamental sandstone balusters and squeezed off two quick shots. The man with the AKS-74 staggered back. As he slumped to the tiles, his weapon fell with him, secured by the nylon sling round his shoulders.

Janson stood atop the balustrade and leapt to the adjoining house. He crawled over to the dead man and wrested the submachine gun from its nylon sling. He also found a small device with two angled mirrors attached to a telescoping rod that resembled the antenna of a transistor radio. It was standard equipment for an urban commando. Janson adjusted the mirrors and pulled out the rod. By extending it over the cornice, he would be able to see what threats he confronted without putting himself in the line of fire.

What he saw was far from encouraging. The deadly brunette was still in position.

A bullet *thwack*ed into the chimney. Janson rotated the periscope-like device to see who was responsible. One roof over, standing with an M40 braced against his shoulder, was a former colleague of his from Cons Op, an old-school specialist named Stephen Holmes.

Janson snaked up the incline of the slate roof. He kept his head down as his hands lifted the muzzle of the AKS-74 over the roof line. He relied on memory as he directed a burst of fire towards the long barrel of the rifle. A clang told him he had succeeded.

Now he raised his head over the roof line and directed a second, more targeted burst: the steel-tipped bullets tore into the barrel of Holmes's M40 until the green-black shaft shattered.

Holmes was now defenceless, and when his eyes met Janson's it was with the resigned, almost weary look of someone convinced he was about to die.

Janson shook his head disgustedly. Holmes was not his enemy, even if he thought he was. He craned round and, peering through a hole in the pediment, was able to glimpse the brunette.

A moment later, Janson saw a flicker of movement behind her, and then an attic door burst open and a giant of a man loomed over her. He smashed the butt of his firearm over her head. The woman slumped limply to the parapet, unconscious. Now the giant squeezed off three shots to his right. The strangled cry from the adjoining roof told him that at least one had hit Stephen Holmes.

Janson sprayed a long fusillade towards the hulk—it would force him into a defensive crouch, at least momentarily—then, using various stone ornaments as handholds, he clambered down the side of the mansion, safely out of range. He hit the paved surface of the shadowed alley with as little noise as he could and, positioning himself behind two trash cans, studied the street scene in front of him.

The giant was astonishingly fast. Already he was charging out through the front door of the building, dragging the unconscious brunette with him like a sack.

A second man, attired in similar drab, raced over, and Janson heard them talking. The language was unfamiliar—but not entirely so. Straining, he could make out that it was Serbo-Croat.

A small, powerful sedan roared up to them and, after another brief, barked exchange, the two men leapt into the back seat, dragging the woman with them. Police sirens screamed in the distance.

Janson staggered to the side street where Barry Cooper, sweating and wide-eyed, remained in the driver's seat of the armoured limo.

For a moment Janson was silent. Concentrating intensely, he returned to the words he had heard. *Korte Prinsengracht . . . Centraal Station . . . Westerdok . . . Oosterdok . . .*

'Get me to Centraal Station,' Janson said. 'Pedal to the metal.'

Cooper set off, the wheels squealing against the slick macadam.

Separating Korte Prinsengracht from the Westerdok, where largely abandoned warehouses stood, was the man-made island on which the Centraal Station was built. But that was not where the giant and his friends were headed. They would be heading towards the vast maintenance buildings to the south of the station, which were sheltered from casual observation. At night, heroin addicts went there to shoot up; during the day, however, it was abandoned.

'Keep going, *straight!*' Janson yelled.

'I thought you said Centraal Station . . .'

'There's a maintenance building to the right, five hundred yards away. Overlooking the wharves of Oosterdok. Now *floor* it.'

The limo powered past the train station and bounded down the rough road of the derelict yards where, years ago, the business of the wharves had been conducted. Most of the commercial harbours had relocated to North Amsterdam; what remained were phantoms of brick and concrete and corrugated steel.

A gated Cyclone fence suddenly loomed before them. Cooper stopped the car and Janson got out. He heard a distant scream.

He opened the gate, waved Cooper through and gestured for him to park the car about a hundred yards away.

Janson himself raced to the side of a huge steel shed and, flattening himself against it, edged swiftly towards the scream he had heard.

Finally, he could see through the dim light into the vast interior. The woman from Cons Op was roped to a pillar with a thick hawser, her clothes crudely torn off her. The giant loomed over her. He belted her with his hand, and her head snapped back against the concrete.

'Don't you touch me, you son of a bitch! she yelled.

The giant laughed. 'What are you going to do about it?'

'I wouldn't get Ratko mad if I were you,' said his companion, who held a long thin blade. 'He prefers 'em alive—but he's not particular.'

Janson strode towards them, only to find the raking fire of an AKS-74 pocking the concrete floor. It had to be directed from a cat-walk above, and it created an impassable zone between Janson and Ratko, who had turned to face him. A .45 handgun looked small in the Serb giant's enormous hand.

Now Janson ducked behind a concrete pillar.

Light briefly flooded the dim warehouse as somebody opened a side door. Another burst came from the AKS-74, directed not at Janson but at the unseen arrival.

'Oh shit! Oh *shit!*' It was Barry Cooper's voice.

'Barry, what the hell are you doing here?' Janson called.

'I got scared in the car. Pretty dumb, huh?''

Another fusillade brought up sparks from the concrete floor.

Janson stepped back from the pillar and saw what was happening. Barry Cooper was huddled behind a large steel drum while the man on the catwalk began to reposition himself.

'I don't know what to *do*,' Cooper said in a half-wail.

'Barry, do what *I'd* do.'

'Gotcha.'

A shot rang out, and the man on the catwalk abruptly stiffened.

'That's *right*, baby. Make love, not war,' Cooper yelled as he emp-tied the entire clip of his pistol into the gunman overhead.

Now Janson could move round the pillar, and he immediately squeezed off a shot at Ratko's companion, who was hovering with a knife near the trussed woman.

The man sank to the ground, dropping the knife.

The Serb giant squeezed off a shot at Barry Cooper.

Cooper bellowed. The bullet had penetrated both his arm and his lower chest. His gun fell to the ground and he retreated, in agony, behind a row of steel drums near the side entrance.

'You OK, Barry?' Janson called out, stepping behind another pillar.

There was a moment of silence. 'I dunno, Paul,' he replied weakly.

'Can you drive?'

'Not the Indy 500 or anything, but, yeah, I guess.'

'Get into the car and drive yourself to a hospital. Now!'

Janson did not dare shoot blindly, for risk of hitting Ratko's captive. He took a few steps back until he could make out his target clearly. Ratko had his back to the woman. A glint of steel told Janson that she was not as helpless as he imagined.

With her free arm, she had reached down, stretching farther than seemed possible, and grabbed the knife, which she had managed to raise to mid-thigh level. Now she was raising it high, keeping the blade horizontal, the better to avoid the ribs, and—

Plunged it into the giant's back.

Shock wiped out the menacing expression on his face.

Janson squeezed off his sole remaining bullet, aiming for the man's heart. The Serb pitched forward, dead.

Janson strode over to the woman captive, withdrew the knife from the Serb's back and sliced through the hawser, freeing her.

She slid to the floor, her back resting against the pillar, seemingly unable to stand. She curled herself up, drawing her knees towards her, and resting her head on her forearm.

He collected her clothes. 'Put 'em on,' he said.

She raised her head, and he saw that her face was wet with tears.

'I don't understand,' she said dully.

'There's a US Consulate General at Museumplein nineteen. If you can get there, they'll take care of you.'

'You rescued me,' she said in a strange, hollow voice. 'You came for *me*. What the *hell* would you do that for?'

'I didn't come for you,' he snapped. 'I came for them.'

'Don't lie to me,' she said. 'If you wanted to interrogate one of them, you could have taken one alive and left. You didn't. You didn't, because they'd have killed me if you did.'

'Get yourself to the consulate,' he said.

'How come you didn't take out Steve Holmes? All you did was disarm him. Why would you do that?'

'Maybe I missed. Maybe I was out of ammunition.'

'You think I can't handle the truth? Well, I don't know if I can. I just know that I can't hear any more lies right now.'

'Museumplein nineteen.' Janson started to walk away. 'Report back to work. Go back to your job.'

'*I can't.* Don't you understand?' Her voice became thick. 'My job is to kill you. I can't do that now. I can't *do* my job.'

She struggled to her feet. 'Listen to me. I met this American in Regent's Park who told me maybe us Cons Op folks had got caught up in some big . . . manipulation. That the bad guy we were supposed to take down wasn't really the bad guy. I ignored that, because if that were true, up was down and down was up. Can you understand that? If you can't trust the people who give you your orders, what's the point of anything? Now I'm thinking if I ever want to learn what's going on in the world, I'm probably not going to get that from my bosses. Now I'm thinking that the only one who can tell me what time it is is the guy I'm looking at.' Trembling, she began to put on her clothes. 'I need to know what's going on. I need to know what's a lie and what isn't.' Tears welled up in her eyes, and she wiped them away, mortified. 'I gotta get somewhere safe.'

Janson blinked. 'You want to be *safe?* Then stay the hell away from me. It's not safe where I am.'

'I want you to tell me what the hell is going on.'

'That's what I'm trying to find out.'

'I can help. I know stuff, I know plans, I know faces—I know who's been dispatched to come after you.'

'Don't make things worse for yourself,' Janson said.

'Please.' She had the air of someone who had never before experienced a moment's doubt in her professional life, and who did not know how to deal with the uncertainties that now thronged her.

'Forget it,' Janson said. 'In about a minute, I'm going to steal a car. This is an act of larceny, and anybody who's with me at the time is legally an accomplice.'

'I'll steal it for you,' she said huskily. 'Look, I don't know where you're going. I don't care. But if you get away, I'll never know the truth. I *need* to know what's true. I need to know what *isn't*.'

Janson's temple began to throb again. To take her with him was madness. But maybe there was some sense in the madness.

CHAPTER EIGHT

'Oh *Jesus!*' Clayton Ackerley, the man from the CIA's Directorate of Operations, was practically keening. 'They're taking us *out*.'

'What are you *talking* about?' Douglas Albright's voice was truculent but alarmed.

'You don't know?'

'I heard about Charlotte, yes. A terrible accident.'

'You don't know!'

'Slow down and tell it to me in English.'

'Sandy Hildreth.'

'No!'

'They fished up his limo. Goddamn armoured limo. On the bottom of the Potomac. He was in the back seat. Drowned!'

'Couldn't have been an accident? Some horrible coincidence?'

'An accident? Oh sure, that's what the police report has it down as. Driver was speeding, eyewitnesses saw the car as it skidded off the bridge. Like with Charlotte Ainsley—some cab driver loses control of his car, does a hit-and-run. And now there's Onishi.'

'*What?*'

'They found Kaz's body this morning.'

'Dear God.'

'Corner of Fourth and L Streets in the near Northeast.'

'What the hell was he doing *there*?'

'According to the coroner's report, there was phencyclidine in his blood. That's PCP—angel dust. And a lot of other shit besides. Officially, he OD'd on the street corner, outside a crack house.'

'Kaz? That's *crazy*!'

'Of *course* it's crazy. But that's how they did it. The fact is, three key members of our programme have been killed in twenty-four hours.'

'Christ, it's true—they're picking us off, one by one. So who's next? Me? You? Derek?'

'We all just joined the goddamn endangered-species list.'

'But it doesn't make sense!' Albright exploded. 'Nobody knows who we are. Nothing connects us! Except the most tightly guarded secret in the United States government.'

'Even if nobody who's not in the programme knows, *he* knows.'

'Now wait a minute . . .'

'You know who I'm talking about.'

'Christ. I mean, what have we done? *What have we done?*'

'He hasn't just cut his strings. He's killing everybody who ever pulled them.'

THE SUN FILTERED through the mulberry trees and tall pines, which spread their boughs over the cottage. It was remarkable how well it blended into its surroundings, Janson noted with satisfaction as he walked through the door. He had just returned from the village, a few miles down the mountain, and carried groceries and an armload of newspapers: *Il Piccolo, Corriere delle Alpi, La Repubblica.*

He entered the bedroom where the woman was still sleeping and prepared a cool, damp compress for her forehead. Her fever was subsiding; time and antibiotics had had their effect. And time had had its healing effect on him, too. The drive to Lombardy had taken all night and some of the morning. She was conscious for little of it, waking up for only the last few miles. It had been picture-perfect north Italian countryside—yellow fields of dried corn stalks, groves of chestnuts and poplars, vineyards, and, behind them, the grey-blue Alps. Yet by the time they arrived, it was clear the woman had been badly affected by her ordeal, much more so than she had realised.

She coughed and opened her eyes. 'Where?' she said.

'We're in a cottage belonging to a friend of mine,' he said. 'In Lombardy. It's a very isolated, private spot.'

'How long . . . here?'

'It's been three days,' he said.

Her eyes filled with disbelief, alarm, fear. Then, gradually, her face slackened, as consciousness ebbed.

While the woman slept, Janson went downstairs, to the room that the house's owner, Alasdair Swift, used as a study. On the desk was a stack of print-outs—articles Janson had downloaded from online newspapers and periodicals. These were the lives of Peter Novak—hundreds of stories about the life and times of the great philanthropist.

Janson pored over them, hunting for a key, a clue, an incidental bit of data with larger significance. Something—anything—that would tell him why the great man had been killed. But it was striking how little the details varied. There were countless renditions of Peter Novak's financial exploits, countless evocations of his childhood in war-torn Hungary, countless tributes to his humanitarian passions. Even Novak's small, homey eccentricities—like his unvarying daily breakfast of kasha—cycled from one piece to another.

Hours later, he heard footsteps, bare feet on terracotta tile.

The woman, wearing a terry-cotton robe, had finally emerged from the bedroom. 'Pretty swank place,' she said.

Janson was grateful for the interruption. 'Three centuries ago, there was a mountainside monastery here. Almost all of it was destroyed, then overgrown by the forest. My friend bought the property and turned the remnants into a cottage.'

'Who's this friend?'

'"Friend" is an exaggeration. If it really belonged to a friend, I wouldn't go near it—the risk would be too great. Alasdair Swift is someone I did a favour for once. Urged me to stay at his place if I were ever in north Italy. He spends July here, otherwise it's pretty much vacant. There's a fair amount of high-tech communication equipment here. Satellite dish, high-bandwidth Internet connection. Everything a modern businessman might need.'

'Everything but a pot of joe,' she said.

'There's a sack of coffee in the kitchen. Why not make us a pot?'

'Trust me,' she said. 'That's a real bad idea.'

'I'm not fussy,' he said.

She held his gaze sullenly. 'I don't cook and I don't make coffee. I'd say it was out of feminist principle. Truth is, I don't know how. No big whoop. Something to do with my mom dying when I was little.'

'Wouldn't that turn you into a cook?'

'You didn't know my dad.'

'I don't even know who you are.'

'The name's Jessica Kincaid,' she said, and extended a hand. 'Make us some joe, why don't you.'

As a pot of coffee made its way into mugs, and into their bellies, accompanied by fried eggs and coarse bread, Janson learned a few things about his would-be executioner. She grew up in Red Creek, Kentucky, a hamlet nestled in the Cumberland Mountains, where her father owned the town's gas station and spent more of his money at the local hunting supply store than was good for them. 'He wanted a boy,' she explained, 'and half the time he forgot I wasn't one. Took me hunting with him first time when I wasn't more'n five. Thought I should be able to play sports, fix cars, and take down a duck with a bullet, not a cartridge full of shot.'

'Little Annie Oakley.'

'Shit,' she said, grinning. 'That's what the boys in high school called me. Guess I had a tendency to scare 'em off.'

'I get the picture. Car would break down, boyfriend would hoof it for a phone box, and meanwhile you'd be communing with the carburettor. A few minutes after they set off, the motor roars to life.'

'Something like that,' she said, smiling. 'I was sixteen when I finished high school. Next day, I lift a handful from the gas station cash register and get on a bus. Got a knapsack filled with paperbacks, and they're all about FBI agents. I don't get off until I'm in Lexington. Go straight to the FBI office there. This young Fed happens by, and he's like, "Somebody got you in for questioning?" I'm like, "Why don't you take me in for some questioning, 'cause you hire me, it'll be the best decision you ever made." And he and another guy in a suit are, like, joshing around with me, since it's a slow day, and I tell 'em I can pretty much hit whatever I aim at. And one of them, as a lark, takes me to the shooting range they got in the basement.'

'Don't tell me. You hit in the X-ring.'

'Four shots, four bull's-eyes. They kept punching up new targets, I kept hitting 'em. They went long-distance, gave me a rifle, I showed 'em what I could do.'

'So the sharpshooter got the job.'

'Not exactly. I got a position as a trainee. Had to get a college-equivalency certificate in the meantime. A pile of book learning. Wasn't all that hard. And Quantico was a piece of cake. I could skedaddle up a rope faster than anybody in my class. So a few years later, I'm on a special National Security Division assignment, and I catch the eye of some Cons Op spooks, and that's that.'

'I think I've got the general idea,' Janson said.

'That's not all,' she said. 'When I joined Cons Op, everyone in my class had to prepare a paper on something or somebody.'

'Ah, yes, the Spy Bio paper. And who'd you pick—Mata Hari?'

'Nope. A legendary field officer by the name of Paul Janson. Did a whole analysis of his techniques and tactics.'

'You're kidding.' Janson built a fire in the stone fireplace, stacking the logs and crumpling sections of the Italian newspapers beneath them. The dry logs caught on quickly and burned with a steady flame.

'That's why they chose me, you know. I mean, for the hit.'

'Because you know my moves better than anybody.'

'Sure. The idea of staking out Berman's place—that was mine. I was sure we'd catch up with you in Amsterdam, too. Lot of people were guessing you'd be lighting out for the US of A. Not me.'

Janson stabbed at the fire with a poker, and the pine logs crackled and hissed fragrantly. The sun had begun to sink over the far mountain peak. 'I hope you won't take offence if I ask you to remind me how old you are, Miss Kincaid,' he asked, watching her face soften in the glow of the hearth.

'You can call me Jessie,' she said. 'And I'm twenty-nine.'

'You could be my daughter.'

'Hey, you're as young as you feel.'

'That would make me Methuselah.' He stirred smoking embers

with the poker. His mind drifted back to Amsterdam. 'Here's a question for you. You ever hear of a company called Unitech?'

'Sure. It's one of ours. Supposed to be an independent entity.'

'But used as a front by Consular Operations.' Dim memories were surfacing: Unitech had played a minor role over the years in a number of endeavours. 'Somebody from Unitech is corresponding with the Liberty Foundation, offering to provide logistical support for its education programmes in Eastern Europe. Why?'

'You got me,' Jessie said. 'What you been reading all this time?' she asked looking at the stack of print-outs.

Janson explained, and they read together until he felt the weight of exhaustion start to press down on him. He stood up and stretched. 'I'm going to hit the sack,' he said.

'Gets chilly at night—sure you don't need a hot-water bottle?' she asked. She held out her hands. Her tone suggested she was joking; her eyes indicated she might not be.

He raised an eyebrow. 'Take more than a hot-water bottle to warm these bones,' he said, keeping his voice light. 'Think I better pass.'

'Yeah,' she said. 'I guess you'd better.' There was something like disappointment in her voice. 'Actually, I think I'll just stay up a little while longer, keep slogging away.'

'Good girl,' he said, and dragged himself up. He was tired, so tired. He would go to sleep easily, but he would not sleep well.

IN THE JUNGLE was a base. In the base was an office. In the office was a desk. At the desk was a man. His commanding officer.

Twelfth-century plainsong came through the small speakers of the lieutenant commander's tape system. Saint Hildegard.

'What did you want to see me about, son?' Demarest's features were settled into bland composure. He looked as if he genuinely had no idea why Janson was there.

'I'm going to file a report,' Janson said. 'Sir.'

'Of course. Standard procedure following an operation.'

'No, sir. A report about you. Detailing misconduct, as in Article Fifty-three, relating to the treatment of prisoners of war.'

'Well, go ahead. I've got a lot on my mind right now. You see, while you're filling out your forms, I've got to figure out how to save the lives of six men who have been captured. Six men you know very well, because they're under your command.'

'What are you talking about, sir?'

'The fact that members of your team have been captured in the vicinity of Lon Duc Than. They were on special assignment.'

'Why wasn't I notified about the operation, sir?'

'Nobody could find you. Still, you're here now, and all you can think to do is find the nearest pencil sharpener.'

'Permission to speak freely, sir.'

'Permission denied,' Demarest snapped. 'You think I was inhumane towards those Victor Charlies in the boonies. But I did what I did for a reason, dammit! I've lost too many men already to leaks between ARVN reps and their VC cousins. What happened to you in Noc Lo? An ambush, you called it. A set-up. Goddamn *right* it was. The operation was vetted by MACV, and somewhere along the lines, Marvin tells Charlie. Maybe it's slipped your mind, but we're in counterintelligence, Janson, and I am not going to let my men be fucked by the VC couriers who have turned MACV into a goddamn Hanoi wire service! An officer's first imperative is the welfare of the men under his command. And when the lives of my men are at stake, I will do anything to protect them. I couldn't give a damn what forms you end up filing. But if you're a soldier, if you're a *man*, you'll rescue your men first: it's your duty. Then pursue whatever disciplinary proceedings your little bureaucratic heart desires.' He folded his arms. 'Well?'

'Awaiting grid coordinates, sir.'

VOICES. No, *a* voice.

A quiet voice. A voice that did not wish to be overheard.

Janson opened his eyes, the darkness of the bedroom softened by the glow of the Lombard moon. An unease grew within him.

A visitor? He got up and found his jacket, felt the pockets for his cellphone. It was missing. He put on a bathrobe, took the pistol from under his pillow and crept towards the voice.

Jessie's voice. Downstairs.

He stepped down the stone staircase. The lights were on in the study. Jessie was in there with his cellphone pressed to her ear.

From the snippets he made out, it was apparent she was speaking to a colleague from Consular Operations in Washington.

'So the status is still "beyond salvage",' she repeated. 'Sanction on sighting.'

She was verifying that the kill orders were still in effect. A shudder ran down his spine.

'*Where* is he?' Jessie Kincaid spoke again. 'Hell, I can tell you that.

Monaco, man. You know Novak's got a house there.' A pause. 'Janson didn't say it in so many words. But I heard him making a joke to his little friend there about playing baccarat—you do the math.'

She was lying to them. Lying *for* him.

Janson returned his gun to his holster, feeling almost light-headed with relief.

'No,' she was saying, 'don't tell anybody I called in. This was a private chat, all right? Just me and you, Pookie. You take the credit, that'll be fine with me. Tell 'em, I dunno, tell 'em I'm in a coma somewhere and the Netherlands national health plan is paying for real expensive treatment, because I didn't have any identity papers on me. Tell 'em that and I bet they won't be in such a rush to bring me back to the States.' A few moments later she clicked off, turned round, and was startled to see Janson in the doorway.

'Who's "Pookie"?' he asked, in a bored voice.

'He's a fat-ass desk jockey at State, Bureau of Research and Intelligence. Sweet guy, though. I think he likes me, but what's really strange is what he told me about Puma.'

'Puma?'

'Shop name for Peter Novak. They don't think he's dead.'

'What, are they waiting for the obituary in the *New York Times*?'

'Story is you took money to arrange his death. But you failed.'

'I saw him die,' Janson said sadly, shaking his head. 'God, I wish it were otherwise. I can't tell you how much.'

'Whoa,' she said. 'What, you trying to claim credit for the kill?'

'I'm afraid your contact is either putting you on or just hasn't got a clue.' He rolled his eyes.

'Mentioned there was a news segment on him on CNN today. We got CNN here? Probably still be showing on the *Headline News* retreads.' She wandered over to the TV, and switched on CNN. Then she located a videotape, popped it in the VCR, and hit RECORD.

A special report on tensions between North and South Korea. Protests against genetically modified foods in Britain. Then came a three-minute segment about an Indian woman who ran a clinic in Calcutta for her countrymen with AIDS. A distinguished-looking man presenting her with a special humanitarian award. The same man who had helped fund her clinic.

Peter Novak. The late, great Peter Novak.

Janson watched with a swirling sense of bewilderment. Either this was some kind of technical trickery or it had been filmed earlier.

They rewound the tape and watched again, frame by frame.

'Stop there,' Jessie said at one point. She pointed towards a magazine, fleetingly glimpsed at a cluttered table. She ran to the kitchen and retrieved Janson's copy of *The Economist*, purchased at the newsstand earlier that day. 'Same issue,' she said.

The same image appeared on the cover, which was dated to expire the following Monday. It was not an old tape that had been broadcast. It had to have been filmed *after* the catastrophe in Anura.

What had they seen? A twin. An impostor?

Had Novak been murdered and replaced with a double? It was diabolical, almost beyond imagining. Who could do such a thing?

When he looked at Jessie he found her staring back at him with wounded eyes.

'I ask only one thing of you,' Jessie said. 'Do not lie to me. As for what happened in Anura, I got your word for it, nobody else's.' Her eyes were moist. '*Who* am I supposed to believe?'

'I know what I saw,' Janson said softly.

'That makes two of us.' She jerked her head at the TV screen.

'What are you saying? That you don't believe me?'

'I *want* to believe you. I want to believe *somebody*.'

'Fine,' Janson said. 'I don't blame you. I'll call for a cab, he'll ferry you to the Cons Op station in Milan, and you can report back in. Trust me, a crack shot like you, they'll be relieved to have you back. And I'll be long gone by the time you get the clean-up crew here.'

'Hold it,' she said. 'Slow down. All right. You saw what you saw.'

Janson turned away, lost in his own whirring thoughts.

'If we're gonna figure out what the hell's going on,' she went on, 'we have to get out of here. How long do you think it's going to take Cons Op before they find us? They've got all that eye-in-the-sky data, and they'll be reviewing video from highway tolls and border crossings. Sooner or later, something's going to lead them here.'

She was right. He thought of the philanthropist's motto: *Sok kicsi sokra megy*. Hungarian folk wisdom. Would their own small efforts yield a larger result? Now he recalled Fielding's words: *It's in Hungary, still, that you'll find his greatest admirers, and most impassioned foes*. And Márta Lang's observation: *For better or worse, Hungary made him who he is. And Peter is not one to forget his debts*.

It made him who he is: Hungary. That had to be Janson's destination. It was his best chance at flushing out Peter Novak's blood enemies—the ones who had known him longest and, perhaps, best.

CHAPTER NINE

The National Archives were housed in Budapest. Jessie Kincaid had taken to heart Janson's idea of beginning at the beginning.

She had a list of missing information that might help them unravel the mystery of the Hungarian philanthropist. Peter Novak's father, Count Ferenczi-Novak, was said to have been obsessively fearful for his child's safety. Fielding had told Janson that the count had made enemies who, he was convinced, would seek to revenge themselves against his scion. Is that what had finally happened, half a century later? The most important information they could get would be genealogical: Peter Novak was said to be concerned with protecting the surviving members of his family—yet who *were* these relations? The family history of Count Ferenczi-Novak might be mired in obscurity, but it would repose somewhere in Hungary's National Archives. If they found the names of these unknown relatives and could locate them, they might get an answer to the most vexing question of all: was the real Peter Novak alive or dead?

Janson dropped Jessie off in front of the National Archives building; he had some dealings of his own to conduct. Years in the field had given him an instinct for locating the black-market vendors of false identity papers and other instruments that could come in handy. He might or might not get lucky, he told Jessie, but decided he might as well give it a try.

Now Jessica Kincaid, dressed simply in jeans and a forest-green polo shirt, found herself inside a large room filled with catalogues, tables and, along the walls, perhaps a dozen counters. Over one counter was a sign in English, indicating that it was an information desk for English-speaking visitors. There was a short line in front of the desk, and she watched a bored clerk deal with his supplicants.

When Jessie reached the counter, she simply handed him a sheet of paper on which she had neatly written precise names, locations, dates. 'You're not going to tell me you're going to have a hard time finding these records, are you?' Jessie gave him a dazzling smile.

'The necessary information is here,' the clerk admitted, studying the paper. He disappeared into an annexe behind his counter, and returned a few minutes later. 'Sorry,' he said. 'Not available.'

'How do you mean, not available?' Jessie protested.

'Regrettably, there are certain . . . lacunae in the collections. There were serious losses towards the end of the Second World War—fire damage. And then to protect it, some of the collection was stored in the crypt of St Stephen's Cathedral. Unfortunately, the crypt was very damp, and much was destroyed by fungus. These records of Count Ferenczi-Novak's—they belonged to a section that was destroyed.'

'Isn't there some way you could double-check?' Jessie wrote a cell-phone number on the paper. 'If anything turns up, I would be just so grateful . . .' Another dazzling smile. 'So grateful.'

THREE HOURS LATER, the clerk called the number.

Jessie listened to him with mounting excitement. 'You mean to say you've turned the records up? We can get access to them?'

'Well, not exactly,' the clerk said. 'For some reason, the records were removed to a special section. I'm afraid access to these files is strictly regulated. It would be simply impossible for a member of the public to be allowed to see this material. All sorts of high-level ministerial certifications and documents would be required.'

'But that's plain silly,' Jessie said.

'I understand. Your interests are genealogical—it seems absurd that such records are treated like state secrets. I myself believe it to be another instance of misfiling—or miscategorisation, anyway.'

'Because it would just break me up, having come all this way,' Jessie began. 'You know, I can't tell you how *grateful* I'd be if you could see a way to help.'

'An American woman alone in this strange city—it must all be very bewildering.'

'If only there was somebody who could show me the sights. A real native. A real Magyar man.'

'For me, helping others isn't just a job. It's—well, it's who I am.'

'I knew it as soon as I met you . . .'

'Call me Istvan,' said the clerk. 'Now, let's see. What would be simplest? You have a car, yes?'

'Sure do.'

'Parked where?'

'At the garage across the street from the Archives building,' Jessie lied. The five-storey garage complex was a massive concrete structure of striking ugliness.

'Which level?'

'Fourth.'

'Say I meet you there in an hour. I'll have copies of these records in my briefcase. If you like, we might even go for a drive afterwards. Budapest is a very *special* city. You'll see how special.'

'*You're* special,' said Jessie.

WITH A RELUCTANT mechanical noise, the elevator door opened on a floor two-thirds filled with cars. It was shortly before the appointed time, and nobody else was around.

Or *was* there somebody? As she looked around, she noticed in her peripheral vision a darting motion—someone's head ducking down, she realised a split second later.

She walked casually between an aisle of cars, and suddenly dropped to the ground, cushioning her fall with her hands. Crawling, she made her way between two cars to the adjoining aisle and scurried towards where she had seen the ducking man.

She was behind him now, and as she approached she could see his slender figure. He was not the clerk; presumably, he was whoever the clerk's controller had arranged to send in his place.

She sprang up and flung herself at him from behind, throwing the man down on the concrete, gripping his neck in a hammerlock. There was a crunch as his jaw hit the floor.

'Who else you got waiting for me?' she demanded.

'Just me,' the man replied. Jessie felt a chill. He was American.

She flipped him over and dug the muzzle of her pistol into his right eye. 'Who's out there?'

'Two guys on the street, right in front,' he said.

'Tell me what they look like.' The man said nothing, and she pressed the muzzle in harder.

'One's got short blond hair. Big guy. The other . . . brown hair, crew cut, square chin.'

Jessie eased up on the pressure. An interception team outside. She recognised the stake-out. The thin man would have a car: he was here to observe, and if Jessie drove out he would be in his car, a discreet distance behind her. '*Why?*' she asked. 'Why are you doing this?'

A defiant look. 'Janson knows why—he knows what he did,' he spat. 'We remember Mesa Grande.'

'Oh Christ. Something tells me we ain't got time to get into this shit right now,' Jessie said. 'Now here's what's going to happen. You're going to get into your car and drive me out of here.'

'What car?'

'No wheels? If you won't be driving, you won't be needing to *see*.' She pressed the pistol into his right eye socket again.

'The blue Renault,' he gasped. 'Please stop!'

She got into the back seat of the sedan as he got into the driver's seat. She slumped out of sight, but kept her Beretta Tomcat pointed at him. They sped down the spiralling ramp until they approached the orange-painted wooden lever-gate blocking the way.

'Crash it!' she yelled. 'Do just what I said!'

The car rammed through the insubstantial barrier and roared out onto the street. She heard the footsteps of racing men.

Through the rearview mirror, Jessie was able to make out one of them—crew cut, square-jawed, as described. As the car hurtled away from him, he spoke into some kind of communicator.

Suddenly the windshield spiderwebbed, and the car careened out of control. Jessie peered between the front seats and saw a large blond-haired man several yards off to the side in front of them, holding a long-barrelled revolver. He had just squeezed off two shots.

The American at the wheel was dead; she could see blood oozing from an exit wound in the rear of his skull. They must have figured out that what had happened was not according to plan—that the thin man had been taken hostage—and resorted to drastic action.

There was a deafening cacophony of blaring horns, squealing brakes as the car, moving ever more slowly, rolled through an intersection, across four lanes of traffic, and crashed gently into a parked car. Jessie opened the door on the side nearer the street—and ran along the sidewalk, weaving in and out of groups of pedestrians.

THEY REJOINED each other in the spartan accommodations of Griff Hotel, a converted workers' hostel on the street Bartók Béla.

Jessie had with her a volume she'd picked up on her wanderings. It was a tribute to Peter Novak, and though the text was in Hungarian, there wasn't much of it: it was basically a picture book.

Janson picked it up. 'Looks like it's for die-hard fans. A Peter Novak coffee-table book. What'd you find out at the Archives?'

Haltingly, she told him what had happened. It had become obvious that the clerk was on the payroll of whoever was trying to stop them, that he'd sounded the alarm and then set her up.

He listened with growing dismay. 'You shouldn't have done it alone. A meeting like that—you had to have known the risks, Jessie.

It's reckless . . .' He broke off, trying to control his breathing.

'So,' she said after a while, 'what's Mesa Grande?'

'Mesa Grande,' he repeated, and his mind became crowded with images that time had never faded. *Mesa Grande:* the high-security military prison in the eastern foothills of California's San Bernardino Mountains. The dark blue outfit the prisoner had been made to wear, with the white cloth circle attached by Velcro to the centre of his chest. Demarest had insisted on execution by firing squad, and his preference had been accommodated. Janson took a deep breath. 'Mesa Grande is where a bad man met a bad end.'

Janson had *asked* to witness the execution, for reasons that remained murky even to him, and the request had been granted.

Had the monster's devoted followers decided to avenge his death all these years later? Perhaps Demarest's Devils were among the mercenaries that Novak's enemies had recruited. How better to counter one disciple of Demarest's techniques than with another?

He knew that Jessie wanted to hear more from him, but he could not bring himself to speak. All he said was, 'We need to make an early start tomorrow. Get some sleep.' And when she placed a hand on his arm, he pulled away.

IT WAS THREE decades ago, and it was now. It was in a jungle far away, and it was here. Always, the sounds: the mortar fire more distant and muffled than ever, for the trail had led them many miles from official combat zones.

Janson checked his compass, verified the trail had been leading in the correct direction. The six men in his team moved in pairs, each spaced a good way apart, the better to avoid the vulnerability of clustering in hostile territory. Only he travelled without a partner.

'Maguire,' he radioed, quietly.

He never heard the response. What he heard was automatic rifle fire, the overlapping staccato bursts of several ComBloc carbines.

Then he heard the screaming of his men and the barking commands of an enemy patrol. He was reaching for his M16 when he felt a blow to the back of his head. And then he felt nothing at all.

He opened his eyes to find himself trussed to a chair. A large-boned man wearing steel-framed glasses approached him.

'Where . . . others?' Janson's mouth was cottony.

'Members of your death squad?' the man answered in English. '*Dead.* Only you safe.'

'You're Viet Cong?'

'That is *not* correct term. We represent Central Committee of the National Liberation Front. Why you not wear dog tags?'

Janson shrugged, prompting an immediate whack with a bamboo stick across the back of his neck. 'Must've got lost.'

Two guards stood to either side of the scowling interrogator. They each carried AK-47s.

'You lie!' The interrogator's eyes darted towards the man standing behind Janson, and a crushing blow struck Janson's side. The barrel of a rifle, he guessed. A bolt of agony shot through him.

A two-inch-thick bar was inserted through the heavy irons round his ankles. Next, the unseen torturer tied a rope round the bar, looped it over Janson's shoulders, and pulled his head between his knees, even while his arms remained bound to the arms of the chair. The torque on his shoulder was a growing agony.

He waited for the next question. But minutes elapsed, and there was only silence. The gloom turned into darkness. Breathing became more difficult, as his diaphragm strained against his folded body and his shoulders felt as if they were in a vice. Janson passed out, and regained consciousness, but it was consciousness only of pain.

Another day passed. And another. And another.

It was either evening or morning when he heard a voice, once more, in English. His bonds were loosened, and he could now sit up straight once more—a postural shift that initially caused his nerve endings to scream in renewed agony.

'Is that better now? It soon will be, I pray.'

A new interrogator, a small man with quick, intelligent eyes.

'My name is Phan Nguyen, and I think that, really, we are privileged to know each other. Your name is . . .'

'Private Kevin Jones,' Janson said. 'US Infantry.'

The small man flushed as he boxed Janson on his right ear, leaving it bruised and ringing. 'Lieutenant Junior Grade Paul Janson. Do not undo all the good work you have done.'

How did they know his true name and rank?

'You *told* us all this,' Phan Nguyen insisted. 'You told us *everything*. Have you forgotten, in your delirium? I think so.'

Was it possible? Janson locked eyes with Nguyen, and both men saw their suspicions confirmed. Both saw that the other had lied. Janson had revealed *nothing*—or nothing until now. For Nguyen could tell from his reaction that his identification was correct.

'Just for now, I'm not going to press you for answers. I want you to ask *yourself* the questions.' Phan Nguyen sat down again, looking intently at Janson. 'I want you to ask yourself how it was you were captured. We knew just where to find you. What you faced wasn't the response of surprised men, was it? If you did not divulge the details of your identity to me, then who? How is it that we were able to intercept your team and capture an officer of the legendary Navy SEALs counterintelligence division? How?'

How indeed? There was only one answer: Lieutenant Commander Alan Demarest had funnelled the information to the NVA or its VC allies. He had wanted Janson out of the way; he had *needed* him out of the way. And so he had taken care of the matter.

MOLNÁR. The town that history erased.

Molnár. Where it all began. It now looked like their last hope of finding any link to Peter Novak's origins.

The rented Lancia groaned and bounced as they drove through the Bükk Hills in northeast Hungary. The village of Molnár was near the Tisza River, deep in the Magyar heartland. Sixty miles to the north was the Slovak Republic; sixty miles to the east was Ukraine and, just beneath it, Romania. The countryside was beautiful, filled with emerald-like knolls, foothills ramping towards low, bluish mountains. Here and there, one of the hills swelled to a lofty peak, lower elevations, terraced with vineyards, ceding the higher altitudes to forest.

They rolled over a small bridge across the Tisza; a bridge that had once connected two halves of the village of Molnár.

'It's unbelievable,' Jessie said. 'It's *gone*. Like somebody waved a magic wand.'

'That would have been a lot kinder than what happened,' Janson said. One winter day in 1945, he had read, the Red Army swept down these mountains and one of Hitler's divisions attempted an ambush. The artillery units had been passing through the road along the Tisza River when the German and Arrow Cross soldiers sought to head them off, failing, but taking many lives in the attempt. The Red Army believed the villagers of Molnár had known all along of the ambush. The village was torched, its inhabitants slaughtered.

When Jessie scrutinised maps of the region, she had found that on the spot where prewar maps showed the small village, contemporary atlases showed nothing. Jessie had pored over the maps with a jeweller's loupe and a draftsman's ruler; there could be no mistake.

They pulled into a roadside tavern. Inside, two men sat at a bar. Neither man looked up as the Americans arrived. The barkeeper followed them with his eyes. His receding hairline and the dark indentations beneath his eyes contributed to an impression of age.

Janson smiled. 'Speak English?' he called to the man.

The man nodded.

'See, my wife and I, we've been sightseeing hereabouts. But it's also kind of an explore-your-roots thing. You follow?'

'Your family is Hungarian?' The barkeeper's English was accented but unhalting.

'My wife's,' Janson said.

Jessie smiled and nodded. 'Straight up,' she added.

'According to family lore, her grandparents were born in a village called Molnár.'

'It no longer exists,' the barkeeper said. He was, Janson saw now, younger than he had first seemed.

'I wonder whether anybody else might have any memories of the old days,' Jessie said.

'Who else is here?' The question was a polite challenge.

'Maybe . . . one of these gentlemen?'

The barkeeper gestured towards one with his chin. 'He's not even Magyar, really, he's Palóc,' he said. 'A very old dialect. I can hardly understand him. He understands our word for *money*, and I understand his for *beer*. So we get along. Beyond that, I would not press.' He shot a glance towards the other man. 'And he's a Ruthenian.'

'I see,' Janson said. 'And there wouldn't be anybody who lives around here and might remember the old days?'

'You are visiting from America? Many fine museums in Budapest. And further west, there are show villages. Very picturesque. Made just for people like you, American tourists. I think this is not such a nice place to visit. I have no postcards for you. Americans, I think, do not like places that do not have postcards.'

'Not all Americans,' Janson said.

'All Americans like to think they are different,' the man said sourly. 'One of the many ways in which they are all the same.'

'Mister,' Jessie said. 'Are you drunk?'

'I have a graduate degree in English from Debrecen University,' he said. 'Perhaps it comes to the same.' He smiled bitterly. 'You are surprised? Tavernkeeper's son can go to university: the glories of communism. University-educated son cannot find job: glories of capitalism. Son works for father: glories of Magyar family.'

'Well, we'd better hit the road now,' Janson said. 'It's getting late.' With a firm hand on Jessie's elbow, he escorted her out of the door.

As they stepped into the sun, they saw an old man seated on a canvas folding chair on the porch, a look of amusement in his eyes.

'My son is a frustrated man,' the old man said equably. 'He wants to ruin me. You see the customers? A Ruthenian. A Palóc. They don't have to listen to him talk. No Magyar would come any more. Why pay to listen to his sourness?'

'I bet the bar was packed when you were running things,' Jessie said. 'I bet there were lots of ladies flocking there especially.'

'Now why would you think that?'

'A good-looking guy like you? I got to spell it out? Bet you *still* get yourself in a heap of trouble with the ladies.' Jessie knelt down beside the old man.

His smile grew wider; such proximity to a beautiful woman was to be savoured. He drew in a deep breath, inhaling her perfume. 'My dear, you smell like the Tokaj of the emperors.'

'I'm sure you say that to all the girls,' she said, pouting.

He looked severe for a moment. 'Certainly not,' he said. Then he smiled again. 'Only the pretty ones.'

'I bet you knew some pretty girls from Molnár once upon a time.'

He shook his head. 'I grew up further up the Tisza. I moved here only in the Fifties. Already, no more Molnár. Just stones and trees.'

Jessie's eyes did not leave the old man's. 'Well, things used to be a whole lot different, I know that. Didn't there used to be some baron from these parts, some old Magyar nobleman?'

'Count Ferenczi-Novak's lands used to stretch up that mountainside.' He gestured vaguely. 'There was once a castle.'

'Gosh, I wonder if there'd be anybody alive who might have known that count guy. Ferenczi-Novak, was it?'

'Well,' he said. 'There's the old woman, Grandma Gitta Békesi. Can speak English, too. They say she learned as a girl when she worked in the castle. You know how it is—the Russian noblewoman always insisted on speaking French, the Hungarian noblewomen always insisted on speaking English . . .'

'Békesi, you said?' Jessie prompted gently.

'Lives in an old farmhouse, up around the bend.'

'Can we tell her you sent us?'

'Better not,' he said. 'She doesn't like strangers much.'

'Well, you know what we say in America,' Jessie said. 'There are no strangers here, only friends we haven't met.'

The son stepped outside. 'That's another thing about Americans,' he sneered. 'You have an infinite capacity for self-delusion.'

SITUATED HALFWAY UP a gently sloping hill, the old two-storey farm-house looked like thousands of others that dotted the countryside. It could have been a century old, or two, or three. Once, it might have housed a prosperous peasant and his family. But as a closer approach made clear, the years had not been kind to it. The roof had been replaced with sheets of rusting corrugated steel. Trees and vines grew wild around the house, blocking off many of the windows. It was hard to believe that anyone lived here.

They pulled their Lancia off to the side of the road—a road that was hardly deserving of the name, for the surface was crumbled and pitted by neglect. Proceeding on foot, they made their way down what had once been a cow path, now almost impassable with over-grown brambles. The house was nearly a mile down the slope.

As they approached the entrance, they heard the growl of a dog, and then a throaty bark. Through narrow slot glass set into the door, Janson saw the white figure springing impatiently. He recognised it as a Kuvasz, an ancient Hungarian breed. It was three feet tall and 120 pounds, he estimated.

'Mrs Békesi?' Janson called out.

'Go away!' A quavering voice floated through the open window; the old woman herself remained in the shadows. They heard the distinctive sound of a shotgun cartridge being chambered.

'Hey, lady,' Jessie said. 'You ever hear of Count Ferenczi-Novak?'

A long silence ensued. In a voice like sandpaper, the woman demanded, 'Who *are* you?'

WITH SUPREME RELUCTANCE, Gitta Békesi finally agreed to let them enter the decaying farmhouse where she now lived alone with her savage dog. The old crone shared the decrepitude of her lodgings. The skin hung loosely from her skull; pale, dry scalp showed through her thinning hair; her eyes were sunken, hard and glittering behind loose snakeskin-like folds. It was the face of a survivor.

In the large sitting room, a fire burned slowly in the fireplace. On the mantel above it, a sepia photograph in a tarnished silver frame showed a beautiful young woman. Gitta Békesi as she once was: a robust peasant girl, exuding rude health, and something else, too—a sly sensuality. It gazed upon them, mocking the ravages of age.

Jessie walked over to it. 'What a beauty you were,' she said.

'Beauty can be a curse,' the old woman said. She made a clicking noise with her tongue and the dog came over and sat at her side. She reached down and rubbed its flanks with her clawlike hands.

'I understand that you once worked for the count,' Janson said. 'Count Ferenczi-Novak.'

'I do not speak of these things,' she said curtly. She sat in a cane rocking chair. Behind her, resting against the wall, was her old shotgun. 'I have let you in. Now you can say that you have sat with the old woman and asked her your questions. Now you can tell everyone concerned that Gitta Békesi says nothing.'

'Wait a minute—"everyone concerned"? Who's *concerned*?'

'Not me,' she said. And staring straight ahead, she fell silent.

'Are those chestnuts?' Jessie asked, looking at a bowl on a small table by the woman's chair.

Békesi nodded.

'Could I have one? I know you just roasted those, 'cause this whole place of yours smells like it, and it's making my mouth water.'

Békesi nodded again. 'They're still hot,' she said approvingly.

'Makes me think of my grandma. We'd come to her house and she'd roast chestnuts . . .' She beamed at the memory. 'And it made every day seem like Christmas.' Jessie peeled a chestnut and ate it greedily. 'This is just a perfect chestnut, worth the five-hour drive.'

The old woman nodded, her manner noticeably less aloof. 'They get too dry when you over-roast them.'

'And too hard when you don't roast them long enough,' Jessie put in. 'But you got it down to a science.'

A small, contented smile settled on the old woman's face.

'Do all your visitors beg you for 'em?' Jessie asked.

'I get no visitors.'

'None at all? Can't hardly believe that.'

'Very few. Very, very few.'

Jessie nodded. 'And how do you handle the nosy ones?'

'Some years ago, a journalist from England came here,' the old woman said. 'So many questions he had. He was writing something about Hungary during the war and after.'

'Is that right?' Janson asked. 'I'd love to read what he wrote.'

The crone snorted. 'He never wrote anything. Just a couple of days after his visit, he was killed in an accident in Budapest.'

'He ask about this count, too?' Jessie prompted.

The old woman regarded Jessie quietly for a moment. 'Perhaps you will join me in a small glass of *pálinka*.'

'Well, if *you're* having some.'

The old woman slowly rose and walked unsteadily to the glass-fronted sideboard. There, she lifted an enormous jug filled with a colourless liquid, and poured a small quantity into two shot glasses.

Jessie took one. The old woman settled back into her chair and watched as Jessie had a sip.

Explosively, she sprayed the liquid out. It was as involuntary as a sneeze. '*Jeez*, I'm sorry!' she got out in a strangled voice.

The old woman smiled mischievously. 'Around here, we make it ourselves,' she said. 'A hundred and ninety proof.' She swallowed her brandy, and looked more relaxed than she had been.

'How did you end up in the castle?' Janson asked after a while.

The old woman smiled, remembering. 'My parents worked the land. They were peasants, but they had hopes for me. They thought if I worked as a servant at the castle, I would learn a thing or two. My mother knew one of the women who helped run Ferenczi-Novak's household, and had her meet her little girl. And one thing led to another, and I met the great man himself, Count Ferenczi-Novak, and his beautiful blue-eyed wife, Illana. Then came the day my mother took me to the castle on the hill.'

'It must be hard to remember something that happened so long ago,' Jessie ventured.

The old woman shook her head. 'Yesterday is sunk in mist. What happened six decades ago, I can see as if it is happening now.'

Janson recalled the ruins that were visible further up the hill: all that remained of the vast estate were jagged remnants of walls that rose only a few feet from the ground.

'And what about the scampering of little feet?' Jessie asked.

'They had only one child. Peter.'

'Peter,' Janson repeated, casually. 'When was he born?'

'His naming day was the first Saturday in October 1937. *Such* a beautiful boy. So handsome and so clever. I can picture him still, in his Peter Pan collar and his little plus fours and sailor's cap.' Her smile drew with it a trellis of wrinkles. 'And his parents were so devoted to him. You could understand that. He was their only child. The birth was a difficult one, and it left the countess unable to conceive.' The old woman was in another world: if it was a lost world, it was not lost to her. 'Such a perfect little boy.' Her eyelids fluttered. 'The fevers were terrible. It was a cholera epidemic, you know. I was one of those who attended him on his sickbed, you see. I can never forget that morning—finding his body, so cold, those lips so pale, his cheeks like wax. It was heartbreaking when it happened. He was just five years old. Dead, before he truly had a chance to live.'

A sense of utter disorientation, overcame Janson. *Peter Novak had died as a child?* How could that be? Was there some mistake—was this another family the old woman was describing, *another* Peter?

There could be no doubt that the old woman was telling the truth as she remembered it. And yet what did it mean?

Peter Novak: the man who never was.

Jessie unzipped her knapsack, took out the picture book on Peter Novak, and opened it to a colour close-up of the great man. She showed it to Gitta Békesi. 'See this fellow? *His* name is Peter Novak.'

The old woman glanced at the picture and shrugged at Jessie. 'I do not follow the news. But, yes, I think I have heard of this man.'

'Same name. Sure it couldn't be the same person?'

'Peter, Novak—common names in our country,' she said, shrugging. 'Of course this is not Ferenczi-Novak's son. He died in 1942.' Her eyes returned to the photograph. 'Besides, this man's eyes are brown. Little Peter's were blue, like his mother's.'

CHAPTER TEN

In a state of shock, the two began the long walk back up the hill to the car. As the house receded into the distance, they began to talk.

'What if there was another child?' Jessie asked. 'A kid nobody knew about, who took on his brother's name. A hidden twin, maybe.'

'The old woman seemed certain that he was their only one. And it wouldn't be an easy thing to hide from the household staff. Of course, if Count Ferenczi-Novak was as paranoid as his reputation had it, any number of ruses are conceivable.'

'But why? He wasn't crazy.'

'Not crazy, but desperately fearful for his kid,' Janson said. 'Hungarian politics was in an incredibly explosive condition.

Reprisals and counter-reprisals were just a way of life back then. Hundreds of thousands of people were killed in late '44 and early '45 after the Arrow Cross took over. Remember, these Arrow Cross were true homegrown Hungarian Nazis. When the Red Army took control of the country, you had another round of purges. People like Ferenczi-Novak were caught in a pincer.'

'So we're back to the old question: how do you bring a child into that world? Maybe these guys thought they couldn't. That any child of theirs would have to be hidden.'

'Moses in the bulrushes,' Janson mused. 'But that raises a lot more questions. Novak tells the world that these are his parents. Why?'

'Because it's the truth?'

'A child like that would have been raised to be afraid of the truth. I don't think they had another child. I think Gitta Békesi told us the truth: Peter Novak, the count's only son, died when he was little.'

Shadows lengthened as the sun dipped behind the distant peak. Minutes later, clearings that had been golden suddenly turned grey.

'This is getting to be a hall of mirrors,' Jessie said. 'Yesterday, we were wondering whether some impostor had taken on Peter Novak's identity. Now it's looking like Peter Novak himself took on somebody else's identity. A dead kid, a wiped-out village—an opportunity.'

'Identity theft,' said Janson. 'Beautifully executed.'

'It's genius, when you think about it. You choose a village that was totally liquidated in the war—so there's practically nobody around who'd remember a thing about his childhood. All the records, certificates of birth and death, destroyed after the place was torched.'

'Making himself an aristocrat's son was a good move,' Janson said. 'It helps deal with a lot of questions that might have arisen about his origins. Nobody has to wonder how he could be so well educated without an institutional record of his schooling.'

'Exactly. Where'd he go to school? Hey, he was privately tutored—a count's kid, right? Why was he off the radar? Because this aristocrat, this János Ferenczi-Novak, had tons of enemies and good reason to be paranoid. Everything fits, real tight.'

'Like dovetailed planks. Too tightly. The next thing you know, he's a big-time currency trader.'

'A man with no past.'

'Oh, he's got a past, all right. It's just a past that nobody knows.'

'Thing I keep going back to is *why*? Why the trickery? Everybody loves him. He's a goddamn hero of the age.'

'Even saints can have something to hide,' Janson parried. 'What if the man came from a family that had been involved with Arrow Cross atrocities? No matter what he did, it would come up again and again—in every interview, every conversation, every discussion.'

A few moments elapsed before he recognised the sound that drifted up the hill. It was faint and nearly imperceptible, and yet as his senses tuned to the auditory stimulus, he recognised the source, and his heart began to thud. It was a woman screaming.

THE THORNY PRIVET and overgrown vines whipped and scratched at Janson as he raced down the winding hillside path. He had ordered Jessie to return to the Lancia; it would be a disaster if their enemies reached it first. Her trek was uphill, but she ran like a gazelle.

A few minutes later, Janson arrived at the old woman's farmhouse. The screams had been replaced by utter silence.

The door was ajar. Inside, the noble Kuvasz lay on its side; it had been disembowelled. Splayed in the nearby rocking chair was Gitta Békesi. Her face was hidden by her coarse muslin frock, which had been yanked up and over her head, exposing her flaccid torso—and the unspeakable horrors that had been visited upon it. Small, red-rimmed wounds—each corresponding to the plunge of a bayonet, Janson knew—crisscrossed her silvery flesh in a grotesque arrangement. The blades of her assailants had plunged into her dozens of times. On her exposed arms and legs he could see a cluster of red weals caused by the pressure of gripping fingers. The woman had been held down and tortured with a plunging blade.

Where were they? Close, very close. Because they were looking for him. They would be up the hill.

Janson needed elevation if he was to get a proper view of the field of operation. At right angles to the farmhouse was a portico with a hayloft above. He ran into the courtyard and climbed a ladder to the tall hayloft. A hinged door in the rough-planked roof allowed him to clamber to its highest point.

A quarter of a mile up the hill, he could see, a small party of armed men were making their way towards Jessie Kincaid. Then Janson saw and heard the flutter of black birds, swooping from the nearby underbrush into the sky, with strident caws; something had disturbed them. A moment later he saw movement in the overgrown trees and bushes surrounding the farmhouse, and realised what it meant. *He had fallen into a trap!*

116

The men had been *counting* on his overhearing the old woman's screams. They had sought to lure him back.

The farmhouse was a gated enclosure, but the armed men had it surrounded on all four sides, and now they edged out of the underbrush and into the yard.

Janson lowered himself from the roof, then let himself down from the loft to the dirt floor. If the men had not rushed the place, it was only because they did not know whether he was armed.

Now he darted across the yard and back into the woman's parlour. The shotgun was gone. Yet if the woman kept a shotgun, she must also have cartridges.

It was in a small pantry that he found what he was looking for. He pulled out a couple of boxes and crawled back to the parlour.

In the iron pan over the fireplace, where the woman had been roasting chestnuts earlier that day, Janson placed a handful of cartridges. Though they were designed to be detonated by the firing pin of a shotgun, sufficient heat would produce a similar effect.

Janson added another small log to the fire, and returned to the kitchen. There he placed a cast-iron skillet on the decades-old electric range, and scattered another handful of cartridges on it. He set the heat on medium low. It would take a minute for the element just to heat the bottom of the heavy skillet.

Now he turned on the oven, placed the remaining fifty cartridges on the rack, and set the temperature on high.

He crept across the yard, climbed to the hayloft again, and waited.

Suddenly, a *bang* shattered the still air, followed, in rapid succession, by four more bangs. Then he heard the return fire of an automatic rifle, and the sound of broken glass.

To Janson, the acoustic sequence relayed a precise narrative. The cartridges over the fireplace had detonated. The gunmen assumed that they were being fired on from the parlour. Urgent shouts summoned men to join the apparent gunfight in the front of the farmhouse.

A series of low-pitched blasts told Janson that the cartridges on the range-top skillet had been heated to the point of detonation. It would tell the gunmen that their quarry had retreated into the kitchen. Through the gap between the slats of the barn wall, he saw that a solitary gunman remained behind; his partners had raced to the other side of the compound to join the others in their assault.

Janson withdrew his Beretta and, through the same gap, aimed it at the burly, olive-clad man. But he could not fire yet—could not risk the gunshot being heard by others and exposing the subterfuge. He waited until he heard the immense boom-roar of fifty shotgun cartridges exploding in the oven before he squeezed the trigger. The sound would be utterly lost amid the blast.

Slowly, the burly man toppled over, face forward.

Janson unlatched a door and strode over to the fallen man.

For a moment he contemplated disappearing into the dark thickets of the hillside. But then he remembered the slain woman, her savagely brutalised body, and any thought of flight vanished from his mind. He removed the dead man's submachine gun and bandolier, and adjusted its sling round his own shoulders.

The team of assailants was now gathered in the house, tramping around, firing their weapons into every conceivable hiding place.

He circled round to the front of the farmhouse, dragging the dead man behind him. In the roving beams of flashlight he recognised a face, a second face, a third. They were hard, cruel faces. The faces of men he had worked with many years ago in Consular Operations, Coarse men. Men for whom brute force was not a last resort but a first. They had no business in government service; in Janson's opinion, they reduced its moral credibility by their very presence.

He placed his jacket on the dead man, then positioned him behind a sprawling chestnut tree. With the man's shoelaces, he tied his flashlight to the lifeless forearm. He pulled tiny splinters of wood from a dead branch and placed them between the man's eyelids, propping his eyes open in a glassy stare. It was crude work, turning the man into an effigy of himself. But in the shadows of the evening, it would pass on a first glance. Now Janson directed a raking burst of fire through the parlour's windows. The three exposed gunmen twitched horribly as the bullets perforated diaphragm, gut, aorta, lungs. At the same time, the unexpected burst summoned the others.

Janson switched on the flashlight laced to the dead man's forearm, and dashed to the boulder ten feet away in the gloom.

The response was as he expected: four of the commandos directed their automatic weapons at the crouching figure. The noise and the gunmen's furious concentration worked to Janson's advantage: with his Beretta, he squeezed off four carefully aimed shots in rapid succession. Each man slumped, lifeless, to the ground.

One man remained; Janson could see his profile shadowed against the curtains on the top floor. He was tall, his hair cut short, his bearing rigid. His was one of the faces Janson had recognised, and he could identify him now simply from his gait, the decisive efficiency of his movements. He was their leader. From what little Janson had seen of their interactions earlier, that much had been clear.

The name came to him: Simon Czerny. A Cons Op operative specialising in clandestine assaults. Their paths had crossed in El Salvador, during the Eighties, and Janson had even then considered him a dangerous man, reckless in his disregard for civilian life.

Janson ran towards the ruins of the parlour, saw the gallon-sized jug of brandy, the poisonous *pálinka*. Frisking one of the slain gunmen, he extracted a Zippo lighter. Then he splashed the 190 proof brandy around the room, extending to the hallway that led to the kitchen, and used the lighter to ignite the volatile spirits.

Janson waited as the flames grew in strength. Billows of smoke funnelled up the narrow staircase.

The commander, Czerny, would have no choice. To remain where he was meant being consumed in an inferno. The only way out was down the stairs and through the front door.

Janson heard the man's heavy footsteps. Just as he reached the threshold, though, Czerny loosed a spray of bullets, sweeping round an almost 180-degree range. Anybody laying in wait for him outside would have been struck by the wildly chattering submachine gun. Janson admired Czerny's efficiency and forethought as he watched the gunman's pivoting torso—from behind.

He rose from where he was hidden, by the staircase on the very floor of the burning parlour, perilously near the gathering conflagration—the one place the gunman would not have expected. Janson lunged, lashing his arm round the gunman's neck, his fingers hurtling towards the trigger enclosure, tearing the weapon from his hands. Czerny thrashed violently, but rage made Janson unstoppable.

With an almost supernatural effort, Czerny reared up and threw Janson off him. He ran down the yard, away from the burning house. Janson raced after him, taking him down with a powerful shoulder tackle, throwing him to the stony ground. Czerny let out a groan as Janson sharply wrenched one of his arms up behind him, simultaneously dislocating the arm and turning him onto his back. Tightening his grip on the man's neck, he leaned in close.

'If you don't tell me what I want to hear, you'll never speak again.' Janson yanked a combat blade from a holster in Czerny's belt. 'You still with Consular Operations?'

Czerny laughed bitterly. 'Goddamn overgrown Scouts—that's all they were. Should have been selling cookies door-to-door, for all the difference they made.'

'But you're making a difference now?'

'Tell me something. How do you live with yourself, you traitor? Somebody once tried to help you, a true-blue hero, and how did you repay him? You turned him in, pushed him in front of a firing squad. That should have been you at Mesa Grande, you son of a bitch!'

Janson pressed the flat of the man's knife against his lightly bearded cheek. 'You part of some Da Nang revenge squad?'

'*Freeze!*' The command came from above him; Janson looked and saw the barkeeper they had spoken to earlier that day. And his hands were clutching a double-barrelled shotgun.

'Isn't that what they're always saying on your crappy American cop shows? I told you that you were not welcome,' the man said. 'Now I will have to *show* you how unwelcome you are.'

Janson heard the noise of a runner, vaulting over boulders and branches, plunging through thickets.

Seconds later, Jessie Kincaid emerged. 'Drop the goddamn antique!' she shouted. She held a pistol in her hand.

The Hungarian cocked the Second World War-era shotgun.

Jessie squeezed one shot into his head. The man toppled back.

Janson grabbed the shotgun and scrambled to his feet. 'I've run out of patience, Czerny. And you've run out of allies.'

'I don't understand,' Czerny blurted.

Kincaid shook her head. 'Drilled four fuckers up the hill. Your boys, right? Thought so. Didn't like their attitude.'

Janson pressed the point of the combat knife to Czerny's face. 'Who do you work for?'

Czerny blinked hard, his eyes watering with pain.

'You'll tell us, sooner or later,' Janson said. 'You know that. What's up to you is whether you . . . lose face over it.'

In a sudden movement, Czerny reached for the hilt of the knife and, with one powerful twist, wrested control of it. Janson pulled back, away from the blade's range, and Jessie stepped forward with the gun, but neither anticipated the man's next move.

He forced the blade down with shaking muscles and, carving deeply, drew it across his own neck. In two seconds, he had sliced through the veins and arteries that sustained consciousness.

The hard ball of rage within Janson subsided, giving way to dismay and disbelief. He recognised the significance of the spectacle before him. Death had been deemed preferable to whatever Czerny knew was in store for him if he were compromised. It suggested a fearsome discipline among these marauders: a leadership that ruled through terror.

And these men, these former members of Consular Operations. Janson had barely known them, but something nagged at his memory. Were they truly *former* Cons Op agents? Or were they *active* ones?

THE DRIVE to Sárospatak took two hours, but they were two hours racked with tension. Janson kept a careful eye out for anyone who might be following them. Finally, they pulled up to a hotel.

The clerk at the front desk barely glanced at them or their documents. 'We have one vacancy,' he said. 'Two beds will be suitable?'

'Perfectly,' Janson said.

In the sparsely decorated room, Jessie spent twenty minutes on Janson's cellphone. She held a piece of paper on which Janson had written the names of the three former Consular Operations agents he had identified. When she clicked off, she looked distinctly unsettled.

'So,' Janson said, 'what does your boyfriend tell you about them?'

'Boyfriend? If you ever saw him, you wouldn't be jealous. He makes wide turns, OK?'

'Jealous? Don't flatter yourself.'

Jessie rolled her eyes. 'Look, here's the thing. According to official records, these guys have been dead for the better part of a decade. Remember the Qadal explosion?' Qadal had been the location of a US Marines installation in Oman. In the Nineties, terrorists set off a blast that cost the lives of forty-three US soldiers. A dozen State Department 'analysts' had also been on site, and had perished as well.

'One of those "unsolved tragedies",' Janson said, expressionless.

'Well, the records say those guys you mentioned died in the blast.'

Janson tried to assimilate the information. The terrorist incident in Oman must have been a cover. It enabled an entire contingent of Cons Op agents to conveniently disappear—only to reappear, perhaps, in the employ of another power. But what power?

Jessie paced for a while. 'They're dead, but they're not dead, right? Is there any chance—any chance whatever—that the Peter Novak we saw on CNN is the same Peter Novak as ever? Never mind what his birth name might have been. Is it conceivable that—I don't know—he somehow wasn't on the aircraft that exploded?'

'I was there, I observed everything . . . I simply don't see how.' Janson shook his head slowly. 'I can't imagine it.'

'Unimaginable doesn't mean impossible. There must be a way to prove it's the same man.'

On a table, Jessie spread out a stack of Novak images from the past year, downloaded from the Internet back in Alasdair Swift's Lombardy cottage. One of them was from the CNN web site and showed the philanthropist at the ceremony they had watched on TV, honouring the woman from Calcutta. Now she took out the jeweller's loupe and ruler she had acquired for analysing the maps of the Bükk Hills region, and applied them to the images in front of her.

Ten minutes later, she interrupted a long silence. 'Well, you got to take into account things like lens distortion. But depending on the photo, the guy seems to be slightly different heights. Subtle—no more than half an inch difference. Here he is, standing next to the head of the World Bank. Here he is again, separate occasion, standing next to the same guy. Looks like everybody's wearing the same shoes in both shots. And he's got slightly different forearm spans. And the ratio between forearm span and femur span . . .' She jabbed at a picture that showed him walking alongside the prime minister of Slovenia. She pointed to a similar configuration in another photograph. 'Same joints, different ratios.' She riffled through the picture book she'd bought in Budapest, and busied herself with the ruler again. 'Ratio of index finger length to forefinger length. Not constant.'

With the loupe and the ruler, she continued to look for and find tiny physical variances. Scepticism melted as examples multiplied.

'The question is, Who is this man?' She shook her head bleakly.

'I think you mean the question is, *Who are these men?*' Janson said. 'I can't get to Peter Novak, or whoever is calling himself that. Who else do we know who might know the answer?'

'Maybe not the people trying to stop you, but whoever's giving the orders.'

'Exactly. And I've a strong suspicion I know who that is.'

'You're talking about Derek Collins,' she said. 'Director of Consular Operations.'

'Lambda Team doesn't get dispatched without his direct approval,' he said. 'Let alone the other teams we've seen deployed. I think it's time I paid the man a visit.'

'Listen to me,' she said urgently. 'If Collins wants you dead, don't count on leaving his company alive.'

'I've got no choice,' Janson said.

Heavily, she said, 'When do we leave?'

'There's no "we". I'm going by myself.'

'You don't think I'm good enough?'

'You know that's not what I'm talking about,' Janson said. 'You're good, Jessie. Top-drawer. The point remains: what I've got to do next, I've got to do alone. It's not a risk you need to take.'

'It's not a risk *you* need to take.'

'Trust me, it'll be a walk in the park,' Janson said with a smile.

'Tell me you're not still sore about London. Because—'

'Jessie, I need you to reconnoitre the Liberty Foundation offices in Amsterdam. I'll rejoin you there shortly. We can't ignore the possibility that something, or somebody, might turn up there.'

'I think you're *scared* of putting me at risk,' Jessie said.

'You don't know what you're talking about.'

'Hell, maybe you're right.' She was silent for a moment, averting her gaze. 'Maybe I ain't ready.' Suddenly, she noticed a small splotch of blood on the back of her right hand. As she examined it more closely, she looked a little sick. 'What I did today, in those hills . . .'

'Was what you needed to do. It was kill or be killed.'

'I know,' she said in a hollow voice.

'You're not supposed to like it. There's no shame in what you're feeling. But sometimes lethal force is the only thing that will defeat lethal force. You did what had to be done, Jessie.'

She disappeared into the bathroom, and Janson heard the shower run for a long time. When she returned, a terry-cloth bathrobe was wrapped round her slim yet softly curving body. She walked towards the bed nearest the window. Janson was almost startled at how delicately feminine the field agent now appeared.

'So you're leaving me in the morning,' she said after a moment.

'Not the way I'd put it,' Janson said.

'Maybe we'd better seize the day—or the night.' He could tell she was afraid for him, and for herself, too. 'I got good eyes. You know that. But I don't need a sniper scope to see what's in front of my face.'

'And what's that?'

'I see the way you look at me.'

'I don't know what you mean.'

'Oh, come on now, make your move, soldier. Now's the time you tell me how much I remind you of your late wife.'

'Actually, you couldn't be less like her.'

She paused. 'I make you uncomfortable. Don't try to deny that.'

'I don't think so.'

'You flinch when I come too close.' She stood up and moved towards him. 'And your eyes widen and your face flushes and your heart starts to race.' She reached over, and pressed his hand to her throat. 'Same with me. Can you feel it?'

'A field agent shouldn't make assumptions,' Janson said, but he could feel the pulse beneath her warm, silky skin, and it seemed to keep rhythm with his own.

'I remember something you once wrote, about interagency cooperation between nations. "To work together as allies, it is important that any unresolved tensions be addressed through a free and open exchange." ' There was laughter in her eyes. 'Just close your eyes and think of your country.' She stood closer and parted her bathrobe. Her breasts were two perfectly shaped globes, the nipples swollen with tension, and she leaned towards him, cupping his face now with her hands. Her gaze was warm and unwavering.

As she started to remove his shirt, Janson said, 'There's an ordinance in the reg book prohibiting fraternisation.'

She pressed her lips to his, smothering his halfhearted demurrals. 'You call this fraternisation?' she said, shouldering off her robe.

He became aware of a delicate fragrance that emanated from her body. Her lips were soft and swollen and moist, and they moved across his face to his mouth, inviting his into hers. Her fingers gently stroked his cheeks, his jawline, his ears. He could feel her breasts, soft yet firm, pressed against his chest, and her legs thrust against his.

Then, abruptly, she began to tremble, and convulsive sobs came from her throat as she gripped him more fiercely. Gently, he pulled her face back, and saw her cheeks were now stained with tears.

'Jessie,' he said softly. 'Jessie.'

She shook her head, helplessly, and then cradled it against his chest. 'I've never felt so alone,' she said. 'So frightened.'

'You're not alone,' Janson said. 'And fear is what keeps us alive.'

'You don't know what it's like to be afraid.'

He kissed her forehead tenderly. 'You've got it wrong. I'm always afraid. Like I say, it's why I'm still here. It's why we're here together.'

She pulled him to her with a savage intensity. 'Make love to me,' she said. 'I need to feel what you feel. I need to feel it now.'

Two intertwined bodies rolled over on the still-made bed, flushed with an almost desperate passion, flexing and shuddering towards a moment of fleshly communion. 'You're not alone, my love,' Janson murmured. 'Neither of us is. Not any more.'

CHAPTER ELEVEN

Less than an hour from Dulles Airport, Janson found himself on small winding roads that took him through some of the most tranquil territory on the Eastern Shore. Chesapeake Bay covered 2,200 miles of coastline, more if one counted the 150 tributaries. The bay itself was shallow, ranging from ten to thirty feet.

Janson drove over a bridge, and finally to the long spit of land known as Phipps Island. As he drove the rented Camry along the narrow road, he could see fishing sloops moving slowly along the bay, hauling in nets laden with crabs and rockfish.

He saw why Derek Collins had chosen Phipps Island for a vacation home, a retreat from the pressures of his Washington existence. Though only a short distance from Washington, it was isolated, peaceful; it was also, by dint of the land formation, secure. A skinny strip of land connected it to the main peninsula, making a surreptitious land approach difficult. An amphibious arrival would be impeded by the shallowness of the water surrounding the land.

Janson pulled off the road, nosing the car into a particularly exuberant growth of bayberries and marsh willows. The remaining mile he would traverse on foot. If Jessie's contacts had provided her with accurate information, Collins should be in his cottage, and by himself. A widower, Collins had a penchant for spending time alone.

Janson walked through the grass to the shoreline, a strip of rocks and sand and battered shells.

He heard the sound of boots on the planked walkway just twenty feet away, where the land formed a crown near the top of the beach. A young man in a uniform of green and black camouflage, cinched trousers, a weapons belt: standard-issue National Guard attire.

'Hey, you!' The young guardsman had spotted him, and was walking towards him. 'You see the signs? You can't be here.'

Janson turned to face him, stooping slightly, *willing* himself to appear older and feebler. 'Shoreline here is public property.' He made his face muscles slack, and his voice developed a slight quaver suggestive of infirmity. He spoke with the vowels of the Eastern Shore accent. 'You think you're going to tell me I can't go where the law says I can, you got a whole 'nother think. I know my rights.'

The guardsman scowled, half amused at the old salt's line of blather. But his orders were clear. 'Fact remains, this is a restricted area, and there's a dozen signs saying so.' He stood directly in front of the other man. 'You got a complaint, write to your congressman.'

Suddenly, Janson sprang at him, clamping his right hand round his mouth, his left round the back of his neck. Even before they hit the ground, Janson had grabbed the man's holstered M9 pistol.

'Nobody likes a smart ass,' he said, dropping the accent, jabbing the M9 into his trachea.

The young man's eyes widened.

'You got new orders: a sound out of you and you're dead, greenhorn.' Janson undid the guardsman's belt and used it to bind his wrists to his ankles. Next, he ripped strips of cloth from his camouflage tunic and stuffed them in the man's mouth, finally securing the gag with the guardsman's bootlaces. After pocketing the M9, he left the man hidden amid a thick growth of cordgrass.

Janson pressed on, and when the beach disappeared he walked up the grass. After five minutes he found himself on the south side of a sparsely grassed dune, the cottage just out of view.

He looked at at the placid water of Chesapeake Bay. In the distant glare he could just make out Tangier Island, several miles to the south.

'My wife Janice used to love that spot.' The familiar voice came without warning, and Janson whirled round to see Derek Collins.

The only thing that was unfamiliar was the bureaucrat's garb: a man he had always seen in three-button suits was wearing khakis, a madras shirt and moccasins—his weekend attire.

Collins was standing only ten feet from Janson, but his voice was far away. He stood with his hands in his pockets. 'She loved watching the birds. You see that one near the Osage orange tree? Pearl grey, white undersides, black mask like a raccoon round the eyes? That's a loggerhead shrike.'

'Better known as the butcher bird,' Janson said.

The bird trilled its two-note call.

'Figures,' Collins said. 'Because it preys on other birds. But it doesn't have any talons. That's the beauty part. It takes advantage of its surroundings—impales its prey on a thorn or barbed wire before it rips it apart. It doesn't need claws.' Collins turned and looked at Janson. 'Why don't you come inside?'

'Aren't you going to frisk me?' Janson asked. 'See what weapons I might have on me?'

Collins laughed. 'Janson, you *are* a weapon. What am I supposed to do, amputate all your limbs?' He shook his head. 'Besides, I'm looking at somebody who has folded his arms beneath a jacket, and that bulge a foot below his shoulder is quite likely a handgun, aimed at me. I'm guessing you took it off Ambrose. Young kid, reasonably well trained, but not the sharpest knife in the drawer.'

Janson said nothing but kept his finger on the trigger.

'Come along,' Collins said. 'We'll walk together. A two-man demonstration of mutual assured destruction, and the deep comfort the balance of terror can bring.'

Janson said nothing. Collins was not a field agent; he was no less lethal in his way, but through more mediated channels. Together, they traipsed over a boardwalk of cedar and into Collins's cottage.

In the kitchen, gleaming with stainless steel and high-end appliances, Collins made coffee. He took care to pour it in front of Janson, tacitly letting him verify that his coffee had not been spiked. Similarly, when he brought the two mugs to the granite counter, he let Janson choose the one he would drink from.

They sat together at the counter, each perched on a high stool.

Collins took a sip of coffee. 'The shrike we saw earlier—it's a hawk that thinks it's a songbird. I think both of us remember an earlier conversation we had along those lines. One of your "exit interviews". I told you you were a hawk. You didn't want to hear it. I think you wanted to be a songbird. But you weren't one, and never will be. You're a hawk, Janson, that's your nature.' Another sip of coffee. 'One day, I got here and Janice was at her easel, where she'd been trying to paint. She was crying. Turns out she'd watched as this songbird—that's how she regarded it—impaled a small bird on one of the hawthorn and let it hang there. Sometime later, the shrike came back and started to rip it apart with its curved beak. A butcher bird doing what a butcher bird does. What could I tell her? That a hawk with a song is still a hawk?'

'Maybe it's both, Derek. Not a songbird pretending to be a hawk, but a hawk that's also a songbird. A songbird that turns into hawk when it needs to. Why do we have to choose?'

'Because we have to.' He placed his mug down hard on the granite counter. 'And *you* have to choose. Which side are you on?'

'Which side are *you* on?'

'I've never changed,' Collins said.

'You tried to kill me.'

Collins tilted his head. 'Well, yes and no,' he replied.

'Glad you're so mellow about it,' Janson said. 'Five of your henchmen in the Tisza valley seemed less philosophical.'

'*Not* mine,' Collins said. 'Look, this really is awkward.'

'I wouldn't want you to feel you owe me an explanation.' Janson spoke with cold fury. 'About Peter Novak. About me. About why you want me dead.'

'That was a mistake, the Lambda Team dispatch, and we feel terrible about the whole beyond-salvage directive. Big-time product recall on that order. But whatever hostiles you encountered in Hungary— well, they weren't ours. Maybe once, but not any more.'

'So I guess everything's squared away,' Janson replied.

'Look, I didn't institute the order, I just didn't countermand it. Everybody thought you'd gone rogue, took a sixteen-million-dollar bribe. For a while, I thought so, too.'

'Then you learned better.'

'Except I couldn't cancel the order without an explanation. Otherwise, people would assume I'd lost it or somebody had got to me, too. And the thing was, I couldn't offer an explanation without compromising a secret on the very highest levels. The one secret that could never be compromised. You're not going to be able to look at this objectively, because we're talking about your own survival here. But my job is all about priorities, and where you've got priorities, you're going to have sacrifices to make.'

'Sacrifices? You mean a sacrifice for me to make. I *was* that goddamn sacrifice.' Janson leaned closer, his face numb with rage.

'You can remove your curved beak. I'm not arguing.'

'Do you think I killed Peter Novak?'

'I know you didn't.'

'Let me ask you a simple question. Is Peter Novak dead?'

Collins sighed. 'Well, again, my answer's yes and no.'

'God*dammit!*' Janson exploded. 'I want answers.'

'Shoot,' Collins said. 'Let me rephrase that: ask away.'

'Let's start with a pretty disturbing discovery I've made. I've studied dozens of photographic images of Peter Novak in detail. There are variances, subtle but measurable, of fixed physical dimensions.'

'Conclusion: these are not pictures of one man.' Collins's voice was flat.

'I went to his birthplace. There *was* a Peter Novak born to Janós and Illana Ferenczi-Novak. He died five years later, in 1942.'

Collins nodded, and his lack of reaction was more chilling than any reaction could have been. 'Excellent work, Janson.'

'Tell me the truth,' Janson said. 'I'm not crazy. *I saw a man die.*'

'That's so,' Collins said.

'And not just any man. Peter Novak—a living legend.'

'Bingo.' Collins made a clicking sound. 'A living legend.'

Janson felt his stomach drop. A living legend. A creation of intelligence professionals.

Peter Novak was an agency legend.

Collins stood up. 'There's something I want to show you.'

He walked to his office. A Sun Microsystems UltraSPARC workstation was connected to racked tiers of servers.

'You remember the ending of *The Wizard of Oz*? I've always thought it's the moment when we lose our innocence. Up there is the great and powerful Oz, and down there is the schmuck beneath the curtain. But it's not just him, it's the whole goddamn contraption, the machinery. You think that was easy to put together? And once you had that up and running, it's not going to make much difference who you've got behind the curtain, or so we figured. It's the *machine*, not the man, that matters.'

The director of Consular Operations was babbling; the anxiety he displayed nowhere else was making him weirdly voluble.

'Start making sense,' Janson said, gritting his teeth.

Collins gestured towards the computer system. 'You might say *that*'s Peter Novak. That, and a few hundred interoperable, omicron-level-security computer systems elsewhere. Peter Novak is a composite of bytes and bits and digital-transfer signatures with neither origins nor destinations. Peter Novak wasn't a person. He's a project. An invention. A legend, yeah. And for a long time, the most successful ever.'

'Please,' Janson said calmly, quietly. 'Go on.'

'Best if we sit somewhere else,' Collins said. 'The system here has so many electronic security seals and booby traps, it goes into auto-erase mode if you breathe on it hard.'

The two settled into the living room.

'Look, it was a brilliant idea,' Collins said. 'Such a brilliant idea that, for a time, people were feuding over who had the idea first. Except that the number of people who knew about this was tiny. Had to be. Obviously, my predecessor Dan Congdon had a lot to do with it. So did Doug Albright, a protégé of David Abbott.'

'Albright I've heard of. Abbott?'

'The guy who devised the "Caine" gambit, back in the Seventies, trying to smoke out Carlos. Same kind of strategic thinking went into Mobius. Asymmetrical conflicts pit states against individual actors. Mismatched, but not the way you'd imagine. Think of an elephant and a mosquito. If that mosquito carries encephalitis, you could have one dead elephant, and there's really not much Jumbo can do about it. Abbott's insight was that you really couldn't mobilise anything as unwieldy as a state against substate baddies. You had to counter with a matching stratagem: create individual actors who, within a broad mandate, had a fair level of autonomy.'

'Mobius?'

'The Mobius Programme. A small group at the State Department are tossing around ideas, and somehow they hit on this scenario. What if they assembled a small, secret team of analysts and experts to create a notional foreign billionaire? They like the idea because it means they can advance American interests in a way that America just can't. They can make the world a better place. Totally win–win. Which is how the Mobius Programme was born.'

'Mobius,' Janson said. 'As in a loop where the inside is the outside.'

'In this case, the outsider is an insider. This mogul becomes an independent figure in the world, no ties whatever to the United States. Our adversaries aren't his adversaries. They can be his allies. He can leverage situations we wouldn't be able to go near. First, though, you've got to create a "he", and from the ground up. Molnár was perfect for the programme's purposes, especially when you added to that the short, unhappy career of Count Ferenczi-Novak. Made perfect sense that our boy was going to have a sketchy early childhood.'

'There'd have to be an employment record,' Janson said, 'but that would have been the easy part. You restrict his "career" to a few front organisations you control.'

'Anybody makes enquiries, there's always some silver-haired department head, maybe retired, to say, "Oh yes, I remember young Peter. A brilliant financial analyst. The work was so good, I didn't mind that he preferred to do it from home." And like that.'

These men and women, Janson knew, would have been generously compensated for uttering a lie perhaps once or twice to an enquiring reporter, and perhaps never. They would not be aware of what else the bargain would entail: the around-the-clock monitoring of their communications, a lifelong net of surveillance—but what they didn't know couldn't hurt them.

'And his incredible humanitarian assistance?'

'Isn't it *messed up* that no matter how much good this country does, so many people round the world hate our guts? Yes, it meant offering balm to the world's trouble spots. Look, the World Bank is a lender of last resort. This guy's a lender of *first* resort, ensuring that he has enormous influence with governments the world over. Peter Novak: your roving ambassador for peace and stability.'

'Oil on troubled waters.'

'Expensive oil, make no mistake. But "Novak" could mediate, resolve conflicts that we could never go near. He's been able to deal with regimes that consider us the Great Satan. He has been a one-man foreign policy. And he's so effective precisely because he appears to have no connection to us.'

'But who is—was—Peter Novak?' Janson asked.

'Three agents were assigned to the part. They were all similar-looking to begin with, close to one another in build and height. And then surgery made them near identical. We had to have replicas in place: given our investment, we couldn't afford to have our guy drop dead from a stroke. Three seemed like good odds.'

Janson looked at Collins. 'Who would ever agree to allow his entire identity to be wiped out, to become dead to everyone he ever knew, his very countenance transformed . . .?'

'Someone who had no choice,' Collins replied cryptically.

Janson felt a gorge of anger. He could hardly stand to look at the bureaucrat, and his eyes drifted towards the glittering bay, towards the fishing boat that had moved into view, safely beyond the security zone that began half a mile from the shore, marked off by warning buoys. 'Someone who had no choice?' He shook his head. 'You mean the way I had no choice when you set me up to be killed.'

'*That* again.' Collins rolled his eyes. 'Calling off the termination order would have raised too many questions. The cowboys at the CIA got credible reports that Novak had been killed and that you had something to do with it. Cons Op got hold of the same info. The last thing any of us at Mobius wanted bruited about, but you play the cards you're dealt. At the time, I did what I thought was best.'

A scrim of red momentarily suffused Janson's vision. Which was the greater insult, he wondered—being executed as a traitor, or being sacrificed as a pawn? Once more the fishing vessel caught his attention, but this time the sight was accompanied by a wrenching sense of danger. It was too small to be a crabber, too near the shore to be after rockfish, and the thick staff that extended from the tarpaulin on the deck was not a fishing pole.

The shell smashed through the window and hurled into the opposite wall, spraying the room with splinters of wood, chunks of plaster and fragments of glass. The blast was so intense that it registered on the ears less as sound than as *pain*. Black smoke began to billow and Janson understood the fluke that had saved them. The shell had burrowed into the cottage's pine and plaster construction before it exploded. Only this had spared them a deadly blast of shrapnel. Janson realised, too, that an artillery gunner's first shell was fired in order to zero in on the mark. The second shell would not arrive ten feet above their heads.

Janson leapt from the couch and raced to the attached garage. The door was open and he stepped down to the concrete floor, where a convertible stood. A yellow Corvette.

'Wait!' Collins called out breathlessly, winded from having followed Janson's sprint. 'I've got the keys right here.' He held them out.

Janson grabbed them and jumped into the driver's seat.

Collins pressed the garage-door opener, and leapt in beside Janson, who revved the motor in reverse and shot out of the garage, executed a J turn and gunned the car down the narrow road.

At eighty miles per hour, the tall grass and thorn trees zipped past in the rearview mirror. The roar of the motor seemed to grow louder, as if the muffler was cutting out. Janson reduced speed slightly.

The sound of the motor did not subside.

It was not the sound of his motor.

Janson turned to his right and saw the hovercraft, an amphibious military model, skimming along the surface of the bay. It was gaining on them. And, perched just below and to the left of the rear fan encasement, someone was fumbling with an M60 machine gun.

Janson hunched down as low as he could in his seat without losing control of the car, and the car's body jarred to a jackhammer rhythm as a spray of bullets tore into the Corvette's steel body.

The hovercraft eased onto the beach and then to the cambered road itself. It was just a few yards away, and the powerful sucking propellers seemed to loom over the tiny sports car. As the antiplough skirts struck the car's rear fender, Janson had a horrible realisation: *It was trying to climb over them.*

He glanced to his right and saw Collins doubled forward in his seat, his hands over his ears, trying to protect them from the din.

Janson swung the steering wheel abruptly to the left, and the car veered off the road, its wheels spinning into the sand and scrub as it rapidly lost traction and speed. The hovercraft zoomed past, then came to a halt and reversed course without turning round. The man with the M60 now had a direct line of fire at driver and passenger alike.

Then Janson heard the sound of yet another craft—a speedboat, veering towards the shore. And in the speedboat he saw a figure, arranged in prone firing position, with a rifle. Aimed at them.

Janson steered the Corvette back onto the road, heard the chassis scrape as it lurched from the sodden earth to the hard macadam.

Crouching below the fan, the machine gunner in the hovercraft, grinned evilly. Seconds remained before he served them with a lethal fire hose of lead. Suddenly the man pitched forward, slack, his forehead dropping like a deadweight against the bipod-propped gun.

There was an echoing sound—on the waters of Chesapeake Bay, it sounded oddly like a cork popping—and then another, and the hovercraft came to rest just a few feet from the car. As it fell to earth, Janson saw that the pilot, too, was sprawled, limp, on the windshield. Two shots, two kills.

A voice called across the waters of Chesapeake Bay, as the engine of the speedboat sputtered to a halt. '*Paul!* Are you all right?'

Janson got out of the car and raced to the shore. He saw Jessica Kincaid in the boat only ten yards away. It was the closest she could bring the speedboat without grounding it.

'Jessie!' he shouted. He felt suddenly, absurdly lighter.

'Tell me I did good,' she said, triumphant.

Derek Collins approached, his sweaty face coated with sand.

Janson turned and faced his adversary. 'Were those two your henchmen as well?'

'Goddammit, I had nothing to do with it! They almost killed *me*, for Christ's sake! They wanted *both* us of dead.' His voice rose with the unabated terror that his whole body exuded.

He was probably speaking the truth, Janson decided. But who *was* behind this latest attempt? And something about Collins's manner bothered Janson: for all his candour, he was holding too much back.

'Maybe so. But you seem to know who the attackers were.'

Collins blinked hard. 'There's a lot you need to know, but I'm not authorised to tell you. You've got to come with me, to meet the Mobius team. We need you to get with the programme, OK?'

'You want me to "get with the programme"? Let me ask you a

question first. You told me about a surgical team that performed procedures on three agents. I'm wondering about the members of that surgical team. Where are they now?'

Collins was silent, bowing his head slightly.

Something burned within Janson, though Collins had done nothing more than confirm his suspicions. They had probably allowed themselves a twelve-month period for the mop-up. It would not have been difficult. A car crash, an accidental drowning, perhaps a deadly collision on a double-diamond ski slope.

Janson's eyes drilled into Collins's. 'Small sacrifices for the larger good, right? That's what I figured. No, Collins, I'm not going to get with the programme. Not *your* programme, anyway.'

Janson looked out towards the water, saw Jessie Kincaid in the idling craft, saw her short hair ruffled by the gentle breeze, and all at once his heart felt as if it might burst. Maybe Collins was telling him the truth about the role of Consular Operations in what had gone down; maybe he wasn't. The only verifiable truth was that Janson could not trust him. *There's a lot you need to know . . . Come with me.* That's just the sort of line Collins would use to lure him to his death.

Janson bolted down the beach, first wading into the shallow water, then propelling himself to Jessie's boat with powerful crawl strokes.

As he climbed aboard, Jessie reached for him, took his hand.

'Funny, I thought you were in Amsterdam,' Janson said.

'Let's just say its charms ran thin.'

He put his arms round her, feeling the warmth of her body. 'OK, my questions can wait. You've probably got some of your own.'

'I'll start with one,' she said. 'Are we partners?'

He pressed her close to him. 'Yeah,' he said. 'We're partners.'

CHAPTER TWELVE

'**Y**ou don't understand,' said the courier, a straitlaced black man in his twenties, with rimless glasses. 'I could lose my job for that.' He gestured towards the patch on his navy jacket with the distinctive logo of his company: Caslon Couriers. Caslon: the extremely expensive, top-of-the-line, ultrasecure courier service to which select individuals and corporations entrusted highly sensitive documents.

He was sitting at a small table at the Starbucks on 39th Street and Broadway, in Manhattan, and the grey-haired man who had joined him there was politely insistent. He was, he had explained, a senior officer of the Liberty Foundation; his wife was a staff member of the Manhattan office. Yes, the approach was irregular, but he was at the end of his rope. The trouble was, he had reason to believe she was receiving packages from a romantic suitor.

The courier grew visibly uncomfortable until Janson began to peel off hundred-dollar bills. After twenty of them, his eyes began to warm behind his glasses.

'I'm not asking you to divert anything,' the grey-haired man said, 'All I'm asking is to see copies of the invoice slips. And if I learn something, if it's the guy I think it is, nobody will ever know how.'

The courier nodded. 'How about you meet me at the atrium of the Sony Building, Fifty-fifth and Madison, in four hours?'

At the Sony atrium, four hours later, Janson was finally able to look through the invoices. There were dozens of packages that arrived from cities corresponding to the major Liberty Foundation branch offices. Yet there were also a handful of packages that were sent to Márta Lang from a location that corresponded to nothing at all. Why was Caslon Couriers making regular pick-ups from a small town in the Blue Ridge Mountains?

A little additional research—several hours in the New York Public Library—was suggestive. Millington, Virginia, turned out to be the nearest town to a vast pastoral estate that was built by John Vincent Astor in the 1890s, a place that, by several architectural accounts, rivalled the legendary Biltmore estate in its elegance and attention to detail. And now? Who owned it now? Who lived there now?

Only one conclusion suggested itself: a man the world knew as Peter Novak. Control *required* communication. 'Novak' was still in command of his empire; he would have to be in communication with his deputies. People like Márta Lang. Janson's plan called for breaching the channels of communication. By tracing the subtle twitchings of the web, he might find the spider.

JANSON SPENT the following morning on the road, eventually shifting from the turnpike to the smaller roads that webbed across the Blue Ridge Mountains. A few miles past a camping exit, he saw a turnoff marked for the town of Castleton, and he knew that Millington would not be much further.

JED SIPPERLY'S PRE-OWNED AUTO—BUY YOUR NEXT CAR HERE! read a garish roadside sign. Janson pulled into the lot.

Switching vehicles was standard procedure during long trips. He was confident he was not being followed, but there was always the possibility of 'soft surveillance': a purely passive system of observation, agents instructed to notice, not to follow.

A 120-pound dog lunged at a Cyclone fence as Janson got out of his Altima and made his way towards the trailer office. The large animal—a mongrel whose ancestors seemed to include a pit bull, a Doberman and a mastiff—was penned into one corner of the lot.

A thirtyish man with a cigarette in the corner of his mouth sauntered out of the trailer. 'I'm Jed Sipperly,' he said, with a handshake.

There was another cage-rattling lunge from the dog.

'Don't you mind Butch.' Jed Sipperly stooped down to pick up a small Raggedy Ann cloth doll. He tossed it into the enclosed area. It turned out to be what the mammoth dog was pining for; he bounded over to it and began to cradle it between huge paws.

Jed returned to his customer with an apologetic shrug. 'Dog's so attached to that doll, it ain't wholesome. A real good guard dog, 'cept he won't bark. That your Nissan Altima?'

'Thinking of a trade,' Janson said.

'How many miles you got on it?'

'Fifty thou,' Janson said. 'A little more.'

'Good time for a trade, then. Because those Nissan transmissions start making trouble once you reach sixty. If what you're looking for is reliability, I can steer you towards one or two models that'll probably outlast *you*.' He pointed towards a maroon sedan. 'See that Taurus? One of the all-time greats.'

Janson looked grateful as the salesman fleeced him, taking the late-model Altima in trade for the ageing Taurus and asking for an additional $400 on top. 'A sweet deal,' Jed Sipperly assured him. 'Tell you what, you give me another fiver and you can have the damn dog in with it!' A long-suffering laugh: 'Or maybe I should *pay* you to take it off my hands.'

Janson smiled, waved, and got into the seven-year-old Taurus.

IT DIDN'T TAKE Janson long to size up Millington. Perched on a rocky slope of Smith Mountain, it was a town that was dark by ten o'clock. The biggest single employer produced glazed bricks and did a side business in unrefined mineral by-products; and the downtown diner served eggs and fries and coffee all day. Janson's kind of place.

Yet if the decades-old accounts were accurate, there was a vast estate hidden somewhere in the hills, as private a residence as you could hope for—legally as well as physically. For even its ownership was completely obscure.

Janson entered the diner, where he started a conversation with the counterman. The man's sloping forehead, close-set eyes and jutting, square jaw gave him a slightly simian appearance, but when he spoke he proved surprisingly knowledgeable.

'So you're thinking of moving nearby?' the counterman asked. 'Let me guess. Made your money in the big city and now you want the peace and quiet of the country, that it?'

'Something like that,' Janson said. 'Possible to build round here?'

'Possible to build on the moon, people say.'

'What about transportation?'

'Well, you're here, ain't you?'

'I guess I am,' Janson said. 'Airport?'

'Nearest real airport's probably Roanoke.'

'"Real" airport? There another kind round here?'

'There used to be, back in the Forties and Fifties. Some sort of tiny training airport the army air force built. About three miles up Clangerton Road, a turnoff to the left. I don't think it's much more than an airstrip any more.'

'So what happened to that airstrip? Ever get used?'

'Ever? Never? I don't use those words.'

'Reason I ask, you see, is an old business associate of mine, he lives near here, and he said something about it.'

The counterman looked uncomfortable. Janson pushed his empty coffee cup forward to be refilled, and the man pointedly did not do so.

'Then you'd better ask him about it, hadn't you?' the man said.

The town grocery was just down the street. Janson stopped in and introduced himself to the manager, a bland-looking man with light brown hair. Janson told him what he had told the man at the diner. The store manager evidently found the prospect of a new arrival lucrative enough that he was downright encouraging.

'That is a great idea, man,' he said. 'It's real beautiful here. You get a few miles up the mountain and look around and it's totally unspoilt. Plus you got your hunting and your fishing and your . . .' He trailed off, seemingly unable to think of a third suitable item.

'And for everyday stuff?' Janson prodded.

'We got a video store,' he volunteered. 'Laundromat. This store right here. I can do special orders, if you need 'em. Do that once in a while for regular customers.'

'Do you, now?'

'Oh yeah. We got all kinds round here. There's one cat—we've never seen him, but he sends a guy down here every few days to pick up groceries. Super-rich—gotta be. Owns a place somewhere up in the mountains, some kind of Lex Luthor hideaway, I like to think. People see a little plane touching down near there most every afternoon. But he still uses us for groceries.'

'And you do special orders for this guy?'

'Oh, sure,' the man said. 'It's all real secure. Whatever he wants, it's not a problem. I order it and a Sysco truck comes by and delivers it, and he has a guy come get it, he don't care what it costs.'

A grey-haired woman at the refrigerated section was calling to him. 'Keith? Keith, dear?'

The man excused himself, and went over to her.

'Is this sole fresh or frozen?' she asked.

'It's fresh frozen,' Keith explained

As the two carried on an earnest conversation about whether that signified a way of being fresh or a way of being frozen, Janson wandered to the far end of the store. The stockroom door was open, and he stepped into it, casually. At a small metal desk was a stack of pale blue Sysco inventory lists. He flipped through them until he reached one stamped SPECIAL ORDER. Towards the bottom of a long row of foodstuffs in small print, he saw an order of buckwheat groats.

A few seconds elapsed before it clicked. Buckwheat groats—also known as kasha. Janson felt a stirring of excitement as thousands of column inches from press profiles whirred through his head. *Every day starts with a spartan breakfast of kasha . . .*

It was true, then. Somewhere on Smith Mountain lived a man the world knew as Peter Novak.

IN THE HEART of Manhattan, the bag lady stooped over the steel-mesh trash can with the diligent look of a postal worker at a mailbox. Her clothes were torn and filthy, her shoes were oversize sneakers, the soles beginning to split. On her hands were dirty cotton gloves, and as she rummaged through the plastic bottles, apple cores, banana peel and crumpled advertising flyers, the gloves grew even dirtier.

Yet Jessica Kincaid's eyes were not on the refuse; they returned regularly to the small mirror she had propped against the trash can, which allowed her to monitor those departing from the Liberty Foundation offices across the street. After days of a fruitless watch, one of Janson's former confederates, Cornelius Eaves, had called last night: Márta Lang seemed finally to have made an appearance.

It was not a mistaken sighting, Jessie now knew. A woman matching Janson's description of Deputy Director Márta Lang had been among the arrivals at eight o'clock that morning.

It was six when the elegant, white-haired woman appeared again, striding through the revolving door of the lobby. As she stepped into the back seat of a waiting Lincoln Town Car, Jessica radioed Cornelius Eaves, whose vehicle—a yellow taxi cab with its OFF DUTY lights on—had been idling in front of a hotel at the other end of the block.

Eaves, who had been retired from active duty for a few years and was eager to have something to occupy his time, did not know the purpose of his assignment. The only authorisation he required was Janson's personal entreaty.

Jessica dived into the back seat of Eaves's cab, wriggled out of her rags and changed into her ordinary street clothes. Ten minutes later, they had an address: 1060 Fifth Avenue.

DRIVING THE MAROON Taurus up the winding mountain path known as Clangerton Road, Janson found the unmarked turnoff that the counterman had mentioned. He continued a short distance past it, pulling the car off the road and into a natural cave of greenery.

He walked into the woods and doubled back towards the small lane he had driven past. And then he found the airstrip.

It was a sudden clearing in the forest, and disturbingly well maintained: the bramble and bushes had been clipped back recently and a long oval strip of grass was neatly trimmed. It was empty except for an SUV with a tarpaulin over it.

Janson nested himself in the middle of an old pine, concealing himself behind its trunk and the profusion of needle-laden fronds. He steadied his binoculars against a small branch, and waited.

He was convinced there would be a flight today, not only because of what the grocery-store manager had reported but because packages, couriers, *people*, would all have to come in and out.

He was not wrong. The plane was a Cessna, a twin-engine craft, and its pilot, as Janson could tell by the grace with which it touched down and came to a stop, was an extremely skilled professional.

The pilot, dressed in a white uniform, emerged from the cockpit and folded down the aluminium steps. The sun glared off the fuselage, obscuring Janson's vision. All he could make out was that a passenger was quickly ushered off the plane by an assistant, this one in a blue uniform, and brought to the SUV. The assistant yanked the tarp from the vehicle, revealing a Range Rover—armoured, he surmised, from the way the body rode low on the chassis—and held open the back door for the passenger. Moments later, the car sped off.

And then it disappeared.

Janson slid from his perch and set off towards the drive. It was overhung by branches about six feet off the ground—just high enough to allow clearance for the Range Rover. The tree-sheltered drive had been recently resurfaced—a driver who knew the road could make good time—yet could not be seen even from overhead.

Janson followed the drive, staying parallel to it, ten yards away, lest he activate any surveillance equipment. It was a long walk, and a strenuous one. An hour passed before he climbed up the last rocky ledge and saw the Smith Mountain estate. It took his breath away.

It was a plateau—perhaps 1,000 acres of rolled Kentucky bluegrass. And tucked away was a shimmering mansion. It was the perimeter defences, however, that inspired Janson's awe. As if the natural impediments surrounding the site were not sufficient, a high-tech obstacle course made the house resistant to any intrusion.

Ahead of him was a nine-foot chain-link fence. Janson could see the array of pressure detectors built into it. Tensioned wire threaded its way through the chain links, connecting to a series of boxes. A taut wire intrusion-detection system reinforced with vibration detectors. Beyond the chain-link barricade he saw a series of stanchions—four-foot-high poles. Each received and transmitted a microwave flux. They were staggered, with overlapping beams protecting the stanchions themselves. Janson scanned the grassy fairway beyond until he identified the small box near the gravelled driveway with the logo of TriStar Security on it. There, beneath the ground, was a buried-cable pressure sensor.

A wave of despair overcame him. So near and yet so far.

IT WAS DUSK by the time he found his way back to the Taurus. He drove back towards Millington and then north on Route 58.

At a roadside flea market, he bought an electric egg-beater, though all he wanted was the solenoid motor. A strip-mall Radio Shack sufficed for a cheap cellphone. At the Millington grocery store, he bought a steel can of butter cookies. Next was the hardware store on Main Street, where he bought glue, a roll of electrical tape, a pair of heavy-duty scissors and a locking extensible curtain rod. His final stop was Sipperly's car lot.

'You know all sales are "as is", don't you?' Sipperly said warily.

Janson took five dollars out of his billfold. 'For the dog.'

'Come again?'

'You said I could have the dog for a fiver,' Janson said.

'Well, joking aside, I'm really very fond of that dog,' Sipperly insisted. 'He's truly one-of-a-kind. Excellent guard dog—'

'Except he doesn't bark,' Janson pointed out.

'But he's really a great dog. I don't know if I could part with him.'

'Fifty.'

'A hundred.'

'Seventy-five.'

'Sold,' Jed Sipperly said. 'And you'd better take that mangy puppet along with it. The only way you'll ever get the beast in the car.'

The mammoth dog sniffed Janson and, indeed, got into the vehicle only when Janson tossed the Raggedy Ann onto his back seat.

'Thank you kindly,' Janson said. 'And, by the way, can you tell me where I can pick up a radar detector?'

Sipperly grinned. 'If you're interested in a sweet deal on one of those babies, all I can say is, you asked the right guy.'

It was early evening when Janson returned to his motel room, assembled his equipment and loaded it into a knapsack. By the time he set out again for the estate, he and the dog had to walk by moonglow.

Just before Janson approached the final ridge, he removed the dog's collar, scooped up a few handfuls of soil and smeared it into the dog's already muddy coat. The dog now looked feral, a large version of the mountain dogs that occasionally roamed the slopes. Next, Janson took the Raggedy Ann doll and flung it over the chain-link fence. Then he stepped back into the dense stand of trees.

The dog lunged against the fence, crashing against the vibration sensors and the taut-wire system. With an electronic chirp, both systems registered the presence of an intruder, and a row of blue diodes lit up, marking out the segment of the fence.

Janson heard the motorised pivot of a closed-circuit video camera mounted on a high pole within the grounds. A cluster of lights above the camera blinked on, directing a halogen blaze towards the section of the fence where Butch was launching his repeated assaults.

Janson could see the camera's lens elongate. It was operated, it seemed, from within one of the guard stations. Having pinpointed the intruder, its operators could zoom in and make a determination.

That determination did not take long. The halogen light was switched off, the camera swivelled away from the fence, and the blue diodes of the section went black.

The next time Butch sprang against the fence, no diodes illuminated. The segment was deactivated, the false alarms forestalled. Janson knew what conclusions had been reached. No doubt the dog was chasing a squirrel; no doubt its enthusiasm would soon pass.

Now Janson threw his knapsack over the fence. Moving hands and feet in tandem, he swiftly propelled himself towards the top of the fence, and flung himself over.

There was something soft beneath him as he landed. The rag doll. Janson tossed it back over the fence; the dog gently picked it up and crept away somewhere behind the tree line.

Janson made his way towards the stanchions. He unzipped his knapsack and removed the police radar detector. It was a Phantom II, a high-end model. What made it so effective was that it was both a detector and a jammer, aiming to make a motorist's car 'invisible' to speed-detecting equipment. It worked by detecting the signal and bouncing it back towards the radar gun. Janson used duct tape to fasten the device near the end of the long telescoping steel rod. If it worked as he hoped, he would be able to exploit an inherent design feature: the necessary tolerance for wildlife and weather.

He studied the configuration of the stanchions. In his head, he drew an imaginary line connecting a pair of adjacent stanchions, then an imaginary line connecting the next pair. Midway between those two parallel lines would be the point where the area of coverage was at its minimum. Holding the steel rod, Janson moved the Phantom II towards that spot. The system would have detected the appearance of an object, but it would also determine that the waveform patterns did not correspond to that of any human intrusion.

He kept the Phantom II steadily in position, moving himself down the pole, hand over hand, keeping it aloft without shifting its position. Then he rotated the rod and continued to back away from the microwave barrier. And . . . he was through.

He looked at the dimly illuminated LCD display of his black Teltek voltmeter, holding it in cupped hands. Nothing. No activity.

He travelled another ten feet. The digits began to climb; he took another step, and they surged.

He was approaching the subterranean pressure sensors. Though the voltmeter indicated that the buried cable itself was still a way off, he knew that the electromagnetic flux of TriStar's buried-cable sensors created a detection field that was more than six feet wide.

Janson locked the telescoping rod in its fully extended position. He walked some way back towards the microwave poles and, keeping the rod extended in his hands, raced towards the buried sensor cables, imagining the invisible six-foot-wide band to be a physical barrier.

He held the pole as he ran, then plunged the end of it in the ground, just above where he believed the cable to be buried. He swung his right knee up and jumped, swinging upwards as he held on to the pole. If all went well, his momentum would carry him, and he would land a safe distance from the cable. The volumetric detector would have been alerted only to the thin pole twitching in the ground—nothing even approaching the volume, or flux disturbance patterns, consistent with a human being.

Janson tumbled to the ground and rolled away from the zone.

He stood and looked up at the mansion that loomed before him. The windows were dark except for a dim glow of what might be standard night-time illumination. Were its inhabitants in the back rooms? It seemed too early for anyone to be asleep.

He crept over to a narrow side entrance. Its door was alarmed. With the help of a penlight, Janson scanned the door until he saw the tiny screws on the topmost section: evidence of the contact switch. Within the door frame, the contacts of a ferrous-metal switch were kept together—the circuit kept closed—by a magnet recessed in the top of the door. As long as the door was shut, the magnet would keep a plunger within the door frame depressed, completing the electric circuit within the switch unit. Janson withdrew a powerful magnet from his knapsack and, using a fast-drying adhesive, fastened it to the lower part of the door frame.

Then he went to work on the door lock. There was no keyhole. The door was opened by means of a magnetic card. His magnetic picklock was not an impressive-looking piece of equipment, having been jury-rigged with electrical tape and epoxy. He had removed the core of the solenoid and replaced it with a steel rod. At the other end of the rod he had attached a thin rectangle of steel, cut from the cookie tin using heavy-duty scissors. The electronic part was a circuit of transistors he had extracted from the Radio Shack cellphone. Once he connected a pair of AA batteries to the apparatus, a quickly oscillating magnetic field was created: it was designed to pulse at the sensors until they were activated.

Janson inserted the metal rectangle in the slot and heard the click of the lock's own solenoid being activated. The door's bolts and latches were swiftly retracted. He opened the door.

As long as the house was occupied, any internal photoelectric alarms would be deactivated. Janson quietly closed the door behind him and, in the gloom, proceeded down a long hall.

After a few hundred feet, he saw a crack of light. It was seeping beneath a panelled door to his left. What kind of lair was this? An office? A conference room?

He removed his pistol and strode into the room.

He was in the middle of a magnificent drawing room. And in the middle of it, eight men and women were seated, facing him.

They had been waiting for him.

'What the heck took you so long, Mr Janson? Collins here told me you'd make it here by eight o'clock. It's practically half past.'

Janson felt flash frozen by the shock. He blinked hard at his questioner, but the evidence of his eyes remained unchanged.

He was staring at the president of the United States.

Next to him sat the director of Consular Operations. And the others? Janson recognised most of them. There was the secretary of state. The U.S. Treasury Department's undersecretary for international affairs. The chairman of the National Intelligence Council. The deputy director of the Defense Intelligence Agency. Also a few colourless, nervous-looking technicians: he knew the type immediately.

'Have a seat, Paul,' said Derek Collins. 'Apologies for the programmed misdirection.'

'The courier was on your payroll,' Janson said, toneless.

Collins nodded. 'We'd had the same thought as you about getting access to the incoming documents. As soon as he reported your contact, we knew we had a golden opportunity. Look, you weren't exactly going to respond to an engraved invitation. It was the only way I could bring you in.'

Glances were exchanged between Collins and the president. 'And it was the best way to show these other good people you still have what it takes,' Collins said. 'That your abilities live up to your reputation. That was one impressive infiltration. And before you get all hurt and sulky, you better understand that the people in this room are pretty much the only ones left who know the truth about Mobius. For better or worse, you're now a member of this select group. Which means we've got an Uncle Sam Wants You situation here.'

'God*damn* you, Collins!' Janson reholstered his pistol.

The president cleared his throat. 'Mr Janson, we really are depending on you. Our creature has become—well, not our creature any more. We've lost control of the asset.'

'Paul?' Collins said. 'Have a seat. This is going to take a while.'

Janson lowered himself into a nearby armchair.

President Berquist glanced at Douglas Albright, the man from the Defense Intelligence Agency. 'Doug, why don't you start?'

'I gather it's already been explained to you that we had three extremely dedicated agents trained to play the role of Peter Novak.'

'Right,' Janson said. 'What about the wife, though?'

'Remember Nell Pearson?' Collins asked quietly.

Janson was thunderstruck. No wonder there was something about Novak's wife that seemed familiar. His own affair with Nell Pearson had taken place a couple of years after he joined Consular Operations. Like him, his fellow agent was single, young and restless. They had both been working undercover in Belfast, assigned to play husband and wife. It didn't take much for them to add an element of reality to the imposture. Those long elegant fingers—the one thing that could not be altered. And the eyes. There had been something between them, had there not? Some frisson, even in Amsterdam?

Janson shuddered, imagining the woman he knew being reshaped, irreversibly, by the cold steel edge of a surgeon's scalpel. 'But what do you mean you've lost control?' he persisted.

The Treasury Department's undersecretary for international affairs spoke. 'Start with the operational challenge: how do you secure the funding necessary to sustain the illusion of a world-class tycoon-philanthropist? The Mobius Programme couldn't simply divert funds from a closely monitored US intelligence budget. So the program drew upon our intelligence capabilities to create its *own* fund. We put to use our signals intercepts . . .'

'Jesus *Christ*—you're talking about Echelon!' Janson said.

Echelon was a complex intelligence-gathering system comprising a fleet of satellites: every international phone call, every form of telecommunication that involved a satellite could be intercepted by the orbiting spy fleet. Its mammoth download was fed into an assortment of analysis facilities, all controlled by the National Security Agency. The NSA had repeatedly denied rumours that it used the intercepts for purposes other than national security, in its strictest sense. Yet here was the shocking admission that even the most conspiracy-minded sceptics didn't know the half of it.

The Treasury undersecretary nodded sombrely. 'Echelon enabled us to gain secret intelligence about central-bank decisions around the world. Our creation was armed with that inside information. Through him we placed a few massive, highly leveraged currency bets. In rapid order, twenty million became twenty *billion*—and then much, much more. Here was a legendary financier. And nobody had to know that his brilliant intuition was in fact the result of—'

'The abuse of US government surveillance,' Janson said.

'Needless to say, Mobius was a programme that was in place long before I took office,' President Berquist said. 'It had created a highly visible billionaire . . . yet we hadn't counted on the human factor: the possibility that access to and control of all that wealth and power might prove too great a lure to at least one of our agents.'

Janson turned to Collins. 'I asked you, when we spoke earlier, who would agree to play such a role—to have his entire identity erased. What kind of man would do such a thing?'

'Yes,' Collins said, 'and I answered, "Someone who had no choice." The fact is, you *know* that someone. A man named Alan Demarest.'

CHAPTER THIRTEEN

'No,' Janson said. He shook his head slowly. 'It's impossible.'
Alan Demarest had been executed. *And Janson had watched.*

Collins shrugged. 'Blanks, squibs. Basic stagecraft. I'm sorry you were lied to for all these years, but material like that doesn't come along very often in our line of work. So Demarest was presented with a choice. He could face execution. Or give his life to us.'

'*Damn* you!' Janson cried out. He saw it now. Demarest had been the first Peter Novak: *primus inter pares*. The others would be matched to the frame of his body. He had been the first because of his redoubtable gifts, as a linguist, an actor, a brilliantly resourceful operative. Demarest was the best they had. Had the thought even arisen that there might be risks in giving this responsibility to someone so utterly devoid of conscience—to a *sociopath*?

Derek Collins continued. 'Demarest has seized the assets created for the Mobius Programme, changed all the banking codes—and foiled the measures we'd taken to prevent such an eventuality.'

'And the United States can't expose him,' said the secretary of state. 'Not without exposing itself.'

'And Anura?' Janson demanded.

'His masterstroke,' said the chairman of the National Intelligence Council. 'When we heard our man was imprisoned there, we panicked, and acted precisely as Demarest knew we would. We entrusted him with the second set of codes, the ones that would normally have been under the control of the man the guerrillas were about to execute. It seemed necessary, as a stopgap. What we didn't realise was that Demarest had *arranged* the hostage taking. Evidently he used a lieutenant of his named Bewick as the cut-out, a cut-out the Caliph knew only as the "Go-Between".'

'Jesus.'

'For that matter, we failed to realise that he was also responsible for the death of the third agent, a year earlier.'

'Why did Demarest bring *me* into it?'

Collins spoke first. 'The man loathes you, blames you for taking away his career, his freedom, almost his life—turning him in to a government he thought he'd served with incredible devotion. He didn't just want to see you dead. He wanted you to be accused, humiliated, killed by your own government. What goes around comes around—that's how he must have seen things.'

'And now the puppet is killing off the puppet masters,' said Doug Albright. 'He's erasing the programme. Erasing Mobius.'

'It's become apparent that Demarest has been planning his *coup d'état* for years,' the secretary of state said. 'As the recent killings have revealed, Demarest has assembled a private militia, recruited dozens of his former colleagues to use as his personal enforcers and protectors. These are operatives who know the codes and procedures of our most advanced field strategies. And the corrupt moguls of the former Communist states—the ones who pretend to be opposed to him—are actually in league with the guy. They've made their own centurions available to him.'

'You called it a *coup d'état*,' Janson said to him. 'A term usually reserved for toppling and supplanting a head of state.'

'The fact is,' the president said, 'Demarest can blackmail us into doing whatever he demands. If the world ever found out that the US had been surreptitiously manipulating global events—not to mention using Echelon to bet against the currencies of other countries—it would be a devastating blow. You'd get revolutions all over the Third World and we'd lose every ally we have. He's sent us a message demanding we turn control of Echelon over to him. And that's just for starters. Nuclear codes could be next.'

'What did you tell him, Mr President?'

'We refused, naturally.'

'So now he's given us a deadline along with the ultimatum,' Collins said. 'And the clock is ticking.'

'And you can't take him out?'

'If we could find the son of a bitch, he'd be dead meat,' Collins said. 'But we can't. Plus, any person we bring in represents another potential blackmail threat. *It's just us.*'

'And you,' said President Berquist. 'You're our best hope.'

'What about people who genuinely oppose "Peter Novak", the legendary humanitarian? Fact is, he's not without enemies. Isn't there some way to mobilise a fanatic, a faction . . . ?'

'The truth is, we've tried that,' Collins said. 'But the crazy terror king can't find him, either.'

Janson squinted. '*The Caliph!* Jesus. But how are you in a position to steer him at all? *Every* Westerner is satanic, in his book.'

'There's somebody in Libyan military intelligence who works with us occasionally. If you can think of a way to use him, go for it. But the problem remains: we can't get Demarest in our sights.'

'Which means you're our best hope,' President Berquist repeated.

'There's nobody better in the field than you, Janson,' Collins said.

'Except . . .' Doug Albright was worrying aloud, then thought better of it.

'Yes?' Janson was insistent.

The DIA man's eyes were pitiless. 'Except Alan Demarest.'

THE HANDSOME silver-haired West African looked out of the window of his thirty-eighth-floor office and waited for his calls to be returned. He was the secretary-general of the United Nations, and what he was about to do would shock most of the people who knew him. Yet it was the only way to ensure the survival of everything he had devoted his life to.

The sun was low on the horizon, giving the East River a rosy tinge, when the secretary-general's assistant notified him that Peter Novak was on the phone. He picked up at once.

'*Mon cher* Mathieu,' the voice said, with crystalline clarity.

After a few pleasantries, Mathieu Zinsou began to hint at what he had in mind. The United Nations, he told the great man, was running out of money. 'In many respects, our resources are enormous,' the secretary-general said. 'We have thousands of soldiers seconded to us, proudly wearing the blue helmets. UN officials operate freely in just about every country on the planet. We see the suffering of people victimised by the incompetence and greed of their leaders. Yet *we* cannot reshape their policies, their politics. Our rules and regulations, our bylaws and systems—they hamstring us into irrelevance! The successes of your Liberty Foundation have put the United Nations to shame. And meantime our ongoing financial crisis has crippled us. A partnership with the Liberty Foundation is a matter of common sense—a pooling of resources and competencies.'

'I've always thought your reputation for foresight was well earned,' Novak said. 'But so is your reputation for strategic ambiguity, *mon cher*. I wish I had a better sense of what you're proposing.'

'Simply put, there can be no salvation for us except through partnership with you. A special joint division can be established—joint between the Liberty Foundation and the UN—devoted to economic development. It will be a powerful, invisible directorate within the United Nations. I can serve as the bridge between the two empires, yours and mine.'

'You intrigue me, Mathieu,' said Novak. 'But we both know the rules of bureaucratic inertia. You admire the extraordinary effectiveness of the Liberty Foundation, but there's a reason for our record: the fact that I have always retained absolute, top-to-bottom control.'

'I am aware of that fact,' said the secretary-general. 'And when I speak of "partnerships", I need you to understand my meaning. Ultimate control would be exercised by you, Peter.'

A mirthless laugh came from the phone: 'Sounds like you're offering to sell me the United Nations.'

'I hope I didn't say *that*!' Zinsou exclaimed lightly. 'It is a treasure beyond price. But yes, I think we understand each other.'

'And what about you, Mathieu? You'll be serving out your second term—and then what?' The voice on the phone grew friendly. 'You have served your organisation selflessly for so many years.'

'You're kind to say so,' the secretary-general said, catching his drift. 'The personal element is a subsidiary one, you appreciate. My real concerns are for the survival of this institution. But yes, I will be frank. The UN job does not exactly pay well. A job as, let us say, a director of a Liberty Foundation institute . . . with salary and benefits to be negotiated . . . would be the ideal way to continue my work.'

'I believe I'm coming to a better understanding, and find it all very encouraging,' said the man who was Peter Novak.

'Then why don't we have dinner. The sooner the better.'

'*Mon cher* Mathieu,' the man on the phone repeated. 'I'll get back to you.' And the line went dead.

'*Alors?*' The secretary-general turned to Paul Janson, who had been sitting in the corner of the darkening office.

'Now we wait,' said Janson.

WITH A NUMBER of calls, Jessica Kincaid had learned more than she needed to know about the inhabitants of 1060 Fifth Avenue.

'We've got one Agnes Cameron on the floor above Márta Lang,' Kincaid told Janson. 'Serves on the board of the Metropolitan Museum of Art. I called the office of the director, pretending to be a journalist writing a profile of her. Said I was told she was in a meeting there, and I needed to double-check some quotes. A snotty woman said, "Well, that's impossible, Mrs Cameron is in Paris."'

'That the best candidate?'

'Seems to be, yeah. According to the phone company records, she had a high-speed DSL Internet connection installed last year.'

She handed Janson a cotton-knit shirt emblazoned with the logo of the phone company Verizon, matching hers. Next came a leather instrument belt and a bright orange test phone. Rounding out the costume was a grey metal toolbox.

As they approached the doorman, Jessie Kincaid did the talking. 'We've got a customer, she's out of the country, but her DSL line is on the fritz and she asked us to service it while she's gone.' She flipped a laminated ID at him. 'Customer name is Cameron.'

The doorman went inside and consulted with the guard. 'Repair guys from the phone company. Mrs Cameron's apartment.'

They followed him into the elegant lobby.

The second doorman had been sitting on a stool, talking to the guard. Now he sprang to his feet. He was evidently senior to the other doorman. He lifted an internal phone and pressed a few digits.

'Repairmen from Verizon,' he said. 'To fix a phone line.' He put his hand over the mouth of the phone and turned to the two visitors. 'Mrs Cameron's housekeeper says why don't you come back when Mrs Cameron's in town. Be another week.'

'When you see Mrs Cameron, tell her it'll be a few months before we'll be able to schedule another appointment,' Janson replied. 'The backlog is incredible. When an appointment is cancelled, you go to the end of the line. Just be sure to tell Mrs Cameron that.'

The senior doorman flinched. Now, speaking into the phone, he said confidingly, 'You know what? I think you'd better let these guys do their job.' Then he jerked his head in the direction of the elevator bank. 'Eighth floor. The housekeeper will let you in.'

Janson and Kincaid walked to the elevators and entered a cab.

They pressed the button to the seventh floor and waited impatiently as the small cab rose and then slowly shuddered to a halt. The doors parted directly onto the apartment's foyer.

Janson and Kincaid stepped quietly into the hallway and listened. A clink of china, but distant.

To the left, at the end of the hallway, a staircase led to the floor below—the main floor, it seemed. Janson signalled to Jessie: remain behind. Then he descended the stairs. In his hands was a small pistol.

To his left: a sort of double parlour. Janson progressed through the first room and reached the entrance to the adjoining parlour. There, in front of him, was a housekeeper in a pale blue uniform.

She turned towards him, holding an old-fashioned feather duster.

Suddenly the housekeeper's chest erupted in a spray of scarlet and she toppled forward onto the carpet.

Janson whirled round and saw the silenced gun in Jessie's hand, a wisp of cordite seeping from its perforated cylinder.

'Oh, *Jesus*,' Janson breathed. 'Do you realise what you just did?'

'Do you?' Jessica strode over to the body and, with a foot, nudged the feather duster in the housekeeper's hand. Artfully concealed beneath the fan of brown feathers was a high-powered SIG Sauer.

At the end of the second parlour was a doorway with a swing door. Suddenly, there was a series of loud blasts, and the swinging door was perforated by several magnum-force bullets, spraying splinters of wood and paint. Janson looked at Kincaid, verifying that she, like him, was out of the line of fire, safely to the side of the doorway.

There was the sound of quiet footfalls. Janson knew whoever it was was going to peer through the bore holes their gun had drilled.

Janson threw himself against the swinging door. With a thud, it connected, sending the person on the other side sprawling.

It was Márta Lang he saw as the door swung all the way open. The door had knocked her against a dining-room table. The weapon in her hands had been sent flying, too, clattering beyond her reach.

As she got to her feet, Janson picked it up. 'A Suomi burp gun. Impressive. You have a licence for this toy?'

'You've broken into my house,' she said. 'I'd call it self-defence.'

'Don't waste our time and we'll try not to waste yours,' Janson said. 'We know the truth about Peter Novak. Give him up. It's your only chance. They've pulled the plug on him. An executive directive from the President of the United States himself.'

The white-haired woman's contempt was magnificent. 'Peter Novak is more powerful than he is. The US president is only the leader of the *free* world.'

'You're deluded. He's somehow brought you into his own madness. And if you can't break free, you're lost.'

Something between a grin and a grimace flashed on her face. 'Has it never struck you that he's been three steps ahead of you all along? He knows just what you're capable of doing, and just what you'll decide to do. For all your derring-do in the Stone Palace, he was playing with you like a kid with a goddamn action figure. We knew every element of your plan and we'd prepared contingencies for every anticipated variant. Of *course* Higgins—oh, that was the fellow you sprang—was going to insist on saving the American girl. And of *course* you were going to give up your seat to the lady. Perfectly *predictable*. The craft was wired to blow by remote, needless to say. Peter Novak was practically waving a baton—he could have been conducting the whole goddamn operation.' She flashed a strangely ethereal smile. When Janson had met her in Chicago, she seemed the picture of a highly educated foreigner. Her accent was now decidedly American; she could have come from Darien.

'Alan Demarest—where is he?'

'Not telling,' she said lightly.

Janson stared. 'If you know where he is, then, God help me, I will extract the information from you. After a few hours on a VERSED-scopolamine drip, you won't know the difference between your thoughts and your speech. Whatever comes into your head will come out of your mouth. If it's in your head, we'll extract it.'

He grew aware of choral music in the background. Hildegard von

Bingen. The hairs on his neck stood erect. '"The Canticles of Ecstasy,"' he said. 'The long shadow of Alan Demarest.'

'Huh? *I* turned him onto that,' she said, shrugging. 'Back when we were growing up.'

Janson stared at her, seeing her as if for the first time. Suddenly, a series of small nagging details snapped into place. The movement of her head, her sudden, bewildering shifts of affect and tone, her age, even certain lines and locutions.

'Jesus Christ,' he said. 'You're—'

'His twin sister.' She started to massage the loose skin beneath her left collarbone. 'The fabulous Demarest twins. Double trouble. The Mobius morons never even knew that Alan brought me into the picture.' As she spoke, her circular movements became more insistent, seemingly responding to an itch deep beneath the skin. 'So if you think I'm going to "give him up", you'd better think again.'

Lang's movements grew smaller, more focused; with her fingers she started to dig at something to the side of her clavicle. 'Ah,' she said. 'That's it. Oh, that feels so much better . . .'

'Paul!' Jessica shouted. '*Stop* her!'

It was too late. There was the barely audible pop of a subdermal ampoule, and the woman threw her head back, as if in ecstasy, her face flushing to a purplish red as she fell to the ground. Her jaw fell open, and saliva dribbled from her mouth. Then her eyes rolled up, leaving only the whites visible through her half-parted lids.

Janson put a hand on Márta Lang's long neck, feeling for a pulse, even though he knew there would be none. The signs of cyanide poisoning were hard to miss.

THE SECRETARY-GENERAL picked up the phone. A few clicks and electronic burps, and Peter Novak's voice came on: '*Mon cher* Mathieu.'

'*Mon cher* Peter,' Mathieu Zinsou replied. 'Your munificence in even *considering* what we discussed must be honoured—'

'Yes, yes,' Novak interrupted. 'I'm afraid, though, that I'm going to decline your invitation to dinner. I have something more *ceremonial* in mind. I hope you'll agree. We have no secrets, have we? Transparency has always been a paramount UN value, no?'

'Well, up to a point, Peter.'

'I understand that there will be a meeting of the General Assembly this Friday. It has always been my fantasy to address that body. Foolish vanity perhaps, but nobody would begrudge me the right and privilege—I think I can say that without fear of contradiction.'

'*Bien sûr.*'

'Given that a great many heads of state will be present, the level of security will be high. Call me paranoid, but I find that reassuring. If the US president is present, as seems possible, there will be a Secret Service detail on the case as well. All very reassuring. And I shall probably be accompanied by the mayor of New York, who has always been so friendly towards me.'

'An extremely public and high-profile appearance, then,' Zinsou said. 'That is not like you, I must say.'

'Which is exactly why I suggest it,' the voice said. 'You know my policy: always keep them guessing.'

'But our . . . dialogue?' Confusion and anxiety roiled within him.

'Not to worry. I think you'll find that one never has more privacy than when one is in the public eye.'

'GOD*DAMN* IT!' Janson yelled. He was reviewing the tape recording of Demarest's last phone call.

'What do you make of this request?' Zinsou asked.

'It's ingenious,' Janson said bluntly. 'He knows the forces against him are ultracompartmentalised. There's no way the Secret Service could ever be let in on the truth. He's using our own people as a shield. And he'll be walking up the ramp to the General Assembly Building with the mayor of New York by his side. Any attempt on his life would endanger a well-known politician. He's entering an arena of incredibly tight security. If an American operative tried to take a shot, the resulting inquiry would blow everything sky-high.'

'Now what?'

'Either I'll figure something out . . .'

'Or?'

'Or I won't.' Janson walked out of the secretary-general's office without another word, leaving the diplomat alone with his thoughts.

THE CALIPH REREAD the cable he had just received, and felt a glow of anticipation. Peter Novak was going to address the UN General Assembly. The man would show his face at last. He would be greeted by gratitude and acclamation. And, if the Caliph had his way, by something more.

He turned to the Mansur minister of security—plainly little more than a jumped-up carpet merchant, despite the rhetorical inflation of his title—and spoke to him in tones both courteous and commanding: 'This meeting of the international community will be an important moment for the Islamic Republic of Mansur.'

'But of course,' replied the minister, a small, homely man who wore a simple white head wrap. On matters that did not concern Koranic orthodoxy, the leadership of this desolate little country was easily impressed.

'Your delegation will be judged by its professionalism and comportment. The very highest level of security must be maintained.'

The minister bobbed his head. He was out of his depth and, to his credit, realised there was no point in pretending otherwise, at least in the presence of the master tactician who stood before him.

'Therefore, I shall myself accompany the delegation. You need only provide the diplomatic cover, and I shall *personally* ensure that everything happens as it should.'

'Allah be praised,' the small man said. 'Your dedication will be an inspiration to others.'

The Caliph nodded slowly, acknowledging the tribute. 'What I do,' he said, 'is merely what must be done.'

THE TOWN HOUSE was anonymous-looking, a brownstone like hundreds of others in New York's Turtle Bay. But its thick leaded glass was proof against even heavy-calibre bullets. It was a safe house.

Janson sat in the study. He phoned Derek Collins.

'The good news is, the cobra's en route,' Collins said. 'The bad news is, Nell Pearson's body was discovered yesterday. The Mrs Novak of record. Supposedly a suicide. Slit her wrists in her bathtub. So that thread's been snipped.'

'What a damn waste,' Janson said. There was lead in his voice.

'Moving right along,' Collins said bleakly, 'nobody's sighted Puma. The fact is, our guy might not be arriving from overseas—he might already be in the country.'

Janson hung up. Almost immediately, the silver-grey phone on the desk rang. It was the line reserved for White House communications. He picked up the phone. It was the president.

'Listen, Paul. This address Demarest's giving before the General Assembly—there could well be an implicit ultimatum here.'

'Sir?'

'As you know, he asked for the control codes to the entire Echelon system. I think the message he's sending is pretty unambiguous. If he doesn't get what he wants, he's going to appear before the General Assembly and lay the thing out, with the whole world listening.'

'Ergo?'

'I've decided to meet with him just beforehand. Capitulate. Give in to his first round of demands.'

'You'll be putting yourself in harm's way.'

'Paul, I'm already in harm's way. And so are you.'

'*SOME PEOPLE wanna fill the world with silly love songs*,' the Russian crooned tunelessly.

'Grigori?' Janson said into his cellphone. 'You doing OK?'

'Never better!' Grigori Berman said stoutly. 'Back in own home. Private nurse named Ingrid! Second day, I keep dropping thermometer on floor just to watch her bend over.'

'Listen, Grigori, I've a request. If you're not up to it, though, just let me know.' Janson spoke for a few minutes, providing a handful of details; either Berman would work out the rest or he wouldn't.

Berman was silent for a few moments when Janson finished talking. 'Now it is Grigori Berman who is shocked. What you propose, sir, is unethical, immoral, illegal—is devious violation of standards and practices of international banking.' A beat. 'I *love* it.'

'Thought so,' said Janson. 'And you can pull it off?'

'*I get by with a little help from my friends*,' Berman crooned.

CHAPTER FOURTEEN

The motorcades started arriving at the UN Plaza at seven the next morning. Among the delegations was a man wearing a kaffiyeh, a full beard and sunglasses: typical attire among certain ruling-class Arabs. He looked like any of a hundred diplomatic representatives.

In fact, the ample beard not only altered Janson's appearance but disguised a small microphone. He had placed a microphone on the secretary-general as well. Mounted within a nodule on his gold collar bar, it was hidden behind his wide four-in-hand knot.

A barrage of camera flashes signalled the legend's arrival. The man known to the world as Peter Novak entered the West Lobby, and was hustled by his aides into the executive suite behind the Assembly Hall.

This was Janson's cue to retreat to the central security booth, located behind the main balcony of the Assembly Hall. An array of monitors displayed multiple camera angles on the hall itself. At his request, hidden cameras had also been placed in the suites tucked away behind the dais. The secretary-general's new security consultant wanted to be able to keep an eye on all the principals.

Adjusting the control panel, he zoomed in, looking for the table where the delegation from the Republic of Mansur would be seated.

There, beside the aisle, was a handsome man in robes that matched those of the other men in the Mansur delegation. Janson pressed buttons on the console and the image appeared on the large central monitor. He enlarged the image further and watched, mesmerised, as the monitor filled with the unmistakable visage of Ahmad Tabari. The man they called the Caliph.

Janson pressed several buttons, and the central screen feed switched to the hidden camera in the executive suite.

A different face. The full head of hair, still more black than grey, the high cheekbones, the elegant three-button suit: Peter Novak. Yes, Peter Novak—it was who the man had become, and it was the way Janson had to think of him.

Now the door to the suite opened, and two members of the Secret Service made a visual inspection of the room. Peter Novak stood up. Smiled at his visitor. The president of the United States, looking ashen. There was no audio feed, but it was clear the president was asking the Secret Service detail to leave the two of them alone.

Wordlessly, the president withdrew a sealed envelope from his breast pocket and handed it to Peter Novak. He walked out.

Novak slipped the envelope into his own breast pocket. That envelope, Janson knew, could change the course of world history.

THE METAL DETECTORS made it impossible to carry firearms; this was as the Caliph expected. Yet securing such a weapon would be elementary. There were hundreds of them in the building, the property of the UN security guards and other such protectors.

The aura of invincibility he had lost that dreadful night at the Stone Palace he would regain, redoubled even, once he had completed this, his most daring act. He would do the deed and, in the ensuing uproar, make his escape in the speedboat docked at the East River, just a hundred feet east of the building. The world would learn that their righteous cause could not be ignored.

According to the schedule, Peter Novak would commence his address within five minutes. This member of the Mansur security detail would have to take a quick trip to the bathroom. He pushed out through the door that led from the hall.

The Caliph caught the attention of a dark-suited Secret Service agent. 'Sir,' he said to the agent, 'I protect the leader of the Islamic Republic of Mansur. We have received a report that someone is hiding—in *there!*' He gestured towards the chapel.

'We had the whole place turned over a few hours before.'

'But you'll take a look? Doubtless there's nothing to the report, but if we are mistaken on this score, we shall be hard-pressed to explain why we did nothing.'

A grudging sigh. 'Show the way.'

The Caliph held open the small wooden door to the chapel and waited until the Secret Service man walked through.

'Ain't no place to hide here,' the man said. 'There's nothing.'

The heavy, soundproofed door closed behind them.

'What would it matter?' the Caliph said. 'You have no weapon. You'd be helpless against an assassin!'

The Secret Service man grinned and opened his navy jacket, allowing the long-barrelled revolver to show from his shoulder holster.

'Apologies.' The Caliph turned round, his back to the American, seemingly captivated by a mural. Then he took a step back.

'You're wasting my time,' the American said.

Abruptly, the Caliph whipped his head back, cracking into the American's chin. As the agent reeled, the Caliph's hands snaked towards his shoulder holster and pulled out the revolver, a Ruger. He slammed the butt down on the agent's head, ensuring that smug infidel would be unconscious for many hours.

Now he dragged the American behind an ebonised light box, where he would be invisible to a casual visitor.

IN THE EXECUTIVE SUITE, the light on the black slimline phone started to glow. It was the speaker's 'ready in five' notification—standard procedure, alerting him a few minutes before he would be asked to step out in front of the assembled leadership of the planet.

Novak reached for the phone, listened, said, 'Thank you.'

And as he watched, Janson felt a jolt of foreboding.

Urgently, desperately, he jammed on the REWIND button and replayed the last ten seconds of video feed.

The light glowing on the black phone. Peter Novak reaching for it with his right hand. Holding the handset to his right ear.

Janson's mind filled with a cascade of images. Demarest at a desk in Khe Sanh, reaching for a phone. Holding the phone against his ear for a long while. Demarest in the swampy terrain near Ham Luong reaching for the radiophone, listening intently. Reaching with his *left* hand, holding the phone to his *left* ear.

Alan Demarest was left-handed. Invariably so. Exclusively so.

The man in the executive suite was not Alan Demarest.

He had sent a double. An impostor.

Demarest had gained his freedom by destroying his own duplicates, but then he had been planning his takeover for years. During that time he had created a duplicate of his own—one under *his* power.

The man who was on his way to address the General Assembly was the Judas goat, leading them to their slaughter. He was the cat's paw, drawing out their fire. In a few minutes, the man, this copy of a copy, would take his position before the podium. And be shot dead.

That would not be Novak's undoing. It would be their own undoing. Alan Demarest would have confirmed his most paranoid suspicions: he would have flushed out his enemies, would have discovered that the whole invitation had indeed been a plot.

The scheme they had set in motion could not be stopped. It was not in their control. That was its great recommendation—and, possibly, its lethal flaw.

Frantically, Janson flipped to the camera angle on the Mansur delegation. There was the aisle seat that had been occupied by the Caliph. Empty.

Janson ran down the stairs and through the hallway that bounded the Assembly Hall. He had to find the fanatic from Anura. This assassination would not save the world; it would doom it.

The Caliph had disappeared from the Assembly Hall—which meant that he was retrieving a weapon he or a confederate had somewhere managed to stow earlier. The South Lobby was vacant. The giant escalator was empty. He bounded towards the delegates' lounge. Nothing. Where could he be? Janson's mind desperately sorted through possibilities.

Ask it differently: where would you be, Janson?

The chapel. A space that was almost never used but was always open. It was the one room in the building where one was guaranteed to be unobserved.

Janson pushed open the door and saw a man in white robes bending down behind a large ebonised box. As the door closed behind Janson, the man whirled round. The Caliph.

For a moment Janson was so convulsed with hate that he could not breathe. He composed his face into a look of friendly surprise.

The Caliph spoke first. '*Khaif hallak ya akhi.*'

Janson remembered his beard and Arab headdress and forced himself to smile. In his best Oxbridge English—an Arab royal might well have been educated at such an institution—he said, 'My dear brother, I hope I wasn't intruding. It's just that I've such a migraine, I was hoping to commune with the Prophet.'

The Caliph strode towards him, scrutinising him closely. He placed a hand on Janson's shoulder. It was a gentle, friendly, confiding gesture—from the man who had killed his wife.

Involuntarily, Janson flinched. His mind filled with a flood of images: a cascade of destruction, the ruined office building in downtown Caligo, the phone call informing him that his wife was dead.

The Caliph's face suddenly closed. Janson had betrayed himself.

The muzzle of a long-barrelled revolver was jabbed into Janson's chest. The Caliph had made his decision: his suspicious visitor would not be permitted to escape.

'I have offended you,' Janson said plaintively. Suddenly, he grabbed the wrist of the Caliph's gun arm with both hands. With a powerful upward wrench, he locked the man's arm. Then he lashed out with his left leg, and the two men landed hard on the slate floor.

Janson slammed the Anuran's gun hand against the floor, causing him to loosen his grip on the weapon. In a lightning-fast movement, Janson grabbed it and scrambled to his feet.

Then he felt a staggering blow from behind. The assassin had leapt from the ground and snaked a forearm round Janson's throat. Janson bucked violently, twisting and thrashing, hoping to throw off the younger, lighter man, but the terrorist was all coiled muscle.

Now, instead of trying to dislodge the Caliph's grip, Janson hurled himself to the floor, landing heavily on his back—yet cushioning his impact with the body of his assailant, who was slammed against the floor as he fell.

Winded and aching himself, Janson rolled over and began to rise to his feet. As he did so, the Caliph rose, with incredible endurance, and threw himself at him.

Janson held out his arms, as if in an embrace—and squeezed the

Caliph to his body, locking his arms around the other man's chest.

Then, in a sudden, convulsive effort, he dropped his armlock and *lifted* the Anuran into the air horizontally. In an equally abrupt movement, Janson fell into a crouch, his left knee bent to the ground, his right knee angled upward. At the same time, he slammed the lithe-bodied assailant down against it.

The Caliph's back snapped with a horrifying sound, and his mouth contorted into a scream that would not come.

Janson seized him by the shoulders and slammed him against the slate floor. He did so again. And again. The Caliph's eyes grew unfocused, glazed.

Janson jammed the Ruger into his shoulder holster, adjusted his beard and kaffiyeh and made sure there were no visible bloodstains on his person. Then he walked out of the chapel and into the General Assembly Hall.

For years he had fantasised about killing the man who had killed his wife. Now he had done so. And all he felt was sick.

THE BLACK-HAIRED man stood at the podium, giving a speech about the challenges of a new century. He looked like Peter Novak. He would be accepted as Novak. Yet he lacked the sense of command associated with the legendary humanitarian. His voice was thin, wavering, the delivery atypically hesitant and tentative.

And only Janson knew why.

As the man at the podium finished his remarks, the audience rose in a standing ovation. What his address lacked in delivery, it made up for in rhetorical appeal. Besides, on such an occasion, who could begrudge the great man his proper due?

Janson walked out of the hall. If Demarest wasn't at the United Nations, where was he?

The secretary-general had walked off the dais together with the clamorously applauded speaker, and now, as a twenty-minute recess began, both would repair to the chamber behind the hall.

Janson realised that his earpiece had been dislodged by his struggle; he repositioned it and, crackling, heard snippets of dialogue. The microphone on Mathieu Zinsou's collar bar was transmitting.

'No, I thank *you*. But I *would* like to have that tête-à-tête you mentioned after all.' The voice was fuzzy but audible.

'Certainly,' Zinsou answered.

'Why don't we go to your office, in the Secretariat?'

'You mean *now*?'

'I'm rather pressed for time, I'm afraid. It'll have to be now.'

'Then follow me. The thirty-eighth floor.' Janson wondered if the secretary-general had added the specification for his sake.

He made a dash for the eastern ramp of the General Assembly Building, and then lumbered towards the Secretariat Building.

Inside the lobby, he flashed the ID card that had been prepared for him, and a guard waved him through. He pressed the button for the thirty-eighth floor, and rode up.

A minute later, the elevator stopped at the thirty-eighth floor. Because of the special meeting, the floor was almost entirely vacant; every staff member was attending to the visiting delegations.

Now Janson removed his headdress and his beard and waited round the corner from where the elevator banks opened.

THE ELEVATOR CHIMED.

'And this will be our floor,' said Mathieu Zinsou to the man who looked, for all the world, like Peter Novak.

As Zinsou opened the door to his office, he started as he saw a man seated behind his own desk, silhouetted by the ebbing light.

What the hell was happening?

He turned to his companion: 'I don't know what to say. It seems we have an unexpected visitor.'

The man at Zinsou's desk rose and stepped towards him, and Zinsou gaped in astonishment.

The thick black hair, only lightly flecked with grey, the high, almost Asiatic cheekbones. A face the world knew as Peter Novak's.

Zinsou turned to the man at his side.

The same face. Essentially indistinguishable.

Yet there *were* differences, Zinsou reflected, just not physical ones. Rather, they were differences of affect and mien. There was something hesitant and cautious about the man by his side: something implacable and imperious about the man before him. The marionette and the marionette master.

Now the man at Zinsou's side handed an envelope to the man who could have been his mirror image.

A subtle nod. 'Thank you, Laszlo,' said the man who had been waiting for them. 'You may go now.'

The impostor by Zinsou's side turned and left without a word.

'*Mon cher* Mathieu,' said the man who had stayed behind.

JANSON HEARD ZINSOU'S voice distinctly in his earpiece: '*My God.*' At the same time, he saw the Peter Novak who was not Peter Novak press the DOWN elevator button.

In Janson's earpiece, another man's voice: 'I must apologise for the confusion.'

Janson raced to the elevator and stepped in. The man who was not Peter Novak wore an expression that was startled—but devoid of recognition.

'I SIMPLY DON'T UNDERSTAND,' said the secretary-general.

The other man was magnetic, utterly confident, utterly relaxed. 'You'll have to forgive me for taking special precautions. That was my double, as you've no doubt figured out. I'm afraid there had been rumours of an assassination attempt in the General Assembly. I couldn't risk it.'

'I see,' said Zinsou, who didn't.

'So let's get our business done,' said Novak. 'Here are instructions for getting in touch with me.' He handed the secretary-general a white card. 'It's a number you can call to get a return phone call within the hour. As our plans develop, we'll need to be in regular touch. Your Swiss bank account has, you'll find, already been enhanced—simply an advance on a package of benefits that we can finalise at a later point. And there will be regular monthly payments, which will continue as long as our partnership remains on a solid footing. It will be very important that you do not make any errors of judgment.'

Zinsou swallowed. 'I understand.'

'It's important that you do. In your speeches as secretary-general, you've often maintained that there's a thin line between civilisation and savagery. Let's not put that proposition to the test.'

JANSON KEPT a foot in the elevator door, preventing the elevator from moving. 'Give me the envelope,' he said.

'I don't know what you're talking about,' the man said.

Janson formed his right hand into a spear and delivered a crushing punch to the man's throat. As the man fell to the floor, Janson struck the Ruger against his temple. A quick frisk verified that there was no envelope on his person.

Now Janson crept towards Zinsou's office. He turned the knob, threw open the door, and rushed in, the Ruger in his right hand. Demarest's reaction to the intrusion was deft: he repositioned himself behind Zinsou. There was no line of fire that would reach him and not strike the secretary-general.

All the same, Janson fired—wildly, it seemed: three shots high overhead, three slugs smashing into the window, causing the whole pane to buckle and then disintegrate into a curtain of fragments.

And there was silence.

'Alan Demarest,' Janson said. 'Love what you've done with your hair.'

'A poor shot, Paul. You shame your teacher.' Demarest was holding a Smith & Wesson .45.

'Zinsou! Walk. Now. *Get out of here!*' Janson's instructions were crisp. The secretary-general moved from between the two blood enemies. To Demarest, Janson said, 'Shoot him and I shoot you.'

Janson waited, Ruger in position, until he heard the door close.

Demarest's gaze was steady. 'We were the same, you and I. In many ways, we still are. And you presumed to judge me? Oh, Paul, don't you know *why* you took it on yourself to destroy me? Are you that devoid of self-insight? How comforting it must be to tell yourself that I'm the monster and you're the saint. You're afraid of what I showed you.'

'Yes—a profoundly disturbed individual.'

'Don't delude yourself, Paul. I'm talking about what I showed you about *yourself*. Whatever I was, you were.'

'*No!*' Janson flushed with rage and horror. Violence was indeed something he excelled at, he could no longer run from that truth. But for him it was never an end in itself; rather, violence was a last resort to minimise further violence.

Demarest took a step closer. 'It's time to be truthful with yourself,' he said gently. 'There's always been something between us. Something very close to love.'

Janson looked at him, mentally imposing Demarest's features over the famous countenance of the legendary humanitarian, seeing the points of resemblance even on the recontoured visage. He shuddered. 'And a lot closer to hate,' he said at last.

'I *made* you. Accept it. Accept who you are. Once you do, *the nightmares will cease*, Paul. Take it from me. I always sleep well at night.'

Janson took a deep breath. 'You sleep well because something inside you—call it a soul, call it what you like—is dead. Maybe something happened that snuffed it out one day, maybe you never had it, but it's the thing that makes us human.'

'*Human?* You mean *weak*. People always mix those two words up.'

'My nightmares are *me*,' Janson said, in a clear, steady voice. 'I have to live with the things I've done on this earth. I don't have to like them. I've done good and I've done bad. As for the bad—I don't *want* to be reconciled with the bad. You tell me I can take that pain away? That pain is how I know who I am and who I'm not. *That pain is how I know I'm not you.*'

Suddenly Demarest lashed out, batting the gun out of Janson's hand. It flew clattering to the marble floor.

Demarest looked almost mournful as he levelled his pistol. 'I tried to reason with you. I tried to reach you, to bring you back in touch with your true self. All I wanted from you was an acknowledgment of the truth—the truth about us both.'

'The truth? You're a monster.'

A heavy sigh. 'It's time for me to be going. I have great plans for the world, you know. Truth is, I'm *bored* with conflict resolution. Conflict *promotion* is the new order of the day. Human beings *like* battle and bloodshed. Let man be man, I say.' He smiled as he levelled the pistol two feet from Janson's forehead. 'Bon voyage,' he said as his finger curled round the trigger.

Then Janson felt something warm spray against his face. Blinking, he saw that it came from an exit wound at Demarest's forehead. Undeflected by window glass, the sniper's shot was as precise as if it had been fired point-blank.

For a moment, Demarest's expression was perfectly blank: he could have been in meditation; he could have been asleep. Then he crumpled to the ground with the utter relaxation of life surrendered.

When Janson peered out from the secretary-general's antique brass telescope, he found Jessie precisely where he had stationed her: across the East River, her rifle positioned on the roof of an old bottling plant. She was disassembling the weapon with practised movements. Then she looked up at him, as if she could feel his gaze upon her. All at once, Janson had a feeling, an odd, lighter-than-air feeling, that everything would be all right.

'THANK YOU for joining us, Mr Janson,' said President Charles W. Berquist Jr, seated at the head of the oval table. 'Your nation owes you a debt of gratitude that it will never know about. But I know. I don't think it'll be any surprise that you'll be receiving another Distinguished Intelligence Star.'

Janson shrugged. 'Maybe I should go into the scrap-metal business.'

'But I also wanted you to hear some good news, and from me. Thanks to you, it looks like we're going to be able to resurrect the Mobius Programme. Doug and the others have walked me through it and it's looking better and better.'

'Is that right?' Janson said impassively.

'You don't seem surprised,' President Berquist said.

'When you've been around the planners as long as I have, you stop being surprised by their combination of brilliance and stupidity. Anyway, you can just forget about it.'

'The question is, where do you get off talking to the president like that?' Douglas Albright, the DIA deputy director, interjected.

'The question is whether you people ever learn anything,' Janson shot back.

'We've learned a great deal,' Albright said. 'We won't make the same mistakes twice.'

'True—the mistakes will be different ones.'

The secretary of state spoke. 'To jettison the programme at this point would be to scuttle tens of thousands of man-hours of work.'

'We've got control over Demarest's understudy,' said a grey-faced technician. 'A fellow named Laszlo Kocsis. Used to teach English in Hungary. He went under the knife eighteen months ago. Make a long story short, if he went along with Demarest's plans, he'd get ten million dollars. If he didn't, his family would be slaughtered. He's under our thumb now.'

'My game, my rules,' said Janson. 'Gentlemen, the Mobius Programme is over.'

'On whose orders?' President Berquist snorted.

'Yours.'

'What's gotten into you, Paul?' he said, his face darkening.

'A question for you, Mr President. You have just received and accepted an illegal personal contribution of one and a half million dollars.' As Janson spoke, he imagined Grigori Berman guffawing back in Berthwick House. It had been the sort of outsize mischief that pleased him beyond measure. 'How are you going to explain that to Congress and to the American people?'

'What the hell are you *talking* about?'

'I'm talking about a big-time scandal—Watergate times ten. I'm talking about watching your political career go up in flames. A seven-figure sum was wired to your personal account from an account of Peter Novak's at International Netherlands Group Bank. The digital signatures can't be faked—well, not easily. So it's looking like a four- or five-column headline in the *Washington Post:* IS PRESIDENT ON PLUTOCRAT'S PAYROLL? INVESTIGATION PENDING. You know those media feeding frenzies—there'll be such a din, you won't be able to hear yourself think.'

'That's *bullshit!*' the president exploded.

'And we'll all enjoy watching you explain that to Congress. The details will arrive by email tomorrow to the Justice Department as well as the relevant members of the House and the Senate.'

'You're kidding me,' the president said.

'Call your banker,' Janson repeated.

The president stared at Janson. His personal and political instincts had gained him the highest office of the land. They told him that Janson was not bluffing.

'You're making a terrible mistake,' said Berquist.

'I can undo it,' Janson said. 'It's still not too late.'

'Thank you.'

'Though soon it will be. That's why you need to decide about Mobius.'

'But—'

'Call your banker.'

The president left the room. A few minutes passed before he returned to his seat.

'What you're proposing amounts to nothing less than blackmail.'

'Let's not get sidetracked by the formalities,' Janson said.

'Derek,' the president said, turning to the director of Consular Operations and the one man at the table who had said nothing so far. 'Talk to your guy. Make him understand.'

'I kept trying to tell you—you don't know this man,' Collins said.

'Derek?' The president's request was clear.

Collins looked at Janson. 'There's one person in this room who's gone a long way on common sense and common decency. He's a tough son of a bitch, and as true a patriot as they come, and, agree with him or not, at the end of the day, this has to be his call . . .'

'Thanks, Derek,' President Berquist said, solemn but pleased.

'I'm talking about Paul Janson,' the undersecretary finished. 'And if you don't do what he says, Mr President, you're a fool.'

'Undersecretary Collins,' the president barked, 'I'd be happy to accept your resignation.'

'Mr President,' Collins said, 'I'd be happy to accept yours.'

President Berquist froze. 'Goddamn it, Janson. Do you see what you've done?'

Janson stared at the director of Consular Operations. 'An interesting song for a hawk,' he said with a half-smile. Then he turned to the president. 'You know what they say: "Consider the source." The advice you've been given may say more about your advisers' concerns than your own. As far as they're concerned, you're just passing through. They've been around before you, they'll be here after you. Your interests don't really mean a whole lot to them.'

Berquist was used to making the cold, hard calculations that political survival depended on. He forced a smile. 'Paul,' he said, 'I'm afraid this meeting got off to a bad start. I'd love to hear you out.'

'Mr President,' Douglas Albright protested. 'This is *entirely* inappropriate. We've gone through this again and again, and—'

'Fine, Doug. Why don't you tell me that you know how to nullify what Paul Janson's gone and done? I haven't heard anybody here bother to address that particular matter.'

'These aren't comparables!' Albright stormed. 'We're talking about the long-term interests of this geopolitical entity, not the greater glory of the second Berquist administration! There's no comparison! Mobius is bigger than all of us. You *cannot* sacrifice this programme on the altar of political ambition.'

'Call me a stick-in-the-mud,' Berquist said. 'I kinda have a hankering for the scenario where I'm still president.' He turned to Janson. 'Your game, your rules,' he said. 'I can live with that.'

'Excellent choice, Mr President,' Janson said neutrally.

Berquist gave him a smile that combined command and entreaty. 'Now give me my goddamn presidency back.'

The New York Times
PETER NOVAK TO YIELD CONTROL OF THE LIBERTY FOUNDATION
By Jason Steinhardt

In a press conference held at the Amsterdam headquarters of the Liberty Foundation, the legendary financier and humanitarian Peter Novak announced he would be relinquishing control of the Liberty Foundation, the global organisation that he created and ran for more than fifteen years. He also announced he was turning over all his capital assets to the foundation, which would be reconstituted as a public trust with an international board of directors under the chairmanship of the UN secretary general, Mathieu Zinsou.

Sources close to Mr Novak suggest that the recent death of his wife catalysed his decision to retire from the operations of the foundation. Others point out that the financier's reclusive habits were in conflict with the exposed and highly public position that his work at the foundation demanded. Novak was sketchy about his future plans, but some aides suggested he planned to remove himself from the public eye entirely.

EPILOGUE

The lithe woman with the spiky brown hair lay prone, the four-foot rifle braced by sandbags fore and aft. The shadows of the belfry rendered her invisible from a distance. Beneath the bell tower where she had been positioned for the past several hours, there was a sea of faces that continued several hundred yards to the wooden platform that had been erected in the centre of Dubrovnik.

The Pope had decided to start his visit to Croatia by addressing an audience in a city that had come to symbolise the suffering of its people. Word had got out that he intended to address a history that most Croatians preferred to forget.

His moral courage had seemingly only increased the devotion of his throngs of admirers here. It had also—Janson's suspicions had recently been confirmed by his contacts in the capital city of Zagreb—resulted in a carefully organised assassination plot. An embittered secessionist movement of minority Serbs would avenge their historic grievances by murdering the figure whom this predominantly Catholic nation venerated above all others.

As a gentle breeze filtered through the medieval buildings of the city's old town neighbourhood, an unexceptionable-looking man with short, grey hair—nobody who would ever get a second look—walked down the street Bozardar Filipovic. 'Four degrees off the median,' he said softly. 'The apartment block on the middle of the street. Top floor. Got a visual?'

The woman repositioned slightly, and adjusted her Swarovski 12×50: the gunman lying in wait filled the scope. The scarred visage was familiar from her face book: Milic Pavlovic. A seasoned and highly skilled assassin. The terrorists had sent the best.

But then so had the Vatican, which sought to eliminate the assassin without the world knowing what it had done.

The executive security business was only formally a new pursuit for Janson and Kincaid. For that matter, it was only formally a business. As Jessica had pointed out, the millions that remained in Janson's Cayman Islands account were his to keep—if he hadn't earned it, who had? Still, as Janson had said, they were too young to put themselves out to pasture. He had tried that—tried to run from who he was. That was not the answer for him, for either of them; he knew that now. For better or worse, neither of them had been made for a peaceable existence. The bountiful cash reserves simply meant that the partnership could be selective in choosing its clients and there would be no need to stint on operating expenses.

Now Kincaid spoke in a low voice, knowing that the filament mike carried her words straight to Janson's earpiece. 'Goddamn Kevlar body armour,' she said, stretching her long, loose-jointed body beneath the layers of bulletproof mesh. She always found it uncomfortably hot, protested his insistence that she wear it. 'Tell me the truth—do you think it makes me look fat?'

'You think I'm gonna answer that while you've got a bullet in the chamber?'

She found her spot-weld—stock to cheek—as the craggy-faced assassin assembled his bipod, and inserted the magazine into his long rifle. The Pope would be making his appearance in minutes.

Janson's voice in her ear again: 'Everything OK?'

'Like clockwork, snookums,' she said.

'Just be careful, right? Remember, the back-up shooter's in the warehouse at location B. If they get wind of you, you're in his range.'

'I'm on top of it,' she said, suffused with the deep, glowing calm of a perfectly positioned marksman.

'I know,' he said. 'I'm just saying, be careful.'

'Don't worry, my love,' she said. 'It'll be a walk in the park.'

ROBERT LUDLUM

Don't ever begin a Ludlum novel if you have to go to work the next day, a critic once advised, and few fans would argue with this assessment of Ludlum's labyrinthine and addictive plots, in which a hero of James Bond-style cleverness and daring escapes from a succession of extreme situations in order to see justice done. So successful is the formula that the Ludlum name continues to sell books even though he died in 2001. His publishers say that in the years before his death he had been working on several novels, all of which will be published posthumously.

Ludlum started his working life as an actor, appearing in a Broadway production called *Junior Miss* in 1943 when he was sixteen. A two-year stint in the Marines was followed by a degree course in Fine Arts at Wesleyan University. He graduated in 1951 and in the same year married actress Mary Ryducha, with whom he had three children. During the 1950s he embarked on a successful career as a television and stage actor. He then moved on to directing and producing, and during this time staged over 300 plays for New York and regional theatres.

Although he claimed to have always been a 'closet writer', scribbling away whenever he got the chance, it wasn't until he was forty that he decided to try writing a novel. 'I was the most paralysed guy in the world when I made that decision. I knew what I wanted to do but I didn't know if I could do it,' he once said in an interview. It was a risk that paid off, because his first novel, *The Scarlatti Inheritance*, published in 1971, became an immediate best seller. He attributed his success to his work in the theatre. 'I was heavily involved with putting on new plays and understood about dialogue and the architecture of scenes instinctively . . . If I had tried to write ten years before I did, I wouldn't have gone anywhere.'

His subsequent books, which include *The Osterman Weekend*, *The Prometheus Deception*, *The Sigma Protocol* and the recently filmed novel *The Bourne Identity*, have sold over 220 million copies in forty countries and thirty-two languages. Not bad for an author who wasn't sure if he could write.

Winter's End
John Rickards

For Alex Rourke, returning to Winter's End in Maine to help investigate a murder proves far from straightforward. He finds questioning the suspect an unnerving process and before long realises that the pale, gaunt figure before him is playing a sinister game.

Alex begins to think the unthinkable—that the key to solving the crime lies buried in his own past.

PROLOGUE

'I don't know why Jimmy insists on playing him,' Sheriff Dale Townsend says, raising his voice over the hammering rain and the swish of the Jeep's wipers. 'It's obvious the guy just isn't on form. His confidence is gone, he's tensed up and he's gripping the bat too hard. Jimmy should rest him a couple of games, give him a chance to get his head right, then bring him back for the end-of-season run-in.'

His companion, Deputy Andy Miller, keeps both hands on the wheel and his eyes firmly on the pool of light in front of the vehicle. 'Rendall hit three-eighty last year,' he says. 'You can't write off a guy like that. He'll come good.'

'Maybe.' Dale stares absent-mindedly out at the darkened landscape. A flash of lightning shocks the trees bordering the highway, a jumble of drenched foliage and stark blue shadows. Darkness returns as a shift in the tone of the wind tells him that they have left the woods behind. Four miles of flat grassland before the road reaches the town. Four miles to home. He checks his watch.

'Your wife give you hell when you get in?' asks the deputy.

'Naw, she knows I'm going to be home late, even if I can't be sure of the exact time when the weather's so goddamn miserable.'

'When's your car going to be finished in the shop?'

'Tomorrow. That's what they tell me, anyway.'

'Well, if it takes longer, you're welcome to keep hitching a ride with me. Until my shift changes next week, anyhow.'

Sheriff Townsend is about to reply when the lightning flashes again and his attention is grabbed by something ahead on the highway. 'What the hell?' he says.

The deputy eases off the gas and, on reflex, hits the blue and red strobes.

The twin headlight beams pick out a man who is bare from the waist up with rain dancing from his exposed skin. Townsend's first, almost unconscious thought is that he must be freezing cold. The man is staring calmly at the ground in front of him, absolutely still, with his hands at his sides. In each of them he holds a hunting knife. At his feet is the naked body of a woman, her flesh white in the glare.

'Andy, call Dispatch,' Townsend says.

He draws his pistol and reaches for the door, then steps out into the downpour. The water hits him like a cold shower as he raises the comforting weight of his gun and carefully sights up on the figure in front of him.

'Aroostook County Sheriff's Department!' he shouts. 'Put down the knives and step slowly over to the vehicle with your hands where I can see 'em.'

To his left, the other door opens and Andy steps out, the dim crackle of the radio still faintly audible behind him. The deputy mirrors Townsend's movements, keeping his gun trained, ready to shoot.

The man, who Townsend guesses is young, no older than his mid-twenties, looks up and his gaze settles on the sheriff. Face pale from the cold. Dark hair drenched. Eyes black pits reflecting the blue and red flashes from the Jeep's lights. A slow, almost mocking smile spreads across his face as he gently places the knives on the ground. Then he strides calmly to the Jeep, keeping his hands in the air.

Andy cuffs him and frisks him for other weapons while Townsend goes to check on the woman. She looks to be in her late thirties, with shoulder-length dark hair and a trim build. Her face is familiar and quite attractive, despite the unreal presence death brings. Her chest is a welter of slashes and stab marks washed clean by the rain. Townsend has little real hope of finding her alive, but checks for a pulse as a matter of procedure. Nothing. Lightning flashes again and, if anything, the rain gets harder.

'Arrest this guy on suspicion of murder,' he calls out to the deputy behind him. 'And notify the Chief Medical Examiner's Office. We'll need to get someone out here.'

1

The morning is well under way by the time I reach the red-brick building in Boston's Fenway district that serves as my office, workplace and home away from home. I can feel the glare of the May sunshine on my back, warm despite the cool air. The sky is glacial blue with scattered flecks of distant cloud. I've just crossed the road from Rick's, my local coffee bar, and a cup of the establishment's finest is nestled warmly in my hand. I need it this morning. I'm tired, breakfast was four hours ago in a cramped diner full of construction workers on the early shift, and I had one too many drinks last night.

All in the line of duty.

I climb the steps and push my way into the burgundy-carpeted foyer. Five companies share the building with mine, our names picked out in silvered lettering on a board by the twin elevators.

Inside the elevator, I examine my appearance in the mirrored walls. I look exactly like I feel: dog-tired and in need of a shave, a shower and a decent night's sleep. On better days, I'm told I bear a vague resemblance to a gaunt version of Cary Grant. Today, I'll settle for a vague resemblance to a member of the human race.

As the elevator doors slide open, I manage to fumble a cigarette one-handed out of the pocket of my battered tan leather jacket and into my mouth. I make a left into reception and wave good morning to Jean, our secretary, as I bring up the lighter, spark and inhale. My lungs flood with nicotine, carcinogens and black oozing crap.

The sign on the open door behind me reads: ROBIN GARRETT ASSOCIATES. In smaller writing underneath it adds: LICENSED PRIVATE INVESTIGATORS, BUSINESS SECURITY AND CRIMINAL CONSULTANTS.

I amble through the interior door next to Jean's desk and into our spacious squad-room-style office. Five desks, a coffee machine and water cooler, lines of steel shelving and filing cabinets, faded leather swivel chairs, a few framed photos on the walls. Only two of our trio of junior staff are in at the moment, and both are busy on the phone. I place my coffee on the worktop and settle into my chair.

The man whose desk faces mine across the room calls out, 'Made it at last, I see.'

Robin Garrett is, technically, my boss, but in reality we're more like partners. He started out as a lone operator, but since I joined him three years ago, we've added Jean, three more investigators and our relatively plush office to the company.

'Morning, Rob,' I say as I leaf through the mail on my desk.

'What kind of time do you call this?'

He's not really annoyed; he just likes playing the overbearing boss every once in a while. It's a routine we're both well used to.

'I call it half past ten,' I say. 'If it's got another name, I haven't heard it.'

'Overslept or hung over?'

'Neither of the above. Working.'

He raises a sarcastic eyebrow. 'Well I'll be damned. Who are you and what have you done with Alex?'

'Nothing a month's sleep and a couple of painkillers won't solve. We can tell the Ingrams that Little Jamie is living with his girlfriend, Chrissie Evans, in an apartment on Bedford Avenue. She's still studying at university; he's currently Employee of the Month at Miss Mona's Fried Chicken on Douglas. Having been there, I can only say that he can't have had much competition for the award. He's not keen on getting back in touch with his folks, but I did manage to extract his permission to give them his number.' I take a long gulp of the gritty, extra-strong espresso. 'I spent yesterday evening with some of Chrissie's friends, and the night in the company car outside her apartment, waiting for her or Jamie to show. Eight thirty they got in. We talked. Nice enough kid, I guess.'

'So we can hand the Ingrams our final bill. Another satisfied customer,' Rob says with a contented smile on his face.

'I wouldn't call them that until they've *seen* the bill,' I retort, flashing him a tired grin. 'Anything new doing down here?'

'A couple of bread-and-butter jobs. The kids are working on them now. Oh, and you had a call from some Hicksville County Sheriff's Department. Name and number's on your desk.'

Rob is from Chicago and never ceases to look down his nose at everything from anywhere not covered by city concrete, including my own roots in what he likes to think of as the 'Great White North'. There's no malice in his opinions; it's just part of his repertoire.

I scan the desk until my eye picks out a scrap of envelope bearing a number and the name Dale Townsend. I know Dale. We grew up in the same small town and Chris, his younger brother, was my best friend when we were kids. I haven't seen Dale since I left to go to college seventeen years ago, but I spoke with him a year and a half ago, when he called me about a burglary case he was working on and asked me to look at what his office had turned up. I was happy to help out.

I wonder what Dale wants now. Maybe he has something else to throw at me. I pick up the phone and punch in the number. It rings once, twice, before a voice says, 'Sheriff Townsend.'

'Dale? This is Alex Rourke. You tried getting in touch with me earlier. How are things?'

'Alex! Long time, no see. Things aren't too bad up here. A little hectic right now.' His voice is gruff and throaty. I have no idea how much Dale has changed from when I last saw him. From the voice, I find myself imagining him with a beard and a truck driver's physique.

'How's Chris?' I say. 'Still in the Coast Guard?'

'Yeah. He says he'll be home for a few weeks sometime in September. You'll have to come up and get together for a drink.'

'I'll do that. What's on your mind?'

'We've got a funny situation on our hands and I figured you might be able to help out like you did with the Sharp case.'

'Sure,' I say. 'Fire away.'

'On the night of the 15th we took a guy in on a murder charge. We found him standing on the highway four miles south of town, with the victim's body at his feet and two knives in his hands.'

'South of Winter's End?'

It's where Dale and I grew up, a small town in the wooded hills of northeastern Maine that make up the tail end of the Appalachians. I can't remember hearing of a single case of murder in the eighteen years I lived there. This must be a hot crime locally.

'Yeah,' Dale continues. 'According to the medical examiner, the knives were the right dimensions to be the murder weapons. The victim had been dead less than an hour when we found her.'

'OK, so you've got the suspect at the scene at around the time of death, with the murder weapons in his hands and the vic at his feet. Sounds pretty open and shut.'

'It does, doesn't it? That's where the complications come in,' Dale says. 'Firstly, we haven't been able to find the guy's prints on the body or the weapons. That might be because of the way the knives' hilts are dimpled, and could have been made worse by the rain.'

'It was raining?'

'Like you wouldn't believe. I nearly drowned making the arrest.'

'So what else was there?'

'In two days we haven't been able to find any blood traces on the guy or his clothing—he was wearing nothing from the waist up, by the way. Nothing on the road either, thanks to the downpour, so we're not certain that it actually *was* where the murder took place.'

'Were there any marks on either of them? Any signs that she put up a fight?'

'Not a scratch. Some bruising on her right arm, looks like grip marks from where she'd been held by someone. She was naked and we haven't been able to find her clothes.'

'Who was she?'

'Angela Lamond, forty, a nurse at the doctor's in town. We checked her house, turned up nothing.'

I nod to myself. 'Who's the guy?'

There's a pause at the other end of the line and a long-drawn breath. 'That's the biggest problem. We don't know, and he won't tell us. There was no ID on him. We ran his prints, no dice. He doesn't have a record. We've tried what checks we can do through the National Crime Information Center and the Violent Criminal Apprehension Program and also drawn a blank so far. I've sent out the guy's photo and details direct to the rest of the state's agencies, as well as posting them further afield. Nothing as yet.'

'DNA?'

'There wasn't any evidence of sexual assault, so I'm not expecting him to show up on the CODIS Forensic Index. We're checking through the State Crime Lab in Augusta anyway.' There's another pause, shorter this time. 'We've got the guy at the scene, but without knowing anything about him we don't have a motive unless he tells us why he did it. I was wondering if you ever handled anything like this while you were with the Feds. You do lectures on difficult interrogation for local law enforcement down in Boston, don't you?'

'Not very often but, yeah, I do. I took courses on it when I worked for the Bureau's National Center for the Analysis of Violent Crime.' A long time ago, I add in the privacy of my own head.

'Good. If you can, I want you to come up to Houlton and have a talk with our John Doe to see if you can get anything out of him. He hasn't said a damn thing about himself or the murder as yet.'

'Don't the State Police have someone who can question him?'

'They're not involved in the interrogation. They did the scene investigation, but he's our suspect.'

I hesitate for a moment. It's not often a county sheriff has such a personal involvement in a murder investigation. Normally, most of the work would be carried out by the State Police Criminal Investigation Division. Dale must be under a lot of pressure for his department to solve the crime. If he had to call in the State or another outside agency he'd lose serious face, and perhaps his job.

'Sure,' I say. 'It's going to be a long drive, so I'll leave first thing tomorrow morning and aim to get there about lunchtime. Can you arrange a room for me?'

'No problem.'

'Is this going to be sworn or non-sworn work, Dale?'

'Sworn, I think. It'll look better on interview transcripts if you've been deputised, and if you have to do any asking around it'll give you a badge to flash.'

As I thought, he wants this to look like his department's work as much as possible. 'OK. Fax me copies of everything you've got on the case and I'll go over it before I leave.'

'Thanks, Alex. I'll see you tomorrow.'

'Yeah. Bye.'

As I hang up, Rob looks at me with his eyebrows raised and his arms folded. 'Trouble in the wilds, huh?' he says.

'They want me to go and talk to a guy they've got for a murder near my home town. Sounds interesting.'

He grins. 'I'm happy so long as they pay the fee. Just make sure you take your phone with you. We might get busy all of a sudden.'

I spend the next few hours clearing up some small details on other cases. The fax machine finally stops whirring and disgorging paper just shy of three in the afternoon. I bundle Dale's reports together and leave the office for home.

Unsure how long the trip will last, I pack a bag with enough clothes for a week. An electric razor and toiletries. A couple of blues CDs for the journey. My old but well-tended Colt M1911 with a couple of spare clips. A crowbar, some bolt cutters, a torque wrench and a couple of files in my car's toolbox for letting myself into places I'm not supposed to be.

Packing complete, I settle back on my black felt sofa, Sonny Boy Williamson II on the stereo and a bottle of Mexican beer in hand. I start leafing through the files.

AT AROUND 7.45AM on May 15, two days ago, forty-year-old nurse Angela Lamond left her house on Altmayer Street, Winter's End, on the short walk to the doctor's office on Main Street where she worked. She was seen by her neighbour, Walter Sarrell, who exchanged morning greetings with her. Nothing in her manner indicated anything amiss. At 8.00am she opened up the office as normal, arriving shortly before Dr Nathan Vallence, the town's physician.

The working day passed normally. None of the people coming for their appointments reported anything strange. Dr Vallence didn't notice anyone suspicious in or around the office. At around 1.00pm, Angela Lamond took her lunch break, leaving the other nurse on duty to cover, and had lunch with two friends in Martha's Garden, a diner not far down the road. Neither friend noticed anything unusual in Angela's manner. She made a quick stop at a convenience store to buy some milk before returning to work. The afternoon passed much the same as the morning, and Angela left the office just after its official closing time of 4.45pm. No one saw her alive again.

At 9.40pm, almost five hours after she left the office, Sheriff Dale Townsend and Deputy Andy Miller found Angela Lamond's naked corpse on Route 11 some three and a half miles south of town. The best estimate placed her time of death somewhere after 8.40pm.

Canvassing failed to turn up anyone who remembered seeing Angela on the route she would have taken home. There were no reports of suspicious individuals or vehicles in the area. Police found no indications of intrusion or any kind of struggle at Angela's house. The driver of a logging truck heading south passed the spot at around 9.15pm. He said he saw nothing, unusual or otherwise.

Forensic investigation of the crime scene was hampered by heavy rain. Highly diluted blood traces were found in the immediate vicinity of the body, and rapidly decreasing in the direction of water flow. The small amount found made it impossible to determine whether this was the actual murder site. Neither of the two weapons recovered at the scene retained detectable quantities of the victim's blood.

Examination of the wider site provided little of apparent worth. There were no tracks visible in the tall grass bordering the highway. The police concluded that the victim arrived at the scene by travelling along the highway, not by walking through the fields.

There were no blood traces or foreign fibres on the suspect's clothing, and no hairs belonging to the victim. The tread of the suspect's shoes contained three pieces of highway gravel and a minute amount of soil local to the area. There were no traces of leaf litter on them. This came as a surprise to the forensic techs, and to me. My shoes would pick up more than that just going for a walk round the block.

The site where the body was found lies within what was once sheep pasture, a grassy rectangle roughly four miles long and two wide, cut out of the local forest. Route 11 bisects it almost perfectly. There are no derelict buildings on site, and no drainage ditches save for small culverts either side of the road, limiting the available cover to the long grass alone.

The county's part-time medical examiner, Dr Gemma Larson, carried out the post-mortem examination on the morning of May 16. Cause of death was two stab wounds, cutting some four and a half inches into the victim's chest cavity. One penetrated the right ventricle of the heart, the second punctured the left lung between ribs six and seven. Entry angles of the wounds suggested they were made from behind, by someone reaching over the victim's shoulder, or from the right-hand side by a right-handed attacker.

There were fourteen other, shallower injuries to the victim's chest and upper abdomen. All were made post-mortem.

There were no defence wounds on the victim's arms or hands, although there was faint bruising on her right arm, consistent with grip marks. There was no evidence of sexual assault.

Scrapings taken from beneath Angela's fingernails revealed nothing. Hair and fibre checks also drew a blank. There were no palm or fingerprints found on her skin. Preliminary results from toxicological testing of her blood indicated nothing out of the ordinary. Angela's stomach and upper digestive tract were almost empty, indicating that her lunch was almost certainly the last food she ate.

AT THIS POINT I'm interested only in the facts of the case, not the suspect. I can see why Dale is looking for help; this guy is a *ghost*. No prints, trace evidence, blood or anything. We have him at what may or may not be the murder scene, holding what may or may not be the murder weapons. And yet if he hadn't stood around waiting for the police to show up, we'd never have known he was there.

My thoughts turn to the murderer, and what strikes me first is the extent of overkill injuries to the victim. Whoever did this must have had a lot of anger, perhaps against women in general, or against the victim in particular. She's naked, degraded, and mutilated in death.

The killer snatched Angela unseen shortly after she left the doctor's office for home. That, and the fact that her clothes, and the second crime scene where he presumably kept her, still haven't been found, indicate that the killer planned his deed. He must have known the route she took and found a good hiding place to strike from, along with a safe way to smuggle her away from public view.

If we were still hunting for a suspect, I'd suggest checking the people who lived along and around Angela's route, since grabbing her and whisking her inside would be one easy way to hide her quickly. I'd also look at people whose vehicles might have been in the area on a regular enough basis not to arouse suspicion.

I'd like to know how the killer brought a naked woman three and a half miles out of town on a public highway without being spotted. I scribble 'Vic's route' and 'Highway walk?' on a piece of paper. Then I turn to the transcripts of the interviews Dale and his people have had with the suspect since his arrest two days ago.

Transcript #1—May 16
Interrogation of subject (SUB) conducted by Sheriff Dale Townsend (DT) and Lt. B. Watts (BW).

DT: Time is 0035 hours at start of interview. Present are Sheriff Dale Townsend and Lieutenant Bruce Watts, Aroostook County Sheriff's Department, and interview subject. I remind you that you have the right to remain silent. Anything you do say can be used against you in a court of law. You have the right to speak with an attorney and have them present during questioning. If you cannot afford an attorney one will be appointed for you free of charge. Do you understand these rights that I have read you?

SUB: Of course.

DT: You do not currently have an attorney representing you. Are you waiving your right to legal representation?

SUB: I have all the lawyers I could want. I just don't think I need them here.

DT: So you are—

SUB: (interrupting) Yes, I am waiving my right to an attorney.

DT: Please state your name for the record.

SUB: (short pause) I'm afraid I won't be adding my name to the record. Did you know people used to believe that knowing someone's true name gave you all sorts of power over them, if you were so inclined? A nice idea, if a little outdated.

BW: You know you could face additional penalties if you fail to provide a name for the record?

SUB: I'll bear those in mind, although given that you've brought me here to question me about murder, I wonder why you think additional charges would frighten me. Has obstruction of justice become punishable by death?

DT: All right, we'll forget it for now. Subject will be a John Doe until we know his proper identity. Let's start with what you were doing on the highway, Mr Doe.

SUB: Waiting.

DT: Waiting for what?

SUB: You'll know when it happens.

BW: Did you kill the woman at the scene, or did you carry her there from town?

SUB: Winter's End?

BW: Yeah.

SUB: Do you know how the town got its name, Lieutenant?

BW: I don't know how it's relevant.

SUB: A group of settlers were caught by the onset of winter some way south of the St John River. They tried waiting it out, but supplies were low, and they eventually had to turn south.

DT: Let's get back onto tonight's events.

SUB: They kept going for weeks. The going was slow, especially after they killed their pack animals for meat.

DT: Could you describe your movements tonight until the point where you were arrested?

SUB: Starving and with their numbers dropping, they stopped when they saw the first signs of spring thaw. They called the settlement they founded Winter's End.

BW: Fascinating. You're familiar with the town then?

SUB: An astounding deduction. At the very least, I might have read a tourist pamphlet about it once.

BW: You got any favourite places to hang out there? Me, I grab a beer at Larry's if I'm passing through. Not everyone's type of place, though.

SUB: (quiet laughter) That was almost clever, Lieutenant. I'm impressed.

DT: Look, friend, it's late and we're all tired. Why not just tell us what happened so we can all get some sleep?

SUB: If I remember rightly, in the beginning was the word. There's more, but it's a long story.

DT: (sighs) Forget it. We'll try again in the morning. Interview terminated at 0105.

Transcript #2—May 16
Subject (SUB) waived his right to an attorney.

DT: Time is 0945 hours at start of interview. Present are Sheriff Dale Townsend and Lieutenant Bruce Watts, Aroostook County Sheriff's Department, and interview subject, currently referred to as John Doe.

BW: Let's start with what happened yesterday, Mr Doe. How did you spend the day?

SUB: I'm surprised to see you here again in person, Sheriff. I would have thought a busy man like you would have had better things to do this morning.

DT: As it happens, John, I do have better things to do. It's your pig-headedness that's keeping me from them. Why not give us your side of the story? At least then we'll have two ways of looking at the situation, and not just our reconstruction from the evidence, which I have to say looks pretty bad for you.

SUB: Since I doubt you'd believe anything I say, would there be a point in telling you my side of the story? I could say I spent the entire day at a twenty-four-hour New England Steak Lovers' Association whist drive, but what use would that be?

BW: We could check your story. If you were telling the truth, we'd have to look again at the evidence.

SUB: Well, thank you for explaining that to me, Lieutenant. Before today I had no idea what the word 'alibi' meant.

DT: Did you know Angela Lamond?

SUB: Do you have a family, Sheriff Townsend? Wife? Kids?

DT: Is that some sort of threat?

SUB: Simple curiosity. I'm locked firmly in jail, hardly a position from which to be making threats. So, do you?

BW: Let's stick to the events of the 15th.

SUB: I'd rather talk about something else.

There's more but I skip through it. The suspect doesn't give anything away, dodging questions whenever he's asked about the crime, occasionally digressing onto other subjects: history, sport, religion. I have what's necessary. I know the case and I have a feel for the suspect. Everything else will come later.

2

It's six o'clock the following morning when I step, yawning, out of my front door and trot down the steps towards my car. The day is cool and still has the fresh, undisturbed air that comes with the dawn. I slide into the leather driver's seat, dropping my bag in the passenger footwell. The immobiliser, a retrofit since my car is too old to have one as standard, switches off as I turn the key in the ignition. When the engine growls into life, I reflect for the millionth time that I'm driving an anachronism given form.

The car that eases north towards the bridge over the Charles River is a 1969 Stingray Corvette. Pale metallic-blue bodywork hides a seven-litre V8 throwing out somewhere over 400 horsepower. If I had a shrink, he'd probably say I was compensating for something.

Maybe so. My 'Vette takes a lot of work to look after and is expensive to run. In many ways, it compensates for not having a family.

Like my choice of attire and my personal appearance, it also represents a complete break with my time at the FBI. Agents are expected to be smart and presentable at all times. The requisitioned unmarked brown sedan is a little clichéd, but it's not far from the truth. When I quit, I dropped the look of a Bureau man, and when I happened to spot the 'Vette at a collectors' auction, I couldn't resist.

I cruise up the interstate at sixty-five with Hound Dog Taylor's 'Sitting at Home Alone' wailing above the roar of the engine. The highway cuts relentlessly north, through Massachusetts and New Hampshire, then dives a short way inland from the picture-postcard Maine coast, which even now will be starting to fill up with tourists.

Winter's End itself never gets many visitors. There's usually some hikers, snowmobilers and people who come for the fishing or hunting, but nothing like the infestation that the coast and the mountain resorts endure. Hell, the whole eastern chunk of Aroostook County is the same. Nothing but woods, cold weather and potato farms.

I've not been back to my home town since I started at college down south. I wonder whether anyone will remember me. I also wonder how many would remember my parents—my dad a lawyer and one of the town's volunteer fire-fighters, my mom a kindergarten assistant—and how many of those would know about the crash. It happened two years into the quiet life of retirement in the Florida sun. I was visiting, driving them into town, when my car was T-boned and wrecked by a stolen sedan. The cops never caught the driver. I was thirty-one when I buried my parents. Six months later came the breakdown that finished me as a federal agent.

I found the NCAVC—the FBI's violent crime subdivision whose staff help local police forces on request—a hectic, pressure cooker of an assignment. People's lives were on the line in almost every job we took, and we never seemed to have enough staff to cover everything as we would have liked. Quantico's internal politics didn't help matters. Maybe I don't handle pressure very well. Maybe my parents' death was just one thing too many.

One October morning I suffered complete physical and mental collapse. For weeks I'd been growing more and more irrational. I wasn't sleeping or eating properly, drinking too much coffee and smoking almost continuously. I'd had several full-blown psychotic episodes, thankfully while no one was around to see, and when I did manage to sleep I'd have terrible nightmares, seeing the victims of the people we were trying to stop: murder, pain and torture like some horrible late-night cable channel. Eventually, it all became too much.

I found myself in a hospital in Kansas City. The early days were a haze of tranquillisers, antidepressants and antipsychotics. I drifted in and out, from zombie to human and back again. After a while, the drugs were phased out and I could go home for a few months' less intense therapy. Then, just as I was starting to wonder about my future as a thirty-two-year-old FBI burnout, Rob Garrett, who I'd first met as a rookie FBI field officer in Atlanta, got in touch. He offered me a job with his agency in Boston. Easiest decision I ever made.

A lot of water has passed under my particular bridge, then, since the last time I pulled off I-95 at Exit 62, not far short of the Canadian border, and turned south into the town of Houlton.

The engine hums to itself as I cruise towards the town centre. Well-kept brick houses with the slightly bleached look to them that comes with the climate. Rows of box-shaped stores selling groceries, outdoor wear. The people are dressed for late spring—bright hues and lighter cloth. Couples chat to one another and kids play on the sidewalk, enjoying the freedom that Saturday brings.

I hit Military Street and the red brick of the Houlton Superior Court building is right in front of me, a stone's throw from the smaller District Court and the Aroostook County Jail. I swing the 'Vette into the Superior Court parking lot and pull up next to a Jeep Grand Cherokee with the six-pointed star of the Sheriff's Department on the side. There's a State Police blue-and-white not far away. I climb out of my car, which looks as out of place here as a ski shop on a Pacific island, and haul on my leather jacket.

I push through the courthouse doors. A wooden sign on the wall inside directs me up to the Sheriff's Department offices on the first floor. There, a pair of open doors lead into a small but tidy room occupied by a handful of polished wooden desks set with computers, filing trays and assorted personal clutter. A man wearing a uniform shirt marked with a DISPATCH badge looks up from behind a short wooden counter. Aside from him and a deputy staring at a glowing monitor, the place is empty. There are two closed doors at the far end of the room, each marked with letters too small for me to make out.

'Can I help you, sir?' the dispatcher says neutrally.

'Yeah, my name's Alex Rourke. I'm here to see Sheriff Townsend.'

The man nods as if he'd already guessed my response and gestures at the left-hand door. 'The chief's in his office, go right on through.'

'Thanks,' I tell him.

'Alex!' says Dale as I step into his office. He's not quite as I pictured him when we spoke on the phone. His gruff voice suggested a beard—he has a moustache—and a gut, which is just beginning to protrude as he heads for forty on a carbohydrate-heavy diet. His dark hair is thinning on top, lines show around his eyes and his cheeks have begun to sag. The resemblance to his father is startling.

We have that moment that all people experience when they meet someone they haven't seen for years: studying, judging, remembering.

'Good to see you, Dale,' I say. 'It's been too long.'

'You too. You're looking well. Good trip?'

'All right,' I say. 'I could do with a coffee, though.'

I take a seat while Dale goes out into the squad room. 'Has there been any change in our guy's story since you sent me the transcripts?' I ask him when he returns with two mugs.

He shakes his head. 'No. He gives us the same stuff every time; still no name. You ever encountered anything like this before?'

'Yeah, but they've always given in after a few hours. Since most of them that do it are trying to hide the fact that they've been busted before, their prints are on file anyway.' I swallow a mouthful of black coffee. 'Has the guy been arraigned?'

'Yep,' Dale says, 'the day before yesterday. The judge slapped him with contempt of court since he wouldn't identify himself.'

'He refused to do it in court?'

'Same performance. They won't set a trial date for a while; they're giving us a chance to find out who he is.'

I nod. 'Where am I staying? I might as well drop my stuff off before I talk to the guy.'

Dale looks a little sheepish. 'Well, I figured you might want to see the old town again, so I got you a room at the Crowhurst Lodge in Winter's End instead of somewhere here in Houlton. It's less than an hour's drive. I still live up there.'

'That's OK.' I polish off the last of my coffee, and say, 'Let's go meet your mystery man.'

I WATCH from behind the one-way glass as two deputies wearing Corrections Division uniform escort the guy into the interview room and sit him at the table. Although I've seen his mugshots, photos never compare with seeing a suspect in the flesh. Untidy straight black hair. Guarded oval eyes coloured a blue so deep it's practically black. A narrow nose and thin mouth. He's a couple of inches shorter than I am, and I can see that beneath his orange County Jail overalls he's well built. Mid to late twenties, I guess. He moves without any hint of rancour for his captors, even nodding at them when they show him to the chair. Then he just sits and stares, Zen-like, at the wall.

He glances up as I open the door to the interview room carrying a fresh cup of coffee and a manila file. I walk to the seat opposite him, turn on the tape recorder and identify myself as Deputy Alex Rourke.

Then I begin. 'Well, John . . . That's kind of a silly-sounding name —"John Doe". Is there something else I could call you? I'm not asking for your real name, not if you don't want to give it to me.'

The guy regards me calmly, head cocked slightly to one side as if I'm a new lab rat whose quirks he finds interesting. Dark blue eyes reach out to me like they can see my thoughts.

'If you'd prefer, Deputy, you can call me Nicholas.' He smiles faintly. 'Not my true name, of course.'

'Sure. And you don't need to call me Deputy. Mr Rourke, Alex, whatever you want.' I spark up a Marlboro and take a drag on it to give him a chance to respond, but he stays silent and still. His eyes continue to track mine. 'How are you finding the jail? It's been reno-vated since I last saw it. Used to be pretty drab.'

'I can think of worse places.'

The eyes continue to stare at me. I change tack.

'It's got to be tough,' I say. 'Being stuck in a place like this on your own. No family to speak to, no friends. I take it you aren't a local?'

'You can take whatever you want, Mr Rourke.'

'Is there anyone you'd like us to contact for you, just to let them know you're OK? Even if it's just to cancel the morning papers.'

Nicholas smiles faintly again. 'I'm not a great reader of the news. I prefer to stick to less salacious subject matter. It's more stimulating.'

'Well, a man should always try to broaden his horizons.' I finish the contents of my polystyrene cup. 'You study history?'

'Not specifically, no.'

'You know how Winter's End came to be founded, though.'

'I see one of the sheriff's people has been hard at work typing up our earlier conversations.'

I nod as if that's obvious. 'Of course. I wasn't going to come here without knowing what to expect.'

'And what did you expect?' Although his tone is steady, Nicholas pauses slightly before the final word. The effect is one of disdain.

'An apparently intelligent man who, for some reason, hung around a murder scene until the cops found him. There's three thousand miles of public highway in the county, Nicholas, and the Sheriff's Department has three patrol cars. Strange stroke of luck that Dale came along when he did.'

'Are you saying my timing was deliberate?'

The eyes are still fixed on me, but I just stare back. 'I'm not saying anything in particular. Maybe you were just unlucky. Maybe you wanted to get caught so people could marvel at what you'd done.'

'So what else did you learn from the transcripts, Mr Rourke?'

'Nothing definite,' I reply, brushing off the question. 'If you wouldn't mind, though, I'd like to hear why you were standing in the middle of the road on the night Angela Lamond died.'

'I've already given an answer to that.'

'Waiting. What were you waiting for?'

'Do you believe I'm a murderer?'

'That's what I drove all this way to find out.'

'Ah yes, how is Boston, Mr Rourke?' Nicholas leans forward

slightly, the only movement his frame has made since he first sat down, and for some reason the change unsettles me. 'Or should it be Agent Rourke?' he continues. 'Tell me, why did you leave the FBI?'

The question takes me aback, but I try not to let it show. 'You know I was in the FBI? What else do you know about me?'

'Why did you *leave*, Agent Rourke?'

I take a long, soothing drag on my cigarette. Most successful interviews are based on trust. Suspects open up to you because they want to justify their actions. Trust is the hook on the end of the fishing line, with confession the nice fat trout.

'Health reasons,' I say. 'Then someone I knew from the Bureau offered me a job in the private sector.'

'Health reasons?' Nicholas has returned to his original posture. The sneering half-smile has become a permanent fixture. The tip of one ivory-white incisor is visible through the gap between his lips.

'Stress. Too many cases, not enough time. I had a breakdown.' I stub out the cigarette. 'I spent some time in an institution.'

'I would have thought the Bureau prepared you for the effects of the job while you were in training,' Nicholas says.

'They do, but anyone can snap.'

'True.'

I sense an opening. 'Has that kind of thing ever happened to you, Nicholas?'

'Not as such, no.' His voice softens even more, barely louder than a whisper. 'I came close once, a long time ago.' His eyes are no longer looking at me, but back through time.

'What happened?' I ask, my voice as low as his.

'I could feel myself starting to go. Then I made a decision, set myself a goal. Everything became clear again.'

'What did you decide?'

Nicholas seems to snap out of his reverie. 'That's private, Mr Rourke. I doubt you'd understand it, either.'

'You could try me.'

'I don't think so.'

This seems like a reasonable time to take a quick break. 'Do you want a coffee, Nicholas?' I ask him. 'I'm going to get one for myself.'

'No, thanks.'

'Fair enough.' I stand and walk out of the interview room.

First I head to the coffee machine and help myself to a cup. Then I let myself into the darkened viewing room, where Dale is watching the suspect from behind the mirrored glass. 'How does this compare with your earlier chats?' I ask him.

'Good,' he says. 'I'm impressed.'

'Get someone to send his pictures to mental institutions all over the northeast. There might be something in the breakdown angle that could identify him.'

'Sure.'

I walk back into the interview room and sit back down. 'Did you know Angela Lamond, Nicholas?' I say.

'What was there to know?' By now, his face has resumed its Zen-like façade.

'She was a forty-year-old nurse who'd lived in Winter's End for her entire life. She was a smart, attractive woman with no steady boyfriend, but plenty of friends and no enemies. She wasn't rich, didn't hang around in bad company and, as far as we know, had no reason for anyone to hate her. Yet someone abducted her, stripped her and stabbed her to death on a lonely highway.'

The half-smile makes another fleeting appearance. 'By "someone", I assume you think it was me.'

'I just want to understand why it happened. Her family do too.'

'Why do you want to understand?' The question is posed so flatly, I can't tell whether he's being sarcastic or whether there is a real reason for asking.

'Their peace of mind. Besides, the more people understand, the more we can stop things like this happening in the future.'

Nicholas's face stays impassive as he stares at me in silence for a moment. Eventually he says, '*Eripere vitam nemo non homini potest, at nemo mortem; mille ad hanc aditus patent.*' When I remain blank, he translates. '"Anyone can stop a man's life, but no one his death; a thousand doors open onto it."'

'Who are you quoting?'

'Seneca. I don't suppose you had much of a chance to study Seneca at college, Mr Rourke. Criminology and law, wasn't it?'

I stay silent.

'And at high school I suspect you were too busy chasing cheerleaders. Not the sort to spend all your time in the library, were you?'

'True enough.'

Nicholas smiles at me, like an indulgent parent at his child. 'I'm feeling tired, Mr Rourke. I wonder if we could continue this later.'

For a moment I think of denying this request, forcing him to stay until he answers my questions. However, something tells me that his resentment wouldn't make my job easier. A break will also give me a chance to find out how he knows so much about me.

'Sure,' I say. 'We'll stop here.'

I note the time, and turn off the tape recorder. Then I call for the two deputies to take Nicholas back to his cell. As he heads for the door, he stops and looks back at me. 'You asked what I was waiting for,' he says. 'I was waiting for you, Mr Rourke. You.'

3

The sun is dipping towards the distant Appalachians by the time I reach a spot on Route 11 marked with a couple of small bouquets of flowers. I bring the 'Vette to a halt at the side of the road and climb out. Dale slams the door of his Jeep shut and leads me to a spot in the middle of the northbound lane no more than twenty feet from the hood of my car.

'Here,' he says. 'Head to the north, lying on her right side.'

'I need to check the scene,' I say, 'then walk the route Angela would have taken from work. I'd also like to look at her house, and anything you have on her personal history.'

'You think her personal details are important?'

I bend to touch the asphalt. 'Always try to know the victim, Dale.'

'Speaking of which, our suspect seems to know a lot about you. What do you think he meant by "waiting" for you?'

'I don't know.'

Dale's coat rustles as he wedges his hands in the pockets to keep off the chill. 'He sounds educated,' he says. 'You think we should try asking colleges and universities whether they recognise him?'

I shrug. 'You can try, but I don't think it'll work. For one thing, you're talking about remembering one student in thousands. For another, I don't think he is well *educated*. To me he sounds more well *read*; no formal teaching, just what he's picked up for himself.'

'How do you get that?'

'The way he talks.' I stand and take a summary of the crime scene notes out of my jacket. 'He quotes stuff and brings out information, but there's no pattern to it. It's like having someone read poetry without giving it any sense of rhythm.'

Dale nods uncertainly.

I glance briefly at a couple of police photos taken at a wide enough angle to show her entire body. Then I let my gaze wander over the roadway and the narrow concrete-lined culvert and fields to either side. 'You say there were no tracks in the grass?'

'No.'

The thigh-high stalks that fill the former farmland bordering the road are now bent and twisted into tufts by the crime scene unit's inch-by-inch search of the area round the site. The edge of the forest surrounding the oblong patch of grassland is visible as a dark line in the distance, three and a half miles north, half a mile south and a mile to the east and west. A breeze blows down from the west, setting the pale green strands dancing in rippling waves.

'Why did he choose here?' I say, ostensibly to Dale, although we both know it's a rhetorical question. 'This is either a really stupid place to dump a body, or it's really clever and we've missed something. Fingernail scrapings on the vic turned up nothing?'

'No. What have you got in mind?'

I gesture up the road, towards town. 'If he didn't come across the fields, he must've come along the road. He couldn't walk openly with traffic going past. If he walked her along the culvert, he could've laid them both flat whenever a vehicle came by. But if he did, she'd have grit and mud under her nails. Did the ME examine her toes?'

'I don't know.'

'OK. I'll ask her tomorrow. Let's check out Angela's route home. Drive slow—I'd like to scope out the woods around town.'

The thin belt of spruce and birch trees that separates the fields from the town itself offers no obvious sign that they were used as cover by the murderer. The area beneath the brilliant green canopy is open and airy. Dog-walkers' countryside.

Then I'm through and driving past houses of red brick and white-washed wood. Wide lawns carpeted with the thick emerald grass that always sprouts after the spring thaw. Four-by-fours in driveways. Pick-up trucks and sturdy sedans. To a tourist, this would simply be one more picture-postcard Maine town. But I can see peeling paint, loose boards, curtains in need of a wash. Winter's End is just an ordinary town with ordinary people and ordinary problems.

Ordinary in part because it's so familiar. I've been away for seventeen years and—if you allow for certain changes in fashion—it seems as though nothing has changed. Street names and buildings evoke surprisingly strong memories. Skinner Street, where Rhona Garde lived when we were at high school. Making love while her parents were away—the first time for both of us—was probably the scariest five minutes of my life. Renfrey's Liquor where my friends and I used to buy six-packs before heading for Boynton Campground, just north of the town, to get wasted. The grocery store, now a chain 7-Eleven, where I got my first part-time job to help pave my way to college. I push the memories aside and park outside the doctor's office on Main Street. It's past closing time and the building is locked. I light a cigarette while Dale clambers out of his Jeep.

I turn to the south and begin walking down Main Street under the indigo sky. The shops are typical small-town fare: a couple of grocery stores, a place selling outdoor wear, a tiny bookstore. Nothing large, and most of them pretty much as they've been for years.

A block from the doctor's office, I make a right onto Carver. 'She went this way?' I say to Dale.

'As far as we know.'

Carver is a curving road flanked by identical red-brick houses, all with tidy little front yards. Windows are shut for the most part, and the curtains framing them give the buildings a dark, walled-off aspect. Every time we pass one, though, I get the feeling that someone inside is watching. Twitches at the curtain. A shadow moving out of the corner of my eye. Carver hits Altmayer after a couple of minutes' walk. Altmayer used to be where the town's better-off folk lived, and many of the houses here have painted wooden boards covering the stonework. Now it just holds most of Winter's End's oldest houses. Angela lived a few doors down from the junction. Her salary can't have been bad to afford one of these places. Half a dozen bouquets lie by the porch and the front door has a strip of police tape across it. Dale unlocks the door and ducks underneath the tape. I follow.

There are notes—reminders and friends' phone numbers—stuck to the mirror in the hallway. A couple of spare coats hang on hooks behind the door. The living-room furniture is well kept but starting to show threads. A TV, the remote control on the coffee table, and a TV guide on the sofa. Hi-fi with stacked CDs—Mozart, Vivaldi, some late-sixties soul and a couple of modern compilations.

The kitchen at the back is tidy, although there's an unwashed mug and cereal bowl in the sink. I glance through the kitchen window at the back yard. Shrubs along the borders, a neat lawn. Dale follows my gaze and tells me that the state crime scene people checked it.

Upstairs, the picture is much the same. The bed is unmade, and there are a couple of stray items of clothing discarded on a chair. On top of the dresser is a wilted rose in a glass vase.

'Present from an admirer?' I ask.

'She didn't have a boyfriend,' Dale replies. 'Forensics checked it for latents and fibre *in situ* but all they got was a partial print from her left thumb on one of the leaves. Guess she bought it herself.'

'Uh-huh. I guess.'

A shoebox in the closet contains certificates, employment records and thankyou notes from patients. The trappings of a life that's over. I start to replace them. Then a thought strikes me and I flick through the bundled papers.

'Did Angela ever work anywhere where they got mental patients?' I ask. 'Just in case our boy Nicholas does turn out to be a nut.'

'I doubt she has—we don't have anything like that round here. As far as I know, she used to be the in-house nurse at the children's home before she worked at the doctor's office.'

I pause in my flicking. 'St Valentine's? Just outside of town?'

'Yeah,' Dale says. 'It closed after a fire about six years ago.'

'After my time,' I tell him. 'My dad used to visit the home occasionally when I was young, taking presents for the kids. I went with him a couple of times. I never heard about a fire.'

'The staff quarters burned to the ground one night, taking the director and a couple of others with it. The insurance company wouldn't pay up, so the home closed down. Come to think of it, your dad must have been one of the ones called out to tackle the blaze.'

I shrug and replace the papers. 'That's what volunteer fire-fighters do, Dale. Are there any records of the kids who lived there?'

He shakes his head. 'Up in smoke. The county might have copies, though. You think there's a chance Nicholas spent time there?'

'Maybe. It's certainly worth a look.'

We head back downstairs and I wait on the porch while Dale locks up. The shadows of evening are beginning to deepen.

'So what do you think?' Dale asks when he's finished.

I glance at him. His face is expectant, as if he's hoping I've learned something that will help get Nicholas to talk.

'Nothing definite,' I say. 'As far as I can see, there's still no clear reason for anyone to want Angela dead, so still no clue to Nicholas's motive.' I let my gaze wander down the road. 'But there *is* something.'

'What's that?'

'What if Nicholas had an accomplice?' I say, as we wander back towards the cars. 'Someone local working with him.'

Dale frowns at this suggestion. 'Is this just a hypothesis, or something you want me to take a serious look at?'

'It's a hypothesis. What have we got?' I start counting off fingers. 'A woman disappears on a journey that would've taken five or six minutes at most. She vanishes for nearly five hours, during which time she's stripped naked. Then she turns up three and a half miles down the road, still naked, and we're fairly certain she hasn't come across country. The suspect we've got doesn't have a car that we know of, so presumably he snatched her in the middle of a residential area. He takes her somewhere and gets rid of her clothing. Then he walks her out of town along a public highway without being spotted.'

'So where does the accomplice come in?'

'Let's say that Angela is walking home when someone living on Carver or Altmayer calls at her from his front door. He asks if she can give him a hand with something. She goes inside, Nicholas grabs her and strips her and they keep her inside for a few hours. Then they take her down to the garage, stick her in the accomplice's car and together they all drive out to the highway. The accomplice drops her and Nicholas off, then turns round and heads back into town.'

Dale thinks for a moment, then shakes his head. 'Suppose someone saw her going into the house?' he says. 'It'd be too risky. And we'd have picked up fibre traces from the car's seats on her body.'

'Plastic covering. Hell, keep her clothed, then strip her off when she gets to the place you found her. Take the clothes away in the car. The house is trickier, but suppose the accomplice picked her up in his vehicle rather than calling her into his home. He could pick a spot on the road where he knew as few people as possible would see.'

'True, though no one acted funny when we did door-to-door along her route the morning after.' He pauses for a moment. 'How about if Nicholas stole one of the locals' cars and used it to snatch Angela?'

'You'd have a report of a stolen car.'

'Not if he left her unconscious somewhere while he returned it.'

Now it's my turn to shake my head. 'That's more risky than someone calling her into their house. Anyone could have seen him stealing or returning the vehicle, and he'd have to leave the body unattended while he did it. What if Angela's corpse got found?'

'OK, maybe it doesn't quite fit. Let's leave it until you talk to Nicholas tomorrow. Maybe he'll let something slip. Oh, before I forget, Laura wants you to come for dinner tomorrow. She'd make it tonight but her sister's down from Presque Isle.'

'Sure, no problem.'

'You remember where the Crowhurst Lodge is?'

I smile as I watch him get back into his Jeep. 'The town hasn't changed that much. I'll see you tomorrow.'

I decide to check into the hotel and leave my car there while I get something to eat. The evening gloom is deepening. What traffic there is hurried and purposeful, as if people are anxious to be off the streets before nightfall. The same is true for pedestrians, walking quickly, heads bowed.

Then one calls out to me. 'Alex? Alex Rourke?'

I turn to face a guy with short dark hair, glasses and the beginnings of a double chin. I feel I should recognise him. 'Yeah?' I say.

'Cochrane, Matt Cochrane. We were at high school together.'

'Oh, hell, yeah! How's it going?' The memories are slower to return than my voice implies. Cochrane. Cochrane. A damp, slightly nerdy kid who was good at maths. Hand-me-down clothes. Not enough of a target to be bullied, not fun enough to have a lot of friends.

'It's good, good. I'm an accountant. Up in Ashland.'

That figures. 'Yeah? Good work?'

'I do all right.' A touch of pride in his voice. Without meaning to, we've entered the game of one-upmanship all old acquaintances fall into. 'I heard you became a cop.'

'FBI. I left to go private three years ago,' I say, trying not to make it sound like a challenge, another item to be trumped.

'Are you here on the nurse's murder case? Terrible business.'

'Dale Townsend called me in. It must be big news round here. I don't remember there ever being a murder in town.'

Matt nods. Then his face changes as he thinks of something else. 'What are you doing tonight?' he says.

'I've got to check into the hotel and get something to eat, but aside from that I've got no plans. A few notes to write up, maybe.'

'How about a drink with my wife and me? You remember Rhona, don't you? Her surname was Garde when we were at school.'

I concede the game to him. Sure, Matt's an accountant who never managed to escape the smallsville we grew up in. But he's the one who married Rhona Garde, my high-school girlfriend.

'Great,' I say. 'What time, and where?'

'Meet you in the Sawmill at half eight?'

'OK, I'll see you then.'

Matt waves goodbye and I head for my car once more, helping myself to a cigarette to stave off the feeling of defeat. I wonder whether Matt and Rhona have any kids. Then I'm back in the 'Vette's welcoming interior and the smell of motor oil, old smoke and leather banishes such thoughts. I drive to the hotel.

The Crowhurst Lodge has been a hotel and guesthouse for almost its entire life. It is a 1920s building fashioned in neogothic style, with high windows and scattered chunks of decorative masonry around its ledges and cornices. Its white limestone facing seems to glow in the twilight. Twin mosaics, each depicting a smiling face, indistinct in the shadows, look down on me as I park, like grimacing circus clowns picked out in green and terracotta tiles.

The outer door, double-glazed frosted glass, is open and leads into a short, stubby porch lined with pamphlets, some of them practically antique. At the end of the porch is a second door, solid wood blackened through age, with a cast-iron knocker moulded to look like a snarling . . . whatever. I push the door open and step into a warmly lit foyer, which has the same neogothic leanings as the exterior.

'Yes?' says an elderly man in a faded cardigan as he emerges from the doorway behind the desk.

'My name's Alex Rourke. Sheriff Townsend booked me a room.' I notice that my voice echoes faintly but the old man's, perhaps because of its different timbre, does not.

'Hm.' The man opens a ledger that looks no younger than himself and leafs through it. He finds the most recent page and runs his finger down the list. 'Mr Rourke, yes. Room fourteen, at the top of the stairs. Sign in, please. Do you have any other baggage?'

'No,' I say, as I sign. 'The room's at the top of the stairs?'

'First door on the right,' he says as he hands me a fob with two keys on it. One of them looks like it fits the front door. 'Breakfast is from seven to nine, dinner from six to eight thirty if you request it.'

I thank him and head up the stairs to my room. The building is deathly quiet. I unlock my door and find myself in a small but clean and tidy room with a single bed, TV, dressing table and closet. There's a phone on the dressing table. A door leads to the toilet and shower.

I use the phone to send out for pizza—the number of the only place in town was in the porch—then take a quick shower and get changed. A buzzer sounds just after I flick on the TV and I assume this means the pizza guy has arrived. I look through the window and see his bike parked out front. As I'm about to turn away, I spot what looks like a figure lurking in the shadows beneath the trees that surround the hotel's small parking lot. I can't make out any details, just a dim silhouette and a glint of what could be a face. The shape remains still as I stare at it. Then I blink and it's gone.

I go downstairs and collect my dinner. The scent of melted cheese, tomato and basil wafts from the warm box in my hand. The parking lot is empty save for the delivery boy's bike and my Corvette. The hotel is silent, too. It looks as if I'm the only one here.

Once I've finished the pizza—which is pretty good, given that Winter's End isn't exactly Little Italy—I sling on my jacket and make my way down to the Sawmill, one of the town's two bars. Winter's End isn't silent, but has an edgy quiet amplified by the swish of the trees around the parking lot and the faint murmurings of TVs glowing behind lit windows on the streets leading off Main. Life is taking place behind closed doors tonight.

I push through the door of the Sawmill, a nondescript building with few windows, and into the quiet Saturday-night hubbub inside. The faint *clunk* of pool balls comes from the back, and the jukebox is playing softly. People are talking, socialising. Normality. Matt is sitting at a table near the wall and with him is a woman facing away from me. Shoulder-length black hair and a violet sweater are the only details I can make out. He waves at me and I walk over.

'Alex!' he says as I reach the table. 'You and Rhona know each other, of course. See,' he says to her, 'not changed a bit, I told you.'

'How are you, Alex?' she asks. 'It's been a long time.'

'Too long.'

'Drinks are on me,' says Matt. 'What'll it be?'

'Beer, thanks.'

'Rum and Coke,' says Rhona.

Matt goes to the bar, giving me a chance to study my former girlfriend. She hasn't aged badly; the beginnings of laughter lines round her eyes are the only sign of her years. Her dark eyebrows are still fine and arched high over deep brown eyes that have a slightly dead, flat look to them; resignation, perhaps. I knew her as a cheeky cheerleader-type, slightly too sure of herself, always ready with an acid put-down if she thought you deserved it. Surprisingly tender behind the public façade.

'So, how have you been?' I say. 'Matt seems to be doing well.'

She nods. 'He is. I'm teaching English at the elementary school. Where did you get to after high school?'

'College, then the FBI. Now I work with an old Bureau buddy of mine down in Boston.'

'How are your parents? I haven't seen them since their going-away party.'

'Dead. Car accident about three and a half years ago.'

'Oh, Alex, I'm sorry,' she says.

'Don't worry, it happened a long time ago.' I pull out a cigarette and light it, then hesitate. 'Sorry, I should've asked if you minded me smoking. I've picked up some bad habits over the years.'

'It doesn't bother me.'

At this point, Matt returns with the drinks. He's on what looks like whiskey sour. 'So,' he says, 'have you two caught up yet?'

'Rhona says she's become a teacher.' I grin, trying not to look like I'm faking. 'Who would have seen that coming?'

We laugh. 'I just wonder how she'll handle it when Seth's old enough to go to school,' says Matt.

'Seth?'

'Our boy.' Rhona looks at Matt, almost as if she's sheepishly admitting some shared secret. 'He's nearly five. How about you, Alex? Are you married? Any kids, a family?'

'I had a cat once.'

We chuckle. I can see that they're both being a little hesitant, unsure whether this is a sensitive subject for me. I swill some beer and decide to expand further. 'His name was Rusty. Got hit by a truck about eighteen months ago.'

What else can I tell them? That I never formed any successful long-term relationships while I was with the Bureau? That even if I had, I wouldn't have wanted kids? I didn't want to leave them with only half of my life, the part outside the job. That since I left, I haven't made a serious effort to start a family because I'm not sure that any sensible woman would want a failed FBI agent as the father of her children?

'Whereabouts are you living now?' I ask, changing the subject.

'Spruce Street, not far from the library. We've got more space than we know what to do with. Rhona thinks we could do with a couple more kids just to fill up the place.'

'Oh, Matt, stop it,' she says, slapping him playfully on the arm.

'Sounds nice,' I tell him and mean it, pretty much. I take a long gulp from the bottle and finish my cigarette. 'I live in a shoebox with a bed. But I still get residents' parking, so it's not all bad.'

'What do you drive these days?'

I pause for a moment, reflecting that perhaps there's still a last round of one-upmanship to be played. 'A '69 Stingray Corvette.'

Rhona laughs. 'You always were one for flashy cars, Alex. Maine's answer to Don Johnson.'

'Well, if I'm going to be remembered for something, that's an image I can live with.' I grin and finish my beer. 'Same again?'

I fetch another round of drinks from the bar. The jukebox starts playing 'Ramblin' Man' by Hank Williams.

'Matt told me you're here working for the Sheriff's Department,' Rhona says when I return. 'To do with Angela being killed, I take it.'

'That's right. Dale Townsend asked me to help him out.'

Rhona sips her rum and Coke. 'It must have been awful for poor Angela. Has the man they arrested given you any idea why he did it?'

'I can't say. You know how it is with police work.' I light another cigarette. 'How many of our old classmates are still in town?'

'There's a few,' says Matt. 'Jimbo's a mechanic, Brooke married Tristan Maitland—they've got two kids now—and Grant owns the pizza place. There's more, but I can't remember who right now.'

Rhona is about to cut in with some additions of her own when a hand slaps me firmly on the shoulder and a voice behind me says, 'So you're Alex Rourke. Dale told me you were coming.'

I turn to look up at a floury man in his mid to late forties. Brown hair shot with grey, combed neatly back from a widow's peak. A suit but no tie. The firm handshake of someone who likes to make out that he's as tough as the next man and won't stand for any bullshit. His eyes are constantly moving, assessing. 'Byron Saville, mayor,' he says. 'I see you're catching up with old friends.'

'That's right. Do you know Matt and Rhona Cochrane?'

Saville nods. 'Sure. How's the case coming?'

'Well, this is the first day I've been on it. I'm fairly confident of having everything settled in a few days, though.'

'That's good, Alex, very good. The murder's got the whole town rattled. The sooner we can all put it behind us, the better. Remember now, if you need anything while you're here, just give me a call and I'll see what I can do.' He hands me a business card. 'In the meantime, I'll leave you to your drinks. Good night.'

'Good night, Mr Mayor.'

Saville struts away as if he's having a hard time keeping his inflated ego tethered to the ground. A big man in a small town; I know the signs. 'Word gets around fast,' I say to my two former classmates.

'Angela's death is a big thing,' says Matt. 'No one can believe something like that could happen to someone like her. She was always so quiet. Not like the other seniors. Did you hear about the time Scott Robson dared her and a couple of her friends to go with him to Mason Woods after nightfall? She got so freaked out by his spook stories that he had to drive the lot of them home.'

'No, I don't remember. I remember Scott, though.' An asshole, if I recall correctly, though my opinion may have been coloured by the natural disdain and fear younger kids hold towards their elders.

I also remember Mason Woods, an area of forest east of town. Every kid growing up in Winter's End hears the various ghost stories set beneath its tangled boughs. A massacre of one of the local Indian tribes by French colonial troops in the eighteenth century; a lynched trapper and his wife who committed suicide when she found his body; the spirit of a priest from the town who fell into a ravine.

Back in fifth grade, Dale's younger brother Chris and I spent a night camping out in Mason Woods. I told my folks I was going to be sleeping over at his place, and he told his folks the opposite.

A week or so before, Dale had told Chris a bunch of ghost stories about the Blue Axeman, and suggested he'd be too chickenshit to spend a night out in the woods. It was the kind of challenge that a couple of kids like me and Chris couldn't help but take up.

The Blue Axeman was supposed to be the ghost of a tribesman who'd been pressed into service as a scout by a French officer back in colonial times. He soon deserted to return to his family. The officer who recruited him took a handful of soldiers and headed back to their homestead, making it there first. He hung the Axeman's wife and daughter from a tree to punish him, then his men ambushed the Axeman as he tried to cut them down. According to Dale's stories, the Axeman's ghost had prowled the woods ever since, hunting the French officer so he could avenge his family. His spectre was supposed to appear on nights when the moonlight made the night sky appear a deep blue rather than black, hence the name, and to kill all who stood in his path.

There was a lot more to the tales, most of it pretty gory, but I've forgotten it down the years. The crucial point made by Dale was that the Hanging Tree, where the Axeman would begin his nightly rampages, was the ancient fir that stood in the clearing outside Thachel Burrow, a cave underneath Golson Ridge. It was in this clearing, full of the scent of pine resin, that we were going to spend the night.

We got there an hour or so before nightfall, laid out our sleeping-bags and lit a small fire. We huddled by its meagre flames, eating chocolate, drinking Coke and talking kid stuff. Then darkness fell. We tried to get to sleep, but between the chill of the night, the sounds of the forest and the Axeman stories, it was impossible.

Then, around midnight, there was a noise from the cave behind us. A kind of snorting growl. Something moved in the darkness.

I don't think we stopped running until we made it home.

Smiling inwardly at the memory, my attention returns to the Sawmill and I realise that the conversation has—unsurprisingly—petered out. Matt and Rhona are both sitting uncomfortably, sipping their drink, reading the beer mat, anything to make it look as though they're silent through choice and not necessity.

Rhona eventually finds a way to break the deadlock. 'How long do you think you'll be up here for?' she says.

'At least another day, probably more,' I say. 'Dale's invited me to dinner tomorrow night.'

'Did you know that Chris joined the Coast Guard?'

I nod. 'Yeah, Dale filled me in the last time I worked with him, a year or two back.'

'I didn't know you were in town back then.'

'I wasn't. We did it over the phone.'

Things go quiet again. Then Matt makes a show of checking his watch. 'It's getting late,' he says. 'We'd better be going. It was nice seeing you again, Alex. We'll have to keep in touch.'

'Sure,' I say. We both know it's bullshit. I hand him my card anyway. 'It was nice seeing the two of you again.'

Rhona leans close and kisses me on the cheek. 'Take care, Alex,' she says. Then she and her husband leave.

As I finish my drink, I reflect on how it took just an hour to get seventeen years of catching up out of the way. I find that depressing.

I wedge a Marlboro between my lips as I step out of the bar and into the night. The lighter flame leaves bright blue spots dancing in front of my vision. It's a chilly evening, with no moon as yet. Traffic is almost non-existent and the town is even quieter than it was before, as if the people safely tucked away indoors are now talking in whispers with their TVs muted. A breeze I can't feel blows ghostly notes on the telephone lines spanning the street. I glance at my watch. It is 9.40pm. The same time that Dale came upon Angela Lamond's body.

I walk home with nothing but the night's imaginary demons for company. A movement in the shadows: just a cat on the prowl. Footsteps that echo my own, but quieter and more hollow: someone walking the same path as me, too far behind to be visible. It's the kind of night when the superstitious subconscious fights with the rest of the brain to see who rules the roost, and actually has a chance of winning. When I can almost hear a lone, dead voice calling for revenge like a wolf howling in the distance. When I can almost hear others, victims of past crimes I never knew about or couldn't solve. When I can almost feel their anger.

I tell myself not to be so stupid, pull my collar up and quicken my pace. I don't want to be outside any longer than I need.

The Crowhurst Lodge is in darkness when I arrive. There isn't even a welcome light over the front door. The hotel's limestone facing has a sickly look to it, and the mosaic faces leer hungrily. I manage to slide my key into the lock on the second attempt, then find myself in almost complete blackness in the porch. Relying on memory, I avoid tripping over anything and push the inner door open, using the snarling face of the old iron knocker as a convenient handle.

A single candle-effect bulb in a socket above the main desk illuminates reception. Its feeble glow and my night vision, by now well developed, are enough to guide me up the stairs to my room. The instant brightness as I switch on the lights is a welcome relief.

I drop my jacket on the bed, then turn on the TV and splash some water on my face. I sit up for over an hour, skipping through random channels, before I douse the lights and fall into bed.

I can't sleep.

It's a combination of factors, but they add up to several hours of insomnia. I'm in new surroundings; primal instincts latch onto the building's unfamiliar smell and heighten my alertness. The trees outside keep up a continuous whispering, loud enough to hear and not regular enough to lull me to sleep. I'm not comfortable lying on my left. I'm not comfortable lying on my right. Back. Front. I run through conversations in my head—the afternoon interview with Nicholas, the questions I'm going to ask him tomorrow.

The last time I remember seeing the clock by the bed, it reads four fifteen. Finally, sleep claims me.

4

Seven o'clock. The grating beep of the alarm drags me out of a surreal dreamscape I can barely remember. Something about snow-covered trees, but the details are fading fast. Perhaps it was a throwback to my youth; I used to have a recurring nightmare about the winter when I was growing up. Maybe it was the first sign of the trouble I've always had with sleeping, maybe not. No matter how many times I had it, it was always enough to wake me in the middle of the night. I'd sit in bed, arms wrapped round my knees, and try to clear my head so I could go back to sleep. It rarely worked.

The nightmare would always begin as something else. If I was a soldier in some far-flung country, for instance, I'd start to notice snow on the leaves of the jungle I was marching through. Pretty soon the foliage would be rimmed with ice and I'd be trudging through the bitter cold, an icy wind peppering my face with grains of snow. Then I'd hear a rasping voice behind me. 'You said we'd be somewhere safe by now,' it would say. I'd turn to see a man with a straggly beard, dressed in leather and tattered furs. His face was always pale, his skin looked raw and his eyes were cold and desperate. Behind him would be a line of battered wooden wagons and gaunt, ragged people, all staring at me. 'We should never have come this way,' the man would say, stepping closer, his face hardening. 'This is all your fault! We're dying because of you.'

I couldn't take the stares of the people in rags or the fury of the bearded man. I would turn and run blindly through the forest, crashing through the snow and ice. I'd hear the man chasing me, his footfalls smashing through the undergrowth. Usually, I'd catch my foot on something and fall headlong into the snow. Cold would smother me and I'd wake up with a pounding heart.

If I did have this dream last night, at least it didn't wake me. Zombie-like, I head for the bathroom. I shower and shave, then dress, slowly and mechanically. Have my first cigarette of the day. Then I make my way downstairs to grab breakfast.

The building is lighter now, and quite airy. There's still no evidence of anyone other than myself in residence, although the smell of cooked food emanates from the doorway next to the reception desk. There's no sign of the old man I saw yesterday. A buffet off to one side of the dining room holds a surprisingly good range of breakfast offerings on hot plates, although the amounts on offer bolster my belief that I'm alone in the hotel. I help myself to cereal and orange juice, then a big plate of fried stuff and an entire pot of coffee.

Finished, I leave the silent dining room and cross the foyer. Outside, the day is bright but the sky is peppered with small clouds. There are darker patches of grey over the rugged foothills to the west, which make the green-clad peaks look as though they're frowning at me, showing their displeasure for some misdemeanour I'm not even aware I've committed.

As my car leaves the gravel driveway and turns onto the road, the engine its usual comforting snarl, I catch sight of a dark-haired girl. She's young—seventeen or eighteen—with short hair and neat, colourful clothing. The girl watches my 'Vette as I drive by, and continues to stare at it until she becomes too small in the mirror to make out. Just a small-town kid, maybe, gawking at a big-town car.

Perhaps because of my tiredness, I drive fairly slowly as I cut through the old fields, past the murder scene, and on towards Houlton. A few hundred yards beyond where the woods begin again, an overgrown track winds away to the left, disappearing as it passes behind ranks of dead-looking brown trunks and thick, matted undergrowth. The silhouette of a building is just visible at the far end of the trail, maybe half a mile away. The old Wade House, later the St Valentine's Home for Children. I wonder whether Dale and the crime scene unit checked it. I make a mental note to ask him.

The primeval forest, dark with new spring growth, continues almost unbroken along miles of rolling hills before turning abruptly into grass and farmland as I head east on Route 212. From here, it's half an hour through empty country to reach Houlton. I leave my car in the lot by the Superior Court, then walk back up to Houlton Regional Hospital to see Dr Gemma Larson, the medical examiner who carried out the post-mortem on Angela Lamond.

The morgue is situated in the bowels of the hospital, well away from the areas frequented by patients. At least, those frequented by living patients. I walk through a double set of aluminium doors and into an office containing a couple of desks, computer terminals, lockers and a coffee machine. A second set of doors leads into a spacious chamber lined on one side by a chiller cabinet with its drawers marked by name and number, and on the other by three examination tables. Through one of the windows looking into the mortuary proper, I can see a woman in a lab coat supervising the loading of a fresh addition to her collection. I tap on the glass and she turns round, then beckons me inside.

I hang back a couple of paces while a pair of morgue assistants place the body of an elderly man in one of the drawers. Then, once the two have wheeled their empty gurney away, Dr Larson turns to me. She has high cheekbones, eyes like smooth jade and blonde hair tied back in a ponytail. She's tall, slim and pretty with a delicate elfin look to her. I guess that she's three or four years younger than I am.

'You must be Mr Rourke,' she says, her eyes giving me the same quick once-over mine have just given her. She extends her hand, which I shake. 'I'm Gemma Larson.'

'Call me Alex, Dr Larson.'

'Gemma,' she says, giving me a bright smile. 'How can I help you?'

'Angela Lamond, a murder victim from a few days ago. When you worked on her, were scrapings taken from underneath her toenails as well as her fingers? I know it's not something that often comes up.'

She stares into space for a moment, then says, 'I'm not sure. Come into my office and I'll check my notes.'

I follow her back into the outer room and over to one of the computers. After a moment of scanning the screen, she says, 'I did check her toenails during the exam. Two specks of tar-covered gravel, almost certainly from the road, but nothing else. It's possible other traces may have been washed away.'

I nod. 'Were there any kind of dimple marks on the soles of her feet, like she'd been walking barefoot on the road?'

'There's nothing in my notes, but the feet weren't my main area of interest.' Gemma dips one eyebrow, half frowning. 'With surface water there could well have been dimpling anyway, like you get after you've been in the shower or bath. I could check again. There might still be tiny pinpricks if the edges of the stones dug in.'

'What about blood toxins?' I say, then give an embarrassed laugh. 'Sorry, I'm being very officious. I didn't sleep well last night. Normally I'm much more easy to get on with.'

Gemma flashes me her smile again, then her gaze shifts down at the desktop. 'That's all right. I have mornings like that. Doesn't look like the lab found anything out of the ordinary in her blood.'

'Ah, nuts. An otherwise good theory out the window.'

'If you give me your phone number, I'll give you a call when I've checked the feet again,' she says, finished with the monitor screen.

'Do you normally work on Sundays?'

She shrugs and tucks a stray hair back behind one ear with her fingertips. 'My shifts vary, but it does happen when the hospital's busy.'

'Irritating, isn't it?'

'I don't know; sometimes it has its moments.' Her eyes meet mine, then quickly look away again. 'Anyway, you were going to give me your phone number,' she says.

'Sure. In fact, if we swap numbers I'll be able to get in touch if there's anything else that jumps to mind.'

Hastily scribbled notes are exchanged. 'If my phone's switched off, it's because I'm in interrogation,' I say once I have her number safely in my pocket. 'Leave a message and I'll call you back.'

'OK. I'll call you later.'

I grin involuntarily. 'That'd be great, thanks. Bye for now, then.'

She waves at me and smiles again. 'Goodbye.'

As I head for the County Jail, a voice in the back of my mind points out that there weren't any photos on her desk, and no wedding ring on the hand that touched her hair. For now, though, there are more important matters at hand.

Nicholas is waiting calmly in the interview room when I walk through the door. 'Mr Rourke,' he says. 'How nice to see you again.'

'Good morning, Nicholas.' I drop into the chair facing him and turn on the tape recorder, then run through the usual identification procedure and read him his rights.

'How was your return to Winter's End?' he says.

'What's to say I've been back?' I light a cigarette.

He permits a half-smile to break the stillness of his features. 'You came all this way and didn't visit your home town? I don't think so.'

'As it happens, I have been back. I took a look at the spot where you were arrested. What route did you take there? North or south?'

'How do you know I didn't come from the east or west?'

'The police didn't find any tracks through the fields. How could you have avoided leaving a trail?'

'I'm *relying* on you to work that out, Mr Rourke. Believe me when I say that there's nothing to be gained by revealing all.'

I take a long drag on my cigarette and regard the man in front of me. His ability to sit like a statue makes him infuriatingly hard to read. I have no idea what he means by 'relying' on me, but I let it pass and say, 'I've done some checking and I still can't work out why Angela was chosen as a victim. Assuming she was chosen.'

'Have you ever been fishing, Mr Rourke?'

I shrug. 'I've been once or twice.'

'Taught by your father? Where did you go?'

'Claye Lake. Why?'

Nicholas ignores my question. His eyes meet mine and he says, softly, 'Claye Lake. A small cabin thirty yards or so from the lake. Trees running all the way down to the water's edge. A young boy with his adoring daddy. Pleasant picture.' A trace of emotion passes over his features, a twinge at the corner of his mouth. 'Did your father explain why there are different types of fishing, with different types of bait and different techniques?'

I pause for a moment. His description of the cabin where my father and I used to fish is startling in its accuracy. But then I figure, trees down to the water and small cabins are a dime a dozen in these parts. 'Not really, no,' I say.

'I'll use a different example. Do you believe in God, Mr Rourke?'

I shake my head. 'Not really, Nicholas. I've never seen the point. A pleasant afterlife might be something to look forward to, but I'd rather make the best of the one I've got right now.'

'I can't imagine a policeman who wouldn't take comfort in the idea of heavenly judgment whenever the bad guy walks free.'

'I've always preferred to get the judgment correct here on earth.'

Nicholas smiles, showing the tips of his teeth again. 'I admire your faith in man's efforts at justice.'

'You prefer divine retribution?' I say.

He chuckles drily. 'I never said anything about *divine* retribution. Sometimes people's actions put them in the service of the Devil. If God won't forgive them, the Devil will eventually come to collect.'

'What do you mean?'

'Say, for example, that I committed a murder and got away with it. Then one day, I get hit by a car and killed. My borrowed time is up.'

'Did Angela Lamond get away with some crime that no one knew anything about? Was she living on borrowed time?'

Nicholas smiles. 'Until you know the answer to that yourself, I'm afraid I can't help you,' he says.

'Well, I've looked at her history but I didn't see anything she'd done to put her onto borrowed time.' It's my turn to smile. 'If she had, I doubt it would have been to anyone important.'

There's a moment of silence. When Nicholas replies his face stays emotionless but his tone is different, more controlled. I can't tell whether he's angry or laughing. 'Importance is relative. But you're in no position to know.' He relaxes again. 'Trust me on that.'

'I'd like to trust you, Nicholas, but at the moment I don't understand what happened. To me, it looks like any other random killing by a nut who needed to vent his anger on someone. I can't see any bigger picture. Perhaps you could show it to me.'

'I've already told you I won't do that. But believe me, by the time you return to Boston, you'll know why the nurse died.'

'Are you saying you killed her?'

'I'm saying I know why she died. You will too.'

The promise is spoken as flatly as if he had just said he was going to buy the next round of drinks. Normally, I'd start pushing my suspect at this point, driving forward to get a confession. But although he's no longer being so evasive, I don't have the feeling he's about to break. A gut instinct tells me to hold back for the time being.

I help myself to another cigarette and change tack. 'You said you believe in God, Nicholas. Are you a follower of a particular faith?'

'Why do you ask?'

'We can try to accommodate any individual religious leanings at the jail. Are you a Christian?'

Nicholas smiles at me. 'I'm not a Christian. Nor a Muslim, Jew, Buddhist or anything of that nature, but I am a great admirer of God's sense of humour. Even if His jokes are sometimes a little cruel. Did you learn about Charles Ryland at school?'

'I never paid much attention in class.'

'He was a rich businessman who spent a year building a new church for your home town when the inhabitants had barely finished hacking land out of the forest. At the height of the first sermon in the chapel, the building was struck by lightning and Ryland, the priest and eighteen others died in the fire that followed.'

'So you believe in God and the Devil. And you think Angela Lamond is, what, burning in the fires of Hell?'

'The "fires" of Hell aren't really appropriate here, Mr Rourke. Do you know where the Bible was written? The eastern Mediterranean. A hot climate. Deserts. Sandstorms, drought. Hot weather evils. I suspect that's where the association comes from. In this part of the world, I'd say that "icy wastes" would sum it up better.'

'And that's where Angela Lamond is?'

'Yes.'

'What did she do to deserve it?'

'You're repeating yourself, Mr Rourke.' Nicholas sighs.

'That's because I seem to be wasting my time,' I say. Maybe it's the way he sighs, or maybe I'm just getting fed up with the bullshit he's spouting. 'I'm hoping that you're eventually going to be smart enough to realise that giving me your side of the story is the only chance you have of avoiding jail. Now why don't you stop being an asshole and actually give me something useful?'

'Language, Mr Rourke. I'm sure your parents didn't bring you up to swear at people.'

'You obviously didn't know my parents, Nicholas. They'd swear like anyone else if they got annoyed.'

He smiles like I've said something funny. 'And you're annoyed?'

'Smartass pricks always do that to me. So why not help me out?'

'I already have, Mr Rourke. You just don't know it yet. Come back and see me tomorrow, or perhaps later today. As you become more aware of your destination, I'll illuminate more of the path for you.'

I think for a moment, then nod and stub out my cigarette. 'OK. I'll see you later. Let's hope you can start talking to me then.'

I have the deputies outside take the suspect back to his cell, then I go to find Dale. He's in his office, talking to another man in uniform.

'Alex Rourke,' he says, 'this is Owen Marsh, Chief Deputy. He's been handling most of my civic duties while I focus on the Lamond case.'

'Owen,' I say, extending my hand.

Dale's second-in-command looks about the same age, with a slimmer build and a nose rouged by burst capillaries just beneath the skin. 'Mr Rourke,' he replies, then nods at Dale and walks out.

'How's our man coming along?' Dale asks me.

'I'm starting to feel I'm getting somewhere,' I say, 'but it's not going to happen quickly. On my way here I caught sight of St Valentine's,' I say, changing to the subject I came to talk about. 'Was it checked when the murder site was examined?'

Dale thinks for a moment, then shakes his head. 'No. We didn't have any information to suggest it might have been relevant. Why?'

'It struck me that the turnoff for the old building is only half a mile from the crime scene. We've been assuming the guy brought Angela to the scene from town. What if he came the other way, from the south? He wouldn't even have been on the highway at the time the truck driver passed through.'

'You want to go up there?'

'Yeah. Just in case.'

Dale nods and I catch something in his eyes, a glimpse of a fleeting thought or emotion, quickly gone. 'Do you want me to go with you?'

'Shouldn't be necessary. I've got my badge to flash if anyone asks what I'm doing. I'll give you a call if I find anything. Otherwise, I'll see you for dinner tonight. Whereabouts do you live?'

'Francis Street, number fourteen. Come by about half six or seven.'

'OK, Dale, I'll see you later.'

I've just stepped out of the building when my phone rings. 'Alex,' says a woman's voice, 'it's Gemma Larson at the hospital. I've just checked Angela Lamond's feet again.'

'Hi, Gemma. What did you find?'

'A few pinpricks of broken skin. I'd say she'd been walking on the road barefoot.'

'I don't suppose there were any grit traces in the breaks?'

'No such luck, sorry.'

'Can't win them all, I guess. Thanks for getting back to me so fast, Gemma. I'll give you a ring if anything else comes up.'

'Sure,' she says. 'You're welcome. Bye for now.'

'Goodbye.'

I breathe out slowly, then slide into my car and start back towards Winter's End.

THE GRAVEL of the St Valentine's Home for Children driveway crunches beneath my tyres as I coax my Corvette up the slope towards the building's hunkering mass. Grass and weeds are slowly establishing themselves between the stones as the forest embarks on reclaiming the land carved out of it years before. The trees around are in full spring bloom and the drive is roofed by a green vault of birch and ash leaves. A hundred yards from the derelict hulk, I come across a set of wrought-iron gates in the crumbling remains of a wall which seems to surround the establishment. The gates are yawning open, rusted in place, and I park the car just inside, in what was, I guess, the gravel parking lot. A couple of cherry trees in blossom rise out of the overgrown lawn, occasionally dropping petals in the breeze. It looks as though it would once have been a pleasant place to live.

I step out of the car and a single feature immediately draws my attention: a double set of tracks, lines of bent and crumpled grass across the former parking lot. I think about calling Dale and getting him to send for a crime scene unit, but since the trail doesn't mean a thing by itself, I decide to leave it until I've checked the building.

I check my gun, just in case, and drop my bolt cutters in my belt before picking up my flashlight and heading for the building.

St Valentine's looms above me, a four-storey edifice of red brick and aluminium siding with the lines of the original house still visible beneath. Several windows are broken. A padlock and chain that once barred the front doors have been wrenched out of place, taking the handles with them, but I notice that there are no scrape marks in the leaf litter on the top step. Leaving the doors as I found them, I switch my flashlight on and clamber in through a window.

From what little I remember of my last visit, St Valentine's used to be a clean place, if somewhat clinical and spartan. Now the structure smells of old sawdust, damp, and years of neglect. Wind-blown leaves are scattered on the mouldering carpet tiles near the window, mingling with items left over from when the children's home closed—a couple of plastic bags, a discarded stuffed bear. Somewhere deep within the gloomy structure I hear something patter over the floor. I move through the room and further inside, searching for evidence of recent visitation. The entire building sighs whenever the breeze passes through its shattered windows; the noise makes it seem as if the old house is breathing long and slow, asleep.

The main house seems to have consisted mostly of facilities for the kids staying here. I walk through a number of dormitories with many bunks still intact. A dining room and kitchen, showers, and what looks to have been a small classroom. Something I recall from my few childhood visits to St Valentine's as being a playroom, now empty save for the broken shards of a toy robot. Store cupboards. A staff room. There's a small administration office on the top floor, littered with empty filing cabinets and galvanised drawers.

Downstairs, soot streaks the walls of the corridor leading to what were the staff quarters. The door at the other end is shut, and when I open it I find myself in the ruins of the old staff wing. The walls of the building continue for a little way in each direction, albeit dark and buckled. Charred beams crisscross above me, and I can glimpse patches of the sky beyond. A few yards into what remains of this extension to the building, I can only guess at its shape by the height of each jumbled pile of masonry, charcoal and debris. Nothing has disturbed the ashen silt on the floor in a long time, and my footprints cut a lonely path through the blackened rubble.

The basement is the last place I check. It's occupied mostly by disused laundry equipment. A large gas boiler is tucked in one corner, dead and dusty. Past it is a steel door hanging temptingly ajar. Opening it, I scan my flashlight over a short brick-lined corridor with two doors on either side. All are sturdy and, like the corridor itself, plainly an addition to the original house. They have equally sturdy steel locks on them, like prison cells. The air is stale and cold.

I return to the outside to see if I can find where the tracks went. At the back of the building I catch sight of the twin dark lines in the grass again, leading towards the tree line to the north. At the point where the marks vanish into the trees, I catch sight of something glittering in the leaves. A heart-shaped locket, looped over a twig at head height. Tempting though it is to remove it, I head back towards my car and call the department on my cellphone.

THREE HOURS LATER, when the forensics truck containing the crime-scene technicians loaned by the State Police is vanishing down the drive, the locket nestles in an evidence bag in my pocket. Inside, one photo is missing and the second shows a slim young woman with dark hair, smiling uncertainly at the camera. I don't recognise her, but I'm planning to show the locket to Angela's friends and colleagues in the hope that they might.

I take one last look at St Valentine's, then start up the 'Vette and drive into town, my earlier weariness beginning to return. The Sunday streets are almost deserted. I'm about to head for the Crowhurst Lodge when a thought strikes me and I hang a sudden right onto Verger Street. Fifty yards or so down is the small public building that houses Winter's End Museum. I park the car and make my way up the weather-beaten paving towards the building.

The old woman behind the desk looks up as the door tinkles shut behind me. 'A dollar for adults,' she says, blunt but not unfriendly, then stops to look me over. 'Don't get many tourists out here this early in the year.'

'I didn't expect you to be open, not today. I only tried on impulse.'

'Spring's here. We're just about in season. You from out of town?'

I fish around for the money. 'I'm a local boy just returned home. Came here on a class trip with my school once when I was a kid.'

'Local, huh? What business are you in these days?'

'Sheriff's Department.'

The woman looks at me afresh. 'Alex Rourke, right? News travels fast, even getting as far as me,' she adds when she sees my expression. 'Don't remember you when you were a kid, but I remember your parents. Good people. So, you here for some catching up? I don't reckon cops have too much use for history.'

'Actually I am here on police work. Kind of,' I add. 'Someone mentioned something about the town's past and I thought I might as well check it out. Say, you wouldn't remember if you'd had a visit from a white guy in his mid-twenties, slim, about so tall, with short dark hair, dark blue eyes, would you? Probably on his own.'

The woman thinks for a moment, then shakes her head. 'We don't get many lone visitors, and most of those are older guys up here for the area's "atmosphere".'

'Oh well, it was a long shot anyway.'

'If you think of anything else, sonny, just holler.'

I thank her and move off to examine the small collection of glass cases and framed photographs that fill the museum's three rooms. The first has as its centrepiece a model depicting a wagon train.

Our community began as 100 people heading for the rich forests near the St John River to find somewhere they could log and trap in peace. They were led by Samuel Parnell and Nathan Laroche of L&P Milling and Mining Co., says the card stuck to the case.

According to the notes that accompany a battered diary from the period, a string of minor mishaps delayed them and they were still well to the south of the river by the time winter set in.

Our ancestors made camp and tried to wait out the months of cold. But before long, the ice and snow, dwindling supplies, exposure and frostbite facing the settlers were bad enough to drive them back south-wards, the card next to a moth-eaten pair of leather gloves reads. *By the time they saw the first signs of thaw the following year, 1806, and stopped at the place that would become Winter's End, Parnell and Laroche had only sixty folk with them.*

Another glass case in the corner of the room holds a couple of pieces of period costume as well as an old map, a faded copy of land deeds, and a model of the town as it was to begin with. The sixty seem to have been busy, clearing the forest, building a mill, homes, and a small chapel dedicated to St Francis. A second case holds another set of costume and a musket, noting that the discovery of a skeleton clad in rotting native-style leathers and a musket started rumours of a massacre of local tribes by French or British troops.

I'm pleased to see that the ghost stories I learned as a kid had some basis in fact, if only a loose one. I read on. *Charles Ryland, apparently one of the early settlers' more affluent members, further fuelled these rumours when he cleared some of his land and found a patch of forest scattered with bones.*

Ryland must be the guy Nicholas was referring to. There's a small and rather dusty portrait of him hanging in a corner. A chubby guy with bushy sideburns and narrow eyes. In 1815 he apparently decided that Ryland Hill, the place where the bones were found, would make a fine site for a proper church for the town. The Chapel of St Valentine was finished in spring the following year. The first service in the newly consecrated church took place on an April evening during a thunderstorm. At the height of the sermon, the chapel was struck by lightning and burnt to a cinder. Twenty people died, including Charles Ryland and the priest, and thereafter plans for a church outside Winter's End were abandoned.

Bad luck, or God's sense of humour, as Nicholas called it, didn't stop with Ryland's death. Winters were ferocious for the next two years, and in December 1818 the L&P mill burned to the ground with Samuel Parnell and half a dozen workers inside. Some said it was Nathan Laroche moving to gain sole control over the company, others said it was a curse on the town. Laroche himself died in 1821, a bitter and miserly man.

Winter's End held its breath in 1827 when Boston businessman Gabriel Wade bought Ryland's land. He demolished Ryland's run-down house and built a new home up the hill, on the site of the old chapel. There were no more strange happenings and the town prospered, mostly as a supply stop for the big lumber camps in the north.

I pass quickly on, looking for more information on the house that would become St Valentine's. In the last room, amid the pictures of town festivals and small-time news, I find it. The Wade family evidently moved out in the 1960s, but the place wasn't sold to become a children's home until a few years after I was born. There's a photo of some of the original staff. Henry Garner, director. Sarah Decker, night manager. Dorian Blythe, day manager. Deborah Pierce, nurse. I vaguely remember Garner from the couple of times I visited the home with my father, when we took toys for the kids.

There's a bunch of stuff on the fire that led to the home's closure: news clippings, photos, interviews. The blaze started in the middle of the night, quickly taking hold of the staff quarters, but everyone got out save for Garner and a couple of other workers. By the time the volunteer fire crews arrived from town, they could do little more than stop the blaze from spreading to the rest of the building. My father was one of those called out; I spot him in a couple of photos.

The remains of those who died were never properly identified. The newspapers don't say why, but my guess would be that if the emergency crews found a burnt skull crushed by fallen masonry, even dental records wouldn't be much help. Arson was the verdict of the official investigation, though no one was ever charged with the crime. The insurance company cited a loophole in the home's cover and refused to pay up, and St Valentine's closed for good.

'Find anything?' The woman's voice startles me out of my thoughts.

'Yeah, thanks,' I say, turning to face her. 'More than I expected.'

She taps the glass case. 'I've heard it said that the place was cursed. Nothing good ever came of anything built on that land.'

'Two fires in nearly two hundred years doesn't mean a curse, not to my mind,' I say.

She shrugs. 'They're just stories. I don't know if there's any truth to them. Don't much care, either. So long as people still want to hear them. Kids, mostly.' She laughs, dry and rattling. 'Probably told them to you and your classmates when you came here way back. It's not often I get to try them on the same audience twice.'

'I seem to remember you gave me nightmares last time. I'm hoping you don't manage it again.' I make my way towards the door, trying not to seem impolite. 'Well, thanks for your help. Most informative.'

'Just be sure to recommend this place to your friends,' she calls after me, then laughs again.

The drive back to the Crowhurst Lodge takes five minutes in the slowly advancing evening. The sun is already touching the horizon, turning the sky a deep orange and lighting the scattered clouds a brilliant yellow. The forest that blankets the hills around town is already in shadow. As I approach the turnoff, I again see the girl who watched me leave this morning. She's standing a little way down the road and stares at me as I drive past and make the turn.

The hotel itself is already starting to glow faintly in the failing light. Inside, the air is flat and lifeless, like that of some long-forgotten tomb. Back in my room, I drop into bed with the intention of snatching an hour's shuteye before making my way round to Dale's house. Instead, I spend a sleepless sixty minutes staring at the locket and letting my mind wander. The face of the woman whose photo lies inside floats before my vision, tantalisingly out of reach. I wonder who she is, or was. My weary mind, perhaps returning to last night's dream, mingles her image with thoughts of the biting cold, of the feeling of plunging into the snow, of ice cutting into my skin.

THE WOMAN'S FACE is still lurking at the back of my mind when Laura Townsend opens the door of the house she shares with her husband.

'You must be Alex,' she says, standing aside to let me in. 'I don't know if you remember me from school. I was in the year above you.'

I smile politely, trying to remember as I step into the hallway. Something stirs in the attic of memory and I say, 'Laura Redfern?'

'That's right.' She turns and yells, 'Dale! Alex is here!'

'How long have the two of you been married?'

'Twelve years,' Laura replies, 'and I'm still trying to civilise him.'

I grin, as always a little uncomfortable around others' apparent domestic bliss. 'That's not a job I'd want to take on.'

'Hey, Alex,' says Dale, finally emerging from the depths of the house. 'You want a beer?'

Bottles in hand, we make our way into the dining room. As we help Laura to get the table ready, I run through what I found at the hospital, along with the results of the crime scene technicians' work.

'No usable impressions?' Dale asks once I've finished.

'They got enough to say that there were two sets of footprints, moving from the north, round the building, and then away to the west. One set, which might be Nicholas, may have stepped up to the front door to break the padlock. But they couldn't find a single identifiable tread-mark that we could match with a shoe.'

'What about the locket?'

'No prints, no hair, no fibre. I don't recognise the girl inside.'

At this point, Laura emerges bearing plates of steaming fish stew with potatoes and the conversation breaks up somewhat to accommodate chewing and swallowing. I steer clear of 'shoptalk', and let Laura run through the usual questions—Do I have a family? How's Boston? Have I run into any of my old school friends?—and I give all the usual answers. Once the stew, which is excellent, and the fudge cake dessert are out of the way, I take out the locket and show it to Dale and Laura. Keeping it in its bag, I flick the catch with my thumbnail to reveal the picture within.

'No,' says Laura after a moment's thought, 'I don't recognise her.'

Dale shakes his head too. 'Doesn't ring any bells with me either, Alex. Are you going to ask Nicholas about it?'

'Yeah. But I'll check with people who knew Angela whether she owned a locket like this first, though.' I stifle a yawn.

'You look tired,' says Laura.

'I didn't sleep well. Hopefully I'll have better luck tonight. Say, do either of you know a girl, about seventeen, eighteen, with short dark hair, about so tall? Slim, pale, dark make-up.'

Dale nods. 'Sounds like Sophie Donehan, maybe. Why?'

'I've seen her up near the hotel a couple of times. Staring at me.'

'She's a messed-up kid,' says Laura. 'Sophie's mom killed herself, what, six years ago. Overdosed. They never found out why she did it, but Sophie's dad hasn't been the same since.'

'Six years ago?' I say. Around the time of the St Valentine's fire.

'I've heard she pesters tourists from out of state, trying to get them to take her away with them,' Dale chips in. 'Maybe she thinks you might be another potential ticket out of town.'

'Just the souvenir I've been looking for—a screwed-up adolescent.'

We chuckle and the conversation moves on. Around half past ten, tiredness begins to tell and I say my farewells. I leave Dale's warm, tidy house and walk back through deserted streets towards the pallid glow of the hotel and the sighing of the wind in the trees.

I'M WALKING THROUGH TOWN and it's the middle of the night. I don't know what hour it is exactly, nor how long I've been out wandering, unable to sleep. The moon is up, though, casting a silver sheen on the mist that drifts through the streets. Winter's End is utterly silent. Even the breeze and the distant sound of the trees are no more.

I have no idea what I'm doing out here. Everything's hazy. I don't even remember leaving the hotel.

Then I catch movement out of the corner of my eye, away to the right. A whitewashed stone church is visible behind a couple of stunted trees, the mist smudging its pale outline. As I glance at the building, the low gate at the end of the path leading to its doors clicks shut. I wonder who could be about so late at night; the good folk of Winter's End seem to hide away from well before midnight until daybreak. Images of Nicholas's hypothetical accomplice drawing me into a trap spiral through my mind. They are followed by more fantastic scenarios—fresh murders, new killers, demons of the subconscious—that no amount of rationalisation can banish.

Nothing lurks by the gate, which I allow to swing shut behind me. The small church rises before me in the fog, and as I crunch cautiously up the path, between carved cherubs, crucifixes and other burial markers, I catch sight of a woman's figure silhouetted in the moon's thin light. She turns her head briefly towards me before she steps behind a cluster of stones, and for some reason I feel certain she is the woman depicted in the locket.

I turn left round the corner of a mausoleum-type structure and she's right there in front of me. Cold arms clad in a rotting shroud reach up towards me as the woman smiles, mouth turned up at the corners but eyes dead and clouded. Hands scrabble at my feet and I can feel their scratching nails through my shoes. One finds flesh beneath the leg of my jeans, and cold pain flares from my shin.

I turn and run wildly, pursued by a hideous high-pitched keening, like screaming infants or cats in heat. Out through the gate and into the town, buildings and streets blurring through fright and fatigue.

Eventually, exhaustion triumphs over panic and I collapse onto the sidewalk, fighting for breath. My head swims and my vision whirls drunkenly before going completely black.

5

I wake up in bed, my head a confusion of thoughts and memories, my heart thudding audibly in my ears. My throat is dry but I'm sweating and the pillow beneath my head is damp. I check the clock next to the bed. It's 2.30 and I'm wide awake. I go to the bathroom to get a glass of water, down it, and take a refill back into the room. Then I sit on the edge of the bed and wait for my system to relax.

I remain like that for half an hour, sipping the water. Once I'm feeling tired again, I try to get back to sleep. It doesn't work. Three o'clock becomes four o'clock, and I can feel a point of bright light developing behind my eyes, an oncoming migraine. I find a couple of ageing paracetamol on the bathroom shelf and swallow them in the optimistic hope that they'll do something. They don't, as ever.

Five o'clock turns into six turns into seven. Two more hours spent lying like a beached dolphin, staring blankly at my surroundings as the migraine makes sections of my vision blur and wheel. I take a brief shower, keeping my eyes closed and my head as still as possible, then dress and head downstairs.

I eat another lonesome breakfast in the Crowhurst Lodge's empty dining room, but my weary senses are in no state to enjoy whatever flavour it may have. After my warm but tasteless meal, I walk into town. My first stop is Martha's Garden, the diner where Angela used to have lunch. It's a pleasant enough place, simple, unpretentious. I order a coffee and ask the staff on duty if they knew Angela and whether they've ever seen the locket before. I also ask whether they recognise the woman depicted inside. They don't.

I arrive at Dr Vallence's office almost as soon as it opens. I show the nurse my badge and tell her I'm with the Sheriff's Department.

'Oh, you'd be the one investigating Angela's death,' she says. Her eyes take in my haggard expression. 'I work . . . worked with Angela.'

I show her the locket. 'Did you ever see Angela wearing this?'

'No, I've never seen it before.'

'How about the woman inside? Do you recognise her?'

'No, sorry.'

'That's all right. Is Dr Vallence available?'

She buzzes the intercom and informs the doctor of my presence, then sends me through.

Nathan Vallence is white-haired, with a lined face and a long, haughty nose. 'Good morning, Deputy Rourke,' he says. His voice is dry and cultured but wavers slightly. 'How can I help you?'

I shut the door behind me and sit in the chair at the far side of his desk. 'I'm looking into Angela Lamond's death. I was wondering if you recognised this locket as belonging to her.'

'I was under the impression that the man responsible had been arrested,' he says as he briefly regards the battered gold in front of him. 'No, I never saw Angela wearing anything like this.'

'Do you recognise the woman inside?'

He peers at it again, swallows once, then slides it back to me, jerkily shaking his head. 'No, I'm afraid not.'

'Was there anyone Angela might have encountered while working here who might have had a reason, however mistaken, to hate her? Do you ever treat mental illnesses or anything like that?'

'Rarely, and never anything serious. I usually refer them to Houlton where they're better equipped. As to Angela making enemies . . .' He shakes his head. 'Not that I can recall.'

I shrug and clamber to my feet. 'Thanks for your time, Doctor. If anything else comes to mind, get in touch.'

As I turn to go, Vallence draws breath and calls hurriedly after me,

'If I may say so, you don't look well, Deputy Rourke. Is there anything I can help you with on a professional basis?'

'As it happens, there is,' I say, glad of the invitation. I sit back down. 'Insomnia—I have attacks occasionally, which my doctor down in Boston prescribes me stuff for. I've also got a thundering migraine and I left the pills I take for them at home.'

'If you can give me the name and number of your doctor, I'll give him a ring and see what I can do.'

I rattle off Dr Hansen's phone number. Vallence calls him up and the two talk briefly. Then he writes a couple of prescription notes.

'Thanks,' I say, and hand him one of my business cards. 'If you think of anything, give me a ring. My cellphone number's there.'

Fifteen minutes later, I emerge from the town's dispensary with two sets of pills. The first are ergotamine tablets for my headache, to be taken once every half-hour until the migraine is gone. The second bottle contains lorazepam, to deal with my insomnia.

I start on the first of six migraine capsules as I head back to the hotel to pick up my car. Then I set off south to Houlton.

On the way through town, I catch sight of the Church of St Francis down a side street. While my dream had the building itself correct, the cemetery around it is smaller and far simpler. I guess I should have remembered that, but accuracy is a rare commodity in dreams.

'Jesus, Alex,' says Dale when I clamber out of my car in the Superior Court parking lot. 'You look like shit.'

'Thanks, Dale,' I reply. 'I appreciate the sympathy.'

'I'm serious. You're not coming down with something, are you?'

I shake my head. 'Just another bad night's sleep. Had a migraine this morning, too. Dr Vallence gave me some stuff for both.'

'Are you sure you want to speak to Nicholas right now? We can ask him about the locket tomorrow if you want.'

'No. A cigarette and some coffee and I'll be OK.' I change the subject to something other than my health. 'I spoke to Angela's colleagues about the locket. They don't remember her owning anything like it. They don't recognise the woman in the photo either.'

'So maybe it's just coincidence,' Dale says, frowning.

I spark up a cigarette and suck contentedly on the filter. 'I don't think so. You know what this whole thing looks like to me? One big case of staging. Everything that we've been able to learn about the crime itself looks like a set-up. Hell, we only have the guy in custody because he stuck around to get arrested. We look into what he did and find tracks leading towards the house. Someone breaks the lock to make it look like he went inside, but doesn't actually bother to do so. Someone hangs a piece of jewellery, which seems significant but which we can't identify, at the place where he emerged from the woods.' I puff a couple of times more, then flick the butt into the gutter. 'It's like we're following breadcrumbs, but don't know where we're being led.'

Dale just shrugs as I head for the interview room where Nicholas awaits me. If it wasn't for the fact that I see the deputies taking him away every time, I could almost believe he never moved from his seat.

Once the usual legal pleasantries are out of the way, I begin. 'Good morning, Nicholas. How are you?'

His eyes gaze flatly back at mine. 'I'm well, Mr Rourke. You look a bit under the weather, though. Nothing catching, I hope.'

'Insomnia. Sometimes I can't sleep if something's bugging me.'

'And what is the cause of your little problem, Mr Rourke?' Nicholas asks. His pitch has become higher, his tone almost amused.

I light another cigarette. 'You. I can't figure out why you won't give us a name if you're not someone who's already got a record. I also can't figure out what you were doing with a dead body on a highway in the middle of the night.'

'You must have a theory.'

'To me it looks as though you abducted Angela Lamond, walked her through the woods to the old St Valentine's children's home, and then down to the road. Then you killed her.' I blow smoke at the lights above us. 'It fits the facts, even if I can't see why you would do that. Maybe I'm wrong. Maybe you were just out for a walk and you came across the body and the knives. But unless you tell me something, my theory is what's going to put you away for murder.'

Nicholas's eyes don't so much as twitch.

'I went for a stroll up near St Valentine's yesterday, Nicholas.'

'Really?' he says. His eyes are even darker, more empty than usual.

I take the plastic bag out of my pocket and place it on the table. 'I found this at the edge of the woods. Do you recognise it or the woman in the photo?'

Nicholas smiles. 'Yes, I know who the woman is.'

'Who?'

'I say "is", but I suppose "was" would be more appropriate. She was a victim, Mr Rourke. A victim.'

I light a Marlboro. 'One of yours?'

Nicholas does something unexpected. He laughs, long and loud.

Eventually he calms down, wipes his eyes and looks at me. 'I'm sorry, Mr Rourke,' he says. 'You'd have to be sitting on this side of the table to see how funny that question was. No, not one of mine.'

'Then what happened to her?'

The blank mask returns, and he changes the subject. 'Tell me a little about your childhood, Mr Rourke. I'm interested in the small-town boy who ended up chasing murderers for the FBI.'

'The locket, Nicholas,' I say, trying to keep him on track.

'Son of a lawyer and a part-time teacher, weren't you? Daddy part of the volunteer fire department in Winter's End?'

My instinctive reaction is to ask him how he knows this, but I don't. Try to keep focused, stay on track. I maintain an emotionless façade and correct him. 'My mom wasn't a teacher, she helped out at the kindergarten. But so what?'

'Childhood events shape the rest of our lives, Mr Rourke. Basic psychology. Did your father ever have any near misses as a fireman? Stress as a kid might have made you prone to stress as an adult.'

I stub out my cigarette. 'No, nothing like that.'

'And where are mom and dad now?'

Bile rises and I feel the muscles at the sides of my neck tense. Perhaps it's his tone of voice, perhaps it's just because I'm tired, but for a brief moment I consider slamming his smart-ass face into the table until his nose splits and his mouth fills with blood. Three years ago, right before the breakdown, I might have done it. Today I satisfy myself with the glare, force the anger back. 'That doesn't concern you, Nick,' I say, keeping my voice steady.

'I'm sorry if I hit a nerve,' he says, and I'm certain that he's not. 'But you're wrong: it does concern me, insomuch as I'm now real curious to know what happened to your parents.'

In my mind, I hear the sound of the sedan screaming towards me from the right a split second before a mind-numbing collision. Glass rains around me as my car grinds along the road on its side. I don't know at the time, but the passenger door has been shredded and driven inwards. Something sprays onto my face; it might be blood.

'They're dead,' I say. 'They died more than three years ago.'

Either he detects something in my reply that satisfies him, or his digression is at an end, because he sighs and relaxes a little. 'The woman in the locket was a victim of a crime that went unpunished for a long time,' he says. His tone is different, direct and focused, as if we have dispensed with the trivia and are only now getting to the serious business at hand. 'As we discussed before, sometimes the Devil comes to collect. He did so in this case. You won't find what happened to her in police records, Mr Rourke.'

'So what does she have to do with Angela Lamond's death?'

'It's a belief in some religions that our actions are all connected to each other in a myriad tiny ways. The Devil collected on Ms Lamond, Mr Rourke. He never acts without a reason.'

'What does the marker mean? Did you put the locket there?'

'I wouldn't like to say.'

'So you did?'

Nicholas stays silent. His body language, leaning back in his seat with his mouth firmly shut, seems to suggest that he regards the interview as over. At other times, I'd try to press him further, but I'm too tired right now. Instead, I have the deputies take him away.

I step out of the room and go to find Dale, who as before has been watching from the viewing booth, hidden behind the one-way glass.

'What do you make of that?' he asks.

I shrug. 'Nicholas seems to think he had a reason to kill Angela, and I get the impression he'd be willing to spill everything if we can figure out what that reason is. Let's make a copy of the photo in the locket and send it out around the state to see if anyone recognises the woman. It's probably a good idea to get hold of the records from the doctor's in town to see if there were any deaths while Angela worked there. It might be that this woman died after she went for treatment and Nicholas blames the staff. See if you can dig up any records of parents who had their kids taken away by the authorities and put in St Valentine's as well. Maybe she was an unfit mother or something.'

'For all we know, she might have been killed in a hit-and-run.'

'That's not a bad thought. Let's ask the State Police about fatal accidents over the past few years, while I'll check the records we've got here. Her face might be there somewhere.' I stop Dale as he's about to turn and leave. 'Have any of the guards at the jail been talking to Nick, do you think?'

He frowns. 'What do you mean?'

'I just wondered how come he knows so much about me. Some of the things he's said run very close to the truth.'

'I doubt any of our people could tell him much at all about you, even if they did chat to one of the inmates. Which they wouldn't.'

Lunchtime and the early afternoon tick away while I plough through old accident reports, looking for the woman in the locket.

Crash photos, drivers' licences, victim details. She isn't there.

Half past three comes round and I start the drive back to Winter's End. I'm feeling somewhat light-headed, as if I'm stoned or suffering from a concussion. I don't know whether this is a result of general fatigue or an aftereffect of the migraine pills. I concentrate as best as I can on the road, thankful it's not raining and I don't have to worry about slippery conditions.

Since I could do with a pick-me-up, I stop off at Martha's Garden and order a coffee. An old guy with thick white hair and a beard takes the seat next to me. In a red checked jacket and well-worn jeans, he looks like an ageing lumberjack or a country musician. Something about him is familiar.

'Hey,' he says, gesturing at the waitress for a coffee, 'you're Alex Rourke, aren't you?'

'That's me.'

'Ben Anderson.' He extends his hand, which I shake. 'Last time I saw you, you were still at high school.'

'You were one of my dad's friends?'

'Sure was. Used to go fishing with him and Josh and a couple of others back when I was a lot younger.'

I light a cigarette and offer him one. 'I remember you, I think. You came round to our house a couple of times at Thanksgiving.'

'That's right. I helped your dad build a new porch, too.'

'Yeah. I remember now. Did you hear what happened to my parents?'

Ben nods and slurps at his coffee. 'Terrible shame. They were good people, both of them.' He nods to himself. 'Come to think of it, they left some things with me when they moved away. Just a couple of boxes of junk, probably. You can have them if you want.'

'Sure.'

He downs what's left in his cup and fumbles for some change. 'I'll give you a ride down to my house and you can pick them up.'

'Only if it's OK with you.'

'I'm retired, son,' he says as we walk outside. 'Don't have anywhere to be in a hurry. What about you, what are you up to these days?'

'You haven't heard?' I finish my Marlboro. 'The way gossip spreads around here, you must be about the only one. Right now, I'm working with the Sheriff's Department on the Lamond murder. Normally, I'm a private detective down in Boston.'

'I don't hear much gossip these days,' Ben says. 'I spend most of my time patching up my RV'—he gestures to where a battered but obviously well-tended vehicle is parked by the side of the road—'or fishing. By the time you hit my age, you've got plenty of time for gossiping but you find you don't care since none of it concerns you.'

I grin. 'I thought you old-timers did nothing else except wag beards on your driveways.'

'Not me, son. I keep to myself.'

Ben's house stands at the end of a muddy track that joins the northern end of Altmayer Street. When we pull up outside the two-storey building, I see the hand-painted sign that hangs from the door handle: GONE FISHIN'. I shake my head as Ben climbs out of the RV and unlocks the door. In anywhere bigger and not as quiet as Winter's End that message might just as well read: HOUSE EMPTY. BURGLE AT WILL.

Inside, the house displays the habitual quasi-neatness of most long-time bachelors. It has a character of its own only because it's plainly been lived in for a good many years.

'It's not much,' he says as if acknowledging my thoughts. 'But it's enough.'

'I like it. It's nicer than my place in Boston.'

We make our way upstairs while I get the usual feeling of vague disorientation I always have when entering someone else's home. At the top of the attic ladder Ben pulls the cord to switch the light on and says, 'They're in here somewhere.'

Shadows scatter and run into the corners of the room like a carpet of bugs disturbed by the sudden glare. They lurk behind the bags and boxes, waiting for a chance to reclaim the floor for themselves, as we hunt through Ben's collected detritus for my dad's things.

Eventually, he drags out two rather desiccated cardboard boxes. My chest tightens involuntarily as I rest my hands on top of them. I'm curious as to what lies inside, but I catch myself wondering whether I should open them at all. What's within might be personal. Then I tell myself not to be so stupid and slide the boxes over to the hatch where the light is better.

The first, the heavier of the two, contains a couple of faded high-school yearbooks, a collection of crinkled papers from my dad's legal work, and some books on fly-tying. A flurry of dust kicks up from the second as I open it. Inside, I find a couple of old photo albums scattered with blank white spaces where my parents took favourite pictures away with them, as well as a bundle of loose prints held together with string. I flick quickly through the musty-smelling

photos out of curiosity. Family members, some people I don't recognise—presumably distant relatives or old friends—and a couple of
shots from what look like fishing trips.

I've got fond memories of my own times at Claye Lake and other
places with my dad. After all these years I can still picture the first
time he took me with him.

I watch the water shimmering as it laps beneath my feet. Light
glints with every wavelet that reaches the battered wooden jetty. The
cooler behind me feels rough where I'm leaning against it.

'You're not getting bored, are you?'

I lift my head and turn to look at my dad. His expression is part
genuine concern, part hope that I'm not getting fed up only a day
into our fishing trip. 'I'm fine,' I say, raising the rod in my hands to
emphasise my interest. 'I was just watching the water.'

He grins. 'Hypnotic, isn't it? I always like the way the lake looks in
the sun. It's relaxing.'

'Uh-huh.'

'It's nice to get away from everything for a while.'

'Why doesn't Mom come?' I ask with a six-year-old's grasp of
married life.

Dad smiles. 'It's as much a break for her as it is for me. Besides,
don't you like it just being you and me?'

'Yeah. You think we can catch dinner?'

'It doesn't matter if we don't. I brought a couple of steaks with us.'
He leans conspiratorially towards me. 'Don't tell Mom. I'm supposed to be watching what I eat.'

I smile at the shared secret. 'Sure, Dad.'

'Reach behind you and get me a beer, would you?'

I place the rod on the wooden planking and stand to open the
cooler. The catch is difficult for my small hands and when it finally
pops up the sudden release is enough for me to lose my balance. I
stagger for a moment, trying to hold myself upright by rocking on
the balls of my feet, then topple backwards into the water.

Cold. A burst of pressure and a roaring in my ears.

Then my feet bite into the stony bottom of the lake and I stand, a
little unsteadily, uncomfortable with the water sloshing against my
chest and the sudden weight of sodden clothes. I look up at the jetty
and see my dad leaning over, sudden worry pinching his face.

'Alex! Are you all right?' he says, trying to keep from yelling.

'Yeah,' I nod, hair plastered to my forehead.

For a moment more he stands, looking at me, then he stifles a chuckle. Seeing me glaring with childish outrage at his expression, he says, 'I'm sorry, Alex. It's just—you should have seen your face.' A snigger escapes. 'I'm sorry,' he says again, eyes creasing.

I do what most kids would in my position. I hurl an armful of water up at my dad. He throws up his arms in mock panic and I slosh another load up towards him.

Dad is laughing out loud by the time he jumps off the jetty, fully clothed, and joins me in the lake as the water fight begins in earnest.

That evening we ate steak by the fire, wrapped up in sweaters. I fell asleep on the sofa, curled up by my father.

At least, that's how I remember it. How I like to remember it.

Years later, and I'm sitting in my room at college with the phone against my ear. At the other end of the line, my dad's asking me whether I'll be home for the summer. He's being very polite about it; we had a string of arguments about my future career direction before I left. I haven't been back since.

'Sorry, Dad,' I tell him. 'Kurt's invited Howard and me out to Rochester to stay at his aunt's place. We're going to work at her diner for a while to get money together and hang out there all summer.'

'You're not going to be home at all?'

The answer is 'no'. Things are OK between us, but I'd prefer to stick with my friends right now. 'Maybe. It depends how things go.'

'Well, give me a ring if you can make it back to see your mom and me. Do it anyway, just to let us know how you're getting on.'

'Sure, Dad.'

There's a pause which I use to take a swig from the beer in my other hand. Then my dad says, 'I'm still proud of you, whatever you do. You're my only son.'

I didn't go home that summer. I never went home again. My parents visited me at Thanksgiving, then again the year after. By the next time I actually went to see them, for the first time in fourteen years, they'd moved down to Miami.

I sigh and close the boxes again before the two of us manhandle them out of the attic and down to the waiting RV. Back in the centre of town, Ben helps me get them into the trunk of my 'Vette, then stands back and brushes the dust from his fingers.

'Thanks,' I tell him. 'I never got round to sorting through most of my folks' things after the crash. I'll go through these properly.'

'No problem, son. Just a favour for old friends. Say, if you find yourself with some spare time, I'm heading for a few days' fishing on the McLean River. There's a dirt road meets Route 11 a short way north of Ashland. I'll be parked a few miles down. If you fancy taking a break for a while, feel free to drop by.'

'That'd be nice,' I say, nodding. 'I'll do it if I get a moment. Haven't been fishing since Dad took me up to Claye Lake when I was a kid.'

A strange look passes across his eyes. Sadness, perhaps. He then scribbles his number on a scrap of paper. 'Give me a ring if you can't find my truck. It was good seeing you again, Alex. Take care.'

'You too.'

Ben clambers back into his RV, and heads north. I'm about to climb into the 'Vette when I hear a voice calling my name. I look round to see Mayor Saville walking briskly towards me.

'Mr Rourke,' he says, a little out of breath. 'How's things?'

'OK, I guess. What can I do for you, Mr Mayor?'

Saville smooths his hair back against his scalp. 'I'm just on my way to a meeting—well, an informal get-together—with some of the town's business folk. It'd be good to give them some reassurance about the murder. You know, tell them it'll all be wrapped up and forgotten before long. I wonder if you've got time to meet them?'

I think of my room at Crowhurst Lodge. All I want to do is get back there and sleep. 'I'm kind of tired right now,' I say. 'Maybe tomorrow?'

'I'd be really grateful if you could, just to show them everything's going to be OK,' he persists. There's a hint of desperation in his eyes; the once-easy process of re-election suddenly appearing much more of a challenge. Cold-blooded murder in a place as small as Winter's End carries a lot more weight than it does in the city.

'All right. But only for half an hour,' I say.

The Sawmill is quiet, the jukebox turned off. The collection of the town's business leaders amounts to less than a dozen people, gathered round a couple of tables in a far corner. Otherwise, the place is empty. Saville leads me over and makes the introductions. Someone gets me a beer. Someone else says, 'So, are you guys going to be finished soon so we can all go back to normal?'

I smile, nod, answer, reassure. Yes, we caught the suspect red-handed. Yes, he's going to go to jail for a long time. No, I doubt tourist numbers are going to be affected.

The conversation moves on to other matters, and after a while I take advantage of a break in the discussion to ask Saville a couple of questions, on the off chance he can tell me anything useful.

'What is it, Mr Rourke?' he says, stepping back from the table and lowering his voice so we can talk in relative privacy.

'Did you know Henry Garner?' I ask.

He nods. 'Yeah, for a few years before the fire; he wasn't a local. I was a teenager back then, of course.'

'He must have been pretty young for someone running his own children's home. What kind of person was he?'

'Orderly, I guess you could call it,' he says after a moment's thought. 'He liked everything to be nice and neat, whether it was business dealings or eating lunch.'

'Quite a stern guy, then?'

Saville nods. 'I recall he once nearly went to court after an argument over a maintenance bill for St Valentine's. In the end the company just backed down and he got his way.'

'Was he that strict with the kids?' I ask the question quickly and directly, the verbal equivalent of attacking out of the sun.

'I don't know,' Saville says before he's had a chance to think. He pauses before continuing. 'Some of them used to shift schools now and then, but I guess children in that kind of situation can have problems. He didn't strike me as the sort who'd stand for trouble, though.'

'Was there ever any hint of scandal about St Valentine's?'

'Never, nothing.' He shrugs. 'Sorry I can't be more help. Is this because of what you found at St Valentine's yesterday?'

'More or less, Mr Mayor,' I say. 'Just some background information, that's all. I don't suppose you recognise this woman, do you?'

He looks at the locket as I hold it up in front of him. He stares at the picture for a moment, half frowning and chewing his lip, then eventually shakes his head. 'I don't think so,' he says. 'Sorry.'

After another ten minutes or so, I make my excuses and leave. The town's Great and Good murmur their goodbyes and I trudge back down the road to where my 'Vette is parked.

The Crowhurst Lodge is a dirty white beneath the grey-studded sky. I make my way up through the deserted hotel to my room, I get undressed and take two of the sedative pills I acquired this morning. Then I lie on the bed, listening to the faint rush of the breeze through the trees outside. Fifteen minutes later, I pass out.

I'M DRAGGED OUT of blissful sleep by the sound of muffled voices coming from further down the hall. I blink blearily, and check the clock to find that it's two in the morning. I've been under for about eight hours, and I don't want to miss out on a single minute of the other five that will pass before the alarm goes off. I lie in bed for a moment, hoping the sounds will die away. Once that hope has been dashed, I struggle out of bed and haul on my shirt, jeans and shoes, then go looking for those responsible.

The stairwell is unlit and I can see bright light streaking round the edges of a door on the far side of the landing. It is from here that the noise emanates.

I'm more than a little taken aback when my knock is answered by Rhona Cochrane in a black cocktail dress. In the room behind her I can see Matt, Dale, Laura, Dr Vallence, the pharmacist and others, all holding drinks and dressed for a dinner party. On the wall behind them are portraits of Angela Lamond and the woman in the locket.

'Alex!' Rhona exclaims, ushering me inside. 'We were afraid you weren't going to make it. It's almost time.'

'Time?'

Dr Vallence presses a martini into my unresisting hand. 'Borrowed time,' he says, looking down his nose at me.

'Borrowed?'

'That's why we're all here.'

The movements of those around me whirl me further inside the room, no matter how hard I try to stop. A blur of faces from around town, almost every one of them recognisable.

'You got a cigarette?' Rhona asks.

I pat my pockets, now thoroughly confused and feeling somewhat underdressed. 'No,' I say. 'I must have left mine in my room.'

'Never mind, you can have one of mine.'

Beyond her shoulder, I see Sophie Donehan, wearing a dress of emerald crushed velvet and rings of dark make-up round her eyes. She flashes a look of eager, razor jealousy at me as Rhona hands me the white stick of tobacco.

'If you like,' says Rhona, 'we could go out on the balcony while we're waiting. The others will call us in when it's time.'

She's close enough to me for me to feel her body heat. She tilts her face up towards mine. When the kiss happens, it does so with surprising force. The tip of her tongue whirls around and against mine like it's dancing the tango.

Then I break it off and pull away. 'This is all nuts,' I say.

I push forward into the throng, through to where the portraits are hanging. Staring at them with the look of an art critic on her face is

Gemma Larson. 'What are you doing here?' I say. 'You're not from Winter's End. Why should your time be up?'

'It's not,' she says, giving me her delicate smile. 'I'm here to get everyone's particulars for the morgue.'

I see then that she's not dressed like the others, but is still wearing her lab coat. 'Oh,' is all I can think of by way of a reply, and before I come up with something else, there's a knock at the door.

Rhona shushes the crowd, who watch the door with their glasses in hand, then goes to open it. She claps with glee and the other guests cheer when they see Nicholas standing there, naked from the waist up and carrying a pair of knives.

'Hello, everyone,' he says. 'It's time. I'm here to claim my souls.'

As the cheering continues, the killing starts. The twin blades carve through smiling guests, slicing throats and lancing into chests. Rhona is the first to drop, then the pudgy form of the mayor. After that, I can't make out the individual victims. I turn and run, pushing my way through people still standing as if celebrating New Year. At the back of the room are a set of French windows, which open onto a patio at the rear of what has now become St Valentine's Home for Children. Hearing someone behind me, I keep running, across the grass and into the woods. Thorns and twigs whip at me as I plunge on, through the undergrowth. Footsteps grow closer, gaining on me no matter how hard I try to escape.

Beep. Beep. Beep.

The alarm, hauling me back to the waking world.

6

It's just gone eight o'clock as I complete another solitary breakfast in the Crowhurst Lodge's lonely dining room, greatly refreshed after my night's slumber despite the unsettling dreams. My chest feels as if something is burning inside, like bad indigestion, but I ignore it and do my best to bury it in cigarette tar.

The day outside is grey and blustery. Gusts packed with the scent of rain whip at my clothes as I head for my car. I stop when I see a piece of paper tucked beneath one of the 'Vette's wiper blades. I glance around the deserted parking lot, looking for movement. Nothing.

I pick up the note. *Meet me at Martha's at five*, it reads. *I can help you.* The writing is tight and controlled, but the well-rounded curves of the letters suggest a female hand. The final full stop sits in a noticeable dent in the paper, which suggests that the author has a serious point to make. The one name that jumps to mind straight away is Sophie Donehan, more because I know she's been watching me than from any solid suspicion.

Then my cellphone rings.

'Don't bother heading straight into Houlton,' Dale says at the other end of the line. 'Something's happened here in town.'

'What?'

'A dead body has been found at the bottom of Black Ravine in Mason Woods this morning. A guy out walking his dog noticed some bones sticking out of the bottom of one side of the gully.'

'Anything connected to our case?'

'No way to tell, but there's always a chance. Officially, the remains haven't been identified yet. Unofficially, it looks like this is Henry Garner, the director of St Valentine's at the time of the fire. His wallet was on the corpse. If you drive down to the old picnic spot I'll have Andy show you where we are.'

From Main Street I hang a left and make for a dirt track that dives into the woods on the eastern periphery of town. The picnic area is over half a mile through the trees, which seem strangely gloomy despite their spring greenery. Eventually the track splits, each arm heading for a different parking spot. A deputy is waiting for me at the junction and I follow his outstretched arm to park where two Jeeps from the Sheriff's Department, a State Police crime scene services van and an unmarked station wagon are already waiting.

'Hi,' the deputy says. 'I'm Andy Miller. Sheriff's this way.'

I follow him into the underbrush. Through a gap in the foliage, I catch sight of one of the other clearings. In it is a red car; I'm not sure of the model but I can just make out the Toyota logo on its radiator. The dog-walker's, I suppose.

Some 300 yards later, the sound of voices reaches me. Gemma, Dale and another guy in deputy's uniform are standing in the leaf litter on the edge of Black Ravine, a twenty-foot-deep gash in the forest floor lined with charcoal-coloured stone. The stream responsible for carving it gushes happily at the bottom. Three forensic technicians are huddled at the base of the cliff opposite, well into the painstaking process of removing the unfortunate Mr Garner from the rock wall.

'What have they found so far?' are the first words I say to Dale as I step into the small patch of clear ground at the edge of the drop.

'Morning, Alex,' he says. 'Very little, beyond basic ID. The cliff is undercut at the base and the body was packed in there. Rock and earth; must have been pretty solid to keep out the stream whenever it flooded.' Dale grins wryly at me. 'We're not far from Blue Axeman territory here. You don't suppose he had something to do with it?'

I smile back. 'I doubt it. Not really his style.' I look back down at the ravine. 'Seriously, though, this is definitely homicide?'

Gemma nods and I notice how nice her hair, damp and a little bedraggled, looks in the early morning. 'I'll know more after the post-mortem, but there's no way he got there by accident.'

'Anything else? How was the body found?'

'Some of the debris surrounding it seems to have fallen away,' she says. 'It revealed one of the arms.'

'The CSU has come up with a few pieces of evidence that might be usable,' Dale adds. 'Nothing instantly helpful, though. I'll run through it once the scene's been cleared.'

I frown. 'So we're dealing with a death from, what, six years ago. Why am I here, Dale?'

'Everyone assumed Garner died in the fire at St Valentine's along with two others. We found some remains, but we couldn't ID everything for sure. If that's Garner down there'—Dale gestures at the ravine—'it means that's not the way it happened. Someone killed him, then covered it up with the fire. Angela Lamond worked at the kids' home too, and your guy killed her. What if he'd had practice before?'

'The St Valentine's blaze was arson, wasn't it?'

He nods. 'That's what the investigators reckoned. We never nailed anyone for it. Sheriff Kennedy was a friend of Garner's. He was pretty worked up about it and had us check anyone with a box of matches who was within fifty miles of here at the time.'

'And you reckon Nicholas was behind it? I don't see a connection.' My irritation mounts and the heartburn sensation in my chest grows.

'It's a theory, Alex.'

'I don't want you to try to pin this on Nicholas just to save yourself having to face another unsolved murder in your jurisdiction.'

Dale scowls. 'I don't like what you're implying, Alex.'

My irritation still won't go away, even though I feel like it should. 'You know how it goes with cops. You've got two murders, one murderer. If he did one, why not both? It's the easiest outcome.'

'Don't be an asshole, Alex.' He waves a finger at me. 'Don't forget that it was your theory that there might be a connection between Nicholas and St Valentine's.'

I sigh and rub my face. 'I'm sorry, Dale. It's not your fault; I haven't exactly been on peak form over the past couple of days.'

'Yeah, I know.' He puffs out his cheeks. 'I'm going to check on Andy. I don't want him being overwhelmed by sightseers while we're still working the scene. I'll see you back at the cars.'

I nod and he shoulders his way into the woods. Gemma lifts her gaze from the stream beneath her, at which she had been staring intently and rather awkwardly while Dale and I argued. 'I'll do the post-mortem when I get back to Houlton. Identification might take a while longer.'

I hold her gaze. 'Any thoughts on what might have happened? I don't know how much of a look you've had at the body.'

'Not enough to suggest anything, I'm afraid. I do know that the techs think someone might have disturbed the burial site. They've got a partial shoe-print for the Sheriff's Department to check. To me, it didn't look like a running shoe, but more like something you'd wear if you were in a suit or dressed smartly.'

I grin. 'I didn't realise you were a tracker as well as a pathologist.'

'You say the sweetest things,' she says, laughing softly.

'Well, I've never been very good with the classic compliments to pay a lady,' I admit. 'The words are there, they all make sense, but when the time comes to say them, they turn to garbage. I try to stick to what I know, and leave the lines of poetry to the experts.'

'You could maybe try them over dinner tonight. If you'd like, that is,' she adds. Her cheeks flush as she says it, pink rising on cheeks left pale by the morning chill.

I smile, but it's just an attempt to mask a sudden attack of nerves. 'Are you asking me out on a date?'

'Um, yes.' Gemma plays with her fingers, keeping her eyes from meeting mine. 'I mean, I don't even know if you're married or some-thing, or whether you'd want to or not, but . . .'

'I'm not married. And yeah, I'd like to have dinner with you.'

'Come by my house at eight?' She scribbles her address on a spare piece of notepaper and hands it to me. 'There's a nice little place not far down the road.'

'OK, yeah, that'd be great. Eight. I'll see you later.'

We have one of those awkward goodbyes where neither one of us is quite sure how to end the conversation. Then I'm trudging back through the trees, reflecting that one possible reason I've never managed to keep up a long-term relationship is that my store of witty conversation is, at best, limited.

When I reach the cars, I find Dale and Andy Miller dealing with a couple of interested dog-walkers and a woman of indeterminate age with wide, crazy eyes. I step towards my car and it's then that the woman with the staring eyes screeches, 'It's the curse of the Devil! He's come for you! He's come for us all!'

I stare at her for a moment, taking in the wild locks of dark hair and the hands clenched into fists at her sides. 'It's the Devil!' she wails again, and this time I just shake my head and slide into my car.

The countryside is quiet and disturbingly still as I cruise south towards Houlton. An atmosphere of brooding seems to have settled on the land around Winter's End. The sky seems darker, the clouds thicker and more menacing.

Back in his office, Dale puts a steaming cup of coffee in front of me. 'How much do you know about the fire?' he asks.

'Just what you've told me and what I saw in the museum. Arson, three presumed dead, bodies never fully found, no arrests.'

'That's about it. There were a few things that came after, though. A couple of people in town got crank letters, anonymous threats, nothing much. We figured it was just one of the nuts that always come crawling out of the woodwork after any crime like this.'

'Who received the letters?'

'I remember Sheriff Kennedy got one.' Dale smiles. 'Opened it here in the office, right in front of me. Read it, screwed it up and tossed it in the trash. "Got no time for dumb assholes," he said.' Dale takes a mouthful of coffee. 'If memory serves, the town clerk and Dr Vallence also had letters. I don't think we kept it on record.'

I nod. 'You ever find out who sent them?'

'No, we didn't. There wasn't anything in them that suggested the author knew any more than he could have read in the papers. I never heard of anything more happening to any of the recipients.' Dale looks up as one of his deputies knocks and walks in.

'Initial crime scene report,' he says, placing a file on the desk.

'Thanks, Jack. You want a look, Alex?'

I open the file. A batch of photos taken by the CSU this morning are the first things that grab my eye. Glossy shots of the bottom of Black Ravine. In one, a skeletal hand and forearm can be seen protruding from the rock and packed dirt that had hidden the body at the base of the cliff. A chunk of this mud lies overturned beneath it. I stare at it for a moment, then pass the photo over to Dale.

'Take a look at this,' I say. 'What do you see?'

'Nothing special,' he replies after a moment's thought. 'What is it?'

'Look at the earth that came away to reveal the hand. Look at the cut. It's very clean, aside from a couple of places. To me, that looks like it was made by a shovel. Someone dug that body up.'

IT'S HALF PAST ONE in the afternoon when the initial results of Gemma Larson's examination of the remains come through.

'The victim's knees and wrists were both broken,' Gemma's voice floats over the speakerphone. 'There's also a couple of fine cracks round an impact point at the base of his skull. Not enough to kill, but it would have been enough to knock him out. We've done a pre-liminary match of Henry Garner's dental records with the teeth of the victim. It looks like they're the same.'

'What about cause of death?' Dale says.

'His hyoid bone is intact, so strangulation is unlikely. There are a pair of scrapes on his ribs just below the solar plexus. I'll be more certain when the remains are examined by the forensic pathologist in Augusta, but I'd say he was most likely stabbed.'

'The arm that was exposed,' I chip in. 'How clean was it? Any moss or other signs that it had been out in the open for some time?'

'The bones were muddy, with no greenery on them.'

I nod. 'Probably fresh out of the ground, then. Thanks.'

'Yeah, thanks, Dr Larson,' says Dale.

'No problem. I'll let you know when I've found out more.'

The line goes dead. Dale checks his cup and says, 'I could do with another coffee. You want one while I'm going?'

I nod and he ambles out into the squad room. He returns a couple of minutes later with two fresh mugs.

'What are your thoughts on this whole Garner business?' he says as he sips his coffee.

I pause a while before answering, running scenarios through my mind. 'Why do you break someone's arms and legs?'

'To hurt them. Like kneecapping someone if they owe you money.'

'Or to leave them crippled and powerless, so you can do other shit to them, like locking them up or torturing them, without them being able to stop you or get away. If whoever killed Garner just wanted him dead, they'd have cut his throat and left his body to turn to ash in the fire. Instead, they wanted to spend some quality time with him, then stabbed him when they were done.'

'Something personal?'

'Or the killer was a proper nutcase,' I say, shrugging. 'But since the burial site was obviously carefully chosen I think personal is more likely. The fire was simply cover for the abduction—'

Dale interrupts, 'Unless the killer's motives had something to do with the staff at St Valentine's.'

'Sure,' I say, nodding. 'So we've got a careful, methodical murderer who acts for personal reasons and who's smart enough not to be caught. He's physically tough enough to break someone's limbs and stab them to death.' I swallow a mouthful of coffee. 'If it wasn't Nicolas that killed Garner, I'd say we're looking at someone with a similar mindset.'

Dale smiles faintly. 'I guess I must've won you over to that way of thinking then. So why would the killer dig the corpse up?'

'If it was the killer that did it, God knows. Maybe it was an accomplice acting on instructions.' I knock back another slug of coffee.

Dale slides a piece of paper over to me. 'I made a list of Garner's known acquaintances, mostly from memory.'

The names are few. I look at the list. *Town clerk Joshua Stern, Ian Rourke, Dr Vallence, Earl Baker.*

I look up at Dale. 'Ian Rourke? Not much point including my dad here, since he's been dead for just over three years.'

'I was just scribbling down ideas. Stern won't be any help either; he died in a crash four years ago. I checked.'

'What about Baker?'

'He runs a building firm. Done some work around here. He and Garner used to go hiking together. No idea where he is now.'

'Garner didn't have any family?'

'Not up here; he wasn't a local and he wasn't married,' Dale says. 'I can't remember if we managed to reach any next of kin at the time of the fire. But if they don't live locally they're not likely to know of anyone who might have wanted him dead.'

'What about the rest of the home's management? I saw a photo in the museum of'—I rifle through my memory—'Sarah Decker, someone Pierce and Dorian Blythe. Where are they now?'

Dale shrugs. 'No idea. Moved away when St Valentine's shut, I guess. I'll look into it, see if I can turn them up.'

I finish my coffee. 'Fair enough. And I'll go and have a word with Nicholas. Let's see if he knows anything about Garner or the fire.'

'HELLO, MR ROURKE,' Nicholas says once we've assumed our familiar places in the interview room. 'You look like you've recovered from whatever was ailing you yesterday. Your eyes still seem a little bloodshot, though.'

'Thanks for the appraisal.' I light a Marlboro out of habit. 'Tell me again about the first St Valentine's, up on Ryland Hill.'

'I didn't think you were interested in history.' No detectable sarcasm in his voice, which is flat and even.

'Maybe it's growing on me.'

'The chapel was struck by lightning during the first sermon there. Twenty people died and the building burned to the ground.'

I lean forward. 'Now tell me about the second St Valentine's.'

'What about it?' Nicholas smiles.

'It also had a fire in which people died.'

'What makes you think I know anything about it?'

I continue to fix him with my eyes. 'You've been there. You left this.' I pull the locket from my jacket and place it on the table. 'What happened there that was so important you left a marker for us to find?'

The smile stays, though if anything it becomes a little more condescending. 'There was a fire several years ago, like you said. Was your father called out to deal with it, Mr Rourke?'

'Why would it matter if he was?'

'So he was there.' The smile broadens, as if Nicholas is appreciating a joke I haven't noticed. 'Did he talk about the difficulty they had evacuating everyone inside? Perhaps that was why people died.'

'I never heard they had trouble clearing the building.'

'You haven't listened to the right people.' Nicholas leans back slightly as if settling into his seat. 'What did you see when you went to St Valentine's, Mr Rourke?'

'A building, corridors. A lot of mould. A lot of burnt rubble.'

'Did you see the locked doors?' The question is quick and direct.

'Yeah.'

'And what did they remind you of?'

'Cells. You're not going to suggest—'

'If there was a fire at a prison, Mr Rourke, do you think the evacuation would be easy? Do you think it would be any easier if only a few people had keys to the cells?'

'None of the kids at St Valentine's died in the fire, Nick, as you should know. Is there a point to all this?'

'Were you ever caught doing anything bad and told to go to your room without any dinner?'

I sit in silence for some time, watching his face and taking an occasional drag on my cigarette. Once I've finished it, I speak. 'You're suggesting the staff used to lock up children if they were naughty, I guess. I'm willing to entertain the possibility, but how do you know?'

'Plenty of people would know if they did, Mr Rourke. The kids at the home and the staff both would.'

'Do you know any of the staff?'

'Is there anything to suggest that I might?' Like a politician or psychiatrist, answering one question with another.

'You seem to know a lot about the place, and about Winter's End as a whole.' I lean forward, resting my arms on the table as I ask, 'Have you ever met Henry Garner, the director of the home?'

Nicholas raises his eyebrows, but the look in his eyes tells me he is anything but taken aback by the question. 'According to the stories people tell, he died in the fire, Mr Rourke.'

'His remains were found in Black Ravine this morning, several miles from St Valentine's. He was murdered and his body hidden. He didn't die in any fire, Nicholas. Do you know anything about it?'

The suspect's smile returns and a smug look creeps across his features. 'Death is such a personal subject. Our opinions of a particular person's demise vary according to our perspective.'

'And your opinions are?'

'How did you feel when your parents died, Mr Rourke?'

Anger pumps through me like battery acid. 'That's none of your damn business. Stick to the subject, Nicholas.'

'Did you know when you lifted your head from the steering wheel that their lives were over, or did you still harbour some hope that they had survived? Did you hate the driver whose car collided with yours, or did you hate yourself?'

The ashtray rebounds from the wall opposite, scattering its contents in a cloud of grey powder. Only my training stops me from vaulting across the table and pounding Nicholas's smiling face against the floor. Instead, I march past him and out of the room. The two deputies watch me, but don't ask questions.

I give myself a couple of minutes to calm down, grab a can of Coke from a machine down the hall, then return to the interview room.

'Let's go back to the subject,' I say as I sit opposite Nicholas. 'Did you or didn't you know Garner? Did you or didn't you have anything to do with the fire at St Valentine's? Did you or didn't you have a reason to hate the staff there, like Garner and Angela Lamond?'

'Those like Garner and the nurse abused their positions, Mr Rourke. Plenty of people had reason to hate them.' He grins, but his eyes are cold and glittering. 'The Devil came to claim them when their time was up, just as he did with others who were equally deserving. You were lucky in your upbringing, Mr Rourke. You've never been the victim of anyone like that.'

'And you were?'

He chuckles. 'Still looking for a motive, Mr Rourke? Casting your bait this way and that, you remind me of the boy struggling to catch fish on Claye Lake under the watchful eye of his beloved father.'

'Just cut the crap and answer the damn questions, Nicholas,' I say through clenched teeth. 'Tell me about what happened on the 15th. Where did you take Angela when you grabbed her? Is there a patch of Mason Woods where we'll find her missing clothes?'

'This is getting tiring, Mr Rourke.'

'Maybe it is, but if I don't start getting some answers soon, I'm going to give up on this whole case and go back to Boston. You'll go to jail for murder and the rest of our investigation will be forgotten about. You want that?'

Nicholas sighs. 'I understand your frustration, but I need you to work this through. *I* won't allow you to go just yet.'

I ask the question even though I've already guessed at the answer. 'What do you mean?'

'Everything that has happened here has done so because I willed it. I am arrested but refuse to talk, forcing the Sheriff's Department to bring in outside help. You used to specialise in interrogating difficult suspects, and you're a friend of Dale Townsend. You've even worked for him in the past. Who better for him to turn to now? You find the children's home, and the tracks and signs I so carefully left. You check out the building, you follow my footsteps, you find the locket *I* left for *you*.' His voice is growing steadily in intensity if not in volume. 'I told you I was waiting for you, and so I was. Now you're here and you're not going anywhere until I'm through. It's rare for a man to be able to make up for the injustices he suffers and punish those who have stolen the life he should have had.'

His dark blue eyes burn into mine and I'm almost certain that I'm in the presence of a lunatic. 'Is that what you're here for, Nicholas,' I ask, 'to punish the people who ruined your life?'

'That's not an issue, Mr Rourke. Remember when I told you that people's actions sometimes put them in the service of the Devil, and that he eventually comes to collect?'

I nod, mouth strangely dry.

'*That's* the issue here. I'd look to yourself, Mr Rourke. It's a rare man indeed who can bargain with the Devil without losing his soul.'

The silence in the room is broken only by the faint hiss of the tape recorder. We sit, staring at each other, as I try to determine what is going on behind the mask Nicholas presents to the world. Did he come to Winter's End for revenge? Does he believe he's the Devil, or just the Devil's agent? Either seems possible.

Finally, I break the stillness. 'Why should I look to myself? What have I done?'

'If you can't answer that question yourself, I won't do it for you.' Nicholas smirks wolfishly. 'One can't be given absolution unless one first confesses one's sins.'

I return his smile. 'It's interesting to hear you talking about confession, given the sins you've yet to admit yourself.'

'Yes?'

'Thou shalt not kill, Nicholas. But you did just that to Angela Lamond, and perhaps Henry Garner too.'

He shakes his head. 'I didn't kill the nurse. She was already dead.'

The look in his eyes tells me that there's an unspoken 'she just didn't know it' at the end of his denial. I try to get him to say it anyway. 'Really?'

'In some ways, her fate was similar to that of the woman in the locket. She wasn't killed either.'

'Who was she, Nicholas? A local? What was her name?'

'You'll have to discover that for yourself.' He sighs, and the change in his posture tells me that, as far as he's concerned, the interview is over. I won't be sorry to get out of the room myself, so I stop proceedings there and wait for the deputies to take him to his cell.

IT WAS A HOT DAY, not quite into the full swing of the Florida summer, but pretty close. I was in Miami to spend a week visiting my parents and relaxing. At least, that's what I told myself. In reality, I had a pile of case folders on my desk, all needing my attention, and wanted some support, someone to talk to. So I took a week off and headed for the sun and the only people I thought would understand.

Three days into the holiday and I was driving my mom and dad down to a little restaurant by the waterfront they visited every Wednesday. My dad was sitting next to me and the two of us were holding forth on our views on the Red Sox, past and present, with my mom occasionally chipping in with comments from the back.

Traffic was light, but there were quite a few people out on the streets. Tourists, mostly, to look at them. Everyone was strolling with the same easy-going air, almost sedated by the warmth.

I think that was what told me something was wrong. As I approached one intersection of many on the drive south, the light up ahead green, I could see that most of the pedestrians on the sidewalk to my right were looking away, down the road that was about to meet my own, paused in mid-stroll.

As I passed beneath the traffic lights I heard the roar of an engine running fast and hard, no longer muffled by the buildings that had blocked the noise. I glanced to the right.

Here, the memories get a little confused. I saw a dark car screaming towards me, and I remember slamming on the brakes. I was thrown about like a matador hit by a charging bull, held only by my seat belt, and I felt sharp fragments, probably glass, scatter against my flesh. As the car shrieked sideways under the impact and my view began to tilt as its passenger-side wheels left the road, my air bag fired, smothering me briefly in whiteness. Then I felt the door next to me shudder and buckle as it hit the ground; my car was now on its side. Liquid dripped against my skin. Either I passed out, or I was too dazed to know what happened for a while. Next thing I knew, there were flashing lights outside. I looked across, no, *up*, and saw my father hanging limply in his seat, blood running across his face. The side of the car next to him was shredded and punctured.

The cops told me later that none of the people they spoke to could remember seeing the driver of the other car. It was a kind of 'situation blindness' I was familiar with. They also said there had been extra padding material in the remains of the stolen sedan, and asked if I had any enemies who might have wanted to kill me. In a daze I rattled off some names—stay with the Bureau for long enough, and anyone makes enemies. Most of those I could think of were in jail.

The cops eventually decided that the driver might have been planning to ram-raid somewhere nearby and had wanted to make sure he didn't get hurt. Tragic accident, colliding with someone on their way to commit a crime. I accepted the theory at the time.

From there, I couldn't see any way of avoiding the inevitable. My life as an FBI agent effectively ended on that day, even though the full breakdown took another six months to overcome me completely.

'SO WHAT DO YOU THINK?' Dale asks, leaning back in his chair as I spark up a cigarette and settle into the seat opposite in his office, glad to be away from the jail.

I spend a few moments rolling the tobacco smoke around my mouth before answering. 'I think Nicholas has a serious grudge against Garner as well as Lamond. He talked about them "abusing their positions" and about people stealing the life he should have had. Both victims worked at a children's home, and Nick is certainly familiar with the place.'

'Angry ex-inmate?'

'It would fit everything we have,' I say with a shrug.

'And you'd buy him as the guy that torched St Valentine's and killed Garner?'

'Yeah, I would. It happened six years ago, which would make him between twenty and twenty-four at a guess.'

'Young enough to have been at the home during the time Angela worked there,' Dale observes, nodding. 'Which would only leave the question of who dug up Garner's body and why. Forensics report on the partial shoe-print we found in the ravine says it was a size ten man's shoe, probably Hush Puppies, not heavily worn. It doesn't match those of the guy who found the body, so we're probably looking at the digger.'

'That's good, but we still don't know why he was there.' I pause for long enough to finish my cigarette. 'Has Nicholas sent or received any mail since he's been here?'

'No. Didn't even take his phone call. You figure he might have someone on the outside?'

'Perhaps.' I lean across and pick up the list of Garner's associates. 'I'll speak to Vallence and this Earl Baker guy and see if they know anything,' I say. 'Have you managed to track down any of the rest of the home's management?'

'Not yet. Charlie's still working on it.'

I pocket the list as well as a copy of Nicholas's photo and stand to leave. 'I'll phone you when I'm done.'

'Sure. And, Alex,' Dale calls after me as I reach the doorway, 'don't let Nick get under your skin. He's not worth getting worked up over.'

I nod once, then let the office door swing shut with a click.

THE BLUSTERY WEATHER turns to rain, a squall charging in from the west, as I head north to Castle Hill, home of Earl Baker. Droplets splash from a heavy sky, keeping my wipers working overtime.

I run up the driveway of 12 Pulver Street without bothering to stop and check out the house, an indistinct brown shape in the watery murk. By the time Baker opens the door, I'm busy shaking myself off in the shelter of his porch.

'Can I help you?' he says, raising his voice to be heard over the hammering. He's a thickset man in his early fifties.

I raise my badge in my left hand. 'Sheriff's Department. I'd like to speak with you a moment.' I glance behind me. 'Inside, if possible.'

'What's up?' Baker asks, once I'm ensconced in the relative comfort of his home.

'It's about Henry Garner,' I say. 'I don't know whether you've heard, but his remains were found this morning.'

'I heard on the radio that they found a body.'

'Well, I've got a couple of questions to ask, if you don't mind.'

'Sure.'

I'm about to say more when a woman steps in through the doorway in the far right-hand corner of the room. 'Who was it, Earl?'

'Deputy Alex Rourke, ma'am,' I say.

Earl turns to look at the newcomer, who appears to be about the same age, and is of a lighter build, with short hair dyed coppery-ginger and casual clothes. 'He's here about Henry's death,' Earl says, turning back towards me as the woman joins him.

'Deborah Pierce,' she says, extending a cold, clammy hand. I recognise the name—she was the nurse at St Valentine's when it opened. 'That was a long time ago. What's happened?'

'They found his body, Deb. He didn't die in the fire after all.'

'You both knew Garner well?'

Earl nods. 'For years.'

'He was such a nice man,' Deborah coos. 'I couldn't believe it when they said he'd died in the fire.'

'You worked at the home. Were you there on the night of the fire?'

'No, I'd been gone for a good ten, twelve years by then.'

I turn to Earl. 'How about you, Mr Baker? Were you there?'

'No, I never worked with Henry. I was in construction and maintenance. Did a few jobs jobs at St Valentine's.'

'Did either of you know anyone who might have had any kind of
grudge against him?'

They both shake their heads, so I take the locket and the photo of
Nicholas from my jacket pocket. 'How about these two people?' I
say. 'Do you recognise either of them?'

They look at the jewellery nestling in the plastic bag in my hand.
My eyes follow theirs, gauging their reactions. I'm disappointed.

'I'm sorry, Deputy Rourke,' Earl says.

'I don't know,' Deborah adds. Then she takes a further look at the
locket. 'She seems a bit familiar, maybe. Like someone I might have
seen around town a few times or something.'

I jump on this. 'Around Winter's End? While you were working at
the home?'

'Maybe. I might be wrong, though. It was a long time ago.'

'What about the guy?'

She purses her lips. 'No,' she says at last, shaking her head. 'No. I
thought his eyes looked familiar, but I can't place him.'

It's something, but not much. 'There's one more thing,' I say. 'St
Valentine's had a reputation for strictness. To your knowledge, were
kids who misbehaved ever locked up? We've heard a couple of stories
that it used to happen, and I noticed some rooms that looked like
they could have been used that way while I was there.'

Earl and Deborah look at one another and *there*, there it is. That
meeting of stares, the way their eyes twitch as if unspoken thoughts
are being exchanged. I see it, and I know that Nicholas spoke the
truth. Children who were bad were locked away in cells that were
probably put together by Earl during his construction days.

Deborah breaks eye contact with me before she answers. 'No, not
that I know of.'

'Well, they were just stories I heard. Thank you both for your help.'

'What's your theory on Henry's death? Do the police have any
leads?' asks Earl as he shows me to the door.

'It's a little early to say,' I reply. 'But at the moment, we're treating
it as suspicious.' I don't know what prompts me to add what I do
next, giving Earl a steady, almost knowing glance as I say it. I guess I
just don't like people mistreating children. 'We're treating a lot of
things as suspicious right at the moment.'

I return my eyes to the driveway in front of me. 'What do you know,' I say, more friendly. 'The rain's moved on. I'll be seeing you.'

I leave the beefy form of Earl standing statue-like in the doorway, Deborah dangling at his shoulder, a guilty conscience with weak, watery eyes. When I'm back in the privacy of my car, I fumble for and light a cigarette, mostly to give my free hand something to do while my brain ticks over. If the woman in the locket lived in Winter's End, even if it was years ago, someone must remember her. I make a note to ask Vallence about her again when I see him, as well as trying the older folk in town.

It's getting late by the time I reach Winter's End, but on impulse I pull up at the Church of St Francis. My eyes take in the whitewashed stone building, a simple construction in the style of the nineteenth century. As I noticed yesterday, the graveyard of the church is small, consisting mostly of bare turf with a couple of lonely-looking trees and a gravel path cutting through it. The church doors are open a crack, just enough to let prospective visitors know that the building is available to them without letting out the warmth within.

The locket, which shares a pocket with my left hand, seems to grow hotter as I trudge along the gravel. I'm about to put it down to no more than body heat when my vision blurs and I again see a woman in the church grounds. Black hair, pale face, and now with no darkness to conceal her, I can see that she *is* the one from the photograph, still clad in her rotting shroud. This time, she points away to the south, eyes imploring. I turn and look, but see nothing except houses and the tops of the trees bordering town.

When I look back, she's gone. My nerves crackle, a quivering that has nothing to do with the damp. I quicken my pace up the path, worried that I'm seeing things. I've had hallucinations before, during my breakdown, when the fear and paranoia that gnawed at the root of my mind suddenly exploded to the surface.

Once I'm at the doors I pause, some inner force suddenly very reluctant to step over the threshold. You're not a believer, I tell myself. What are you doing here? I don't have a good answer, but I turn the handle and walk in anyway.

Aside from me, there seems to be only one other person here, kneeling in one of the front pews near the simple altar. I walk softly down the aisle, unconsciously adopting the habit of trying to make as little noise as possible when in a place of worship, as if God is sleeping next door and would be extremely annoyed to be woken.

Getting closer, I recognise the tangled hair and the faded clothing the kneeling woman wears. I saw her in the woods this morning. Hearing my approach, she turns to face me and says, 'You've come, then. I warn them all, but they pay no heed.'

'What do you mean?'

'You've come to pray for forgiveness for your soul.'

I let it pass; I have a feeling she'd react badly if I argue with her. 'What did you mean this morning, about what happened to Garner being the work of the Devil?'

The woman's eyes seem to be focused on something other than me as she says in a calm voice, 'The Devil has come for us. This town is drenched in spilt blood, but the only reward he gives for our sins is everlasting damnation.'

Her words are striking in their similarity to those of Nicholas. 'What exactly has gone on here?'

'They built this place on the bodies of the slain. They murdered one another for greed. They schemed and they worked their evil.'

She seems to be referring to the town's early years, so I ask, 'Isn't that all ancient history?'

'Not all of it,' the woman says. 'He's cursed this place. He took the woman who died on the highway. Like he took those others.'

I take out the locket, which still feels strangely warm, and show it to the woman. 'Do you know who this is in the picture?'

The woman brushes the plastic covering the photo with a single fingertip. 'Poor thing,' is all she says.

'What do you mean?'

'You know, or else you wouldn't be asking me. Now you must pray.'

'I'm not a believer.' I turn to walk away. Behind me, I hear the woman stand up, although she doesn't come after me.

'Throw yourself on the Lord's mercy,' she calls out. 'If you don't, the Devil will take you too!'

I glance at the locket. 'No, he won't,' I reply. 'He needs me here.'

I MAKE IT to Martha's Garden and my meeting with the mystery note-writer with a quarter of an hour to spare. I take a stool and order a coffee, thankful for the reassuringly ordinary human bustle after my experience at the chapel. At five Sophie Donehan walks in. She's wearing a dark green shirt and a pair of tight trousers a little lighter in hue than her bobbed black hair. The dark lines round her eyes make her look like I feel. She orders a coffee, then moves to a table near the window, watching me as she does so. I pick up my own cup and follow.

'You wrote the note?' I ask, sitting opposite.

She nods, then fixes me with eyes the colour of dark chocolate.

'Did you know that Angela, y'know, the dead one, used to work at the kids' home in the woods?'

Sophie blows on her coffee to cool it. Her eyes never leave mine.

'Yeah, I knew that. What about it?'

'Do you know what they were like there?' Sophie practically spits out the question in the same kind of tone a priest might use when talking about practitioners of black magic.

'I'm sorry, but no one's said much about it.'

'They *all* know,' she hisses. 'They pretend they don't, but they do.'

'Know what?'

The teenage emotional thermostat moves down a couple of notches and Sophie's face settles again. Her eyes continue to burn into mine, hard and piercing. 'If I tell you, will you help me?'

I take a mouthful of coffee by way of slowing the pace. 'Help you how?' I ask once the cup is back on the table.

'Get me out of here. Take me down to Boston with you. I've got money. I can get a place there and find a job.'

'And your parents would probably try to charge me with kidnapping if I did. Why can't you talk it over with them?'

'My mom's dead, so there's just my dad. But they weren't my parents,' she says, hatred in every word. 'Not my real ones, anyway.'

'How about trying to find your real parents, then?'

'I don't want to find my real parents. I hope they're rotting in hell!' The hiss is back and, as far as I can tell, her anger at both sets of people is genuine. 'And I hate this place and everyone in it.'

'Why?' I ask softly, hoping to calm Sophie down.

'My foster-father doesn't care about me, and I don't care about him. He spends most nights drinking in front of the TV. When he says anything to me it's usually to yell at me to fix him dinner or something. I've had enough.'

'All right, I'll think about it,' I say with a sigh, not knowing if I'm being truthful. 'But only if you're honest with what you know.'

She hesitates, as if making up her mind whether to trust me or not. Eventually, she says, 'Do you have kids?'

'No,' I tell her. 'Never got round to it.'

'Uh-huh. But you know that parents are supposed to love their children, right? I guess my real ones must've died or something, 'cos if they loved me they wouldn't have left me in *that* place.' She shows little emotion as she speaks, although she seems relieved to have found someone willing to listen to her at last.

'You were at St Valentine's? What was so bad about it?'

'I got out when I was five or six, I guess. Something like that.' She makes it sound like she'd been given parole from jail. 'But it took me ages to get used to living someplace else. It was like the routine they had there. We weren't ever allowed outside the grounds, and they only ever let us out of the *building* in the middle of summer. You imagine that? I guess it would have been harder if I'd been older.'

'What do you mean?'

'If older kids misbehaved, they'd get a beating, or they'd be locked in the basement for hours, or days even. They had to do work around the place. I remember one boy getting a beating with a ladle from one of the cooks, just for spilling some gravy he was serving.'

'Do you remember any of the names of the kids there? Especially the older ones,' I say. It's a long shot, but I'm hoping she'll tell me about a boy called Nicholas. In the end, I'm disappointed.

'No, not really. I remember a few that were my age, but that's all.'

'How about the staff? Anything they were known to have done in particular? Any names you can recall?'

She gives me a calculating smile. 'You want to know about the dead woman, right? Sorry, I don't remember much about her, except I think the kids only ever went to see her when they'd been hurt.'

'And no one ever reported what went on at St Valentine's? They could have got it closed down.'

'No. I guess all the staff were happy with it. If the place was still open today, the story would probably have got out. But it's not. Whoever burnt it down saved everyone the trouble.'

I know the question I'm about to ask is on a sensitive subject, but I try it anyway. 'Sophie, Sheriff Townsend told me your foster-mom died about the same time that St Valentine's shut. What happened? I'll understand if you don't want to talk about it.'

'That's OK,' she says, shrugging. 'I don't care about her, and I don't know why she did it, not really. She was pretty uptight most of the time, and her husband's always been an asshole. One day I came back from school and found her dead on the couch, an empty bottle of sleeping pills on the table. My foster-father's been on the bottle ever since.'

I motion for another refill for our cups and light a cigarette, offering her one. She accepts.

'I'll tell you what,' I say once the fresh coffee has arrived, 'if you still want to get away from Winter's End when I'm finished here, you can come with me. But think carefully about this. Leaving home's no small decision, and it won't be all sunshine and roses. OK?'

'OK.'

'Here's my card. If you want to get in touch, my number's on there.'

She glances at the dark blue print. 'Thanks. Alex,' she adds, hesitant in using my first name. She seems to be about to say something else, but then stops herself and walks out with just a plain 'goodbye'.

I CHECK MY WATCH once the rumble of the 'Vette's engine has faded into nothing. Five to eight. Hell. Early. The worst possible time to arrive. It makes you look desperate and forces your date to rush. Under other circumstances, I'd correct this by sitting in the car for five minutes. Unfortunately, this is a quiet residential street and the 'Vette isn't exactly stealth on wheels. I grab the flowers I bought on the way here and climb out of the car, making a lot of effort to breathe slow and easy. It's like prom night all over again. I just hope that the restaurant she has in mind isn't going to require me to wear a tie, since I didn't bring one up from Boston.

Gemma answers my ring on the bell within a few seconds. She's wearing a loose red top and a tight knee-length black skirt, and she looks absolutely gorgeous. Her blonde hair is draped around her shoulders like golden cotton candy. Her smile is bright and pretty, but betrays a nervousness that matches my own. This feeling is so obviously shared in both our initial words that we each relax somewhat; we've found our first piece of common ground.

'They're lovely,' she says when I rather awkwardly present her with the flowers. She places them in a vase on her hallway table, then grabs a slim jacket of brown suede and her handbag.

'I hope they'll let me into the restaurant,' I say, gesturing at my smart-as-possible but still underdressed self. 'My nearest tie is a few hundred miles away.'

I grin and she laughs, a genuine sound, soft and tinkling. I know the evening is going to be fine.

We stroll into the town centre, hands knotted together, talking about nothing in particular. The restaurant Gemma has chosen is a small place of dark wood, frosted glass and soft lighting. Friendly atmosphere and food that's good rather than overpriced culinary art.

In a quiet corner I learn about Gemma's childhood in Bangor, the largest town in northern Maine. Her elder sister, Alice, who moved away to Baltimore while Gemma was finishing medical school, and her younger brother, Ryan, who works at a bank in Augusta. Her student days, her first job as an intern at a pathology lab, the path leading her to the post of part-time medical examiner. I learn that she has friends in town but spends most of her evenings in. I learn that she likes reading so long as it doesn't relate too closely to work, that she watches horror films but likes to have something to cover her eyes at the scary bits, that she listens to music but doesn't have favourites, just whatever comes on the radio.

In return, I try not to bore her with the details of my own sorry life. I cover pretty much everything, good and bad, but don't dwell on anything for long. I wheel out anecdotes from my own student days, then more from my time with the Bureau and after. I tell her that my choice of car is less about keeping up a macho image and more about demonstrating my taste for the ridiculous. She laughs at the jokes; she gets caught up in the serious stuff. I think she likes me, which is good because I certainly like her.

Hours tick past without us noticing and it's soon time to pay the bill and leave. We walk home arm in arm, still talking, smiling. She asks if I'd like to come inside.

'I would,' I say, 'but I never do on first dates. Maybe it's old-fashioned, but I like to give the girl some time and a second chance for her to decide if I'm really a jerk or not.'

I smile, but I'm aware that this is the final test. If she doesn't like it, then I know that this isn't going to work.

Gemma just smiles back and moves closer to me. 'In that case, are you doing anything tomorrow night?' she says, green eyes shining.

I move my hands to her hips, a motion she mirrors, and we kiss, long but softly. Lips like cool satin, breath as sweet as cinnamon. I can feel her hair against my cheek, her body warm against mine.

When we break off, she whispers good night and caresses my hand as she steps through the door. I stand on the doorstep for a moment like a love-struck adolescent, then amble down the driveway to my car. Once I'm inside, I break into a big watermelon grin, happy as I've been in ages. I'd punch the air but it's a low roof. Instead, I turn the ignition and pull slowly, reluctantly, away from the kerb.

On the long, dark journey home, I hum all the way, genuinely buzzing. The grey day has turned into a starless night, and the sole illumination for most of my journey are the twin beams of light spraying from the front of the 'Vette. The damp blacktop has an almost hypnotic TV-static look to it as the tiny cracks and imperfections between every lump of grit in the asphalt flash by, until a feeling of light-headedness steals over me, a sensation akin to having my skull filled with helium and loosely tethered to my shoulders. Elation, doziness, or something altogether different.

I burst out into the empty fields that lie between St Valentine's and Winter's End doing just over sixty, looking forward to getting home. Even the thought of the Crowhurst Lodge and its pale malevolence is a welcome one. Then I catch sight of something reflecting the glow of the headlights up ahead and slam on the brakes.

When the tyres have finished squealing and I've lifted my head from where it rests against the wheel, I'm free to take in the scene in front of me. A man, bare from the waist up and carrying a knife in each fist. Nicholas. In front of him stands a naked woman, Angela Lamond, sobbing, with one hand pressed to her mouth. Phantom rain, translucent in the glow, dances from their skin.

The apparitions stand in front of the 'Vette, oblivious to my presence, afterimages of events already passed into history. I can feel the sharp point of light behind my eyes that signals an oncoming migraine even as I stare at this tableau. Despite this, I step from the car to get a closer look. Nicholas is speaking softly and calmly.

'You understand why this has to be,' he says. 'I wouldn't normally do this sort of thing myself, but I need you to act as a messenger.'

'Please,' Angela whispers. 'Please.'

'I'd tell you that your torment will be less because of the purpose you shall serve,' Nicholas continues. Lightning that exists only for the two actors in the spectral play in front of me flashes from their skin and dances in Angela's eyes. 'But that would be a lie. You must've known how your actions would be rewarded.'

Nicholas gently turns her round so her back is to him and wraps his arms round her in a lover's embrace. Lightning flashes again as the knives in his hands whip out, then back into her rib cage, and blood mixes with the ghostly rain. He lowers her to the floor, waiting until her heart has stopped, then proceeds to cut and slash with abandon at her chest. Then he stands, lowering his hands to his sides. 'Now, to wait,' he says.

It's enough for me. I break out of my stupor and turn and run back to my car. My fingers twitch and shake as I fire up the engine. I hit the gas and don't ease off on the throttle until I reach town.

All I can think about is that I'm seeing things. Again. I desperately want it to be fatigue, or some kind of reaction to something I ate. But every movement of my head produces a tingle at the back of my neck that adds to my fear that I'm falling apart.

The parking lot of Crowhurst Lodge is darkened and empty. I lurch for the front entrance, fumbling my key from my pocket. The ancient iron door knocker at the far end of the porch now wears a mocking grin. I run through, past the reception desk with the single bulb glowing dim and red. Up the stairs, into my room, turn on every light I can find, and then the TV to drown out the noise of the leaves outside.

I pop one of my migraine pills before splashing some water on my face and neck. My head is throbbing and jittering whorls of distortion dance in front of my vision. Take a second capsule. Sit, watch TV, and try to relax again. Take a third. Then a fourth. Knock back my two sedatives for this evening, then follow them up with a fifth treatment for my headache. Shrug out of my jacket and clothes, but make sure my Colt is within reach of the bed.

I pass out to the uncertain noise of the television.

A DREAMLESS SLEEP is brought to an end by the repetitive tone of the alarm clock. I'm cold, lying on top of the covers. I have a headache, but it feels like a hangover rather than anything more serious. I rub my eyes and pop another tablet anyway. Then I edge cautiously over to the window and peep out through the gap in the curtains. What world is waiting for me out there? Awakened or sleeping, dreamscape or nightmare? Has anything changed?

No. It's an ordinary day outside. The clouds are back, sluggishly blanketing the entire sky like mouldy cotton wool, but at least there are no phantoms or strange visitations to plague me.

I shower and dress, lighting my first cigarette as I throw on a shirt. I check myself in the mirror before I leave the room. I don't look well. Skin too pale, eyes bloodshot and red-rimmed, stubble sprouting from a grey chin. I decide not to bother with breakfast today. I can't face another morning in that lonely dining room, feeling like an exiled monarch under house arrest in a foreign land.

Instead I trot outside to the 'Vette and hit the gas.

At 8.15, six miles south of town, my cellphone rings.

'Alex, it's Dale. I've been trying to get hold of you for ages.'

'Sorry,' I say, 'I had my phone turned off. What's up?'

'Nicholas has escaped.'

7

I pass through two roadblocks on my way into Houlton. The first is on I-95, a cordon of State Police blue-and-whites and businesslike cops packing shotguns; the second is on the town limits, not far from the interstate off-ramp. I'm waved through as soon as the officer who taps on my window sees my badge.

The Superior Court parking lot is crowded with police cruisers, badly parked cars and reporters. I find a space a little way away from the media circus, then take a deep breath, and brave the journey to the doors. I'm in luck, and none of the TV, radio and newspaper staff gathered outside seem to know who I am.

Up the stairs, legs already tired by the time I reach the top of the first flight, and into the Sheriff's Department offices. In addition to two regular dispatchers, a pair of the department's part-time staff have been drafted in to help deal with the manhunt effort. Dale, Chief Deputy Owen Marsh, a man in a lieutenant's jacket and two guys in State Police uniforms are in discussion round a desk in the centre of the room covered by a large map of Maine.

'Alex,' Dale calls over to me as I help myself to a coffee before heading to the table. 'Come here and I'll fill you in.' He points at the lieutenant. 'Bruce Watts,' he says. 'He handled the first couple of interviews with Nick before I called you in. The other two are Lieutenant Matheson and Sergeant Austin, both from State.' Dale looks at me while the three men nod in my direction. 'Jesus, Alex, you look rough. Pills not working?'

I shake my head. 'They're fine. I just had a strange night, that's all. What've you got so far?'

Matheson gestures at the map. 'We've had roadblocks on the roads out of town since within an hour of the alarm being raised. We've alerted the Border Patrol and posted the suspect's details to every police department in the state. Houlton PD are checking in case he's still here. We got a K-9 unit on the scene as fast as we could, but we lost the trail just outside the jail. He may have got into a car or truck. We've got dog teams checking the outskirts of town.'

'That's about all we can do without any leads,' Watts adds. 'There's been no reports of auto theft since he escaped, so if he's in a vehicle, he either stole one that no one's missed yet or he had help on the outside; either way we don't know what we're looking for.'

I rub my chin. 'How did he get out?'

'He jumped one of the deputies at the jail just before lights out last night and took his uniform,' Dale says. 'Then he triggered the fire alarm and made his way out during the confusion. They realised what had happened when they took a head-count of the inmates and staff. By that point, he was gone.'

'How easy would it be to plan something like that?' I ask.

Owen Marsh shrugs. 'The County Jail isn't exactly maximum security. We don't take prisoners with sentences over nine months, so it's staffed for that kind of low-risk prison population. If he knew the layout of the building and its fire procedure, it's possible.'

'And he's had a good few days with nothing better to do than get to know the jail layout,' I observe gruffly, annoyed at the ease of Nick's escape. 'It wouldn't surprise me if one of the deputies from Corrections gave him blueprints in trade for a couple of beers.'

'Hey, this wasn't our fault any more than it was everyone else's,' Owen says, like I've hurt his pride.

'Not your fault? It's the department that runs the jail. I don't know who it was that let a prisoner on a murder charge walk out of the front gate during a fire alarm, but if they were any more stupid they'd need to be watered twice a week. Jesus.' I shift my gaze away from Owen, not wanting to get drawn into an argument.

Dale changes the subject while his chief deputy goes to get a refill of coffee. 'You think he's been planning this all along?'

'Why not? He's sure as hell planned everything else.' I glare at the map. 'If he was smart enough to put everything else together, my guess is that he was smart enough to have a car waiting by the jail. Maybe his, maybe someone else's. I'm sorry, Lieutenant Matheson, but your roadblocks aren't going to catch him. He's already gone.'

The State Police man frowns as he regards me. 'We'll see,' he says after a moment's silence. Then he looks back at the map. 'We've got a helicopter sweep of the town due to start in a short while. I think we'll head back to headquarters and see if it turns anything up. Sheriff.' He nods at Dale, then leaves, followed by Sergeant Austin.

'Are you feeling all right?' Dale asks. 'You were pretty blunt with Owen and the lieutenant.'

'I'm fine. Just tense.'

'You think Nick's vanished for good?'

My mind's eye flits over the half-burnt ruins of St Valentine's, the dark and tangled forest of Mason Woods, and with them come the barely discernible face of the woman in the locket.

'No,' I tell Dale, 'I don't believe he's run for good. I think he came here to punish people for their "sins", and from what he told me, he didn't sound like he'd finished yet.' I think of the vast forest, and all the empty hunting lodges scattered within. Nicholas would be the proverbial needle in the haystack.

'Any idea who else he might want to "punish" before he's done?'

'Not really. It doesn't help that we know so little about him.'

'Bruce,' Dale says, 'try to arrange things so that there's always one of our cars within shouting distance of Winter's End. If he tries anything, I'd like to be sure we can respond quickly.'

The lieutenant nods and goes to speak with one of the dispatchers.

Dale turns to his chief deputy. 'Owen, could you handle the press outside when Houlton PD check in with the results of their search?'

The chief deputy looks round from the far side of the room. 'No problem. When are they due to tell us how they got on?'

Dale shrugs. 'Give them an hour or so.' He turns back towards me. 'Nick seemed mightily interested in you. You think you might be one of his targets?'

'No,' I say, 'at least not at the moment. He doesn't like me, I don't think, but it's as if I'm his confessor. If he does anything to finish his business here, it wouldn't surprise me if he wanted to talk to me about it. He doesn't know my phone number, so he might have trouble getting in touch.'

'He knows you're staying in Winter's End, though,' Dale says.

'He doesn't know where.'

'There's only one hotel in town, Alex.'

I shrug. 'No sense getting worried about that now. I can take care of myself.'

'Sure.' Dale puffs out his cheeks and turns back to the map. 'Let's focus on the hunt for Nick.'

'If I could work out why he came here, I might have some inkling of who he is and where he's hiding,' I say. 'I want to keep working on Garner, the kids' home and the woman in the locket. I haven't spoken to Dr Vallence again yet; I'll do that this afternoon. Any luck finding the other management from St Valentine's? I spoke to Deborah Pierce yesterday.'

'Not yet, Alex. We're trying to track them, but with everything else going on we can't throw too much effort at it right now.'

'That's OK, Dale. I might just take a look at your records on Garner and St Valentine's.'

'Fine , but check in with me before you head back to Winter's End, just in case. Once the hunt gets scaled down, I'll be able to help you.'

'Thanks, Dale.' I turn to leave, but he calls after me.

'Sure, Alex. And take it easy on the pills, huh? It's not a good idea to go overboard on that kind of thing.'

I SPEND A COUPLE of hours looking for anything the department has that might be relevant to Nicholas's case. It's hard going, navigating by guesswork and instinct more than logical deduction. Every so often I find something on computer or in the files and print it out or copy it—some light reading for my spare time. It's gone one o'clock by the time I leave the offices. Since Nicholas's escape has left me with nothing to do save skimming my newly acquired material and waiting for the State Police to come up with a lead in their hunt, I decide to pop up to the hospital and speak to Gemma.

A growling noise from my stomach reminds me that I've not had anything to eat since yesterday evening. I grab a sandwich at a place in the market square and munch it on the bridge, looking down at the swirling water below.

I reflect that, with Nick gone, I could say my job here is done. But even as the thought occurs to me, I know that I won't walk away. My instinct, the primeval desire of the hunter, is to be there at the kill. And besides, I have a second reason not to leave, which should even now be coming off her lunch break and going back to work.

I finish my snack and walk to the hospital, heading straight for the elevators to the basement. I see no one else on my way to the mortuary office. Once there, I knock and poke my head through. Gemma is sitting at her desk with a cup of coffee and a computer print-out in front of her. She looks up and smiles when she sees it's me.

'Hi,' I say, stepping into the room, 'I hope I'm not interrupting.'

'We don't often have anything urgent down here,' she says.

'You hear about the escape?'

'On the radio.' Gemma shrugs as she says it, seemingly uncon-
cerned about Nicholas being on the loose. She changes the subject. 'I've just been on the phone to the pathology lab in Augusta.'

'Anything interesting?'

261

She shakes her head. 'Nothing beyond what I'd already found. The remains were those of Garner, and he was probably stabbed to death. It wasn't just this you came down here for, was it?'

'Just the opposite. I thought I'd make sure we were still on for this evening.' I grin. 'I also wanted to see you at work; those doctor's greens are a big turnon.'

Gemma laughs, high and clear. 'I'll have to remember that. Meet me at my place at the same time as last night?'

'Sure. Are we going anywhere nice?'

'I thought I might try cooking something at home.'

'Sounds lovely,' I tell her. 'I'll be there at eight.' I lean down and we kiss once, twice. 'I'll have to do the same for you some day. Of course, that will mean learning to cook first.'

She laughs again and gives me a little wave goodbye as I vanish through the doors.

I DRIVE BACK to Winter's End. The State Police are still out in force on the interstate, and I pass another couple of cruisers on my way up Route 11. I pay them and the rest of the road's other users scant attention, more interested in identifying possible accomplices for Nick, assuming it was an associate of his who dug up Garner's body. And why did they only dig up an arm?

The only scenario I've been able to come up with is that whoever disturbed Garner's grave only dug up an arm because they didn't know they were unearthing a corpse. If I'm right, Nick's accomplice isn't another killer, but someone far more ordinary. I press on to Winter's End feeling sharper than I have all day.

Once parked, I climb out of the car and cross Main Street towards the doctor's office. The town centre is almost deserted, an empty shell shrouded in silence and roofed by low, thick clouds. I find it hard to believe that even a prisoner escape could have made everyone want to stay indoors as much as it plainly has, even if the town was already on edge. On reaching the doctor's, I find a printed note stuck to the inside of its door.

OFFICE CLOSED TODAY DUE TO ILLNESS.
PATIENTS NEEDING TO SEE A DOCTOR URGENTLY SHOULD
CONTACT ASHLAND AMBULANCE SERVICE ON 435–6323

I peer through the glass. The room beyond is dark and unoccupied. Back at the 'Vette, I check my notes for Dr Vallence's home address.

His residence turns out to be a couple of streets away from where I used to live. The driveway is empty, but I ring the bell anyway, three times. No answer. I give up and stroll back to my car.

Then my phone rings. I don't recognise the number. 'Hello?'

'Mr Rourke, how are you?' Nicholas's voice, slightly muffled by the connection, but unmistakable.

'I'm fine, Nicholas,' I say, looking about me, heart thudding. 'How did you get my number?'

'It's on your business cards. Very thoughtful of you.'

A dark blue pick-up cruises across the intersection at the far end of the road. It doesn't make the turn towards me. I fight to remain calm and to keep a lid on my paranoia. Act rationally, check your surroundings, keep him talking. Hope to God he's not behind a parked car with a hunting rifle at the other end of the street.

'Thanks,' I say. 'Pleasure to be of service. I guess you have something you want to say.'

'Maybe I just wanted to see how you were doing, Mr Rourke.'

The windows along the opposite side of the road are either empty or wreathed in net curtains. I tell myself that any scattered movement at the periphery of my vision is just the twitchiness of my eyes.

'Why don't we get together for a drink? We could talk all you want.' It's an old and obvious ploy, but I try it anyway.

'Still fishing for an opening? You can do better than that, surely.'

'What's to say I'm not keeping you talking so the cops can trace your call?'

Nicholas chuckles. 'There's no cops trying to trace this. Until now you didn't have any reason to think I knew your number.'

The street seems empty, but I can't relax. I feel too exposed. Despite that, though, I don't give in to the instinctive urge to get into my car. Outside, I've got a clear 360-degree view of the street. Inside, it's hard to see anything low down and to the back, leaving me open.

'Well, now you've got my number, you want to do something useful with it before I get bored and hang up,' I say, trying not to sound flustered.

'Have they told you how Garner died yet?'

'Stabbed.'

'Stabbed? True enough, and I suppose the other marks would have gone by now,' Nicholas continues.

'You're saying you killed him?'

'Eventually, yes.' He pauses, enjoying himself, knowing that our conversation isn't being taped. 'It was ironic that the path I took with the Lamond woman passed only a short way from his grave.'

'How did you keep us from finding leaf litter on her skin?'

'She stripped before we stepped out of the car. Then I wrapped her feet, hands and hair in plastic bags and covered the rest of her in plastic sheeting. I did the same with my own shoes as well. I got rid of the coverings when we reached the highway.' He pauses for a moment. 'I'm surprised you didn't find them. Still, no one found Garner, either. Do you remember him? You visited the home as a boy.'

'Vaguely. Who dug up his body?'

Nicholas ignores the question. 'Do you remember Garner talking with your father?'

'Who dug him up?' I repeat. Before, I could just about stomach him mentioning my dad. I don't want to talk about it here, particularly since he seems to know so much about him.

'We're not in an interrogation room now, Mr Rourke.'

I decide to change tack. 'I'm surprised at you, Nicholas. It's usually only the dumb killers who phone the police to brag. Did you send a bunch of letters to people after you set fire to St Valentine's, too?'

'Why would I want to do that?'

'To try and scare them. Make yourself seem more important than you actually are.'

'I'm sorry to hear you have such a low opinion of me, Mr Rourke.' He doesn't sound surprised. 'Still, I can't say I didn't expect it.'

'Because I know you're a nut?'

'Because of who you are. Because of your past. Because of what you've done to me. Because of what we have in common.'

'We don't have anything in common, Nicholas.'

'Are you so sure?'

The phone goes dead, leaving me standing on a silent and deserted street, the words of the killer fading in my mind.

For a moment, I don't move, then I check my phone for the number Nick was calling from and ring Dale. 'I've just been speaking with Nicholas,' I tell him as soon as he picks up. 'He was talking on a cellphone. Can you get a fix on the place he made that call from?'

'Jesus, Alex. How did he get your number?'

'Said he read it on a business card. Can you get a fix?'

'It'll take a while,' he says. 'He'll probably be long gone by then.'

'Yeah, but it'll give us an idea of his movements.' I rattle off Nick's number. 'At least we'll know if he's running or not.'

'Sure. I'll let you know as soon as we've got an answer.'

'Good. See if you can get any further calls from that number to my phone diverted someplace else. I really don't want him to be able to ring me up whenever the hell he feels like it.'

'Will do,' Dale says.

I hang up and reach for a cigarette. After speaking with Nicholas, I'm in no mood to go through my bundle of notes surrounding Garner, his associates, and St Valentine's. He talked about taking Angela Lamond through the woods on the day he snatched her. A walk in the fresh air might be a good idea right now.

Or maybe it's not, if he's hiding out in the forest. That doesn't worry me as much as the phone call did. Nick's voice caught me by surprise. Me turning up in the place he's gone to ground would surprise *him*. I take a last look at the empty street, then climb into the 'Vette.

A couple of minutes later I turn onto the rough muddy track that plunges into the blackened, twisted boughs of Mason Woods. I pull into the first parking spot I come to, then sit absolutely still as the echoes of the engine fade and die. It's quite possible that Nicholas could be waiting out here, hoping I'd come. I make sure I have my Colt with me, just in case, and step out of the car.

The woods are utterly quiet. There's no wind to stir the trees, and the birds, insects and other wildlife seem to have fled or been silenced. The noise my feet make as I trudge through the leaf litter towards Black Ravine is the only sound to disturb the dead air.

When I hit the ravine itself, the noise of the stream, confined and amplified by the stony walls of the cleft, sounds harsh and loud in the deathly quiet. The grey skies do nothing to alleviate the close atmosphere of the woods. Below, a thin strand of police tape marks the point where Garner was found.

I clamber down to the bottom of the ravine and spend a few minutes getting a feel for the site, which is overlooked by a giant spruce. The climb, although fairly straightforward now, would have been much trickier in the dark, when the remains were dug up.

There's a sudden burst of movement and a crashing in the leaves above me. I whip my Colt from its holster and wheel round, blood singing. A second burst of movement and a screech like a dying animal and a huge crow or raven, coal-black, bursts out of the trees and lurches into the sky with steady beats of its wings.

Everything falls silent again and I wait, breathing shallowly and running my eyes along the top of the ravine. A minute or two ticks past with no further interruptions and I relax a little.

I turn south, away from the rock face, and follow the stream for a while until I reach a point where the rocks disappear to be replaced by boggy earth on its banks. If my reckoning is correct, it shouldn't be long before the ground starts rising again on the long, gentle slope that will eventually become Ryland Hill. The woods around me have fallen silent again. Only the stream keeps up its noise in the background, and I wish it wouldn't as it could be masking other movement. I feel like I'm being watched—no, *stared* at. My stomach tightens. Maybe I've done enough walking for today.

I head back towards my car, and when I come within sight of the parking spots at the end of the track, I again see, faint through the trees, the red Toyota, sitting as it did yesterday. I check my gun is within easy reach, then cut through the undergrowth towards the car.

Emerging from the greenery at a point next to its rear wheels, I can see no immediate sign of anyone within. A spider has spun a web between the wing mirror and the bodywork and now sits, poised but unmoving, waiting for a catch. I glance quickly underneath the Toyota, then move up to the windows and check inside, ready to dive back at the first sign of trouble.

Empty.

Through the smudged glass, I can see an old blanket on the back seat with something underneath it. Nowhere near large enough to be a man, with an irregular shape.

The door is unlocked and, after a quick look around me, I open it. Reach inside, take hold of one corner of the blanket, then flip it back to reveal some of what's underneath. Cloth. White. A heavy cotton uniform-style shirt. A name badge of dark blue plastic.

A. LAMOND, NURSE.

IT'S OVER AN HOUR before the State Police crime scene unit arrives, and another half an hour before I feel I can leave them to the task of meticulously going over the Toyota and the ground around it. According to the records, the car was stolen in Augusta a few days before Angela Lamond's murder. By the time I call at the convenience store on Main Street for cigarettes, the sky is darkening rapidly. I'll have barely enough time to get ready for my date before I have to leave for Houlton. Reading the files will have to wait.

I walk out of the store and straight into a reporter from the *Bangor Daily News*.

'Mr Rourke,' he says, bounding up to me like a terrier to its master. 'Could I have a word with you?'

'Sure. Fire away. Just make it quick.'

'The escaped prisoner, this "Nicholas" guy. Do you think there's a chance that he could return to the place where he was arrested?'

'Why would he want to do that?'

He shrugs. 'If he killed Angela Lamond, and he killed Henry Garner, isn't there a risk that, for whatever reason, he could have other targets lined up around here?'

I unlock the car door. 'You'd have to ask him, or find yourself a psychic. You're asking questions I can't answer.'

'That's fair enough, Mr Rourke,' he says as I open the door. 'Just one more thing. We're interested in the human side to this story as well. How's this investigation affecting you personally?'

'What are you talking about?'

He shrugs. 'We understand you've had problems with work stress before,' he says. 'How does this compare?'

'Leave it alone,' I say to him, sliding into my car. My fists are itching, but I tell myself that he hasn't said anything to make it worth punching him. 'That's none of your damn business.'

'Come on, Mr Rourke. This is the kind of dimension to a story that the public love.'

'Yeah, maybe. But I don't give a rat's ass about that. Now fuck off.'

He doesn't seem put off by what I'm saying. He just asks, 'Are you threatening me, Deputy Rourke?'

I ignore him and close the door, inwardly kicking myself for getting fired up. More hassle than it's worth, I tell myself as I turn the ignition and head back to the smothering miasma of silence that surrounds the Crowhurst Lodge.

EIGHT O'CLOCK comes round and I'm even more on edge than I was earlier. There doesn't seem to be any sensible reason for it, but the feeling is there nonetheless: a slight tension in every muscle, a taut sensation along every nerve. I only hope that an evening in Gemma's company will be enough to banish those feelings.

As before, Gemma answers the door almost before the chimes of the bell have faded. Tonight she's wearing a cotton blouse and tight blue trousers, both emphasising her willowy figure. She kisses me in greeting, hangs up my jacket, then shows me into the lounge. Her house is neat and, like my own apartment, has a definite sense of solitary occupation. There are none of the little oddments couples pick up down the years—photos, souvenirs and presents.

I follow Gemma through to the kitchen and place a bottle of what I hope is good wine on the worktop, next to a big bowl of salad.

'How did you know to get red?' she asks as she checks something in the oven. The smell of rosemary and garlic wafts past her.

'Well, I nearly brought white as well but I figured it might look kind of excessive. What's in the oven?'

'Italian roast lamb. You do like lamb, don't you?'

'Love it,' I say. 'And it smells great.'

We have a glass of wine and chat about nothing much, continuing where we left off yesterday. I notice a Patriots coffee mug on the draining board. 'I didn't realise you were a football fan,' I say.

'Oh, that. No, I'm not. It was a present. How about you?'

'I had a case once, involving one of the team's staff, got a couple of free tickets out of it. Can't stand the game, though.'

Gemma looks at me as she hands me a couple of plates, perhaps picking up on the vehemence of my tone.

'Still,' she says, 'it must have been a nice job to have on your books. High profile, especially in Boston.'

'High profile isn't all it's cracked up to be. Damn reporters.' I describe my encounter with the man from the *Bangor Daily News*, and what he insinuated. The thought alone is enough to make me feel hot and prickly as the pressure builds up inside. 'He practically came out and said I was cracking under the strain. The son of a bitch.'

'It's just what he does. It didn't sound like he said very much.'

'Well, maybe not now but it did at the time. Asshole!'

Gemma shrugs, looking a little confused at my sudden change in mood. 'He probably didn't mean anything by it.'

'I don't think they understand what it's like,' I snap at Gemma, unable to control my rage. 'I spend hours at a stretch talking with a psycho. I haven't done anything in my spare time since I got here except read police reports. Then my suspect escapes from under everyone's nose and people look at me like it's my fault. That's when they're not trying to say I'm cracking up. If they'd get off my back and leave me the hell alone I'd be fine!'

'They're just concerned. And you do look a bit . . .'

'A bit what? Are you starting as well? I've had Dale hassling me too, saying I should lay off the medication. As if he knows anything.'

Uncertainty creeps into her eyes. 'Alex, what's wrong? I just said I was worried about you. I'm sorry if that bothers you.'

'Worried about me? Why? Do you think there's something wrong with me? Is that it, are you siding with them?'

'Well, yes,' Gemma says. 'Listen to yourself!'

'You don't like what I'm saying?'

'Not the way you're saying it!' she says, eyes blinking rapidly. If I notice how baffled and upset she is becoming, I don't care.

'So how would you like me to say it, eh? Let's hear it,' I snarl.

'Alex, stop.'

'Stop? Yeah, why don't I?' I snap. 'I'll stop bothering you, so you can stop pestering me. I've had enough of your bleeding-heart sympathy! Thanks for a wonderful fucking evening. Have a nice life!'

With those words I storm out of the house, leaving behind a confused and tearful woman who I know I have badly hurt. By the time I've reached the bottom of the driveway the fit of madness has passed. I lean against the car and let my head slump onto the roof, trying to figure out what the hell came over me. I should go back and apologise. Would she believe me? Would it make things better if I did?

I climb into the car, realising as I do so that my jacket is still hanging in Gemma's hallway. Some time spent cold, in nothing but shirtsleeves, is probably no more than I deserve. I take a last look at the house, then turn the ignition and drive away.

BY ELEVEN, not only am I back in Winter's End, but I've ditched the car at the hotel and I'm in Larry's, the bar at the north end of town, frequented by truckers and passing workers for the logging companies. I've been here for two hours, getting hammered, trying to wash away whatever made me flare up at Gemma's house. I want to shoot pool and work out a little aggression. I want to get in a fight with a couple of truckers and have the shit beaten out of me.

Steps one and two are complete. Three gets going when I return from taking a leak to find my bar stool occupied by a big sweaty guy in a check shirt and jeans that could easily fit a couple of trees. In retrospect, I could have chosen something more tactful than my opening line of, 'Get your ass out of my seat.'

Could have, but didn't.

The guy slowly turns to look at me. Dark hair thinning from the temples back. His jowls hang over the line of his chin, unevenly covered with stubble and sweat. His gut mirrors this, dropping down over his belt.

'What?' he says, more a grunt than a word. Over his shoulder, I can see two guys by the pool table taking an interest.

I lean, somewhat unsteadily, towards Fatty's ear and say, louder, 'Get your goddamn ass out of my seat!'

The guy stands up. He's a couple of inches shorter than me but carries a distinct weight advantage. 'You got a big mouth, pal,' he says.

'Not half as big as your butt. What do you do for a living, taste tester at a doughnut factory?'

Fatty's two friends join him to stand at his shoulder. 'I think you've had enough,' the thinner one ventures, still holding his pool cue.

'Yeah, find yourself some fresh air,' number three says.

I'm aware through the haze that our little quartet is now the centre of attention. Off to my right, the barman leans across the counter and says, 'That's enough, pal. Get out of here and sleep it off.'

When I don't budge, he starts making his way round to kick me out by force. I just keep on looking at the Three Stooges.

'Well, c'mon! What are you waiting for?' I snarl.

Just as they look like they've collectively decided my apparent bravado isn't anything they need worry about, a voice yells from the back of the bar, 'Sheriff's Department! Leave it alone, guys, or I'll have every damn one of you off to the cells!'

No one moves as Dale shoulders his way through the throng. 'Take it easy, Alex,' he says to me. Then he turns back to the rest and yells, 'Go on, it's over! Haven't you got drinks to go back to?'

I sigh. 'Hey, Dale. What're you doing here?'

We move further down the bar and order a couple of beers. The barman hesitates to serve me but Dale gives him a nod.

Dale swigs a mouthful of Bud. 'Gemma Larson called me. Said you were acting kind of strange. She asked me to look out for you. I checked the hotel and the Sawmill before I came here.'

I knock back a quarter of the bottle, then watch the light playing off it as I turn it in my hands. Round and round. Self-pity has won out over anger. 'I screwed it up, Dale. Just like I screw up everything.'

Dale considers this for a moment, then has another mouthful. 'You're not a screw-up any more than the rest of us. And you're also not at high school any more, so just deal with it. Go home, sleep this off, and think again in the morning.'

'Ain't going to be able to sleep,' I slur. 'Left my pills in my jacket.'

Dale drags me to my feet. 'Believe it or not, a gallon or two of beer works just as good as any sedative. Let's go. I'm driving you home.'

8

When I finally collapse onto the bed, sleep comes quickly, but it's an uneven and fragmented visitor. As the night goes on and the effects of the alcohol wear off, the periods of waking become increasingly pronounced and uncomfortable.

During one of my too-brief bouts of unconsciousness, I find myself standing in a corridor in St Valentine's. I blink once or twice, for the mildewed run-down present I'm familiar with seems semi-transparent, overlaying the bright paintwork and clean linoleum of the past like a ghostly second skin.

Children's voices echo faintly from the walls, giggling and laughing, the sound high and piping. I move down the corridor to an open doorway. Beyond, in the dusty remains of the playroom, two young boys are kneeling on the floor, their attention caught up in some sort of game. Despite my proximity, I still can't hear what they're saying and their words turn into unintelligible babble as I approach.

Then I see that one boy has twin miniature knives in his hands. The other is holding a toy pistol. They are turning over, one at a time, a stack of photographs that sits between them, and are trying to be the first to stab or shoot the person or place depicted. The images on the photos are in black and white, and hard to make out, so I bend down and pick one up.

It's me. The two boys look up and their eyes, eyes I recognise, meet mine. One has the same deep blue irises as Nicholas. The other has the same as my own.

'Bang,' says the boy with the gun, pointing it at me.

The blue-eyed boy smiles as he thrusts his knives at my gut.

OPENING MY EYES, I find that the night has dragged on long enough to reach half past five in the morning. The sky outside is starting to lighten. I feel tired, but not in the remotest bit sleepy. My mouth is dry and sticky, a leftover of yesterday's drinking binge, but I'm glad to find that I don't have much of a hangover. I take a piss, shower and brush my teeth, then sit in front of the TV for an hour or two with a glass of water.

I eat another breakfast alone, then step out of the still-unoccupied hotel, rubbing in turns at my weary eyes and my stiff neck. I climb into the 'Vette and drive straight to the doctor's office, only to find the same note on the door as yesterday. I try Vallence's home phone, but all I get is his voicemail, leaving me with no choice but to head round to his house again.

The building is the same as when I left it yesterday. I ring the bell twice before I move to the living-room window and cup my hands against the glass, trying to see inside. Everything is still. There's a coffee mug on the table as well as a half-eaten sandwich.

I walk round the side of the house, through an iron gate with hinges that squeal as it swings open, to the tiny back yard. I knock on the door and kitchen window, but neither that nor calling Vallence's name earns a response. I return to the front and try again. When I still haven't had an answer, I try the front door. Unlocked.

'Dr Vallence,' I yell. 'Sheriff's Department. Anyone home?'

Silence. My fingers instinctively reach out and touch my pistol, seeking reassurance. They find it, but I leave the gun holstered. No sense scaring the wits out of him if he's bedridden with flu.

I step into the cream-carpeted hallway. At the far end of the corridor I can see the kitchen. The door to the living room is open at the foot of the stairs and it's here that I head first. The room is devoid of life, but I check the coffee mug on the table to see if it still retains any warmth. It doesn't. I move through to the kitchen, which is tidy, then return to the stairs, walking on the balls of my feet like a burglar.

At the top is a short landing. Ahead, an open door into the bathroom. To the left, two others, both ajar. The first leads into an unoccupied bedroom. The second opens onto what seems to be Vallence's den. There are a pair of wooden bookcases, a set of shelves holding photos and souvenirs, and a desk covered in papers, computer equipment, and the remains of the late Dr Vallence, face down in the dried remnants of a fantail spray of blood. I don't need to check for a pulse to know that he's dead, and it doesn't look like it happened just a moment ago. I call Dale.

'Alex, I was just about to ring you,' he says. 'We've got a fix on Nick's position when he called you.'

'That's great, Dale. I've got a dead body in front of me.'

I hear the hiss of an indrawn breath. I flash a glance over my shoulder in case it didn't come from the phone. I'm alone.

'Who is it?' Dale asks.

'Dr Vallence. I'm at his house right now. It's hard to say from where I am, but it looks like his throat was cut.'

'You might be right. The phone company fix had Nicholas calling from Vallence's address. Is there any sign of him at the house?'

'Aside from the corpse, you mean?' I think back to my conversation with Nick, looking up and down the street in a haze of subconscious paranoia. He was probably watching me from Vallence's window while the doctor's body slowly cooled upstairs. The thought makes my nerves fizz. If I had noticed something wrong, Nicholas might be back in custody. Vallence might even be alive.

'The house seems empty,' I tell Dale. Deep down, I wonder whether I really believe that. 'And I've not found anything to suggest Nick's been back since the phone call.'

'OK, stay there and I'll have a unit join you at the house. The CSU should be with you in an hour or so.'

As I hang up, my eye is drawn by the papers on the desk. At first glance they seem to have been what Vallence was last reading or working on, but I notice that the text faces my side, not his. Wanting to know why this little vignette was arranged, I move closer.

Accidental injury logs marked with the St Valentine's emblem, countersigned by Vallence. Personal records, maybe, or something stolen by Nick when he torched the kids' home. Print-outs of what look like prescriptions issued by the doctor, his copies of the documents given to the pharmacist. Bank statements for at least two accounts in Vallence's name.

A voice calls from downstairs, 'Deputy Rourke? It's Sergeant Elliott.'

'I'll be right with you,' I reply.

As I back away from the desk, touching nothing, a photo on the shelf behind it catches my eye. It shows Dr Vallence standing somewhere in the woods alongside a short man with thinning hair and Henry Garner. All three are dressed in jackets that were last in fashion a good thirty years ago, and are grinning broadly. The short man is proudly holding a heavy-looking fish. A label stuck to the frame reads: 'The gang at Claye Lake—Josh's beauty'.

The short man is familiar from somewhere, and I make a mental note to take a copy of the photo when the CSU has finished here.

Downstairs, a beefy guy in sergeant's stripes is waiting outside beside a Jeep. 'What's the picture?' he says as I walk over to him.

'Victim's in his den upstairs. Looks like a cut throat. You check the back of the building?'

'Jack's keeping an eye on it right now.'

I make my way to the 'Vette and leaf through the police files on Garner I copied yesterday, looking for the short man's face. It takes a couple of minutes of flicking, but I eventually catch sight of someone similar, but older, in a blurry photo taken from a ten-year-old newspaper. The caption underneath names him as Joshua Stern, town clerk for Winter's End. I'm pretty sure I've found a match.

'I'm going to head back to the department's offices in Houlton,' I tell Sergeant Elliott. 'There's something I've got to check. Dale's got my number if I'm needed for anything.'

I drive as quickly as I reasonably can, thinking about the photo. Everyone in it is now dead, two of them murdered and Stern killed in a car crash. I need to know about Stern.

Back in the archived police reports, I find the four-year-old file on the crash that killed him. In it is a much clearer photograph, more recognisable as the same man in Vallence's picture.

Stern was driving home from a get-together with some old friends in Presque Isle when his car skidded off the snow-covered road and went over an embankment. Twenty feet down, it hit a tree. Massive cranial damage was the official cause of death. There was no sign of mechanical failure on the car, so investigators concluded that Stern fell asleep at the wheel. This would have seemed an open-and-shut death on the roads, perfectly common during the winter months. But in my mind's eye, I see another scenario. I can see Stern driving home in the ice-hard darkness. His headlights pick out a car apparently stranded by the side of the road, its driver flagging him down. He stops, and the driver staves his skull in. Then he wedges Stern's foot on the gas and runs the car into the trees at speed.

When I replay the images in my head, over and over again, the driver who stops Stern is Nicholas.

'DALE, IT'S ALEX. What's the situation with Vallence?'

'Forensics are still going over the house, although the ME's left. It looks like he died from a single cut to the neck. We've got some clear latents from around the house, at least two sets, and some other stuff that might be of use. Including his shoes.'

'What about them?'

'The sole of Vallence's right shoe matches the print we found where Garner's body was dug up. There's a spade in the garage, still with mud on it. We're having it analysed, just to check it matches.'

'So Vallence was Nicholas's accomplice?' I say, cradling the phone with my shoulder so I can gather my cup of coffee from across the desk I'm sitting at. 'I guess that's why his car wasn't at his house.'

'Reckon so. No keys, either. I've put out an APB on the car. It might help the State boys in finding him.'

'Still no luck then?'

'Not yet. There's more, too. Vallence had a couple of pictures of Angela Lamond in his bedroom, along with some other things. It looks like they were seeing each other on the quiet.'

'Angela's rose buyer, huh? Why the big secret?'

'I dunno. Maybe they just liked it that way. It might be that Nick killed her as a way of threatening the doctor.' I hear the sound of the breeze across the connection as Dale moves outside. 'While you were at Vallence's house, did you see the papers on his desk?' he asks.

'I had a quick skim. It looked like we were meant to find them.'

'Yeah, I thought the same. Interesting stuff, some of it. Our people are going through his computer to see if there's anything more.'

'What did you find?'

'It looks like the doctor was arranging for people to get hold of drugs on prescription, for a price. Had a few steady customers— enough to give him a healthy bonus on top of his salary. It seems he also received money from St Valentine's, possibly for overlooking the way some of their kids were treated.'

'If Nick knew that, he might have been blackmailing Vallence into helping him. Anything else?'

Dale pauses, and I hear him hold his breath for a moment. 'There is,' he says eventually, 'but you'd be better off hearing it from someone else. Have you spoken with Dr Larson at all today? I mean, did you try and patch things up at all?'

'Not yet. I've been busy and I thought she'd still be at the scene,' I say. I'm also afraid of having the door kicked in my thoroughly deserving face, but I don't want to admit it to Dale.

'Go talk to her at the hospital. She'll explain.'

I puff out my cheeks. 'If you say so. Oh, and thanks for sorting me out last night,' I add. 'I don't know what came over me.'

'No worries. Everyone has that kind of trouble now and again. I'll see you later.' He hangs up.

I pluck up my courage and drive down to the hospital. To my relief, Gemma is alone in her office downstairs. I knock and walk in. She looks up at me without smiling, green eyes unreadable.

'Hi,' I say sheepishly. 'Can we talk?'

'I was worried you wouldn't want to,' she says. I can't detect any hint of blame in her tone; a good sign, or so I hope.

'Oh, I do.' Nerves lend my flow of words speed. 'I'm really sorry for what I did and the things I said last night. I hurt you and screwed up what was going to be a great evening with someone I care about.' I run my fingers through my hair. 'I know you must think I'm a jerk,' I tell her, 'but I want to say how bad I feel, and to ask whether you'd give me another chance.'

For what seems like an hour, Gemma sits in silence, eyes locked on mine. Then she looks away and her face relaxes. 'I don't think you're a jerk, Alex,' she says. 'Not yet, anyway.'

Relief floods through me.

'And I think maybe I know what came over you last night,' she continues. 'You've taken drugs for insomnia for ages, right?'

'Years, yeah. On and off.'

She holds up the bottle of pills I left in my jacket pocket. The jacket itself is on a worktop in the corner. 'And you've been taking these according to the instructions?'

'Two a night, just like it says.' Suspicion of what's been happening begins to creep over me. 'Dr Vallence gave me the prescription after he spoke to my doctor back in Boston.'

Gemma looks at my eyes, checking them as if she's examining something inside. 'How do you feel right now?'

'OK, I guess. What's wrong with the pills? I mean, they get me to sleep and everything like they're supposed to.'

'When the Sheriff's Department read through Dr Vallence's notes this morning they found your name in the prescription records on his desk,' she says, breaking eye contact. 'On the back he'd scribbled a note that suggested he told the pharmacist to give you a different drug than what was on your prescription. I said I had your jacket, with the pills in, so Sheriff Townsend asked the hospital lab to check them.'

She looks back up at me. 'What you've been given is called triazolam. It is used for treating insomnia, but it can have side effects, particularly if you take twice the normal dose.'

'Twice? What side effects?'

'Psychotic behaviour, increased irritability,' she says. 'The label on the bottle says that it contains lorazepam tablets. But you've actually been taking double the limit of something much stronger.'

'That sounds bad,' I say, a deliberate understatement.

Gemma nods. 'It is. Someone was trying to make you overdose, either to kill you or to make you useless as a cop. You're lucky it didn't have any worse effects on you than what I saw last night.'

'Well, I have had some pretty strange dreams.'

'Dreams?'

'And one or two hallucinations. I thought I might be on the way to another breakdown,' I add with an embarrassed smile.

Gemma's eyes widen slightly. 'Hallucinations?'

'Nothing bad, I promise. Look, I am going to be OK, right? I mean, this stuff doesn't fry your brain or kill your liver or anything?'

She smiles, showing the dimples in her cheeks. 'You'll live.'

'Good. And you don't think I'm an asshole?' As I say it, uncertainty blows across the surface of my memory. Did the drugs trigger my episodes, or was I already having them? Did I have the dreams and suffer the visions before I'd seen Vallence?

'No,' says Gemma. 'I don't think you're an asshole.'

I smile too. 'It's a real relief to hear you say that,' I tell her. 'Things have been complicated enough without ruining the one really good thing that's come out of being here. I don't, well . . .'

'Yes?'

Feeling a little bashful, I continue, 'I don't suppose you're free tonight, are you? We could maybe have another go at a second date.'

Gemma answers with a kiss, a lingering touch with little force and a sense of distant sweetness, cotton candy against my lips. When we finally break away she says, 'Eight o'clock again?'

'I wouldn't ask you to cook for us two nights in a row.'

'We'll send out for pizza.'

I HEAD BACK to Winter's End with the intention of grabbing a couple of hours' sleep before getting ready for seeing Gemma. When I pull up outside the Crowhurst Lodge I rest my hands on the wheel for a moment, tired mind still ticking over what I've learned. The foyer is as empty as ever when I walk through the inner door. I am surprised, though, when I discover that the door to my room is unlocked. Perhaps I've caught whoever passes for cleaning staff here at work.

I step inside. The TV is on, playing one of the music channels, and Sophie Donehan is on the bed, lying against the headboard with her knees hitched up in front of her, TV remote by her hand.

'Hi,' she says without looking round. 'I told the guy at the desk that I was a friend of yours and he let me in.'

'I haven't seen anyone at that desk since I got here. You must have struck lucky.' I don't mean to sound suspicious, but I do.

Sophie just shrugs. 'OK. I had a look at the guestbook and took a spare key from behind the desk,' she says in a flat, uninterested voice. 'It doesn't matter. I'll drop the key off on my way out.'

'Which only leaves the question of why you're here.'

'I heard about the doctor and that guy they found in Mason Woods.' I nod slowly, not yet able to see the relevance to her visit. 'And?'

'And I think maybe what I know might help you. Otherwise I wouldn't be here.'

'OK, I'm sorry.' I perch on the end of the bed. 'What've you got?'

Sophie straightens her legs so I'm no longer hidden by her knees. 'There's something else I remembered about that place. Something specific, y'know? It was just before I left. I was in one of the dormitories not far from some of the offices.' Her eyes have the unfocused glaze of reminiscence. 'It was night but I couldn't sleep because I had a cold and my throat hurt. I heard a man yelling, but it was muffled, like there was a thick door in the way. Then there was another voice, not so loud, talking back. I crept out of bed and opened the door a little. There was a light coming from one of the rooms further down the corridor, and I could hear the voices more clearly. The man was shouting, I guess to one of the older kids; I couldn't hear what he was saying back. The man got louder, then the kid said something else, real low, and everything went quiet. Then the crying started. It went on and on, sobbing and stuff, until I finally went to sleep. You don't forget a noise like that, especially in a big old house.'

It's interesting enough, but doesn't seem to be especially relevant. 'What does this have to do with the case?' I ask.

'You asked me if I remembered anything about the older kids,' Sophie says, shrugging. 'Anyway, all next day the nurse's office was shut because she was treating someone. I couldn't get any medicine for my throat.'

That seems to be about it. 'Thanks for telling me what you have, Sophie,' I tell her. 'If you think of anything else, give me a ring.'

'Sure.' Sophie slides her legs off the bed and stands up. 'Thanks for listening to me, Alex,' she says as she passes me on her way out. 'Most people round here think I'm crazy.'

'I know that feeling.'

She glances up at me, scanning my face. 'You look kinda tired.'

'The job's just been catching up on me, that's all.'

'OK.' Sophie shrugs, then reaches up towards me and plants a kiss firmly on my lips before leaving with a wave and a sly smile.

I close the door behind her, shaking my head, but before dropping back onto the bed for some well-deserved rest, I reach for the boxes of stuff my dad left with Ben Anderson. The photo from Vallence's den reminded me of something, and the only place I can think of to check it out is the bundle of pictures in my dad's things.

I untie the yellowed string binding them together and spread the photos out around me, looking for anything that stands out. After a minute or so, I pull two prints out and stare at them.

The first interests me because I don't recognise the person in the photo. A young boy, probably no more than five or six years old, looking at the camera with wide, staring eyes. The second shows my father in outdoor gear, with a belt of trees and a sliver of lake behind him, exactly the same as the picture in Vallence's den. Standing with him are Henry Garner and the doctor himself. A note in pencil on the back says: *Claye Lake. Josh's big catch (his turn with the camera)*.

My skin pricks and tingles as I look at the faces of the men, all of whom are now dead, two almost certainly killed by Nick. And what about the third—my dad? Is that why Nick seemed to know so much about him and the way he died?

Before I pack everything away, I lift up the last couple of items in the box and find, at the bottom, a single sheet of paper, yellow with age, which bears the St Valentine's name and emblem.

Some of Matthew's schoolteachers have complained about his behaviour. While he is not openly disruptive, they report that he has refused to do his homework on several occasions and pays little or no attention in class.

We may have to transfer him to another school. Our staff are doing their best to instil a sense of discipline in him as well as keeping an eye on him in case his behaviour is a symptom of anything more serious.

The note is signed: 'Henry'. I have no idea what it's doing in my father's things. Maybe he did some legal work for St Valentine's, I don't know, but the skin of my hands feels taut and prickly. The image of Vallence's fishing photo dances before my weary eyes. Garner, dead at the bottom of Black Ravine. Stern, in the wreckage of his car. Vallence, pitched forward in his office. My father, in the passenger seat next to me, blood running from his forehead. And the woman in the locket . . .

The woman in the locket was a victim of a crime that went unpunished for a long time . . .

What did those men do, kill her?

I abandon that thought as soon as it strikes me. My dad was about as far from being the murdering sort as it's possible to get. He had his failings, like anyone, but he wasn't a criminal.

That doesn't leave me with much. I need to know who the woman in the locket is, and for that I need Nicholas. I try phoning the cellular number he called me from, but the automatic message tells me that the phone I'm trying to call is turned off.

I lie on the bed, the photo of the three men overlaid by that of the nameless woman. She hovers, just out of reach, eyes wide and trusting, smile strong but somehow uncertain. A face now with a touch of familiarity about it. The cheekbones. The shape of the eyes.

Similar, so much so that I can almost believe there's a family resemblance, to the boy whose picture my father left in Ben's attic.

ANOTHER EVENING, another check on the time, another ring on the doorbell. My hands, damp with nerves, clasp a bunch of flowers and another bottle of wine.

Gemma makes me wait a little longer on the doorstep this time. She's wearing a tight black top, in deep contrast to her blonde hair, and a matching skirt. She smiles to see me and shows me in.

As promised, we send out for pizza. We lie back on the sofa, Gemma nestling in my arms, and watch *Hannibal*, eating take-out and drinking wine. About halfway through, we lose interest in the film, our attention occupied solely by each other. We make love slowly and gently, a tender but passionate entwining of bodies. Then again later, this time beneath her cool-smelling sheets. Gemma dozes off first and for a while I watch her as she lies still against me, feeling my heart beating in time with hers through the warmth of her chest.

I've always thought that it's when we sleep that humanity's true face is revealed. Our daily cares and worries disappear, and our features soften as we find the kind of peace that's a rarity during daylight hours. Gemma, with her tousled hair lying on her cheek and a faint smile on her lips, is perhaps the most beautiful sight I've ever seen.

My sleep that night is natural, blissfully deep and dreamless, something I haven't experienced since returning to Winter's End.

The dawn arrives and for the first time in what seems like for ever, I don't have to face breakfast alone in the echoing confines of the Crowhurst Lodge. Freed, I revel in the rediscovered joy of human company. Gemma and I part on the driveway as we each go our separate ways. The kiss we share is long and deep.

I reach the office to find Dale already there, along with Lieutenant Matheson. Dale gestures at the papers in front of him. 'Here's how things stand,' he says, for my benefit. 'The prints we found at Vallence's belonged to Nicholas. Time of death for the doctor was some time between two and four in the afternoon two days ago, during which time we know Nick called you from the doctor's house. Vallence was killed by a single cut to the throat with a blade we still haven't found. His car is gone, and, according to his neighbours, it's been missing since the afternoon before the prison break. This fits with what else we found at the doctor's home.

'There were three notes in his desk, all delivered by courier firms. One warned him that if anyone came carrying a locket with the photo of a woman in, he was to "take measures"—I figure that's where your fake prescription comes in, Alex. The order was backed up with the threat: "Look at what I did to your girlfriend if you're not convinced of my sincerity." The second note told Vallence to dig at the site of Garner's grave on the night in question, though it didn't tell him what to expect there. The last told him to leave his car in Houlton, half a block from the prison, and go home without it. We found Nick's prints on each of them.

'According to the phone company, the cellphone he called you from hasn't been turned on since, so they can't get its location. No one's reported seeing Vallence's car, anyone matching Nick's description, or anything to narrow down his location. The State Police are no longer setting up roadblocks, though they're keeping their eyes peeled. We've had nothing from the local PDs.

'On the bright side, we now have a much better idea of how he abducted Angela Lamond. The stolen car that Alex found in the woods is the same model and colour as that of one of the residents on Carver Street. She wouldn't have known it wasn't one of her neighbours until she was in a position for him to grab her.

'While that's good, though, we've still got dick to go on until someone spots him.' Dale drains half a cup of coffee in one swallow.

'Who was that nutcase who was out in the woods when we found Garner?' I ask him.

Dale raises an eyebrow. 'That's just Ellie Naylor. Why?'

'I ran into her again at St Francis's. She came out with the same kind of "work of the Devil" shit that Nick did in our interviews and she seemed to recognise the woman in the locket.'

Dale shrugs and reaches for his coffee. 'Just crazy talk, most likely.'

'How did she get like that?'

'She's Sophie Donehan's aunt. She lost it after her sister killed herself. She's harmless.'

'Could she have any connection to Nick, do you think?'

Dale shakes his head. 'She's a nut, Alex. Just like every other nut you've ever run into.'

I sigh, unconvinced, even though he has a point. 'Yeah, I guess.'

'Any other ideas?'

'How about coming up with a list of possible victims?' I suggest. 'Even if he only killed Vallence to tie up a loose end, there might be more to go before he's finished his business.'

Matheson shrugs. 'Surely he'd only kill to cover his tracks or if someone tried to stop him stealing a car or something?'

Dale looks at me, but I shake my head. 'No, he came here to finish something. I don't know what yet, but he's thought this through. When he killed Garner, he did it cleverly enough that no one even knew it had happened. I think there's a chance he's killed since, as well, but made the deaths look like accidents. This time, he got himself caught. Someone like that doesn't show himself unless it's not going to stop him doing what he's set out to do.'

'Who are you thinking of for these previous victims, Alex?'

'Joshua Stern, the town clerk, and'—I hesitate a second or two, a little unwilling to face the possibility—'and my father.'

Dale raises his eyebrows. 'You think he killed your parents?'

'My dad was his target. My mom was probably just a bonus.' I realise what I've said. 'Jesus, I feel bad for making it sound like that.'

I now understand why cops aren't supposed to get involved in personal cases if they can avoid it. Not because the thirst for revenge is too strong—though if Nick did kill my folks, I aim to see him go down for it—but because it becomes harder to think and talk like a cop. And you feel guilty every time you act like you would in any other case. It's a hell of a position to be in.

Dale seems to understand, and continues as if nothing's changed. 'Stern died in a car crash,' he says.

'And my dad was killed in a hit-and-run collision. They were both friends of Vallence and Garner. They all used to go fishing together.'

'Were there any other deaths around that time that might have been connected?' Matheson asks.

'I'd have to check the records,' Dale says. 'If I remember rightly, Stern died in the same year that Bob Kennedy, the Sheriff before me, had his heart attack. He used to know Winter's End pretty well. Had a cabin by the Aroostook River. I don't remember any others.'

'Sheriff Kennedy, huh? Didn't he get one of those notes after the fire at St Valentine's?' I say.

Dale shrugs. 'Yeah, but that was a couple of years before he died. There was no sign of foul play. Guy just had a weak heart.'

'Even so, you don't think there might be a connection?'

I don't get an answer. At the back of the squad room, the dispatcher calls out Dale's name.

'I've got a forest warden on the line, Chief,' he yells, an excited look on his face. 'He says he saw a car matching the one you're looking for up at the McWirren hunting lodge near Purser Lake.'

HALF AN HOUR LATER, rain is beginning to fall as I step out of my car and onto a dirt road hemmed in by rank upon rank of trees heavy with spring foliage. The ground between their thick dark trunks is dim and indistinct, shadows made worse by the gloom of the day. I follow the track for a couple of hundred yards before diving off to the west, towards the lakeside and the McWirren cabin.

I pull my collar up against the cold water that is falling with increasing force and join Dale, two of his deputies and four state troopers next to one of their cruisers. I find him talking with one of the troopers, apparently the first to arrive.

'Where the hell is the forest warden?' he asks. 'Didn't he say he'd meet us here?'

The younger man shrugs. 'He did, but he's not here now. You don't think he might be closer to the cabin?'

'Maybe, but I don't see his truck anywhere, either.'

'What's going on?' I ask Dale.

'The warden said he was going to sit tight and let us know if anyone came or went this way. I guess we'll have to go down to the cabin without him.' Dale raises his voice a little to be heard by everyone. 'There's a chance that if our man is down there, he could have a hostage. We'll walk so as not to alert him to our presence. Don't shoot unless you're sure of who you're shooting at. Let's go.'

I draw my pistol from my jacket and take the safety off. 'I don't like the sound of the warden being missing,' I say quietly.

'Neither do I. He might just have got nervous and bugged out.'

'I hope so.'

We fall silent again. The TV static noise of the rain hitting the leaves is the only sound to accompany us as we walk through the growing mire to the point where the track bends to the left.

The McWirren hunting lodge, a large log cabin of the sort rented out to vacationing families, squats darkly at the bottom of the hill within spitting distance of the grey waters of Purser Lake.

'No car outside,' Dale mutters. 'Could be round the back.'

'Still no sign of the warden, either.'

We fan out into the trees, three of us on either side of the track. The air beneath the leaves is damp and earthy, and pine needles deaden our footsteps as we sidle towards the building.

I reach the last line of trees before the cabin, and notice that the lodge itself still seems to be asleep after the winter lull, with heavy shutters over its windows and a carpet of twigs and old leaves covering the ground outside. If there have been any motor vehicles down here recently, someone must have expertly covered their tracks.

I glance across at Dale as our little force emerges from the greenery and advances cautiously towards the building, guns out.

'He's not here, Dale,' I say, holstering my gun.

'What makes you so sure?'

'Look at this place.' Two state troopers move slowly up to the front door, which turns out to be locked. 'No one's been here in ages. This has been a damn wild-goose chase.' I turn and start trudging back towards the slope alone.

'What about the warden?' he says after me.

I stop and look over my shoulder. 'How the hell should I know? A hoax, maybe, or Nicholas giving us the run-around. I'm going back to the cars. If I'm wrong and there's something here, give me a shout.'

I slog grimly uphill to where my 'Vette sits among the police vehicles. A pair of deputies are perched in their four-by-four, waiting.

'Any news?' one of them asks as I pass.

'Not yet. Place looks deserted.'

I slump into the 'Vette, sitting sideways with the door open and my mud-covered shoes outside while I have a smoke, out of the rain. I feel a little guilty about giving Dale a hard time down by the lake. I should apologise, and probably will once my mood improves.

Then the radio in the deputies' Jeep crackles into life, and one of the deputies calls me over. 'You'd better hear this,' he says.

'What is it?'

'This is Deputy Traynor over in Winter's End,' the voice on the other end of the connection says. 'I got called out to a report that someone was vandalising the graves at St Francis's church.'

'Uh-huh.'

'Turned out it was just one tombstone pushed over, but it had a note addressed to Deputy Alex Rourke laying on it.'

My fingertips begin to tingle. 'Which would be me. Who phoned up with the report? Did you get a description of the vandal?'

'A woman living across the street called it in about half an hour ago. She didn't get a good look, but she said it was a guy with dark hair and casual clothing. He drove off in a red pick-up. You want me to open the note?'

'No, no. It could always be a letter bomb or something. I'll be there in half an hour.'

I tell the two deputies to let Dale know what's happened then jump in the 'Vette and keep my foot down all the way to St Francis's.

So sorry to have missed you, Mr Rourke. Are you enjoying the hunt, or is the pressure starting to get to you? I take it you know about the doctor and how he had your pills switched. I wasn't sure what he'd come up with, but I have to say I admire his efforts.

Don't feel sorry for him, though. The man was scum, a criminal, though his worst offence wasn't in the records I left for you.

Do you know what it's like to have a loved one taken from you? I'm not talking about your parents here; even if that sedan hadn't finished them, old age would have had them soon. No, I'm talking about someone truly close to you, that you'd do anything to protect. Do you know how it feels when they die?

Do you know how it feels when they're killed by your own blood?

I look up from the note, running each sentence through my mind, looking for meanings, suggestions, conclusions. Deputy Traynor is hovering next to me by the open door of his Jeep.

'Bag the note and the envelope,' I tell him, still running its words through my head. 'Where did you find it?'

'There's a turned-over gravestone near the right-hand edge of the churchyard,' he says. 'You can't miss it.'

'Any other witnesses who might have seen him plant this?'

'Not that I could find.'

Through the gate, onto the sodden grass of the graveyard. Near the wall that borders the eastern side of the grounds I find the vandalised tombstone. As I reach it the wind suddenly gusts around me, driving ice-hard specks of rain against my skin. I duck down to get a closer look at the toppled stone.

JOANNA THORNE
BE AT PEACE, FREE AT LAST OF LIFE'S TRIALS

The pale grey stone is spattered with moss and lichen; from that and the lack of fresh flowers I guess that Joanna hasn't had any visitors in a while. So what made Nick choose her grave?

The part of my mind still turning over Nick's words settles on the last section of the note. I turn and jog back to the Jeep, then pick up the sheet of paper and run through it again.

Heart jumping, I reach for my cellphone. 'Dale, it's Alex.'

'We didn't find anything at the cabin, and we haven't been able to trace the warden—'

'Yeah, well it was probably Nick trying to get us haring all over the countryside while he was up here at St Francis's church. I need you to do two things for me, Dale.'

'Sure, Alex. Sounds urgent.'

'It is. I want you to get a couple of people down to the hospital and keep an eye on Gemma for me. We'll have to figure out somewhere safe where she can stay, but that can wait.'

'Nick threatened her?'

'Yeah, maybe.' I read the note out loud for his benefit. 'All that stuff about your loved ones dying sounds pretty threatening to me.'

'How did he find out about you and her?'

'Who knows. Maybe I'm getting worried over nothing but I'm not willing to take that chance.'

'OK, we're getting hold of Houlton PD right now. There'll be a couple of uniforms with her in a few minutes. Now what was the second thing you wanted?'

'Joanna Thorne. Died twenty-one years ago, buried here in Winter's End. Can you get hold of some information for me—who she was, how she died, that kind of thing? I'll come down and do some checking of my own, but it'd help if the ground's been prepared.'

'No problem.'

'Thanks, Dale.' I'm about to hang up when I think of something else. 'Oh, Dale,' I say, 'I'm sorry I was a bit grouchy this morning. Guess it's just eating at me that we haven't caught him yet.'

'Forget it, Alex,' he says. 'We all get like that sometimes. If you like, I'll give you some traffic duty while things are quiet. You could take out your frustration on the travelling public.'

'Tempting, but I'll settle for catching the son of a bitch.'

'You and me both. I'll see you later.'

JOANNA THORNE. Born in Bangor fifty-three years ago. Became a secretary at a law firm in Houlton after leaving college. At first, I think this might prove to be the link between her and my father, along with the rest of his circle of deceased friends, but it turns out that she worked for a rival group of lawyers. Left her job and moved to an apartment above a clothing store in Winter's End four years before she died at the age of thirty-two. Held a handful of low-pay jobs around town—store clerk, cleaner, kitchen assistant—until she became an alcoholic. Eventually passed out drunk in the street one January night and froze to death. Never married but had one child, a son called Matthew, to an unknown father nine months or so before moving to Winter's End. He became a ward of the state after his mother's death, and was sent to St Valentine's Home for Children. Any record of him leaving the home must have vanished in the fire.

Or did it? I think back to the note I found among my dad's things which mentioned a child called Matthew. Could they be the same, and if so, how was my dad involved in his stay at St Valentine's? It could be that his law firm dealt with Matthew when he was placed into care, or it could be that he took a liking to the boy during his visits to the home. And there are other possibilities, far darker, that prowl like sharks in the gloom beneath the surface of my thoughts.

From what little information exists about her, I can't work out why her life changed so dramatically after the birth of her son. Matthew would now be about the age we've estimated for Nicholas. His familiarity with the area, the burning of St Valentine's and his choice of gravestone to leave his note on would all make sense if Nick and

Matthew Thorne were the same. But why desecrate his mother's grave?

'Not interrupting, am I?'

The voice startles me out of my thoughts and whisks my attention back to the Sheriff's Department records office. Gemma, stepping quietly through the door, a half-smile, half-frown on her face.

I stand to meet her, giving her the best smile I can manage. 'No, I was just thinking, that's all.'

She moves as if to kiss me, but instead fixes me with her eyes and says, 'Alex, why am I being escorted everywhere by a pair of cops?'

I can't think of an easier way to put it. 'Because there's a chance that Nicholas knows about you and me, and might try to, well, get at me by doing something to you.'

'Oh,' she says, blinking a couple of times and lowering her eyes.

'He hasn't threatened you outright,' I tell her, trying to cushion things a little. 'But he talked about how it feels to lose a loved one, and I didn't want to leave you in danger. Hence the cops.'

I tell her what the note said.

'What about going home?' she asks. 'Or going to work? Am I supposed to take a break somewhere away from here?'

'At work, you should be OK. It would be hard for him to do anything without being seen. Staying at home is dangerous. He could break in and hide while you were out. So Dale's made up one of the spare rooms here in the courthouse. You should be comfortable enough for a few days. He says the department will even cover the expense of getting breakfast from one of the places down the road.'

She smiles briefly, then says, 'You think it'll be over in a couple of days, by the end of the weekend?'

The image of Nick sending us out on a bogus tip, just so he could tear up a grave and leave me a message, hangs in my mind. 'Yeah, maybe. There's a couple of things I have to find out first, though.'

THAT NIGHT I SIT in the darkened chamber in the Superior Court building, Gemma breathing softly on the couch opposite, and run through everything I've heard. The quiet, controlled tones of Nicholas blend and spill over into the older voice of Dr Vallence, Dale's gruffness, Earl Baker's lies, the woman at the museum.

If Nick was Matthew Thorne, an embittered former inmate of St Valentine's, I could understand why he'd kill Garner on the night of the fire. If Vallence helped the home's management cover up the abuse it inflicted, I'd also understand why he killed the doctor after blackmailing Vallence into helping him. But what about Joshua Stern and my father? Did Nick murder Stern and make his death look like an accident? Was he the driver of the car that killed my parents in Miami? Why would anyone want revenge on my dad?

Anger dies over time, and I've had my therapy and I think I've more or less come to terms with their deaths. I just wish I could somehow make up for all the times I didn't go and see them, or didn't feel like talking to them. I wish I could have patched things up with my dad earlier. I'm not the vengeful sort, but if Nick killed them I'd want to see him stand trial for it. And I'd want him to lose.

Most of all, I want this whole affair to be over so I can go back to my normal life. But to do that, I need to know what happened to make Nick the way he is. What tied Stern and my dad to Matthew Thorne? For that, I'd have to ask someone who knew my dad well.

THE SUN MAY BE UP, but I can't see it through the thick bank of dark cloud that hangs low over the woods near the McLean River. My watch tells me it's just past nine o'clock on a Saturday morning as I push through the thick, leafy foliage with Gemma in tow.

Twenty minutes' hike from where we left the 'Vette next to Ben Anderson's battered RV, and we're standing on a low bank of stone at the outside of one of the river's sweeping curves. I can just make out Ben a good distance downstream and some way out from the water's edge, casting his line expertly into the water.

'Hey, son,' he calls out as soon as we're close enough. 'See you've brought a friend, too.'

'Ben Anderson, Gemma Larson,' I say, making the introductions.

'Pleased to meet you. You two feel like joining me?'

'Afraid not. Are you having any luck?'

He shakes his head. 'Not today. Haven't had time to get a feel for the water, know where the fish are. What's on your mind, son?'

'You and my dad were pretty close, weren't you?'

There's a *swish* as the line arcs back across the water. 'Yeah, we were,' Ben says, keeping his eyes on what he's doing as he speaks.

'Do you remember him ever mentioning a woman called Joanna Thorne?'

The old man turns to regard me. 'What do you want to go asking after her for? No need to go digging up the past now.'

'I think the guy I'm looking for might be her son,' I say. 'I've got a suspicion he was involved in my father's death as well as Joshua

Stern's, and we already know he killed Henry Garner and Dr Vallence. Somehow, Joanna Thorne is linked to them, but only someone like you, who knew them all, can fill in the blanks for me.'

Ben stays still for a moment, just another rock in the river, before he wades towards the bank. 'Let's head back to the van,' he says. 'This kind of talk's better in more homely surroundings.'

The interior of the RV is in better shape than the outside. Gemma and I sit at a table spread with a cream cloth embroidered with tiny geese in flight, while Ben potters around making coffee. Eventually he produces three steaming mugs and sits opposite.

'What do you want to know about Joanna?' he asks.

'How she knew the four men. Anything that could lead her son to murder. I know he grew up in St Valentine's after she died, but that wouldn't explain why he killed Stern or my father. If he did,' I add.

Ben nods. 'First, you have to understand something: your dad loved your mom. He really did. But he had his weaknesses, too.'

'And Joanna was one of them?'

'He had an affair with her what, twenty-five, thirty years ago now. Didn't last long. A couple of months, I think. A few of us knew— Josh, Nathan, Henry, me, a couple of others. I didn't have much to do with it, but some of them used to cover for him, saying they were going up to the cabin for a weekend's fishing. Then they'd head somewhere else while he and Joanna had the cabin to themselves.'

The thought of my father cheating on my mom all those years ago leaves me feeling strange, a little unnerved. 'And that was it?'

'Not exactly,' Ben says, almost apologetically. 'A little while after it was over, she got in touch, said she was pregnant and that he was the father. Guess that'd make her son your half-brother.'

10

A hole opens in my chest and my senses begin to drain away through it. Everything I thought I knew about my upbringing, childhood—hell, my whole life—is falling down and there's nothing to take its place. I thought I was comfortable being Alex Rourke, only child, no living relatives. But I'm not any more because it's not true any more.

I have a brother.

Not only that, but I have a brother who's a killer. A brother who might well have murdered my mom and my—his—*our* dad.

'What did he do?' I ask, gulping down a couple of swigs of coffee to ease the dryness of my throat.

'He wouldn't have anything to do with her. Didn't want to break up his family, I guess, not with a kid of his own already.'

'Which is why she moved from Houlton to Winter's End,' I say quietly. 'She was trying to stay close to him.'

'Used to see her around town sometimes. We never spoke—I don't think she even recognised me—but I used to try to help her out if I could. Generous tips when she was waitressing, that kind of thing. Sweep the path outside her place in winter. Work dried up, I guess, and I stopped seeing her so often.'

'And she hit the bottle.'

'If you say so,' Ben says, shrugging. 'Like I said, I stopped seeing her around after a while. But I heard what happened from Josh. Your dad told him she'd called at his house, desperate for money. He reckoned she was trying to blackmail him, told her to leave him alone, shut the door on her. A couple of days later, she was dead.

'She didn't have no family, so the boy was headed for the children's home. I guess he would've been about five or six by then. Your dad asked Josh, being town clerk, to make sure his name was never mentioned on any of the records. Nathan and Henry kept quiet about what they knew, and I think one of them might have said something to old Bob Kennedy 'cos he didn't look too hard at what she was doing with her evenings before she died.'

I turn the warm mug in my hands. 'My dad used to visit St Valentine's when I was a kid,' I say softly, looking back with new light on old memories. 'He used to take toys and stuff for the children. I thought he was just being kind to less fortunate kids. But he did it because he had a son there?'

'I guess. Your dad was a good man,' Ben says, equally softly. 'He wanted to make sure the boy was all right, but he didn't want to lose your mom and you because of the mistake he'd made.'

'I went with him a couple of times,' I continue. 'Played with some of the kids. It could have been my brother I was playing with, but he never told me.'

'He was trying to work things out as best he could.'

I think of what Nick—Matthew—has become. His words: *Do you know what it's like to have a loved one taken from you? Do you know how it feels when they're killed by your own blood?* He blamed my father for the death of his mother. He hated the others for helping brush the past under the rug and for his treatment at St Valentine's. He said he came back to bring me here. Why? For having the life he didn't?

I sit in silence for an age, staring blankly through the mug, into the distant past. I don't know what prompted Dad to be unfaithful, just as I don't know what made him break off the affair. Did he leave Joanna because he loved my mom, or because of me? I think maybe Ben was right, and that he'd tried to work things out as best he could, but he couldn't turn his back entirely on his offspring, illegitimate or not, after Joanna died. That's certainly what I'd like to think.

Gemma lays a hand on my arm, and says, 'Are you all right, Alex?'

'Hard news to hear now,' Ben adds from the opposite side of the table. 'Some things are best left forgotten. Wish they could have stayed that way.'

'DALE, IT'S ALEX. Any developments?' I'm parked at a gas station not far from Smyrna Mills, having dropped Gemma off at the Superior Court building. I need to go somewhere quiet and clear my head, and there's only one place I've got in mind to do it. Where it all started, and where my dad tried to end it. Gemma isn't happy about it, but she understands. First, though, I guess I should check in.

'Hi, Alex.' Dale pauses. 'Everything OK?'

I stare through the windshield, eyes focused on nothing much. 'Yeah. It's fine. Have you got anything on Matthew Thorne?'

'We're building up quite a life history on him. The banks have been very cooperative.' I hear paper being turned over at the other end of the line. 'Matthew Thorne, twenty-six. We're still tracing his early educational history, but he doesn't seem to have gone to college. First employment records start at the age of sixteen. Mostly low-key stuff—store clerk, delivery driver—but then things get interesting.'

'Yeah?'

'Worked at a locksmith's in Milwaukee for four months, then a stint with a demolitions firm in Detroit. After that he skipped to Atlanta and worked at an auto-wrecking yard, then a library in New Jersey. That takes him almost up to the time of the fire at St Valentine's, and he can already pick locks and knock down buildings. God knows what else he learned.'

'Then what?'

'There's a blank around the fire itself. He pops up about six months later at a mail-order company based in Pennsylvania selling military surplus to wannabe soldiers. A stint as a mountain guide in Nevada, librarian at a college in New York State, then there's another break, but credit cards seem to have him staying at a couple of motels further north for a few weeks.'

'At the time Joshua Stern died, right?'

'Right,' Dale says. Then he pauses, so I ask the inevitable question. 'Where was he when my folks were killed?'

'Miami. Working as an auto mechanic.'

'Oh my God.'

Dale doesn't comment, just continues with his list. 'After that he goes back to wandering again. Store clerk in Virginia, bartender in Kansas City for a while. Small-time stuff.'

I blink once, twice. 'Kansas City? When?'

'About six months after your parents died. Stayed for a few weeks.'

'Jesus. I was in hospital in Kansas City then.' My mind is doing cartwheels, trying to work out how long Nick—Matthew—has been stalking me, working on his revenge.

'Anything you want us to do?'

'Not right now,' I say, shaking my head. 'I just need some time.'

'Sure, Alex.' Another pause. 'The guys said you and Dr Larson took off somewhere this morning. Anything new crop up?'

'I'll tell you later,' I say. Then I hang up. 'Maybe.'

THE STONY TRACK that winds up to Claye Lake. I bring the 'Vette to a halt beneath a slate-grey sky and spend a moment looking through the trees, mostly birch and fir, to where a stream tumbles down the hill in flashes of white foam and silvery water. The cabin is somewhere out of sight beyond the crest of the slope.

I'm not sure why I'm here. Some idea of revisiting the ghost of my childhood at one of its symbolic anchors, maybe. The view from the track leading up the slope is one I've carried with me since the first time I saw it, filled with excitement at the thought of spending a weekend up here with my dad.

Childhood events shape the rest of our lives, Mr Rourke.

Nicholas's words, back in the interrogation room. A shudder runs through my body as other things he said come back to me.

Claye Lake. A small cabin thirty yards or so from the lake. Trees running all the way down to the water's edge.

293

You remind me of the boy struggling to catch fish on Claye Lake under the watchful eye of his beloved father.

Claye Lake, where my father used to take Joanna Thorne for their secret trysts. Where Matthew, now Nicholas, was probably conceived. Where the lies began.

She was a victim, Mr Rourke. A victim. 'One of yours?' Laughter.

Is this the hiding place he prepared before killing Angela Lamond? I think about calling Dale and letting him know my suspicions. But I don't know if he'd be willing to send back-up out all this way on no more than a hunch, particularly after yesterday's wild-goose chase. And there's a part of me that doesn't want him here, if Nick is at the cabin. This is my place, and if anything is to happen here, I don't want to share it. It's as if I owe that to the memory of my father. I take my cellphone out of my pocket and turn it off.

I check my Colt and make sure I'm carrying a spare clip before opening the car door and stepping out into the rain, feeling the same anticipation I did the very first time I was here. Then, gun in hand, I jog in a hunter's half-crouch up the hill towards the cabin.

Still hidden in the sodden, moss-lined woods, I crest the top of the slope not far from where the stream begins its downward journey. In front, Brightwell Mountain vanishes into the clouds at the far end of the granite-coloured waters of Claye Lake. The cabin, tough and seasoned wooden boards over stone, it stands thirty yards or so from the water's edge. Next to it, what looks like Vallence's ageing Honda and a dark red pick-up. Light spills dimly through the windows of the building.

I tighten my grip on the gun and break across the short stretch of clear ground between me and the truck, careful to make as little noise as possible. When I'm safely tucked next to the vehicle I risk a quick look at the cabin before scuttling forward to the shelter of the wall by one of the smaller windows.

Keep low, to the rear of the cabin. The straggle of trees leading down to the water looks empty, and the wooden jetty that runs ten yards or so out onto the lake seems to be deserted.

Back to the front. I lift my eyes cautiously over the edge of the window. No sign of Nicholas, so I try the door.

Unlocked. I cautiously push it open and step inside.

The living room runs all the way to the western wall of the building on my right. Someone has tacked papers up above the mantelpiece, some kind of plans or notes, perhaps. A TV is on, but silent, at the far end of the room. On my left is the door that I remember leads to the kitchen, ahead is another, standing slightly ajar, that takes you to the bedrooms at the back of the cabin. The building is quiet save for the sound of rain thudding on the roof.

First I check the kitchen, pushing the door and swinging through the opening just as I was taught so long ago, gun ready but not held too far from the body, careful to check the corner behind me. The door at the other end of the long kitchen, which leads into the dining room and pantry, is open. The kitchen itself shows signs of occupation: clean washing-up on the draining board, food on the worktop.

I move through and into the dining room. Like the small pantry off to one side, it is empty, but again shows signs of habitation. A pair of muddy boots sits on the mat by the back door.

I return to the living room, intending to head next for the bedrooms, when a voice says, 'It's amazing what you can catch in these waters, if you're patient enough.'

Nicholas. The sound has a scratchy, metallic edge and seems to be coming from the far end of the living room. A speaker, I guess.

'Hello, Nicholas,' I call out. 'Or should I call you Matthew?'

'At last you've managed to work out the truth, brother. I was wondering how long it would take.'

A chill that has nothing to do with my rain-soaked clothes steals over me as I get my first good look at the papers on the walls. Photographs, newspaper clippings, records both typed and written. The black and white mugshot from my high-school yearbook sits next to an article from my college newspaper about baseball. My graduation photograph sits below it. Further along are a string of clippings from local newspapers, all of them about cases I worked on at the Bureau. A couple of blurry pictures of me in my FBI days are interspersed between them. At the top of the display is a set of print-outs from the Robin Garrett Associates web site. Almost my entire life is plastered on the walls, the object of an obsessive's focus. I swallow, trying to get some moisture back in my throat. I feel like my past has been pinned inside a display case like a museum exhibit.

'How did you know I was coming?' I say.

There's a dry laugh. 'Smile, brother. You're on candid camera.'

I look at what I had taken for a TV, in reality a closed-circuit camera monitor, and next to it, the cabin's phone. The light next to the 'speaker' button glows red. It is from here that Nicholas's voice emanates. The glowing screen shows my 'Vette sitting in the rain. He must have called the cabin's number from his cellphone when he saw me coming, and he's just been waiting for me to find his nest, with my life history on display like a hunting trophy.

As I look up from the screen I notice two colour pictures that lie at the heart of Nick's montage. The first shows my parents' headstones up close. The second shows an orderly little crowd wearing black, most of them facing away from the camera. A priest in black robes, reading a passage from the leatherbound book in his hand. And me, standing next to him, looking down past knotted hands to a pair of identical coffins, each of which bears a single wreath.

'You might be my father's son, Matthew,' I say, staring at the photo, 'but you're a long way from being my brother.'

Perhaps it's a whisper of air as the door leading towards the bedrooms opens, perhaps the faint sound of a foot landing on the carpet, but I hear something move behind me.

I turn quickly, but only quickly enough for Nick's fist to hammer into my jaw. I feel a couple of teeth wobbling as my mouth fills with blood and I stagger backwards into the wall. Before I can fight back, Nick follows up with a punch to my gut that knocks all the wind out of me and leaves me slumped on the floor.

'I could have killed you before, Alex,' he says, slamming his foot into my ribs. 'I thought about finishing you off in Miami while you were still passed out in the wreckage of your car.'

'Why didn't you?' I rasp, blood dribbling down my chin. Hearing Nick admit that he killed my parents, coupled with the image on the wall from their funeral, threatens to bring back the pain and anger I felt over three years ago. Somehow, I've managed to keep hold of my gun, but I don't have the strength to lift it.

'I decided to learn more about you, the brother I never knew, who had the life I should have had.'

'I didn't kill your mom,' I say. 'And I never knew you existed.'

'Sins of the father, Alex.' Nick takes another kick at my ribs, but on reflex I bring my knees up and the blow catches me on the shin.

'You didn't have to kill him, you son of a bitch!'

'No, but I hadn't thought of a suitable alternative back then. Besides, I'd already dealt with the others. I figured Vallence might still be useful, particularly once I'd decided what to do with you.'

He turns away from me and walks across to his wall display. I can see the butt of a pistol wedged behind a clock on the mantel, within easy reach of where he stands.

'This is your life up here on this wall, Alex. High school, the FBI, therapy, going private. Your parents.'

I manage to climb to my knees, despite the pain in my ribs. 'Yeah?'

'Your career tanked after your breakdown, didn't it? You've got no family—except me, of course—and few friends. I couldn't ruin your past, but I could dig up some old secrets that would destroy people's memories of it.' He looks back at me and smiles. 'Our father's reputation will be in tatters once they all know what he did.'

I use the wall at my back to help me get to my feet. 'Bullshit, Matthew. You're under arrest,' I say, cradling the Colt in both hands to keep my aim steady. 'Get your hands—'

'My mother, an innocent woman, died because of your father. I was abused for years by people like Garner because of him, and the people who covered for him. Do you have any idea how that feels?' he yells. 'But I'm not done with you, brother. There's one more thing I need you to do for me.'

'Shut up and place your goddamn hands on your head before I blow a hole through it!'

He takes a short step forward, smiling. 'Do it, Alex. Kill me. I want you to. There's no one here to see you.'

'What the hell are you talking about?'

'I want you to become a murderer, a failed cop who shot an unarmed suspect for his own satisfaction. It'll destroy everything you've got left.' He raises his voice a notch, pride and bitterness in equal measure. 'At last you'll have to face everything I did. No life worth speaking about. Trapped for ever, wondering what might have been. I don't know if I'll be able to watch you from where I'll be, but if not we can always compare notes when you get to Hell.'

'Shut the fuck up and stick your hands on your head.'

'I killed your mom and dad, Alex. You wouldn't believe the planning I had to put in to make sure I smashed into your car at that intersection with enough speed to waste them both. I even had to pay some kid to phone me when you were a couple of blocks away.'

I blink as sweat runs past the corner of my eye, struggling to keep focused on the man in front of me.

'I had a look at your car once I'd picked my way out of my air bag. I leaned in through the hole where your windshield was and checked Dad for a pulse. You know what I'd have done if I'd have found one?' His smile widens and hardens. 'I'd have grabbed the back of his head and slammed his face into the dashboard, over and over again until all you'd have seen when you woke up would have been a mass of pulped flesh where his face used to be. And I'd have enjoyed it.'

My pulse sounds loud in my ears, but not loud enough to drown out his voice. The gun feels hot and heavy in my grip. The trigger seems to be drawing itself back beneath my finger.

'Then I would have done the same to your mother,' he says. 'I'd have pounded her shattered skull until it split.'

I can't seem to breathe. Killing Nick seems so easy. Then I start to hear a voice, my father's. I can't make out what he's saying, but the calm, soothing tones are unmistakably his. A fragment of memory, perhaps, synapses firing without reason in my battered brain.

Nick smiles. 'It's a shame you didn't have a wife or some kids I could have dealt with next. Of course, I've got the chance to do that now.' He pulls out a blurred Polaroid of Gemma walking into the Superior Court building with her police escort and adds it to the display on the wall. 'I like her, Alex. I think I'll kill her next.'

I blink and swallow drily, then adjust and tighten my grip on the gun. Nick's smile broadens. I breathe in. 'Maybe I've got more of my father in me than you have,' I say through a parched and sticky mouth. 'Maybe it's something else. But there are places where we differ. I'm not a murderer. I'm taking you in.'

The room bleeds back into view as I breathe out. Nick's smile fades and twists as he realises that I'm serious. 'Perhaps you're right,' he says. 'You might not be a killer. But I am.'

With that he whips round, grabbing his pistol from the mantel, swinging towards me. The rage in my half-brother's face is clear to see as I squeeze the trigger once, then again. Blood blossoms from his forehead and chest and for a moment he seems to hang still, frozen in the split second before his muscles fail and gravity takes over. He slides to the floor, gun falling useless at his side.

I let out a long, shuddering breath, wincing with the pain that flares from my broken ribs. Then I take a last look at Matthew Thorne before trudging towards the front door.

Outside, I take out my phone and turn it on again. I call Dale.

'Alex!' he says as soon as he picks up. 'Where are you? I tried calling but I couldn't get through.'

'I'm at the cabin by Claye Lake. Nick's here.'

'We're on our way.' I can hear his chair scraping back and his footsteps against the floor of his office. 'Does he know you're there?'

'Yeah, no, it doesn't matter.'

I put the phone away and sit on the ground by the front of the cabin. I feel empty, drained. It's a hard thing to kill someone, even more so when they're family. Did I do right? Could I have hit him in the shoulder and disarmed him instead? I lean my head back against the wall of the cabin and let rain splash against my face.

It barely seems a moment later that Dale's Jeep crests the hill, going flat out with its lights blazing. Dale jumps out, followed by one of his deputies. Both men are packing shotguns.

'Alex! Are you all right?' he says as he reaches me.

'I'm alive,' is all I can say in reply.

11

Dale drives me down to the hospital in Houlton. I entrust Deputy Andy Miller with the keys to my 'Vette and he promises to deliver it to the Superior Court without wrecking it. I spend most of the journey staring out of the window in silence, watching the trees flash past and, later, the miles of lonely green fields.

As we approach the I-95 interchange, Dale tries to draw me out of myself. 'He was a murderer, Alex,' he says. 'Whether he was really your brother or not doesn't matter. You did right.'

'Yeah, I guess,' I reply, watching oncoming traffic kicking up spray from the road. I turn to look at Dale. 'Why do you think Nick and I turned out so different? He was so full of anger over things I never even knew about. I don't think I could ever get like that. But we came from the same place and the same source. I don't get it.'

He shrugs. 'You're asking the wrong person. Just be thankful you weren't both the same.'

'I guess.'

GEMMA COMES TO SEE ME while my injuries are being treated at the hospital. She doesn't say much—I guess she knows I'll talk if I want to—but clasps my hand and rests her head on my shoulder. What few words she does share with me are soft and warm, and they haul me out of my melancholy.

Dale drops by again later on, to see if I'm up to answering his questions and filling in the paperwork for the State Attorney

General's Office that follows any police shooting. I tell him I'll do it tomorrow, and he seems happy with that. In fact, he seems pretty happy all round, I suppose because he's managed to wrap up the Lamond case without help from another police department or agency. His stock must have risen quite a bit in the county, and I don't begrudge him his success.

Gemma takes me home and I'm asleep almost from the moment I pull the covers up around me.

The following morning I drive back to Winter's End to collect my things, which gives me the distinct pleasure of checking out of the Crowhurst Lodge. I walk down the silent staircase for the last time, my bag slung over one shoulder. As usual, the front desk is unoccupied. Rather than attempt to summon someone by ringing the bell, I sneak up to the thick wooden door behind the desk, and push it inwards, unsure of what awaits me.

It opens onto a narrow room, cluttered with papers, mouldering ledgers and handwritten notes. At the far end is a table. On it are an old portable TV, an electric kettle and a huge collection of coffee jars and milk powder. The whole room smells dark and sour.

The old man who manages the hotel is sitting in front of the TV, watching reruns of *M*A*S*H*. 'What are you doing back here?' he says, startled by my presence. 'Guests aren't allowed here.'

'Um . . . I'm checking out. Send the bill to the Sheriff's Department; they're paying.' I look at the TV. 'You do this all day, every day?'

'Not always the same programme,' he says, as if that explains everything. Maybe it does. 'Why, what business is it of yours?'

I shake my head. 'It's just . . . nothing. I'll be off now.'

Outside, the clouds have passed and the sun is shining once more. The trees around the parking lot are a vibrant, healthy green. I drive down to the blacktop of the highway and turn southwards. Winter's End seems cheerier, and perhaps a little busier than it was. I can't tell whether it's really that way, or if I'm just looking at it differently.

I'm about halfway through town when I see Sophie Donehan walking down Main Street, dark hair glinting in the sunlight. I pull up in front of her and wind down the window.

'Hi,' she says, her smile an upturned curve of dark lipstick.

'Hi. If you're still set on getting out of here, I'll probably be leaving at the weekend.'

'Yeah, I heard everything was finished. They said you shot a guy.'

I nod. 'I did,' I say. 'Though I don't know if I'm happy or not about killing him. So, do you want to go or not?'

'No, I think now I'll stay for graduation and the summer break. I'm starting college in the fall.'

'Yeah? Whereabouts?'

Sophie gives me a sly smile. 'Boston,' she says, 'so I'll probably see you later, Alex.'

She gives me a peck on the cheek, then walks off with a backward glance and a wave over one shoulder. I pull away from the kerb.

The familiarity of Winter's End still stirs up memories, but no longer with the same force as when I first returned here over a week ago. The streets are just rows of houses, the people just ordinary folk from an ordinary town. The past no longer intrudes on the present.

I SPEND A WEEK attending to the paperwork from Nicholas's shooting, and watching Dale tie up the remaining details of the case. On the Tuesday, the State Police announce that they've arrested Arthur Tilley, the pharmacist who switched my prescription on Dr Vallence's orders. He breaks down completely during questioning and admits changing the pills, working with Vallence in the prescription drugs trade, his morphine addiction, everything. I suspect he'd have confessed to killing JFK if he'd been asked.

The department's efforts to track down the other senior staff from St Valentine's begin to bear a little more fruit. Sarah Decker, under her married name of Sarah Weir, turns up on a missing persons' report filed by her husband nearly four years ago. Dorian Blythe's fate remains a mystery. I may be wrong but my guess is that the remains of both of them are buried somewhere, or lying at the bottom of a lake or river. A couple of other former inmates of St Valentine's come forward as the story hits the press and give their own versions of what life was like there. Dale manages to keep any mention of Matthew being my half-brother out of the papers.

I stay with Gemma at her house in Houlton for the entire week, an arrangement we both find surprisingly comfortable, and one that allows us to learn ever more about one another. The days are glorious, the evenings beautiful and the nights wonderful, aside from some discomfort from my three broken ribs. Our time together is by far the happiest I can remember in a long while.

At noon on my last day in Houlton, I reluctantly lug my bag out to the 'Vette. Gemma and I embrace long and tightly. The colour of her eyes, the brightness of her smile and the warmth of her body are already safely locked in my memory, keeping me going until the next time I see her. Not perfect, but it'll do.

I climb into the car and fire up the engine. As I head west, I find myself wondering once again about Joanna Thorne and the other family, the other past I so nearly had.

I drive up the stony track to Claye Lake again, this time under the brilliance of the springtime afternoon sun. There's some police tape on the door to the cabin, but it's not enough to distract me from the beauty of the place. At the far side of the mirror-smooth water, swaths of evergreens blanket the slopes of Brightwell Mountain, the streams between them resembling flashing rivulets of quicksilver. The forest around the cabin is full of the scent of leaf mould, rising sap and old, healthy wood. Birdsong chimes from the branches.

I walk round to the back of the cabin and onto the jetty. I sit on the weathered wooden planking with a can of my dad's favourite brand of beer and look out across the lake, silver-blue beneath the sky. Then the two of us talk for an hour or so, just like we used to before we fell out, drinking beer and watching the world grow older. It's what we should have done when I left to go to college, and what I never got the chance to do again after the crash. We don't talk about anything much, just father–son stuff, but I feel better for it.

When I'm ready to leave, I take Matthew's locket from my jacket and look at it one last time. I draw back my hand and fling it as far as I can, into the lake. The tiny piece of scratched gold arcs away from me, glinting in the sun until it hits the water. It disappears leaving barely a ripple, taking the past with it.

Then I say goodbye to my dad and walk away.

JOHN RICKARDS

John Rickards guards his privacy closely, but he agreed to tell Condensed Books readers a little bit about his writing career. 'I was studying Environmental Engineering at university when I first started writing. I can't remember what sparked me off; I guess it's just a way of making a living that suits someone with an overactive imagination and an ability to type quickly! After graduation, I walked straight into a job in journalism, working for publications in the UK, the Far East and the US. I still do some freelance journalism, although these days I mostly write books. It already feels strange to be on the other side of an interview!

Winter's End grew out of its opening scene. I could picture that moment in the rain and I had one of those stray thoughts—what can the cops do if the guy won't tell them who he is? Once I started thinking "why is he there?", "why won't he tell them?", "who is he?" everything else followed. In order to keep the story going, there had to be multiple answers to all those questions, plenty of layers for Alex to work through, yet it all had to tie together.

'I've spent some time in Maine and I liked it as a setting, particularly for this kind of story. Southern, tourist-trap Maine has the same old-world feel as much of the rest of New England, while the far north is comparatively desolate and isolated—exactly the sort of thing I was looking for. I've got an eidetic memory, not as good as a photographic one but still handy for picking up impressions of a place. Because I'm not a Maine native, though, I did as much research as I could—I had to be able to go into some detail because Alex grew up there.

'My second novel, currently titled *The Touch of Ghosts*, is with my editor now. Hopefully she likes it! It's similar in tone to the first, and it's about a string of disappearances in a snowbound town where night always falls early. Although I've written other things before, they've mostly been for my own private embarrassment. My first student effort was dreadful; I made every classic first-time-writer error there is. You live and learn.'

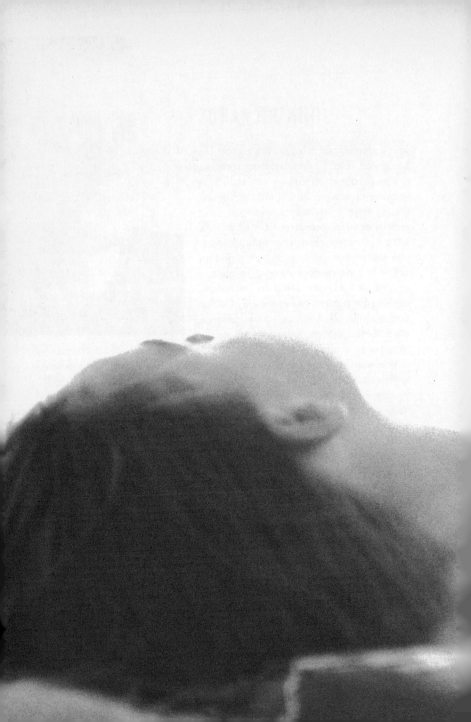

peter lovesey
the **house** sitter

It's an idyllic summer's afternoon
and the beach at Wightview Sands is
crowded with swimmers, sunbathers
and children playing. As the sun
begins to set, everyone is packing
up and starting to drift away.

Everyone, that is, except the young
woman behind the windbreak.
Those nearby assume she is asleep.
Until the tide comes in—and still
she doesn't move. Suddenly, the
awful truth dawns . . .

After lunch Georgina Dallymore, the assistant chief constable at Bath, took an hour off work and drove out to the cattery at Monkton Combe. She'd decided to board Sultan while she was away on holiday. She needed to be sure it was a place where he would be treated kindly. He wouldn't get the devoted attention he got at home, but he was entitled to some comfort, and she was willing to pay.

She expected a better response than she got.

'He's a long-hair, then,' Mrs O'Leary, the cattery owner, noted without a word about his good looks. 'He'll need grooming.'

'Every morning.'

'Getting down to basics, has he been done?'

Georgina frowned. Even an officer of her rank didn't always catch on immediately. 'I don't follow you.'

Mrs O'Leary gave a wink, raised two fingers and mimed the action of scissors. 'I won't have rampant males making nuisances of themselves in Purradise.'

This was the moment Georgina decided there was no way Sultan would be happy in Purradise. 'I don't think I need take up any more of your time,' she said. 'I've several other addresses to visit.'

'Please yourself. You won't find one better than this.'

'I'll make up my own mind, thank you. Good afternoon.' Georgina turned and walked with dignity towards her car.

'Stuck-up cow,' Mrs O'Leary said. 'You'll end up paying through the nose for some house sitter who runs up enormous phone bills and burns holes in your carpet.'

But she wasn't heard.

one

If you were planning a murder and wanted a place to carry it out, a beach would do nicely. Think about it. People lie about on towels with no more protection than a coating of sun screen. For weapons, there are stones of all weights and sizes, pieces of driftwood, rope and cable. After the deed is done, the tide comes in and washes everything clean. Your footprints, fingerprints, traces of DNA, all disappear. Scenes of crime officers, eat your hearts out.

Every half-decent weekend in summer, the shoreline at Wightview Sands on the Sussex coast is lined with glistening (and breathing) bodies. The sand is clean and there is plenty of it, in sections tidily divided by wooden groynes. Lifeguards keep watch from a raised platform. There are no cliffs, no hidden rocks, no sharks.

This Sunday morning in June, the Smith family, Mike, Olga and their five-year-old daughter, Haley, arrived shortly before eleven after an uncomfortable drive from Crawley, paid their dues at the gate, and got a first sight of the hundreds of parked cars on either side of the narrow road that runs beside the beach.

'Should have started earlier,' Mike said.

'We'll have plenty of time to enjoy ourselves,' Olga said.

'If we can park this thing.' The heat had really got to him.

They cruised around for a bit before slotting into a space on the left, sixty yards past the beach café. They took their towels and beachbags from the boot. Mike suggested a coffee, but young Haley wanted to get on the beach right away and Olga agreed. 'Let's pick our spot first.'

They didn't want to sit too close to the lads with shaven heads and tattoos who had several six-packs of lager lined up beside them. Or the howling baby. They found a space between three teenage girls on sunloungers and a bronzed family of five who were speaking French. Mike unfolded the chairs while Olga helped Haley out of her clothes. The child wanted to run down to the sea with her bucket and spade.

'Remember where we are,' Olga told her. 'Just to the right of the lifeguards. Look for the flags. Stay where we can see you. Don't go in the water without us.'

Haley ran off.

'If I don't get my fix of coffee soon, I'll die.' Mike went in the other direction.

Olga sat forward in her chair and watched every step Haley took.

Briefly Olga's line of sight was blocked by a woman choosing the best place to sit. She took a few steps down the beach, spread a large blue towel on the sand, unfurled a windbreak and pushed the posts into the sand to screen herself on three sides. To Olga's relief, she could now pick out the tiny figure of Haley again, jumping in the shallows.

The woman took off her headband and shook her copper-coloured hair loose. She was around thirty, Olga reckoned, watching her delve in her beachbag and take out sun screen and a pair of sunglasses. Finally she sank out of sight behind the windbreak.

Mike returned with his hands full. 'Where's the kid? I got her an ice cream.'

Olga pointed Haley out. 'You'd better take it down to her.'

'My coffee's going to get cold.'

She laughed. 'All right. Give it to me.' She took the ice cream down the beach, threading a route through the sunbathers.

Haley had found two other girls about her own age and was helping them to dig a canal. She didn't want the ice cream.

'Shall I eat it for you?' Olga offered.

Haley nodded.

'You remember where we are? Near the lifeguards. And the flags.'

Another nod.

Olga turned and made her way back more slowly, licking the sides of the ice cream. The beach looked entirely different from this direction. She set a course for the flags above the lifeguard post, beginning to doubt if Haley would have the sense to do the same. Before spotting Mike, she passed the woman with the copper hair, now down to a white two-piece and spreading sun screen on her middle. Their eyes met briefly. She had a nice smile.

'She all right?' Mike asked, propping himself on an elbow.

'She's with some other girls, digging in the sand.'

He lay back on the sand and closed his eyes.

Typical Mike, she thought.

Olga lifted the lid off her less-than-hot coffee, still watching her child. Just ahead, a man in a black T-shirt crossed Olga's line of vision. She could see his top half above the windbreak. He was talking to the copper-haired woman. From the tone of the conversation, they knew each other and he was laying on the charm and not getting the response he was trying for. To Olga's eye, he was rather good-looking, broad-shouldered, with black, curly hair and the cast of face she thought of as rugged—that is to say, strong-featured. His voice was more audible than hers. 'How does it go? Of all the gin-joints in all the towns in all the world . . . What are you doing here?' She made some reply and he said, 'OK, that was pretty dumb. It's a nice surprise, that's all. You don't mind if I join you for a bit?' Then: 'Fair enough. Suit yourself. I'll leave you to it. I just thought—oh, what the fuck!' And he moved off, the smile gone.

In another twenty minutes the tide was going out amazingly fast across the flats. Haley hadn't moved, but she was no longer at the place where the waves broke. She was at the edge of a broad, shallow pool of still water. The other girls were no longer with her.

'I think I'll go and talk to her,' Olga said. Mike murmured something about fussing.

She made the journey down the beach again, marvelling at the huge expanse of sand now opened up. Haley looked up and waved.

After admiring the excavations in the sand, Olga asked if she was ready for some lunch. Hand in hand, they started back.

'Race you.' She let Haley dash ahead and then jogged after her to make it seem like pursuit, until the risk of tripping over a sunbather forced her to slow to a walk. Already Haley had reached Mike and given him a shock by throwing herself on his back. Laughing, Olga picked her way through the maze of legs, towels and beachbags. The copper-haired woman looked over her sunglasses, smiled again and spoke. 'Wish I had her energy.'

'Me, too.'

Olga flopped down beside Mike and reached for the lunch bag.

Mike revived with some food inside him and actually began a conversation. 'Amazing, really, all this free entertainment. Years ago, people would buy tickets to see a tattooed man. One walked by just now with hardly a patch of plain skin left on him. No one paid him any attention.'

'I wouldn't call that entertainment.'

'Then there are the topless girls. Over there. On the sunbeds.'

She took a quick glance. 'Trust you to spot them. When are we going for a swim?'

'Not now, for Christ's sake. It's miles out.'

Haley asked, 'Can I bury you in the sand, Daddy?'

'No chance.'

Haley sighed and went down the beach to look for her new friends. Olga, reassured that the child wouldn't get lost, opened a paperback. The afternoon passed agreeably, more agreeably for Olga when the topless women turned on their fronts.

She may have slept for a while after that. She felt a prod in her back and seemed to snap out of a dream of some sort. The paperback lay closed beside her.

'Time to face it,' Mike said. 'The tide's turned.'

Olga heaved herself onto her elbows and saw what he meant. That big expanse of sand had disappeared. 'Oh, my God. Where's—'

'She's OK. Over to the right.'

Haley and the others were playing with a frisbee.

On the way down to the sea, Olga interrupted the frisbee-throwing to tell Haley they wouldn't be long.

The waves had reached the stretch of beach that shelved, so getting in was a quick process, and the water wasn't as cold as she expected. After the first plunge, the two of them held hands and jumped the waves.

They stayed in longer than they realised. The people closest to the incoming tide were gathering their belongings and moving higher up.

'Where's Haley?'

Mike didn't answer. He took a few quick steps higher up and looked around.

'I can't see the girls she was with. Oh, God. Mike, where is she?'

'If she's lost, someone will have taken her up to the lifeguards. I'll check with them. You ask the people who were sitting near us.'

She dashed back to their spot. No sign of Haley. The woman with copper hair was lying on her side as if she'd been asleep for hours, so Olga spoke to the teenagers.

'No, I'd have noticed,' one of them said. 'She hasn't been back since you ate your sandwiches.'

Olga asked the French family. They hadn't seen Haley either. She looked up to where the lifeguards had their post, a raised deck with a wide view of the beach. Mike was returning, looking about him anxiously. She felt the pounding of her heart.

'The lifeguards are going to help us to find her,' he said when he reached her. 'They say she's probably come up the beach and wandered into the wrong bit. All these sections between the groynes look the same.'

'She'll be panicking by now.'

'Yes, but it's up to us not to panic, right? You stay here. This is the place she'll come back to. One of us must be here,' he said. 'I'll check the next section.'

She remained standing, so as to be more obvious when Haley came back—if she came back. Appalling fears had gripped her. A beach was an ideal hunting ground for some paedophile. Supposedly a non-believer, she started saying and repeating, 'Please God, help us to find her.' She was shivering, more from shock than cold. She folded her arms across her front gripped by fear and guilt. How selfish and irresponsible she had been to stay so long in the sea.

'Isn't that your little girl?'

'What?' She snapped out of her stupor.

One of the teenagers was beside her. 'With the man in the red shorts on the bit above the beach.'

'Oh, my God!' Haley, for sure. She was holding the hand of a strange man. Olga started running up the beach towards them. 'She's mine! That's my child! Haley!'

Haley shouted, 'Mummy!' and waved her free hand. The other was gripped by the man, a shaven-headed, muscled figure in tight-fitting red shorts that reached to his knees. He didn't attempt to leave.

Continuing to shriek, 'He's got my child! That's my child!' Olga scrambled up the steep bank of pebbles.

As soon as she was close enough she shouted, 'What are you doing with my child? Let go of her!'

She heard him say, 'I just found her. I'm the lifeguard.'

The man released Haley, who flung herself at her mother.

'What happened? Are you all right, darling?'

'Oh, Mummy—I was lost. This man found me.'

He said, 'Did you hear me, Mrs? I'm the lifeguard. She was in our hut. One of her friends went there for first aid.'

'One of those girls I was playing with was hit in the face by the frisbee,' Haley said. 'She's all right now. Her mummy came and took her away. I was left. I couldn't see you anywhere.'

Olga felt tears streaming from her eyes. She'd had a big fright. She apologised to the lifeguard and thanked him, then carried Haley back to their spot. Mike hadn't returned but the people around smiled and asked if Haley was all right. Olga explained what had happened.

The tide was coming in. People were packing up all around them. The French family dismantled their windbreak and folded their towels. The teenagers said goodbye and carried the loungers back to the store. Of those around them, only the copper-haired woman appeared intent on staying until the tide forced her to move.

'Where's Daddy?'

'He went looking for you. He'll be back soon.'

Olga started to fold the towels and fill the bags.

Presently Haley asked, 'Why isn't that lady packing up? Her feet must be getting wet.'

Haley was right. The woman hadn't made any attempt to move. Olga couldn't see her properly. The windbreak was round her head and shoulders. Probably if Olga hadn't already made such an exhibition of herself she would have popped her head over the canvas and said, 'You'd better move now, sweetie.' The experience with Haley had temporarily taken away her confidence.

Olga looked around for Mike, and there he was at last, striding towards them.

'Brilliant! She came back, then. Are you OK, Hale?'

Haley nodded.

Mike kissed her forehead. 'Thank God for that.'

Olga started to explain, but was interrupted by Haley.

'Mummy, don't you think we ought to wake the lady up? She's going to drown.'

'God, yes. Mike, you'd better go to her. She's out to the world. I don't know what's the matter with her.'

He said, 'It's none of our business, love.'

'There's something wrong.'

With a sigh that vented all the day's frustration, he stepped the few paces down the beach to where the water was already lapping right around the windbreak. He bent towards the woman. Abruptly he straightened up. 'Bloody hell—she's dead.'

'ISN'T THIS A JOB for the police?' Mike Smith said.

The lifeguard gave him the look he used for people who drift out to sea in inflatables. 'By the time they get here, sport, she'll be three feet under water.'

'Have you called them?'

'Sure.'

Ankle deep in the water, they lifted the corpse and carried it up the shingle and past the lifeguard post to the turf above the beach, watched by a sizable, silent crowd. The lifeguard opened a nearby beach hut.

'We'll take her in there.'

Once the dead woman was deposited on the floor of the narrow wooden building, Mike started to walk away, but the lifeguard said, 'Hold on, mate. You can't leave. You found the body. The police'll want to talk to you. They should be along shortly.'

'I'll tell my wife, then. She's waiting in the car.'

'You're coming back?'

'Sure.'

Mike marched to the car park, got in the car and started the engine.

'Is that it?' Olga asked. 'We don't have to talk to the police?'

'We've had enough hassle for one day. We're leaving.' He put the car in gear and drove across the turf to the exit.

'Are you sure this is right?' Olga asked.

'We can't tell them anything. We don't know who she was or why she snuffed it. All they'll do is keep us here for hours asking idiot questions.'

Inside five minutes they were in a long line of traffic heading away from the coast.

POLICE OFFICERS Shanahan and Vigne stood outside the open door of the beach hut where the woman's body lay. They hadn't gone right in.

'Are we one hundred per cent certain she's dead?' PC Shanahan asked. He seemed to be in charge, young as he appeared with his innocent blue eyes and smooth skin.

'You've only got to look at her,' the lifeguard said.

This they were in no hurry to do.

'It's not up to us. A doctor has to certify she's dead.' Shanahan turned to PC Vigne, who looked at least five years his senior. 'Haven't you sent for the police surgeon, lamebrain?'

Vigne used his personal radio.

'What happened to her things?' Shanahan asked.

'Things?'

'Bag? Clothes?'

'She was lying on a blue towel. Didn't notice a bag.'

'We'd better go and search. We won't know who she is until we find her bag. Where exactly was she lying?'

They closed and padlocked the door of the hut and walked along the path above the beach. The waves were rattling the pebbles and the exact spot where the woman had been found was two feet underwater already.

'Is that the towel?'

'Where?'

Shanahan pointed. He had spotted something blue shifting in the foam at the margin of the tide. 'Would you mind?' he asked the lifeguard. 'We're not dressed for the water.'

So the towel was recovered, a large, plain bath towel. A search of the bank of shingle above the sea produced nothing else.

'Great,' Shanahan said. 'We're supposed to identify this woman from one blue towel and the costume she was wearing.'

The lifeguard was more upbeat. 'At the end of the day you'll find her car standing all alone in the car park. That's your best bet. Most people come by car. This beach isn't the sort you walk to.'

'Unless someone nicked the car as well.' A few years in the police and you expect no favours from fate.

They radioed back to say they were unable to identify the dead woman and some of her property was missing. They were ordered to remain at the scene and wait for the doctor. So the three men sat in the sun on the canvas seats outside the hut, with the wind off the sea tugging at the policemen's shirts.

Some time later, a woman in a suit and carrying a bag stopped in front of the three of them reclining in the sun, and said, 'Nice work, if you can get it.' This was Dr Keithly, the police surgeon.

They all stood up.

'You've got a corpse for me, I was told.'

'In that beach hut,' PC Shanahan said.

The lifeguard explained how the body was found. 'Do you want me to open up, doc?'

'Well, I hate to spoil the fun but . . . please.'

Presently Dr Keithly stood in the entrance to the hut beside the feet of the deceased. 'I could do with some light in here.'

'I'll fetch a torch.'

Torch in hand, she stepped around the outstretched legs. She was silent for some time, crouching beside the body.

Shanahan stood in the doorway. 'What's the verdict, doc?'

Dr Keithly stood up and stepped out, removing her plastic gloves.

'She seems to have been strangled. Didn't you notice the mark around her neck? I'd say it was made by a ligature. And there's some scratching on this side where she tried to tug it away from her throat.'

'Christ.' Shanahan said. 'How could this have happened on a

beach in front of hundreds of people? Wouldn't she have screamed?'

'Not if it was quick and unexpected,' the doctor said.

'I'd better report this,' Shanahan said. 'It's out of our hands if it's murder.'

two

Two hours were left before sunset. The local CID had arrived in force and sealed off the stretch of beach where the body was found, but they need not have bothered. Most visitors had left at high tide when only a small strip of pebbles remained.

Henrietta Mallin, the senior investigating officer, was already calling this case a bummer. A beach washed clean by the tide couldn't be less promising as a crime scene. There was no prospect of collecting DNA evidence. The body itself had been well drenched by the waves.

The SIO was known as Hen, and superficially the name suited her. She was small, chirpy, alert, with widely set brown eyes that checked everything. But it was unwise to stretch the comparison. This Hen didn't fuss, or subscribe to a pecking order. Though shorter than anyone in Bognor Regis CID, she gave ground to nobody. She'd learned how to survive in a male-dominated job. Fifteen years back, when she'd joined the police, she'd been given more than her share of the jobs everyone dreaded, just to see how this pipsqueak female rookie would cope. But she'd always reported for the next shift. Strength of mind got her through. She'd gained respect and steady promotion without aping male attitudes. There was only one male habit she'd acquired. She smoked thin, wicked-smelling cigars, handling them between thumb and forefinger and flicking off the ash with her smallest finger.

She turned to one of her CID team. 'How many cars are left in the car park?'

'About twenty, guv,'

'What time does it close?'

'Eight thirty.'

She checked her watch. 'Get your boys busy, then. Find out who the cars belong to, and get a PNC check on every one that isn't spoken for. The victim's motor is our best hope. I'm tempted to say our only hope. Have you spoken to the guy on the gate?'

'He didn't come on duty until two. He's got no memory of the victim, guv. They just lean out of the kiosk and take the money. Thousands of drivers pass through.'

She went through the motions of organising a line of searchers to scour the beach, now that the tide was on the ebb. They began picking up an extraordinary collection of discarded material: carrier bags, cans, an odd shoe, scrunchies and empty cigarette lighters. Everything was bagged up. She watched with no expectation. There was no telling if a single item had belonged to the victim.

'Did anyone check the swimsuit? Labels? Is it a designer job, or did she get it down the market? Might tell us something about this unfortunate woman.'

'The towel she was lying on is top quality, pure Egyptian cotton,' the one other woman on the team, DS Stella Gregson, said.

'There speaks a pampered lady.'

'I wish,' Stella said. She was twenty-six and lived alone in a bedsit in a high-rise block in Bognor.

'Never mind, Stell. Some day your prince will come. Meanwhile come up to the hut and give me your take on the swimsuit.'

Stella had a complex role in the CID squad, part apologist for her boss, part minder, and quite often the butt of her wit. She'd learned to take it with good humour. Her calm presence was a big asset at times like this. Together they crunched up the steep bank of pebbles.

'We can assume she was murdered some time in the afternoon,' Hen said. 'The lifeguard didn't notice any stiffening of the muscles when they carried the body up the beach. As a rough estimate, rigor mortis sets in after three hours or so. I'd like the opinion of the pathologist but . . .'

'She was strangled here?' Stella said in disbelief. 'On a public beach?'

'I know,' Hen said. She paused to draw breath at the top of the bank. 'My first reaction was the same as yours, Stell, but I'm changing my mind. We can assume she was lying down, like most people on a beach, and she had a windbreak round her head and shoulders. That means the killer was screened on three sides. She'd be relaxed, maybe with her eyes shut. Even asleep. On sand she wouldn't hear him arrive. He flops down as if he's going to sunbathe with her. When he thinks no one is watching, he pulls the ligature over her head and tightens it before she knows what's happening. If anyone did get a look, they could easily think they were snogging. Any sound she makes will be muffled.'

Stella gave a shrug that meant she was dubious, but couldn't supply a more plausible theory.

They found the lifeguard sitting outside his hut. His duties had ended two hours ago, but he'd been told to wait. Hen asked him his name. It was Emerson. He was Australian.

'You were here keeping watch, Mr Emerson,' she said to him. 'Didn't you see what happened?'

'Sorry.'

'You lads have little else to do all day except study the women. Didn't you notice this one?'

'She was some way off. There were a couple of thousand people here, easy.'

'Do you remember *anyone* who was near where she was found?'

'The guy who told us about her.'

'Describe him.'

'About thirty. Tall and thin, with short brown hair. Do you want his name?'

Hen said with more approval, 'You got his name?'

'Smith. And he has a kid called Haley.'

An interested tilt of the head. 'How do you know this?'

'Earlier in the afternoon she was lost. Smith came up here and reported it. He just said his missing child was called Haley Smith, aged five, and he described her. He told me where they were sitting and I said he should try the beach café, where the ices are sold. But I found the kid myself, only a short way from here. I handed her back to her mother.'

'The mother?' Hen said, interested. 'You met her mother as well?'

'Right. A bottle blonde, short, a bit overweight. Red two-piece.'

'So you saw exactly where these people were on the beach?'

'I didn't go right over. The mother ran up when she saw the kid.'

'Where was Haley's father at this time?'

'Don't know. Still searching, I guess.'

'So Haley was returned to her mother? Then Mr Smith comes back and tells you he's found a dead woman?'

'That was a good half-hour after. Around four thirty. I went back with him to look and it was true. She was lying face down, stretched out. The tide was already washing over her. We got her up here and into the beach hut.'

'How did you know she was dead? Did you feel for a pulse?'

'No need.'

She said with a sharp note of criticism, 'You've had first-aid training, I take it? You know you should always check?'

'She'd gone. Anyone could tell she'd gone.'

'That isn't good enough for someone in your job, Sunny Jim.'

The lifeguard didn't answer.

'So you dumped her in the hut and put in a nine-nine-nine call. Why didn't you ask Smith to stick around after the body was brought up here? You must have known we'd want to speak to him.'

'I did. I said, "The police'll want to talk to you." He said he needed to tell his wife what was going on. He promised to come back, but he never did.'

'They hardly ever do,' Hen said. With a knowing glance at Stella, she turned away and the two of them stepped inside the beach hut. Hen directed the torch beam up and down the corpse. 'Any observations?'

'Would you point it at the head, guv?' Stella knelt and studied the line of the ligature, gently lifting some of the long red hair. 'The crossover is at the back here. Looks as if he took her from behind. Difficult to say what he used. Not wire. The mark is too indefinite. Leather, maybe, or some fabric?'

'Let's ask the pathologist,' Hen said. 'I thought you were going to tell me how she rates in the fashion stakes.'

So Stella fingered the hair, looking at the layers. 'It isn't a cheap haircut. She went to a good stylist. And the manicure looks expensive too.'

'The swimsuit?'

'Wasn't from the market, as you put it. See the logo on the shorts? She won't have got much change out of two hundred for this.'

'A classy lady, then,' Hen said. 'No jewellery, I notice.'

'No ring mark, either.'

'Did they find any sunglasses?'

'No. Dropped on the beach, maybe. We can look through the stuff the fingertip search produced. Thanks, Stell. Let's see what the car-park trawl has left us with.'

Soon there wouldn't be much daylight left. The sky over the sea already had an indigo look to it. In the car park, a few of the search team tried to look busy when Hen and Stella approached.

'Eight thirty. Car park closed. So what are we left with?' Hen asked the sergeant in charge. 'How many unclaimed vehicles?'

'Four, ma'am. Two Mitsubishis, a Peugeot and a Range Rover.'

'Did you check with the PNC?'

'Yes, guv. Two have women owners. That's one of the Mitsubishis and the Range Rover.'

'Who owns the four-by-four.'

The sergeant read from his notes. 'Dr Shiena Wilkinson, thirty-seven Pine Tree Avenue, Petersfield.'

'And the Mitsubishi owner?'

'A Ms Claudia Cameron, Waterside Cottage, near Boxgrove.'

'It doesn't prevent a woman from driving the others,' Hen said. 'However, let's start with the obvious.'

Dr Shiena Wilkinson's Range Rover was parked near the entrance gate, a black vehicle in mint condition.

'I need to get inside.'

'We'll have to break in unless you're willing to wait, guv,' the sergeant said.

'As you must have discovered, my darling, there are women who will, and women who won't. I belong to the second group.'

A jemmy did the job, at some cost to the side window. Hen put on gloves and overshoes and stepped inside. In the glove compartment she found a roll of peppermints, a bottle of cologne and a small bag of silver coins, presumably for parking machines. Nothing so useful as an address book or diary. Dr Wilkinson's medical bag was out of sight in the storage space at the rear.

'Order a transporter, Stella. I want this vehicle examined by forensics.'

The Mitsubishi owned by the Boxgrove woman was some distance away, near the beach café and close to the last remaining barbecue. This owner was not as tidy as Dr Wilkinson. The floor of the car was littered with used tissues and parking tickets. A pair of shoes. Sweet wrappings. The tax disc was a month out of date.

The jemmy came into play again, but not for long. From behind them came a scream of, 'What the bloody hell are you doing to my car?' and a woman came running from the barbecue.

'I thought you told me the owner wasn't around,' Hen muttered to the sergeant.

'WE HAVE A POSSIBLE VICTIM, playmates, and I stress that word "possible",' Hen told her team, assembled for the first formal briefing. 'She is Dr Shiena Wilkinson, from Petersfield.'

'Don't we have a positive ID yet, guv?' one of the team asked.

'Later this morning, I hope. One of the other doctors at the health centre where she works is going to the mortuary. Dr Wilkinson's thirty-two and a GP. She'd arranged to take three days off, Saturday to Monday. Likes going to the beach, apparently. But before we all get too excited about Dr Wilkinson, let's get back to what we know for certain.'

She took a drag at her cigar and pointed with it to the colour photo on the board behind her. The woman's wide-open eyes had the glaze of death and the mouth gaped. 'All that was found with our victim was the two-piece swimsuit she was wearing. The towel was recovered from the water not long after. We were told she was partly hidden by a windbreak, but it was missing when our patrol arrived. Going by the quality of the towel and swimsuit, she wasn't short of cash. She had a nice haircut and well-kept nails. No jewellery.'

'Do you think the motive was theft?' George Flint asked. George was the pushy sergeant who wanted Stella's job.

'It has to be considered. But you don't need to commit murder to nick a handbag from a beach. People take amazing risks with their property every time they go for a bathe. She may not even have had a bag with her,' Hen pointed out.

'So where did she keep her car key?' George asked. 'Where were her clothes? In the car?'

'We found no clothes in the car, and no bag either.'

'Then the killer walked off with her clothes, or her bag, or both.'

Hen tilted her head. 'But theft may not be the real motive. The killer may have taken the bag to make identification more difficult.'

'What's left if we rule out theft?'

'Wise up, George. Most killings are carried out by people in a close relationship with the victim. Family, lovers, ex-lovers.'

George Flint had hammered away at this theory for long enough. It was another voice that asked, 'Guv, do we know if she was alone on the beach?'

'We know nothing. The lifeguard on duty claims he didn't see her alive. The witnesses all left before the patrol car arrived.'

'What about this lifeguard? Is he a suspect?'

'He's an Australian named Emerson, and he's not comfortable. I dare say there are things he doesn't want us to know about how he got the job. Maybe he hasn't got a work permit. But to have killed her, he'd have needed to leave his post for a while, and someone might have noticed.'

'He could ask one of his mates to cover for him.'

'For what reason?'

'Who knows? He recognised her as someone who dumped him some time in the past?'

'Not much of a motive,' George Flint commented.

'We need to find this guy who alerted the lifeguard. He was asked to remain at the scene, and didn't. We have a description of sorts. Tall and thin. Short brown hair. Around thirty years of age. And we have his name . . . Smith.' She timed the pay-off like a stand-up comic and got the laugh she expected. 'He has a wife or partner, short, a bit overweight and with dyed blonde hair. Also a five-year-old daughter called Haley.'

'Are we regarding him as a suspect?' a youngish DC asked.

'Because he left the scene, you mean?'

A sergeant across the room said dismissively, 'He called the lifeguard. We can rule him out.'

'Not yet, we can't,' Hen said. 'It's not unknown for the perpetrator to blow the whistle. Let's say Smith is our principal witness. I want to talk to all three members of that family and anyone else who was on that stretch of beach. I'm going to put out an appeal on the local TV news tonight.'

THE SMITHS LIVED on a housing estate in Crawley, close to Gatwick Airport where Mike was manager of a bookshop—the terminal bookshop, as he called it in his darker moods. Monday had been chaotic, with two staff off sick, the phone forever ringing and a problem with one of the tills. He wasn't in a receptive frame of mind when he finally got home at six thirty.

Olga worked in the local Safeway, an early shift that freed her in time to collect Haley from school at three thirty. She had seen the *Sun*'s headline: STRANGLED ON THE BEACH, and was appalled to discover it referred to the dead woman at Wightview Sands.

'I've been waiting all afternoon to talk to you,' she said as soon as Mike came in. 'I tried calling the shop, but I couldn't get through.'

'Something up?' he said without much interest.

'This.' She held the paper up. 'It's the woman we found, Mike. They're appealing for witnesses.'

His manner changed abruptly. 'You haven't phoned the police?'

'Not yet. I thought you'd like to speak to them.'

'Whatever for? We didn't see anything.'

'I *spoke* to her, for God's sake. She was sitting right in front of us.'

'They want witnesses to a murder, not people making small talk. You'd be done for wasting their time.'

'That isn't true, Mike. It says they want anyone who was there to come forward, however little they saw. We can tell them what time she arrived and about the guy who tried to chat her up.'

'I didn't see anyone.'

'You were asleep. She wasn't amused, and he walked off, not too pleased. It didn't amount to anything, but . . .'

'If it didn't amount to anything, forget it. Other people may have seen something. We didn't. We're minor players. They don't want the likes of us wasting their precious time.'

'Do you think so?' The force of his words was starting to tell on Olga.

'I know it. And what can we expect if we call the police? They'll tear us to shreds. They won't believe we sat on the beach all afternoon and saw sod all. The woman was murdered a few yards away from us. How come we didn't notice? We'll look a prize pair of idiots.'

Olga hesitated. She hadn't thought of this.

'You know what I think?' he said. 'I think she was killed while we were swimming.'

Olga was relieved. 'That's what I was thinking, too. When we came back from our swim, and Haley was missing, I thought the woman was asleep,' Olga recalled, picturing the scene. 'She was very still. She could have been dead already.'

'The whole point is that we don't know because we saw nothing,' Mike said. 'I'm keeping out of this, Olga. Our life is heavy enough. We can do without this.'

He'd talked her round. She was uneasy, but she didn't want another argument. There had been too many in recent days.

HEN MALLIN CALLED St Richard's Hospital at eleven thirty and asked if Dr Mears, a colleague of Shiena Wilkinson, had been in as arranged to identify the body recovered from Wightview Sands. He had not. A call to the health centre revealed why. One of the doctor's patients had collapsed with chest pains. Dr Mears was in attendance.

Hen got through two cigars deciding how to pitch the TV appeal. It was a tough decision whether to name the Smiths and their child, Haley. Normally you kept children out of it, but this name pinpointed them and might prompt friends and neighbours into asking if they were the Smith family in the news. On balance, she thought she would go for it. She would also ask for other witnesses. Plenty of the public had been on that stretch of beach when the body was found.

By the time she went in front of the cameras she would expect to know if the dead woman was Dr Wilkinson. She could show a photo —and ask for help in tracking her movements up to the moment of her murder.

Satisfied with what she would say, she went for a late lunch in the station canteen. Hen had a theory that in this job she could never be certain where the next meal would come from, so she stoked up with carbohydrates like a marathon runner packing energy before the race. Steak and kidney pie and chips today, followed by apple tart and custard. She claimed she could go for hours after a lunch like that, though she wouldn't turn down a good supper.

At two thirty-eight, a call came in from a car park attendant at Wightview Sands. Hen was back in the incident room to take it.

'Yes?'

The speaker was self-important, and he obviously had difficulty accepting a woman as chief investigating officer. 'Am I speaking to the senior detective in charge of the murder investigation?'

'Yes. Have you something to tell me?'

'Are you sure you're in charge?'

'Look, do you have something to tell me, squire, or not? We're very busy here.'

'A lady here would like a word with you.'

'Put her on, then.'

The new voice was easier on the ear, low-pitched for a woman, well in control. 'I understand you've taken possession of my Range Rover. My name is Shiena Wilkinson. How do I get it back, please?'

HEN MALLIN'S TELEVISION APPEAL needed some rapid script changes now. So it was Stella who drove out to Wightview Sands and met Dr Wilkinson. Not an easy assignment.

After she'd been on TV, Hen returned to the incident room and told her team they weren't just to sit around and wait for witnesses to get in touch. 'What about the other two cars left there yesterday evening?'

The keeno, George Flint, produced a notebook. 'The Mitsu was registered to a guy by the name of Thomas West, two-one-nine Victory Road, Portsmouth, and the Peugeot is down to a Londoner, Deepak Patel, eighty-eight Melrose Avenue, Putney.'

'Follow it up, would you, George? See if there's any link with a missing woman.'

Stella said, 'Speaking of missing persons, I looked at the Missing Persons Index. You know how it is, guv. Thousands of names. It could take another week before our victim gets on the MPI. We're talking about a missing adult here, not a kid.'

'Keep checking each day. Do we have the list of all the objects picked up on the beach?'

'That's in hand.'

'Get it on my screen by six tonight. And, speaking of tonight, does anyone have a problem working overtime?'

No one did, apparently.

NOTHING STARTLING EMERGED in the next twenty-four hours. The television appeal brought in over seventy calls from people who believed they had seen the victim on the beach on Sunday. As Hen remarked to Stella, 'I'm beginning to wonder if there was anyone on that bloody beach who *wasn't* female with copper-coloured hair and a white two-piece swimsuit.'

George Flint spoke to the owners of the Mitsubishi and the Peugeot. Each had good explanations for leaving their vehicles in the car park overnight. The Mitsubishi had run out of fuel and its owner had got a lift back to Portsmouth from a friend who vouched for him. He'd returned with a can of petrol the next day. The Peugeot owner had gone for a sea trip along the coast to Worthing with some friends in a motorised inflatable and returned too late to collect his car. No women were involved in either case.

The inventory of items found on the beach gave no obvious clue. A pair of Ray-Ban sunglasses with a broken side-piece could have belonged to the victim, but how could you tell without DNA or fingerprint evidence?

'Why does anyone choose to strangle a woman on a crowded beach in broad daylight?' Hen asked Stella. 'I don't buy theft as the motive. I really don't. There's something else at work here.'

'Crime of passion? A man she's dumped gets so angry that he kills her.'

'What—follows her to the beach?'

'Or they drive there together to talk about their relationship, and she tells him it's over. He turns ballistic and strangles her. Then he picks up her bag and returns to the car park and drives off. It

325

explains why we didn't find her car at the end of the day.'

'That part I like. The rest, not so much. The strangling was done from behind, remember, and with a ligature. He took her by stealth.'

Stella didn't see any problem with that. 'So they had their row and she told him to get lost and turned her back on him because she didn't want to argue any more. He used anything that came to hand.'

Hen said, 'It's more likely he brought the ligature with him.'

'I still think this was a spur-of-the-moment thing. If it were planned, he'd have taken her somewhere remote.' A fresh thought dawned on Stella. 'What if she was wearing some kind of pendant on a thin leather cord? He grabbed it from behind and twisted it.'

'Better. You might persuade me this time. But you're making a couple of assumptions here. First, the killer is a man. All right, the odds are on a man. Second, that he drove her there. *She* could have done the driving. Or even a third person. Until we get a genuine witness, all this is speculation. The people we've got to find are the Smiths. Why haven't they come forward?'

THE POST-MORTEM was conducted the following morning by James Speight, a forensic pathologist of long experience, with Hen Mallin in attendance, along with Stella Gregson, two scene-of-crime officers and two police photographers, one using a video recorder.

Hen had to be patient in this situation. Dr Speight gave minute attention to the marks around the corpse's neck, having the body turned by stages and asking repeatedly for photographs. He pointed out some bruising in the nape area, probably made by pressure of the killer's knuckles. He noted the two scratches above the ligature mark on the right side of the neck and said indications of this kind were not uncommon, where the victim had tried to pull the cord away from her.

'I can't see any pattern or weave in the mark, yet it's fairly broad, more than half a centimetre. Not so clear-cut or deep as a wire or string. It could have been made by a piece of plastic cable or a band of leather or an extra thick shoelace. Certainly from behind. That's where the pressure was exerted. Death was pretty quick, going by the absence of severe facial congestion and petechiae.'

'Could she have screamed?'

'Once the ligature was in place, I doubt it.'

'So if he surprised her from behind, under the cover of a wind-break, people nearby wouldn't have known?'

Dr Speight gave a shrug. 'A guttural, choking sound, perhaps.'

'Like waves breaking on a beach?'

The doctor smiled. 'Romantic way of putting it.'

He continued with his task, removing the clothes and passing them to the SOCOs, and taking swabs and samples. The internal examination confirmed that the unknown woman had definitely died of asphyxiation, not cardiac arrest. The findings gave minimal assistance as to identity. She was about thirty to thirty-five and sexually experienced, but had not given birth.

'So what's new?' Hen muttered to Stella as they left. 'Don't know about you, but I need a smoke and a strong coffee.'

By THREE TWENTY each weekday, you couldn't get a parking space in Old Mill Road, where the junior school was. Parents massed outside the gates and waited for their offspring to emerge. Haley Smith was always one of the last, and Olga was always waiting for her.

Today, unusually, the class teacher, Miss Medlicott, walked across the playground with Haley, hand in hand.

'I've done a lovely picture, Mummy,' Haley called out, and waved a sheet of paper so energetically that it was in danger of tearing.

Olga nodded, searching Miss Medlicott's face for some clue as to why she was with Haley. 'Beautiful!' she said without really looking.

'It's the seaside.'

'Isn't it lovely?' Miss Medlicott said with a warm smile at Olga. 'I'd like a word, if you can spare a minute.'

'Of course.' Olga turned to Haley. 'Why don't you have a ride on the swing while I talk to Miss Medlicott?'

'I'll take care of your picture,' Miss Medlicott offered.

Haley ran across to the play area.

'Is there a problem?'

'Not really. At least, I don't think there is,' Miss Medlicott said. 'As you see, we were doing some art work this afternoon.' She held out the painting. There were several horizontal stripes in blue and yellow across the width of the paper. Some of Haley's characteristic stick figures were there, probably done with a marker pen. 'The people are sunbathers or swimmers, depending which bit of the picture they're drawn in, so Haley informed me. The reason I wanted to speak to you is that she insists one of these figures is a dead lady.'

Olga felt her flesh prickle.

'I tried to persuade her that it couldn't be so—that she must have seen someone who was asleep,' Miss Medlicott said. 'But she's adamant that she saw a dead lady when you took her to the beach a few days ago. I'm a bit concerned. I think it troubles her.'

Olga wrestled with her loyalties. This young teacher was concerned only with Haley's mental well-being. 'There was an incident,' she said. 'It was in the papers. Wightview Sands. A woman found dead. I expect Haley overheard us talking about it and linked it to someone she noticed lying near us.'

'That would explain it, then. You'll talk to her?'

'I'll do my best. Thanks.' Ashamed of herself, she handed back the picture and went to collect Haley.

Miss Medlicott strolled back across the playground. The head teacher, Mrs Anderson, was at the school door. 'Was that the child's mother?'

'Yes. The mother is very sensible. She'll be supportive. She looked rather stressed herself, so I'm afraid I ducked telling her the most disturbing part of the child's story.'

'What was that?'

'Well, that her daddy was with this woman who died on the beach.'

three

The breakthrough came on day twelve. The MPI churned out a new batch of names and Stella found one that matched better than most, a thirty-two-year-old unmarried woman from Bath. She was the right height, build and age and, crucially, her hair colour was described as 'auburn/copper'.

Hen Mallin was intrigued by the missing woman's profession. Emma Tysoe was listed as a 'psych. o.p.'.

'What's that when it's at home?'

Stella pressed some keys and switched to a glossary of abbreviations and found the answer: psychological offender profiler. 'She's a shrink. I've seen them on TV telling us how to do our job.'

Hen was more positive. 'Profilers have their uses. Is there a photo? See if you can get one on screen.'

This took some organising with Bath police and when it appeared on the monitor it was in black and white and not the sharpest of images. Even so, it convinced Hen. 'That's our lady. I'll put money on it.'

'All bets are off,' Stella said. 'I agree with you.'

'Have we ever used her?'

'Not to my knowledge.'

Hen merely nodded. 'There's a list of profilers approved by the NCF—the National Crime Faculty at Bramshill. I'll find out what they know about her. And you can get on to Bath police again. Presumably she lives or works there.'

'ARE YOU SURE?' the young-sounding sergeant in Bath queried. 'She only went onto Missing Persons yesterday. It's so quick.'

'Not for us. We've had a body on our hands for twelve days. Can you send someone to look at it?'

'The next of kin, you mean? You'll have to be patient with me. I'm not fully up with it.'

'Why not? It's been on national television. Didn't I tell you she was murdered?'

'Yikes—you didn't.'

'So you'd better get up with it fast. Are you CID?'

'No, ma'am.'

'Why don't you get hold of someone who is and ask him to call me in the next ten minutes? I'm DS Gregson, Bognor police station.'

'*BOGNOR?*' Detective Superintendent Peter Diamond repeated.

'But the body was found at Wightview Sands,' the sergeant who had taken the call informed him.

'A Bath woman?'

'Emma Tysoe. A psychological offender profiler. She helps out in murder enquiries.'

'She's never helped me.'

'All I know is that she was reported missing by the university. She often goes away on cases connected with her work, but she always keeps in touch with the department. This time she didn't get in touch. After some days, they got concerned.'

'Where does she live?'

'A flat in Great Pulteney Street.'

'Posh address. There must be money in profiling, sergeant.'

'It's only a basement flat, sir.'

'How was she topped?' Diamond asked.

'Strangled. It's been in the papers.'

'Strangled on a beach?'

'On a Sunday afternoon when everyone was down there. They don't have any witnesses either.'

'Someone must have seen it. This is weird. You've got me all of a quiver, sergeant.'

He sent a couple of young detectives to Great Pulteney Street to seal the missing woman's flat and talk to the neighbours. One of them was DC Ingeborg Smith, a former journalist, bright, blonde and eager to impress, recently enlisted to the CID after serving her two years in uniform. He asked Keith Halliwell, his trusty DI, to go up to the university and establish that Emma Tysoe was known to the psychology department.

Then he called Stella Gregson. Enquiries into the background and movements of Emma Tysoe were well under way, he told her. He looked forward to full cooperation over this case. He would accompany the identity witness to Bognor and use the opportunity to make himself known to the senior investigating officer.

'HE SOUNDS PUSHY,' Stella told Hen Mallin.

'Peter Diamond? I've heard of him, and he is. I've also heard that he pulls rabbits out of hats, so we'll see if his magic works for us. Don't look so doubtful, Stella. I've handled clever dicks like him before. When they stand up to take a bow, you pull away the chair.'

'I guess we can't avoid linking up with Bath.'

'We're not going to get much further unless we do. That's where Emma Tysoe lived, so that's where we look next.'

Diamond duly arrived that afternoon, a big man of about fifty with a check shirt, red braces and his jacket slung over his shoulder. Going by looks alone, the beer belly, thrusting jaw and Churchillian mouth, he was pushiness personified. With him was a less intimidating individual, altogether smaller and more spry, in tinted glasses.

'This is Dr Seton,' Diamond said. 'He's a professional colleague of Dr Tysoe's, here to see if he can identify the body. No one in Dr Tysoe's family was available,' Diamond said. 'There's a sister, but she's in South Africa.'

'Good of you to come,' Hen said to Dr Seton.

'He was volunteered by the professor,' Diamond said. 'Shall we get on with it?' Considering Dr Seton had given up most of his day, this seemed unnecessarily brusque.

Hen knew Diamond must have quizzed Seton thoroughly on the journey down and could probably have summed up the salient facts in a couple of sentences. However, she intended to hear everything first hand. 'Before we do, I'd like a few words of my own with Dr Seton—that is, if you don't object.'

Diamond shrugged.

She swivelled her chair away from him and asked, 'So, Dr Seton, are you involved in Emma Tysoe's work as a profiler?'

'Absolutely not,' the man said. 'That's something she does independently. I believe it arose out of her Ph.D research into the psychology of violence. She acts as an adviser to the police. She has an arrangement with the university and takes time off when required.'

'And was she currently working on a case?' Hen asked Dr Seton.

'I presume so. We hadn't seen her for a while.'

'But you wouldn't happen to know the details?'

'No.'

'Did she keep it to herself, the offender profiling?'

'It doesn't interest me particularly. We all have different areas of interest.'

'So what's yours, Dr Seton?'

'Masturbation.'

For a full five seconds nothing was said. Diamond, who had spent the last two hours with the man and must have known what was coming, was gazing steadily out of the window. Stella covered her mouth with her hand.

Hen carried on resolutely, 'Do you know Emma Tysoe well?'

'Not particularly. We meet in the staff room on occasions. I'm not sure why the professor picked me for this.'

Diamond said, 'Perhaps he thought you should get out more.'

Stella made a sound like a car braking and went pink in the face.

Hen's glare at Diamond left him in no doubt that she'd had enough. 'All right. Let's go to the mortuary.'

Stella drove them to St Richard's Hospital, and not much was said on the way. Hen asked Dr Seton if Emma Tysoe gave lectures and was told that she did five hours a week and her topic was forensic psychiatry. When she was away on a case, colleagues would cover for her.

In the anteroom of the mortuary the formality of identification was got through quickly.

'That's her.'

'Dr Emma Tysoe?'

'Yes.'

Out in the sunshine, Hen lit up a cigar and said to Stella, 'We passed Outpatients on the way in. Why don't you take Dr Seton there and buy him a cup of coffee? I need to check a couple of things with Mr Diamond.'

So Stella found herself reluctantly paired off with the masturbation expert, while Hen flashed a not-too-sympathetic smile and a promise of, 'We won't forget you.'

Hen took Diamond to the staff canteen where these two strong individuals sat opposite each other like chess-players. They'd collected a pot of tea and Hen was determined not to be the one who poured. After Diamond had eaten a biscuit, slowly, he said, 'Do you take yours white?'

She nodded and reached for the milk. 'Are you going to pour?'

It seemed a fair distribution of the duties. 'OK, I'm sorry about Seton,' he had the grace to say.

'You could have tipped me off.'

'How? It's not the kind of thing you can whisper in a lady's ear.'

She weighed that. 'Probably not,' she conceded finally.

'When I get back to Bath, I'll speak to the prof,' Diamond said, putting down the teapot. 'He should be able to tell me more about the cases this woman was advising on. I'm assuming her death is in some way related to her job.'

'It has to be followed up,' Hen agreed.

'So what's been happening down here?' he asked. 'Do you have anything else under investigation?'

'Nothing we'd need a profiler for, if that's what you're getting at.'

'She must have been down here for a reason.'

'Unless it was a holiday. People do go on holiday.'

'Dr Seton didn't seem to know about it.'

Hen said, 'Dr Seton seems to have narrow vision.'

He smiled. 'It's supposed to turn you blind, isn't it?'

Her real reason for setting up this tête-à-tête had to be faced. 'You'll report back to me on this?' she asked.

'Full consultation,' he said, after a pause. 'It's a joint investigation.'

'It was initiated here,' Hen made clear. 'The incident room is at my nick. I'll take the decisions.'

He said, 'I wouldn't want to pull rank.'

'Then don't. It's a West Sussex murder.'

'She's a Bath woman. You may find the focus of the investigation is off-limits for you. Then you'll need my help.'

'Need it? I'm depending on it,' Hen said. 'Bath nick is my second home from now on.'

He grinned. Without getting heavy, they had reached an understanding. 'And you'll be welcome. So what's happening at this end?'

She told him about the TV appeal and the difficulty in finding the Smith family.

'Haley is better than Smith. Not so many Haleys about. Have you tried the local schools?'

'No joy.'

'People drive miles to the seaside,' he said. 'They could be from anywhere. My way, even. Do you want me to take it on?'

She was guarded in her response. 'For the present, I'd rather you found out what you can about Emma Tysoe's life and work in Bath.' But it had not escaped her that he'd deferred to her. Maybe this man Diamond was more manageable than people said. 'Now that we have her name, it's going to open up more avenues.'

'As you wish,' he said. 'And let's get *our* names into the open. I'm going to call you Henrietta from now on.'

'Try it and see what happens,' she told him with a sharp look. 'I'm Hen.'

'Fair enough. Is it time we rescued your colleague?'

'Stella? Not yet,' she said with a steely gleam in her eye. 'I think I'd like a second cup. How about you, Pete?'

HALEY SMITH'S TEACHER, Miss Medlicott, was telling the class about their project for the afternoon. 'We're going to do measuring. You'll work in pairs with the person sitting on your right. Anyone without a person sitting on his right put your hand up now.'

Without fuss, she made sure everyone had a partner. She explained that they would be measuring the length of their shoes in centimetres, and showed them how to make two marks on a sheet of paper.

After twenty minutes she said, 'Now we'll see what results we have.'

Not all of the kids had fully understood. Aidan, who was Haley's partner, reckoned the length of his shoe was eighty-four centimetres.

'I expect you used the wrong end of the rule,' Miss Medlicott said. 'What about you, Haley? What was your measurement?'

Haley turned and whispered something to Aidan.

Aidan said, 'She says fifteen, miss.'

'Thank you, Aidan, but I'd like to hear it from Haley.'

Again Haley whispered to Aidan, who said, 'She can't, miss. Her daddy said she isn't to speak to you.'

After a moment, Miss Medlicott said, 'Very well. Who's next?'

Something very wrong was happening in that family. She would have another word with the mother.

DIAMOND GOT BACK to Bath just before seven and dropped Dr Seton outside his lodgings, then set off for the university campus at Claverton. Tired from all the driving, he found himself in a slow-moving line of traffic coming down Wellsway and let his attention wander. Halfway down, they had erected one of those mechanical billboards with rotating strips that displayed three different ads. These had the same slogan, BECAUSE IT'S BRITISH METAL, but the pictures altered. He watched an image of Concorde being replaced by the Millennium Bridge—and then jammed his foot on the brake just in time to avoid running into the bus in front of him.

He was relieved to complete the drive without mishap.

The department of behavioural psychology was quiet at this hour, though not deserted. A research student confirmed that Professor Chromik had been in earlier.

'Do you happen to know where he lives? It's important.'

The young man shook his head. 'You might catch him at the end-of-semester bash later tonight.'

'Where's it held?'

'The clubhouse at the Bath Golf Club.'

There was time to go home to Weston and shower. He called the nick and spoke to Keith Halliwell. Nothing more dramatic had happened in Bath than a middle-aged streaker running down Milsom Street. 'He didn't have a lot to show to the world,' Halliwell said. 'Nobody complained.'

Diamond took that shower, and decided on cream-coloured trousers, navy shirt and pale blue linen jacket. As a safeguard, he tucked a tie into an inner pocket. Golf clubs could be sniffy about open necks. The shirt was a favourite, made of a fabric that didn't crease. In the year since his wife Steph had died, he'd scorched a couple of shirts trying to iron them.

It was after eight when he parked his old Cortina outside the club, only for some member to point out that he was in the space reserved for the club captain. He found another berth and decided to put on the tie, a sober-looking black one with a repeat design of silver handcuffs, some wag's idea for a birthday gift for a copper.

Inside, he located the psychology crowd in a private room upstairs. Leather jackets seemed to be *de rigueur* for the men and black trouser suits for the women. Picking a glass of wine from a passing tray, he steered around the groups to where a dark-haired woman in a silvery creation with a plunging neckline stood alone.

'You don't have the look of a trick cyclist,' he told her.

She said, 'Can I take that as a compliment?'

'Of course.'

'I'm Tara, PA to Professor Chromik. And who are you?'

'The unlucky cop who took Dr Seton to the seaside today.'

Tara gave the beginning of a smile, and no more. Like every good PA, she was discreet—which Diamond was not.

He told her his name. 'Which one is Professor Chromik?'

'Over on the right, with his back to us.'

'Frizzy black hair, and half-glasses?'

'That's him. Did he invite you, then?'

'No, but I'm here to talk to him. You must have heard about Dr Emma Tysoe.'

Her features creased. 'It wasn't really Emma?'

'Seton identified her.'

She put her hand to her throat. 'None of us thought it was possible. She went missing, but . . . this!'

He was silent, giving her time to take it in.

'And here we are, enjoying ourselves,' she said.

'Have you any idea what she was doing down at Wightview Sands? Was she on holiday?'

'Not officially. She told us she was on a case. She usually phones almost every day to check in but no one had heard from her for something like three weeks. That was why we got worried in the end.'

'Didn't *anyone* know what case she was on?'

'I assumed she'd told Professor Chromik, but it turned out she hadn't. He asked me if I'd heard from her.'

'Hush-hush, was it?'

'I couldn't say. I can't think why anyone would want to murder her, whatever she was working on. She was only an adviser.'

'What about her personal life? Was there a boyfriend?'

'She never mentioned one. She was a lovely person, but she didn't say much about her life outside the department. Mind, I don't blame her. They're a nosy lot. It goes with the subject.'

'Who were her special friends at work, then?'

'Nobody I noticed. She seemed to stay friendly with everyone.'

'Even the ones who had to fill in when she was away?'

'People grumbled a bit. They do when there's extra work being assigned. A few harsh words were spoken in the last few days. But it's not a reason for murdering anyone, is it?'

'Let's hope not.'

He drifted away from Tara and stood for a while watching the behavioural psychology department socially interacting.

The tragic news circulated rapidly. You could see the stunned expressions as it was passed around. The moment arrived when Professor Chromik was informed. Diamond stepped in fast.

'You've just heard about Dr Tysoe I gather? I'm Peter Diamond, Bath CID.'

The professor's brown eyes were huge through his glasses. 'CID? It's true, then? Appalling.'

'The whole thing is a mystery, and I'm hoping you can help.'

'It's a mystery to me, too,' Chromik said. 'I'm devastated.'

'You must have known why she was away from your department.'

'She came to see me in June and said she'd been asked to advise on a case. She was not at liberty to speak to me about the matter. I can tell you nothing about it.'

'You don't even know who contacted her?'

'No.'

He seemed to be speaking truthfully, but the story sounded wrong. If some senior detective wanted the help of a profiler, surely he wouldn't need to insist on secrecy?

'Are you certain she was honest? Is it possible she wasn't working on a case at all, and simply took time off for a few days by the sea?'

Chromik shook his head forcefully. 'Emma wouldn't do that. She valued her profiling work too much to put it at risk.'

'Did you appoint her to the job?'

'I was on the appointments committee, yes. We were fortunate to get her. A first-class brain, without question one of the most brilliant psychologists of her generation.'

'So where did she come from?'

'She did her first degree in the north. Then she was at one of the London colleges for her Ph.D.'

'Do you know anything about her life outside the university?'

'In what way?'

'Relationships? Any family?'

'I wouldn't know.'

'Is there anyone on the staff she might have confided in?'

'You could speak to one of the women. Before you do, I'd better break the news to them all. I'll make a brief announcement.'

Chromik called his staff to order and said he had just been given some distressing news. Most people had heard, but one or two gasps of horror were provided as he imparted it. Without much subtlety, he went straight on to say he believed Emma would have wished the party to continue. There were general murmurs of assent.

Diamond stepped forward and introduced himself, inviting anyone with information to speak to him. He said he wasn't only interested in the circumstances leading up to Dr Tysoe's murder, but wanted to find out more about her as a person.

As soon as he'd finished, a woman touched his arm.

'I can help with the background. I'm Helen Sparks, a lecturer. We shared an office.' She spoke with a south London accent. She was black, slim and tall, probably the same age as Emma had been.

He took her to a large leather sofa. 'Thanks. I appreciate this.'

'I liked Emma a lot. She had style.'

'Are we talking fashion here?'

'Absolutely. For an academic, she was a neat dresser. She knew what was out there and made sure she wore it. The best. The top designer labels.'

'That must have used up most of her salary.'

'Emma wasn't short of money. I think her parents died a few years ago and left her comfortably off.'

'Did she have a lifestyle to go with it?'

'Depends what you mean. She was living at a good address. Drove a dream of a sports car. But she wasn't one for partying or clubbing.'

'Did she talk about the work she did, the profiling?'

'Once or twice when she got back from a case she mentioned what it was about. There were some rapes in a Welsh town, and she put together a profile of the man that helped them to make an arrest.'

'What about the case she was involved in this time? Did she say anything at all?'

Helen Sparks leaned back, frowning, trying to remember. 'One Thursday, she said she wouldn't be in for a few days. I asked her where she was going this time and she said she wasn't allowed to speak about it. I said, "Big time, then?" and she said, "Huge, if it's true."'

'I wonder what she meant by that. How was she when she told you this? Calm?'

'Yes, and kind of thoughtful, as if her mind was already on the job.'

'Is there anyone else she might have spoken to?'

'Professor Chromik, I suppose.'

'He says she didn't tell him anything,' Diamond said. 'Did Emma have enemies?'

'In the department? Not really. You couldn't dislike her.'

'Students? She graded them, presumably. Her marking might affect the class of degree they got, right?'

'It's not so simple as that. They're being assessed all the time by different people.'

'But one of them could hold a grudge against a member of staff if he felt he was being consistently undervalued?'

'Theoretically, but I don't think they'd resort to murder.'

Diamond disagreed. 'Helen, I have to be suspicious of everyone.'

He asked her to introduce him to more of her colleagues, and he met three others on the staff. All professed to having been on good terms with the saintly Emma. It was obvious no one would admit to being on *bad* terms with her. Maybe he should have delayed the questions until they'd all had a few more drinks.

'THE KEY TO THIS may well be the case she was working on,' he told the small team he'd assembled. They were Keith Halliwell, his main support these days; John Leaman, a young sergeant, and the rookie, Ingeborg Smith. 'The word that was used about it was "huge". What I don't understand is the need for secrecy.'

'Maybe someone is knocking off members of MI6,' Leaman said, not entirely joking.

'Or the royals—and no one is being told,' Ingeborg said.

'The corgis?' Halliwell said.

'Anyone got any more suggestions?' Diamond said with a sniff. 'Whatever she was asked to do, we need to find out. As I understand it, profilers work with serial cases. There can't be that many under investigation. I want you to start ferreting, Keith.'

'Using HOLMES?'

Diamond gave him a glare.

'The computer, guv.'

'Fine. By all means.' In time, he'd remembered that HOLMES was one of those acronyms he found so hard to take seriously: Home

Office Large Major Enquiry System. In theory it collated information on similar serious crimes. Diamond's objection was that as soon as the computer came up with cases in different authorities, some assistant chief constable was appointed to coordinate the various SIOs. One more infliction. 'But ask around as well. Down in Bognor they claim there aren't any serial crimes under investigation.'

'If it's hush-hush . . .'

'Exactly.'

'Are they up to this—the Bognor lot?' Halliwell asked.

'I think so. But they're having trouble finding genuine witnesses.'

'From a crowded beach?' Ingeborg said in surprise.

'They put out a TV appeal and had plenty of uptake, but not one was any use. The only person they can definitely link to the case is the fellow who found the body, and he's done the disappearing act.'

'He has to be a suspect, then.'

Diamond said, 'He is. Said his name was Smith. Bognor police won't make much headway unless we turn up something definite on Emma Tysoe. I didn't get much from her workmates. You went to the home address?'

Ingeborg nodded. 'Great Pulteney Street. There's a big pile of mail I brought back, most of it junk, of course. Various bills. Bank statements. She has a current account with about fifteen hundred in credit, and two hundred grand on deposit.'

'A lady of means. Did you get into the flat?'

'Eventually. It's the garden flat, amazingly tidy. Living room, bedroom, study and bathroom. The main room is tastefully furnished in pale blue and yellow.'

'We don't need the colour schemes,' Diamond said. 'Did you find anything that would tell us what she was up to in recent weeks?'

She said, 'No diary or calendar, but I brought back the answerphone cassette. I've listened to it twice, and I really believe there's nothing of interest on it.'

'Computer?'

'There's one in the office. I arranged for Clive to collect it.'

Clive was the whiz kid who handled all computer queries at the Bath nick.

'Is that it, then?' he asked Ingeborg.

'She drives a sports car, dark green.'

'Registration? Make? Have you checked with the PNC?'

'Bognor are onto it. They expect to trace it down there.'

'I don't mind who checks so long as we're informed.'

He summed up by handing out duties. Ingeborg was to get onto Clive for a speedy report on the contents of the computer. Leaman would set up a mini incident room. Halliwell would see what HOLMES could deliver on serial crimes in Sussex and Hampshire.

Diamond himself would get onto the man at Bramshill who kept the list of profilers. Someone at the top knew what Emma Tysoe had been up to.

THE NATIONAL POLICE STAFF COLLEGE at Bramshill is in Hampshire, an easy run from Bath along the M4. Peter Diamond's eyes glazed over at the name of the place. For years he'd ducked his head whenever anyone mentioned the Bramshill refresher course for senior officers. He pictured himself like Gulliver in Lilliput, supine and tied down by little men who talked another language.

After reporting to an armed officer at the battlemented gatehouse, he was told to drive up to the house. Facing him at the end of the long, straight avenue was a building that made the word 'house' seem inadequate, for this academy for top policemen was one of the stately homes of England, a Jacobean mansion with a south front that in its time had drawn gasps of awe from hardened policemen.

Diamond picked a parking bay well away from the entrance and walked back, pausing only to buff his toecaps on the backs of his trousers. His appointment was with a civilian whose name on the phone had sounded like Hidden Camera. It turned out to be Haydn Cameron.

Inside, he gave his name and was directed to the National Crime Faculty. He stepped through the great hall, panelled from floor to ceiling, into a waiting area.

A bright-eyed young woman with flame-coloured hair came in, asked him his name and invited him up the exquisitely carved stairs. He was shown into the office of an overweight, middle-aged man with a black eye-patch and hair tinted boot-polish brown.

'Good journey?' Haydn Cameron asked.

Diamond tried an ice-breaker. 'The last part was the best.'

'Oh?'

'Following the young lady upstairs.'

'I don't have a great deal of time, superintendent.' Haydn Cameron spoke Diamond's rank as if it were an insult. Probably was, in this place.

'Let's get to it, then.'

He got a sharp look for that. What did the man expect? Yes, sir, no, sir? He was just a civilian.

'We run regular courses on how to conduct murder enquiries for SIOs. According to my records you haven't attended one.'

The old blood pressure rose several notches. Calm down, Diamond told himself. 'No, I haven't found a window of opportunity yet.'

'You could go on the waiting list.'

Diamond tried not to curl his lip. 'The list that interests me is the approved list of offender profilers. I was told you deal with it. This is about the murder of one of the profilers on your list, Dr Emma Tysoe.'

'Which is why I agreed to meet you,' Cameron said. 'We're not unaware of the case.'

'Do you mind telling me how it works when an SIO asks you to recommend someone?'

'The matching of the profiler to the case is far from simple,' Cameron said acidly. 'All kinds of criteria come into play.'

'Such as where they live?'

Diamond got a basilisk stare from the seeing eye. 'That's of trifling importance. You really ought to do the course.'

This was not a comfortable interview. 'You mentioned all kinds of criteria,' Diamond prompted him.

'The term psychological offender profiler is a useful label, but it includes several different types of expert. If you asked each of the twenty-six on my list to provide a job description you'd get twenty-six different answers. Some stress the statistical element and others the clinical. There are those who are more intuitive.'

'How did you class Emma Tysoe?'

'She was one of the latter.'

'Intuitive?'

Cameron sighed and rolled the eye. 'I thought you'd jump on that word. It gives the impression of guesswork.'

'I didn't take it that way.'

A better response, it seemed. A note of conciliation, if not approval, crept into the conversation. 'All right. She was a psychologist, as you know, not a psychiatrist, not medically trained. Her approach was more theoretical than hands-on. But it was based on a remarkable understanding of the criminal mind. She somehow immersed herself in the thinking of the offender and predicted what would happen next.'

'That's the intuitive part?'

'Yes, but only as a result of minute observation of all the data from the previous crimes. To give you an example, she assisted on a case of serial rape in north Wales. By analysing the data—and interpreting the behaviour of the rapist—she decided he had spent most of his youth in custody or institutions and lived with someone of his own sex who dominated him. She said that because of the way he picked his victims it was clear he was in awe of women. He would spend months stalking them, but only rarely choosing to attack them. He was on the lookout for certain women who appeared even more submissive than he was. Dr Tysoe estimated the perpetrator's age, intelligence and the type of work he would do, and it led them to a man they'd disregarded much earlier, a farm worker. Broken home, fostering, youth custody, just as she'd said. On his release he'd ended up living with his bullying elder brother. He confessed straight away. That's only one example.'

'So Emma got to be one of your star performers?'

The staring eye told Diamond he still hadn't clicked with this mandarin. 'Please. This isn't show business. She was exceptionally good. Her name came up more frequently after that. Word travels from one authority to another.'

'Her latest assignment?'

'I'm not at liberty to say.'

'I'm investigating a murder, Mr Cameron.'

'We run this service on the need-to-know principle. Our judgment is that you don't need to know.'

Great, he thought. 'So I've come all this way for nothing.'

Cameron didn't answer. He looked at the ceiling with the air of a bored host waiting for the last guest to leave.

This stonewalling incensed Diamond. 'She was one of your experts. Don't you give a toss what happened to her?'

That touched a raw nerve. 'Of course we care! There's no evidence of a link between her murder and the case she was advising on.'

'The evidence isn't there because it hasn't been investigated. How can you be so sure the two incidents are unrelated?'

'Have you enquired into her personal life?' Cameron asked in an unsubtle shifting of the ground. 'Her work? The university?'

'We're looking at it, of course. The problem is that we have this black hole—the last few days of her life when we don't know what she was doing, who she was meeting or where she was based. How can we conduct a murder enquiry without knowing these things?'

Cameron didn't move a muscle.

Diamond weighed in with another attempt. 'If I don't get answers from you now, I'll start rooting for them. It could be far more damaging than finding out from you today.'

He seemed to have made some impact at last, because Cameron said, 'Sit there, will you? I have to speak to someone.' He got up and left the room.

Trying not to be too encouraged, Diamond amused himself swaying back in the chair, looking for the gleam of a camera lens in the panelled walls. He was sure this interview would be kept for training purposes. How to deal with dickheads from the sticks.

Five minutes at least passed before Cameron returned and invited Diamond to go with him. He was out of that chair like a game-show volunteer. They entered the southeast wing and he was taken through a recessed door into a low-ceilinged office where a small man with a shock of white hair stood looking at a computer screen. Whatever was on the screen was more gripping than his visitors, because he didn't give them a glance.

Cameron stated Diamond's rank and name without any attempt at a two-way introduction. The need-to-know principle in action again. Obviously this was someone pretty high in the Bramshill pecking order. Diamond privately dubbed him the Big White Chief.

Cameron left the room, closing the door after him.

Still without turning from the screen, the Big White Chief said, as if he were continuing the conversation in Cameron's office, 'This black hole of which you spoke, these missing days in Dr Tysoe's life. If I fill in some detail for you, you'll have to treat it as top secret.'

Progress at last. 'Understood.'

The Big White Chief turned, and Diamond was glad to see he possessed two eyes and there was a spark of humanity, if not a twinkle, in each of them. 'All right. Sit down.'

The little man assessed him with a penetrating look, as if still reluctant to go on. 'On June the 14th, a man was murdered in the grounds of his house in Sussex. Nothing was taken. There was a wallet in his pocket containing three hundred pounds. The house was open. It was hung with valuable paintings, and there are cabinets of fine china and pottery. Everything was left intact.'

'Except the owner.'

'Yes. He was shot through the head with a bolt from a crossbow.'

'From a *crossbow*?' Diamond took this in slowly. 'It's a medieval weapon.'

'With modern refinements. Still used in sport for shooting at targets. And killing wild animals.'

'There can't be many around.'

'Actually, more than we ever imagined.'

'You'd still need to be an expert.'

'It's a surprisingly simple weapon to use.'

'Strange choice, though,' Diamond said. 'What kind of person uses a crossbow as a murder weapon?'

'This is where the profiler comes in. Emma Tysoe was consulted as soon as it was clear that an early arrest was unlikely. She was the obvious choice. Her reputation here was second to none.'

'And was she helpful?'

'We thought she could be. She seemed confident. But it all takes time. These experts don't like to be rushed. When she was ready, she would come back with her recommendations.'

'So did she give you any opinion at all?'

'A few thoughts. The killer was methodical, unemotional, and self-confident to the point of arrogance. He, or she, had an agenda, and expected to carry it out.'

'What did she mean by that?'

'There's more. I'll tell you presently.'

Tiresome, but the promise was there, so Diamond didn't press him. 'You said the victim was in the grounds of his house. Was he alone?'

'As far as we know. He was sitting on a wooden seat watching the sunset. That's the presumption, anyway. He liked to do this.'

'Literally a sitting target. When was he found?'

'Next morning, about eight. He had a housekeeper, Aubrey Wood, who lived out. He's in the clear. He was on a pub quiz team that night.'

'His special subject didn't happen to be archery?'

The Big White Chief wasn't amused. 'If you'll allow me to continue, I'll give you the salient facts. Jimmy Barneston, a young Sussex detective who has handled several big investigations, took charge. He was unable to find any obvious motive. The victim was a highly successful film and TV director. Axel Summers.'

Diamond was no film buff, but he knew the name. Summers had been at the top of his profession for over twenty years.

'Summers was in the middle of filming a major project for Channel Four. *The Ancient Mariner*.'

'The poem?'

'Yes. You wouldn't think a poem could be turned into a feature-length film, but Summers decided it would cater very well to the current appetite for fantasy and myth and persuaded the backers to invest over fifteen million.'

'Is that big budget?'

'By UK standards, yes. There's a hefty financial input from industry. They get their corporate message on the credits and in the commercial breaks. Summers had just been away for five weeks shooting the sea sequences off the coast of Spain. He'd told his office he was taking a complete break before the next phase. Convenient for us, as it turned out. It wasn't necessary to announce his death immediately.'

'Why are you suppressing it?'

'Do you know your Coleridge?'

'Do I look as if I know my Coleridge?'

'Inside the house on Summers's desk the murderer left a sheet of paper with five words on it: "he stoppeth one of three".'

'"It is an ancient Mariner, and he stoppeth one of three",' Diamond chanted.

'So you do know it? This was cut from a book and pasted on an A4 sheet of copying paper. Below were three names, cut from newspapers. The first was Axel Summers. The others are equally well known.'

'A death list?'

'We have to presume so.'

Diamond waited. 'So you're not going to tell me who they are?'

He was given a less than friendly stare. 'I'm telling you about Emma Tysoe's part in all this. As a matter of urgency the team investigating the murder wanted to know if the others were under serious threat—in other words, was this a serial murderer at work?'

'What was her answer?'

'After much thought, yes. By naming a list of potential victims he—and she was in no doubt that this was a man—was challenging the police, an act of pure conceit. "Emotionally disconnected" was the phrase she used. He was treating this as a chess game. He had planned it coldbloodedly, and with the advantage of surprise was already several moves ahead in the game. So quite possibly there was no motive in the sense that you or I would understand it. The motive was the challenge of the game.'

'Chilling.'

'Yes, it shows a complete absence of humanity.'

'Are the two other people on his list going to be any safer if it isn't made public?'

'We're sure of it. This man, whoever he is, wants his crime sensationalised. He's picked people in the public domain as his targets.'

'So have you slapped on a D notice?'

'In effect. The local paper discovered something was afoot and we secured their cooperation. The nationals still don't know. The others on this death list have been told, of course. They were offered round-the-clock protection, and they've taken it.'

'Quite a number are in on this, then?'

'Already more than we would wish.'

An ominous statement. 'One more is no big deal, then.'

'You don't need to know.'

'So are you about to tell me that there's no link between the murders of Axel Summers and Emma Tysoe?'

The answer was laced with scorn. 'You can't compare them. This killer is focused, organised. A controller. He's got his agenda and he'll stick to it. He's not going to put his master plan at risk by strangling her on a public beach. He'd hate the idea of so many people around, so much outside his control.'

Diamond refused to be steamrollered. 'If this genius felt his master plan was threatened when Emma Tysoe was called in, wouldn't he do something about it? A cunning bastard like this is going to have heard of your list and know she's the number one choice.'

'Possibly,' he conceded.

'If this killer is as smart as you say, he's going to have a line into the investigation.'

The Big White Chief was quick to say, 'So you think you should have a line as well?'

'We're on the same side, aren't we?'

'I've told you more than I intended already, and I thought you'd have the experience to see that these killings are chalk and cheese.'

'I'd still like to have the full picture.'

'You've got it—apart from names, and they aren't germane to your enquiry. People's lives are threatened, Mr Diamond. I don't suppose you've ever worked with a burden like this, knowing that named individuals will die if you make a mistake. Show some sensitivity towards your fellow officers who carry that responsibility.'

Faced with an argument like that, he couldn't pursue it.

'If it's of interest you can look at other enquiries she advised on.'

Peter Diamond left Bramshill some time later with a sheaf of photocopied material that he slung onto the back seat of his car. He was unsatisfied and unconvinced.

The official line was that the murders of Emma Tysoe and Axel Summers were unrelated. Tell that to the marines, he thought. Emma had been at work on the Summers case when she was murdered. There was a link, and he would find it. He'd root out the truth and the Big White Chief, to put it politely, could take a running jump.

DS STELLA GREGSON arrived in Crawley soon after ten and was driven to the school in Old Mill Road. She hesitated before knocking on the head teacher's door. Childhood conditioning never entirely leaves you. The head introduced Miss Medlicott and left them to it.

'I hope this isn't a waste of your time,' Miss Medlicott said. 'All I've got for you is secondhand.'

'You don't have to apologise,' Stella said. 'We're grateful for any information. This comes from a child in your class, I was told.'

'Haley Smith. She's acting strangely. She drew a picture of a visit to the beach and told me one of the figures on it was a dead lady. I discussed it with the mother. The family were at Wightview Sands on the day that poor woman was found, she admitted that. She thought the child must have heard her talking about the incident with her husband and then assumed some sunbather had been the dead woman. But I felt Mrs Smith seemed rather guarded. And I didn't mention to her something else the child had told me—that her daddy had been with the lady.'

Stella felt goosebumps prickling her flesh. 'Haley said that?'

'Yes. And later in the week one of the other children told me Haley's daddy had said she wasn't to speak to me. I tried to talk it over with Mrs Smith at the end of the day, but she said it was obviously another misunderstanding. I've worried about it since.'

'You did the right thing,' Stella said. 'May I speak to Haley?'

'You can try. In the classroom would be better than here.'

The children were on their morning break as Miss Medlicott escorted Stella along the edge of the playground. Stella entered the classroom and the teacher went to find Haley.

When the small, dark-haired child was brought in with bowed head, Stella invited her to sit in her usual chair and sat beside her and said, 'Haley, my dear, I want to talk to you about what happened that day you spent with Mummy and Daddy at the seaside.

I'm a policewoman, and you don't have to worry, because you're not in trouble. I think you can help me.'

The child's pale face, framed by her bunched hair, registered only apprehension.

'A poor lady was killed,' Stella continued, 'and it's my job to find out about it. Did you see what happened?'

Haley looked up and there was eye contact. She shook her head.

'I was told you did a lovely painting of the beach. May I see it?'

Haley showed she had a voice. 'Miss Medlicott's got it.'

'So I have. I'll fetch it,' the teacher said, going to the cupboard.

In a moment she returned, the painting in her hands.

'My, that's a picture!' Stella said. 'Such colours. What a bright blue sea. That *is* the sea, across the middle?'

A nod.

'And this yellow part must be the sand. Are you in the picture?'

She placed her finger on one of the figures.

'Of course, it has to be you. Is that a ball in your hand?'

'Frisbee.'

'So it is. Silly me. Who did you play with? Some other children?'

A nod. This was chipping at stone, but it had to be done.

'And while you were playing, where were Mummy and Daddy?'

The tiny forefinger pointed to two stick figures on the band of yellow, with circles for heads, and a scribbled representation of hair.

'So they are. I expect they got worried when you were lost?'

The child felt for one of her bunches and sucked the end of it.

'So where were you?'

She was silent.

'Haley, no one is angry with you. I'm sure you can help me if you really try to remember what happened,' Stella said. 'You were playing with the children, were you? That must have been a lot of fun.'

The comment triggered the best response yet. 'A girl I was with got hit in the face by the frisbee and she was bleeding and crying, so we all went up to the hut where they've got bandages and things. Then the girls went back with their mummy, but I got lost, and the man with a whistle and red shorts found me, and then Mummy came.'

'Was that man the lifeguard?'

'Mm.' Haley pointed again, to a horizontal figure immediately above the parents. 'That's the dead lady.'

'How did you know she was dead?'

'Daddy said so. I seed the lady lying on the beach and she wasn't moving and the sea was coming in and I thought she was asleep and Daddy went to look and said she was dead.'

'So before this, Daddy must have been somewhere along the beach looking for you?'

'I 'spect so.'

'I believe you told Miss Medlicott he was with her. Do you mean when he went to see what was the matter with her?'

She nodded.

'And Daddy got some help, did he? Did you notice who helped? The lifeguard—with the red shorts?'

'I think so.'

'Did you drive home after that?'

She nodded.

'And did Daddy say anything about the lady?'

'He said we don't know who she is or why she snuffed it.'

'Did he say anything else?'

'They'll keep us here asking e-dot questions.'

'*E-dot? Idiot* questions? Is that what he said?'

'I 'spect so.'

Stella thanked the little girl, and Miss Medlicott said she could go. She said, 'Are you going to talk to my daddy?'

'Yes, but you don't have to worry. I'll tell him he can be proud of you. You're a clever girl, and helpful, too.'

After the child was gone, Stella said to Miss Medlicott, 'Am I going to talk to her daddy? You bet I am—and fast.'

BACK IN BATH late in the afternoon, Diamond was pleased to find an incident room set up. Sergeant Leaman had found a first-floor office being used as a furniture store. He'd 'rehoused' the furniture (he didn't say where) and installed two computers and a phone. Keith Halliwell was already at work at HOLMES.

Diamond asked if he'd come up with anything.

'It's given me all the unsolved cases of strangling in the past five years. More than I bargained for.'

'A popular pastime is it, strangling—like home decorating?'

'Do you mind, guv? I do a spot of DIY myself.'

'See if there's any record of deaths by crossbow, will you?'

Halliwell swung round.

'I'm serious. Just do it. Is our computer geek about?'

'Clive? He's downstairs with Dr Tysoe's disks.'

Diamond found the whiz kid in front of a screen in his usual corner of the main office, fingertips going like shuttles.

'Any progress?'

'Yes. I got in eventually. She had a firewall on her system.'

'Oh, yes?' Diamond said in a tone intended to conceal his ignorance.

'A lockout device. You get three attempts to guess the password, and then the system locks down for the next hour.'

'So what was the password—"sesame"?'

Clive's fingers stopped. 'As a matter of fact you're right about "sesame". It's always worth a try. I've done a printout. Thought you'd like to see it on paper rather than use the screen.' Clive pointed to a wall to his right stacked high with reams of paper. 'That's the contents of her hard disk.'

'All of that? If I was looking for something in particular—case notes, for instance—is there any way I could find them quickly?'

'Depends. Is there a key word I can use to make a search?'

'Try Summers.'

The quick fingers rattled the keys, apparently without a satisfactory result. 'This could take longer. Give me an hour.'

'And, by the way, Clive, this is under your hat, right? If you find something interesting I don't want it all over Bath nick.'

'Stay cool, Mr D. My lips are sealed.'

Diamond returned to his office and called Hen Mallin. Liberally interpreting the need-to-know principle, he told her everything he'd learned at Bramshill.

'A house in Sussex? That's my manor. I haven't heard a whisper.'

'Shows how seriously they take it. Have you heard of Jimmy Barneston?' Diamond queried. 'He's in charge.'

'That makes sense. He's top of the heap, young, energetic, and his clear-up rate is awesome. Should I have a quiet word with him?'

'I wouldn't trouble him yet. He'll be trying to keep the cap on the bottle. Let's wait until we've got something to trade.'

She said, 'You're a wily old soul, aren't you? Good thinking.' After a pause, she added, 'You really believe she was killed by the man who did Summers, don't you? In spite of what you were told?'

'I wouldn't put it as strongly as that. But I'm not ruling it out just because Bramshill tells me to. One thing I've learned in this job, Hen, is that the people at the top have their own agenda, and it doesn't have much to do with what you and I are working on.'

'Speaking of which, I'd better let you know what's been happening here.' She told him about Stella Gregson's interview with Haley Smith. 'We've established that the father, Michael Smith, manages a bookshop at Gatwick Airport. Stella has gone to interview him.'

'He'd better have a good story. What about his wife?'

'Done. I sent Stella to see her. I wanted the woman's angle first. She confirmed that her husband was the first to do anything about the dead woman. He alerted the lifeguard and helped to carry the body to the hut. Afterwards they cleared off fast in their car. They figured they wouldn't have anything useful to contribute. They hadn't seen anyone with the victim all day. There was also a period when Haley went missing and they were both very taken up with searching for her. Olga Smith says she was far too upset to have noticed whether the woman was alone, or if she was dead at that stage.'

'Makes sense.'

'Yes, Stella believed her, but got a strong impression that she's scared of her husband. She knew we were appealing for information. He seems to have put her under pressure to say nothing. And we know he ordered the child not to speak to her teacher.'

'He's got plenty to explain, then.'

'When we've picked him up, sunshine, I'll let you know.'

'WHAT I DIDN'T APPRECIATE when I printed all the files is that some of them are encrypted,' Clive told Diamond. 'The text is scrambled.'

'You mean we can't read it? So how do you unscramble files?'

'Decrypt them. With blood, toil, tears and sweat. It could take me weeks to crack this.'

'Better make a start, then.'

STELLA GREGSON found the right Gatwick Airport terminal and located the bookshop easily enough. Finding the manager was not so simple. He'd gone for a late lunch, the woman on the till told her, and he should be back soon.

Stella said she'd wait. She'd had no lunch. She had a young male DC with her and she treated him to a toasted sandwich at the Costa shop, which offered a good view of the open-plan bookshop.

After forty minutes Stella asked the woman on the till, 'Where does Mr Smith eat? Somewhere in the terminal?'

The woman thought Smith went home to lunch. He lived nearby, in Crawley. 'Is he in trouble, then?' She added cheerfully.

'We just need to check something with him.'

'I DON'T KNOW WHY,' Stella said to her young colleague as she drove out of the airport, 'but I've got a bad feeling about this.' The feeling got worse when they turned the corner at the end of the Smiths' street and an ambulance sped towards them, siren blaring, lights flashing. A police patrol car was parked outside one of the houses.

'That's the one.'

They drew up outside and went in through the open door.

'Who are you?' a sergeant in uniform asked.

Stella held up her warrant card, 'So what's going on?'

'Some bastard beat his wife unconscious. She was in a right old state. She's on her way to hospital.'

'Is he in there?'

'No, he scarpered.'

four

Very late the same afternoon, Diamond heard from Hen Mallin that Olga Smith had been attacked and was in hospital, and the husband, Michael Smith, was missing.

'I'll come at once,' he said.

'Hold your horses, squire,' she told him. 'She's in intensive care. She won't be talking to anyone until tomorrow at the earliest.'

'The husband did it, I suppose?'

'There's little doubt. His car was seen outside the house between two and three. A white Honda Civic. It was gone when she was found.'

'He'll be miles away, then. What could have triggered this attack?'

A heavy sigh came down the line. 'The most likely sequence of events is that Olga phoned her husband at the airport after Stella's visit and he came straight home in a vile temper and knocked her senseless for blabbing to us. We knew he wasn't willing to help us with the Tysoe murder.'

'But she didn't come to us.'

'Right.'

'What about young Haley? I hope she wasn't at home when this was going on.'

'No, thank God. She has lunch at school. One of the neighbours is looking after her tonight.'

'Poor little kid. So what's being done to find him?'

'Crawley are handling the search and letting me shadow the SIO. They've already held a press conference and issued a photo and announced that Smith is wanted for questioning. The main effort is being put into finding the Honda.'

'I'll come in the morning, then. Which hospital?'

'Crawley General.'

'Would around nine suit you?'

He went to the incident room to update his team. And on his way back home to Weston that evening he called at the library and borrowed a copy of *The Selected Poems of Samuel Taylor Coleridge*.

THE NEXT MORNING Hen Mallin was already waiting in the entrance to intensive care when Diamond arrived. An officer from Crawley, DI Bradley, was also waiting, but unfortunately for all of them the interview with Olga Smith would have to wait. 'There's a definite improvement,' the doctor told them. 'She's conscious now, but I can't have her subjected to the stress of questions. Why don't you come back later this afternoon, say around four?'

Diamond asked about the extent of Olga Smith's injuries and was informed she'd taken a blow to the back of the skull and there was extensive bruising.

'A single blow to the head?'

'Yes, and that could easily have killed her. It's highly likely she'll have no memory of the incident.'

Diamond suggested a visit to see where the attack had happened. DI Bradley looked at his watch.

'Is it far?' Diamond asked.

'It's not so much how far it is—' Bradley started to say.

'It is to me. How far?' And so the hard-pressed DI Bradley drove ahead, and the house was only five minutes from the hospital.

Bradley had a key and let them in. It seemed the Smiths had a taste for period furniture. A rosewood table and a pair of upholstered chairs stood in the hallway. The SOCOs had been through the previous afternoon, leaving a powdering of zinc over the hard surfaces.

'She was found in here,' Bradley said, pushing a door open.

This room was more typical of a young family, with fitted carpet, three-seat sofa and matching armchairs, a wall unit with TV, sound system and a few books. The only period piece here was a mahogany dining table in the bay of the window.

'Where, exactly?'

DI Bradley pointed to a bloodstain at the window end of the room, close to the table. It was the size of a beer mat.

'Was any weapon found?' Diamond asked.

Bradley shook his head. 'If he had any sense, he'll have taken it with him. Villains are wise to DNA these days.'

'I was thinking that if there isn't a weapon she could have cracked her head on the corner of the table.' Diamond stepped closer to the table and assessed its position in relation to the bloodstain.

'Theoretically possible, I suppose.' From his tone, Bradley didn't think much of the suggestion.

'Anyway,' Hen said with diplomacy, 'forensics will find out.' Like Bradley, Hen was in no doubt as to Michael Smith's guilt, and now she threw in more damning information. 'It wasn't Smith who called the ambulance. It was the woman next door, Mrs Mead.'

'How come?' Diamond said.

Hen invited Bradley to explain.

'What happened was that Haley comes home from school, can't get in, so goes next door, knowing Mrs Mead has a spare key. Mrs Mead goes round and finds Olga Smith lying here. It was Mrs Mead who noticed Michael Smith's Honda.'

'I'd like to meet this splendid woman.'

First, they looked into the other rooms. Holiday photos and post-cards around the kitchen. A notice board with reminders pinned to it. A homemade cake under a Perspex cover. Diamond sifted through a batch of photos. The father had the same expression in all of them, with half-closed, ungenerous eyes and only the vestige of a smile.

Upstairs, the Smiths' bedroom didn't have the look of a battle-ground. They shared a kingsize bed. Each had a pile of books. He was reading Jeffrey Archer and she Victoria Beckham's autobiography. Haley's room had a vast collection of stuffed toys and three shelves of books. The third bedroom had been converted into an office, with two filing cabinets and a computer. Diamond picked some letters off the desk. One was a bank statement.

He showed it to Hen. Michael L. Smith had £120,000 on deposit. 'Is that the kind of money a bookshop manager stacks away?'

'Maybe he came into money.' Hen said.

'Regularly, by the look of it. He made two deposits in cash last month, one of fifteen hundred, the other of two grand. *Cash*, Hen.'

'A tax dodge?'

'Or some other scam.'

They went next door to call on Mrs Mead, a short, bright-eyed woman in her sixties with permed silver hair that matched the colour of a yapping Yorkshire terrier held against her chest. 'Let him sniff the back of your hand and he'll quieten down,' she told Diamond, and it worked. Then she put the dog down, said, 'Basket,' and it trotted off somewhere.

Bradley introduced them and asked Mrs Mead to repeat her account of what had happened. She described the day's events as she had seen them: the arrival of Mike Smith's car at two, or soon after, and the sight of him entering the house and leaving some fifty minutes later and driving off again. Haley had knocked at about three forty-five saying her mummy hadn't met her from school and wasn't answering the door.

'I was worried something was wrong.' Mrs Mead went on. 'I let myself in and discovered her lying in the sitting room unconscious. I called an ambulance, and that was it, really. Haley stayed with me last night. An aunt came down from London this morning and collected her.'

'What sort of man is the husband?' Hen asked.

'A good neighbour. I've no complaints.'

'And you've heard nothing?'

'No violence, if that's what you mean. He has his moods, as most men do. A bit inconsiderate at times.'

'When you say "a bit inconsiderate", what do you mean?'

'Small things. For example, he doesn't ever help her with the shopping. She does it all, struggles back from the supermarket where she works laden down with bags. It wouldn't hurt him to pick it up in the car once in a while, would it?'

'Doesn't she have the use of the car?'

'She doesn't drive. She confided to me once that she was banned. I didn't ask her for the details.'

They left Mrs Mead. It was agreed that DI Bradley would meet them again at four at the hospital, while they filled the time having lunch at the Boar's Head, south of the town, on the Worthing road.

Back in his car, Diamond used his mobile to check on the driving career of Mrs Olga Smith. When was she banned and what was the offence? He was given an answer of sorts before he drove into the car park of the Boar's Head. The DVLC at Swansea had no record of Olga Smith.

He got out and ambled across to Hen. They found a comfortable corner seat in a part of the main lounge no one else was using. Hen lit up a cigar while Diamond fetched beer for himself and dry white wine for her.

'You seemed to be back-pedalling this morning over what happened to Olga Smith,' Hen commented.

'Inserting a note of caution, that's all. Just because Michael Smith is a dodgy character, we shouldn't jump to the conclusion that he bashed his wife.'

'If it was an accident and she fell and hit her head on the table, as you were suggesting, his behaviour is still suspicious. You don't leave your wife lying unconscious in a pool of blood.'

'No,' he admitted before taking a sip of beer. 'And when you find large cash deposits like that you have to think this fellow is onto a scam. It could be why he avoids us, and why he did a runner yesterday.'

They looked at the menu. Diamond said he fancied the steak and Guinness pie with chips, and Hen surprised him by saying she'd join him. He hadn't yet heard her ship-of-the-desert theory of nutrition.

'The other thing about Smith,' he said, 'is that I find it difficult to cast a husband and a father as the killer of Axel Summers.'

'You're sure the two killings are connected?'

'I'm not *sure* of anything, Hen. But I don't buy the theory that this killer is so rigid in his thinking that he wouldn't dispose of someone like Emma Tysoe who might have fingered him before he completed his quota of murders.'

'The method was different. It's almost unknown for a killer to use a different MO,' Hen pointed out. 'They find a method that suits them and stick to it.'

'Strangulation was a suitable MO for the beach. This Ancient Mariner guy is out on his own,' he said. 'He's something else, Hen, totally callous. Committed. He kills to make some kind of point.'

'But how would he have known Emma Tysoe was at work on the case? Even her workmates didn't know.'

'He'd expect a case like this to be referred to a profiler. He'll know about the Home Office list. It's circulated. He'll have worked out which of the names were most likely to be consulted. Wouldn't be difficult to find out who was currently off work doing some profiling.'

Their food arrived, pub-sized portions, and he looked at hers wondering where she could possibly stow it all. She was just a sparrow, the shortest officer he'd met in years, and she wasn't chunky, either.

As they tucked in, they talked strategy. Hen was uneasy about Bramshill. 'They've put up the shutters on the Axel Summers murder, so we're right out of order trying to pin these two killings on the same guy.'

'I'm not worried,' Diamond said. 'Let's play it by the book. We're investigating the killing of Emma Tysoe and we've every right to find out what she was doing in the last days of her life. If it takes us into forbidden territory we simply say we're doing our job.'

'Like finding out what's on her computer?'

'Exactly.'

'You're confident we can decrypt her hard disk?'

'I'm confident Clive can—given time.'

A SURPRISE AWAITED them when they returned to the hospital. Instead of DI Bradley, a tall man in a grey three-piece greeted them outside the intensive-care ward. He was about thirty, with dark, swept-back hair making him look as Italian as the cut of his suit, except that he was blue-eyed. Hen shook hands. 'For all that's wonderful! Jimmy the Priest! Peter, meet Jimmy Barneston.'

'The Priest?' Diamond queried, after he'd felt the firm handshake.

'He's always hearing confessions.'

'It's not down to me. It's the Sussex Inquisition. People like Hen Mallin,' Barneston told Diamond. He had an air of confidence it had taken Diamond twenty years to acquire. 'I decided to join you for this. Bramshill brought me up to speed on your investigation and they tell me you know about the case I'm on. Something of interest may be developing here, so I'd like to hear what Mrs Smith has to say.'

Which wasn't the Bramshill line at all. Jimmy Barneston shouldn't be underestimated.

'No problem,' Diamond said cheerfully. 'Let's see if they're ready for us.'

The sister asked them to keep the questioning to five minutes and showed them into the room where Olga Smith lay tubed up, with her head bandaged. Only her eyes moved.

Hen stepped closer and said who they were. 'Olga, we need to know how this happened. Can you remember?'

She mouthed the word 'no'. The voice came feebly.

'Do you recall Sergeant Gregson coming to the house?'

She tried clearing her throat, and winced. 'Yes.'

'She told you she'd spoken to your little girl Haley, right?'

'Is Haley—'

Seeing the sudden concern in Olga's features, Hen said quickly, 'She's fine, perfectly OK. Your sister is looking after her.'

'Ah.' The muscles relaxed a little.

'After my sergeant, Stella Gregson, visited you, I expect you phoned your husband to tell him. Am I right?'

'Yes, I spoke to Mike.'

'Did he come home at once?'

'Yes. He was upset.'

'Upset. You mean angry?'

'Yes.'

'So what happened?'

'I told him what the policewoman said and what I'd said. And then he told me he was going away.'

'Where to?'

'Didn't say. Business things.'

'Was that when he turned violent?'

'Violent?' Olga repeated the word as if it was unknown to her.

'He hit you.'

'No. Mike didn't touch me.'

Hen exchanged a glance with Diamond. Was the episode erased from Olga's memory by the concussion?

'Are you sure of this?'

'He collected some things and left. I saw him drive off.'

'You're certain?' Diamond broke in. 'You were OK at that stage?'

'Yes.'

'But you ended up here, in intensive care. You don't have any memory of being struck on the head? Or breaking your arm?'

A look of panic came into her eyes. Then they closed and her jaw slackened.

Hen said, 'I don't think we'll get much more.' And as if on cue the sister appeared and ushered them outside.

In the waiting area, Jimmy Barneston said, 'What did you make of that?'

'Weird,' Hen said. 'She didn't sound confused. She was very definite. She didn't blame her husband at all.'

'Are we looking at someone else as the attacker, then? Someone who called at the house after the husband had driven away?'

'Hard to believe,' Hen said.

Diamond was unusually silent. A possible explanation was coming to the surface, but he needed to check something first. 'I'll be right back.' He left them and returned to the ward.

The sister stepped forward. 'I'm sorry. No more questions.'

'It's you I want to speak to,' he said. 'When she came in, did you send for her medical records?'

'They're confidential.'

'Absolutely. But we're trying to establish whether the head injury was caused by someone else, or was accidental. I'm wondering if she's epileptic. It may well explain the injury, if she suffered a fit. She was found beside a table. If her head hit the corner as she collapsed . . .'

'That's possible.' She hesitated. Finally she sighed and said, 'Yes, if it helps, I can confirm that Mrs Smith has a history of epilepsy.'

'Thank you.'

When he passed on the news to the others, Hen said, 'Who would have thought it? The husband may not even know his wife is injured.'

Barneston agreed. 'If she saw him drive off. She'll have had the fit after he left. Have you any idea why he came home at all?'

Diamond told him about the bank statement they'd found. 'If the cash deposits are dodgy, as we suspect, he could have panicked.'

'It's got to be followed up,' Barneston said. 'And I'm even more doubtful that Michael Smith has anything to do with the killing of Emma Tysoe.' He held out a hand to Diamond. 'Good luck with the investigation. You need it.'

After he'd gone, Hen asked, 'What do you make of him?'

'Young for a DCI.'

'They're getting younger all the time,' she said, grinning. 'Too brash for your liking? Plenty of people think so, but he gets results.'

He smiled faintly. In his years in CID, he'd seen a few meteors rising high. They looked brilliant for a time, and then they fizzled out. But maybe Jimmy Barneston had more substance to him.

Hen asked, 'What made you suspect Olga might be epileptic?'

'The driving ban. I checked with Swansea, and there's no record of her ever having had a licence. So it crossed my mind that the ban could be on medical grounds. No epileptic can get a licence.'

'Mr D?'

Diamond squeezed the mobile against his ear, as if more pressure would help. He couldn't put a face to the voice. 'Yes?'

'I thought I ought to tell you I had some visitors this afternoon, two heavies from the computer crime unit.'

The penny dropped. This was Clive, the computer expert.

'What did they want?'

'They, em'—a long pause—'they seized Dr Tysoe's hard disk.'

'What—the thing you're working on?' This was devastating. 'For crying out loud, Clive. Didn't you stop them?'

'I couldn't do that. They're part of SO6.'

This was one abbreviation he recognised. 'The Fraud Squad.'

'They said they had authority, waved some piece of paper in front of me. It was no use arguing.'

The moguls at Bramshill were behind this, he guessed. 'We're down the pan, then. And I suppose you were still trying to crack the code?'

'It's all right, Mr D. I can use the zip.'

'The what?'

'The zip disk. It's a back-up of everything on the hard disk. I wouldn't do a job like this without at least one back-up.'

Mightily relieved, Diamond asked, 'Do the Fraud Squad know you've got this copy?'

'They'd expect it. I'd have to be a complete nerd not to back up something as important as this.'

'Get back to it, then. Pull out all the stops, or whatever you do with computers.'

HE TOLD HEN the news over a cup of tea made and served by the WRVS in the main waiting area of Crawley General Hospital.

'I'm not surprised,' she said. 'Bramshill gave Dr Tysoe the job, so they're entitled to know what progress she made.'

'I thought it was a cynical move to stop us finding out stuff they want to keep secret. She could have named the two other targets.'

'Let's hope she did. And let's hope your computer wizard delivers.'

They were on the point of leaving, when one of the tea ladies came over and asked if they were from the police.

'At your service, ma'am,' Diamond said.

'Because we just took a phone call from Sister Thomas in intensive care. She said would you please go back directly?'

Diamond saw the flash of alarm in Hen's eyes. They got up from the table and moved fast to the exit.

The sister was waiting for them outside the intensive-care unit.

'Thank God you're still here.'

'Bad news, sister?'

'We had a man here.'

'What?' Neither of them had anticipated this.

'Just a few minutes ago. He came to the desk insisting he was the patient's husband. She seemed to recognise him. We were very alarmed, knowing the circumstances. I told him visitors weren't allowed. He shouted her name from the door and then he left. I called Crawley police, and then I thought you might still be here.'

'He went which way?' Diamond asked.

She pointed along the corridor. 'And he's in a rather crumpled black or grey striped suit.'

'Can he get to the car park that way?'

'Yes.'

Diamond started running.

Three hundred or more cars were parked in neat rows and others were in the aisles waiting for spaces. A few pedestrians were visible, but nobody remotely like the tall, mean-looking man Diamond knew he ought to recognise from the photo.

He slowed to a walk and stopped altogether, catching his breath.

More cars were streaming in, through a gate system. Diamond watched the striped arm go up and down a couple of times before realising it could be his salvation. Each driver had to pay something at the automatic exit. So there was only one way out—and it was possible Smith hadn't got there yet.

Another dash, this time across the car park among slow-moving but still hazardous vehicles. But it was worth the risk. The fourth in line at the exit was a white Honda Civic. Heart and lungs pounding, Diamond approached the driver. Definitely the man in the photo. And the car couldn't move out of line.

Smith had his window down. One look at Diamond's warrant card said it all. He knew he was caught.

Diamond told him to switch off the engine and step out.

THE QUESTIONING took place in a room normally used by the hospital almoner, with flowers on the desk and holiday posters on the walls—a distinct improvement on the average police interview room. This was a coup for Diamond and Hen. They would hand the prisoner over to Crawley police at the end of the day, but they had first crack at him.

Tired and scruffy, Smith now appeared not so mean, or guarded, as he had in the photographs. He'd evidently slept in the suit. But to his credit he seemed to have some concern about his wife's condition.

'Is Olga going to be all right? I heard someone say on the radio she was injured and in Crawley General and they were looking for me. I drove here to try to see her.'

'They think so,' Hen said.

'She fell and cracked her head, didn't she? Do they know she's epileptic? You can never tell when a fit is going to happen.'

'She's going to be fine,' Diamond said. 'But you're under strong suspicion of attacking her.'

'*Me*, attack Olga? I wouldn't hurt her. I'm not violent, I tell you. You're way off beam if you think I had anything to do with this.'

'Why were you on the run if you're innocent?'

'That's something else.'

'Come on. We're not arsing about here.'

'I panicked. That's all.'

'Why? What is there to panic about?'

'She told me on the phone the police had been to the house.'

'Is that so scary? What have you been up to, Mr Smith?'

He shook his head. Suddenly the eyes were more defiant than panic-stricken. It was obvious he wasn't going to roll over easily.

Diamond gave Hen an enquiring look, a slight lift of the eyebrows that said, in effect, shall we pursue this? Whatever racket Smith is in, there are more urgent matters to discuss before DI Bradley arrives.

Hen nodded. They had a good understanding already.

Diamond said, 'You know the dead woman who was found on Wightview Sands beach? We're in charge of that investigation.'

Smith stared back in alarm. 'You're not trying to swing that on me?'

'You're a key witness. You called the lifeguard, I understand. And then you quit the scene. And you haven't responded to any of the calls for help.'

'I couldn't tell you anything. I didn't want to get involved.'

'For the same reason you spent last night on the run?'

'Well, yes.' He held out his hands in appeal. 'All I did was tell the life-guard guy she was down there and then help him to lift her to the hut.'

'Now we've got you here, can you tell us anything else about the dead woman? Did you notice her earlier on?'

Smith took his time over the question. 'She was there most of the day. Arrived alone not long after we did, around eleven thirty.'

'Do you remember what she was carrying?' Hen asked.

'She had a windbreak with her, blue, I think. The first thing she did was put it up.'

'Quite near you?'

'Just in front. But we couldn't see her without standing up.'

'That was because the windbreak was in the way? But you'd have noticed if anyone joined her at any stage?'

'I guess I would have done. No, I don't remember anyone joining her.' He shrugged, and he seemed to be genuinely trying to think of an explanation. 'Wait a bit. Olga said something about a guy who tried to chat the woman up, and she wasn't having any of it.'

'She did?' Diamond leaned forward eagerly. 'When was this?'

'Going by what Olga said not long before lunch.'

'Did you see him?'

'No, I had my eyes closed. Well, I was probably sleeping.'

'Did she describe this man?'

'Something about a black T-shirt. That's all I recall.'

'Come on. She must have noticed more than that.'

'I didn't ask. He didn't interest me.'

'He could be really important,' Hen said.

Smith obviously didn't think so. 'I wouldn't make too much of it if I were you. The woman was OK when he came by. And after.'

'So when do you think the murder happened?'

'I've no idea, unless it was when Olga and I went for a swim.'

'What time was that?'

'Some while after the tide had turned. Towards four o'clock.'

Diamond asked, 'How long were you away? Any idea?'

'For the swim? Half an hour to forty minutes. We stayed in for some time. When we got out, the tide had covered a lot of the beach. And that was when we couldn't see where Haley, our little girl, had gone. We'd left her playing with some other kids. My wife went back to our place in case Haley came back. I went up to the lifeguards. I told them my kid was missing and gave them a description and they promised to make a search. They suggested I looked for her in the sections of beach either side of us.'

'You say "they", as if there was more than one lifeguard,' Hen broke into his narrative. 'But when the police arrived there was only one present. And I've only ever interviewed one, an Australian called Emerson.'

'There were two when I first told them Haley was missing. A shaven-head one in red shorts and a tall, blond guy with a ponytail. But you're right about the blond guy. He wasn't around later, when I reported finding the woman. I expect he'd gone off duty.'

'I'm going to follow this up,' Hen said. 'Tall, blond ponytail . . . anything else?'

'An earring, I think. Yes. He was well tanned, as you'd expect, and built like an ox—well, an athlete, anyway.'

'So it was Emerson who found Haley?' said Diamond, putting the story back on track.

'Must have been. I was still flogging up and down the beach looking for her when Olga brought her back. It seems one of the other children got a nosebleed from a frisbee or something, and all of them went up to the first-aid hut. Then Haley got confused when she was left alone.'

'You heard this from your wife?'

'Yes, when I got back.'

'Was that when you noticed the dead woman?'

Smith nodded. 'Yes. Haley drew our attention to her. Olga asked me to look and I went over and realised she was dead. Christ, that was a shock.'

Hen asked, 'Did you notice anyone else sitting close enough to have seen what was happening?'

'There was a French family on our right. Mother, father and three kids, but they'd packed up and gone by the time the body was found.'

'That's one reason why people haven't come forward,' Diamond said. 'They'd left the beach before the body was found, so didn't have the faintest idea they'd been sitting a few yards away from it.'

Diamond glanced towards Hen. They'd covered everything except the real reason for Smith's avoidance of the police. Smith was a deeply worried man, almost certainly into something criminal. But as a killer so cool that he'd strangled a woman within yards of his own wife and child, Michael Smith just didn't cut it.

five

Diamond's voicemail had been building up while he was in Sussex. He wasn't bothered. Much of it could be ignored now. And being out of the office had other advantages. He'd missed a meeting called by Georgina Dallymore, the assistant chief constable, to discuss some desks and chairs that had mysteriously been dumped in the executive toilet upstairs. 'Couldn't have helped, anyway,' he said, as he called her to give his apologies.

Georgina said, 'Would you have any use for some extra desks?'

'Not really, ma'am.'

'I had to have them moved, and now they're cluttering the corridor. I'm worried about fire regulations.'

If that's all you have to worry about, he thought, it's not a bad old life on the top floor. 'Someone will have a use for them, ma'am.'

'I hope so. I'm going on holiday next week. When I come back, I don't want to find them still there.'

His interest quickened. Georgina off the premises was good news. 'Anywhere nice?'

'A Nile cruise.'

'Sounds wonderful. How long?'

'Ten days.'

Back to the voicemail. The one message that stood out was from Clive: 'Mr D, I've got a result.'

CLIVE'S HOURS OF WORK spoke of long nights on the Internet. He never came in before eleven. Today, it was twenty minutes after, and he looked spent when he and Diamond got together with black coffees and doughnuts in a small office in the basement. While the computer was booting up, Diamond told the young man he'd done well. 'I just hope this is worth all the hours you put in.'

'It will be.'

'Hot stuff?'

Clive grinned. 'From what I saw.' He took something not much bigger than a cigarette lighter from his shirt pocket and attached it to a lead at the back of the computer tower.

'What's that?'

'A USB—portable storage device. I had to work on this at home.'

'That's all there is?' Diamond couldn't disguise his disappointment.

'Mr D, this little item is a hard drive. Five hundred and twelve megabytes. Enough to keep you busy for the rest of the morning.' Clive explained that there had been three encrypted files on Emma Tysoe's hard disk, each allotted a number that he thought represented the date it was created. The first, 1706, was the 17th of June. The next was the 22nd. The last was the 25th.

'Two days before she was murdered,' Diamond said. 'And we can now read it off the screen? Let's go.'

Clive gave him a quick lesson with the mouse, showed him how to access the files and left him to it.

Magic. Suddenly Diamond was right where he wanted to be, inside the mind of the murdered woman, getting that precious insight he'd been denied up to now.

Had this 8.30am call about a profiling job. Bramshill won't give me any details except an address in Sussex. All very cloak and dagger. Just to cover my rear end, I'm going to keep this personal record of what happens. I can't keep everything in my head.

I'm flattered to get this assignment, but it's a nuisance too, if I'm going to have to make up excuses for not going out with Ken. We're supposed to be eating at Popjoy's tomorrow night. Even if I get there it takes the pleasure out of a beautiful meal when you've looked at a mangled corpse the day before.

The upside is that I get out of the university for a bit. I called the office and fixed it with Tara to take indefinite leave.

I dressed for the country and drove to a house overlooking Bramber, a village tucked away below the South Downs in Sussex. In fact there wasn't much to see of the murder scene except police photos. It all happened three days ago, so they'd already removed the corpse and finished their forensics. Victim was Axel Summers, that smooth old (fiftyish?) film director. He'd been hit through the head with a nine-inch arrow—a bolt, they call it—from a crossbow. I had no idea a crossbow packed such force. In the photos you could see the point sticking out of the other side of his head.

The reason they asked for a profiler is that the killer left a note with a quote from *The Rime of the Ancient Mariner*, 'he stoppeth one of three', and two extra names. So, is this a serial murderer declaring himself? they want to know. Strictly between you and me, Computer, one of the names is the glamour-boy golfer, Matthew Porter, and the other is gorgeous, pouting Anna Walpurgis, the one-time pop star. The police have already warned them both and steps have been taken to safeguard them.

'Get away!' said Diamond aloud. These were huge names.

Media people. My first thought is that this killer must be some kind of attention-seeker. Egocentric, and either extremely stupid to announce his plan, or brilliant. Summers has been filming a big-budget movie of *The Ancient Mariner*. The SIO—a literate policeman!—reminded me that the Ancient Mariner in the poem uses a crossbow to kill the albatross. Coincidence? I don't think so. This is someone using murder as a melodramatic statement.

Does he have to be an insider to know what the victim was filming? Not necessarily. The project has been getting plenty of publicity. The budget runs to millions. They managed to get some of Britain's industrial giants to back it, companies like Superglass and British Metal.

If the killer—the police team call him the Mariner—is just an attention-seeker he may have thrown in a couple more juicy names to see the effect. Somehow, I doubt it. I think he really means to get Porter and Walpurgis as well. I get the impression of a cold-blooded killer untroubled by conscience or emotion, figuring he's so far ahead of the game he can safely post his intentions.

Motive? We'll see. At this stage it doesn't look like theft. According to the housekeeper everything in the house is intact. Housekeeper, by the way, has an alibi for the evening of the murder. He knows of no feuds, no obvious enemies. Actually, Summers had the reputation of being a charming bloke, always willing to help people out. There are no women in the frame. The police think Summers was probably gay by inclination, but sexually inactive. He put a lot of energy into his work.

What does the method tell us about the murderer? I'm relying on what I've been told here. The crossbow is an eccentric choice of weapon, as accurate and deadly as any gun, the only drawback being . . . the drawback. Unlike a handgun it takes time to load but one shot should be enough. I gather the dishy detective is pinning his hopes on finding where it was obtained. There aren't more than a couple of hundred regular crossbowmen, he's been told. You don't need a licence and anyone can learn to use a crossbow easily and quickly.

I wouldn't mind DCI Jimmy Barneston, the SIO, showing me how to hold a crossbow. Tall, a smart dresser, broad-shouldered, mid-thirties (I'd say), with amazing blue eyes.

Predictably, this hunky cop wanted an instant opinion and I had to tell him sweetly that certain things can't, and shouldn't, be rushed. I fed the poor lad a few first thoughts to keep him sweet. I warned him to expect surprises and gave him a bit of a look. I'm sure the blue eyes twinkled.

I drove back to Gt Pulteney St still thinking about it all. Didn't even bother to garage the car, I was so hyped up. This, I feel strongly, has the hallmarks of a ground-breaking case and I don't want to put a foot wrong.

Am I dealing with a boaster or is he a committed killer? Obviously there's pressure on me to provide a profile before someone else is murdered. So let's assume the Mariner intends to kill again. I can't duck the question any longer: is this a psychopath? How I hate this word with all its colourful associations, suggesting a biological propensity to kill, when in reality there's no explanation for such behaviour.

All we can say for sure is that certain individuals who persistently commit violent crimes are able to function at two contradictory levels. They appear 'normal', with an ability to participate in human relationships. Yet they have a detachment that allows them to carry out random acts of violence without pity or guilt. If the Mariner fitted this profile I would expect him to have a history, a trail of cruelty and suffering. Murder is part of a process that begins early.

Then there's the other kind of serial killer, acting not on impulse, but from a motive such as revenge, or ambition, or greed, probably deriving from some seminal incident in his life. He has an agenda and the killing of his victims is purposeful. He's not at all the same as the random killer who may claim to have a 'mission' to kill prostitutes, or gay men, or people of a certain racial group, to rectify what he sees as personal injustices.

I don't know yet where to place the Mariner.

This evening I cooled off in the bath and drank lager and lolled around in my Japanese dressing gown listening to Berlioz and thinking. Just before ten the phone went. Only Ken, making sure I was still on for Popjoy's tomorrow. Couldn't get too excited about the prospect. He's getting clingy and I'm not sure I like that.

And now it's another day and I'm spending the morning at home with my books, checking on the kinds of serial killers. I've yet to find any who actually named their victims in advance. This must be arrogance without precedent.

The police are looking for links between the victim, Summers, and the 'targets', Porter and Walpurgis, in the hope this will lead them to the killer. I wish them luck, but I fear they may be wasting their time. What matters is their link to the Mariner, if any.

The meal was the best part of the evening, a wonderful breast of pheasant as my main course and the most delicious crème brulée I've ever tasted to follow. Unfortunately, Ken picked a red Californian wine, Zinfandel, that always makes my head ache. I wish he'd asked me first. Stupidly I drank a glass or two with the meal, not wanting to mess up the evening. My head started splitting before we got to the desserts. He was really miffed when the waiter asked if we would take coffee and I said what I really wanted was a glass of still water with two Alka-Seltzers. Yes, I embarrassed him horribly.

Then he proposed to walk me home—me in a pair of strappy high heels!—all the way from Sawclose, at least half a mile. He claimed it would be romantic. Stuff that, I told him, I want a taxi. Unfortunately the theatre crowd had just come out and we spent the next twenty minutes trying to beat other people to a cab. Result: I wasn't in the mood for the shag he expected when we finally got back here. Ugly things were said, entirely by me.

Things went wrong in the restaurant and they weren't really anyone's fault, but it helped me to face facts. I happen to have a bigger-than-average appetite for sex and I needed a bloke and Ken came into my life at the right time and did the necessary. We had five or six good weeks. Now it's time to draw a line under them. Basically, it's over. And to be honest, I'm relieved.

Diamond sat back in the chair, trying to catch the implications for both murders. On one level it was a fascinating insight into Emma's analysis of the Summers case. It was a definite advance to have the names of the two 'targets' Bramshill wanted to keep to themselves. Equally, it seemed to open the way to new lines of enquiry in her own murder. Ken, the lover on the skids, was a real discovery. He had to be traced—and soon.

I got in touch with Jimmy Barneston today, wanting to follow up on a few matters. The main thing I wanted to get across was that I now believe the Mariner really does intend to kill those two he named. The police should keep them under twenty-four-hour surveillance. Jimmy said I was welcome to sit in on one of their case conferences and I've agreed to drive down to Horsham tomorrow. I'll make another visit to Bramber in the afternoon without the murder squad in attendance.

Ken left a message asking me to call him. He wants to start over, I suppose. I'm going to ignore him. Our fling is over. Now that it's done and dusted I can see there was never very much emotionally. I was keeping it going for the sex on tap, my personal demon, the tyranny of the hormones. Let's be honest, he was rather good at it, but not world class.

This will not be easy, this case. You can't make too many inferences from a single crime. It's quite on the cards that he has carried out crimes in the past, maybe even murders. But I can't access them unless the police pick up some piece of evidence that links him to their records.

What age might he be? The trouble he took to pick out the crossbow suggests someone reasonably mature, calculating, rather than impulsive. Not a youth, I would say.

The choice of 'targets' is intriguing. They're all huge names, but apart from that they don't have much in common. Summers was creative and intelligent and over fifty. Porter is precocious, little more than a kid, certainly under twenty-one. Walpurgis is past thirty and very rich, still a celeb, but past her prime as a pop singer.

So off I drove to Sussex again, for a day that was to surprise me. Just as I hoped, no one was on duty at the Summers house, so I let myself into the garden and tried to think myself into the Mariner's brain as he stalked his victim that fine evening. I'm certain, looking at the scene, that he would have made a dummy run—maybe without the weapon—some previous evening. I know from Jimmy Barneston where the bolt appeared to have been fired from, a position fifteen yards or so away, behind a small rhododendron bush. Actually tried it. Lay on my tummy and looked down an imaginary telescopic sight at the wooden seat where the body was found. He must have been in place before Summers appeared with his G&T. And after the bolt was fired, he calmly entered the house and left his note.

Here is a killer who is painstaking, yet audacious. By choosing to leave a note, he issues a challenge, and takes a huge risk. He relishes the thrill of taking us on.

Aubrey Wood, the housekeeper, lives alone in the village. He was willing to talk to me. He'd worked for Summers for nearly ten years, cooking and cleaning and doing jobs about the house. He saw various friends of his boss when they came to the house. He never detected any bad vibes.

On the evening of the killing, Wood served a light evening meal about six, loaded the dishwasher and left sharp at seven. He noticed nothing unusual. He left Summers in a good frame of mind. Wood met his friends at seven fifteen and was driven to Plumpton for the pub quiz they'd entered as the local team. I'm satisfied he's incapable of anything so callous as this killing.

After that chat, I had to get to the 4.00pm case conference in Horsham. Met the entire murder team and a couple of people from Bramshill. Jimmy Barneston chaired it. Watching him in action, I was more smitten than ever. He has a way of energising everyone, encouraging them to chip in and picking out the salient points.

Jimmy went through the various lines of enquiry. Forensic reports on the fingertip search (little of interest). Crossbow manufacturers and retailers (more promising, although they don't all keep records of customers). He spent some time going over Summers's career, pointing out that even a man so popular and friendly must upset people when he makes decisions on casting and scripts. An embittered actor or writer might fit the profile of the killer. At the use of the 'p' word, heads turned to see if I had any comment. I made clear it was too soon to give them anything reliable.

Two of Jimmy's senior people gave similar run-downs on Porter and Walpurgis. Was there some deeply wounded person who had been damaged by all three? Nothing to connect them had so far been discovered.

It was after seven when the meeting ended. Jimmy asked if I'd like to eat. I took this to mean several of them would be going to some local pub and it seemed a good idea, because by the time I got back to Bath it would be getting late for a meal. Then would you believe it? He used his mobile and booked a table for two at a local Italian restaurant. Wow!

Mild panic. I'm in my denim jacket and designer jeans, still dusty at the knees from lying on the ground simulating the shooting. So I nip into the ladies and brush myself down and do some repair work on the face.

Wasn't sure if Jimmy fancied me or just thought I might give out some more about my thoughts on the case. In ten minutes we're in the window seat at Mario's looking at each other by candlelight. No, we weren't there to talk shop. We spend the next hour getting to know each other the way you do on a first date. He's a graduate (business administration at Reading) and he shares quite a few of my tastes in music and film.

We share a bottle of Orvieto and have chicken and pasta, and at the end he suggests coffee at his place. So I find myself next in his gorgeous stone-built house beside the River Arun. Real coffee and Mozart's flute and harp concerto, and I just know I won't be driving back to Bath that night.

Jimmy is a natural. Knows without asking what gets me going and goes for it with such a sense of sharing the excitement. Talk about hitting the spot!

Was it a one-night stand, or can it develop into something more permanent? Each of us played it cautiously over breakfast, not wanting to seem possessive, and no commitment was made. But I honestly think he finds me more adventurous (exciting?) than the average girl, so I'm hopeful of another invitation. It won't be easy keeping a relationship fresh when we live a couple of hours from each other, but this case requires close and frequent consultation!

Here, the file ended. Just as well, because Diamond was at the point of spontaneous combustion. Jimmy Barneston and Emma Tysoe! Barneston knew the dead woman's private life was fundamental to the investigation and he'd said bugger all when they'd talked about the case. It wasn't as if he needed to feel guilty. He wasn't having a fling with a suspect, or a witness, or even one of his team. She was a profiler, an extra. Diamond thought he wouldn't care to be in his shoes when the Big White Chief at Bramshill read the files.

IN THE INCIDENT ROOM he found Keith Halliwell and Ingeborg Smith.

He gave them all the facts he knew about the murder of Summers, ending with a warning that Bramshill wanted to keep the lid on it.

'I haven't finished reading the files, and I'll give you a fuller run-down when I'm through. Meanwhile there are two things you can do. Ingeborg.'

'Guv?'

'Dr Emma Tysoe wasn't the shrinking violet her colleagues made her out to be. She had an above-average appetite for sex and a lover she dumped called Ken. It's pretty obvious he lives locally. He took her for a meal at Popjoy's the evening after she was given this job. Do some ferreting, will you? Ken has to be regarded as a suspect.'

'Because she dumped him?'

'Right. Now, the other matter I want you to follow up, Keith, is the whereabouts of her dark green sports car. She mentions in the file that she didn't put it in the garage one evening when she got back home. But Great Pulteney Street doesn't have garages so she must have rented one nearby. That's my assumption, anyway. I dare say one of her neighbours would know. And I want to know if the car is still in there. They didn't find anything belonging to her in the beach car park. What make is it?'

Halliwell glanced towards Ingeborg, saw the startled look in her eyes. She attempted to cover up. 'As you recall, guv, Bognor were doing the index check.'

'And none of you thought to ask?' Diamond said. 'I give up! Get on that bloody PNC yourselves. If anyone wants me, I'll be in the basement, catching up on the next instalment.'

I'm keener than ever to make an accurate profile of the Mariner [Emma's second file began]. I'd love to amaze Jimmy with my findings. The problem is there's so little data to go on. I'm beginning to firm up on certain assumptions:

(a) The killer is above average in intelligence, educated to a pretty high level. [The Coleridge quote]

(b) He's methodical and cool under stress. [The absence of any traces at the scene]

(c) He must have had some practice with the crossbow and knowledge of its firepower. [One bolt had to be enough]

(d) He has an exalted opinion of himself and his ability to outwit the police. [The naming of future victims]

(e) He may feel he is underrated, or cheated by some failure in his own career. [Choice of famous victims suggests he envies people in the limelight]

Not enough to be of use to the police, unfortunately. It's still too theoretical. What Jimmy needs from me are notes that will pin this man down as an individual.

The way forward must be to look more closely at the choices

the killer has made. Why pick Summers, by all accounts a charming, well-respected man? What is it about the others that singles them out for slaughter? Is it only that they are so well known? I definitely need to know more about Porter and Walpurgis.

A few minutes ago I phoned Jimmy. Glad to say he sounded pleased to hear from me. You can tell straight away when a man wants to back off and when he doesn't. But this was strictly business: I was putting my case for a meeting with Matthew Porter. I made the point that while Porter is alive we have the chance to question him about people he may have crossed and threats he may have received. He saw the sense in this. He said he'd need to talk to the high-ups. He promised to get back to me.

(Later, in bed) I've had Ken on the mobile wanting to start over, giving me the hard sell about how he really loves me and can't face life without me. What a wimp. So I bit the bullet and told him I was seeing someone else—which gave him a seismic shock and showed him in his true colours. This guy who really loves me called me a slag and a whore and lots of other disgusting names. I just said, 'Grow up,' and switched off.

Better news. A message on the answerphone from Jimmy saying I should meet him in the coffee shop at Waterloo Station at 2.30 today. And I should erase the message after listening to it—real cloak-and-dagger stuff which was as good as saying he'd fixed the meeting with Matthew Porter. Brilliant.

I got to the station early and sat on one of those tall stools drinking an Americano. I'd put on the style for this, the dark red number with the split skirt. Black pashmina and matching tights. My Prada shoes. I got some looks.

Jimmy showed up dead on time. He kissed me on the cheek and steered me to the taxi rank. In the cab, I sat close to Jimmy and slipped my hand under his arm and squeezed it. He smirked a little, but of course we were on a serious mission, so things didn't get any more intimate than that.

He told me we were going to a Special Branch safe house. The cab put us down at the war memorial in Streatham High Road. We walked for ten minutes or so through the backstreets, me beginning to think I should have worn something less conspicuous, but no complaint from Jimmy.

The house is in as quiet a road as you're likely to find in London, old Victorian buildings with sash windows. I noticed a video camera quietly rotating under the eaves.

The front door was opened by an unsmiling honcho in a track suit and we were shown straight into a back room where Matthew Porter, a young man in a green polo shirt and white jeans, was sitting in an armchair with a can of lager watching the racing on TV. He turned his head briefly to give us a glance, but didn't get up or shift his feet from the coffee table in front of him. Jimmy gave my name and explained my reason for wanting to meet him. This achieved some eye contact, no more.

Case-hardened by all those seminars with grouchy students, I wasn't going to take any of this personally, was I? I launched straight into my questions. I began by asking him if he'd ever met Axel Summers. He shrugged and continued to look bored, but then he muttered something about always meeting people and not remembering them unless they were players.

I probed gently into his background and by degrees he loosened up. He was more comfortable talking about his start in golf. His father had taught him to play when he was eleven. Their house backed onto a golf course in Broadstairs and he would practise shots early in the morning before anyone else was about. The club professional gave him lessons. At fourteen the club rules were changed for him to become a member. A year later, he won the club championship. He'd turned professional at eighteen and started winning minor tournaments right away. His win in the British Open at the age of nineteen made him famous overnight.

His parents had separated four years ago. His mother was now living in France with another man. His father was an 'alkie'. He said he didn't want to talk about them. So who were the main people in his present life? His manager, Sid Macaulay, who looked after everything—his travel around the world, his interviews, his endorsements, even paid his tax. Girlfriends? He hadn't time, he said, adding—with a smirk—apart from one-night stands. He was travelling most of the year—normally.

By now I was getting wiser about Matthew Porter. This looked like a case of arrested development. Golf had taken over his life before he had had a chance to mature. He did as he was told by the manager, lived in cocooned comfort and performed on the golf course when required. He couldn't relate to other people unless they talked to him about golf.

He said it was the manager who'd ordered him to come to this place for his own safety. He didn't like it much, he confided, and he ought to be practising instead of sitting indoors.

Jimmy interrupted to say a move was planned to another safe house, away from London, with better facilities and maybe even the chance to get out and strike a ball from time to time.

I asked if he could think of any link with Anna Walpurgis. He pulled a face and said her music was crap. I asked if he'd met her—which brought the strongest response so far. He thought I was suggesting he might have dated her. Just for the record, young Matthew Porter thinks of the celebrated Anna as 'that old boiler'. Let's hope no one has the bright idea of putting those two in a safe house together.

I switched back to golf. With so much money at stake, I said, was there any pressure to fix results? He went purple protesting that he always played to win. He said he wasn't a cheat and I'd better shut my face. To restore calm, I reminded him that some-body meant to kill him and my job was to find out if the threat came from a complete stranger or somebody he'd upset. At this, the protest melted.

All in all, the visit wasn't the success I'd hoped for. At least I'd satisfied myself there was no obvious link with Axel Summers or Anna Walpurgis.

We walked back to Streatham High Road and Jimmy waved down a taxi. Much to my surprise, he asked the driver to take us to Crystal Palace. 'Something I've laid on,' he said mysteriously. My imagination went into overdrive. Love in the afternoon? A luxurious hotel suite, with caviar and chilled champagne?

Dream on. He'd arranged for someone from the British Police Archers to demonstrate the crossbow. The guy waiting for us had brought two Swiss target bows. They are very like a rifle in appearance, with a wooden stock shaped to fit against your shoulder. You have a trigger and telescopic sight, and a groove along the centre of the stock to guide the bolt when it's released. The 'cross' part, making the shape of the bow, is the prod.

The power of these things was a revelation. The bowstring is made of steel cable, but the force of the pull, at least 200 pounds, is in the prod. He demonstrated what happens when the trigger is pulled. The snap of the cable was awesome. The bolt thudded into a target thirty yards away.

Our instructor told us he preferred a kneeling position with the elbow supported on the knee. So my assumption that the Mariner was belly-down may have been wrong. Provided you hold the bow steady you should hit the target.

As we walked back across the park, I linked my arm through Jimmy's and asked what other surprises he had in store, and he knew exactly what was on my mind. But he said he had to get back to Horsham. He gave me a peck on the cheek.

Bloody men.

The second file ended there. Diamond closed it and switched off. He sat for a moment, reflecting on what he'd learned. He'd taken to Emma with her Prada shoes and her lively love life. Earlier, he'd assumed her reputation as a top profiler had put her in the path of her killer. Now it seemed possible it was a crime of passion. Reading the journal, it was difficult to accept that she was dead.

The glimpse of Porter, too, was valuable . . .

A voice interrupted his thoughts.

'Finished, Mr D?' It was Clive.

Diamond swung his chair round. 'Is it possible for me to press a couple of keys and send a copy of these red-hot files to someone I know? A DCI Mallin, at Bognor Regis?'

KEITH HALLIWELL had tracked down the registration details of Emma Tysoe's car. It was a dark green 2000 Lotus Esprit.

'We also found the garage she rents, in Pulteney Mews.'

'Surprise me, Keith. Was there anything in there?' Diamond said.

'Not even a bike, guv.'

'Put out an all-units call on this. London and everywhere south and west. The thing must be somewhere. Where's Ingeborg?'

'She's up at Popjoy's, looking at their reservations book, trying to work out the name of the ex-boyfriend.'

'She'll be lucky. Restaurants usually make bookings with sur-names alone.'

'Yes, but we know which evening it was, so we'll have the names of everyone who made a reservation. How many would you say— twenty maximum?'

Diamond raised a thumb in tribute. 'Good thinking, Keith.'

HE RETURNED to the basement to finish reading Emma Tysoe's files. The third was dated two days before her death.

Can't get Jimmy Barneston out of my mind. I know he's working all hours on the case and I can't expect him to call me, but I keep wondering if he thinks of me as nothing more than an easy lay. It didn't seem like that at the time. The sex was special (I ought to know) and I've never felt so good as I did lying beside him afterwards. And there's a whole lot more about Jimmy that I find attractive. I want a real relationship.

Computer, what can I do? I could ask to meet Anna Walpurgis, I suppose, but I doubt if she can tell me anything useful. I sense I'll get nothing more from her than I did from Matthew Porter. I'm thinking they were chosen because of their fame, to create more of a sensation when they are killed.

But hold on, is the Mariner a true serial killer? Maybe he does know them personally. The fact that he has named his second and third 'victims' in advance makes the whole process more difficult for him. Why take the risk? Is it because he wants to strike fear into these people's hearts? Is there a personal grudge behind all this?

If so, I should insist on a meeting with Walpurgis. She may tell me some detail of real importance. She's the one I know least about, but I've looked her up on the Internet. She topped the charts in Britain and America in her best years and had a huge three-album contract with one of the record companies. And when the first album flopped they paid her off with about twenty million. She married one of the super-rich kings of industry and came into all his money when he fell off the perch not long after. She has the controlling interest in her old man's company, so she can't be a total airhead.

(Later) Jimmy isn't sure if he can fix an early meeting with Walpurgis. He says she's in a panicky state, close to a breakdown, and finding the security hard to take. I reminded him that I have a Ph.D in psychology, but it cut no ice. 'Maybe in a couple of days,' he said. I told him the profile can't progress until I've spoken to her. I said if I couldn't get to see her myself, could I give him a list of questions to put to her? He agreed, so I jumped in with both feet and said in view of her fragile state I'd need to brief him personally about the way it was done, and debrief him afterwards (I have no shame), and how was he fixed this weekend?

He sounded slightly ambushed, but that's it. Perfecto! He's agreed to see me tomorrow morning (Saturday), and I'm off (or on) for the weekend, I hope. The weather's going to be glorious. I shall pack my swimsuit, just in case I can tempt him out of the nick and down to the coast.

Wish me luck, Computer

Diamond smiled at the last line, then shook his head and sighed. Emma's luck had run out on Wightview Sands.

HEN MALLIN HAD READ the files overnight. 'I learned a sight more than I expected,' she said on the phone next morning to Diamond. 'Almost enough to bring a blush to my innocent cheek. And I thought profiling was all about maps and diagrams.'

'Like so much else it comes down in the end to people making judgments about other people,' he said, in a rare reflective vein.

'So what's next?' Hen asked.

'We're still trying to trace this guy Ken.'

'He's right in the frame,' Hen said as if Diamond needed more convincing. 'The jilted lover, consumed by jealousy. It's one of the oldest motives around. I'm willing to bet he was the guy in the black T-shirt that Olga Smith saw.'

A bit sweeping, ma'am, Diamond thought. 'If that was Ken, what took him all the way down to Wightview Sands?'

'Car, obviously. Guessing there's another guy in Emma's life, he follows her to Horsham and sees her cosying up to Jimmy Barneston. While those two spend Saturday night together, the luckless Ken is sitting in his car thinking murderous thoughts. In the morning he trails her down to Wightview Sands and tries to talk her round. When he doesn't succeed, he gets mad and strangles her.'

'Maybe,' he said, leaving plenty of room for doubt. 'We don't know for certain if she spent another night with Barneston.'

'So are you going to ask Jimmy?'

'We'll have to, obviously. Indeed, you know the bloke better than I do. If you'd prefer to have a word with him yourself . . .'

'Nice try, matey,' she said in a tone that was not impressed at all. She wasn't fully tuned in to the Diamond sense of humour.

'All right, let's see him together.'

'He won't like it one bit.'

'We're entitled,' Diamond emphasised. 'He's become a crucial witness. He could be a suspect, in fact.'

'Hold on, Peter. That's pushing it. He's one of us.'

'He's got to be treated like anyone else. We don't know what passed between them that last night.'

'Let's do it, then.'

There was a danger of being carried away by Hen's get-up-and-go. 'Before we do, I'd really like to hear from Olga Smith, if she's recovered enough to talk.'

'She's at home now. Her sister is looking after her.'

'Any news on the husband?' Diamond asked.

'He's facing charges of smuggling cigarettes. Big-time smuggling, a profitable scam at the airport with some baggage handlers. They delivered them to his stockroom and he acted as a conduit to the criminal trade right across the southeast. Which explains the large cash deposits. He'll go down for a spell.'

They agreed to meet at midday at the Smiths' house in Crawley. Hen would call Olga Smith and arrange an interview. Later they would drive to Horsham and speak to Jimmy Barneston.

A SMALL, SOLEMN GIRL with her hair in bunches came to the door.

'You must be Haley,' Hen said. 'We've come to see Mummy, my darling. Can we come in?'

Olga Smith, pale and tight-lipped and wrapped in a black dressing gown, was sitting in the living room. Another woman sat near her.

Olga said, 'My sister Maud is here to support me.'

Hen said, 'Whatever you wish.'

So the sister remained. Haley had already nestled close to her mother on the sofa.

'We're grateful to you for seeing us, Mrs Smith,' Diamond opened up. 'You're looking much better than when we saw you last.'

'I've been advised not to discuss the trouble my husband is in.'

'That's fine by me. We're here on another matter entirely, the woman at Wightview Sands. Just tell us what you remember of that Sunday on the beach.'

'I'll do my best. We got there at about eleven, I think, and we found a spot on that part of the beach near where the lifeguards have their lookout. We hadn't been there long when she arrived and sat more or less in front of us.'

'Do you remember what she was carrying?'

'A blue towel and a windbreak for sure. And some kind of beach-bag, blue, like the towel, with a dolphin design, about the size of the average carrier bag, but not so deep.'

This was new, and possibly important. Olga Smith had made the journey worthwhile already.

'I think she was in denim shorts and a top that she took off later. She spread out the towel on the sand and set up the windbreak. She took her sunglasses out of the bag and put them on. And she had a bottle of sun screen. After that, she settled down behind the windbreak and I couldn't actually see her. But later I went down the beach to Haley, and when I returned I had a different view and the woman was sunbathing in a white two-piece.'

'She didn't speak?'

'Not that time. She smiled at me. And quite soon after that, a man came by and spoke to her. They seemed to know each other, from what I overheard.'

'What did you overhear?'

Olga Smith blushed. 'I'm not nosy. You can't help picking up bits of conversation on a beach. He was trotting out that line about all the gin-joints in all the world.'

'"Of all the gin-joints in all the towns in all the world, she walks into mine." Humphrey Bogart in *Casablanca*.'

'That's it. Anyway, as a chat-up line, it didn't seem to work very well. I couldn't hear what she was saying, but I heard his side of the conversation. He asked to join her and she obviously gave him a short answer because he said something like, "Suit yourself, then. I'll leave you to it." Then he swore and walked away.'

'What were the words?'

'The swearing?' She blushed again. 'He said, "Oh, what the fuck."' She mouthed the final word, unseen by her small daughter.

'He was angry, then?'

'Annoyed, anyway. After he'd gone, he didn't look back.'

'This is really helpful,' Diamond told her. 'Can you remember what the man looked like?'

'I'd say he was around thirty. He had a black T-shirt and I think he was wearing jeans. His hair was black, quite curly. Latin looks, I think you'd call them.'

'Was he tall?'

'Not specially. About average, I think, with wide shoulders and

PETER LOVESEY

narrow hips. He was nice-looking, a broad, strong face.'

'You seemed to suggest just now that the woman spoke to you at some stage of the day.'

'Yes, it was when I went down to the sea to collect Haley for lunch. Haley and I had a little race up the beach and I was some way behind. The woman said she wished she had such energy, or some such. That was all.'

'But she seemed relaxed?'

'I thought so. And I can't remember any more about her until later when we had a crisis of our own, with Haley going missing. I was asking people if they'd seen her, but the woman looked as if she'd been asleep for hours, so I didn't disturb her.'

'Obviously you know she was strangled at some stage of the afternoon. You didn't notice anyone else with her?'

'Nobody. Didn't hear anything or see anything. It must have happened while we were swimming. That's all I can think.'

'So the last time you saw her alive was just before you had your lunch?'

'Yes, about one thirty, I think.'

He thanked her, and looked to Hen to see if she had anything to ask. She obviously hadn't. And it was no use questioning the child, because she'd spent most of the day playing near the water's edge.

THEY DROVE to the Green Dragon at Horsham, Hen leading the way in her car, for a pub lunch.

'Fish and chips suit you?' she suggested when Diamond reached her at the counter where the food was ordered. 'We've plenty of time. A little bird told me Jimmy is out of the office until three.'

So he found a table in the main eating area, and fetched the drinks, two half-pints of Tanglefoot. He usually drank cheap lager, but this seemed the kind of place where you went for a full-bodied beer. Tom Jones was coming over the sound system.

'It's not too loud, is it?' he remarked to Hen.

'I like it. But they don't let you smoke in this area,' she said. 'Before you sit down, do you mind if we move to the patio?' She led him to a table outside.

'Will they find us with the lunch?' he said.

'No problem.' She took out her cigars and lit one. 'I told them I'd be with the Sean Connery lookalike.' She paused before saying, 'How do you want to play this with Jimmy?'

'Straight bat. I've brought my copy of the files. I think we should let him have a read before we say a thing.'

'Good thinking. But then what?'

'We simply ask what happened next. We're entitled to know if he slept with her the night before she was murdered. And anything she said that might throw light on it. There's another thing I'd like to find out from JB. When Emma Tysoe was first brought in on the case, how many people knew? Bramshill, obviously. Jimmy. But who else?'

She stared at him for a moment. 'So you're still holding on to the possibility she could have been killed by the Mariner?'

'I haven't excluded it.' From the beginning, everyone had told him the cases were unconnected, so his stubborn personality wanted to prove the opposite.

Their food arrived shortly after. Hen slid the vinegar towards him. 'I expect you're quite a connoisseur of fish and chips.'

'Living alone, you mean? Actually I'm a pizza specialist.'

'Do you cook for yourself at all?'

'Pizzas from the freezer. I sometimes open a tin of beans. I could be asking you these questions.'

'Me?' Hen said. 'The canteen at Bognor nick is second to none.'

They finished their food and left on foot for the police station, a ten-minute walk through the park.

He asked how the Wightview Sands end of the investigation had been going, and she told him she hadn't yet traced the second life-guard, but she had a name and a mobile phone number—which had not helped, as they couldn't make contact with it. The assumption was that the phone needed recharging.

'What's his name?' Diamond asked.

'Laver.'

'Straight up?'

She frowned. 'What's wrong?'

'Just that the lifeguard we met is called Emerson, or claimed to be. Laver and Emerson were two of the biggest names in Australian tennis in the sixties. They won God knows how many Grand Slam titles between them.'

'You think they were having us on?'

'Having someone on for sure. It could be about work permits, rather than what happened on the beach that day. Is Emerson still working there?'

'The last I heard, he was,' Hen answered. 'I'll follow this up.'

At the police station, they were asked to wait in an office, because DCI Barneston was still not back. They had an upstairs room to themselves. It was typically barren of anything of interest. There were three plastic chairs and a table stained with tea. On the wall facing the door was a map of West Sussex.

'A bloody ashtray would help,' Hen said as she lit up.

Diamond was looking at the map. 'If Emma Tysoe was here with JB the night before she was murdered, she had a drive of thirty-five miles to Wightview Sands. From what I can see, Worthing or Brighton would have been nearer. It looks as if she went to Wightview because she knows the place. It was what she wanted. Somewhere to relax.'

'Presumably. Unless she'd agreed to meet someone.'

'Doesn't appear so. We have a short list of four suspects. The ex-lover, Ken. The two lifeguards. And the Mariner.'

Hen was brooding. 'There are problems with each of them. We don't know how Ken or the Mariner knew she was on that beach on that particular morning.'

'They could have followed her. What about the guy in the black T-shirt who tried to chat her up and got nowhere? He could have been Ken. He got the brush-off, but he could have come back later.'

'The two suspects we know for certain were on that beach are the two Australian guys,' Hen said, doggedly working through the possibilities, 'but we don't have a motive for them.'

'Theft? Her beachbag was missing.'

'It's dead simple to steal a bag on a beach. However, we haven't found her car yet.'

'Good point, Hen.' He snapped his fingers. 'A Lotus Esprit might be a prize worth having for a young guy living on a shoestring without a work permit. He steals the bag because it contains her car key. He's seen her park this beautiful car—'

'People have been killed for less.'

'A lot less. I rather like it, Hen. There's only one problem with it.'

'Yes?'

'Any one of a couple of thousand others who were on that beach could have done it.' Diamond yawned and checked the time on his wristwatch. 'It's bloody near four o'clock. Where is Barneston? I'll see if they can get a message to him.'

The desk sergeant apologised. 'You're waiting for DCI Barneston, sir? He won't be coming back. He's dealing with an incident.'

'Well, I'm going to need his mobile number. I've come from Bath to see him, and another officer with me has come up from the coast.'

Not so simple. Getting Barneston's number was like trying to steal meat from a pride of lions. By sheer force of personality he eventually obtained it on the say-so of a CID inspector.

When he finally got through, he found Barneston incensed at being troubled. 'Who put you onto me? Didn't anyone tell you there's an emergency here?'

Diamond gritted his teeth. 'We're coming to see you.'

'You're joking. I'm dealing with a crisis here.'

'So are we, and you'd better listen up, Jimmy, because it concerns you. Emma Tysoe came to see you the day before she was strangled.'

After a long hesitation, Barneston said, 'I'm at Littlegreen Place, South Harting. It's laughingly described as a safe house.'

six

Littlegreen Place was a large, brick-built house standing in chain-fenced grounds on the northern escarpment of the South Downs. There was no other building within sight. When Diamond drove up with Hen Mallin, the electric gates were open and three police minibuses, two patrol cars and a Skoda were parked in the drive.

Someone with a camera came from the open front door, and Diamond asked him if DCI Barneston was about. The man nodded towards the interior. They went inside, through a sizable entrance hall, in the direction of voices. Jimmy Barneston was slumped at the kitchen table, his head in his hands. Two others in plain clothes, holding mugs, were standing together watching a uniformed inspector speaking urgent orders into a mobile phone.

Diamond asked what was happening.

Barneston gave a groan that was part threat, part protest.

Diamond put a hand on his shoulder. 'You cocked up, is that it?'

This got a response. Barneston said with a heavy emphasis, 'Not me.'

'The people on duty?'

He nodded, all too ready to shift any blame. 'Two hours ago, a call was made to this place, a scheduled call, to the two Special Branch officers supposed to be guarding, em, a person under threat.'

'Matthew Porter,' Hen said.

She wasn't supposed to know the name. Barneston took note with a twitch of the eyebrows. 'This was only a routine check. It's done at regular intervals. There was no response. They kept trying. Still nothing. So a rapid response vehicle was sent here. The officers found the front gate wide open. The double doors at the front of the house were also open. No one was inside. The bulk of the security system was disabled. Two armed SO12 officers had vanished.'

'And Matthew Porter?'

'Yes. The Range Rover used by one of the officers is also missing. There's no sign of a struggle, nothing out of place.'

'Video cameras?' Diamond enquired.

'All disabled from the control room upstairs.' Barneston scraped his fingers through his thick black hair. 'We moved him here from another address because it was allegedly more secure. The Mariner has found it and strolled in and out as if it were a public toilet. Someone's going to swing for this.'

'Are you certain this is the Mariner?' Hen asked.

'How could it be anyone else?'

'Matthew Porter didn't like being cooped up in Streatham. What if he didn't like it here and walked out?'

Barneston glared at her. 'What do *you* know about Streatham? We've had a major balls-up in security and you people know too much for my liking. Tell me now. It could be relevant.'

Hen flushed bright pink. She shouldn't have mentioned Streatham.

Diamond felt the muscles tighten across his shoulders. This wasn't the moment he would have chosen, and there was no way now of putting it off. He let his eyes meet Barneston's. 'Emma Tysoe—whose death we are investigating—kept some files on computer. I have a copy with me, as decrypted by a lad in my nick.'

'Oh shit.'

It wasn't Jimmy Barneston's day. Hen tried to divert him. 'Coming back to the present emergency, don't you think it possible Porter simply made a break for it?'

'No, I don't,' he said. 'Come and see this.' He led them upstairs. He pushed open the first door on the landing. 'Porter's bedroom.'

The interior was in pretty good order. On the bed was a sheet of A4 paper with words in newsprint pasted to it.

Diamond took a step closer and bent over to read the message.

'"Three under par."'

'You know what that is?' Barneston said.

'A reference to golf, I suppose.'

'Three under par is an albatross. The albatross is the bird the Ancient Mariner killed. Now tell me the bastard wasn't here.'

They stood in silence, absorbing the force of the words and feeling a chilling contact with the mind of their author. The note dashed any hope that Porter would survive.

'Have you got roadblocks in operation?' Diamond asked.

'Full-scale alert, but it could have happened four hours ago. The last check-in we logged was at noon.'

'And the building has been searched?'

'From top to bottom.'

They returned downstairs. In the kitchen, Barneston seemed to be getting a grip again. 'Was there anything useful in those files?'

'We've learned a lot more about our murder victim and the job she was on,' Diamond told him.

'Does she say anything that will help me right now? Did she put together a profile I can use?'

'How do I know what's going to be helpful to you?' Diamond told him testily. 'Read it yourself. Is there a computer here?'

'Upstairs. There's sod all happening, so I might as well make use of the time. Where's the disk?'

Diamond handed him the tiny USB drive.

They remained downstairs, leaving Barneston to read Emma's files in private. Hen went outside for a smoke. Diamond got on the mobile to Ingeborg and asked how the hunt for Ken was progressing.

'Still trying, guv. I went through the credit card receipts. No Kens. Do you think he could have paid cash?'

'It's possible, I suppose. You'd be better off asking Popjoy's, not me. Have you talked to the neighbours?'

'The thing is,' she said, 'she had her own entrance, living, as she did, in the basement flat. The people upstairs didn't see much of her.'

'You're going to have to track down everyone who dined at Popjoy's the evening they were there, and see how much they remember about the other guests. A description would be a start, even if we don't have his name. You've talked to the waiters, I hope?'

'I'll get onto that,' she promised. Apparently she'd been talking to the management, not the waiters.

Diamond joined Hen outside. Garden maintenance wasn't high priority in Special Branch. Across a stretch of meadow that had once been a lawn, a line of officers searched the undergrowth near the fence. Somewhere overhead the police helicopter buzzed.

'What's his game, Peter?' Hen asked.

He gave a shrug. 'Whatever it is, I'm certain it's just as he planned it.'

'He brought that message with him like a calling card, the bastard. Bloody arrogance. It doesn't give any grounds for hope.'

'No.'

They returned to the kitchen. One look at the others told them no news had come through. Diamond picked up someone's *Daily Mail* and looked for news of the rugby. Bath were slipping in the league.

THERE WAS STILL nothing to report to Barneston when he came downstairs and found them in the garden again. He had the look of a man in deep shock, thoughts whirling in his brain. He made a visible effort to focus on the immediate problem. 'He'll be clean away by now.'

'It doesn't look good,' Diamond agreed.

A short nervy sigh. 'It bears out what she wrote in the files—he knows he can outwit the police.'

'She didn't put it quite like that, if I remember,' Hen said. 'It was something like "has an exalted belief he can outwit us". There's a difference. He'll get overconfident.'

'Breaking into this place will have done his confidence a power of good,' Barneston said gloomily. 'Mine is at rock bottom.'

Diamond took a head-on approach. 'We need to know if she spent the night with you, the last night of her life.'

Barneston confirmed it with a nod.

Diamond had never scored points for sensitivity. 'So she came to Horsham with a list of questions for Anna Walpurgis?'

'Yup. Emma came to my house and we went out for a meal and spent the night together.'

'Did she say anything to you about this man Ken she mentions?'

'Not directly. She told me she'd been in another relationship that was finished. She didn't give a name.'

Hen said, 'Jimmy, can you remember anything she said about him that will help us to identify him?'

'Nothing at all. She only mentioned him in passing.'

Diamond said, 'We know she dumped him. Do you think it's possible he could have found out about you?'

'I don't see how. I didn't visit her in Bath.'

'We're wondering if he followed her to Horsham and saw you

together. Did you have a sense of anyone watching you?'

'No.'

'Was Emma relaxed?' Hen asked.

'I thought so. She seemed to be enjoying herself.' He spread his hands in a gesture of openness. 'Listen, if there was anything I could think of to help you, I would. She was a sweet girl. I really enjoyed being with her. I freaked out when I heard what happened to her.'

This little tribute didn't melt Peter Diamond's heart. 'But you didn't come forward and say you spent the night with her. You just hoped we'd make an early arrest and leave you out of it?'

No answer. Diamond had hit the mark. He said, 'Tell us about the morning of the day she was murdered. Did she talk about her plans?'

Barneston looked down at the ground. 'She did her best to persuade me to spend the day with her at the beach. Said I'd function better for a few hours away from the Mariner enquiry.' He paused and sighed. 'I was almost persuaded, too.'

'So what happened, exactly?'

'I gave her breakfast in bed and told her to take her time getting up. When I left around nine, she was about to take a shower.'

'Did she say anything about going to the beach alone?'

'Yes. It was a beautiful day. She was going, with or without me.'

'She must have driven there,' Diamond said.

'Yes, her car was on my drive. And that's about all I can tell you.'

'There is something else,' Diamond said. 'Would you mind telling us how you actually spent the rest of the day?'

Barneston frowned, glared and then gave a hollow laugh. 'You're not asking me to account for my time?'

'You've got it in one, Jimmy,' Diamond said with a look as unrelenting as his voice.

Barneston hesitated for a long time, perhaps to show dissent. Diamond's eyes, unblinking, had never left his. Finally, he submitted. 'I went to the nick and worked on the case.'

'Until when?'

'I don't know. Late morning, early afternoon. I had a canteen lunch. Then a stroll around the park.'

'Alone?'

Barneston's face reddened. 'I don't have to take these innuendoes. Who do you think you are questioning here?'

'Alone, then,' Diamond said. 'How about the rest of the afternoon?'

'Didn't you hear me? I've had enough of this crap.'

Hen put in gently, 'He's doing his job, Jimmy. He's got a duty to ask.'

Making every word sound like an infliction, Barneston said, 'I returned to my office for about an hour and finished the job I was on. Then I went home. It was about two thirty when I left. No, I didn't make any phone calls, and nobody knocked on my door, so it's perfectly feasible that I could have driven to Wightview Sands inside an hour, found Emma and strangled her. Of course, you have the minor problem of the motive—establishing how we fell out after a night together—but I guess that's not beyond your fertile imagination.'

'Probably not,' Diamond said evenly, 'but there is another problem. How would you drive two cars away from the scene? Hers hasn't been seen since the murder.'

Barneston was silent while he played this over in his mind. After a longish interval he saw the point. 'So you're not about to caution me?' It was an attempt to recoup, a feeble joke.

Diamond indulged him with a grin.

After the tension of the past minutes it was a relief to go inside and check developments. But nothing *had* developed. The Mariner had come and gone leaving no clue except his newsprint taunt.

'How could he have conned his way in?' Diamond asked.

'God only knows,' Barneston said. 'The guards have entry codes that even I don't know. Anyone at the gate is under video surveillance from the control room upstairs.'

'Are you sure of the guards?'

'Special Branch is. One hundred per cent. And the system is the best they have. Infrared sensors in every room, lasers, cameras, the lot.'

A personal radio gave off the sound of static and a voice came through clearly enough for everyone to hear. 'Oscar Bravo to Control, reporting a sighting from the chopper. A four by four, possibly Range Rover, stationary in Caseys Lane, reference six-eight-five-eight-zero-three. Shall we investigate? Over.'

'Give me that,' Barneston said to the officer holding the radio. He touched the press-to-talk switch. 'We're on our way. Over and out.'

There was a stampede to the cars.

THE MAP REFERENCE wasn't required. The helicopter marked the spot by hovering over it. The convoy of three police vehicles travelled at speed in emergency mode, blue lights flashing.

'One thing's certain,' Diamond said to Hen, some distance in the rear in a fourth car, his own. 'We're not going to surprise anyone.'

A short distance ahead was the gate to a field where sheep were grazing, indifferent to the activity. Beside an oak tree, a dark green Range Rover stood in front of the gate on turf, just off the lane.

The convoy stopped about thirty yards short and two armed officers were detailed to make an approach. A few people got out and crouched behind the vehicles, but Diamond and Hen chose to wait in the car. The Range Rover looked unoccupied, but there was no telling what was below window level.

The two armed men separated, one taking a wide arc through the field on the far side of the Range Rover, while the other remained in the lane. The man in the lane flattened himself to the ground and began a crocodile-like approach to the rear of the vehicle, using his knees and elbows for leverage, but still gripping his short-barrel machine gun. He finally got right up to the rear bumper of the Range Rover. For about half a minute he did nothing, listening, no doubt, for a voice or a movement inside the vehicle. Then he slowly stood high enough to look through the rear window. Abruptly he turned towards the others. 'Go, go, go!'

The response was immediate. Everyone got out and started running towards the Range Rover.

The officer was shouting, 'They're on the floor.' He smashed the side window with the butt of his gun—which activated a loud alarm. He put his arm through, swung back the door and dipped inside.

In a moment he emerged with a body trussed with plasticuffs and a leather belt. Others helped to lift the man out and onto the grass. He was breathing. He opened his eyes. A second man was removed from the space behind the back seat. He, also, had been tied up and handcuffed, and he, also, was alive. Like his companion, he looked dazed and ill. Neither of the rescued men was Matthew Porter.

'Somebody kill that bloody alarm!' Barneston yelled.

A uniformed inspector disabled the mechanism.

The men's groans could now be heard by everyone. Jimmy Barneston wasn't too concerned by the state of them. He wanted information. 'Where's Porter?' Barneston asked the more animated of the two. 'What happened to him?'

The man shook his head.

Barneston asked again, 'What happened? I need to know.'

The man's mouth was moving soundlessly, like a beached fish.

Hen said, 'He's dehydrated. Give him a drink, for pity's sake.' Someone produced a bottle of water, which she snatched up and held to the man's mouth. They fetched another bottle for the second man. 'Can't we get them out of these cuffs?' Hen asked. 'The poor guys are in pain.'

One of the police gunmen unhitched cutters from his belt and snipped through the plasticuffs.

The man who seemed in slightly better shape sat up, and immediately vomited, throwing up all the water he'd swallowed and more. It definitely wasn't Jimmy Barneston's day. He'd taken some of it on his shoes. The man was trying to splutter out a word.

'Gas?' Barneston said. 'Did you say gas? Did he put it to your face?'

A nod. He managed a few connected words. 'Took me from behind. I was coughing. Couldn't breathe. Don't remember any more.'

'So the gas knocked you out. Did you see him?'

He shook his head.

'What about Matt Porter? Was he in the room with you?'

'Another room.'

Barneston turned to the second guard and tried to question him. But the gas had affected him more seriously. He was talking gibberish.

This was a medical emergency. Up to now Diamond had thought of himself as an observer, but someone had to take some initiative here because there was no telling how seriously these men were affected. Barneston was entirely taken up with extracting any information he could, so Diamond told the nearest man with a mobile to call an ambulance.

When Barneston stood up, Diamond told him what he'd arranged. But the message didn't seem to register. JB was extremely keyed up. He turned his back on Diamond and returned to the more coherent of the two men.

'This isn't getting anywhere,' Diamond confided to Hen.

'He's poleaxed. He's lost the man he was supposed to be protecting. He's got a neurotic woman in another so-called safe house. He knows Bramshill will come down on him like a ton of bricks, and what's more they're going to decrypt those deeply embarrassing files any time. He's in shock,' she said. 'I've never seen him like this. If there's stuff he should be doing, you'd better tell him.'

Every incident brings its own problems, and the challenge is to stay cool and deal with them. Barneston wasn't shaping up at all. So Diamond tapped him on the shoulder and discreetly suggested he order everyone off the grass and onto the lane.

'What's the problem?' Barneston asked. 'What's up now?'

'Crime scene procedure. You've dealt with the incident. Now it's a matter of preserving what you can of the scene.' For a man who had never been a slave to the rule book this was rich, but Diamond was putting it in language the new generation of CID should understand. 'Particularly the treadmarks. The Mariner had his car waiting here.'

'You think so?' Those blue eyes showed little understanding.

It was obvious Barneston's brain hadn't made the jump, so Diamond laid out the facts as he saw them. 'He gassed these blokes and Porter and put them in the Range Rover and drove here. He must have had a vehicle waiting, right? So he transferred Porter into his own motor and drove off, God knows where. The least we can do is find the treadmarks his tyres made.'

Barneston nodded his head sagely as if it had always been in his plans, and ordered everyone onto the lane. Crime-scene tape was fetched and used to seal off the area.

Hen said, 'That's better. Feel as if we're getting a grip.'

'He's away,' Barneston said bleakly. 'He's hung us out to dry.'

'Snap out of it, Jimmy,' Diamond told him.

'Have you sent for the SOCOs yet?'

'I'd get one of those sergeants onto it if I were you.'

'Good point.' Barneston went over to arrange it.

When he came back, he was still in the same fateful frame of mind. 'We can check the motor inside and out and every inch of the field, but let's face it we're up shit creek.'

That kind of talk didn't go down well with Diamond. 'Haven't you heard of DNA?'

'What use is that without a suspect? We don't know a thing about him.'

'We know several things,' Diamond said. 'He's extremely well informed on our security. Somehow he found out Porter was transferred here. He must have had some kind of inside information. He has access to gas. He's very focused. He could have killed the guards, but he chose not to.'

'Christ, that's not bad,' Barneston said, the interest reviving in his eyes. He asked Diamond what he recommended next.

'The Mariner's car is the thing to concentrate on,' the big man answered. 'There's a chance someone noticed it parked in the lane. A farm hand, maybe. I'd order a house-to-house on all the inhabited places in the vicinity, asking (a), if they saw anyone along the lanes, or crossing the field, and (b), if they noticed a vehicle.'

'I was thinking along those lines myself,' Barneston said.

'Great minds,' Hen said with a wink that only Diamond saw.

Barneston moved off to speak to one of his team.

Diamond and Hen remained there while the paramedics arrived and took the two SO12 guards away for treatment.

Barneston eventually came back to where Diamond and Hen were watching the action from behind the tapes. 'All the farms and houses in the area are being visited.' He cleared his throat. 'You suggested this could be an inside job, seeing that the Mariner found out about Porter being moved here.'

Diamond lifted his shoulders a fraction. 'He must have got it from somewhere.'

'You're right and it's a bloody nightmare,' Barneston said. 'I don't know who I can trust any more. And the worst of it is that I've got someone else under protection. Well, you've read the files, so you know who she is.' Barneston looked about him to make sure no one else was close enough to overhear. 'You see, this story is going to break in the press any time. I can't keep the lid on much longer. Questions are being asked about both Axel Summers and Matt Porter.'

Diamond said, 'In that case, you'd better go public right away. Take control. Call a press conference and tell all.'

'Jesus Christ!' Barneston looked stunned.

'What's the value of secrecy? You can't rely on safe houses being safe for anyone any more. The Mariner will get to Anna Walpurgis, whatever high-tech security you have protecting her.'

'Yes, but what's the alternative? Let her swan around the country? That's as good as handing her over to the bastard.'

'Not this guy. He's a planner. He works everything out, down to the last detail. The killing of Summers and today's murder were both precision-planned. So isn't it a sure-fire bet that he has a plan drawn up for Miss Walpurgis?' Diamond warmed to his theme. 'Do you see what I'm driving at? Up to now, he's remained ahead of us because he knows we're an institution that works along predictable lines, as easy to see as a mail train coming up the line. Now I haven't met Anna Walpurgis. I haven't had that pleasure.'

'Plenty have,' murmured Hen.

'OK, she's a lively lady. Not the type to sit at home every night. That could work in her favour. She'll be safer from the Mariner in the arms of some admirer than she will be in a safe house.'

Barneston was still under the cosh. 'It's too big a risk. Huge.'

'Not so huge as leaving her in a safe house,' Diamond said.

'Even if I believed you, it's not my decision. She's in the care of SO12. Special Branch call the shots.'

'Come off it, Jimmy. After this cock-up, they're in disarray. You can seize the initiative. Tell them you've lost confidence in their security.'

'I'm not sure if I want her on my plate.'

'She is already. When this is over, do you think SO12 are going to put up their hands and say it was their fault?'

Barneston let out a long, troubled breath. He knew Diamond was right; this was obvious in his expression. He'd carry the can if things went wrong. For a while he was silent. Finally he came out with a kind of confession. 'I thought I could take this on and win. Listening to you, I think you've got a better handle on this case than I have. Your way of thinking is different. Would you do me a favour?' he asked Diamond. 'Would you meet Anna and tell me if you still think I should give her a free rein?'

He couldn't say more clearly that he was floundering.

'Sure,' Diamond said, 'but not in a safe house, right? Get her out of there fast. Send her to me in Bath. I'll see she comes to no harm. Then you can get down to what you're good at—detective work.'

After Barneston had gone off to see the SOCOs, Hen asked Diamond, 'Do you think that's wise?'

'In terms of my career, definitely not. I'll have Special Branch wanting my head on a plate. But as a way of wrong-footing the Mariner, it's the best I can think of, and that's the priority now.'

'I hope you know what you're taking on, squire, because I'm foxed.'

'Walpurgis is the bait. The Mariner's going to have to adjust his master plan now. He expected her to be under Special Branch protection. Instead, she's coming to Bath. He'll find out and follow her.'

'You don't have to look so happy at the prospect.'

He raised his forefinger. 'Right. But Bath is my patch. I know it better than he does. The odds have changed a bit. That's how we'll pinch him, Hen.'

She pondered that for a moment. 'It's bloody dangerous.'

'So what's new? Walpurgis is under threat of death already.'

MOST OF HIS TEAM were in the incident room in Bath police station when Diamond arrived the next morning. They were clustered around John Leaman, who was telling a joke. At the sight of their burly superior, people sidled back to their desks.

Diamond looked to his right. 'Ingeborg, what's been happening?'

'Well, I finally nailed Ken. His name is Bellman—Kenneth Bellman. He works as a consultant for an IT firm called Knowhow and Fix based in Batheaston. Lives in digs in a house on Bathwick Hill, about halfway up on the left-hand side.'

He nodded. 'So have you spoken to him?'

Keith Halliwell said, 'We thought you'd want first crack at him.'

'You thought right.' He showed an upturned thumb to Ingeborg. 'Nice work.'

'Can I bring him in, guv?' She couldn't conceal her eagerness.

Diamond shook his head. 'Not yet. I promised DCI Mallin, our colleague from Bognor, that I'd give her the chance to come in on this. More important than that, I want the background on this guy before we see him. Keith, see what you can get. Do it discreetly.'

He called Hen and told her the news. 'I'll keep you posted.'

'I wish I could report some success at this end,' Hen said. 'I was hoping my lot would have found Mr Laver by now, but he's vanished into thin air. And to make matters worse, Emerson has not been seen on the beach for a couple of days. I've got visions of chasing Aussies in camper vans all over Europe. Let's hope your Ken puts his hand up to the murder and saves me the trouble.'

If only it were so simple, Diamond thought.

LATER IN THE MORNING Diamond took a call from Jimmy Barneston. The shell-shocked Jimmy of yesterday sounded more in control.

'I thought you'd like to know I slept on your advice and decided it made sense. I've called a press conference for this afternoon.'

'Good move. Take the initiative away from the killer.'

'I'm going to tell them everything except the third name on the Mariner's list. You know who I mean?' Clearly he didn't trust the phone.

'I'm a detective. I can work it out,' Diamond said. 'Speaking of that person, have you told her about Porter being snatched?'

'Not yet. She doesn't know anything yet. I'll have to now, won't I? Don't want her hearing it first on the telly.'

'Have you told her about my offer?'

'Not yet. She doesn't know anything yet.'

'When you break the bad news about Porter being snatched you can tell her my offer is the good news.'

'All right.'

'I guess there's nothing new on the Mariner? Did the house-to-house achieve anything?'

'No. And the treadmarks aren't sharp enough to help. Forensics told me not to expect much. They tested the steering wheel for DNA and they reckon he wore gloves. He's ultra-careful.'

'Are both of the guards recovering?'

'They were sent home last night. I've spoken to them but they added nothing to what we know already.'

'You may get some help from the public after the media get to work on it.'

'I won't hold my breath,' Barneston said.

KEITH HALLIWELL was back by lunchtime and Diamond took him for a bite and a pint at Brown's, just up the street on the site of the old city police station in Orange Grove, an Italianate palazzo-style building so much easier on the eye than their present place of work. 'So what do we know about Ken Bellman?' he asked, when they were settled.

'There's not a lot to report, guv,' Halliwell told him. 'He's been around for about six months. Gets his paper from a shop on Bathwick Hill, and also buys computer magazines and chocolate. He dresses casually in polo shirts and baggy trousers.'

'Where's he from?'

'The north, I was told. He boasts a bit about the life up there being better than anywhere else.'

'Why come south, if it's so much better up there? Anything else? Is he a driver?'

'Yes, he has an old BMW that he services himself.'

'Description?'

'He's thirtyish, about five nine, with a mop of dark hair.'

'You mean curly?' Diamond said, thinking of the man in the black T-shirt.

'It's what *they* mean, not me, guv. And they said a mop.'

'You didn't catch a glimpse of him, I suppose?'

'He wasn't about.'

It was decision time. 'Wait for tomorrow and then bring him in late morning. I want to give DCI Mallin a chance to get here.'

'When you say "bring him in", do you mean by invitation?'

'Oh, yes. No coercion, Keith, unless he's really stroppy. We need cooperation at this point, help with our enquiries, right? Another thing, Keith.'

'Guv?'

'Some office furniture found its way to the top corridor. It was stored originally in the room we're using as our incident room. Georgina isn't happy about it. See if you can shift it somewhere else.'

'Right.'

'And can you get the team together around three? There's some news about to break that I want you all to hear from me.'

THEY LISTENED in silence to Diamond's account of the Mariner's murderous agenda. When he started telling them about the gas raid on the safe house the interest quickened significantly. This was pretty sensational and they were curious to know where it was leading. Like the best storytellers, he kept them in suspense to the very end. 'I think I've convinced DCI Jimmy Barneston that Anna Walpurgis isn't safe any more in a so-called safe house. A radical rethink is necessary, to take the initiative away from the Mariner. I suggested bringing Ms Walpurgis to Bath.'

He paused, letting this sink in. No one was ready to say that the boss had flipped, but doubt was in the air.

Halliwell was the first to speak. 'Do we have a safe house in Bath?'

'No—and that's the point, Keith, to do something he isn't expecting. It buys us a little time.'

'Don't you think he'll find out and follow her here?'

'I'm sure he will. That's OK by me. He'll be on our territory.'

'It's a hell of a risk, guv.'

He nodded. 'That's why I'm telling you. Any of you could get involved as well. The man is dangerous and single-minded. Stand in his way, and you risk being eliminated.'

'Where will she stay?' Leaman asked.

'Yet to be decided. She'll have a say in the decision. Any other questions?'

'How does all this link up with Emma Tysoe?' Ingeborg asked.

'We don't know. She was working on a profile of the Mariner, so in a sense she was shoved into the firing line. That was my early assumption. Now I've veered in the other direction.'

'Because of Ken?'

'Not especially. No, I've come to think of the Mariner as the kind of murderer who plans his crime like an architect, every detail worked out. But the strangling of Emma Tysoe wasn't planned. Couldn't have been. She only made up her mind to go to the beach the evening before she visited Jimmy Barneston. It had to be an opportunist killing. The variables would have horrified the Mariner.'

He brought the meeting to a close. In his office, he reached for the phone and called Hen to let her know Ken Bellman was being brought in for questioning.

'I was just about to call you,' she said. 'We've all been glued to the TV, watching the news breaking. Petersfield police have found the body of a young white male on a golf course.'

'Matthew Porter?'

'Nobody is saying yet, but of course it's him. They haven't said what he died of, but they're treating it as murder.'

seven

Hen Mallin agreed with Diamond that the questioning of Ken Bellman had to take priority over what was happening in Petersfield. Best leave Jimmy Barneston to sift the evidence.

That evening she drove straight from work to the beach at Wightview Sands, partly because she wanted to refresh her memory of the scene, and also because a lone walk (and smoke) by the sea is as good a way as any of getting one's thoughts in order.

She drove up to the car-park gate just before seven. The man on duty asked for a pound and she said she was a police officer.

'How do I know that?' he asked.

'For God's sake, man. I'm investigating the murder. I've been here on and off for a couple of weeks.'

'I was on, you know,' he said. 'The day when the woman was murdered. But I can't tell you who did it. Can't see a thing from here.'

She was hearing an echo of a voice she seemed to know. Familiar, too, was the self-importance. She looked at him sitting in his cabin, and didn't recognise his brown eyes and black hair.

'I'll show you my ID, if you insist,' she said.

He did insist. She produced it, and he pressed the gate mechanism.

'And what's your name?' Hen asked, before driving through.

'I'm Garth. Don't be too long, will you? We close at eight thirty.'

It came to her as she was cruising up the narrow road that runs alongside the beach. She did know the voice. He was the jobsworth who'd phoned in when Dr Shiena Wilkinson had turned up looking for her Range Rover. The reason she hadn't seen him was that she'd sent Stella to deal with it.

After parking near the beach café she found the gap between beach huts that led to the lifeguard lookout post, above where Emma Tysoe's body had been found. You wouldn't have known it was a murder scene now. Children were busy playing in the sand where the body was found, digging a system of waterways, their shadows long in the evening sun. Most of the day's visitors had left.

Hen picked her way carefully over the children's digging and out to a stretch of sand beyond the breakwaters, where she could walk freely. She lit one of her small cigars and let her thoughts turn to Peter Diamond. He'd proved less of an ogre than she'd expected. He was brusque at times, but funny, too, and willing to listen. She couldn't fault the way he'd conducted the case so far, keeping her informed of each development. Mind, he was a risk-taker. This plan of his to take over the protection of Anna Walpurgis could so easily go wrong. It gave him what he'd wanted all along, a legitimate reason to be involved. But what resources did he have in Bath? Hen could only hope he had a strategy.

She continued her walk as far as the flagpole at East Head. If she walked any farther she'd be late getting back to her car, and she had no confidence Garth would let her out of the car park.

GEORGINA DALLYMORE, the assistant chief constable, was on her guard that morning. It wasn't like Peter Diamond to ask if she could spare a few minutes. He avoided her at all costs.

She folded her arms. 'To what do we owe this, Peter?'

'I expect you noticed the furniture disappeared from the corridor?'

'No,' she said with a faint flush of pink. 'I hadn't noticed. Do I have you to thank for that?'

'No problem. You can enjoy your cruise now. When are you off?'

She relaxed a little. 'Tomorrow, actually.'

As if it was mere politeness, he asked, 'What's happening to Sultan? That handsome white Persian?'

Everyone knew about Sultan. There was a photo on her desk of this mound of fur with fierce blue eyes and a snub nose.

'He has to go into a cattery, unfortunately. He doesn't care for it at all, but you can't let them run your life.'

'Shame.' He paused. 'I don't suppose he'll suffer.'

'*Suffer?*' A cloud of concern passed across Georgina's face. 'I should hope not. The place is very expensive.'

'Poor old Sultan.' Diamond picked up the photo in its gilt frame. 'Personally, I favour having a house sitter. It's nicer for your pet and you can relax knowing someone is there.'

'Ideally, that sounds a good solution,' Georgina agreed.

'Bit of a holiday for the sitter as well. In a city like Bath, house sitting is no hardship. You're convenient for everything in Bennett Street. A house sitter would jump at the chance.'

'It's too late for me to start looking for someone now.'

'I wouldn't say that.'

Georgina tried to appear unmoved, but he could see she was all attentiveness.

'If you'd like one, I may be able to help,' he offered. 'I know of a lady shortly coming to Bath who would gladly look after your home—and Sultan—for no charge at all.'

'Well, I don't know,' Georgina said. 'Who is she?'

'You may have heard of her—Anna Walpurgis.'

The eyes widened. 'The pop star?'

'As was. More a lady of leisure now. Some maniac threatened her life and she's been stuck in a safe house being looked after by Special Branch for some time. She got so bored. It would do everyone a good turn if she could escape to Bath for a week.'

'Anna Walpurgis.' Georgina repeated the name, and there was a discernible note of awe. 'She wouldn't give parties?'

'Good Lord, no. She's keeping a low profile.'

'Is she under guard?'

'Not any more. It's a step towards a normal life. I can keep an eye on her, make sure she's able to cope.'

'Let me think about this.'

'Yes, of course.'

BELLMAN HAD A PAPER CUP of coffee in his hands. He slopped some on his jeans as his interrogators came in.

'Careful,' Hen said. 'You could ruin your prospects that way.'

'It's OK.' He didn't smile. He looked nervous. He placed the coffee to one side.

The description they'd had from Olga Smith was spot on. Latin looks, definitely. Strong features. Broad shoulders, narrow hips, dark, curly hair that looked as if it never needed combing.

Hen and Diamond took their seats. Hen thanked him for coming in and apologised for the formality of asking his name and stating for the tape that he had been invited to attend of his own free will to assist with the enquiry into the death of Dr Emma Tysoe.

He blinked twice at the name.

'So you live locally, I gather. Do you work in Bath?' Hen asked after she'd identified herself and Diamond.

'Batheaston. I'm an IT consultant.'

'Forgive my ignorance. What's that exactly?'

'I'm with a firm called Knowhow and Fix. Kind of troubleshooters really. If a firm has a computer problem we do our best to sort it.'

'I suppose you need a car in this job. What do you drive?'

'A BMW.'

'Nice. How long have you owned it?'

'Five or six years. I bought it secondhand.'

'When did you come to Bath?'

'Just before Christmas.'

'And where were you before that?'

'The job? London. SW1.'

'What sort of work? Similar?'

'Not quite the same. I was a technical support programmer.'

'You've been doing this sort of work for some time, then?'

'Since university.'

'Where was that?'

'Liverpool.'

'Computer science, I suppose?'

'Pretty close. Electronic engineering. I picked up my computer skills later, when I was doing my M.Sc.'

Hen nodded. 'Ken, how long have you known Emma Tysoe?'

His hands felt for the arms of the chair and gripped them. 'About ten years. I met her when we were students at Liverpool. She read psychology there. We went out a few times. I liked her.'

'And it developed into something?'

He shook his head. 'Not at the time. We were friendly, and that was all. After she left, we lost touch. I didn't know she was living in Bath until I met her one day in the library a few months ago. We went for a drink together, caught up on old times, and well, we got serious, if you know what I mean.'

'And it lasted some time?'

He frowned. 'Six or seven weeks, probably.'

'Was it a loving relationship?'

'I thought I loved her, yes.'

'Did love come into it on her side?'

'I don't know what was in her mind. She said she enjoyed being with me.'

'Is it fair to say, Ken, that you were keener than she was?'

He frowned a little. 'Is that a trick question?'

'Why should it be?' Hen said.

'Let's face it. Emma was murdered. If I come across as the guy who pestered her for sex, it doesn't look good, does it? We were good friends, we slept together a few times because we wanted to.'

'I'm not trying to trick you, ducky. We just want to get the picture right. Did she have other friends? Did you go round in a group?'

'She wasn't the kind of person who enjoyed being in company.'

'So you and she spent the time doing what?'

He shrugged. 'Pubs, the cinema, a meal out sometimes.'

'Not long before her death, you took her for a meal at Popjoy's. Is that right?'

He gave a nod.

'Would it be true to say the evening didn't go according to plan?'

There was a delay before he responded. 'How do you know that?'

'We're detectives. We'd like to hear your take on the evening.'

He stared into the palm of his left hand. 'It started well enough. It was a very good meal. Towards the end she complained of a headache and blamed the wine. She said some wines had that effect on her, letting me know, in a way, that I should have let her see the list. She asked the waiter for an Alka-Seltzer, which I found deeply embarrassing. Then we had to wait a long time for a taxi. I thought we could walk home but she was wearing unsuitable shoes. I seemed to be saying the wrong thing at every turn.'

Diamond said, to keep the confidences coming, 'We've all had evenings like that.'

Bellman gave a sigh. 'Well, it got no better. Back in her flat I asked if the headache was easing off and she said I was only asking because I wanted my money's worth, which was pretty hurtful. I think I told her so. I left soon after.'

Hen asked, 'Was it a break-up?'

'I didn't think so at the time. I tried calling her next day to see if I was still in the doghouse. I had to leave a message on the answerphone. I think I just said I hoped she was feeling better and would she call me. But she didn't. When I eventually got through to her, she told me that she didn't want to see me any more because she was seeing someone else. I was gutted.' The pain of the memory showed in his face. 'I reacted badly. I'm ashamed now. I called her some ugly names. She slammed the phone down and I can't blame her.' He shook his head. 'Wish I could take back what I said.'

The self-recrimination didn't impress Diamond. He took up the questioning. 'So did you regard the break as final?'

'No. I'd lost control. I wanted her back. Thinking about it after that phone call, I wondered if she'd invented another man to hurt me. I thought if I handled it right we could get back together again.'

'So did you do any more about patching it up?'

'Not immediately. As I said, I was slightly suspicious about this other man she'd met.' He coloured noticeably. 'This doesn't reflect very well on me, but I'd better tell you. The next Saturday morning she drove off in her sports car and I followed her, to try to find out.'

'Didn't she know your car?'

'We'd never been out in it. She drove all the way to Horsham and drove south of the town until she came to a house near the river. I parked some distance off so I didn't actually see her go in, but her Lotus was parked outside. I watched and waited. Around six thirty she came out with a tall bloke, dark, in a suit, hair brushed back. He opened the garage and backed his car out, a red Renault, I think. She got in and they drove off, leaving her car on the drive.'

'Confirming your worst fears?'

'Absolutely.'

'So what did you do?'

'I waited for them to come back. I had to find out if she would spend the night with him.'

'So did they return that evening?' Diamond asked.

'About ten. And she went into the house with him and didn't come out again. I know because I slept in my own car that night.'

Diamond didn't press him. The man couldn't have been more candid, and every detail chimed in with information they already had.

'Next morning, the Sunday,' he resumed, 'the man left his house alone, dressed in his suit again, and drove off in his car. She came out half an hour later and drove away. I got in my car and followed. She headed south and eventually ended up in Wightview Sands.'

'It must have been obvious you were behind her.'

'I don't know. I was never close enough for her to recognise me.

And when we got closer to the beach, and everything slowed down, I made sure I was at least two cars behind,' Bellman added. 'As it happened, that almost threw me. There was a barrier system at the beach car park. You paid a chap in a kiosk. He was chatting to Emma and then she drove off. All I could do was watch her car disappear. It's a very large car park.'

'Large beach,' Diamond said.

'You're telling me. By the time I'd got up to the barrier, I was resigned to having to walk along the beach looking for her.'

'What did you intend when you found her?'

'By this time, I'd decided to try and talk her round.'

'Even after you knew she'd spent the night with someone else?' Hen said in disbelief.

'If there was any sort of romance between them, he wouldn't have allowed her to spend the day by herself on the beach.'

'He could have had a job to go to,' Diamond said, finding himself in the unlikely role of Jimmy Barneston's spokesman. 'Some of us work Sundays.'

Hen said without catching Diamond's eye, 'I'm with Ken on this. Any boyfriend worthy of the name would take the day off. So what did you do? Park your car and go looking for her?'

'Yes. I set off slowly along the promenade above the beach. It was really crowded. So I went right down on the sand, and that was how I found her.'

'Was she surprised?'

'Very.'

'How did you explain that you were there?'

'Coincidence. I made a joke out of it. I was doing my best to put her at her ease. I thought if I could persuade her to let me sit with her on the beach, we could talk through our problem.'

Diamond said, 'So you chatted to her.'

'I tried. She wasn't pleased to see me, and she made it very clear she didn't want me there. Basically, she told me to piss off.'

'Bit of a blow.'

'Well, yes. I was upset.'

'Angry?'

He gave Diamond a defiant look. 'Not at all. I was unhappy, yes, but I couldn't blame her. I'd hurt her more than I realised when I called her those names. Give her time, I thought, and she may yet come round. So I walked off, just as she asked.'

'Are you sure about this? A witness heard you swear at her. You were heard to say something like, "Suit yourself, then. I'll leave you to it. Oh, what the fuck?"'

He frowned. After some hesitation, Bellman said, 'If that's what I said—and it may be true—it doesn't mean I swore at *her*. I was disappointed. You say something like that when you're pissed off.'

'Then what?'

'I returned to the car and drove back here to Bath.'

'Are you certain you didn't return to Emma in the afternoon?'

'No way. If this witness of yours told you that, they're lying.'

'What were you wearing that day?' Diamond moved on smoothly.

'Probably a black T-shirt and jeans.'

'And you drove straight back? Any idea what time this was?'

'Early afternoon, I suppose. I was home by four.'

'Can you prove this? Did you see anyone in Bath?'

'I told you I drove straight home. When I got in I crashed out for a few hours. I was short of sleep.'

'Did you stop for fuel on the way home?' Hen asked.

'What's that got to do with it?'

'The receipt. They usually show the time you paid.'

His tone softened. He'd realised she was being helpful. 'Right. I'm trying to think. I may have stopped for petrol, but I can't think where. I keep the receipts in my car. I can check.'

'If you can find one that places you somewhere on the road to Bath that afternoon, it will save us all a lot of trouble.'

'OK.'

'But you don't remember stopping at a garage?' Diamond said.

'You've got to understand I had other things on my mind.'

Diamond's frustration began to show. 'And you've got to understand we're investigating a murder, Mr Bellman. By your own admission you'd been following Emma Tysoe for twenty-four hours or more. You trailed her all the way to Wightview Sands. When you found her, she rejected you again. In your own words, you were pissed off. And some time the same afternoon, she was strangled. Is it any wonder we're interested in you?'

Troubled, he raked his hand through his curls. 'You've got me all wrong. I'm cooperating, aren't I?'

'I hope so. You didn't come forward when we first appealed for information. It's been in all the papers and on TV.'

'I didn't want all this hassle and being under suspicion. I hoped you'd find the killer without involving me. You should speak to the guy she spent the night with. I can take you to the house if you like.'

'We've spoken to him.'

His eyes widened. 'Then you know what I told you is true.'

'Yes, your account of your movements fits most of the facts,' Diamond said. 'What I find unconvincing is what you say about your intentions. She dumped you. You tried calling and still she wouldn't see you. For most men, that would be enough. They'd swallow their pride and get on with their lives. You didn't. You stalked her.'

'That's not right,' he blurted out.

'You were angry and jealous. You decided to kill her.'

'No.'

'You tracked her down. She was lying on the sand, maybe face down, so you spoke to her, just to be sure you'd got the right woman. But this wasn't a suitable moment to kill. Too many people were about. You went away—but not far. You waited for a time when the people around her left the beach or went for a swim. You went looking for something to use as a ligature, something like a strap or piece of plastic tape or a bootlace. This time you crept up from behind. She was probably asleep. You slipped the ligature under her head and crossed it behind her neck and tightened it.'

'This just isn't true,' Bellman said, white-faced.

'Can we speak outside?' Hen said to Diamond.

'Now?' He was incensed by her interference at this critical stage.

'Yes, now.'

He listened, but only because she'd won his respect in all their dealings up to now. They left Ken Bellman, looking dazed, in the interview room in the care of a uniformed officer.

Out in the corridor, Hen said, 'I have to say, Peter, I'm not happy where this interview is leading. I wouldn't mind you accusing him of the crime if he was being obstructive. He was talking freely in there. His story fitted the facts.'

'Up to when he met her on the beach and was given his marching orders. Then it departs from what we know to be true. I had to remind him he said "What the fuck!" as he walked away.'

'He's not going to have perfect recall of every phrase he used.'

'He wasn't going to admit to us that he was in a strop. The man had stalked her since the morning of the day before. Do you really believe he gave up and went home? I could crack him now.'

'I'm certain you could. He's brittle. They're the ones you treat with caution, Peter. They confess to anything. Only later, when you're being cross-examined by some tricky lawyer do you discover the flaws. Let's soft-pedal.'

This was the first real difference of opinion with Hen.

Diamond shook his head. 'I'm not happy with this.'

She said, 'I want a result as much as you. I've had a two-hour drive this morning and I'll have to come back for another go, but it's worth it to get everything buttoned up—properly.'

There was a silence as heavy as cement. 'I can only agree to this if we take him home now and ask him to produce the petrol receipt.'

THEY USED DIAMOND'S CAR, driving directly to the garage Ken Bellman rented on Bathwick Hill. Little more was said until he unlocked the up-and-over door and opened his BMW to look inside.

'I slot everything down the pocket in the door.' He scooped out a handful of scraps of paper. He handed a bundle to Hen.

Hen started separating the petrol receipts. They went back at least eighteen months. She passed a batch to Diamond. He went through them steadily and found nothing. He shook his head. Hen finished checking hers. She sighed.

'It's not looking good, Ken,' Diamond commented.

Bellman said, 'I'm not a hundred per cent sure I stopped for petrol.'

'How do you pay for your petrol?' Hen asked. 'With a credit card?'

'Cash, usually. You hear so much about fraud.'

'Well, my friend, we're going to have to ask you to rack your brains for something else to confirm the story you gave us,' Diamond said.

Hen asked, 'Is it possible you put the receipt in your trouser pocket? Could it be somewhere in your flat?'

'I suppose.'

Diamond twigged at once that Hen's suggestion would get them into Bellman's living quarters without a search warrant. He closed the garage and they walked the short distance to the house.

He rented the upper floor of a brick-built Victorian villa, with his own entrance up an ironwork staircase at the side. It was tidy inside, as Diamond discovered when he began strolling through the rooms without invitation, saying benignly, 'Have a good look for that receipt. Don't mind me.'

There were two computers, one in an office, the other in the living room. Any number of manuals with titles in IT jargon were lined up on shelves. Diamond followed Bellman into the bedroom and watched him take several pairs of jeans from the wardrobe and sling them on the double bed. The search of the jeans' pockets produced a crumpled five-pound note and some paper tissues, but no receipt.

'I can't think where else it's going to be,' Bellman said. 'What happens if I can't prove I was on the road that afternoon?'

'We go through it all again, asking more questions.'

'If you do,' Bellman said, 'I want a solicitor. I came in today to make a statement as a witness, not to be accused of the crime.' He was getting more confident here, on his own territory.

'Show me some proof that you aren't involved.'

'So I'm guilty, am I, unless I can prove I'm innocent?'

'In my book, you are, chummy. There isn't anyone else.'

Hen had been listening, and not liking the drift. 'Peter, as the SIO on this case, I'm calling a halt for today.'

Diamond didn't argue. She had the right. It was, officially, her case.

ON THE DRIVE back to the police station, he spoke his mind to her.

'Ten minutes more in the interview room and he'd have put his hand up to the crime.'

'That's exactly what I objected to. Confessions don't impress the Crown Prosecution Service. We need proof. It's up to you and me to make a case that stands up in court.'

'You're asking for the moon,' he said. 'You know as well as I do that there's no DNA. We've bust our guts making appeals for witnesses. No one else is going to come forward now. He admits he was at the scene on the day of the murder.'

Hen said, 'I want to know what happened to her car, the Lotus he says was in the car park. Emma didn't drive it out for sure, yet it wasn't there at the end of the day when I arrived on the scene.'

She'd scored a point. He'd given very little thought to the missing car. 'Stolen?'

'But who by? Someone who acquired the key?'

'There are ways of starting a car without a key.'

'Yes, but it's more likely, isn't it, that the person picked up the beachbag Olga Smith described, and used her key?'

He weighed that. 'That is relevant,' he finally said. 'Bellman couldn't have pinched her car if he drove his own. Why hasn't it turned up?'

'Not for want of searching,' Hen said. She was quiet for a moment. 'You know, there could be something in this. We've had cars taken from the beach car park before now. Nice cars usually, like this one. They're driven around and then abandoned.'

'Joyriders.'

'Right. Teenagers we assumed.'

'But they don't murder the owners?'

'Well, not up to now.'

'You're certain it wasn't left in the car park that night?'

'Totally sure. I know the cars that were there.'

'And they were abandoned?'

'Left overnight. The owners picked them up later.'

'You see what I'm thinking?'

'I do,' she said. 'If one of those two was a car thief, they could have driven away the Lotus during the afternoon and returned for their own car the following day.'

'A bit obvious, leaving their own vehicle overnight,' Diamond reflected. 'A professional car thief wouldn't be so stupid.'

'Maybe this was an opportunist crime,' Hen said. 'They picked up her bag after she was dead.'

There was a flaw here and Diamond was quick to pounce. 'But they wouldn't know which car the key fitted, unless they'd watched her drive in. Which brings us back to Bellman. He's the only one who knew she owned a Lotus. Could he have nicked it after killing her and acquiring the bag?'

'And returned for his own car before the car park closed? I can't think why he'd do it. If he's the killer, it was jealousy, or passion, or frustrated pride, not a wish to own a smart car.'

Stalemate.

'We made some headway,' Diamond said after they'd parked behind the police station. 'It's not all disappointment.'

'Far from it,' she agreed.

Inside the nick, a sergeant spotted Diamond and came over at once. 'You're wanted at the Bath Spa Hotel, sir, by an inspector from Special Branch and a lady by the name of Walpurgis.'

'What the hell are they doing at the Bath Spa?' He turned to Hen. 'Want to back me up?'

They returned to the car.

THE BATH SPA, on the east side of the city in Sydney Road, vies with the Royal Crescent for the title of Bath's most exclusive hotel. It is a restored nineteenth-century mansion in its own grounds, with facilities that include a solarium, indoor swimming pool and sauna.

Diamond and Hen announced themselves at Reception and a call was put through to one of the guest suites.

'The gentleman said he's coming down, sir.'

'Special Branch being careful,' Hen murmured to Diamond.

The 'gentleman', when he arrived, was in jeans and a black leather jacket, worn, without a doubt, to conceal a gun. 'Tony,' he said to Diamond. 'Special Branch.' Pale and red-eyed, he looked as if life in the security service was taking a heavy toll.

'Whose decision was it to bring Walpurgis here?' Diamond said.

'Her own. She expects the best.'

'I'm against it,' Diamond said. 'Isn't she aware of the risk?'

'You haven't met her yet.' Tony said with a persecuted look. 'I'm not sure if she's aware of anything except herself.'

Before going upstairs, Diamond phoned Halliwell. It was agreed that Detective Sergeant John Leaman should be assigned to guarding Walpurgis for the time being.

TONY FROM SPECIAL BRANCH admitted them to the sitting-room section of the Beau Nash Suite. There was no sign of the main guest.

'Taking a shower,' he explained. 'As soon as she's out, I'm off.'

'Anything we should know about her?' Diamond enquired.

'She'll tell you.'

'Does she have luggage?'

'Five cases and a garment bag.'

'*Five?*'

'Can't be seen in the same thing more than once.'

'Are you confident nobody knows she's here?'

'In a word, no. Fortunately that's not my problem any more.'

A door opened and a woman emerged from the bathroom wrapped in a white silk dressing gown. She was stunningly pretty, with blue eyes and dead-straight blonde hair. 'Are you the replacements?' she asked.

Before Diamond could introduce himself, Tony said, 'I'm off, then.' He was through the door and gone.

Diamond gave their names and ranks. 'More of a welcoming committee,' he explained. 'Someone else will be with you shortly.'

'Another kid, I suppose,' Anna Walpurgis said. 'I so prefer mature men. My husband—rest his soul—was well over sixty when I married him. And to save you asking, we were a perfect match and the sex was wicked. Do you like shopping?'

'Depends,' said Diamond.

'Don't be coy, big man. I'm addicted. I want to hit those Bath shops before they close tonight.'

'That may not be such a good idea. There's a man who means to murder you. We take the threat seriously, and so should you.'

'The only thing I'm taking is a taxi to the town centre,' she said, refusing to be sidetracked. 'After two weeks banged up, I'm suffering serious withdrawal. What's your first name anyway? Let me guess— something nice and codgery. Barnaby?'

'If we're going to get on, Miss Walpurgis—'

'Anna.'

'Anna, it's not a good plan to go shopping. You'll be recognised.'

She said as if she hadn't heard, 'Not Barnaby? How about Humphrey, then?'

'It may be necessary for you to stay here for the first night,' he explained. 'After that, we move you to a private address with a guard.'

'Another safe house? No way will I spend my life locked away.'

Hen said, 'It's not your life, Anna. It's just until this killer is caught. This won't be anything like the regime in a safe house. If you're willing to help us, it can be over in a short time.'

'They all said that.' She turned to Hen. 'Is he married?'

Hen hesitated, then shook her head.

'Funny,' Anna said to Hen, 'but I'm quite attracted by the stiff upper lip. Sort of brings up all those old British movies on cable, Kenneth More and Jack Hawkins.' She flashed a look at Diamond. 'That you, is it? Cool in a crisis? The sort I could trust with my life?'

He said, 'This isn't about me. It's about you.'

'Yeah, you know all about me. Everyone knows about me, the gold-digger who married an elderly millionaire when her singing career was on the slide. The tabloids have done it to death. Nobody ever asks me if I loved Wally. That's not in the script. I shut my eyes to the wrinkles and went for the wedge, wrote off two years of my life for the legacy. It's in the papers, so it must be true.'

The bitterness was inescapable. Diamond had to respond. 'I never read that stuff. I've heard you sing. I respect you for that.'

'Perlease,' she said. 'You obviously know how to press all the right buttons. Why don't we do a deal, Humph? If I keep my head down today, will you come shopping with me tomorrow?'

'All right,' he said at once. It was the best trade he would get. 'And the name is Peter.'

LATER IN THE AFTERNOON, Georgina, the ACC, was tidying her desk, her thoughts on that Nile cruise, when Diamond knocked on her door.

'You sent for me, ma'am?'

'So I did, Peter. It was mainly about my house sitter, Ms Walpurgis. Is that a firm arrangement now?'

'Couldn't be firmer,' he said. 'You're still OK with it, I hope?'

'I'm depending on it. I've cancelled the cattery arrangement for Sultan. I've been home,' she said, 'and written out some instructions about his routine. There's enough tinned food for the ten days, but if Ms Walpurgis would be so good as to collect a fillet of lemon sole from Waitrose every two or three days and steam it he'll be her friend for life. I've left some money in an envelope.'

'You've thought of everything,' Diamond said. He doubted whether Sultan had much prospect of his steamed lemon sole. Anna Walpurgis didn't seem the sort of person who cooked.

'I've also cleared a space at one end of my wardrobe and found a couple of spare hangers.'

With difficulty, he suppressed a smile. 'I can guarantee she'll make use of those, ma'am.'

'And be sure to ask her to sign the visitors' book. I've left it open on the table by the front door.'

The visitors' book. Georgina *would* have a visitors' book.

'Table by the front door. Sorted.'

Diamond wished Georgina a wonderful holiday and she entrusted him with the spare key to her house in Bennett Street.

BACK IN THE INCIDENT ROOM, Halliwell told Diamond that Jimmy Barneston had been trying to reach him on the phone.

He returned the call. Barneston was under stress again.

'I've had Bramshill on to me demanding to know what the hell is going on. Special Branch told them you've taken over responsibility for Anna Walpurgis. They told me I made a mistake handing her over to you.'

'Pillocks. They should be grateful someone is willing to take her on board. How's the Porter investigation going?'

'The PM results are in. Death was definitely caused by a missile the shape of a crossbow bolt. He was killed elsewhere some hours before and the body was transported to the golf course.'

'Traces?'

'This time we got lucky. They found some fibres on the victim that could have come from whatever the killer was wearing. While he was manhandling the body he must have rubbed against the clothes. I wonder why he bothered moving it out to the golf course.'

'Making a point, Jimmy. The Mariner has an agenda, and he's carrying it out to the letter.'

'So are you taking good care of Anna Walpurgis?'

'Star treatment.'

'You want to watch out,' he said with a definite note of relish. 'I don't mind betting the Mariner finds his way to Bath.'

eight

If the threat from the Mariner was uppermost in Diamond's thinking, the matter of Emma Tysoe's murder was not to be shelved. He called Ingeborg to his office.

'Have you listened to the tape of the Ken Bellman interview?' he asked her.

'Yes, guv.'

'I want to put this bugger away, Ingeborg.'

'Are you going to have another go at him?'

'You bet. Only I need more to work with. Do some digging for me. Go right back to when he first met Emma as a student at Liverpool. What about the years since then? Did they stay in touch? He claims he just met her in the library one day. Can that be true?'

'I'll get on to it right away.'

'I haven't finished. We didn't get much out of Bellman's employers, either. Have a session with them. In particular find out where he worked previously. I want the authentic life history.'

'Understood.'

Eyes shining with so much responsibility, she returned to the incident room.

SHORTLY AFTER TEN next morning Diamond took the lift to the top floor of the Bath Spa Hotel. John Leaman, looking tired but comfortable, was seated in an armchair outside the Beau Nash Suite with the *Daily Mirror* across his knees.

Leaman rose like a startled pheasant. 'Morning, guv.'

'How's it been? She is still in there, I suppose?'

'Well, she hasn't come out, guv. The breakfast went in about nine.'

Diamond said in a taut voice, 'What do you mean—went in? You allowed someone to go in there? And you didn't go in with him? Christ almighty, man. He could have been the Mariner. What do you think you're here for?' Diamond pressed the bell on the door.

There was an agonising delay before it was opened. Anna Walpurgis, triumphantly still of this world, looked out. 'My shopping escort! What a star!' she said. 'Five minutes to finish my face, guys. Come in, and wait.' Leaving the door ajar, she vanished inside.

Diamond said curtly to Leaman, 'She survived, then. Go home and get some sleep.'

Diamond assumed her five minutes would mean at least twenty, and that was an underestimate by ten. But he didn't complain. He was comfortable looking at the papers with half an eye on the TV.

When she did emerge she was in skintight black velvet trousers. Her small, sleeveless gypsy top announced to the world that she was not wearing a bra. To top it off, a black hat with a vast floppy brim.

'What do you think?' she asked him.

Tact was wanted here, he thought. 'Amazing.' He cleared his throat. 'Allowing that we're trying to keep a low profile, maybe the hat is just a little too eye-catching.'

'A fashion statement,' she told him cheerfully, as if that answered his objection. 'I'll be wearing my shades.'

'Before we do any shopping, we'll be moving you to your new address in Bennett Street.'

'You're not going to spoil my day before we even start on the shops?'

'This will be your own pad, a beautiful Georgian house in one of the most exclusive areas of the city.'

She linked her arm under his. 'I know you mean well, Pete, but I'm comfortable here. So let's you and me chill out a little and take a hike around the shops.'

'I've got to insist.' he said, disentangling himself. 'The move has to be done before we see a single shop.' He picked up a phone. 'I'm having your cases sent up.'

'Masterful,' she said with irony.

Tony from Special Branch had not exaggerated. Five large cases presently came up on a trolley. Their owner, uninterested, was sitting on the sofa watching *Tom and Jerry*.

'I'm going to make a start.' Diamond opened the hanging space behind the door and unhooked several coats.

She said, 'Do you blow fire as well?' Swinging her legs off the sofa, she got up and carried one of the cases into the bedroom.

He'd won the first round.

DOWN IN THE LOBBY, the receptionist checked for mail. 'There is a letter for you, Ms Walpurgis.'

'So soon?' She ripped open the envelope and took out a single sheet, unfolded it, went pale, and said, 'What sicko sent this?'

Diamond took it from her.

> Like one, that on a lonesome road
> Doth walk in fear and dread.
> And having once turned round walks on,
> And turns no more her head;
> Because she knows, a frightful fiend
> Doth close behind her tread.

He knew the lines. He'd read them recently in *The Rime of the Ancient Mariner*. Slightly altered to make the subject female, they were picked to strike terror into Anna Walpurgis.

'I'm afraid he knows you're here.'

'The killer?' She put her hand to her throat. 'How could he?'

'The point is it's happened.'

'God! What can we do?'

He felt like saying, What I've been trying to do for the past hour—move you out of here. But seeing how shaken she was, he calmly told her they were doing the right thing. Mentally he was reeling, at a loss to understand how the Mariner could have penetrated the security.

He showed his ID and asked the desk staff if they recalled who brought the letter in. There was no stamp.

Nobody had any memory of a letter being handed in.

He took some rapid decisions. 'Is there a goods entrance?'

Anna, ashen-faced and silent, was taken through a door marked PRIVATE—STAFF ONLY. Diamond moved his old Cortina to the rear of the hotel and the cases were stowed. He asked Anna to huddle up, head down, in the back. He covered her with the garment bag. Then he drove out. He went twice around the perimeter roads of Sydney Gardens before deciding no one was in pursuit. Taking the Bathwick Street route, he crossed the Avon at Cleveland Bridge and, satisfied he was still alone, he made his way up to Bennett Street.

He took a long look up and down the street. There were parked cars in plenty, but not one appeared to be occupied. He unlocked Georgina's front door, then he returned to the car and opened the rear door. 'OK. Go.'

Anna emerged with head bowed, and hurried inside.

Diamond allowed himself a sigh of relief.

Then she came straight out again, just as quickly, and got back into the car. 'There's a big white cat in there.'

'Flaming hell!' he said. 'I'm trying to save you from a killer!'

'I'm not going in there. I can't stand cats.'

'Get your head down. I'll deal with it.'

He marched into Georgina's house and spotted Sultan reposing in a circular bed made of padded fabric. Diamond scooped up the bed with the cat inside and carried it through the house to the patio door. He opened the door and set cat and bed on the paving.

Anna was persuaded into the house with extreme reluctance.

'What is it about you and cats—an allergy?' he asked.

'A phobia,' she said, her arms protectively across her chest. 'You'll have to find me some other place.'

There was only one option. He said, 'I'll take the cat home with me. I'm going to fetch your cases now. Why don't you go through to the kitchen and put the kettle on for a coffee?'

'Sod coffee. I need a tequila. Where's the cocktail cabinet?'

Leaving her to go exploring, he spent the next minutes struggling upstairs with the luggage. He was short of breath when he finished. In the living room, he grabbed the Scotch she'd poured him.

'Whose gaff is this?' Anna asked in a calmer voice. She'd settled into one of Georgina's armchairs.

'One of my female colleagues.'

'Her taste in music sucks. Have you seen the CDs? It's all Gilbert and Sullivan and Verdi.'

It would be. 'It's a comfortable house,' he said.

'And I'm stuck in it,' Anna said. 'How did this frigging killer suss that I was in the hotel?'

'You're famous. Were you recognised when you registered?'

'Who knows? There were people around. No one took a picture or asked for my autograph, but that doesn't mean they didn't spot me.'

'That's probably what happened, then.'

'And you think the killer got wise to it? How?'

'He's a very smart operator.'

She shuddered. 'He wouldn't know I've moved here . . . would he?'

He shook his head. 'Only you and I know where you are at this minute. You'll be safe if you don't go out.'

With a touch of spirit he admired, she said wistfully, 'No shopping today? I'll call AmEx, tell them to relax.'

'Some other time.'

'Pete,' she said, 'you're doing a fine job.'

'And you can help me to find him. You may know him,' he pointed out. 'There's got to be a reason why he targeted you.'

She said, 'There are freaks out there who hate anyone who makes it big in the music industry.'

'Do you do any singing at all these days?'

'No, I called time on that. I don't need to work any more.'

'You're still a name. Do you get asked to do charity work?'

'All the time. I cut the appearances right down after Wally, my husband, died. Financially I still have a big stake in British Metal and I wanted to contribute in the best way I could.'

'British Metal, you said?' He was on high alert now. He'd heard of British Metal in another context.

'Wally's empire. I invented this role for myself, chairing a committee that looks at the public profile of the company. We sponsor events. Good causes, and celebs, if they're big enough. The aim is to give us a higher profile in the media. When Wally was alive he dealt with it all. He'd give thousands of pounds away without asking what the firm got back in publicity. When I came in, I made sure the money was used for projects that put our name before the public.'

He was deeply intrigued, his brain racing. 'What sort?'

'Don't ask me about the nitty-gritty. My committee does all the hard work. I just use my eyes. I see the racing on TV and I go back to my committee and say I want to see British Metal in large letters along the finishing straight, and they see to it. I watch a new film on TV and I look out for the little commercial the sponsor gets in every break just before the show begins again.'

'So you moved into film sponsorship?' Diamond could scarcely contain his excitement. 'You put a large amount of finance into the *The Ancient Mariner* film that Axel Summers was making.'

'Did we? You've got me there,' she said, shaking her head.

'It's a fact. British Metal had a big stake,' he told her.

'If you say so. My committee could tell you.'

'Do British Metal sponsor golf?'

'I guess,' she said vaguely. 'We do endorsements of sports people now. My sports person on the committee is Adrian,' she said. 'We only endorse the best. Ade is ace at picking future champions.'

'If he picks the best, it's likely he picked Matt Porter. Could you check with Adrian?'

'Any time.'

'Now.' Diamond picked up the cordless phone from the table in the corner and handed it to Anna. She pressed out the number.

She got through. It soon became obvious from her end of the conversation that his guess was right.

Diamond prompted her, 'Has it been reported in the press?'

It had, widely. The reason Diamond hadn't seen it was that he only ever looked at the rugby reports.

'Cheers, Ade,' Anna said. After she'd handed back the phone, she said to Diamond, 'There you go. We sponsored the two guys who were killed. Is that a help to you?'

'Enormous help.' This, at last, was progress.

'But nobody sponsors me. Why am I on the hit list?'

He had no answer to that. There was more to be unearthed. 'Did your late husband have enemies?' he asked.

'Wally?' She shook her head. 'He was the sweetest guy in the world. Everyone loved him.'

'He had the power to hire and fire.'

'That's business for you,' she said. 'Anyone who was laid off was given a fair settlement. He'd bust a gut to keep people in work.'

'Did he lay off any in the year before he died?' Diamond persisted.

'I doubt it. I don't remember lay-offs.'

'OK, let's talk about something else. How did you two meet?'

She sighed and stretched her legs out. 'We both went for the same taxi one wet night in Dean Street, Manchester. I told him the cab was mine and slagged him off. He thought it was a great laugh. We ended up sharing the cab and telling each other jokes. Before getting out he said he'd like to take me to dinner.'

'When did you marry?'

'Six months after. His fourth marriage, my second.'

'He had family?'

'No children. A sister and three ex-wives, all getting handouts. Like I say, Wally wasn't mean to anyone.'

'After he died, did the payments continue?'

'Still do. It was written into the will.' She suddenly became attentive. 'What's that noise?'

He listened. A rustling and scraping. For a moment, he thought the Mariner was breaking in somewhere. He got up from his chair, looked across the room and then breathed more easily.

'It's only the cat scratching on the patio door.'

She was not greatly reassured. 'You will get rid of him?'

'I'll take him with me when I go.' *Getting rid* of Sultan might be a step too far. 'You mentioned your husband's will. To your knowledge, was anyone upset by the contents?'

'Only the pressboys. They gave me a predictable roasting. "His bride of six years, the former pop singer Anna Walpurgis, comes into a cool eighty-five million pounds. Not bad for a performer with maximum hype and minimal talent." Stuff like that can hurt. I do have talent. I made it to the top before I met Wally.'

'No question,' Diamond said. He chose his next words with care. 'But the sad fact is that some people believe everything they read in the papers. The person behind all this could be someone who resents the power you wield through that committee. I want you to cast your mind back and tell me if you received any kind of complaint or threat about the decisions you made.'

She shook her head. 'I don't bother with that shit. We have a publicity officer. She deals with it.'

'I'll need to speak to her. It would speed things up if you made the call now, and put me through to her.'

A call from Ms Walpurgis was given top priority at British Metal. No listening to canned music. She was put through to the publicity officer, a Mrs Poole. Diamond was put on.

Yes, Mrs Poole told him, there was a small file of letters of complaint. Each one was answered, and in most cases the matter ended there. A few complainers prolonged the correspondence.

'Do you get any about sponsorships?' he asked. 'In particular the money given to Axel Summers, or Matthew Porter?'

'I'll check, but I can't say I remember anything so specific,' Mrs Poole said. 'Each time a sponsorship is announced, it triggers some letters from people who feel they have a more worthy cause needing money.'

'That's different,' he said. 'I'm thinking of the sort of letter that's written by someone so angry that he'll carry out acts of violence.'

'I've never seen a letter like that.'

'You'll double-check for me?'

She sounded efficient and her memory was probably reliable. He didn't expect to hear any more. Another theory withered and died.

He told Anna he would arrange for someone to bring in lunch and keep her company during the afternoon.

'Do you have to go?' she said, flicking the blonde hair. 'I was just getting to know you, and, like I told you, I still dig older men.'

He saw the funny side. 'I promised to deal with a pissed-off Persian cat. I wonder if there's a box somewhere in this house I can put him into.'

KEITH HALLIWELL arrived with Anna's order for lunch: a salad, an apple and some mineral water. 'Doesn't look like a lunch to me, guv,' he confided to Diamond when they met at the door.

'This is what beautiful blondes are made of, Keith.'

'What's in the box?' Halliwell asked, eyeing the large carton Diamond was about to carry to his car.

Diamond sighed. 'OK. Don't mention this to anyone else. Georgina's cat is coming home with me. Anna will tell you about it. How many men do you have as a back-up?'

'Three. They're across the street in the unmarked Sierra.'

'That's not enough. I'll have more sent up. For God's sake be alert, Keith. The Mariner is in Bath already. He won't wait long.'

INGEBORG SMITH was alone in the incident room when Diamond looked in.

'Hi, guv.'

'Any progress on Ken Bellman?' he asked, forcing his mind back to the Emma Tysoe investigation.

'Quite a bit, actually. What he said about being at Liverpool University in the same year as Emma is true. He was reading electronic engineering and she was a psychologist. They both got firsts. He stayed on to do a higher degree and she transferred to University College, London, to do hers. I'm trying to find someone who would remember how friendly they were. No success so far. I may get something from the hall of residence. I'm waiting for a phone call.'

'Is that it, then?'

'As far as I've got. I haven't yet talked to the people at Knowhow and Fix. That's next.'

'In short, we haven't come up with anything that conflicts with what he told us at the interview?'

'Not yet.'

'Keep at it,' he said.

He went out to get lunch and buy some lemon sole. On his return he was told there had been a call from Bognor CID. He got through to Hen and he told her about the note from the Mariner.

She was shocked. 'So he's in Bath already?'

'Yes—sooner than I expected. Still ahead of the game.'

'Could he know where Anna Walpurgis is?'

'I don't see how.'

She switched to the matter she'd originally called about. 'Want to hear my news? We've found Emma's car.'

'The Lotus? Where?'

'A couple of miles from the beach, in a caravan park. The key was still in the ignition. It was hidden under one of those fabric covers people put over cars. It's being examined for fingerprints and DNA.'

'A breakthrough at last.'

'We hope so. Have you fingerprinted Ken Bellman?'

'We will now, Hen. We will now.'

'So how was it for you?'

'If you're asking me is she still alive, the answer is yes.' After a night on watch outside the ACC's house, Keith Halliwell was in no mood to trade humour with his boss. 'I checked at nine. She wasn't thrilled to get a wake-up call, but at least she knows we care.'

'Any signs of suspicious behaviour in the street?'

Halliwell shook his head. 'It was dead quiet.'

'You checked the parked cars?'

'Made a list of all the numbers. I know a lot about Bennett Street I never knew before. And I can tell you how many chimney pots there are. The average is nine.'

Diamond said, 'What I really want to know is how the Mariner found out she was in Bath.'

'I can give you the answer to that.'

This downbeat statement almost passed Diamond by. He grabbed the arms of his chair. 'Go on, then.'

Halliwell said, 'It was on the radio. One of the young guys on watch with me heard it the night she arrived. Some DJ on Galaxy 101 played one of her hits, saying he'd heard a rumour she'd been spotted in Bath. The next thing of course is that a listener calls in to say he saw her checking in to the Bath Spa Hotel.'

'And the Mariner happened to be tuned in.'

'Or heard of it from someone else.'

'As simple as that,' Diamond murmured. 'It wouldn't have happened if Special Branch were doing their job,' he complained. 'They should have smuggled her in through the back entrance.'

One mystery solved, then.

TOWARDS THE END of the morning Diamond looked into the incident room. Soon the least experienced member of the squad would have to take a shift on the Bennett Street roster. He'd kept Ingeborg busy, shielding her from front-line duties. It wasn't good practice. In theory, she should face the same risks as anyone else.

'Did you get out to Knowhow and Fix?' he asked her.

'Yes, guv. Bellman is one of about ten consultants on their list. They're satisfied with his work. He seems to be up with the latest technology, which is what counts in IT.'

'Previous employment?'

'Like he said, he was with a London firm in SW1 as a technical support programmer.'

'SW1. That's very central. Westminster, Downing Street, St James's. Scotland Yard is there. Not many computer firms, I would think. It's all government departments.'

'They use computers, guv.'

'I suppose they do. Why did he move to Bath?'

She shook her head. 'His bosses say he's quiet. Doesn't talk about himself or anything personal. He came with good references.'

'For a young man with a good job in IT in central London, a move to the provinces seems a strange career choice.'

'Did he move to be nearer to Emma?' Ingeborg asked.

'He said they met by chance in the library—as if he didn't expect it.'

'I can believe *she* didn't.'

'You're thinking he was lying—that he followed her here? Good point, Ingeborg. We've only got his version of the way it happened. He certainly pursued her for the last hours of her life. He could have been obsessed with her for much longer.'

'Does it make a difference?' Ingeborg said. 'I mean, if he was the killer anyway, does it matter how long he knew her?'

'It strengthens the motive. That helps the prosecution.' Slipping into his superintendent mode, he told her, 'Something you're going to have to learn, constable, is that we have to make the case to the

CPS, and if it isn't rock solid they won't prosecute. I wouldn't mind questioning him again.'

The opportunity came sooner than either of them expected, in fact within twenty minutes. The desk sergeant called up to say a Mr Bellman had walked into the station and asked to speak to the officer in charge of the Emma Tysoe investigation.

Diamond asked Ingeborg to join him. She was starry-eyed at the prospect. 'Do you think he's ready to cough, guv?'

'We can always hope.'

In the interview room, Bellman sat completely still, studying his fingernails. On Diamond's instructions, he'd already been brought coffee—in a cup and saucer because china is a suitable surface for collecting fingerprints.

'You don't mind if we tape this?' Diamond said.

'Whatever you want. It won't take long.'

Ingeborg spoke the formal preamble for a voluntary statement, and then Diamond said, 'You've got something to tell us, Ken?'

'To show you, more like,' he answered. His mouth drew wide in a triumphant grin. 'I found a petrol receipt.' He opened his right hand to show a slip of paper lying on his palm.

'Where did you find this?' Diamond asked as he took it, his voice betraying nothing of the plunging anticlimax he felt.

'Down in the slot where the handbrake is fitted. I thought I'd have another search and there it was, stuck there, out of sight.'

Diamond studied the receipt. Beyond dispute, it showed someone had bought 35.46 litres of petrol from pump five at a cost of £25.50 at the Star service station, Trowbridge Road, Beckington, Bath, at three forty-seven on the afternoon of the murder. A kick in the guts. Trying to salvage some respect, he said, 'Pity you didn't use a card. There's nothing to link this receipt to you personally.'

Bellman was unmoved. 'What are you suggesting—that it's someone else's receipt? That's a long shot, isn't it?'

'We'll examine it, anyway,' Diamond said, passing the receipt to Ingeborg. 'Thanks for bringing it in.'

'I'll be off, then,' Bellman said.

'Before you are,' Diamond said, 'I wonder if you'd clarify a couple of things you said at your previous interview. You said you worked in London prior to coming to Bath. In SW1. But you didn't name your employer.'

'You didn't ask. Mitchkin Systems Limited.'

'Good job, I should think, based in central London. I'm wondering why you left. What brought you to Bath?'

He answered smoothly, 'I'd had enough of London by then. I'm single. With my training I can work pretty well where I choose.'

'But why Bath, of all places?'

A shrug and a smile. 'Nice city. Clean air. Less hassle.'

'Are you sure there wasn't another attraction—the fact that Emma Tysoe moved here.'

A touch of colour sprang to his cheek. 'Oh, no. No way.'

'Before you say any more,' Diamond came in, sensing a hit, 'I don't buy your story that it was pure chance you met in the library. She was an old friend from your student days. You had every right to seek her out.'

The man was silent.

This line of questioning had been a fishing expedition, no more, and now there was the promise of a catch. Diamond continued. 'I'm not suggesting you harboured romantic feelings about her for all those years, checking what happened to her, where she lived, and so on. But I can't help wondering if you were reading your paper one day, and happened to see her name. She was well known in her professional life—as a psychological offender profiler.'

He said firmly, 'I don't have time to read the papers. All my reading is technical. Computer magazines.'

'So you didn't know about the profiling?' Diamond paused, apparently to exercise his thoughts on this mistaken assumption. 'Maybe I was wrong, then. Maybe you did still carry a torch for her after all those years.'

Bellman's eyes flicked rapidly from side to side as if he knew he'd been led into a trap. 'I don't know what you're on about.'

Keen, it would appear, to move on to things of more importance, Diamond said, 'It's simple enough. We know you were attracted to Emma. You've just handed us the proof that you couldn't have killed her. All I'm asking is if you kept tabs on her ever since university.'

'And if I say yes?'

'Then I'll ask you again: did you get your job in Bath just to be nearer to Emma?'

After a pause worthy of a Pinter play, Bellman said, 'Yes.'

Diamond beamed and sounded amiable. 'Even an IT consultant is allowed to be a romantic. Thanks for coming in, Ken. I'll show you out.'

THERE WAS NO DENYING the disappointment. They'd devoted many hours to Bellman that could have been put to better use.

Ingeborg tried to console him by pointing out that it wouldn't be all that difficult to forge a petrol receipt. 'He's a computer geek. He'd have no trouble reproducing the right font and printing it on the sort of paper they use.'

'It looks like the real thing to me.'

'What's more,' Ingeborg continued, 'many garages have security videos running. If we tell them the date and the time, it shouldn't be any problem to check. We even know it was pump five.'

'Do it, then,' he told her. 'I'll see to the fingerprints. Go out to Beckington and collect any video evidence the garage have for the time he claims to have been there. Let's call his bluff—if we can.'

Hen Mallin had already sent through the fingerprints lifted from Emma Tysoe's car. Diamond went in search of a SOCO.

In truth, he wasn't optimistic. Ken Bellman had been caught out in a lie about the circumstances of the reunion with Emma, but this didn't automatically indicate guilt. He *was* a weirdo and a stalker, but not necessarily a killer. They seldom are.

A call to John Leaman brought reassurance. Anna Walpurgis was still in the house and had ordered a long list of videos. 'So it sounds as if she's resigned to staying indoors, guv.'

'Make sure she does. What's happening in the street? All quiet?'

'So quiet I can see parking spaces.'

'Is there any way he could gain access from the back of the house?'

'I can't see how. The back gardens are enclosed. Sealed off.'

'Make quite sure, John. Have someone check.'

Diamond called Hen and told her that Bellman seemed to be in the clear.

She said, 'In your shoes, darling, I'd have my suspicions about a bloke who produced his alibi as late as this. Sounds dodgy to me.'

'We're checking. If it's a try-on, we'll know shortly. He probably had the sodding receipt all the time and just wanted to hit us with this at the last minute. That's the impression I get.'

'Dickhead. Do the fingerprints match?'

'Don't know yet. They could be my last throw.'

'With *this* guy, perhaps,' she said. 'You haven't heard my latest. Remember the lifeguards? Those two who called themselves Emerson and Laver? Stella has spent the past week trying to track them down. Finally, she found an ex-girlfriend, and now we know their real names, Trevor Donald and Jim Leighton, both from Perth, Western Australia, as well as their mobile numbers. They were travelling west, towards Dorset. The local police are on the case.'

'You'll keep me informed?'

'Depend on it.'

INGEBORG RETURNED from the Star service station late in the afternoon with the news that the cashier had found the duplicate receipt for the one Bellman had produced.

'They gave me the video for pump five.' She patted her bag.

They slotted the cassette into the machine in Georgina's office and sat on the leather sofa to watch the rather tedious images. Fortunately a digital record of the time was displayed.

'What was the time on the receipt?'

'Three forty-seven.'

'Can you fast forward it?'

Ingeborg worked the remote control and figures darted out of cars like Keystone Cops in an old movie.

'We must be getting close. Slow up.'

The pictures reverted to normal speed. The time was showing three forty-one. A Toyota was at the pump. The elderly driver filled up, went to pay, and returned. The man drove away and a BMW glided into its place. The man who got out to use the pump was in a black T-shirt and jeans. He had dark curly hair. There was no mistaking Ken Bellman.

Further proof followed at the end of the afternoon. When the fingerprints were compared, it was obvious that the last person to drive Emma Tysoe's stolen car was not Ken Bellman. They could forget him.

THAT SAME EVENING, Hen drove along the coast to Swanage. She'd had a call from Stella to say that the two Australian lifeguards, Trevor Donald and Jim Leighton, had been traced to a campsite a mile outside the town.

Hen's reliable assistant was waiting for her as she arrived at Swanage police station. Stella had a glow about her, and it was more elation than sunburn. 'They're in a pub only five minutes away, guv. The local CID have had them under observation. How would you like to play this?'

'I'm not interviewing them in a pub. Invite them here for questioning about the stolen car. We'll split them up. If they don't cooperate, we book them. Which is the guy we haven't seen at all?'

'That's Jim Leighton.'

'We'll take him first.'

Jim Leighton certainly looked the part in a yellow singlet and faded denim shorts that set off the seaside tan. He was a handsome hunk of maleness, too, Hen didn't fail to notice: blue-eyed, with a swimmer's meaty shoulders and a thick blond ponytail.

'For the record, this will be a voluntary statement,' Hen started to say for the tape.

'I said nothing about a statement, lady,' he said with the Aussie twang.

'You're here of your own free will?'

'You're joking. My own free will is to be in the pub. I came because I was asked, to let you know I didn't swipe anyone's car.'

'How long were you in Bognor?' Hen asked.

'Three, maybe four weeks, doing the lifeguard bit with my mate Trevor. Piece of cake, that is, until you get an east wind.'

'Were you on duty on the day the woman was killed?'

'Sure. But look, you don't think I topped the poor lady? I was told this was about a car, for Christ's sake.'

'The car belonged to the woman who was killed,' Hen said. 'So what time did you go off duty?'

'Who can say? If I felt like a break at the end of the day, I'd take one. The job gets easier with the tide in. Trevor could manage without me. Mid-afternoon I guess.'

'Where were you when the body was found? Between four and five.'

'You really think I remember? It's a beach and I was there every day. Maybe I was chatting up crumpet. Or eating a burger.'

'If you went for a burger, did you go through the car park?'

He grinned. 'Trick question. To save you the bother of asking, I didn't see the Lotus at all.'

'But you know it was a Lotus?'

'Trick question number two. Give me a break, will you? Everyone knows her car went missing and it was a Lotus Esprit.'

'It must have been parked quite close to where you were. She was on the same stretch of beach.'

'I know that,' Leighton said. 'I spoke to her.'

'You did?' Hen leaned forward. 'When was this?'

'"What time? When?" Lady, I'm a beach bum. I don't look at my watch each time I speak to a woman. After I went off duty.'

'So what was said?'

'One of my standard pick-up lines, I reckon. Like "Excuse me, is that a tattoo on your ass or a love-bite?"'

'I'm sure that goes down a treat. Did she have a tattoo?'

He flashed the teeth in a wide smile and shook his head. 'But they always check.'

'What was her response?'

'Told me to get lost, if I remember right. It's all a blur. One day is like another in the lifeguard profession.'

Hen was losing patience. 'Get a grip, will you, Mr Leighton? That day wasn't like any other. A woman was strangled. You were there, or somewhere nearby. I think you know she was murdered. I think you saw an opportunity to take a joyride in a Lotus.'

He nodded. 'Now we're coming to it.'

'I'm giving you the chance to come clean over this. Joyriding isn't a major crime so long as no one gets hurt. Where were you staying in Wightview?'

'In a camper van in a field behind the village.'

'You moved out of there pretty fast after the murder. Trevor stayed on for a few days, but you were nowhere to be found.'

'Didn't he tell you? I was touring the British Isles in a Lotus Esprit.'

Hen stabbed her finger at him. 'Don't come it with me, sonny. Where did you clear off to?'

'Bournemouth. I kicked around with a fifteen-year-old blonde from Amsterdam for a few days until it got boring. End of story.'

'So you deny ever taking the Lotus?'

'How the hell would I do that without the key?'

'Her bag was missing.'

'Nothing to do with me.'

'OK,' Hen said. 'Prove it. The car thief left his fingerprints behind. With your permission, we can take yours and compare them.'

He sneered. 'Oh, sure—and I'm in your records for ever more.'

'No. They'll be destroyed. You'll sign a consent form saying it was voluntary and I'll sign to say they're destroyed. You get a copy.'

'What's the alternative?'

'We carry on with the questions until I'm satisfied.'

Leighton went quiet, fingering the earring. Hen could almost track the process of his thoughts. He wanted to get back to the pub.

Finally he yawned and said, 'Looks like it's the prints, then.'

NEVER A MAN to shirk responsibility, Diamond took his turn that evening keeping watch over Anna Walpurgis. He relieved John Leaman soon after nine, when Bennett Street was as quiet as a turkey farm on Christmas Day. Leaman told him the lady had remained inside all day.

He left and Diamond strolled across to speak to the officers with him on the night watch. There were six of them, all eager to impress. If only Georgina knew, she'd be well satisfied with the house-sitting arrangements, he thought.

He looked up at the top-floor window of the house and saw that the light was on behind closed curtains. A phone call first, to let Anna know he was outside.

She must have been close to the phone. 'Holloway Prison.'

He asked how she was doing.

'Dying from boredom, Sparkle,' she told him.

'Diamond, actually.'

'I know that, dumbo. I'm being playful. You coming to see me?'

'Yes, I thought I might call in. I'll be right over.'

He went over to the house and the door opened before he touched the bell. 'You want to be careful,' he said to Anna. 'I could be anyone.'

'The way I'm feeling, anyone will do.'

She offered coffee and he followed her into Georgina's kitchen. What a mess since he'd seen it last. Unwashed dishes cluttered the table, with eggshells, spilt coffee and used tea bags.

'I don't go in for cordon bleu,' Anna said superfluously. 'I'd never manage in this poky kitchen. What happened to the kettle?'

'Did you take it to another room?'

'Sharp thinking, Sparkle.'

He winced. She fetched the kettle from the front room while he rinsed a couple of mugs.

Before Anna indulged in more games with his name, he asked about hers. 'I presume it's a showbiz touch, to add some interest.'

'Righty. I'm plain Ann Higgins in real life.'

'Why Walpurgis? Something to do with spooks, isn't it?'

'Witches,' she said 'Walpurgis Night is the one before May Day, when all the witches are supposed to have a rave with the Devil somewhere in Germany. Walpurgis herself was an English nun.'

'You named yourself after a *nun*?'

She pointed the kettle at him like a gun. 'Don't say another word. When I found out the nun part of the story, it was too late to do anything about it.' A more solemn note came into her voice. 'What I want to know from you, Pete, is how much longer this pantomime is going on. When are you going to catch this psycho?'

'Soon,' he said with all the confidence he could dredge up. 'I've got a team of trained officers on the street. All I want from you is the same cooperation you've given us up to now.'

'I'm only being good because I'm scared rigid. You know that?'

He gave a nod, and took the opportunity while she was serious to clarify a couple of points. 'When we talked last time about British Metal, you said there weren't any lay-offs you could remember towards the end of your husband's connection with the company. I checked with your people, and your memory is right. The only redundancies in that time—and since—were by agreement. Some people took early retirement on generous pension arrangements.'

'We're a good firm to work for.' The kettle came to the boil and she poured water onto the grains of Nescafé in Georgina's Royal Doulton cups.

'Thanks.' Diamond picked his off the table. 'So I've got to look elsewhere for someone really embittered, someone who wants to get back at the company. You said before you took over the sponsorship committee, that the handing out of funds was all rather disorganised.'

'And it was,' she said.

'But your idea was to sponsor events and people that put the name of British Metal before the public, so you backed high-profile projects like the Coleridge film and top sportsmen like Matt Porter.'

'Darn right we did.'

'It obviously got up the Mariner's nose, because he set out to sabotage your programme in a vicious way.'

'I guess.'

'As he doesn't appear to have been a disgruntled employee, he could be one of the people who lost out through these changes you introduced. You mentioned bursaries in particular.'

'Yes, we were giving big, big sums to support nerds studying the behaviour of ants, for Christ's sake. British Metal was getting nothing back from it.'

'You know what I'm thinking?' he said. 'What if one of these nerds, as you call them, was so angry about losing his bursary that he decided on revenge? Do British Metal have a list of the people who lost out?'

'We must have,' she said.

'Who would I ask? Mrs Poole, the lady I spoke to before?'

'She's the one.'

He looked at the time. 'I must get back to the lads downstairs. You have our number in case of a problem?'

'Does being without a man count as a problem?'

He winked. 'Surely not to someone who named herself after a nun.'

ONLY A SHORT TIME after he was back in Bennett Street, a call came through on his mobile. 'Is this the nunnery?' he said playfully.

'No, matey,' said Hen's husky voice, 'it's Bognor CID.'

'*You?* You're working late.'

'I thought I'd pass on the bad news. Neither of those Australian boys matches the fingerprints in Emma's car. They're back in the pub now. What am I going to do? I've run out of suspects.'

He tried to give it some thought. Difficult, when he was focused on the Mariner. 'Do you still think she was killed for the car?'

'Ninety per cent sure. Did I tell you her key was in the ignition?'

'Was it definitely her personal key?'

'The evidence is pretty strong. It had a Bath University keyring.'

'You said ninety per cent sure, what's your ten per cent theory?'

'That he killed her for some other reason and took the bag and drove away the car to make identification difficult.'

'That isn't bad, Hen. He *did* hold us up. I'd give it better than ten per cent. If this guy was only interested in nicking the car, why would he abandon it so soon after?'

'Panic. He went for a joyride, used up all the petrol in the tank—'

'Is that a fact?'

'Yes. The needle was well down in the red section. And if you're in doubt whether someone would kill for a car, just read the papers. People are killed for their phones, their purses, their clothes.'

He needed no convincing. 'I didn't know about the empty tank. That does alter things. Your joyrider theory looks the best. Can I get back to you tomorrow on this? There's something stirring in my brain and it's not going to surface right away.'

'I'll listen to anything from your upper storey, my old love, even your fantasies about nuns.'

THINKING TIME was a luxury in the modern police. It had been largely replaced by high-tech intelligence-gathering computers and DNA samples. So this silent night was a rare opportunity to bring

some connected thought to bear on the mysteries of the beach stran-
gler and the Mariner. He sat in his car across the street from
Georgina's house and mused. Sherlock Holmes would have smoked
a pipe—Diamond had a flask of coffee and five bars of KitKat.

He was fairly certain that the Mariner had declared a private war
on British Metal and its beneficiaries. It looked increasingly as if this
murderer could have been a loser in the changes Anna had introduced. The peculiar character of the crimes suggested an obsessive,
embittered personality willing to take risks to make his point. This
was a killer with a monstrous grudge. Two hapless people had died
in a bizarre way simply because they were sponsored by the company. To use a chilling, but apt phrase, he'd made examples of them.

In the morning, he would obtain that list of academics who had
been deprived of their bursaries under Anna's new regime. It looked
the most promising avenue now.

He screwed the top back on the flask and got out of the car.

He strolled towards the Assembly Rooms at the end of the street,
where one of the team was stationed in a doorway just out of the
lamplight.

'How's it going?'

'Nothing to report, sir. A couple of people across the street came
home ten minutes ago. That's all.'

'Stay tuned, then.'

The man at the Saville Row turn gave him a similar response. Most
of Bath was asleep.

AT TEN PAST THREE, the intercom in Diamond's car beeped.

'A guy on his own, coming up Lansdown Road, sir. He's got a
backpack with something in it. Looks heavy. Shall I stop him?'

'No. Stay out of sight. Just watch him and report.'

'He's made the turn into Bennett. Coming your way.'

Another of the team, at the corner of Russell Street, announced
that he could now see the man. Diamond turned in his seat and he
had him in sight, too. Average height, baseball cap, both hands at his
chest under the straps of the backpack.

'What's he carrying—a computer he's knocked off?' the man on
Russell Street said.

'If it is,' Diamond said, 'we're not interested.' This was a focused
operation. 'Just watch where he goes.'

The man remained on the side of the street opposite Georgina's.

He went down some steps to a basement flat and let himself in. If he had been out burgling, he would never know how lucky he was.

At 8.00am, the new team arrived to take over.

'Everything's under control,' he told Ingeborg. 'But you know my number. Keep me informed. Anything at all. And stay in regular touch with Anna.'

He left her in charge. He was tired, but there were things to be done.

BACK IN HIS OFFICE in Manvers Street, he phoned Hen.

She said with heavy disapproval, 'Is the world coming to an end? Have the Martians landed in Bognor? No one calls me before nine.'

'Hen, I've been trying to get a grip on a vague idea about Wightview Sands that seemed to be hovering somewhere in my brain. It came to me a short while ago.'

'Be my guest,' she said with a sigh.

'This joyriding theory of yours. You said it's not the first time at Wightview. Other cars—nice cars—have been nicked and later found abandoned. So what if we're dealing with a serial joyrider who follows owners onto the beach and waits for them to go for a swim, leaving their bag or clothes unprotected. Then he helps himself to the car keys. On this occasion, the owner didn't go for a swim. By all accounts, Emma Tysoe remained where she was on the sand. Our thief watches her and waits . . . and waits. He's tantalised. He really covets that car. In the end he decides to go for the bag while she's still there. He moves in. There's a struggle. She hangs onto her bag. Trying to get it away from him, she passes the strap over her head. He grabs it, twists and strangles her. Are you with me?'

'Some kid, you mean?' Hen said.

'Maybe someone slightly older, but still nuts about cars, the man in the perfect position to pick out the one he wants, someone who sees every car drive in.' He waited, wanting her to make the connection.

Finally she said, 'The car-park attendant?'

'We know he was on duty in the morning when she drove in, because Ken Bellman saw him chatting with her.'

'That was Garth,' she said. 'A weird guy with slicked-back hair. But we didn't consider him because he was on duty.'

'All day?' Diamond said. 'I don't think so. Someone will have taken over by the afternoon.'

She was so long reacting that he wondered if the line had gone. Finally she said, 'You're right. I was told on the day of the murder.

Someone else came on duty at two. When I spoke to Garth he tried to give the impression he didn't leave the kiosk all day.'

'Giving himself an alibi?'

'When actually he was free to murder Emma. Oh my God! Peter, you're not so dumb as I thought.'

nine

By nine, Hen and Stella were heading for the caravan park at Bracklesham. They'd been informed by his employers that Garth (now revealed as Garth Trumpington, twenty-six, unmarried) had a mobile home there.

Caravans and tents occupied most of the field. The more permanent homes were lined up on the far side. Hen steered a bumpy route around the edge and came to a stop near a woman who was hanging out washing behind her van, and asked if Garth was about.

'Third one from the end, if he's in,' the woman said.

They drove the short way to Garth's residence, a medium-sized, cream-coloured trailer secured to the ground at each end. A red Renault was parked close by.

The man was at home. He answered Hen's knock right away, opening the door a fraction to look out. From what Hen could see through the narrow space he was in khaki shorts and a white T-shirt. 'Garth, we've met at the beach,' Hen reminded him. 'DCI Mallin, Bognor CID, and this is DS Gregson.' They showed their IDs.

'What's up?' he said in a shocked tone.

'A few simple questions. May we come in?'

His brown eyes widened in alarm. 'No. It's not convenient.'

'Untidy, is it? Don't worry, Garth. We're used to that.'

'You can talk to me here.'

'Certainly we can, but it's going to be overheard by some of your neighbours. What's your problem, Garth? Something to hide?'

He folded his arms. 'No.'

'OK, if you're going to insist, we'll take you down to the nick.' Hen turned to Stella. 'Give the young man his official caution.'

Stella spoke the approved words.

'I've got something cooking,' he said on an inspiration.

'Better see to it, then,' Hen said, putting her foot on the step.

He tried shutting the door, and she said, 'Naughty,' and slammed the flat of her hand against it. Stella gave the door a kick and so it was that they gained admittance, forcing him back inside.

Of course there wasn't anything cooking, except possibly an alibi. Hen stepped through to the living section and said, 'Now isn't this something? What do you make of the decor, Stell?'

Every portion of wall space was taken up with colour photos of cars. The ceiling was covered with them, too. And a large stack of motoring magazines stood in one corner.

'Let's all sit down,' Hen said.

Stella brought a stool from the kitchen and they started, Hen seated in the only armchair, Garth tense on the edge of a put-you-up.

'Cars are obviously your thing,' Hen commented. 'Is that your Renault outside?'

He nodded.

'I'd have thought a man like yourself would have gone in for something more flash, but I guess it's what you can afford. You see some really smart motors drive past your kiosk at Wightview Sands, I reckon. Do you ever get the urge to drive one of them?'

'No.' His conversational knack had temporarily deserted him.

'We've had a spate of joyriding over recent months—from your car park, so I'm sure you know all about it. You're well-placed to see what goes on. Would you know anything about it?'

'No. I'm too busy issuing tickets while I'm there,' he said, finding something to say.

'How long is that? A couple of hours at a time?'

'Longer,' Garth said. 'Four, five hours.'

'Then what do you do? How do you spend your time off?'

'I don't know,' he said. 'I might get something to eat. If it's nice, I could go on the beach.'

'And match up the drivers to the cars you fancy?'

'No.'

It was said a shade too fast. Hen paused, letting him squirm mentally. She was playing a tactical game here. Nothing had been said about the murder. The aim was to manoeuvre him first into admitting the joyriding episodes.

'You know a lot about cars. That's obvious. You must be an expert, Garth. You could probably tell me the makes of cars that were taken for joyrides in recent weeks. An MG. A Lancia. A Porsche.'

'No,' he said. 'You're wrong. There was never a Porsche.'

'You'd remember, I'm sure. It must have been something else in the sports-car line. But you confirm the MG and the Lancia, do you?'

'I didn't say I took them.'

'We're inclined to be lenient if people admit to joyriding, and haven't been caught before,' Hen continued. 'We issue an unofficial warning. It's too much trouble to take them to court. Mind you, if they deny it, we don't have much difficulty proving their guilt. They leave their fingerprints all over the cars. Remind me, Stella, did we find prints in the MG?'

'And the Lancia,' Stella said, nodding.

Garth wiped some sweat from his forehead.

'Did you go for a spin in the MG, Garth?'

'No.'

'The Lancia?'

He shook his head.

'So you're in the clear. You won't mind letting us take your finger-prints down at the nick just to remove all suspicion?'

She watched his hands clench. He was trapped.

'What if I said I took those cars for a ride?' His face had gone white. 'Would you let me off with a warning, like you said?'

Hen said, 'Let's get this clear, then. You've been taking cars from the car park without the owners' consent and driving them just for the pleasure of being at the wheel?'

'That's it,' Garth said, nodding vigorously. 'Just the pleasure. I wasn't stealing them.'

'What's the system? You chat to them from your kiosk, to get a good look at them?'

'Usually, yes.'

'Go on, then.'

He was forced to explain. 'When I go off duty, I go looking to see where the car I fancy is parked. Then I make a search for the owner. I observe them and wait for them to go for a swim. Then I choose my moment to pick up a bag or some clothes with the keys.'

'What about the people around? Don't they say anything?'

He shook his head. 'Not if you do it with confidence. I go directly to it. The stuff goes into a beachbag and then I'm away.'

Stella said, 'What about when you go past the barrier to get out? Aren't you afraid of one of the other attendants spotting you?'

'They're facing the other way, checking the incoming cars.'

'You've got it all worked out,' Hen said.

'I'll stop now,' he said, desperate to draw a line under this. 'I knew it was wrong. It was getting to be a habit. I'm sorry. It was stupid.'

'Unfortunately, Garth, we all know it's far more serious than you make out,' Hen said. 'The last time it happened, things went wrong, didn't they? You killed the woman.'

'No,' he said vehemently. 'No, no—I didn't do that!'

'This joyriding was a compulsion. She didn't leave her bag unattended for one second. So you snatched it and she wasn't asleep, as you thought. She tried to hang onto her bag, and you panicked, thinking she would make a scene, and you killed her.'

'No,' he said, his eyes stretched wide.

'OK,' Hen said calmly. 'We've got the fingerprints on the car—the dark green Lotus Esprit—and we'll check them against yours. You're under arrest, Garth. We're taking you for fingerprinting now.'

He gave a sob and sank his face into his hands. Any uncertainty was resolved in that moment.

DIAMOND FINALLY GOT to bed at ten fifteen that morning and sank immediately into a deep sleep. So when Ingeborg phoned him from Bennett Street twenty minutes later, he slept through the sound. After an hour, the phone beeped again, this time with more success. He groaned, swore and reached for it.

'Guv, are you there? This is Keith Halliwell. It's an emergency.'

'Mm?'

'We just heard from one of the lads on watch in Bennett Street. Ingeborg put in a routine call about ten thirty to make sure Anna Walpurgis was all right and got no answer. She tried several more times. Nothing. She tried calling you as well, and you didn't answer. In the end she acted on her own and used the key to let herself in.'

'Oh, Christ.' He was fully awake.

'And now we can't raise her, either.'

He felt as if the floor caved in and he dropped a hundred levels. 'Tell them to go in after her—all of them. I'm coming at once. Get everyone there you can. This is it, Keith!'

Recharged and ready to go, he threw on some clothes, dashed out to the car and drove to Bennett Street at a speed he would normally condemn as suicidal.

Two response vehicles had got there before him. Halliwell was also there, ashen-faced, standing in the open doorway.

'Come and look at this, guv.'

In the hallway of Georgina's house someone had used a red marker pen to write on the wall in large letters:

THE GAME IS DONE! I'VE WON, I'VE WON!

Diamond stood blankly before it, shaking his head.

He knew the line, and he was certain who'd written it. There was a scene in *The Rime of the Ancient Mariner* when Death was dicing with Life-in-Death for the ship's crew and everyone except the Mariner himself dropped dead. Think ahead, he urged himself. It's the only chance I've got now. I have to out-think him for once.

Halliwell said, 'We've been right through the building. There's no one in there, guv.'

'I don't know how, but he's beaten us. He's got to Anna, and he's got Ingeborg as well.'

One of the team on duty said in his own defence, 'We've had round-the-clock surveillance, sir. No one went in except DC Smith.'

'You *saw* no one go in,' Diamond said.

'But the place is empty. He got out as well, with the two women. Nobody saw them leave. He'd need transport. Every car in the street has been checked. It's a bloody impossibility!'

'Then they're still here.'

'No, guv. I promise you, I went through every room myself.'

'Including the basement?'

Halliwell nodded. 'It's filled with cartons and, believe me, we looked in every box. The door to the street was locked and bolted.'

'I'm going to take a look myself.'

Diamond stepped into the hall. An internal door was fitted at the top of the basement stairs. The lock had obviously been forced. 'Who did this?'

'We did. She keeps it locked. There wasn't time to look for the key.'

'What if the key was in the lock and the Mariner locked it himself and took the key with him?'

Halliwell stared back with a slight frown, failing to see what difference it would make.

Diamond pulled the door open, switched on the light and went down into the basement. Just as it had been described to him, the back room, the largest, was in use as a box room, each box labelled. In the front room was a second door. 'What's this—a cupboard?'

'It's a kind of cellar. Goes right under the street.'

Diamond opened the door. 'Someone get me a torch.'

One was handed to him and he probed the interior with the beam. A single arch constructed of Bath stone, it was tall enough to drive a bus through, except that a wall blocked off the end. Diamond moved towards the back wall. He swung the torch beam over the stonework and bent down to look at some chips of broken mortar.

'Some of these blocks of stone have been drilled out and moved. The wall isn't surface-bearing here. It's just a screen to separate this side of the street from the house opposite. Someone has broken through and then replaced everything later.'

Halliwell crouched down to look. 'Sonofabitch!'

'He must have got in from the house across the street and cut his way through. And that's the way he got out with his prisoners. He shoved the blocks back into position from the other side.'

'Cunning bastard,' Halliwell said. 'I can shift this lot, no trouble.'

'Not yet. We'll go in from across the street. Get some men down here, but have them in radio contact, ready to go when I say, and not before. I don't want a shoot-out in a confined space. He's got his hostages and he'll have his crossbow with him.'

He ran upstairs and out to the street. Exactly as he expected, there were signs of a break-in when he went down the basement steps of the house opposite. Like several of the basements along the street, this one was unoccupied.

With two armed officers close behind him, Diamond entered as silently as possible, stood in the passageway and listened. The place was ominously quiet. He waited a moment. Then he reached for the handle of the door to the front room.

Nobody was in this unfurnished room, so he crossed to the door to the vault and cautiously opened it. One glance confirmed that no one was inside. However, there were tools lying against the wall. Any lingering doubt that the Mariner had been here was removed.

There remained the back room, presumably used as a bedroom when the flat was occupied. He gestured to the back-up men with a downward movement of his hand. The door was slightly ajar, so he put his foot against it and gently pushed it fully open.

A crossbow was targeted at his chest. The Mariner, in baseball cap and leather jacket, stood against the wall. Beside him, on the floor, were two motionless bodies.

Diamond's heart raced and a thousand pinpricks erupted all over his skin. With a huge effort to keep control he managed to say, 'It's all over, Ken. I wouldn't shoot if I were you. Killing me isn't in the script.'

But Ken Bellman kept the crossbow firmly on target.

Boring old Ken, the lover Emma Tysoe had dumped without ever realising he was the killer she'd been asked to profile. Ken—the wrongly accused, the man who'd proved beyond doubt that he didn't carry out the murder on the beach. Ken Bellman was the Mariner.

Diamond's best—his only—option was to talk, steadily and as calmly as he could manage 'You're not going to shoot that thing. You've settled the score. If you take me out you'll be gunned down yourself. The men behind me are armed.'

'Hold it there,' Bellman said, his eyes never shifting from Diamond. He, too, was in deep shock. This was a petrifying humiliation for him and he was dangerous. He'd believed himself invincible.

'The game is done, just as you wrote on the wall,' Diamond said, 'and if you say you won, well who am I to argue? You had me on a string until a few minutes ago. I watched you arrive last night with your rucksack full of tools, and still I wasn't smart enough to twig who you were, or what you were up to. Now I'm asking you to call it quits.' He took a step towards the crossbow.

Bellman warned in an agitated cry, 'Don't move!'

But Diamond took another step. This had become a contest of will-power. 'I'm going to ask you to hand me the crossbow, Ken. Then we'll have a civilised talk.'

'I won't say it again!'

Diamond was almost level with the feet of one of the bodies. He said, 'You know you're not going to shoot now.'

Then there was a moan from one of the women. Bellman swung the crossbow downwards and released the bolt.

In the same split second, Diamond threw himself forward and grabbed at the bow with both hands. The bolt missed Anna Walpurgis's head by a fraction and ricocheted off a couple of walls. The two armed response unit men hurled themselves on Bellman.

Suddenly the room was full of noise and people. Hands gripped Diamond's arms and hauled him upright. The women were both alive. Their arms and legs were bound. Anna vomited when the straps came off her. Ingeborg said, 'It's the chloroform. He used it on both of us, several times.'

'But you're OK?'

Anna said in a croak, 'Thanks to you, Sparkle. Man oh man, that was bloody heroic!'

KEN BELLMAN was forced to wait twenty-four hours before having the satisfaction of telling his story to the chief investigating officers. Diamond needed to catch up on his sleep. Hen Mallin wanted to tie up another case before leaving Bognor. And Jimmy Barneston had been called urgently to the staff college at Bramshill.

A lot more happened in that twenty-four hours.

Anna Walpurgis, quickly and fully restored, moved back into the Bath Spa Hotel. From there, she made a series of shopping trips, contributing handsomely to the economy of the city. As well as buying five new outfits for herself, there was a present for Diamond: a wide-screen TV and DVD player combined, with a disc of herself in concert. 'Just so you don't ever forget the broad whose life you saved, Pete.'

Red-faced, he thanked her.

Keith Halliwell's skills as a home decorator were put to good use in Georgina's house, repapering the wall the Mariner had defaced. A team of professional cleaners went through, restoring the place to inspection order.

In Bognor, Garth Trumpington was charged with the murder of Dr Emma Tysoe. His fingerprints matched those in the stolen car. A check with the duty roster at Wightview Sands car park showed he'd been in the kiosk when Emma arrived and off duty at the time she was killed. He asked if he would get a lighter sentence if the court was told he hadn't meant to strangle her. He claimed that the shoulder strap of her bag got entangled round her neck while he was struggling with her. No one would venture an opinion on that one.

SO IT WAS EARLY on Thursday afternoon when Ken Bellman and his solicitor were ushered into interview room two at Manvers Street, where Diamond, Hen and Barneston were already seated. The solicitor's presence was only a formality. One glance at Bellman told them he was as eager as the Ancient Mariner himself to tell his story, all they wanted to know, and much they didn't. He made no attempt to conceal his guilt. He intended to justify his actions now.

'None of this would have happened if British Metal hadn't pulled the rug from under my research project,' he said with control, taking his time. 'The electronics work I was doing up at Liverpool was the culmination of years of study. It was my purpose in life.' He paused to register the impact of the outrage against him. 'Imagine how I felt when I was told by the head of department that I'd lost my funding. I was out. Overnight. Later, I was told about Anna Walpurgis being the new broom at British Metal and wanting to make sure the sponsorship money brought a return for the company. Sickening.'

'Did you try for some funding from anywhere else?' Hen asked.

'Wasted a hell of a lot of energy writing to other firms. "We're fully committed for the next eighteen months." "We regret to say we're cutting back on sponsorship." Blah, blah, blah. I gave up and came south and got a job in London in electronics, a security firm installing anti-theft systems.'

'And I suppose they had the contract for Special Branch?'

He said with a superior smile, 'You're catching on. We won the contract to upgrade the security on all their properties. I designed the circuits. I had to be vetted, of course. But I'm cleaner than clean. I was given the top security rating.'

Jimmy Barneston muttered, 'Bloody hell.' Special Branch had blamed him for their failings. He'd come here straight from a roasting by the Bramshill overlords.

'That's how I got to know the codes for all the safe houses.'

Barneston's eyes flickered keenly. 'So you had all this planned from way back?'

'No, I only decided to get my revenge on British Metal when I saw an item on TV about them putting a huge amount of money into a film. That really got to me. I mean, my bursary was peanuts to what Summers was given. These ponces who make films are burning up millions on things that add nothing to people's knowledge. My work was important, and real, a notable contribution to computer science. A few days later I saw in the paper that this kid Porter had been handed a fortune by British Metal just because he can roll a small white ball into a hole. I flipped.'

'But you didn't kill in anger,' Diamond said.

A note of pride came into Bellman's voice. 'That isn't my style at all. I approached it as a scientist should, starting by assembling all the information I had and then deciding how to maximise its potential. The objective was to damage British Metal and its sponsorship programme.'

Hen said, 'Couldn't you have done that without resorting to murder?'

'How? I needed to make an impact with newspaper headlines. Sudden death is the only thing that gets through to people. I'm not squeamish. I can do what's necessary to get attention.'

'Taking life?' Hen said, making clear her revulsion.

'How about *my* life?' he said, his voice rising. 'My research was

443

trashed, my hopes and dreams and all the work I'd already put in. Nobody gave a damn about me. As I was telling you, I worked from my strengths. First, my inside knowledge of the security arrangements. Second, I'd seen a former university friend on TV.'

'Emma Tysoe.'

'Emma, yes.' He grinned at Diamond. 'You tried to pin the wrong murder on me, didn't you? Got it all wrong. Emma was far too useful to me. But I mustn't jump ahead. One evening I happened to watch this programme about psychological offender profilers and there was a face I knew from my student days. Based at Bath University. I decided to renew the friendship. So I applied for the IT post with Knowhow and Fix. Easy little number for me. And I started going out with Emma. I knew she was likely to be brought into the investigation, and even if they used someone else, Emma was close enough to the police to feed me some inside knowledge.'

'Luckily for you, she *was* assigned to the case,' Diamond said.

But Bellman didn't want anything to sound easy. 'Luck didn't come into it. I went to no end of trouble to revive that friendship.'

'I follow you,' Diamond said, indulging him. 'It was deliberate.'

'Well, I got my plan under way. I put down Summers, the first of the fat cats, and seeing how everything comes down to presentation these days, I decided to dress up the action with an Ancient Mariner theme. A lot of that poem could have been written with me in mind.'

'The crossbow?' Diamond prompted. 'Where did you get that?'

'A man in Leeds who works in the Royal Armouries Museum and makes replicas as a hobby. I heard of him through the Internet. You've seen the bow, haven't you?'

'Pointing at my chest, thank you.'

He nodded. 'It's a beautiful weapon, easy to use, quick and efficient. I guess it will end up in the Black Museum. It deserves no less.'

'So . . .'

'The blueprint was there from the beginning, as you know, because I gave you people the names of the second and third victims. Has that ever been done before in the history of crime? I don't think so. The whole point was to force you to send Porter and Walpurgis to the high-security safe houses I could break into, and it worked. I knew a lot about the thinking of Special Branch.'

'Through Emma?'

'She was brought in very soon, as I calculated. She confided her thoughts to her computer—which, naturally, I updated and made secure for her—so, knowing her password, I could hack in and read her latest findings. Highly instructive, even down to the progress of our relationship. I have to admit it wasn't all complimentary. In fact, my plans began to go adrift when that oversexed detective on the case started his own relationship with her.'

Barneston blinked and sat forward, jerked out of his introspection. 'What did you say?'

Bellman continued. 'Emma did her best to dump me, as you know. That's how I nearly got my fingers burnt, trying to cling onto her. She was my window on you people, so I didn't intend to lose her.'

'You followed her to the beach and tried to talk her round,' Hen said.

'And so became your number one suspect. I had to keep my nerve then. Poor Emma! She didn't deserve that, even though she was stupid enough to give me the brush-off.'

'You had your alibi, the petrol receipt,' Diamond said. 'All that stuff about losing it under your handbrake wasn't true, was it? You were stringing me along.'

'Dead right, Mr Diamond, and do you know why? Thanks to your interest in me, I was on the inside again, getting a sense of what was going on here, in the police station. I knew Walpurgis was in Bath at that hotel, and I guessed you would move her to some other house when you discovered I was on the scent. I was perfectly willing to spend time at your nick listening out for the gossip. When I was first brought in, the news was just going around that the ACC was going on holiday. When I came back, I had a nice chat with the desk sergeant, a bit of a joke about the boss being away. He got very cagey when I mentioned her. It didn't require rocket science to find out where you were holding Walpurgis.'

'Where did you get her address? She's ex-directory.'

'Her name is often in the local press. She's in the electoral register. People forget how simple it is to check up on them.'

'We know you got into the house opposite during the night. You'll admit you were lucky the basement wasn't lived in?'

'No,' he said, affronted by the suggestion. 'Empty basements are the norm if you walk along Bennett Street. Let's be frank. Your so-called security was rubbish.'

'We caught you, didn't we? Where did you get your chloroform?'

'My old university. They kept a row of bottles in one of the labs. It's still widely used as a solvent.'

'I told you all this was on tape,' Diamond said. 'You've admitted to everything.'

'I'm not ashamed of it, either. I look forward to my day in court, when I shall repeat it all for a wider audience.'

Such self-congratulation was hard to stomach. The entire performance had been repellent. True, he had a genuine grievance at the beginning. But the vengeance he took was out of all proportion. He had expressed not a word of remorse for the killing of people who had done nothing to damage him.

DIAMOND WALKED to the car park with Hen.

'I feel as if I need a shower after that,' Hen said. 'And he still thinks he's the bee's knees.'

'But none of that came out when we interviewed him for the beach murder,' Diamond said. 'I thought he was a weak character. He fooled us, Hen, and I blame myself. I was doing the interview.'

'Don't knock yourself, Peter. You got everything else right. The British Metal connection and the fact that he was a pissed-off academic. Did you ever get that list of the people who lost their bursaries?'

'On my desk. His name is on it. I just didn't get a chance to see it on the morning we nicked him.'

'But you would have got there,' Hen insisted. 'And I hate to say that you solved my murder for me, by fingering Garth, but let's face it, you did.' She opened her car door and then held out her hand to him. 'But don't let it go to your head. You're still a pushy bastard.'

ON THE DAY Georgina Dallymore returned from her Nile cruise and let herself into the house in Bennett Street, Sultan was curled up as usual in his basket in the hall. The big ball of fur opened both eyes briefly but didn't get out to greet her.

'Exhausted, are you, my darling?' she said. 'That makes two of us. I've had such an exciting time.'

The place looked immaculate, maybe even better than she'd left it. When she opened the visitors' book, there was the name of Anna Walpurgis with the comment, 'I'll always remember my visit here.' How good it was to come home to a tidy house and a famous name in the visitors' book and a contented cat, she thought. The house sitter had been one of Peter Diamond's better suggestions.

PETER LOVESEY

In his thirties, Peter Lovesey was working in London, as a department head at a college of further education, when an advert in *The Times*, offering £1,000 for a first crime novel, caught his eye. At the time Lovesey was missing the contact with his students in the classroom, and the value of the prize was a lot more than his annual earnings, so with nothing to lose he thought he'd submit an entry. To his delight, *Wobble to Death*, featuring the Victorian Sergeant Cribb, won the competition. Seven more Cribb mysteries and two television series later, Lovesey decided to make writing his full-time career, and his life changed dramatically. 'For a while it was strange to spend so much time alone. I had to make an effort to get out and meet people and join things.'

Lovesey continued to write historical crime novels and short stories, but in 1991 he shifted gears and wrote his first modern-day mystery, *The Last Detective*. Set in Bath, close to where Lovesey lived, it was intended to be a stand-alone novel featuring Inspector Peter Diamond of Bath's CID. But the likable detective caught readers' imaginations, and *The House Sitter* is now Diamond's eighth case and marks his second appearance in Condensed Books (the first was in *Diamond Solitaire* in 1993).

Some years ago, Lovesey moved to Chichester but he often returns to Bath when researching his books. 'It's the only setting for Diamond, I can't possibly visualise him anywhere else,' he says. 'And it's a wonderful excuse to return. I can walk from one location to the next, and I know all the best places to stop for refreshment.'

In the course of his career, Lovesey has been the recipient of many awards, among them the prestigious Crime Writers' Association Gold Dagger and three Silver Daggers. In 2000 he was honoured with the Cartier Diamond Dagger in recognition of his lifetime achievements. How has he managed to sustain this level of success? 'I suppose it's being alert to what is going on and what other people are doing. And I've always been willing to take risks and to try another type of writing. Apart from that, I'm not sure.' He smiles. 'I've got a loyal bunch of readers, perhaps, who've grown old with me!'

NICCOLÒ AMMANITI

I'M NOT SCARED

Acqua Traverse.
A remote hamlet lost in the
wheatfields of the parched
Italian South, consisting of
just four small houses and an
old country villa. Home to a
handful of families, a small
gang of children—and one
terrible secret.

ONE

I was just about to overtake Salvatore when I heard my sister scream. I turned and saw her disappear, swallowed up by the wheat that covered the hill.

I shouldn't have brought her along. Mama would be furious.

I stopped. I was sweaty. I got my breath back and called to her: 'Maria? Maria?'

A plaintive little voice answered me: 'Michele.'

'Have you hurt yourself?'

'Yes, come here.'

'Where've you hurt yourself?'

'On the leg.'

She was faking, she was tired. I'm going on, I said to myself.

But what if she really was hurt?

Where were the others?

I saw their tracks in the wheat. They were rising slowly, in parallel lines, like the fingers of a hand, towards the top of the hill, leaving a wake of trampled stalks behind them.

THE WHEAT WAS HIGH that year. In late spring it had rained a lot, and by mid-June the stalks were higher and more luxuriant than ever. They grew densely packed, heavy-eared, ready to be harvested.

Everything was covered in wheat. The low hills rolled away like the waves of a golden ocean. As far as the horizon nothing but wheat, sky, crickets, sun and heat.

I had no idea how hot it was—degrees centigrade don't mean much to a nine-year-old—but I knew it wasn't normal.

That summer of 1978 has gone down in history as one of the hottest of the century. The heat got into the stones, crumbled the earth, scorched the plants and killed the livestock, made the houses sweltering. When you picked tomatoes they had no juice and the zucchini were small and hard. The sun took away your breath, your strength, your desire to play, everything. And it was just as unbearable at night.

At Acqua Traverse the grown-ups shut themselves up indoors with the blinds drawn till six in the evening. Only we children ventured out into the fiery deserted countryside.

My sister Maria was five and followed me as stubbornly as a little mongrel rescued from a dog pound.

'I want to do what you do,' she always said. Mama backed her up.

'Are you or are you not her big brother?' And there was nothing for it, I had to take her along.

No one had stopped to help her. After all, it was a race.

'STRAIGHT UP THE HILL. No following each other. No stopping. Last one there pays a forfeit,' Skull had decided and he had conceded to me: 'All right, your sister's not in the race. She's too small.'

'I'm not too small!' Maria had protested. 'I want to race too!'

And then she had fallen down.

Pity, I was lying third.

First was Antonio. As usual.

Antonio Natale, known as Skull. Why we called him Skull I can't remember. Maybe because once he had stuck a skull on his arm, one of those transfers you bought at the tobacconist's and fixed on with water. Skull was the oldest in the gang. Twelve years old. And he was the chief. He liked giving orders and if you didn't obey he turned nasty. He was no Einstein, but he was big, strong and brave. And he was going up that hill like a bulldozer.

Second was Salvatore.

Salvatore Scardaccione was nine, the same age as me. We were classmates. He was my best friend. Salvatore was taller than me. He was a loner. Sometimes he came with us but often he kept to himself. He was brighter than Skull, and could easily have deposed him, but he wasn't interested in becoming chief.

His father, the Avvocato Emilio Scardaccione, was a big shot in Rome. And had a lot of money stashed away in Switzerland.

That's what they said, anyway.

Then there was me, Michele. Michele Amitrano. And I was third that time, yet again. I had been going well, but now, thanks to my sister, I was at a standstill.

I was debating whether to turn back or leave her there, when I found myself in fourth place. On the other side of the ridge that duffer Remo Marzano had overtaken me. And if I didn't start climbing again straight away Barbara Mura would overtake me. That would be awful. Overtaken by a girl. And a fat one too.

'Hey, aren't you going back for your little sister? Didn't you hear her? She's hurt herself,' Barbara grunted happily. For once it wasn't going to be her who paid the forfeit.

'I'm going, I'm going . . . And I'll beat you too.' I couldn't admit defeat to her just like that.

I turned and started back down. 'Maria! Maria! Where are you?'

'Michele . . .'

There she was. Small and unhappy. Sitting on a ring of broken stalks. Rubbing her ankle with one hand and holding her glasses in the other. Her hair was stuck to her forehead and her eyes were moist.

'Maria, you've made me lose the race! I told you not to come, damn you.' I sat down. 'What have you done?'

'I tripped up. I hurt my foot and . . .' She threw her mouth wide open, screwed up her eyes, shook her head and exploded into a wail: 'My glasses! My glasses are broken!'

I could have thumped her. It was the third time she had broken her glasses since school had finished. And every time, who did Mama blame?

'You've got to look after your sister, you're her big brother.'

'Mama, I . . .'

'I don't want your excuses. It hasn't sunk into your head yet, but I don't find money in the vegetable garden. The next time you break those glasses I'll give you such a hiding . . .'

They had snapped in the middle, where they had already been stuck together once before. They were a write-off.

I put the glasses in my pocket. Without them my sister couldn't see a thing, she had a squint and the doctor had said she would have to have an operation before she grew up. 'Never mind. Up you get.'

She stopped crying and started sniffing. 'My foot hurts.'

'Where?' I kept thinking of the others. They must have reached the top of the hill ages ago. I only hoped Skull wouldn't make me do too tough a forfeit. Once when I had lost a bike race he had made me run through nettles.

'Where does it hurt?'

'Here.' She showed me her ankle.

'You've twisted it. It's nothing. It'll soon stop hurting.'

I unlaced her trainer and took it off very carefully. 'Is that better?'

'A bit. Shall we go home? I'm terribly thirsty. And Mama . . .'

She was right. We had come too far. And we had been out too long. It was way past lunchtime and Mama would be on the lookout at the window. I wasn't looking forward to our return home.

But who would have thought it a few hours earlier.

THAT MORNING we had gone off on our bikes. Usually we cycled as far as the edges of the fields, the dried-up stream, and raced each other back.

My bike was an old bone shaker, with a patched-up saddle, and so high I had to lean right over to touch the ground. Everyone called it 'the Crock'. Salvatore said it was the bike the Alpine troops had used in the war. But I liked it, it was my father's.

If we didn't go cycling we stayed in the street playing football, or steal-the-flag, or lounged under the shed roof doing nothing.

We could do whatever we liked. No cars ever went by. There were no dangers. And the grown-ups stayed shut up indoors, like toads waiting for the heat to die down.

That morning we had been talking about Melichetti's pigs.

Rumour had it old Melichetti trained them to savage hens, and sometimes rabbits and cats he found by the roadside.

Skull spat out a spray of white saliva. 'I've never told you till now. Because I couldn't say. But now I *will* tell you: those pigs ate Melichetti's daughter's dachshund. Alive. Completely alive.'

'It's not possible!'

Skull nodded. 'Melichetti threw it into the pigsty. The dachshund tried to get away, but Melichetti's pigs didn't give him a chance. Torn to shreds in two seconds.'

Maria stood up. 'Is Melichetti crazy?'

Skull spat on the ground again. 'Crazier than his pigs.'

We were silent for a few moments imagining Melichetti's daughter with such a wicked father.

'We could go and see them!' I suggested suddenly.

'An expedition!' said Barbara.

'It's a long way away,' Salvatore grumbled.

'No, it isn't, it's not far at all, let's go . . .' Skull got on his bike. He never missed a chance to put Salvatore down.

I had an idea. 'Why don't we take a hen from Remo's chicken run, so when we get there we can throw it into the pigsty and see how they tear it apart?'

'Brilliant!' Skull approved.

'But Papa will kill me if we take one of his hens,' Remo wailed.

It was no use, the idea was a really good one.

We went into the chicken run, chose the thinnest, scrawniest hen and stuck it in a bag. And off we went, all six of us and the hen, to see those famous pigs of Melichetti's, and we pedalled along between the wheat fields as the sun rose and roasted everything.

SALVATORE WAS RIGHT, Melichetti's farm was a long way away. By the time we got there we were parched and our heads were boiling.

Melichetti was sitting, with sunglasses on, in a rusty old rocking chair under a crooked beach umbrella.

The house was falling to pieces and the roof had been roughly patched up with tin and tar. In the farmyard there was a heap of rubbish: wheels, some bottomless chairs, a table with one leg missing.

A great big dog, all skin and bone, barked on a chain.

Behind the house were some corrugated-iron huts and the pigsties, on the edge of a gravina. Gravinas are small canyons, dug by the water in the rock. White spires, rocks and pointed crags protrude from the red earth. Inside, twisted olive trees and holly often grow, and there are caves where the shepherds put their sheep.

Melichetti looked like a mummy. His wrinkled skin hung off him, and he was hairless, except for a white tuft in the middle of his chest. Round his neck he had an orthopaedic collar fastened with green elastic bands, and he was wearing black shorts and brown plastic flip-flops. He had seen us arrive on our bikes, but he didn't move. We must have seemed like a mirage to him. Nobody ever passed by on that road, except the occasional truck carrying hay.

There was a smell of piss. And millions of horseflies. They didn't bother Melichetti. They settled on his head and round his eyes. Only if they got on his lips did he react, puffing them away.

Skull stepped forward. 'Signore, we're thirsty. Have you any water?'

I was worried, because a man like Melichetti was liable to shoot you, throw you to the pigs, or give you poisoned water to drink.

The old man raised his sunglasses. 'What are you doing here, kids? Aren't you a bit far from home?'

'Signor Melichetti, is it true you fed your dachshund to the pigs?' Barbara piped up.

I could have died. Skull turned and gave her a glare of hatred. Salvatore kicked her in the shin.

Melichetti burst out laughing, had a fit of coughing and nearly choked. When he had recovered he said: 'Who tells you these daft stories, little girl?'

Barbara pointed at Skull: 'He does!'

Skull blushed, hung his head and looked at his shoes.

I knew why Barbara had said it.

A few days earlier we had had a stone-throwing competition and Barbara had lost. As a forfeit Skull had ordered her to unbutton her shirt and show us her breasts. Barbara was eleven. She had a small bosom, just fleabites, nothing to what she would have in a couple of years' time. She had refused. 'If you don't, you can forget about coming with us any more,' Skull had threatened her. I had felt bad about it, the forfeit wasn't fair. I didn't like Barbara, but showing her tits, no, that seemed too much.

Skull had decided: 'Either show us your tits or get lost.'

And Barbara, without a word, had gone ahead and unbuttoned her shirt.

Barbara had been brooding on that episode and now she meant to get even with Skull.

'So you go around telling people I fed my dachshund to the pigs.' Melichetti scratched his chest. 'Augustus, that dog was called. Like the Roman emperor. Thirteen he was, when he died. Got a chicken bone stuck in his throat. Had a Christian funeral, proper grave and all.' He pointed his finger at Skull. 'I bet you're the oldest, aren't you, little boy?'

Skull didn't reply.

'You must never tell lies. And you mustn't blacken other people's names. You must tell the truth, especially to those who are younger than you. The truth, always. Before men, before the Lord God, and before yourself.' He sounded like a priest delivering a sermon. He pointed towards the drinking trough. 'If you're thirsty there's water over there. The best in the whole area. And that's no lie.'

We drank till we were bursting. It was cool and sweet. Then we started spraying each other and sticking our heads under the spout.

Skull said Melichetti was a piece of shit. And he knew for a fact the old fool had fed the dachshund to the pigs. He scowled at Barbara and said: 'I'll get you for this.' He walked off muttering and sat down on the other side of the road.

Salvatore, Remo and I set about catching tadpoles, and my sister and Barbara perched on the edge of the trough.

After a few minutes Skull came back, all excited. 'Look! Look! Look at the size of it!'

We turned round.

It was a hill. It looked like a panettone. A huge panettone that some giant had placed on the plain. It rose in front of us a couple of kilometres away. Golden and immense. The wheat covered it like a fur coat. There wasn't a tree, a crag, a blemish, to spoil its outline. The sky around it was liquid and dirty. The other hills, behind, were like dwarfs compared to that huge dome.

Goodness knows how none of us had noticed it till that moment. We had seen it, but without really seeing it. Maybe because it blended in with the landscape, or maybe because we had been looking out for Melichetti's farm.

'Let's climb it.' Skull pointed at it. 'Let's climb that mountain.'

I said: 'I wonder what's up on top.'

It must be an incredible place, maybe some strange animal lived there. None of us had ever been up so high.

Salvatore screened his eyes with his hand and scanned the top. 'I bet you can see the sea from up there. Yes, we must climb it.'

We gazed at it in silence.

Now that *was* an adventure, damn Melichetti's pigs.

'And we'll put our flag on the summit. So if anyone climbs up there, they'll know we got there first,' I said.

'What flag? We haven't got a flag,' said Salvatore.

'We'll use the hen.'

Skull grabbed the bag with the bird in it and whirled it round in the air. 'Right! We'll wring its neck, then we'll put a stick up its arse and fix it in the ground. I'll carry it up.' Skull pulled out his ace. 'Straight up the hill. No following each other. No stopping. Last one there pays a forfeit.'

We were speechless. A race! Why?

It was obvious. To get his own back on Barbara. She would come last and would have to pay.

I thought of my sister. I said she was too small to race and it wasn't fair, she would lose.

'So what? A race is a race. She came with us. Otherwise she has to wait for us down here.'

That wasn't on. I couldn't leave Maria. Melichetti had been kind, but it didn't do to be too trusting. If he killed her, what was I going to tell Mama?

'If my sister stays behind, I stay behind.'

Skull settled it. She could come, but she wouldn't be in the race.

We dumped our bikes behind the drinking trough and set off.

THAT WAS WHY I was up on that hill.

I put Maria's trainer back on. 'Can you walk?'

'No. It hurts too much.'

'Wait a minute.' I blew twice on her leg. Then I dug my hands in the hot earth. I picked up a small amount, spat on it and spread it on her ankle. 'That'll make it better.' I knew it wouldn't work. Earth was good for bee stings and nettles, not twisted ankles, but Maria might fall for it. 'Is that better?'

She wiped her nose with her arm. 'A bit.'

I took her hand. 'Let's get going then. Come on, we're last.'

We set off towards the top. Every five minutes Maria had to sit down to rest her leg. Luckily a bit of wind had got up, which improved things. It rustled in the wheat, making a noise that sounded like breathing.

The climb was steep and never-ending. All I had in front of my eyes was wheat, but when I started to see a slice of sky I understood that it wasn't far now, the top was there, and without even realising it we were standing on the summit.

There was absolutely nothing special about it. It was covered with wheat like all the rest. Under our feet was the same red, baked earth. Above our heads the same blazing sun.

I looked at the horizon. A milky haze veiled things. You couldn't see the sea. But you could see the other, lower hills, and Melichetti's farm with its pigsties and the gravina, and you could see the white road cutting across the fields, that long road we had cycled down to get there. And, tiny in the distance, you could see the hamlet where we lived. Acqua Traverse. Four little houses and an old country villa lost in the wheat. Lucignano, the neighbouring village, was hidden by the mist.

My sister said: 'I want to look too. Let me look.'

I lifted her on my shoulders, though I was so tired I could hardly stand. Who knows what she saw without her glasses.

'Where are the others?'

Where they had passed, the regularity of the ears of wheat had gone, many stalks were bent in half and some were broken. We followed the tracks that led towards the other side of the hill.

Maria squeezed my hand and dug her nails into my skin. 'Ugh! How horrible!'

I turned.

They had impaled the hen. It was there on top of a stick. Legs dangling, wings outspread. Its head hung on one side like a ghastly, blood-soaked pendant.

We went on and after crossing the backbone of the hill we began to descend. Where had the others got to? Why had they gone down that way? We walked another twenty metres and found out.

The hill wasn't round. Behind, it lengthened out into a kind of hump that wound its way gently down till it joined the plain. In the middle there was a narrow, enclosed valley, invisible except from up there or from an aeroplane.

The strange thing was that inside that concealed hollow some trees had grown. Sheltered from the wind and sun there was a little oak wood. And an abandoned house, with a ramshackle roof, brown tiles and dark beams, stood out among the green foliage.

WE WENT DOWN the path and entered the valley. It was the last thing I would have expected. Trees. Shade. Cool. You couldn't hear the crickets any more, only the twittering of birds. There were purple cyclamen. And carpets of green ivy. And a pleasant smell. It made you feel like finding yourself a cosy little spot by a tree trunk and having a nap.

Salvatore appeared suddenly, like a ghost. 'What do you think of this place then? Isn't it great?'

'Fantastic!' I replied, looking around. Maybe there was a stream to drink from.

'What took you so long? I thought you'd gone back down.'

'No, my sister's foot was hurting, so . ... I'm thirsty, I need a drink.'

Salvatore took a bottle from his rucksack. 'There's not much left.'

Maria and I went halves. It was barely enough to wet our lips.

'Who won the race?' I was worried about the forfeit. I was worn out. I hoped Skull, for once, might let me off or postpone it to another day.

'Skull.'

'Where did you come?'

'Second. Remo was third.'

'What about Barbara?'

'Last.'

'Who's got to do the forfeit?'

'Skull says Barbara's got to do it. But Barbara says you've got to do it because you came last. I don't know, I went off for a walk. I'm fed up with all these forfeits.'

We started walking towards the farmhouse.

It was a really tumble-down place. It stood in the middle of a clearing covered by the branches of the oaks. Deep cracks ran up from the foundations to the roof. All that was left of the window-panes were a few shards. A fig tree, all tangled, had overgrown the stairway that led up to the balcony. The roots had dismantled the stone steps and brought down the parapet. At the top there was still an old light blue door, rotten to the core and peeled by the sun. In the middle of the building a big arch opened onto a room with a vaulted ceiling. A cowshed. Rusty props and wooden poles sup-ported the upper floor, which in many places had fallen through. The ground was littered with heaps of broken tiles and brick. The walls had lost most of their plaster and showed the dry stonework behind.

Skull was sitting on a water tank. He was throwing stones at a rusty drum and watching us. 'You made it.'

I was pushed forward and nearly fell flat on my face. I turned round. Barbara, with red face, dirty T-shirt and ruffled hair, came at me, spoiling for a punch-up. 'You've got to do it. You came last!'

I put up my fists. 'I went back. Otherwise I'd have been third. You know that.'

'So what? You lost!'

'Who's got to do the forfeit?' I asked Skull. 'Me or her?'

He took his time before answering, then pointed at Barbara.

'See? See?' I loved Skull.

Barbara started kicking at the dust. 'It's not fair! It's not fair! Always me! Why's it always me?'

I didn't know why. But even then I knew that someone always gets all the bad luck. During those days it was Barbara Mura. I was sorry, but I was glad I wasn't in her shoes.

Barbara stomped round among us like a rhinoceros. 'Let's vote on it, then! He can't decide everything.'

Even after twenty-two years I still don't understand how she put up with us. It must have been the fear of being left on her own.

'All right. Let's vote on it,' Skull conceded. 'I say it's you.'

'So do I,' I said.

'So do I,' parroted Maria.

We looked at Salvatore. No one could abstain when there was a vote. That was the rule.

'So do I,' said Salvatore, almost in a whisper.

'See? Five-one. You've lost. You do it,' Skull concluded.

Barbara tightened her lips and her fists. I saw her swallow a lump the size of a tennis ball. She dropped her head, but she didn't cry. I respected her.

'What . . . do I have to do?' she stammered.

Skull rubbed his throat. His sadistic mind got to work. He wavered for a moment. 'You've got to . . . Last time you showed us your tits. This time you're going to pull down your knickers and show it to us.' He burst into raucous laughter, expecting that we would do the same, but we didn't.

The forfeit was too harsh. None of us wanted to see Barbara's slit. It was a punishment for us as well. My stomach tightened. I wished I was far away. And I didn't like my sister being there.

'Forget it,' said Barbara. 'I don't care if you hit me.'

Skull got up and strolled towards her with his hands in his pockets. Between his teeth he had an ear of wheat.

He stood in front of her. He craned his neck. He wasn't all that much taller than Barbara. Or stronger. I wasn't so sure he would beat her all that easily if they had a fight. If Barbara threw him on the ground and jumped on him she might even smother him.

'You lost. Now pull down your trousers.'

'No!'

Skull slapped her across the face. Barbara opened her mouth like a trout and rubbed her cheek. She still wasn't crying. She turned towards us. 'Haven't you lot got anything to say?' she whimpered. 'You're just as bad as him!'

We remained silent.

'All right then. But you'll never see me again. I swear it on my mother's head.'

'What's the matter, are you crying?' Skull was revelling in it.

'No, I'm not,' she managed to say, suppressing her sobs.

She was wearing green cotton trousers with brown patches on the knees, the sort you could buy at the flea market. They were too tight for her and her flab bulged out over the belt. She opened the buckle and started to undo her buttons. I caught a glimpse of white knickers with little yellow flowers.

'Wait! I came last,' I heard my voice saying.

Everyone turned.

'Yes,' I gulped. 'I want to do it.'

'What?' Remo asked me.

'The forfeit.'

'No. She's got to,' Skull snapped at me. 'It's nothing to do with you. Shut up.'

'Yes, it is. I came last. I've got to do it.'

'No. I decide.' Skull came towards me.

My legs were shaking, but I hoped nobody would notice. 'Let's have another vote.'

Salvatore spoke up. 'Second votes are allowed.'

We had rules and one of them was that second votes were allowed.

I raised my hand. 'I do the forfeit.'

Salvatore put up his hand. 'Michele does it.'

Barbara fastened her belt and sobbed. 'He does it.'

Skull was caught by surprise, he stared at Remo with his mad eyes. 'What do you say?'

Remo sighed: 'Barbara does it.'

'What shall I do?' asked Maria.

I nodded to her.

'My brother does it.'

And Salvatore said: 'Four-two. Michele's won. He does it.'

GETTING UP to the first floor of the house wasn't easy. The stairway no longer existed. The steps had been reduced to a heap of stone blocks. I was working my way up by holding on to the branches of the fig tree. The brambles scratched my arms and legs. One thorn had grazed my right cheek. This was the forfeit I had landed myself with by playing the hero.

'You've got to climb up to the first floor. Get in. Go right across the house, jump out of the end window onto the tree and climb down.'

I had been afraid Skull would make me show my dick or poke a stick up my arse, but instead he had chosen to make me do something dangerous, where the worst that could happen was that I might get hurt. That was something, anyway.

I gritted my teeth and went on without complaining. The others were sitting under an oak enjoying the spectacle of Michele Amitrano risking his neck.

Every now and then a bit of advice came: 'Go that way.'

'You've got to keep straight on, it's full of brambles round there.'

I took no notice.

I was up on the balcony. The doorway was fastened with a chain but the padlock was eaten away by rust and had come open. I pushed one flap and with a metallic groan the doors gave way.

A great fluttering of wings. Feathers. A flock of pigeons took off and flew out through a hole in the roof.

'What's it like? What's it like inside?' I heard Skull ask.

I didn't bother to reply. I went in, watching where I put my feet.

I was in a big room. A lot of roof tiles had fallen off and a beam was hanging down in the middle. In one corner there was a fireplace with a pyramid-shaped hood that was blackened by smoke. In another corner some furniture was piled up. An overturned rusty cooker. Bottles. Bits of crockery. Roof tiles. A broken bedspring. Everything was covered in pigeon shit. And there was a strong smell, an acrid stench that got right into your nose and throat. A forest of wild plants and weeds had sprung up through the tiled floor. At the other end of the room was a closed red door, which no doubt led to the other rooms of the house. That was the way I had to go.

I put one foot down; under my soles the beams creaked and the floor lurched. At the time I weighed about thirty-five kilos. About as much as a tank of water. I wondered if a tank of water, placed in the middle of that room, would bring the floor down. I didn't think I'd try it. To reach the next door it was more prudent to keep right against the walls. Holding my breath, on tiptoe like a ballerina, I followed the perimeter.

In the next room, which was about the same size as the kitchen, the floor had completely gone. At the sides it had collapsed and only a sort of bridge now connected my door to the one on the other side.

I couldn't follow the walls. I would have to cross that bridge.

I was paralysed in the doorway. I couldn't turn back. They would taunt me with it for evermore. What if I jumped down? Four metres separated me from the cowshed below . . .

Then I remembered reading in one of Salvatore's books that

lizards can climb up walls because they have perfect weight distribution. They spread their weight over their legs, stomach and tail, whereas human beings put all theirs on their feet and that's why they sink into quicksand.

Yes, that was what I must do. I knelt down, lay flat and started to crawl along. At every movement I made, bits of masonry and tiles fell down. Light, light as a lizard, I repeated to myself. I felt the beams quiver. It took me a full five minutes but I reached the other side safe and sound.

I pushed the door, the last one. At the other end was the window that overlooked the yard. A long branch snaked across to the house. I had made it. Here, too, the floor had fallen through, but only half of it. The other half had held. I used the old technique, walking flat against the wall. Below I could see another dimly lit room. There were the remains of a fire, some opened cans of tomatoes and empty packets of pasta. Somebody must have been there not long ago.

I reached the window without mishap. I looked down. There was a small yard skirted by a row of brambles and the wood behind it pressing in. On the ground there was a cracked cement trough, a rusty crane jib, piles of masonry covered in ivy, a gas cylinder and a mattress.

The branch I had to get onto was close—less than a metre away. Not close enough, however, to be reachable without jumping. It was thick and twisty like an anaconda. It would carry my weight. Once I reached the other end I would find a way to get down.

I stood up on the windowsill, crossed myself, and threw myself arms first, like a gibbon in the Amazon forest. I landed face down on the branch. I tried to grip it, but it was big. I used my legs but there was nothing to get hold of. I started to slip.

Salvation was right in front of me. There was a smaller branch just a few dozen centimetres away, and with a sudden lunge I grabbed it with both hands.

It was dry. It snapped. I landed on my back. I lay there, petrified, with my eyes closed, certain I had broken my neck. I couldn't feel any pain.

I opened my eyes. I gazed at the vast green umbrella of the oak that loomed over me. The glittering of the sun between the leaves. I must try to raise my head. I raised it. I touched the ground with my hands. And I discovered I was on something soft. The mattress.

I moved my feet and realised that under the leaves, the twigs and the earth there was a green corrugated sheet, a transparent Fibreglass roof. It had been covered up, as if to hide it. And that old mattress had been put on top of it.

It was the corrugated sheet that had saved me. It had bent and absorbed the force of my fall. So underneath it must be hollow.

It might be a secret hiding place or a tunnel leading to a cave full of gold and precious stones. I got onto my hands and knees and pushed the sheet forward. It was heavy, but gradually I managed to shift it a little. A terrible stink of shit was released. I swayed, put one hand over my mouth and pushed again.

I had fallen on top of a hole. The further I shifted the Fibreglass sheet the lighter it became. The walls were made of earth, dug with a spade. The roots of the oak had been cut. I managed to move the sheet a bit further. The hole was a couple of metres wide and two, two and a half metres deep.

It was empty.

No, there was something there. A heap of rolled-up rags? No . . . An animal? A dog? No . . . What was it?

It was hairless . . . white . . . a leg . . . A leg?

I jumped backwards and nearly tripped over.

I took a deep breath and had a quick look down. It was a leg. I felt I was going to pass out. I sat down, shut my eyes, rested my forehead on one hand, and breathed in. I was tempted to run away, but I had to have another look first. I went forward and peered over. It was a boy's leg. And sticking out of the rags was an elbow.

At the bottom of that hole there was a boy, lying on one side, his head hidden between his legs. He wasn't moving. He was dead. I stood looking at him for God knows how long. There was a bucket too. And a little saucepan. Maybe he was asleep.

I picked up a small stone and threw it at the boy. I hit him on the thigh. He didn't move. He was dead. Dead as a doornail. A shiver bit the back of my head. I picked up another stone and hit him on the neck. I thought he moved. A slight movement of the arm.

'Where are you? Where've you got to, you pansy?'

Skull was calling me.

I grabbed the corrugated sheet and pulled it over the hole. Then I spread out the leaves and earth and put the mattress back on top.

'Where are you, Michele?'

I went away, but first I turned round a couple of times to check that everything was in place.

I WAS PEDALLING ALONG on the Crock. The sun behind me was a huge red ball, and when it finally sank into the wheat it disappeared, leaving behind it something orange and purple.

They had asked me how I had got on in the house, if it had been dangerous, if I had fallen down, if there were any strange things in there, if jumping onto the tree had been difficult. I had answered in monosyllables.

Finally, bored, we had started back. A path led out of the valley, crossed the ochre fields and reached the road. We had collected our bikes and were pedalling along in silence.

I looked at Maria, who was following me on her Graziella with its tyres worn by the stones, Skull, out in front, with Remo beside him, Salvatore zigzagging along, Barbara on her oversize Bianchi, and I thought about the boy in the hole. I wasn't going to say anything to anyone. If I told them, Skull, as always, would take all the credit for the discovery. Not this time. I had done the forfeit, I had fallen out of the tree and I had found him. He wasn't Skull's. He wasn't Barbara's either. He wasn't Salvatore's. He was mine. He was my secret discovery.

I didn't know if I had discovered a dead person or a living one. Maybe the arm hadn't moved. I had imagined it. But what was he doing in there?

'What are we going to tell Mama?'

I hadn't noticed my sister was riding beside me. 'What?'

'Will you tell Mama about the glasses?'

'OK, but you mustn't tell her anything about where we went. If she finds out she'll say you broke them because we went up there.'

'All right.'

'Swear.'

'I swear.' She kissed her forefingers.

NOWADAYS ACQUA TRAVERSE is a district of Lucignano. In the mid-eighties a local building surveyor put up two long rows of houses made of reinforced concrete. Then a Co-op arrived and a bar-cum-tobacconist's, and an asphalted two-way road that runs straight to Lucignano. In 1978 Acqua Traverse was so small it was practically non-existent. A country hamlet, they would call it nowadays in a travel magazine.

No one knew why it was called Acqua Traverse, not even old Tronca. There certainly wasn't any water there, except what they brought in a tanker once a fortnight.

There was Salvatore's villa, which we called the Palazzo. A big house built in the nineteenth century, long and grey with a big stone porch and an inner courtyard with a palm tree. And there were four other houses. Just four. Four drab little houses made of stone and mortar with tiled roofs and small windows.

Ours. The one belonging to Skull's family. The one belonging to Remo's family, who shared it with old Tronca. Tronca was deaf and his wife had died, and he lived in two rooms overlooking the vegetable garden. And then there was the house of Pietro Mura, Barbara's father. Angela, his wife, had a shop on the ground floor where you could buy bread, pasta and soap. And you could make phone calls. Two houses on one side, two on the other. And a road, rough and full of holes, in the middle. There was no piazza. Just two benches under a pergola of strawberry vines and a drinking fountain which had a tap so that water wouldn't be wasted. All around, the wheat fields.

'PAPA'S HOME!' my sister shouted. She threw down her bike and ran up the steps. Parked in front of our house was his truck, a Fiat Lupetto with a green tarpaulin.

At that time Papa was working as a truck driver and would be away for weeks at a time. He collected the goods and carried them to the North. He had promised he would take me with him to the North one day. I couldn't imagine this North very clearly. I knew the North was rich and the South was poor. And we were poor. Mama said that if Papa kept working so hard, soon we wouldn't be poor any longer, we would be well off. So we mustn't complain if Papa wasn't there. He was doing it for us.

I went into the house still out of breath. Papa was sitting at the table in his vest and pants. He had a bottle of red wine in front of him and a cigarette in its holder between his lips and my sister perched on one thigh.

Mama, with her back to us, was cooking. There was a smell of onions and tomato sauce. The television, a big boxlike black-and-white Grundig, which Papa had brought home a few months earlier, was on. The ventilator fan was humming.

'Michele, where've you been all day? Your mother was at her wits' end. Haven't you got any consideration for the poor woman? She's always having to wait for her husband, she shouldn't have to wait for you too. And what happened to your sister's glasses?'

467

He wasn't really angry. When he was really angry his eyes bulged like a toad's. He was happy to be home.

My sister looked at me. 'We built a hut by the stream.' I took the glasses out of my pocket. 'And they got broken.'

He spat out a cloud of smoke. 'Come over here. Let's see.'

Papa was a small man, thin and restless. When he sat in the driving seat of his truck he almost vanished behind the wheel. He had black hair, smoothed down with brilliantine. A rough white beard on his chin. He smelt of Nazionali and eau de cologne.

I gave him the glasses.

'They're a write-off.' He put them on the table. 'That's it. No more glasses.'

My sister and I looked at each other.

'What am I going to do?' she asked anxiously.

'Go without. That'll teach you.'

My sister was speechless.

'She can't. She can't see,' I interposed.

He said to Mama: 'Teresa, give me that parcel on the kitchen cabinet.'

Mama brought it over. Papa unwrapped it and took out a hard velvety blue case. 'Here you are.'

Maria opened it and inside was a pair of glasses with brown plastic frames.

'Try them on.'

Maria put them on, but kept stroking the case.

Mama asked her: 'Do you like them?'

'Yes. They're lovely. The box is beautiful.' And she went to look at herself in the mirror.

Papa poured himself another glass of wine. 'If you break these, next time you'll go without, do you understand?' Then he took me by the arm. 'Come here.' I sat on his knee too and tried to kiss him.

'Don't kiss me, you're all dirty. If you want to kiss your father, you've got to wash first. Teresa, what shall we do, send them to bed without supper?' Papa had a nice smile, perfect white teeth. Neither my sister nor I has inherited them.

Mama replied without turning round. 'It'd be no more than they deserve! I can't stand any more of these two.' *She* really was angry.

'Let's say this. If they want to have supper and get the present I've brought them, Michele's got to beat me at arm-wrestling. Otherwise, bed with no supper.'

He'd brought us a present!

'You and your jokes . . .' Mama was too happy that Papa was home again. When Papa went away her stomach hurt, and the more time passed the less she talked. After a month she went mute.

'Michele can't beat you. It's not fair,' said my sister.

'Michele, show your sister what you can do. And keep those legs apart. If you sit crooked you'll lose and there'll be no present.'

I got into position. I clenched my teeth and gripped Papa's hand and started to push. Nothing. He didn't budge.

'Go on! Have you got ricotta instead of muscles? You're weaker than a gnat! Put your back into it, for God's sake!'

I murmured: 'I can't do it.' It was like bending an iron bar.

'You're a sissy, Michele. Maria, help him, come on!'

My sister climbed on the table and together, gritting our teeth and breathing through our noses, we managed to lower that arm.

'The present! Give us the present!' Maria jumped down from the table.

Papa picked up a cardboard box full of crumpled-up newspaper. Inside was the present.

'A boat!' I said.

'It's not a boat, it's a gondola,' Papa explained.

'What's a gondola?'

'Gondolas are Venetian boats. And they only use one oar.'

It was really beautiful. Made of black plastic. With little silvery pieces and at the end a little figure in a red-and-white-striped shirt and a straw hat. But we discovered that we weren't allowed to handle it. It was made to be put on the television. And between the television and the gondola there would have to be a white lace doily. Like a little lake. It wasn't a toy. It was something precious. An ornament.

'WHOSE TURN IS IT to fetch the water? It'll be suppertime soon,' Mama asked us.

Papa was in front of the television watching the news.

I was laying the table. I said: 'It's Maria's turn. I went yesterday.'

Maria was sitting in the armchair with her dolls. 'I don't feel like it, you go.'

Neither of us liked going to the drinking fountain so we took turns, one day each. But Papa had come home and to my sister this meant the rules no longer applied.

I gestured no with my finger. 'It's your turn.'

Maria folded her arms. 'I'm not going. I've got a headache.'

Whenever she didn't want to do something she said she had a headache. It was her favourite excuse. She started massaging her forehead with a pained expression on her face.

I felt like throttling her. 'It's her turn! She's got to go!'

Mama, exasperated, put the jug in my hands. 'You go, Michele, you're the eldest. Don't make such a fuss.'

'It's not fair. I'm not going.' I went over to Papa to complain. 'Papa, it's not my turn. I went yesterday.'

He took his eyes off the television and looked at me as if it was the first time he had ever seen me, stroked his mouth and said: 'Do you know the soldier's draw?'

'No. What is it?'

'It's what the soldiers did during the war to decide who went on the dangerous missions.' He took a box of matches out of his pocket. 'You take three matches'—he took them out of the box—'one for you, one for me and one for Maria. You remove the head from one of them.' He took one and broke it, then he gripped them all in his fist and made the ends stick out. 'Whoever draws the headless match goes to get the water. Pick one, come on.'

I pulled out a whole one. I jumped for joy. 'Maria, it's your turn.'

My sister took a whole one too and clapped her hands.

'Looks like it's me.' Papa drew out the broken one.

Maria and I started laughing and shouting: 'You go! You go! You've lost! You've lost! Go and get the water!'

Papa got up, rather crestfallen. 'When I get back you must be washed. Do you hear me?'

'Would you like me to go? You're tired,' said Mama.

'You can't. It's a dangerous mission. Besides, I've got to get my cigarettes from the truck.' And he went out of the house with the jug in his hand.

We got washed, ate pasta with tomato sauce and *frittata*, and after kissing Papa and Mama we went to bed without even begging to be allowed to watch television.

I WOKE UP during the night. I had had a nightmare. Jesus was telling Lazarus to rise and walk. But Lazarus didn't rise. Rise and walk, Jesus repeated. Lazarus just wouldn't come back to life. Jesus lost his temper. He was being made to look a fool. When Jesus tells you to rise and walk, you have to do it, especially if you're dead. But

Lazarus just lay there, stiff as a board. So Jesus started shaking him like a doll and Lazarus finally rose up and bit him in the throat. Leave the dead alone, he said with blood-smeared lips.

I opened my eyes wide. I was covered in sweat. Those nights it was so hot that if you were unfortunate enough to wake up it was hard to get back to sleep. The bedroom I shared with my sister was narrow and long. It had been converted from a corridor. The two beds were laid lengthwise, one after the other, under the window. On one side was the wall, on the other about thirty centimetres to move in. Otherwise the room was white and bare.

In winter it was cold and in summer you couldn't breathe.

Behind my feet I saw Maria's dark head. She was sleeping with her glasses on, face upwards, completely relaxed with her arms and legs apart. She used to say that if she woke up without her glasses on she got scared. Usually Mama took them off as soon as she fell asleep because they left marks on her face.

Next to our room was our parents' room. I could hear Papa snoring. The fan blowing. My sister breathing. The monotonous hoot of a little owl. The buzz of the fridge.

I knelt on the bed and leaned on the windowsill to get some air. There was a full moon, high and bright. You could see for a long way, as if it were daytime. The fields seemed phosphorescent. The air was still. The houses dark, silent. Maybe I was the only person awake in Acqua Traverse. It was a good feeling.

The boy was in the hole. I imagined him dead in the earth. Cockroaches, bugs and millipedes crawling on him, and worms coming out of his blue lips. I had never seen a dead body. Except my grandmother Giovanna. On her bed, with her arms crossed, in her black dress and shoes. Her face yellow like wax.

But what if the boy was alive? If he wanted to get out and was scratching at the walls of the hole with his fingers and calling for help? If he had been caught by an ogre? I looked out and far away on the plain I saw the hill. It seemed to have appeared out of nothing and stood up, like an island risen from the sea, tall and black, with its secret that was waiting for me.

I lay for a long time staring at the ceiling before I got back to sleep. Papa wasn't going away again, he had come home to stay. He had told Mama he didn't want to see the autostrada again for a while and he was going to look after us. Maybe, sooner or later, he would take us to the seaside for a swim.

TWO

When I woke up, Mama and Papa were still asleep. I gulped down some milk and some bread and marmalade, went out and got my bike.

Another scorching day. At eight o'clock in the morning the sun was still low but was already beginning to roast the plain. I was pedalling along the road we had come down the previous afternoon, trying to get there quickly. I took the road through the fields, the one that skirted the hill and led to the valley. Every now and then magpies rose from the wheat with their black and white tails. I was finding it hard going; the tyres slipped on the stones and the clods of dry earth. The closer I got to the house, the bigger the yellow hill grew in front of me, and the heavier the weight that crushed my chest, taking my breath away.

What if I arrived and found witches or an ogre there? I knew witches met at night in abandoned houses and had parties, and that ogres ate children. I must be careful. If an ogre caught me, he would throw me in a hole too and eat me bit by bit. First an arm, then a leg and so on. My parents would weep in despair. And everyone would say: 'Michele was such a nice boy, we're so sorry.' I didn't want to die. I didn't have to go up there. Was I out of my mind?

I turned my bike round and started for home. After a hundred metres I braked. What would Tiger Jack do in my place? Now there was a serious person. Tiger Jack, Tex Willer's Indian buddy. And Tiger Jack would go up that hill even if an international conference of all the witches, bandits and ogres on the planet was taking place there, because he was a Navaho Indian, and he was fearless and invisible and silent as a puma and knew how to lie in wait for his enemies and then stab them with his knife. I'm Tiger. Even better, I'm Tiger's Italian son, I said to myself. Pity I didn't have a knife.

I hid my bike, as Tiger would have done with his horse, ducked into the wheat and crawled forward on hands and knees.

When I reached the valley I flitted from tree to tree like a Sioux, with my ears pricked up for any suspicious sound. I scanned the house. It was silent and still. Nothing seemed to have changed. If the witches had been there they had tidied up afterwards. I squeezed through the brambles and found myself in the yard. Hidden under the corrugated sheet and the mattress was the hole. It hadn't been a dream.

I couldn't see him clearly. It was dark and full of flies and a sickening smell welled up. I knelt on the edge. 'Are you alive?'

Nothing.

'Are you alive? Can you hear me?'

I waited, then I picked up a stone and threw it at him. I hit him on the foot. A thin, slender foot with black toes. A foot that didn't move a millimetre. He was dead. And he would only get up from there if Jesus ordered him to. My flesh crawled. I must see his face. The face is the most important thing. From the face you can tell everything.

But going down there scared me. I could turn him over with a stick. I went into the cowshed and found a pole, but it was too short. I went back. A small, locked door gave onto the yard. Above the door there was a little window. I climbed up, supporting myself on the jambs, and got through headfirst.

I found myself in the room I had seen while I was crossing the bridge. There were the packets of pasta. The opened cans of tomatoes. Empty beer bottles. The remains of a fire. A drum full of water. I had the same feeling I had had the day before, that someone came here.

Under a grey blanket there was a big box. Inside I found a rope that ended in an iron hook. I took it and chucked it through the little window and climbed out.

On the ground there was the rusty crane jib. I tied the rope round it. But I was afraid it would come undone and I would be left in the hole with the corpse. I tied three knots, like the ones Papa tied on the tarpaulin of his truck. I pulled as hard as I could, it held. So I threw it into the hole.

'I'm not scared of anything,' I whispered to hearten myself, but my legs were wobbly and a voice in my brain was screaming at me not to go. I crossed myself and went down.

INSIDE IT WAS COLDER. The dead boy's skin was dirty, caked with mud and shit. He was naked. About the same height as me, but thinner. He was skin and bone. His ribs stuck out. He must be about my age.

I touched his hand with my toe, but it remained lifeless. I lifted the blanket that covered his legs. Round the right leg he had a big chain fastened with a padlock. The skin was scraped and raw. Transparent liquid oozed from the flesh and ran onto the rusty links of the chain, which was fixed to a buried ring.

Tentatively, I stretched out my arm and with two fingers took hold of one edge of the blanket. I was trying to lift it off his face when the dead boy bent his leg. I clenched my fists and opened my mouth wide as terror gripped me. Then the dead boy raised his torso as if he was alive and with eyes closed stretched out his arms towards me. My hair stood on end, I let out a yell, jumped backwards and tripped over the bucket and the shit spilled all over the place.

I landed on my back screaming. The dead boy started screaming too. I thrashed about, then at last with a desperate lunge I grabbed the rope and shot out of the hole like a flea gone berserk.

I PEDALLED, I swerved between holes and ruts at the risk of crashing, but I didn't slow down. My heart was exploding, my lungs were burning. One knee was grazed and bleeding, my T-shirt was spattered with shit, a leather strap on my sandal had snapped. Breathe, I told myself. I breathed and felt my heart calming down, my breathing returning to normal, and suddenly I felt sleepy. I got off the bike and lay down. I closed my eyes. The fear was still there, but it was just a slight burning way down in my stomach. The sun warmed my frozen arms. The crickets sang in my ears. My knee throbbed.

When I opened my eyes again some ants were crawling over me. How long had I slept? It might have been five minutes or two hours.

I got on the Crock and rode on homewards. As I pedalled I kept seeing the dead boy rising up and stretching out his hands towards me. That gaunt face, those closed eyes, that open mouth, kept flashing in front of me. Now it seemed to me like a bad dream.

He was alive. He had pretended to be dead. Why? Maybe he was ill. Maybe he was a monster. A werewolf. They kept that boy chained up under a Fibreglass sheet covered with earth so that he wouldn't be exposed to the moon's rays. But werewolves didn't exist.

'Stop all this talk about monsters, Michele. Monsters don't exist. Ghosts, werewolves and witches are just nonsense invented to frighten mugs like you. It's men you should be afraid of, not monsters,' Papa had said to me one day when I had asked him if monsters could breathe under water. But if they had hidden him there, there must be a reason. Papa would explain it all to me.

'PAPA! PAPA!' I pushed the door and rushed in. 'Papa! I've got something to . . .' The rest died on my lips.

He was sitting in the armchair, looking at me with toad's eyes. The worst toad's eyes I had seen since the day I had drunk the Lourdes water thinking it was *acqua minerale*. He squashed his cigarette end in his coffee cup.

Mama was sitting on the sofa sewing; she raised her head and lowered it again.

Papa drew in air through his nose and said: 'Where have you been all day?' He looked me up and down. 'Have you seen yourself?' He grimaced. 'You stink like a pig! And you've broken your sandals too!' He looked at the clock. 'Do you know what time it is? Twenty past three. You didn't turn up for lunch. Nobody knew where you were. I went all the way to Lucignano looking for you. Yesterday you got away with it. Not today.'

When he was furious Papa didn't shout, he spoke in a low voice. That terrified me.

He pointed towards the door. 'If you want to do as you please, you'd better go away. I don't want you. Get out.'

'Wait a minute, I've got something to tell you.'

'I don't want to hear it.'

I pleaded. 'Papa, it's important . . .'

Suddenly he raised his voice: 'Get out!'

I nodded. I felt like crying. My eyes filled with tears, I opened the door and went down the steps. I got on the Crock again and cycled down to the stream.

THE STREAM WAS ALWAYS DRY, except in winter, when it rained hard. It wound its way between the yellow fields like a long albino snake. After a steep part between two hills, the stream widened out to form a pond which in summer dried up into a black puddle. The lake, we called it. There were no fish in it, nor tadpoles, only mosquito larvae and water boatmen. If you put your feet in it, you took them out covered in dark, stinking mud. We went there for the carob tree.

It was big, old and easy to climb. I felt good up there in the shade, hidden among the leaves. You could see a long way; it was like being at the top of a ship's mast. I climbed up to my usual place, astride a thick branch, and decided I would never go home again. If Papa didn't want me, if he hated me, I didn't care, I would stay there. I could live without a family, like the orphans.

I took off my T-shirt, rested my back against the wood, my head in my hands, and looked at the hill where the boy was. It was far away, at the end of the plain, and the sun was setting beside it. It was an orange disc that faded to pink against the clouds and the sky.

'Michele, come down!'

I woke up and opened my eyes.

'Michele!'

Under the tree, on her Graziella, was Maria. I yawned. 'What do you want?' I stretched. My back was all stiff.

She got off her bike. 'Mama said you've got to come home.'

I put my T-shirt on again. It was beginning to get cold. 'No, tell her I'm staying here!'

'Mama said supper's ready.'

It was late. In half an hour it would be dark. I wasn't too happy about that. 'Tell them I'm not their son and you're their only child.'

My sister frowned. 'And you're not my brother either?'

'No.'

'So I can have the room to myself and all your comics?'

'No, that's got nothing to do with it.'

'Mama says if you don't come, she will. And she'll spank you.'

'I don't care. Anyway, she can't get up the tree.'

She got on her saddle. 'She'll be cross, you know.'

'Where's Papa?'

'He's gone out. He won't be back till late.'

'Where's he gone?'

'I don't know. Are you coming?'

I was starving. 'What's for supper?'

'Purée and eggs,' she said as she rode off.

Purée and eggs. I loved both of them. Especially when I stirred them together and they became a delicious mush. I jumped down. 'All right, I'll come. Just for this evening, though.'

AT SUPPER NOBODY TALKED. It was as if there had been a death in the family.

I finished and put my plate in the sink. 'Won't Papa ever get over it?'

Mama said: 'If he finds you asleep he might.'

Mama never sat at table with us. She served us and ate standing up. With her plate resting on the fridge. She was always on her feet. Cooking. Washing. Ironing. If she wasn't on her feet, she was asleep. The television bored her. When she was tired she flopped on her bed and went out like a light.

At the time of this story Mama was thirty-three. She was still beautiful. She had long black hair that reached halfway down her back and she let it hang loose. She had dark eyes as big as almonds, a wide mouth, strong white teeth and a pointed chin. She looked Arabian. She was tall, shapely, she had a big bosom, a narrow waist and wide hips. When we went to the market in Lucignano I saw how the men's eyes would be glued to her. I held her hand, I clutched onto her skirt. She's mine, leave her alone, I felt like shouting.

'Teresa, you give a man evil thoughts,' said Severino, the guy who brought the water tanker.

Mama wasn't interested in these things. She didn't see them. Those lecherous looks just slipped off her. She was no flirt.

IT WAS SO HUMID you couldn't breathe. We were in bed. In the dark.

'Good night,' said Maria.

'Good night,' I replied.

I tried to sleep, but I wasn't sleepy, I tossed and turned in bed. I looked out of the window. The moon was no longer a perfect ball and there were stars everywhere. That night the boy couldn't turn into a wolf. I looked towards the mountain. And for an instant I thought a light was glimmering on the top. I wondered what was happening in the abandoned house. Maybe the witches were there, naked and old, standing round the hole laughing toothlessly and maybe they were dragging the boy out of the hole and making him dance. I wished I could turn into a bat and fly over the house. Or put on the old suit of armour that Salvatore's father kept by the front door and go up onto the hill. Wearing that I would be safe.

IN THE MORNING I woke up calm, I hadn't had nightmares. I stayed in bed for a while, with my eyes closed, listening to the birds. Then I started seeing the boy rising up and stretching out his arms again.

'Help!' I said.

What an idiot I was! That's why he had sat up. He had been asking me for help and I had run away. I went out of the room in my underpants. Papa was tightening the coffeepot. Barbara's father was sitting at the table.

'Good morning,' said Papa. He wasn't angry any more.

'Hello, Michele,' said Barbara's father.

Pietro Mura was a short, stocky man, with a big black moustache that covered his mouth. He was wearing a black suit with thin white stripes and a waistcoat. He had been a barber in Lucignano for a number of years, but when a new salon had opened with manicuring and modern hairstyles he had shut up shop and now he was a farmer. But in Acqua Traverse he was still known as the barber. If you needed a haircut you went round to his house. He would sit you down in the kitchen, in the sun, open a drawer and take out a rolled-up cloth in which he kept his combs and his well-oiled scissors.

He looked at me and said: 'What're you trying to be, a longhair?'

I shook my head.

Papa poured the coffee into the good cups.

'He drove me up the wall yesterday. If he carries on like this I'm sending him to the friars.'

The barber asked me: 'Do you know how friars have their hair cut?'

'With a hole in the middle.'

'That's right. You'd better be good then.'

'Come on, get dressed and have breakfast,' said Papa. 'Mama's gone to market and left you the bread and milk.'

'Papa, I've got something to tell you. Something important.'

He put on his jacket. 'You can tell me this evening. I'm going out. Wake up your sister and warm the milk.' He downed his coffee.

The barber drank his and they both went out of the house.

After getting Maria's breakfast I went down the steps into the street. Skull and the others were playing soccer in the sun. Togo, a little black and white mongrel, was chasing the ball and getting under everyone's feet. Togo had appeared in Acqua Traverse at the beginning of the summer and had been adopted by the whole village. Everybody gave him leftovers and he had become a great fat thing with a stomach swollen like a drum. He was a nice little dog.

'You go in goal,' Salvatore shouted to me.

But the hill was calling me. I could go. Papa and Mama were out. As long as I was back by lunchtime. 'I'm not in the mood for football,' I said and went off.

Salvatore ran after me. 'Where are you going?'

'Nowhere.'

'Shall we go for a ride?'

'Later. There's something I have to do now.'

I HAD RUN AWAY and left everything like this: the corrugated sheet thrown to one side with the mattress, the hole uncovered and the rope hanging down inside.

If the guardians of the hole had come, they must have seen that their secret had been discovered and they would get me. What if he wasn't there any more? I must pluck up courage and look.

I leaned over. He was rolled up in the blanket. I cleared my throat. 'Hi . . . Hi . . . Hi . . . I'm the boy who came yesterday. Remember?'

No reply.

'Can you hear me? Are you ill? Are you alive?'

He bent his arm, raised his hand and whispered something.

'What? I didn't catch that.'

'Water.'

'Water? Wait a minute.'

Where was I going to find water? There were a couple of paint buckets, but they were empty. In the washing trough there was a little water, but it was green and crawling with mosquito larvae. I remembered that when I had gone in to get the rope I had seen a drum full of water.

'I'll be right back,' I said, and climbed through the little window over the door.

The drum was half full, but the water was clear and didn't smell. It seemed all right. In a dark corner, on a wooden plank, there were some cans, some candles, a saucepan, a basket and some empty bottles. I took one bottle, walked two paces and stopped. I went back and picked up the saucepan. It was a shallow, white enamel pan with a blue rim and handles, and red apples painted round the outside. It was just like the one we had at home. We had bought ours at Lucignano market. This one looked older. It hadn't been properly washed; there was still some stuff stuck on the bottom. I ran my forefinger over it and brought it up to my nose. Tomato sauce. I put it back and filled the bottle with water, closing it with a cork stopper. Then I took the basket and climbed out.

I grabbed the rope, tied the basket to it and put the bottle inside.

'I'll lower it down to you,' I said. 'Take it.'

With the blanket round him, he groped for the bottle, uncorked it and poured the water into his saucepan without spilling a drop, then he put it back in the basket and gave a tug on the cord. As if it was something he always did, every day. Since I didn't take it back he gave a second tug and grunted something angrily. As soon as I had pulled it up he lowered his head and without lifting the saucepan started to drink, on all fours, like a dog. When he had finished he crouched down on one side and didn't move again.

It was late.

'Well . . . goodbye.' I covered up the hole and went away.

WHILE I WAS CYCLING towards Acqua Traverse, I thought about the saucepan I had found in the kitchen. I found it strange that it was the same as ours, maybe because Maria had chosen it from so many, because she liked the apples.

I arrived home just in time for lunch.

'Hurry up, go and wash your hands,' said Papa. He was sitting at the table next to my sister. I dashed into the bathroom and rubbed my hands with the soap, parted my hair on the right and joined them while Mama was filling the plates with pasta. She wasn't using the saucepan with the apples on it. I looked at the dishes drying on the sink, but I couldn't see it there either. It must be in the kitchen cabinet.

'In a couple of days somebody's coming to stay with us,' said Papa with his mouth full. 'You must both be good. Don't show me up.'

I asked: 'Who is this somebody?'

He poured himself a glass of wine. 'A friend of mine. Sergio.'

'Sergio,' Maria repeated. 'What a funny name.'

It was the first time anyone had ever come to stay with us. At Christmas my uncles and aunts came but they hardly ever stayed the night. There wasn't room. I asked: 'And how long is he staying?'

Papa filled his plate again. 'For a while.'

Mama put a little slice of meat in front of each of us. It was Wednesday. And Wednesday was meat day. The meat that's good for you, the meat my sister and I couldn't stand. I, with a great effort, could get that tough tasteless bit of shoe leather down, but my sister couldn't. She would chew it for hours till it became a stringy white ball that swelled up in her mouth. And when she really couldn't stand it any more she would stick it on the underside of the table. There the meat fermented. Mama just couldn't understand it. 'Where's that smell coming from? What can it be?' Till one day she took out the cutlery drawer and found all those ghastly pellets stuck to the boards like wasps' nests.

But now the trick had been rumbled.

Maria started moaning: 'I don't like it!'

Mama lost her temper at once. 'Maria, eat up that meat!'

Now she'll get sent to bed, I thought.

But Papa looked Mama in the eyes. 'Leave her alone, Teresa. So she won't eat it. It doesn't matter. Put it away.'

After lunch my parents went to have a rest. The house was an oven, but they managed to sleep anyway. It was the right moment to search for the saucepan. I opened the kitchen cabinet and rummaged through the crockery. I looked in the chest of drawers and went outside and looked behind the house where the washing trough was. Sometimes Mama washed the dishes out there and left them to dry in the sun. Nothing. The saucepan with the apples had disappeared.

WE WERE SITTING under the pergola waiting for the sun to go down a bit so we could have a game of football, when I saw Papa going down the steps, wearing his good trousers and a clean shirt. He was carrying a blue bag that I had never seen before.

Maria and I got up and reached him as he was getting into the truck. 'Papa, Papa, where are you going? Are you going away?' I asked him, clinging onto the door.

'Can we come with you?' begged my sister.

He turned on the ignition. 'Sorry, kids. Not today.'

I tried to get into the cab. 'But you said you wouldn't go away again, you'd stay at home . . .'

'I'll be back soon. Tomorrow or the day after. Out you get, now.' He was in a hurry. He wasn't in the mood to argue. We watched him depart in the dust, sitting at the wheel of his great green box.

I WOKE UP during the night. And not because of a dream. Because of a noise. I lay there, with my eyes closed, listening. I seemed to be on the sea, except that it was a sea of iron, a lazy ocean of bolts, screws and nails that lapped on a beach.

I looked out of the window. A combine harvester was clattering along the moonlit crest of a hill. It was like a huge metal grasshopper, with two bright round little eyes and a wide mouth made of blades and spikes. A mechanical insect that devoured wheat and shitted out straw. It worked by night because in the daytime it was too hot. That was what was making the sound of the sea.

I looked towards the hill. Papa was there. He had taken my sister's meat to the boy and that was why he had pretended to be going away and that was why he had a bag, to hide it in.

Before supper I had opened the fridge and the meat wasn't there any more. 'Mama, where's that slice of meat?'

She had looked at me in amazement. 'Do you like meat now?'

'Yes.'

'It's not there any more. Your father's eaten it.'

No, he hadn't. He had taken it for the boy. Because the boy was my brother. Like Nunzio Scardaccione, Salvatore's big brother. Nunzio wasn't a bad lunatic, but I couldn't bear to look at him. I was scared he would infect me with his madness. Nunzio tore out his hair with his hands and ate it. His head was all pits and scabs and he dribbled. His mother put a hat and gloves on him so he wouldn't tear his hair out, but he had started biting his arms till they bled. In the end they had carried him off to the mental hospital. I had been glad.

Maybe the boy in the hole was my brother, and he had been born mad like Nunzio and Papa had hidden him there, so as not to frighten my sister and me. Not to frighten the children of Acqua Traverse. We were the same height and we seemed to be the same age. Maybe he and I were twins.

Papa had put him in a sack and taken him onto the hill to kill him, he had put him on the ground, in the wheat, and he should have stabbed him but he couldn't bring himself to do it, he was his son after all, so he had dug a hole, chained him inside and brought him up there.

Mama didn't know he was alive.

I did.

THREE

I woke up early. I stayed in bed while the sun began to glow. Then I couldn't bear to wait any longer. Mama and Maria were still asleep. I got up, cleaned my teeth, filled my schoolbag with some cheese and bread and went out.

I had decided that in the daytime there was no danger on the hill, it was only at night that nasty things happened.

I raced across the deserted countryside, on the Crock, heading for the house. If I found even a scrap of the meat in the hole it would mean the boy was my brother. I was nearly there when a thick red dust cloud appeared on the horizon. The sort of cloud that can be raised by a car on a sunbaked earth track. It was a long way off but it wouldn't take long to reach me. It was coming from the abandoned house. I didn't know what to do. If I turned back it would catch up with me, if I went on they would see me.

Hide, I told myself. I swerved, the bike reared up on a stone and I flew like a crucifix into the wheat. The car was less than 200 metres away. The Crock was lying at the edge of the road. I grabbed the front wheel and dragged it over beside me. I flattened down on the ground. Not breathing. Not moving a muscle. Asking Baby Jesus not to let them see me.

Baby Jesus granted my request. Lying among the stalks, with the horseflies feasting on my skin and my hands dug into the burning clods, I saw a brown 127 shoot past. Felice Natale's 127.

FELICE NATALE was Skull's big brother. If Skull was bad, Felice was a thousand times worse.

Felice was twenty. And whenever he was in Acqua Traverse life was hell for me and the other children. He would hit us, puncture our football and steal things from us. He was friendless, womanless. A guy who bullied children, a soul in torment. And that was understandable. No twenty-year-old could live in Acqua Traverse without ending up like Nunzio Scardaccione, the hair-tearer. Felice in Acqua Traverse was like a tiger in a cage.

That year the fashion was flared trousers, tight-fitting brightly coloured T-shirts, sheepskin coats and long hair. Not Felice—he had his hair cut short and combed it back with brilliantine, he shaved perfectly and wore combat jackets and camouflage trousers. And he tied a bandanna round his neck. He drove around in that 127, he liked guns and said he had been in the parachute regiment at Pisa and had jumped out of planes. But it wasn't true. Everyone knew he had done his military service at Brindisi. He had the pointed face of a barracuda and little gappy teeth like a baby crocodile's. As long as he didn't open his mouth he was almost good-looking, but if he opened up, if he laughed, you took two steps backwards. And if he caught you looking at his teeth you were for it.

Then, one blessed day, without saying a word to anyone, he had left. If you asked Skull where his brother had gone he would reply: 'To the North. To work.' That was all we wanted to know. But now he had popped up again like a poisonous weed. In his diarrhoea-coloured 127. And he was coming down from the abandoned house.

He had put the boy in the hole. That was who had put him there.

HIDDEN AMONG THE TREES, I checked that there was nobody in the valley. When I was sure I was alone, I came out of the wood and climbed into the house through the usual window. As well as the packets of pasta, the bottles of beer and the saucepan with the apples, on the floor there was an army sleeping-bag. Felice. It was his. I filled a bottle with water, got the rope out of the box and took it outside. I tied it to the crane jib, moved the corrugated sheet and mattress and looked down.

He was curled up like a hedgehog in the brown blanket. I didn't want to go down there, but I had to find out if there were any remains of my sister's slice of meat. Even though I had seen Felice coming from the hill I couldn't get it out of my head that the boy might be my brother.

I took out the cheese and asked him: 'Can I come down? I'm the one who gave you the water. Do you remember? I've brought you something to eat. It's good. *Caciotta.*'

He didn't reply. Maybe Felice had cut his throat.

'I'll throw the *caciotta* down. Catch it.' I threw it near him. A black hand shot out of the blanket and started to feel about on the ground till it found the cheese, grabbed it and whipped it back underneath. While he was eating his legs quivered, like those stray dogs when they come across a bit of leftover steak after days without food.

'I've got some water too . . . shall I bring it down?'

He made a gesture with his arm. I let myself down. As soon as he felt I was near him, he cowered back against the wall. I looked around; there was no trace of the meat.

'I won't hurt you. Are you thirsty?' I held out the bottle. 'Drink it, it's good.'

He sat up without taking off the blanket. He looked like a ragged little ghost. His thin legs stuck out like two spindly white twigs. One was chained up. He put out an arm and snatched the bottle from me and, like the cheese, it vanished under the blanket. He drained it in twenty seconds. And when he had finished, he even gave a burp.

'What's your name?' I asked him.

He curled up again without deigning to reply.

'What's your father's name?' I waited in vain. 'My father's name's Pino, what's yours? Is your father called Pino too?'

He seemed to be asleep. I stood looking at him, then I said: 'Felice! Do you know him?' I didn't know what else to say. 'Do you want me to go? If you want I'll go.' Nothing. 'All right, I'll go.' I grabbed the rope. 'Goodbye, then . . .'

I heard a whisper, a breath, something came out of the blanket. I moved closer. 'Did you speak?'

He whispered again.

'I don't understand. Speak louder.'

'The little bears . . . !' he shouted.

I jumped. 'The little bears? What do you mean, the little bears?'

He lowered his voice. 'The little wash-bears . . . If you leave the kitchen window open the little wash-bears come in and steal the cakes or the biscuits, depending on what you're eating that day,' he said very seriously. 'If you, for example, leave the rubbish in front of the house, the little wash-bears come in the night and eat it up.'

He was like a broken radio that had suddenly started transmitting again. 'It's very important to shut the bucket properly, otherwise they'll spill everything out.'

What was he talking about? I tried to interrupt him. 'There aren't any bears here. Nor wolves. There are some foxes.'

'The little wash-bears bite because they're scared of humans.'

Who the hell were these little wash-bears? And what did they wash? Clothes? I didn't like this little wash-bear business . . . I persisted. 'Could you please tell me if you had a slice of meat yesterday? It's very important.'

And he replied: 'The little bears told me you're not scared of the lord of the worms.' A little voice in my brain was saying I mustn't listen to him, I must run away. I grasped the rope, but I couldn't bring myself to leave, I kept staring at him spellbound.

He persisted. 'You're not scared of the lord of the worms.'

'The lord of the worms? Who's he?'

'The lord of the worms says: "Hey, little sap! I'm going to send down the stuff now. Take it and give me back the bucket. Otherwise I'll come down and squash you like a worm. Yeah, squash you like a worm, I will." Are you the guardian angel?'

'What?' I stammered: 'I . . . I, no . . . I'm not the angel . . .'

'You *are* the angel. You've got the same voice. The little bears talk, but sometimes they tell lies. The angel always tells the truth. You're the guardian angel.' He raised his voice. 'You can tell me.'

I felt weak. The smell of shit stopped up my mouth, my nose, my brain. 'I'm not an angel . . . I'm Michele, Michele Amitrano. I'm not a . . .' I murmured and leaned against the wall and slid down to the ground and he got up, stretched out his arms towards me like a leper asking for alms and he stayed up for a few moments, then took one step and fell down, on his knees, at my feet.

He touched one of my fingers, whispering. I let out a yell. As if I had been touched by a disgusting jellyfish, a venomous spider. With that bony little hand, with those long, black, twisted nails of his.

He was speaking too quietly. 'What, what did you say?'

'I'm dead!' he replied.

'What? Speak louder. Please . . .'

He gave a hoarse, voiceless scream, as piercing as a fingernail on a blackboard. 'Am I dead? Am I dead? I'm dead.'

I fumbled for the rope and pulled myself up, kicking out and knocking earth down on him. But he kept shrieking: 'Am I dead? I'm dead. Am I dead?'

I PEDALLED ALONG pursued by horseflies. And I swore I would never, never go back onto that hill. Never, even if they blinded me, would I speak to that lunatic again. How on earth could he think he was dead? When you're dead, you're dead. And you live in heaven. Or maybe in hell.

But what if he was right? If he really was dead? If they had brought him back to life? Only Jesus Christ can bring you back to life. And no one else. But when you wake up, do you know you've been dead? Do you remember about heaven? Do you remember who you were before? You go mad, because your brain has rotted and you start talking about little wash-bears.

He wasn't my twin and he wasn't even my brother. And Papa had nothing to do with him. The slice of meat had nothing to do with him. The saucepan wasn't ours. Mama had thrown ours away. And as soon as Papa came back I would tell him the whole story. As he had taught me. And he would do something.

I had almost reached the road when I remembered the corrugated sheet. I had run away and left the hole open again.

If Felice went back up he would know at once that someone had been there poking his nose where he shouldn't poke it. If Felice found out it had been me, he would drag me around by the ear.

I turned back, cursing myself. The clouds had gone and it was scorching hot. I took off my T-shirt and tied it round my head, like an Indian. I picked up a stick. If I met Felice I would defend myself.

I TRIED NOT to get any nearer than necessary to the hole, but I couldn't resist looking. He was kneeling under the blanket with his arm stretched out, in the same position I had left him in. I felt like jumping on that damned sheet and breaking it in a thousand pieces, but instead I pushed it and covered the hole.

WHEN I GOT HOME Mama was washing the dishes. She threw the frying pan in the sink. She was so angry her jaw was quivering. 'Where on earth did you get to? You gave me the fright of my life . . . The other day your father didn't give you a spanking. But this time you're going to get one.'

I didn't even have time to think up an excuse before she started chasing me. I jumped from one side of the kitchen to the other like a goat while my sister, sitting at the table, watched me, shaking her head.

'Where are you going? Come here!'

I dived behind the sofa, crawled under the table, clambered over the armchair, slithered along the floor into my bedroom and hid under the bed.

'Come out of there!'

'No, you'll smack me!'

'I certainly will. If you come out of your own accord you'll get fewer smacks.'

'No, I'm not coming out!'

'Very well, then.'

A vice clamped on my ankle. I grabbed hold of the leg of the bed with both hands, but it was no use. Mama was stronger than Superman. I let go and found myself between her legs. She pulled me up by the trousers and tucked me under her arm as if I were a suitcase. I screamed: 'Let me go! Please! Let me go!'

She sat on the sofa, put me over her knees, pulled down my trousers and pants while I bleated like a lamb, threw back her hair and started to tan my backside. Mama always had heavy hands. Her spanks were slow and well aimed and made a dull thud.

'I was looking for you everywhere.' One. 'Nobody knew where you'd got to.' Two. 'You'll be the death of me.' Three. 'They must have thought I'm a bad mother.' Four. 'And that I don't know how to bring up kids.'

'Stop!' I shouted. 'Stop! Please, please, Mama!'

On the radio a voice sang: '*Croce. Croce e delizia. Delizia al cor.*' I remember it as if it were yesterday. All my life, whenever I've listened to *La Traviata*, I've seen myself lying with my bottom in the air, over my mother's knee, as she sat beating the living daylights out of me.

'WHAT SHALL WE DO?' Salvatore asked me.

We were sitting on a bench throwing stones at an old boiler that had been dumped in the wheat. If you hit it you scored a point. I threw too far. 'I don't know. I can't go cycling, my bum hurts. My mother smacked me because I'm always coming home late.'

Salvatore hit the boiler with a good bang. 'Point! Three-one.'

I picked up a smaller stone and hurled it. This time I nearly hit the target. 'Listen,' I said. 'Do you remember when Signorina Destani told us the story of the miracle of Lazarus?'

'Yes.'

'Do you reckon Lazarus knew he'd been dead when he came back to life?'

Salvatore thought about it. 'No. I reckon he thought he'd been ill.'

'But how could he walk? Dead people's bodies are all hard. Remember how hard that cat we found was.'

'What cat?' He threw and hit the boiler again. His aim was infallible.

'The black cat, by the stream . . . do you remember?'

'Yes, I remember. Skull broke it in half.'

'If somebody's dead and they wake up, they don't walk right and they go crazy because their brain's rotted and they say weird things, don't you think?'

'I suppose so.'

I threw and finally hit the target. 'Point! Four-two.'

I WOKE UP because I needed a pee. My father had come back. I heard his voice in the kitchen. There were visitors. They were quarrelling, interrupting each other, trading insults. Papa was very angry.

My sister was asleep. I knelt on the bed and looked out of the window. The truck was parked beside a big dark car with a silver front. A rich man's car. I was dying for a pee, but to reach the bathroom I would have to go through the kitchen. With all those people I felt embarrassed, but I was practically wetting my pants. I got up and went to the door. I grasped the handle. I counted. 'One, two, three . . . four, five, six.' And I gently opened it.

THEY WERE SITTING at the table. Italo Natale, Skull's father. Pietro Mura, the barber. Angela Mura. Felice. Papa. And an old man I had never seen before. He must be Sergio, Papa's friend. They were smoking. Their faces were red and tired and their eyes were bleary.

The table was covered with empty bottles, ashtrays full of cigarette stubs, breadcrumbs. The fan was spinning, but it wasn't doing any good. The heat was suffocating. The television was on, without the volume. There was a smell of tomatoes, sweat and insecticide burners.

Mama was making the coffee. I looked at the old man, who was taking a cigarette from a packet of Dunhills. I later found out that his name was Sergio Materia. At the time he was seventy-seven, and he came from Rome, where he had achieved notoriety, twenty years earlier, as a result of a robbery at a fur shop and a raid on the central branch of the Banca dell'Agricoltura. A week after the robbery he had bought a *rosticceria-tavola calda* in Piazza Bologna. He wanted to launder the money, but the *carabinieri* had busted him on opening day. He had done a long stretch in prison, had been released for good conduct and had emigrated to South America.

Sergio Materia was thin. With a bald head. Above his ears grew some sparse yellowish hair, which he tied back in a ponytail. He had a long nose and sunken eyes and his cheeks were dappled by at least two days' growth of white beard. He was wearing a light blue suit and a brown silk shirt. A pair of gold-rimmed glasses rested on his shiny scalp. And a golden chain with a sun pendant nestled among the hairs of his chest. On his wrist he wore a solid gold watch.

He was in a rage. 'Right from the start, you people have made one mistake after another. And this guy's a moron.' He pointed at Felice. He looked at him the way you look at a dog turd. He picked up a toothpick and started cleaning his yellow teeth.

Felice was bent over the table drawing patterns on the tablecloth with his fork. He was the spitting image of his brother when he got told off by his mama.

The old man scratched his throat. 'I told them up North we couldn't rely on you. You're incompetent.' He threw the toothpick in his plate. 'I sit here wasting my time . . . If things had gone as they should have done I'd have been in Brazil by now. Instead of that I'm stuck here.'

Papa tried to argue. 'Sergio, don't worry . . . Things aren't yet—'

But the old man shut him up. 'What things? You're worse than the others. And you know why? Because you don't realise it. You're incompetent. All calm, sure of yourself, and you've fucked up one thing after another. You're an imbecile.'

Papa tried to answer, then swallowed and lowered his gaze.

I felt as if I'd been stabbed in the side. Papa was the boss of Acqua Traverse. And that disgusting old man was insulting him in front of everyone. Why didn't Papa throw him out?

They sat in silence, while the old man started picking his teeth again. He was like the emperor. When the emperor's in a black mood everyone has to keep quiet. Including Papa.

'The news! Here's the news!' said Barbara's father. 'It's starting!'

'Turn it up! Teresa, turn it up! And switch off the light,' Papa said to Mama. At my house the light was always switched off when we watched television. It was compulsory. Mama rushed to the volume control and then to the light switch. The room fell into half-light. Everyone turned towards the TV set. Hidden behind the door, I saw them turn into dark silhouettes tinged with blue by the screen.

It was the right moment to go and have my pee. All I had to do was reach my parents' bedroom. From there I could get into the bathroom and do it in the dark. I imagined I was a black panther. I crawled out of the room on all fours. I was a few metres from safety when Skull's father got up from the sofa and came towards me. I squashed down flat on the floor. Italo Natale fetched the cigarettes from the table and went back to sit on the sofa. I breathed a sigh and started moving forward. The door was within reach, I had made it, I had got there. I was starting to relax, when they all shouted at once: 'Here it is! Here it is! Quiet! Quiet, everybody!'

I craned my neck over the sofa and nearly had a heart attack. Behind the newsreader was a picture of the boy. The boy in the hole. He was blond. Well washed, his hair neatly combed, smartly dressed in a checked shirt, he was smiling and clutching an engine from an electric train set.

The newsreader went on: 'The search goes on for little Filippo Carducci, son of the Lombard businessman Giovanni Carducci, who was kidnapped two months ago in Pavia. The *carabinieri* and the investigating magistrates are following a new trail which is thought to lead . . .'

I didn't hear any more. They were shouting. Papa and the old man jumped to their feet.

The boy's name was Filippo. Filippo Carducci.

'We are now broadcasting an appeal, recorded this morning, from Signora Luisa Carducci to the kidnappers.'

'What's this cow want now?' said Papa.

A lady appeared. Elegant. Blonde. She was neither young nor old, but she was beautiful. Her eyes were glistening. She was squeezing her hands as if they might escape from her. She sniffed and said, looking us in the eyes: 'I'm Filippo Carducci's mother. I'm appealing to my son's kidnappers. Please don't hurt him. He's a good boy, polite and very shy. Please treat him well. I'm sure you know what love and understanding are. Even if you haven't got any children I'm sure you can imagine what it means when they're taken away from you. The ransom you've asked for is very high, but my husband and I are prepared to give you everything we own to have Filippo back with us. You've threatened to cut off one of his ears. I beg you, I implore you not to do it . . .' She dried her eyes, got her breath back and went on: 'We're doing all we can. Please. God will reward you if you are merciful. Tell Filippo that his mama and papa haven't forgotten him and that they love him.'

Papa made the scissors sign with his fingers. '*Two* ears we'll cut off. *Two*.'

The old man added: 'Yeah, that'll teach you to talk on TV, you tramp!'

And they all started shouting again.

I SLIPPED BACK into my bedroom, shut the door, climbed up on the windowsill and did it outside. It had been Papa and the others who had taken the boy away from that lady on television.

The pee drummed on the tarpaulin of the truck and the droplets shone in the light of the streetlamp. 'Be careful, Michele, you mustn't go out at night,' Mama always said. 'When it's dark the bogeyman comes out and takes the children away and sells them to the Gypsies.'

Papa was the bogeyman. By day he was good, but at night he was bad. Why didn't they give him back to her? What use was a barmy little boy to them? Filippo's mother was distressed, you could see that. She cared a lot about her son. And Papa wanted to cut off his ears.

FOUR

I found the old man in the bathroom next morning. I opened the door and there he was shaving, bent over the washbasin, with his face up against the mirror and a cigarette hanging from his lips. He wore a threadbare vest and some yellowed long johns. On his feet he had black half-boots with the zips down. He had a pungent smell, hidden by the talc and aftershave.

He turned towards me and looked me up and down with puffy eyes, one cheek covered with foam, the razor in his hand. 'Who are you?'

'Michele . . . Michele Amitrano.'

'I'm Sergio. Pleased to meet you.'

I stretched out my hand. 'How do you do.' That's how they had taught me to reply at school.

The old man rinsed the razor in the water. 'Don't you know you're supposed to knock before going into the bathroom? Didn't your parents teach you that?'

'I'm sorry.'

He started shaving his neck. 'Are you Pino's son?'

'Yes.'

He scrutinised me in the mirror. 'Are you a quiet child?'

'Yes.'

'I like quiet children. Good boy. You don't take after your father, then. And are you obedient?'

'Yes.'

'Then go out and shut the door.'

I RAN TO FIND MAMA. She was in my room taking the sheets off Maria's bed. I tugged at her dress. 'Mama! Mama, who's that old man in the bathroom?'

'Let go of me, Michele, I'm busy. That's Sergio, your father's friend. He told you he'll be staying with us for a few days.'

'And where's he going to sleep?'

'In your sister's bed.'

'What about her?'

'She'll sleep with us.'

'And where do I sleep?'

'In your bed.'

'You mean the old man's going to sleep in the bedroom with me?'

Mama took a deep breath. 'Yes.'

'Can't Maria sleep with him? And I'll sleep with you.'

'Don't be silly.' She started putting on the clean sheets. 'Go outside, I'm busy.'

I threw myself on the ground and clung to her ankles. 'Mama, please, I don't want to sleep with that man. Please, I want to be in the bed with you.'

She breathed hard. 'There's not enough room. You're too big.'

'Mama, please. I'll curl up in the corner. I'll make myself really small.'

'I said no.'

'Please,' I implored her. '*Please*. I'll be good. You'll see.'

'Stop it.' She stood me up and looked me in the eyes. 'Michele, why do you never do as you're told? I can't stand it any more. We've got so many problems and now *you* start. You don't understand. Please . . .'

'I don't want to sleep with that man. I'm not going to.'

She took the pillowcase off the pillow. 'That's how things are. If you don't like it, tell your father.'

'But he'll take me away . . .'

Mama stopped making the bed and turned. She peered at me with her black eyes. 'What do you mean?'

'You want him to take me away . . . You hate me. You're nasty. You and Papa hate me. I know you do.'

'Who tells you such things?' She grabbed me by the arm but I wriggled free and fled.

I RAN OFF to the stream and climbed up the carob. I would never sleep with that old man. He had taken Filippo. And as soon as I went to sleep he would take me too. He would put me in a sack and whisk me off. And then he would cut off my ears. Was it possible to live without ears? Wouldn't you die? Papa and the old man must have already cut Filippo's off. While I was up in my tree, he, in his hole, was earless. I wondered if they had bandaged up his head? I must go. And I must tell him about his mother, that she still loved him and that she had said so on television, so everybody knew it. But I was scared. What if I found Papa and the old man at the house? I looked at the horizon. The sky was flat and grey and weighed down on the fields of wheat. The hill was over there, gigantic, veiled by the heat. If I'm careful they won't see me, I said to myself.

BY THE TIME I reached the edge of the valley I was exhausted. A bit of shade and a drink of water were what I needed. I went into the wood. But something was different from usual. I stopped. Under the birds, crickets and cicadas you could hear the sound of music. I dived behind a tree trunk. I couldn't see anything from there, but the music seemed to be coming from the house.

I should have got out of there fast, but curiosity drove me to take a look. Hiding among the oaks I moved in closer to the clearing. The music was louder. It was a well-known song. I had heard it dozens of times. It was sung by a blonde lady with a smartly dressed gentleman. I had seen them on television.

There was a boulder covered with green tufts of moss right at the edge of the clearing, a good shelter, I crawled up behind it. I craned my neck and peered over. Parked in front of the house was Felice's 127, with the doors and the boot open. The music came from the car radio. It wasn't very clear, it crackled.

Felice came out of the cowshed. He was in his underpants. He had army boots on his feet and the usual black bandanna round his neck. He was dancing with arms outspread, grinding like a belly dancer.

'You never change, you never change, you never change . . .' He sang in falsetto, with the radio. Then he stopped and went on in a deep voice. 'You are my yesterday, my today. My always.' And in the woman's voice: 'Now, at last, you can try. Call me tormentress, sigh. While you're about it.'

He was very good. He did it all on his own. Male and female. And when he was the man he acted tough. Narrowed eyes and barely parted lips. 'Words, words, words . . . I swear to you.' Then he threw himself on the ground, in the dust, and started doing press-ups. Two-handed, one-handed, with clap, and he went on singing, jerkily.

I left.

IN ACQUA TRAVERSE they were playing one-two-three-star. Skull, Barbara and Remo were standing still, under the sun, in strange positions.

Salvatore, with his head against the wall, shouted: 'One, two, three, staaaaar!' He turned and saw Skull. Skull always overdid it, instead of going three steps he went fifteen and got caught.

I passed between the houses, pedalling slowly. I was tired and angry. I hadn't managed to tell Filippo about his mother.

Papa's truck was parked outside the house, next to the old man's big grey car. I was hungry. I had run off without having breakfast. But I wasn't too keen on going indoors.

Skull came over to me. 'Where did you get to?'

'I went for a ride.'

'You're always going off on your own. Where do you go?'

He didn't like it when you minded your own business.

'To the stream.'

He eyed me suspiciously. 'What do you do there?'

I shrugged. 'Nothing much. Climb the tree.'

He made the disgusted face of someone who's just eaten a rotten apple. 'Fancy a game of soccer?'

I didn't, but saying no to him was dangerous. 'Isn't it a bit hot?'

He grabbed my handlebars. 'You're being a shit, you know that?'

I was scared. 'Why?' Skull could suddenly flip and decide to pull you off your bike and beat you up.

'Because you are.'

Luckily Salvatore appeared. He was bouncing the ball on his head. Then he trapped it with his foot and tucked it under his arm. 'Hi, Michele.'

'Hi.'

Skull asked him, 'Fancy a game?'

'No.'

Skull lost his temper. 'You're pieces of shit, both of you! Right, you know what I'm doing? I'm going to Lucignano.' And he stomped off in a filthy mood.

We had a good laugh, then Salvatore said to me: 'I'm going home. Do you want to come with me and play Subbuteo?'

'I don't really feel like it.'

He gave me a pat on the back. 'All right. See you later then. Bye.' He went off juggling with the ball. I liked Salvatore. I liked the way he always kept calm and didn't fly off the handle every five minutes. With Skull you had to think three times before you said anything.

I cycled over to the drinking fountain.

Maria had taken the enamelled bowl and was using it as a swimming pool for her Barbies. She had two—one normal, the other all blackened with one arm melted and no hair. That was my fault. One evening I had seen the story of Joan of Arc on television and I had picked up the Barbie doll and thrown her in the fire shouting: 'Burn! Witch! Burn!' When I had realised she really was burning, I had grabbed her by one foot and thrown her in the saucepan where the minestrone was cooking.

Mama had taken away my bike for a week and made me eat all the minestrone by myself.

'Hi, Maria,' I said, getting off my bike.

She put one hand over her forehead to shield her eyes from the sun. 'Papa's been looking for you . . . Mama's cross.'

'I know.'

'You're always making her cross.'

Papa came out onto the balcony, saw me and called to me.

'Michele, come here.' He was wearing a shirt and shorts.

I didn't want to talk to him. 'I can't, I'm busy!'

He beckoned me up. 'Come here.'

I leaned my bike against the wall and went up the steps hanging my head resignedly. Papa sat down on the top step. 'Come and sit here, next to me.' He pulled a packet of Nazionali out of his shirt pocket, took a cigarette and lit it. 'You and I have got to talk.'

He didn't seem all that angry. We sat there in silence. Looking over the roofs at the yellow fields.

'Hot, isn't it?'

'Very.'

He blew out a cloud of smoke. 'Where do you get to all day long, for goodness' sake?'

'Nowhere.'

'Yes, you do. You must go somewhere.'

'Riding around here.'

'On your own?'

'Yes.'

'What's the matter? Don't you like being with your friends?'

'Yes, I do. It's just that I like being on my own too.'

He nodded, his eyes lost in the void. I glanced at him. He seemed older, his black hair was speckled with a few white strands, his cheeks had sunk and he looked as if he hadn't slept for a week.

'You've upset your mother.'

I broke off a twig of rosemary from a pot and started fiddling with it. 'I didn't mean to.'

'She said you don't want to sleep with Sergio.'

'Well, I don't. I want to sleep with you and Mama. In your bed. All together. If we squeeze up, we'll all fit in.'

'What's Sergio going to think if you don't sleep with him?'

'I don't care what he thinks.'

'That's no way to treat guests. Suppose you went to stay with some-one and nobody wanted to sleep with you. What would you think?'

'I wouldn't care. I'd like a room all to myself. Like in a hotel.'

He smiled faintly and threw the dog-end into the street.

I asked him: 'Is Sergio your boss? Is that why he's staying with us?'

He looked at me in surprise. 'What do you mean is he my boss?'

'I mean does he decide things?'

'No, he doesn't decide anything. He's a friend of mine.'

It wasn't true. The old man wasn't his friend, he was his boss. I knew that. He could even call him names.

'Papa, where do you sleep when you go to the North?'

'Why?'

'I just wondered.'

'In a hotel, or wherever I can. In the truck sometimes.'

'But what happens at night in the North?'

He looked at me, breathed in through his nose and asked me: 'What's up? Aren't you pleased I've come home?'

'Yes, I am pleased.'

He squeezed me in his arms, tightly. I could smell his sweat. He whispered in my ear: 'Hug me, Michele, hug me! Let me feel how strong you are.' I hugged him as hard as I could and I couldn't help crying. The tears ran down my face and my throat tightened.

'Hey, are you crying?'

I sobbed. 'No, I'm not crying.'

He took a crumpled handkerchief out of his pocket. 'Dry away those tears. If anybody sees you they'll think you're a sissy. Michele, I'm very busy at the moment so you must do as you're told. Your mother's tired. Stop all this nonsense.'

I gave him back his handkerchief. 'I want to go away from Acqua Traverse. Let's go to the North.'

'What do you want to go away for?'

'I don't know . . . I don't like being here any more.'

He looked into the distance. 'We'll go there.'

I broke off another twig of rosemary. It had a nice smell. 'Do you know about the little wash-bears?'

He frowned. 'The little wash-bears? No, what are they?'

'They're bears that do the washing . . . But maybe they don't exist.'

Papa got up and stretched his back. 'Listen, I'm going indoors, I've got to talk to Sergio. Why don't you run off and play? It'll be suppertime soon.' He opened the door and was about to go in, but he stopped. 'Mama's made tagliatelle. Afterwards, say sorry to her.'

At that moment Felice arrived. He braked his 127 in a cloud of dust and got out as if there was a swarm of wasps inside.

'Felice!' Papa shouted. 'Come up a minute.'

Felice nodded and as he passed me he cuffed me on the back of the head and said, 'How're you doing, little sap?'

Now there was nobody with Filippo.

THE BUCKET OF SHIT was full. The saucepan of water empty. Filippo kept his head wrapped up in the blanket. He hadn't even noticed I had come down into the hole. His ankle looked worse to me, it was more swollen and purple. The flies were homing in on it. I moved closer. 'Hey!' He gave no sign of having heard me. 'Hey! Can you hear me?' I moved even closer. 'Can you hear me?'

He sighed. 'Yes.'

Papa hadn't cut off his ears, then.

'Your name's Filippo, isn't it?'

'Yes.'

I had been rehearsing on the way. 'I've come to tell you something very important. Um . . . Your mother says she loves you. And she says she misses you. She said so yesterday on television. On the news. She said you mustn't worry . . .'

Nothing.

'Did you hear me?'

Nothing.

I repeated. 'Um . . . your mother says she loves you. She says she misses you . . .'

'My mother's dead.'

'What do you mean she's dead?'

From under the blanket he replied: 'My mother's dead.'

'What are you talking about? She's alive. I saw her myself, on TV.'

'No, she isn't, she's dead.'

I put my hand on my heart. 'I swear to you on the head of my sister Maria that she's alive. I saw her last night, she was on television. She was well. She's blonde. She's thin. She's a bit old . . . She's beautiful, though. She was sitting on a high brown armchair. And behind it there was a picture of a ship. Isn't that right?'

'Yes. The picture of the ship . . .' He spoke quietly, the words were muffled by the cloth.

'And you've got an electric train. I saw it.'

'I haven't got that any more. It got broken. Nanny threw it away.'

'Nanny? Who's nanny?'

'Liliana. She's dead too. And Peppino's dead. And Papa's dead. And grandmother Arianna's dead. And my brother's dead. They're all dead. They're all dead and they live in holes like this one. And I'm in one too. Everybody. The world's a place full of holes with dead people in them. And the moon's a ball all full of holes too and inside them there are other dead people.'

'No, it isn't.' I put my hand on his back. 'There aren't any holes on it. The moon's normal. And your mother's not dead. I saw her. You must listen to me.'

He was silent for a while, then he asked me: 'Why doesn't she come here, then?'

I shook my head. 'I don't know.'

'And why am I here?'

'I don't know.' Then I said, so quietly that he couldn't hear me, 'My father put you here.'

He gave me a kick. 'You don't know anything. Leave me alone. You're not the guardian angel. You're bad. Go away.' And he started crying.

I didn't know what to do. 'I'm not bad. It's nothing to do with me. Don't cry, please.'

He kept kicking. 'Go away!'

I sprang to my feet. 'I came out here for your sake, I rode all that way, twice, and you kick me out. All right, I'll go, but if I go I'm not coming back. You'll stay here, on your own, for ever and they'll cut both your ears off.' I seized the rope and started to climb back up. I heard him crying. He sounded as if he was suffocating.

I got out of the hole and said to him: 'And I'm not your guardian angel!'

'Wait . . . Please. Stay with me.'

'No! You told me to go away and I'm going.'

'Please. Just for five minutes.'

'All right. Five minutes. But if you act crazy I'm going.'

I went down. He touched my foot.

'Why don't you come out of that blanket?' I asked him and crouched down beside him.

'I can't, I'm blind . . .'

'What do you mean you're blind?'

'My eyes won't open. I want to open them but they stay closed. In the dark I can see. In the dark I'm not blind. Come here.' He lifted the blanket.

I made a face. 'Under there?' The idea rather gave me the creeps. But at least I would be able to see if he still had both his ears in place.

He started touching me. 'How old are you?' He ran his hands over my nose, my mouth, my eyes.

I was paralysed. 'Nine. What about you?'

'Nine.'

'When's your birthday?'

'The 12th of September. And yours?'

'The 20th of November.'

'What's your name?'

'Michele. Michele Amitrano. What year are you in at school?'

'The fourth. What about you?'

'The fourth.'

'I'm thirsty.'

I gave him the bottle.

He drank. 'That's good. Do you want some?'

I drank too. 'Can I lift the blanket a bit?' The heat and smell were stifling me.

'Only a bit though.'

I pulled it away just far enough to get some air and look at his face. It was filthy. His fine blond hair had mingled with the earth to form a hard dry mat. Clotted blood had sealed up his eyelids. His lips were black and split. His nostrils were blocked up with snot and scabs.

'Can I wash your face?' I asked him.

He craned his neck and raised his head and a smile opened on his battered lips. All his teeth had gone black. I took off my T-shirt, moistened it with the water and started to clean his face. Where I washed, the skin became white, so white it seemed transparent, like the flesh of a boiled fish.

When I bathed his eyes he said: 'Careful, it hurts.'

'I'll be careful.'

I couldn't loosen the scabs. They were hard and thick. I kept bathing them, softening them, till one eyelid rose and immediately shut again. Just an instant, enough for a ray of light to strike his eye.

'Aaaahhhaaa!' he shouted and stuck his head under the blanket.

I shook him. 'See? See? You're not blind! You're not blind at all!'

'I can't keep them open.'

'That's because you're always in the dark. But you can see, can't you?'

'Yes! You're small.'

'I'm not small. I'm nine years old.'

'You've got black hair.'

'That's right. Now I've got to go. I'll be back tomorrow.'

With his head under the blanket he said: 'Promise?'

'Promise.'

WHEN THE OLD MAN came into my room I was in bed. I shut my eyes and pretended to be asleep. The old man made a lot of noises. He rummaged in his suitcase. He coughed. He puffed. I covered my head with one arm and watched what he was doing.

A ray of light lit up one segment of the room. The old man was sitting on Maria's bed. Thin, hunched and dark. He was smoking. And when he inhaled I saw the beaky nose and sunken eyes become tinged with red. I could smell the smoke and the cologne. Now and then he shook his head. Then he snorted as if he was arguing with someone. He started to get undressed. He had flaccid skin that hung from those long bones as if it had been sewn on to them. He threw his cigarette out of the window. The stub disappeared into the night like a burning fragment of volcanic rock. He untied his hair and he looked like an old, sick Tarzan. He lay down on his bed. Now I couldn't see him any more, but he was near. If he stretched out his arm he could grab my ankle. I curled up like a hedgehog.

I mustn't sleep. If I fell asleep he might take me away.

He hawked. 'It's stifling in here. How can you stand it?'

I stopped breathing.

'I know you're not asleep.'

He wanted to get me.

'Crafty little devil, you are . . . Don't like me, do you? My kids didn't like me either.' He picked up from the floor a bottle Mama had put there for him and took a couple of swigs. 'Warm as piss,' he grumbled. 'Good night.'

He lay down on the bed and in two minutes he was asleep and in three he was snoring.

WHEN I WOKE UP the old man had gone. He had left the bed unmade, a packet of Dunhills crumpled up on the windowsill, his underpants on the floor and the bottle of water half empty.

It was warm. The cicadas were singing.

I got up and looked into the kitchen. Mama was ironing and listening to the radio. My sister was playing on the floor. I shut the door.

The old man's suitcase was under the bed. I opened it and looked inside.

Clothes. A bottle of perfume. A flask of Stock 84. A carton of cigarette packets. I also found a lined school exercise book with a coloured plastic cover. I opened it. Written on the first page was: *This exercise book belongs to Filippo Carducci. Fourth C.*

The first few pages had been torn out. I leafed through it. There were some dictations, some summaries and an essay.

Describe what you did on Sunday.

On Sunday my papa came home. My papa lives in America a lot because of his job and he comes back every now and again. He's got a villa with a swimming pool and a diving board and there are little wash-bears there. They live in the garden. I must go there.

After going to the airport me, my papa and my mama went to eat at the restaurant. They talked about where I will have to do middle school. Whether I'll have to live in Pavia or in America. I didn't say anything but I prefer Pavia where all my friends go. In America I can play with the little wash-bears. After lunch we went home. I had another meal and went to bed. That's what I did on Sunday. I had already done my homework on Saturday.

I closed Filippo's exercise book and put it in the folder. At the bottom of the suitcase there was a rolled-up towel. I opened it and inside there was a pistol. I stared at it. It was big, it had a wooden butt and it was black. I lifted it. It was very heavy. Maybe it was loaded. I put it back.

'OVER THE FIELD I chased a dragonfly, forgetting all the cares of days gone by,' they were singing on the radio. Mama was ironing and singing along. For a week she had been worse than a mad dog and now she was singing away happily.

I came out of my bedroom buttoning up my shorts. She smiled at me. 'Here he is! The boy who wouldn't sleep with guests . . . Come and give me a kiss. A real smacker. The biggest kiss you can.'

I took a run-up and jumped into her arms and she caught me in midair and planted a kiss on my cheek. Then she hugged me and whirled me round. I gave her lots of kisses too.

'Me too! Me too!' shrieked Maria. She threw her dolls in the air and clung onto us.

Mama picked up Maria too.

'Both together!' And she started dancing round the room singing at the top of her voice. 'The store has many boxes in a stack, some red, some yellow, and some others black . . .'

From one side to the other. From one side to the other. Till we collapsed on the sofa. We lay close together, slumped on the cushions. Then Mama asked me: 'Didn't Sergio eat you last night then?'

'No.'

'Did he let you sleep?'

'Yes.'

'Did he snore?'

'Yes.'

'How did he snore? Show me.'

I tried to imitate him.

'But that's a pig! That's the noise pigs make. Maria, show us how Papa snores.'

And Maria imitated Papa.

'You're no good, either of you. I'll do Papa for you.'

She did a perfect imitation. Whistle and all. We laughed a lot. She got up and straightened her dress. 'I'll warm the milk for you.'

I asked her: 'Where's Papa?'

'He's gone out with Sergio . . . He said he's going to take us to the seaside next week. And we'll go to a restaurant and eat mussels.'

Maria and I started jumping up and down on the sofa. 'The seaside! The seaside! To eat mussels!'

Mama looked towards the fields then closed the shutters. 'Let's hope so, anyway.'

I had breakfast. There was sponge cake. I had two slices dunked in milk. Without letting anyone see, I cut another slice, wrapped it in my napkin and put it in my pocket. Filippo would be pleased.

Mama cleared away. 'As soon as you've finished, take this cake to Salvatore's house. Put on a clean T-shirt.'

Mama was a good cook. And when she made cakes or *maccheroni al forno* or bread, she always made some extra and sold it to Salvatore's mother.

I cleaned my teeth, put on my Olympic Games T-shirt and went out carrying the baking tin.

FIVE

There was no wind and nobody around. Only the hens scratching about in the dust and the swallows darting under the eaves. The sun was beating down on the houses from directly overhead.

Some noises were coming from the big shed. I went towards it. Felice's 127 had its bonnet up and was tilted on one side. A pair of large black army boots stuck out from underneath. When Felice was at Acqua Traverse he was always tinkering with the car.

'Michele! Michele, come here!' Felice shouted from under the car. 'Help me.'

'I can't. I've got to do an errand for my mother.' I wanted to give the cake to Salvatore's mother, jump on the Crock and dash off to see Filippo.

He growled. 'If you don't come here, I'll kill you . . .'

'What do you want?'

'I'm stuck. I can't move. A wheel came off while I was underneath. I've been under here nearly half an hour!'

I looked inside the bonnet; from above the engine I could see the grease-blackened face and the red, desperate eyes.

I could go off and leave him there. I looked around.

'Don't even think it . . . I'll get out of here and I'll snap you like a stick of liquorice. All that'll be left of you will be a grave for your parents to take flowers to,' said Felice.

'What do you want me to do?'

'Get the jack from behind the car and put it by the wheel.'

I put it there and turned the handle. Slowly the car lifted. Felice moaned with joy. 'That's the way. That's right, so I can get out. Well done!'

He slid out. His shirt was smeared with black oil. He ran his hand through his hair. 'I thought I'd had it. I've done my back in. All because of that fucking Roman!'

'The old man?'

'Yeah, I hate his guts. I told him I can't get up there by car. That road ruins my shock absorbers, but he doesn't give a shit. Why doesn't *he* go up there in his Mercedes? I can't take any more of this. And it's don't do this and don't do that. But I'm getting out . . .' He punched the tractor and vented his anger by smashing up the wooden crates. 'If he calls me an idiot one more time I'm going to hit him so hard he'll stick to the wall.' He stopped short when he remembered I was there too. He grabbed me by the T-shirt and lifted me up and shoved his nose in my face. 'You tell no one what I've told you, got it? If I find out you've breathed one word of this . . .' He took a knife from his pocket. The blade flicked out to within two centimetres of my nose. 'Got it?'

I stammered: 'Got it.'

He threw me down on the ground. 'No one! Now get lost.'

I picked up the cake and got the hell out of there.

THE SCARDACCIONE FAMILY was the richest in Acqua Traverse. Salvatore's father, the Avvocato Emilio Scardaccione, owned a lot of land. Large numbers of people worked for him, especially at harvest time. Papa, too, for many years, before he became a truck driver, had gone to do seasonal work for the Avvocato Scardaccione. To enter Salvatore's house you went through a wrought-iron gate, crossed a courtyard with a stone fountain with goldfish in it, went up a marble stairway with high steps and you were there. As soon as you entered you found yourself in a dark, windowless corridor, so long you could have cycled down it. On one side was a row of bedrooms that were always locked, on the other was the hall, a big room with angels painted on the ceiling and a large shiny table with chairs round it.

In the daytime the shutters were never opened. Not even during the winter. There was a musty atmosphere, a smell of old wood. It was like being in a church. Signora Scardaccione, Salvatore's mother, was very fat and barely five foot high and wore a net over her hair. Her legs were swollen like sausages and always hurt and she only went out at Christmas and Easter to go to the hairdresser's in Lucignano. She spent her life in the kitchen, the only well-lit room in the house, with her sister, Aunt Lucilla, amid the steam and the smell of *ragù*.

They were like a pair of seals. They bowed their heads together, laughed together, clapped their hands together. Two large trained seals with perms. They sat all day long in two armchairs, which they had worn out, checking that Antonia, the maid, wasn't making any mistakes or taking too long rests. Everything had to be neat and tidy for when the Avvocato Scardaccione came back from town. But he hardly ever did come back. And when he did he couldn't wait to get away again.

'LUCILLA! LUCILLA, look who's here!' said Letizia Scardaccione when she saw me enter the kitchen. Aunt Lucilla raised her head from the sewing machine and smiled. On her nose she had some thick specs that made her eyes as small as a fisherman's sinkers. 'Michele! Michele, darling! What have you brought, the cake?'

'Yes, Signora. Here it is.' I delivered it to her.

Then Letizia Scardaccione picked up a bag. 'I've got some clothes here that are too small for Salvatore. Take them. Do take them, I'd be very pleased if you did. Just look at the state you're in.'

I would have liked to. They were practically new. But Mama said we didn't accept charity from anyone. Especially not from those two. She said my clothes were perfectly all right. And she would decide when it was time to change them. 'Thank you, Signora. But I can't.'

Aunt Lucilla opened a tin box and clapped her hands. 'Look what I've got here. Honey drops! Do you like honey drops?'

'Yes, I do, very much, Signora.'

'Help yourself.'

These I could take. Mama never found out because I always ate the lot. I took a good supply. I filled my pockets with them.

I repeated like a parrot: 'Thank you, thank you, thank you . . .'

'Before you go, say hello to Salvatore. He's in his room. Don't stay too long though, he's got to practise. He has his lesson today.'

I WENT OUT of the kitchen and crossed that gloomy corridor, with its black, sombre furniture. I must go and see Filippo; I had promised. I must take him the cake and the sweets. But it was hot. He could wait. Besides, I felt like spending a bit of time with Salvatore.

I heard the piano through his bedroom door. I knocked.

'Who is it?'

'Michele.'

'Michele?' He opened the door, looked around like a hunted criminal, pushed me inside and locked the door. Salvatore's room was big and bare, with a high ceiling. Against one wall there was an upright piano. Along another a bed so high you needed a little stepladder to get onto it. And a long bookcase with lots of books in it arranged according to the colour of their covers. The games were kept in a chest of drawers. A heavy white curtain let through a ray of sunlight in which the dust danced.

In the middle of the room, on the floor, was the green Subbuteo cloth. Laid out on it were Juventus and Torino.

'I brought a cake. Can I stay? Your mother said you've got your lesson . . .'

'Yes, you stay,' he lowered his voice, 'but if they notice I'm not playing they won't leave me in peace.' He picked up a record and put it on the record player. 'This'll make them think I'm playing.' And he added with a very serious air: 'It's Chopin.'

'Who's Chopin?'

'He's one of the best.'

Salvatore and I were the same age, but to me he seemed older. Partly because he was taller than I was, partly because he had white shirts that were always clean and long trousers with a crease in them. Partly because of his placid way of speaking.

'How about a game?' I asked him. Subbuteo was my favourite game. I wasn't very good at it, but I really enjoyed it. In the winter Salvatore and I had endless tournaments, we spent whole afternoons flicking those little plastic footballers around. Salvatore played on his own too. He would move from one end to the other.

'Look,' he said, and took out of a drawer eight small green cardboard boxes. Each box contained a football team. 'Look what Papa gave me. He brought me them from Rome.'

'All these?' I picked them up. The Avvocato must be really rich to spend all that money. Every single year, on my birthday and at Christmas, I asked Papa and Baby Jesus to give me Subbuteo, but it was no use, neither of them heard. Just one team would have been enough. Without the pitch and the goals. Even a Series B team.

Why didn't I get anything? Because my father didn't care about me. He said he loved me but he didn't. He had given me a stupid Venetian boat to put on the television set. And I couldn't even touch it.

I wanted a team. If his father had given him four I wouldn't have said anything, but he'd given him eight. He had twelve now, altogether. What difference would one less make to him?

I cleared my throat and whispered: 'Will you give me one of them?'

Salvatore frowned and started pacing round the room. Then he said: 'I'm sorry, I would give you one, but I can't. If Papa found out I'd given it to you he'd be angry.'

That wasn't true. When had his father ever checked up on the teams? Salvatore was stingy. If I'd had something to swap, perhaps he would have given me one. But I didn't have anything. Wait a minute, I did have something to swap.

'If I tell you an incredible secret, will you give me one?'

'No secret's worth a team.'

'Mine is.' I kissed my forefingers. 'I swear.'

'What if it's just a trick?'

'It's not. But if you say it's a trick I'll give the team back to you.'

'I'm not interested in secrets.'

But now I would stoop to anything. 'I'll even take Lanerossi Vicenza.'

Salvatore goggled. 'Lanerossi Vicenza?'

'Yes.'

We loathed Lanerossi Vicenza. They had a jinx on them. If you played with them you always lost. Neither of us had ever won with that team. And it had one player that had lost its head, another that had been stuck on with glue and a goalkeeper that was all bent.

Salvatore thought it over for a while and finally conceded: 'All right. But if it's a crappy secret I'm not giving it to you.'

And so I told him everything. About when I had fallen out of the tree. About the hole. About Filippo. About his bad leg. About the stink. About Felice keeping guard over him. About Papa and the old man wanting to cut off his ears. About his mother being on television. Everything. It was a wonderful feeling. Like the time I had eaten a jarful of peaches in syrup. Afterwards I had been ill, I felt as if I was bursting. I had an earthquake in my stomach and Mama had first boxed my ears then put my head down the toilet and stuck two fingers in my throat. And I had brought up an enormous amount of yellow acid gunk. And had started living again.

While I talked Salvatore listened silently, impassively. And I concluded: 'And then he's always talking about little wash-bears. Little bears that wash clothes. I told him they don't exist, but he won't listen to me.'

'Little wash-bears do exist.'

I gaped.

'They live in America.' He got out the *Great Encyclopaedia of Animals* and leafed through it. 'There it is. Look.' There was a colour photograph of a sort of fox. With a white muzzle and a little black mask over its eyes like Zorro. But it was furrier than a fox and had smaller legs and could pick things up with them. It had an apple in its hands. It was a very pretty little animal.

'So they do exist . . .'

'Yes.' Salvatore read: 'A bearlike carnivorous genus of the Procyonidae family. It lives in Canada and the United States. It is commonly known as the little wash-bear because of its curious habit of washing food before eating it.'

'It's not clothes they wash, it's food . . . Oh.' I was shaken.

I grabbed his arm. 'Do you want to come and see him? We can go there straight away. It won't take long.'

He didn't answer me. He put the footballers back in their boxes and rolled up the Subbuteo pitch.

'Well? Would you like to?'

He turned the key and then opened the door. 'I can't. My teacher is coming.'

'What do you mean? Don't you want to see him? Didn't you like my secret?'

'Not much. I'm not interested in loonies in holes.'

'Will you give me Vicenza?'

'Take them. They're rubbish anyway.' He thrust the box into my hand and pushed me out of the room. And shut the door.

I PEDALLED TOWARDS THE HILL and I didn't understand.

How could he not care less about a boy chained up in a hole? Salvatore had said my secret was rubbish. I shouldn't have told him. I had wasted my secret. And what had I got out of it? Lanerossi Vicenza, the jinx team. I was worse than Judas who had bartered Jesus for thirty pieces of silver. With thirty pieces of silver just think how many teams you could buy. I wished I could turn the clock back. I would have gone away without even calling on Salvatore.

I WENT UP THE SLOPE so fast that when I got there I felt sick. I had ditched my bike just before the slope and covered the last part on foot, running through the wheat. I felt as if my heart was tearing out of my chest. I wanted to go straight to Filippo, but I had to flop down under a tree and wait till I got my breath back. When I felt better, I looked to see if Felice was around. There was nobody. I climbed into the house and got the rope.

I moved the corrugated sheet and called out to him. 'Filippo!'

'Michele!' He started moving about. He was waiting for me.

'I've come. You see? You see? I've come.'

'I knew you would. You promised.'

'You're right, the little wash-bears do exist. I read about it in a book. I've even seen a photograph. Have you ever seen one?'

'Yes. Can you hear them? Can you hear them whistling?'

I couldn't hear any whistling. There were no two ways about it, he was crazy.

I grabbed the rope and lowered myself down.

They had cleaned up. The bucket was empty. The little saucepan was full of water. Filippo was wrapped in his disgusting blanket, but they had washed it. They had bound up his ankle with a bandage. And he no longer had the chain round his foot.

'They've cleaned you!'

He smiled. They hadn't cleaned his teeth.

I took the cake out of my pocket. 'Look what I've brought you.

It's crumbled—' I didn't even have time to finish the sentence before he snatched the cake and stuffed it in his mouth, then, with his eyes closed, he searched for the crumbs.

He fumbled all over me. 'More! More! Give me more!' He scratched me with his nails.

'I haven't got any more. I swear. Hang on . . .' In my back pocket I had the sweets. 'Here. Take these.'

He unwrapped them, chewed them and swallowed them at an incredible rate. 'More! More!'

He wouldn't believe I didn't have anything else. He kept searching for the crumbs.

I sat down. Filippo wouldn't stop touching my feet and undoing my sandals. Suddenly I had an idea. A great idea. He didn't have the chain. He was free.

I asked him: 'Do you want to go out?'

'Outside?'

'Yes, outside. Outside the hole.'

He fell silent for a moment, then he asked: 'Hole? What hole?'

'This hole. In here. Where we are.'

He shook his head. 'There aren't any holes.'

'This isn't a hole?'

'No.'

'Yes, it is a hole, you said so yourself. You said that the world's all full of holes with dead people in them.'

'You're wrong. I didn't say that.'

I was beginning to lose patience. 'Well, where are we, then?'

'In a place where you wait.'

'And what do you wait for?'

'To go to heaven.'

In a way he was right. If you got into a discussion with Filippo your thoughts got tangled.

'Come on, I'll take you out.' I took his hand, but he stiffened and trembled. 'All right. All right. We won't go out. Keep calm, though. I won't hurt you.'

He stuck his head under the blanket. 'Outside there's no air. Outside I'll suffocate. I don't want to go out there.'

'No, you won't. There's loads of air outside. I'm always outside and I don't suffocate. How do you think that's possible?'

'You're an angel.'

I must get him to see reason. 'Listen carefully. Yesterday I swore to you I'd come back and I have come back. Now I swear to you that if you come out nothing will happen to you. You've got to believe me.'

'Why do I have to go outside? I'm all right in here.'

I had to tell him a lie. 'Because heaven's outside. I'm an angel and you're dead and I've got to take you to heaven.'

He thought about this for a while. 'Really?'

'Truly.'

'Let's go, then.' And he started making high-pitched squeaks. I tried to get him to his feet, but he couldn't support himself. If I didn't hold him up he fell down. Finally I tied the rope round his hips. Then I wrapped his head in the blanket, so that he would keep quiet. I went back up and started hoisting him. But he was like a lead weight and the rope was slipping out of my hands. I stepped back and the rope slackened. I looked down. He had keeled over on his back with the blanket on his head.

'Filippo, are you all right?'

'Am I there?' he asked.

'Hang on.' I ran round the house looking for a plank, a pole, something that could help me.

'Michele?' Filippo was calling me.

'Wait a minute! Just a minute!' I shouted, and there it was, two metres away from the hole. A green-painted wooden ladder lying on the ivy that covered a pile of masonry and earth. It had been there all the time and I hadn't seen it. That was how they got down.

'I've found a ladder!' I said to Filippo. I fetched it and climbed down into the hole.

I had just reached the bottom when the ladder was pulled away. I looked up. On the edge of the hole was a man with a brown hood over his head. He was dressed exactly like a soldier. 'Cuckoo? Cuckoo? April now is through,' he sang and started pirouetting. 'Maytime has returned to the song of the cuckoo. Guess who?'

'Felice!'

'Well done!' he said, and fell silent for a bit. 'How did you guess? Hang on. Hang on a minute.'

He went off and when he reappeared he had his rifle over his shoulder.

'IT WAS YOU!' Felice clapped his hands. 'It was you! I kept finding things arranged differently. At first I thought I was crazy. Then I thought it must be a ghost. And all the time it was you. Little

Michele. Thank God for that, I was going out of my mind.'

I felt my ankle being squeezed. Filippo had caught hold of my feet and was whispering: 'The lord of the worms comes and goes. The lord of the worms comes and goes.'

So that was who the lord of the worms was! Felice looked at me through the holes in his hood. 'Made friends with the prince, have you? See how well I washed him? He put up a bit of a struggle, but I won in the end.'

I was trapped. I couldn't see him. The sun filtering through the foliage blinded me.

'Come on up, move!' Felice got the ladder and lowered it down.

I didn't want to, but I had no choice. He would shoot me. I wasn't sure I would be able to climb up, my legs were shaking.

Filippo whispered: 'Won't you be coming back again?'

Without letting Felice see, I replied in a low voice: 'I'll be back.'

'Promise?'

'Promise.'

'Come on! Up you get, you little runt. What're you waiting for?'

I started climbing. Filippo meanwhile kept whispering. 'The lord of the worms comes and goes. The lord of the worms comes and goes.' When I was almost out, Felice grabbed me by the trousers and with both hands threw me against the house like a sack. I crashed into the wall and crumpled on the ground. A spasm of pain stiffened my leg and arm. I turned. Felice had taken off his hood and was charging towards me pointing the rifle. I saw his tanklike boots growing bigger and bigger.

Now he's going to shoot me, I thought.

I started crawling, all aches and pains, towards the wood.

'Thought you'd set him free, did you?' He gave me a kick in the backside. 'Get up, you little shit. What are you doing down there on the ground? Get up! Haven't hurt yourself, have you?' He lifted me up by the ear. 'You can thank your lucky stars you're your father's son. Otherwise by this time . . . Now I'm going to take you home. Your father'll decide your punishment. I've done my duty. I've kept guard. And I ought to have shot you.' He dragged me into the wood. I was so scared I couldn't cry. I kept tripping over and falling on the ground and he kept pulling me up again by the ear. 'Move, go, go, go!'

We emerged from the trees. In front of us the yellow incandescent expanse of wheat stretched as far as the sky. With the barrel of his rifle Felice pushed me towards the 127.

He opened the door, lifted the seat and said: 'Get in!'

I got in and there was Salvatore. 'Salvatore, what are you . . .' The rest died in my mouth. It had been Salvatore. He had ratted to Felice.

Salvatore looked at me and turned away. I sat down in the back without saying a word.

Felice got behind the wheel. 'Salvatore, old boy, you've done a really good job. Allow me to shake your hand.' Felice grasped it. 'You were right, the nosy parker was there. And I didn't believe you.' He got out. 'A promise is a promise. And when Felice Natale makes a promise, he keeps it. You drive. Take it slowly, though.'

'Now?' Salvatore asked.

'When else? Get into my seat.'

Felice got in at the passenger's door and Salvatore moved over to the wheel. 'It's perfect for learning here. All you have to do is follow the slope and brake now and again.'

Salvatore Scardaccione had sold me for a driving lesson.

'YOU'LL SMASH THE CAR up if you don't watch out!' Felice shouted and with his head up against the windscreen he watched the broken surface of the road. 'Brake! Brake!'

Salvatore could hardly see over the steering wheel and gripped it as if he wanted to break it. He had never told me he wanted to drive a car. He could have asked his father to teach him. The Avvocato never refused him anything. Why had he asked Felice? My whole body was hurting, my skinned knees, my ribs, my arm and my wrist. But especially my heart. Salvatore had broken it. He was my best friend. Once, on a branch of the carob, we had even made a vow of eternal friendship. Salvatore had betrayed me.

Felice shouted: 'That's it, stop! I can't stand any more of this.'

Salvatore braked abruptly, the engine stalled, the car jerked to a halt and if Felice hadn't put his arms out he would have cracked his head on the windscreen.

He opened the door and got out. 'Move!' Salvatore moved over to the other side, without a word. Felice grasped the wheel and said: 'Salvatore, old boy, I must be frank with you, you're just not cut out for driving. Forget it. Your future lies in cycling.'

WHEN WE DROVE into Acqua Traverse my sister, Barbara, Remo and Skull were playing hopscotch in the dust. They saw us and stopped playing. Papa's truck wasn't there. Nor was the old man's car. Felice parked and Salvatore shot out of the car, got his bike and rode off.

Felice pulled up the seat. 'Get out!'

I didn't want to get out. Felice would tell Mama everything and she would tell Papa. And Papa would be very angry. And the old man would take me away.

'Get out!' Felice repeated.

I summoned up all my courage and got out. Barbara put her hand to her mouth. Remo ran over to Skull. Maria took off her glasses and wiped them on her T-shirt. The light was dazzling; I couldn't keep my eyes open. Behind me I could hear Felice's heavy footsteps. Barbara's mother was looking out of the window. Skull's mother was looking out of another. They gazed at me with vacant eyes. There would have been complete silence if Togo hadn't started barking his shrill little bark. Skull gave him a kick and Togo fled yelping.

I went up the front steps and opened the door. The shutters were closed and there wasn't much light. The radio was on. Mama, in her petticoat, was sitting at the table peeling potatoes. She saw me come in, followed by Felice. The knife slipped out of her hand.

'What's happened?'

Felice thrust his hands in his combat jacket, lowered his head and said: 'He was up there. With the boy.'

Mama got up from her chair and turned off the radio. I burst into tears. She ran to me and took me in her arms. She hugged me tightly to her bosom then put me on the chair and looked at my grazed legs and arms, the clotted blood on my knees.

'What happened to you?' she asked me.

'Him! It was him . . . he . . . he beat me up!' I pointed at Felice.

Mama turned, glared at Felice and growled: 'What have you done to him, you bully?'

Felice raised his hands. 'Nothing. What have I done to him? Brought him home.'

Mama narrowed her eyes. 'You! How dare you, you?' The veins on her neck swelled and her voice shook: 'How dare you, eh? You hit my son, you bastard!' And she flung herself at Felice.

He backed away. 'So I gave him a kick up the backside. What's the big deal?'

Mama tried to slap his face. Felice held her wrists to keep her away, but she was a lioness. 'You bastard! I'll scratch your eyes out!'

'I found him in the hole. He wanted to free the boy. Calm down!'

Mama was in bare feet, but she still managed to give him a kick in the balls. Poor Felice let out a strange noise, a cross between a gargle and the sound of water going down a plughole, put his hands to his genitals and fell to his knees.

I, still standing on the chair, stopped blubbing. I knew how much a bang in the nuts hurt. And that was a very hard bang in the nuts. Mama had no mercy. She picked up the frying pan out of the sink and slammed Felice in the face. He howled and collapsed on the floor.

Mama raised the frying pan again, she wanted to kill him, but Felice caught her by the ankle and pulled. Mama fell down. The frying pan shot across the floor. Felice threw himself on top of her with his whole body.

Mama bit and scratched like a cat. Her petticoat had ridden up. You could see her bottom and a shoulder strap had snapped and one breast was coming out, white and big and with a dark nipple.

Felice stopped and looked at her. I saw how he looked at her. I got off the chair and tried to kill him. I jumped on him and did my best to throttle him. At that moment Papa and the old man came in. Papa threw himself on Felice, grabbed him by the arm and pulled him off Mama. Felice rolled over on the ground and I rolled over with him. I banged my temple hard. A kettle started whistling in my head, and yellow lights exploded in front of my eyes.

Papa was kicking Felice and Felice was crawling under the table and the old man was trying to restrain Papa. The hiss in my head was so loud I couldn't even hear my own sobs.

Mama picked me up and took me into her bedroom, shut the door with her elbow and laid me on the bed. I couldn't stop crying. My body was heaving and my face was purple.

She squeezed me in her arms and kept saying: 'Never mind. Never mind. It'll soon be better. It'll soon be better.'

In the kitchen Papa, the old man and Felice were shouting. Then all three of them left the house slamming the door.

And calm returned.

The doves were cooing on the roof. The sound of the fridge. The cicadas. The fan spinning. That was silence. Mama, with swollen eyes, got dressed, disinfected a scratch on her shoulder and washed me, put me under the sheets and lay down beside me. I didn't have the strength to bend a finger. I rested my forehead on her stomach and closed my eyes.

Mama curled up beside me and whispered in my ear: 'When you grow up you must go away from here and never come back.'

I OPENED MY EYES. It was night.

'Michele, wake up.' Papa was sitting on the edge of the bed shaking my shoulder. 'I've got to talk to you.' It was dark. But a patch of light bathed the ceiling. I couldn't see his eyes and I couldn't tell if he was angry. I could hear the voices in the kitchen. The old man, the lawyer, the barber, Skull's father.

'Michele, what did you do today?'

'Nothing.'

'Don't talk nonsense.' He was angry. 'Felice found you with that boy. He says you wanted to free him.'

I sat up. 'No! It's not true! I swear it! He's the one who's lying.'

'Keep your voice down, your sister's asleep.' Maria was lying face down next to me, hugging the pillow.

'If he saw you would he recognise you?'

I thought about it. 'No. He can't see. He always keeps his head under the blanket.'

'Have you told him your name?'

'No.'

'Have you spoken to him?'

'No . . . not much.'

'What did he say to you?'

'He talks about strange things. I can't make head nor tail of it.'

It seemed as if he wanted to go, then he sat down on the bed again. 'Listen to me carefully. I'm not joking. If you go back there I'll give you the thrashing of your life and those people will shoot him in the head.' He gave me a violent shake. 'And it'll be your fault.'

I stammered: 'I won't go back there again. I swear.'

'Say, I swear on your head that I won't go back there again.'

I said: 'I swear on your head that I won't go back there again.'

'You've sworn on the head of your father.' He sat beside me in silence.

In the kitchen Barbara's father was shouting with Felice.

Papa looked out of the window. 'Forget him. He doesn't exist any more. And you mustn't talk about him to anyone. Ever again.'

He lit a cigarette.

I asked him: 'Are you still cross with me?'

'No, I'm not cross with you.' He took his head between his hands and whispered: 'What a bloody mess.' He shook his head. 'There are things that seem wrong when you . . .' His voice was broken and he couldn't find the words. 'The world's wrong, Michele.' He got up and stretched his back and made as if to leave. 'Go to sleep. I've got to go back in there.'

'Papa, will you tell me something?'

He threw the cigarette out of the window. 'What?'

'Why did you put him in the hole? I don't quite understand.'

He gripped the doorknob. I thought he wasn't going to answer me, then he said: 'Didn't you want to go away from Acqua Traverse?'

'Yes.'

'Soon we'll go and live in the city.'

'Where'll we go?'

'To the North. Are you pleased?'

I nodded.

He came back over to me and looked me in the eyes. His breath smelt of wine. 'Listen to me carefully. If you go back there they'll kill him. They've sworn it. You mustn't go back there again if you don't want them to shoot him and if you want us to go and live in the city. And you must never talk about him. Do you understand?'

'I understand.'

He kissed me on the head. 'Now go to sleep and don't think about it. Do you love your father?'

'Yes.'

'Do you want to help me?'

'Yes.'

'Then forget all about it.'

'All right.'

'Go to sleep now.' He kissed Maria, who didn't even notice, and went out of the room, shutting the door quietly.

SIX

I was lying on my bed reading a comic. But I couldn't concentrate. I threw it on the floor. I was thinking of Filippo. What was I going to do now? I had promised him I would go and see him again, but I couldn't, I had sworn to Papa that I wouldn't go. If I went they would shoot him. Filippo was waiting for me. He was there, in the hole, and was wondering when I would come back.

'I can't come,' I said out loud.

The last time I had gone to see him I had said to him: 'You see? I've come.' And he had replied that he had known I would. Not because the little wash-bears had told him. 'You promised.'

All I needed was five minutes. 'Filippo, I can't come here again. If I come back they'll kill you. I'm sorry.' And at least he would know what was happening. Whereas like this he would think I didn't want to see him again and I didn't keep my promises. But that wasn't true. This tormented me.

'It's no good, I must forget him!' I said to the room. I picked up the comic, went into the bathroom and started reading on the toilet, but I had to stop immediately.

Papa was calling me from the street. What did he want from me now? I had been good, I hadn't left the house. I pulled up my trousers and went out onto the terrace.

'Come here! Quick!' He beckoned me down. He was standing beside the truck. Mama, Maria, Skull and Barbara were there too.

Mama said: 'Come down, there's a surprise.'

Filippo. Papa had freed Filippo. And he had brought him to me. My heart stopped beating. I rushed down the stairs. 'Where is it?'

'Wait there.' Papa got onto the truck and brought out the surprise.

'Well?' Papa asked me.

Mama repeated: 'Well?'

It was a red bike, with handlebars like a bull's horns. A small front wheel. Three gears. Studded tyres. A saddle long enough for two people to ride on. Mama asked again: 'What's the matter? Don't you like it?'

I nodded.

On the top of the crossbar were the English words RED DRAGON, in gold letters. 'What does Red Dragon mean?' I asked Papa.

He shrugged and said: 'Your mother knows.'

Mama covered her mouth and giggled: 'Idiot! Since when did I know any English?' Papa looked at me. 'Well, what are you waiting for? Aren't you going to try it out?'

'Now?'

'When else, tomorrow?'

I felt embarrassed about trying it out in front of everyone. 'Can I take it indoors?'

'You really want to take it inside?' Papa asked me.

'Yes.'

'Can you carry it?'

'Yes.'

'All right, but just for today . . .'

Mama said: 'Are you crazy, Pino? A bicycle in the house? It'll leave tyre marks.'

'He'll be careful.'

My sister burst into tears. 'It's not fair. All for Michele and nothing for me!'

'You wait your turn.' Papa took out of the truck a package wrapped in blue paper and tied up with a bow. 'This is for you.'

Inside was a Barbie with a crown on her head and a tight-fitting white satin dress and bare arms. Maria nearly fainted. 'The dancer Barbie . . . !' She flopped against me. 'She's beautiful.'

Papa closed the tarpaulin of the truck. 'That's it. No more presents for the next ten years.'

Maria and I went up the front steps. She with her dancer Barbie in her hand, I with the bicycle on my back.

'Isn't she beautiful?' said Maria, looking at the doll.

'Yes, she is.'

Then she looked at me and asked: 'Didn't you like your present?'

'Yes. But I thought it would be something else.'

THE DAYS FOLLOWED one another, scorching, identical and endless. The grown-ups didn't even go out in the evenings. Felice wasn't around any more. Papa stayed in bed all day and only talked to the old man. Mama cooked. Salvatore had shut himself up at home. I rode my new bike. Everyone wanted a go on it. Skull could get right through Acqua Traverse on one wheel. I couldn't even get two metres.

I often went out on my own. I cycled along the dried-up stream, I rode down dusty little tracks between the fields that took me far away, where there was nothing but fallen posts and rusty barbed wire. Away in the distance the red combine harvesters shimmered in the waves of heat that rose from the fields.

When I was in the street I felt as if everyone was watching what I was doing. Even when I was alone, sitting on a branch of the carob or on my bike, that feeling didn't leave me. Even when I forced my way through the remains of that sea of wheat ears soon to be packed into bales and I had nothing but sky around me, I felt as if a thousand eyes were watching me. I won't go there, don't worry, everybody. I've sworn I won't.

But the hill was there, and it was waiting for me. I started to ride along the road that led to Melichetti's farm. And every day, without realising it, I went a bit further.

Filippo had forgotten about me. I felt it. I tried to call him with my thoughts. Filippo? Filippo, can you hear me? I can't come. I can't. He wasn't thinking about me. Maybe he was dead. Maybe he wasn't there any more.

ONE MORNING we had woken up and everything was veiled with grey. It was cold, it was damp, and sudden gusts of wind shifted the sultry air. In the night some large clouds had piled up on the horizon and started to advance on Acqua Traverse. We watched them spellbound. We had forgotten that water could fall from the sky.

Now we were under the shed. I was stretched out on the sacks of wheat, with my head in my hands, quite relaxed. The others had sat down in a circle by the plough. Salvatore was lounging on the iron seat of the tractor, with his feet on the steering wheel.

The others were chatting, but I wasn't paying attention. Skull as usual was talking in a loud voice and Salvatore was listening.

I wished it would start raining, everyone was fed up with the drought.

I heard Barbara say: 'Why don't we go to Lucignano and have an ice cream? I've got the money.'

'Have you got the money for us, too?'

'No. It's not enough. Might be enough for two tubs.'

'What are we supposed to do in Lucignano, then? Watch you stuffing yourself with ice cream and getting even fatter?'

My sister came over to me and said: 'I'm going home. What are you going to do?'

'I'm staying here.'

'All right. I'm going to make myself some bread and butter and sugar. Bye.' She went off followed by Togo.

'Well?' asked Remo. 'What about a game of steal-the-flag?'

Skull got up, kicked the ball and sent it across to the other side of the road. 'Hey, I've got a great idea. Why don't we go where we went that time?'

'Where?'

'Up on the mountain. To the abandoned house. Near Melichetti's farm.'

My body suddenly awoke, my heart started marching in my chest and my stomach tightened.

Barbara wasn't convinced. 'What do you want to go there for? It's a long way. And what if it starts raining?'

Skull mimicked her: 'And what if it starts raining? We'll get wet! Nobody asked you to come anyway.'

Remo didn't seem very keen either. 'What could we do there?'

'Explore the house. Last time only Michele went in.'

Skull asked Salvatore: 'Shall we go?'

'No, I don't feel like it,' Salvatore shook his head. 'Barbara's right, it's a long way.'

'I'm going. We can make it our secret base.' Skull got his bike. 'Anyone who wants to come, come. Anyone who doesn't want to come, don't come.' He asked Remo: 'What are you going to do?'

'I'll come.' Remo got up and asked Barbara: 'Are you coming?'

'As long as there are no races.'

'No races,' Skull assured her and asked Salvatore again: 'Aren't you coming then?'

I waited, without saying anything.

'I'll do whatever Michele does,' said Salvatore and, looking me in the eyes, he asked: 'Well, are you going?'

I got to my feet and said: 'Yes, I'll go.'

Salvatore jumped down from the tractor. 'Right, let's go then.'

WE WERE CYCLING, all of us, just like the first time, towards the hill. We rode in single file. Only my sister was missing.

The atmosphere was close and the sky was an unnatural scarlet colour. The clouds were now gathering above us, large and sombre. The air was neither hot nor cold, but it was windy. At the sides of the road and on the fields the hay was packed up in bales that were arranged like pawns on a chessboard.

Remo eyed the horizon anxiously. 'It's going to rain any moment.'

The closer I got to the hill the worse I felt. A weight pressed on my stomach. I felt breathless and a veil of sweat bathed my back and my neck. What was I doing? Every turn of the pedal was a piece of oath crumbling away.

'Say, I swear on your head that I won't go back there again.'

'I swear on your head that I won't go back there again.'

I was breaking the oath, I was going to see Filippo and if they found me they would kill him. I wanted to turn back, but my legs pedalled and an irresistible force dragged me towards the hill. A distant rumble of thunder ripped the silence.

'Let's go home,' said Barbara, as if she had heard my thoughts.

I panted: 'Yes, let's go home.'

Skull passed us guffawing. 'If a few drops of rain scare you, you better had go home.'

Barbara and I looked at each other and kept pedalling. The wind increased. It blew on the fields and raised the chaff in the air. It was hard to keep the bikes on line, the gusts drove us off the road.

'Here we are,' said Skull, braking to make his wheels skid on the grit.

The path leading to the house was there in front of us.

Salvatore looked at me and asked: 'Shall we go?'

'Yes, let's go.'

We started the climb. I had trouble keeping up with the others. Red Dragon was a rip-off. I didn't want to admit it, but if you stood up on the pedals you got the handlebars in your mouth and if you changed gear the chain came off. The only way to avoid being left behind was to stay in top gear.

From the fields, on our right, a flock of rooks rose. They cawed and wheeled with outspread wings. The sun was swallowed up by the grey and suddenly it seemed like evening. A clap of thunder. Another.

In front of us the valley opened up. It was sombre and silent. The birds and the crickets were mute. When we arrived at the oaks a big heavy drop hit my forehead, another my arm and another my shoulder and the storm broke over us. The rain teemed down. The downpour lashed the tree tops and the wind whistled among the leaves. The earth sucked up the water like a dry sponge and the drops rebounded on the hard earth and vanished and the lightning struck on the fields. 'We'd better get some shelter!' shouted Skull. 'Run!'

They went into the cowshed. The hole was there, behind the brambles. I wanted to run and uncover it and see Filippo, but I forced myself to follow them. The others were standing there, jumping up and down, excited by the thunderstorm. Everyone was laughing nervously and rubbing cold arms and looking outside. The clearing, in a few minutes, filled with puddles and from the sides of the valley dirty streams of red earth flowed down. Filippo must be scared to death. All that water was draining into the hole and if it didn't stop soon it might drown him. I must go to him.

'Upstairs there's a motorbike,' I heard my voice saying.

They all turned to look at me.

Skull jumped to his feet. 'A motorbike?'

'Yes. Upstairs. In the last room.'

'What's it doing there?'

I shrugged. 'I don't know.'

'Do you reckon it still works?'

'It might.'

Salvatore looked at me; he had a mocking smile on his face. 'Why did you never tell us?'

Skull cocked his head. 'Right! Why did you never tell us, eh?'

I swallowed. 'Because I didn't want to. I'd done the forfeit.'

A flash of understanding went through his eyes. 'Let's go and have a look at it. Wow, if it works . . .'

Skull, Salvatore and Remo rushed out of the cowshed, sheltering their heads with their hands and shoving each other into the puddles.

Barbara set off, but stopped in the rain. 'Aren't you coming?'

'In a minute. You go on.'

'All right.' She ran off.

I went round the house and made my way through the brambles. My heart was beating in my eardrums and my legs were giving at the knees. I reached the clearing. It had turned into a rain-lashed bog. The hole was open. The green Fibreglass sheet wasn't there any more, neither was the mattress.

The water was dripping down me, trickling inside my shorts and pants, and my hair clung to my forehead and the hole was there, a black mouth in the dark earth, and I went towards it. I closed my eyes and opened them again, hoping something would change. The hole was still there. Black as the plughole in a sink. I staggered closer. I was almost collapsing on the ground, but I kept going forwards. He's not there. Don't look. Go away.

I stopped.

Go on. Go and look.

I can't.

Take one step, I told myself. I did. Take another. I did. Another and then another. And I saw the edge of the hole in front of my feet. You're there. I raised my head and looked. I was right. There was nothing there. Only dirty water and a sodden blanket. They had taken him away. Without telling me anything. Without letting me know. He had gone away and I hadn't even said goodbye.

'There isn't any motorbike.'

I turned round. Salvatore. He was standing there. A few metres away from me, his T-shirt soaked, his trousers spattered with mud. 'There isn't any motorbike, is there?'

I gurgled no.

He pointed towards the hole. 'Is that where he was?'

I nodded, and stammered: 'They've taken him away.'

Salvatore came over, looked inside and stared at me. 'I know where he is.'

I slowly raised my head. 'Where is he?'

'He's at Melichetti's. Down in the gravina.'

'How do you know?'

'I heard them yesterday. Papa was talking to your papa and that guy from Rome. They moved him. The exchange didn't work out, they said.' He swept back his wet fringe. 'They said this place wasn't safe any more.'

THE THUNDERSTORM PASSED. Quickly, just as it had started. A dark mass advancing over the countryside, drenching it and continuing on its way. We were going down the path. The air was so clean that far away, beyond the ochre plain, you could see a thin green strip. The sea. It was the first time I had ever seen it from Acqua Traverse.

I had told Skull it had been a practical joke.

'Ha, ha, bloody hilarious,' he had replied.

A deafening roar, a metallic din shattered the calm and swamped everything.

Barbara shouted, pointing at the sky: 'Look! Look!'

From behind the hill two helicopters appeared. Two big blue iron dragonflies with CARABINIERI written on the sides. They dipped down over us and we started waving our arms and shouting, they came alongside, and turned at the same time, as if they wanted to show us how clever they were, then they skimmed across the fields, flew over Acqua Traverse and disappeared on the horizon.

THE GROWN-UPS had gone. The cars were there, but they weren't. The houses empty, the doors open. We all ran from one house to another.

Barbara was agitated. 'Is there anyone at your house?'

'No. What about yours?'

'There's nobody there either.'

'Where are they?' Remo was out of breath. 'I've even looked in the vegetable garden.'

'What shall we do?' asked Barbara.

I replied: 'I don't know.'

'Michele!'

I turned round. My sister was in vest and knickers, outside the shed, with her Barbies in her hands and Togo following her like a shadow. I ran over to her. 'Maria! Maria! Where are the grown-ups?'

She answered calmly: 'At Salvatore's house.'

'Why?'

She pointed at the sky. 'The helicopters went over, and afterwards they all came out in the street and they were shouting and they went to Salvatore's house.'

'Why?'

'I don't know.'

I looked around. Salvatore wasn't there any more.

'And what are you doing here?'

'Mama told me I've got to wait here. She asked me where you'd gone.'

'And what did you tell her?'

'I told her you'd gone on the mountain.'

THE GROWN-UPS stayed at Salvatore's house all evening. We waited in the courtyard, sitting on the edge of the fountain.

'When are they going to finish?' Maria asked me for the hundredth time.

And I for the hundredth time answered: 'I don't know.'

They had told us to wait, they were talking.

Skull had gone off with Remo. Salvatore was indoors, doubtless hiding away in his room. Barbara sat down beside me. 'What on earth's going on?'

I shrugged.

'Barbara!' Angela Mura was at the window. 'Barbara, go home.'

Barbara asked: 'When are you coming?'

'Soon. Run along now.'

Barbara said goodbye to us and went off looking glum.

'When's my mama coming out?' Maria asked Angela Mura.

She looked at us and said: 'Go home and get your own supper, she'll be home soon.' She closed the window.

I got up. 'Come on, we'd better go.'

She crossed her arms. 'No! I'll stay here all night, I don't care.'

'Give me your hand, come on.'

She straightened her glasses and got up. 'I won't sleep though.'

'Don't sleep, then.'

And, hand in hand, we went home.

SEVEN

They were shouting so loud they woke us up.

'Why are they screaming like that?' Maria asked me, lying on her bed.

'I don't know.'

It was the middle of the night, the room was dark and we were in our bedroom, wide awake.

'Make them stop,' Maria complained. 'They're disturbing me. Tell them to scream more quietly.'

'I can't.'

I tried to understand what they were saying, but the voices mingled together.

Maria lay down beside me. 'I'm scared.'

The door opened. For an instant the room lit up. I saw the black figure of Mama, and behind her the old man.

Mama closed the door. 'Are you awake?'

'Yes,' we replied.

She switched on the light on the bedside table. In her hand she had a plate with some bread and cheese. 'I've brought you something to eat.' She spoke quietly, with a tired voice. She had rings round her eyes, her hair was dishevelled and she looked worn. 'Eat up and go to sleep.'

'Mama . . . ?' said Maria.

Mama put the plate on her knees. 'What is it?'

'What's going on?'

'Nothing.' Mama tried to cut the cheese, but her hand was shaking. She wasn't a good actress. 'Now eat up and . . .' She bent forward, laid the plate on the floor and put her hand to her face and began to cry silently.

'Mama . . . Mama . . . Why are you crying?' Maria started sobbing.

I felt a lump swelling in my throat too. I said: 'Mama? Mama?'

She raised her head and looked at me. 'What is it?'

'He's dead, isn't he?'

She slapped me on the cheek and shook me as if I was made of cloth. 'Nobody's dead! Nobody's dead! Do you understand?' She opened her mouth wide and clutched me to her breast.

I started to cry. Now we were all crying. In the other room the old man was shouting. Mama heard him and pulled away from me. She dried her tears.

'Lie down, both of you.' She pulled away our pillows and put out the light. 'If the noises disturb you, put your heads under these. Here!' She put them on our heads.

I tried to get free. 'Mama, please. I can't breathe.'

'Do as you're told!' she snarled and pressed hard.

Maria was getting desperate. It sounded as if her throat was being cut.

'Stop it!' Mama shouted so loud that for an instant they even stopped quarrelling in the other room. I was scared she would hit her.

Maria went quiet. If we moved, if we spoke, Mama repeated like a cracked record: 'Shh! Go to sleep.'

Mama stayed so long I was sure she was going to spend the whole night with us, but she got up. She thought we were asleep. She went out and shut the door.

We took off the pillows. It was dark, but the dim reflection of the streetlamp lightened the room. I got out of bed. Maria sat up, put on her glasses and, sniffing, asked me: 'What are you doing?'

I put my finger to my nose. 'Quiet.'

I pressed my ear to the door. They were still arguing, more softly now. I could hear Felice's voice and the old man's, but I couldn't make out what they were saying. I grasped the handle.

Maria bit her hand. 'What are you doing, are you crazy?'

'Quiet!' I opened a crack.

Felice was on his feet, near the cooker. He was wearing a green track suit; the zip pulled down below his ribs showed his swollen pectorals. He had shaved his head bare.

'Me?' he said, putting a hand on his chest.

'Yes, you,' said the old man. He was sitting at the table, with one leg resting on the other knee, a cigarette between his fingers and a treacherous smile on his lips.

'Me a pansy? A poof?' Felice asked.

The old man confirmed this: 'Exactly.'

Felice cocked his head on one side: 'And . . . And how do you make that out?'

'It's written all over you. You're a poof. No doubt about it.'

Papa was standing up and seemed to be following the conversation, but he was on the other side of the room. The barber was leaning against the door as if the house was likely to fall down at any moment and Mama, sitting on the sofa, with a vacant expression on her face, was watching the television with the sound turned off.

'Listen, all of you, listen, let's give him back to her. Let's give him back to her,' Papa said suddenly.

The old man looked at him, shook his head and smiled. 'You'll keep quiet if you know what's good for you.'

Felice glanced at Papa, then went over to the old man.

'Reckon I'm a poof, do you, you piece of Roman shit? Well, you can have this fistful from me.' He brought his arm up and punched him in the mouth.

The old man crashed to the floor.

I took two steps backwards and clutched my head in my hands. Felice had hit the old man. I started shaking but I couldn't help looking again.

In the kitchen Papa was shouting. 'What the hell are you doing? Are you out of your mind?' He had grabbed Felice by one arm and tried to pull him away.

'He called me a poof, the bastard . . .' Felice was almost blubbing. 'I'll kill him . . .'

The old man was on the ground. I felt sorry for him. I wanted to help him but I couldn't. He tried to get up again, but his feet slipped on the floor and his arms wouldn't support him. He clutched the edge of the table and slowly pulled himself up onto his feet. He picked up a napkin and pressed it to his mouth.

Felice took two steps towards the old man even though Papa tried to hold him back. 'Well? Did that feel like a poof's punch, then? Call me a poof one more time and I swear you'll never get up again.'

The old man sat on a chair and with his napkin stanched an enormous split in his lip. Then he raised his head and stared at Felice and said in a steady voice: 'If you're a man, prove it.' An evil light flashed in his eyes. 'You said you'd do it and you chickened out. What was it you said? Slit him open like a lamb, I will, no problem, I'm not scared. I'm a paratrooper. I'm this, I'm that. Loudmouth, you're nothing but a loudmouth. You're worse than a dog, can't even keep guard over a kid.' He spat a mouthful of blood on the table.

'You piece of shit!' Felice whimpered. 'I'm not doing it! Why should *I* have to do it, why?' Two trickles of tears ran down his shaven cheeks. 'I'm not doing time for you. Forget it!'

He's going to kill him, I said to myself.

The old man got to his feet. 'I'll do it, then. But don't you worry, if

I go down, you go down. I'll take you down with me. You can be sure of that.'

Felice drove forward, head down. Papa and the barber tried to restrain him but he shook them off and charged the old man again.

The old man took his pistol out of his trousers and put it against Felice's forehead. 'Hit me again. Try it. Do it, go on. Please, do it . . .'

Felice froze as if he was playing one-two-three-star.

Papa got between them. 'Calm down, for Christ's sake! You're a pain in the arse, the pair of you!' And he separated them.

'Try it!' The old man stuck the pistol in his belt. On Felice's forehead there was still a little red circle.

Mama, sitting in a corner, was crying and repeating with her hand over her mouth: 'Quiet! Be quiet! Be quiet! Be quiet!'

Papa managed to get them to sit down. But he himself kept walking to and fro. A mad gleam had ignited in his eyes. 'Right. Let's take a count. How many of us are there? Four. In the end, of all that number we started out with, there are just four of us left. The dumbest ones. Well, all the better. The loser kills him. It's so easy.'

'And gets life,' said the barber, putting his hand on his forehead.

'Good man!' The old man clapped his hands. 'I see we're beginning to use our heads.'

Papa picked up a box of matches and showed it around. 'Right. Let's play a game. Do you know the soldier's draw?'

I shut the door. I knew that game.

IN THE DARK I found my T-shirt and trousers and put them on. Where had my sandals got to? Maria was on her bed watching me. 'What are you doing?'

'Nothing.' They were in a corner.

'Where are you going?'

I put them on. 'Somewhere.'

I got onto the bed and from there onto the windowsill.

'What are you doing?'

I looked down. 'I'm going to see Filippo.' Papa had parked the Lupetto under our window, luckily.

'Who's Filippo?'

'He's a friend of mine.'

It was a long way down and the tarpaulin was rotten. Papa was always saying he must buy a new one. If I fell on it feet first it would tear and I would crash down onto the floor of the truck.

'If you do that I'll tell Mama.'

I looked at her. 'Don't worry. You go to sleep. If Mama comes . . .' What was she to tell her? 'Tell her . . . Tell her anything you like.'

I crossed myself, held my breath, stepped forward and let myself fall open-armed. I landed on my back in the middle of the tarpaulin completely unscathed. It held.

Maria put her head out of the window. 'Come back soon, please.'

'I won't be long. Don't worry.' I climbed onto the driver's cabin and from there got down to the ground. The sky was overcast again and Acqua Traverse was wrapped in a thick black mantle of darkness. I would have to enter it to get to Melichetti's farm.

I must be brave. Tiger Jack. Think of Tiger Jack. The Indian would help me. Before making any move, I must think what the Indian would do in my place. That was the secret. I ran round to the back of the house to get my bike. My heart was already hammering at my chest. Red Dragon, bold and brightly coloured, was resting on top of the Crock. I was on the point of taking it, but I said to myself, am I crazy? How far am I going to get on that stupid contraption?

I WAS FLYING ALONG on the old Crock.

I urged myself on. 'Go, Tiger, go.' I gritted my teeth and counted the turns of the pedal. One, two, three, breath . . . The tyres crackled on the grit. The wind stuck to my face like a warm cloth.

'Filippo . . . I'm coming . . . Filippo . . . I'm coming . . .' I repeated, panting with the effort.

As I drew nearer to the farm a new, suffocating terror grew inside me. On the back of my head the hair stood up as straight as needles.

Melichetti's pigs. Unlike the lords of the hills and other monsters, they really existed and they were hungry. For living flesh. 'The dachshund tried to get away, but the pigs didn't give him a chance. Torn to shreds in two seconds.' That's what Skull had said.

Maybe Melichetti let them out at night. They prowled around the farm, huge and vicious, with sharp fangs and noses in the air. The further I kept away from those brutes the better. In the distance a dim light appeared in the gloom.

The farm. I was almost there. I braked.

The wind had dropped. The air was still and calm. I got off the bike and dumped it among the brambles, beside the road.

You couldn't see a thing.

I moved swiftly, hardly breathing, and kept looking over my

shoulder. All around me was a thick black mass that pressed against the road. I wet my dry lips. I had a bitter taste in my mouth. My heart was pounding in my throat. I hadn't even brought a torch. I could have taken the one in Papa's truck.

When I reached the edge of the farmyard, I hid behind a tree. The house was about 100 metres away. The windows were dark. There was just a little lamp hanging beside the door, lighting up a bit of flaky wall and the rusty rocking chair.

Just beyond, in the darkness, were the pigsties. Even from there I could smell the revolting stench of their excrement. Where could Filippo be? Down in the gravina, Salvatore had said. I had been down in that long gully a couple of times in wintertime with Papa, looking for mushrooms. It was all crags, holes and rock faces.

If I went across the fields I would come out on the edge of the gravina without having to go too near the house. It was a good plan. I ran across the fields and stopped at the top of the gorge. Below it was so black I couldn't make out how steep the rock was, whether it was smooth or whether there were footholds. I kept cursing myself for not bringing the torch. I couldn't go down that way. I might get hurt. The only thing for it was to get closer to the house. At that point the gravina was shallower, and there was a little track that went down between the rocks. But that was also where the pigs were.

I was covered in sweat. 'Pigs have a better sense of smell than any other animal, hounds are nothing like as good,' Skull's father, who was a hunter, used to say. I couldn't go that way. They would smell me. What would Tiger Jack do in my place? He would face them. He would mow them down with his Winchester and make them into sausages to roast on the fire with Tex and Silver Hair.

No. That wasn't his style. What would he do? Think, I told myself. Try. He would try to get the human smell off himself, that's what he would do.

The Indians, when they went buffalo-hunting, smeared themselves with grease and put furs on their backs. That was what I must do: smear myself with earth. Not earth, shit. Much better. If I smelt of shit they wouldn't notice me. I got as close as possible to the house, keeping in the dark. The stink got worse.

As well as the crickets I could hear something else. Music. Someone was sitting on the rocking chair. On the ground, next to it, there was a radio.

The person looked dead. I moved closer. It was Melichetti. His wizened head lolling on a filthy cushion, his mouth open and his double-barrelled shotgun on his knees. He was snoring so loud I could hear him from there.

The coast was clear. I came out into the open, took a few steps and the shrill barks of a dog shattered the silence. For a moment the crickets stopped singing.

The dog! I had forgotten the dog. Two red eyes ran in the darkness. He was pulling the chain behind him and emitting strangled barks. I dived headfirst into the stubble.

'What is it? What's up? What's got into you?' Melichetti said with a start. He sat on the rocking chair and rotated his head like an owl. 'Tiberius! Quiet! Be quiet!' But the brute just wouldn't stop barking, so Melichetti stretched, put on his orthopaedic collar and got up, turned off the radio and switched on his torch.

'Who's there? Who's there? Is anyone there?' he shouted into the darkness and made a couple of listless circuits of the farmyard with his shotgun under his arm, pointing the band of light around. He went back grumbling. 'Stop making that row. There's nobody there.'

Melichetti went into the house slamming the door. I kept as far away as possible from the dog and approached the pig enclosure. The pungent smell increased and burned my throat.

I must camouflage myself. I took off my T-shirt and shorts. Dressed only in pants I dipped my hands in the piss-soaked earth and screwing up my face I spread that foul muck over my chest, my arms, my legs and my face.

'Go, Tiger. Go and don't stop,' I whispered and started crawling forward. It was a struggle. My hands and knees sank into the mud.

I found myself between two pigsties. I could hear them. They were there. They made deep low noises that resembled the roar of a lion.

Keep going and don't turn round, I ordered myself. I prayed that my armour of shit would work. If one of those beasts put its snout through the bars it could tear my leg off with one bite.

I couldn't help looking.

A metre away, two vicious yellow eyes were watching me. Behind those little headlamps there must be hundreds of kilos of muscles, flesh and bristles and fangs and hunger. We stared at each other for an endless moment, then the creature gave a sudden jerk.

I shouted and jumped to my feet and ran and slipped in the dung and got up again, I started running again, open-mouthed, in the blackness, clenching my fists as tight as could be and suddenly I was in the air, I was flying, my heart was in my mouth and my guts closed in a fist of pain. I had gone over the edge of the gravina. I was plunging into the void. I fell, a metre below, into the branches of an olive that grew out at an angle among the sheer rocks.

I clung onto a branch. If that blessed tree hadn't been there to break my fall I would have been smashed to a pulp on the rocks. A segment of moon had opened a gap through the bluish clouds and I could see, below me, that long gash in the countryside. I tried to turn round but my hands and legs were shaking and at every moment I felt I was going to slip down. When at last I gripped the rock between my fingers I breathed again. I climbed back up onto the edge of the gravina. It stretched right and left for several hundred metres. It was all holes, gullies and trees. Filippo could be anywhere.

To my right was the beginning of a path that wound steeply down between the white rocks. There was a pole fixed in the ground, and tied to it was a worn rope that Melichetti evidently used to help him get down. I grabbed hold of it and went down the precipitous track. After a few metres I came to a terrace covered in dung. Some clothes, ropes and scythes were hanging on a projecting rock. Further on there was a pile of wooden stakes. Three small goats and a larger one were tethered to a root that protruded from the earth. They stared at me.

I said to them: 'Don't just gawp at me, tell me where Filippo is.'

A silent black shadow dropped down on me from the sky, passed over me; I shielded my head with my hands. A little owl. It rose again, dissolved in the blackness, then swooped towards the terrace again and went back up into the sky.

Strange, they were friendly birds. Why was it attacking me?

'I'm going, I'm going,' I whispered.

The track continued and I went on down holding the rope. I had to walk crouching down and feel with my hands the obstacles that appeared in front of me, as blind people do. When I reached the bottom of the gully I was astonished. The holly bushes, the thistles, the moss and the rocks were covered with luminous dots that pulsed like tiny lighthouses in the night. Fireflies.

I couldn't find any holes, any dens to hide a boy in.

When I had jumped out of the window it hadn't even crossed my mind that I might not find him. All I would have to do was go through the dark and not get eaten by the pigs and there he would be.

It wasn't like that. The gravina was very long and they might have put Filippo somewhere else.

I was disheartened. 'Filippo, where are you?' I shouted. Nothing.

It wasn't fair. I had come all that way, I had risked my life for him and he was nowhere to be found. I started running backwards and forwards between the rocks and the olives, at random, as desperation gripped me. I felt so angry I seized a branch from the ground and started banging it against a rock, till my hands were sore. Then I sat down. Papa must be furious. He would give me a thrashing. They must have noticed I wasn't in my bedroom. And even if they hadn't, they would soon be arriving there to kill Filippo.

I had done what I could and he had been impossible to find. It wasn't my fault.

I must move quickly, they could arrive at any moment. If I ran, without stopping, I might get home before they went out. Nobody would have noticed anything. That would be good.

I climbed quickly among the rocks back up the path I had come down. Now there was a bit of light it was easier. The little owl. It was wheeling above the terrace, and when it passed in front of the moon I could see its black silhouette, its short broad wings. I ran across the terrace, near the goats, and the bird swooped again. I went on a little way and turned back to look at that crazy owl. It kept wheeling over the terrace. It skimmed the heap of poles resting against the rock, wheeled round and returned, stubbornly. Why was it behaving like that? Was there a mouse there? No. What, then? Its nest!

Of course. Its nest. Its young. Swallows, too, if you knock down their nest, keep wheeling round and round till they die of exhaustion. They had covered up the little owl's nest. And little owls make their nests in holes. Holes! I turned back and started shifting the piled-up stakes with the owl brushing past me. 'Wait, wait,' I said to her. There was an opening in the rock, roughly concealed. An oval cleft as wide as the wheel of a truck.

The owl darted in. It was pitch-black. And there was a smell of burnt wood and ash. I stuck my head in and called, 'Filippo?'

I was answered by the echo of my voice.

'Filippo?' I leaned further in. 'Filippo?'

I waited. Not a sound. He wasn't there. I turned away and had taken three steps when I thought I heard a cry, a low moan.

Had I imagined it? I turned back and put my head into the hole. 'Filippo? Filippo, are you there?'

And from the hole came 'Mmmm! Mmmm!'

He was there!

I felt a weight dissolving in my chest, I leaned against the rock and slid down. I sat there, slumped on that terrace covered with goats' droppings, with a smile on my face. I had found him.

I started crying. I dried my eyes with my hands and got up. 'I'm coming. I won't be a moment. You see? I've come, I kept my promise.'

A rope. I found one, coiled up near the scythes. I tied it to the root where the goats were and threw it into the hole. 'Here I come.'

I lowered myself down inside. My heart was pumping so hard that my chest and arms were shaking. The darkness made me giddy. I couldn't breathe. I felt as if I was swimming in petroleum and it was cold. I hadn't even gone two metres when I touched the ground. It was covered with stakes, pieces of wood, piled-up crates of tomatoes. On all fours I groped in the dark with my hands. I was naked and shivering with cold.

'Filippo, where are you?'

'Mmmm!'

They had gagged him.

'I'm . . .' One foot got caught between the branches. I fell, with my arms forward, on top of some thorny twigs. A sharp pain bit my ankle. I cried out and a hot acid flood of bile came up to my throat.

With shaking hands I pulled out my trapped foot. The pain pressed me inside my ankle. 'I think I've sprained my ankle,' I gasped. 'Where are you?'

'Mmmm!'

I dragged myself, with gritted teeth, towards the moan, and found him. He was under the bundles of wood. I took them off him and felt him. He was lying on the ground. Naked. His arms and legs were bound with packing tape.

'Mmmm!'

I put my hands on his face. He had tape over his mouth too.

'Wait, I'll take it off. It might hurt a bit.'

I tore it off. He didn't shout, but started to pant.

'How are you?'

He didn't say anything.

'Filippo, how are you? Answer me!'

I touched his chest. It was swelling and subsiding too quickly.

'Now we'll get out of here. We'll get out. Hang on a moment.'

I tried to untie his wrists and ankles. It was tight. Finally, with my teeth, desperately, I started to saw through the tape. I freed first his hands, then his feet.

'That's it. Let's go.' I tried to pull him up, but he fell back down like a puppet. There wasn't a scrap of energy left in that exhausted little body. The only difference between him and a corpse was that he was still breathing. 'I can't carry you up. My leg hurts! Please, Filippo, help me . . .' I grasped him by the arms. 'Come on!'

I sat him up, but as soon as I let go he flopped down on the ground. 'Don't you realise they'll shoot you if you stay here?' A lump blocked up my throat. 'Die like this then, you fool, you stupid fool! I came here for your sake, I kept my promise and you . . . and you . . .' I burst into tears. I was shaken by my sobs. 'You . . . must . . . get . . . up . . .' I tried again and again, stubbornly, but he sprawled back in the ashes, with his head all bent, like a dead chicken. 'Get up! Get up!' I shouted, and I pummelled him.

I didn't know what to do. I sat down, with my head on my knees. 'You're not dead yet, do you understand?' I sat there, crying. 'This isn't heaven.'

For an instant he stopped panting and whispered something. I put my ear to his lips. 'What did you say?'

He whispered: 'I can't do it.'

I shook him. 'Yes, you can. Yes . . .'

He wasn't speaking any more. I embraced him. Covered in mud, we were shivering with cold. There was nothing more to be done. I felt tired out, dead beat, my ankle was still throbbing. I shut my eyes, my heart started to relax and, without wanting to, I fell asleep.

I OPENED MY EYES again. It was dark. For an instant I thought I was at home, in my bed.

Then I heard Melichetti's dog barking. And some voices.

They had arrived.

I tugged him. 'Filippo, they're here! They want to kill you. Get up.'

He panted: 'I can't.'

'Yes, you can.' I knelt down and with my hands pushed him forward, regardless of the pain. Mine, his. I must get him out of that hole. The bundles of wood scratched me but I kept pushing, gritting my teeth, till we were under the mouth of the hole.

The voices were close by. And a glare flashed on the branches of the trees. I gripped him by the arms. I pulled him up, he clung to my neck. He straightened up. 'You see, stupid? You see, you have got up, haven't you? But now you've got to climb up. I'll push you from below, but you must hold on to the edge.'

He started coughing. It sounded as if stones were shooting around in his chest. When he finally stopped, he shook his head and said: 'Without you I'm not going.'

'Don't be stupid. I'll be right behind you.'

Now they seemed to be there. The dog was barking above my head. 'No.'

'You're going, do you understand?' If I let go of him he would fall down. I took him in my arms and pushed him up. 'Grab the rope, come on.'

And I felt him become lighter. He had got hold of the rope! He was on top of me. He was resting his feet on my shoulders. 'Now I'm going to push you, but keep pulling yourself up with your arms, all right? Don't let up.' I saw his small head surrounded by the pale light of the hole. 'You're there. Now pull yourself out.' He tried. I felt him straining unsuccessfully. 'Wait. I'll help you,' I said, grasping him by the ankles. 'I'll give you a push. You jump.' I pushed at his legs and gritting my teeth I threw him out and saw him disappear, swallowed up by the hole. At the same moment I felt as if a long pointed nail had been driven into my ankle bone right through to the marrow and a spasm of pain ran like an electric shock through my leg up to my groin. I collapsed.

'Michele! Michele, I've done it! Come on.'

I tried to get up but the leg no longer responded. From the ground I tried to grab the rope but I couldn't reach it.

I heard the voices coming nearer and nearer. The sound of footsteps.

'Michele, are you coming?'

'Just a moment.' My head was spinning, but I got on my knees. I couldn't pull myself up.

I said: 'Filippo, run for it!'

He looked down. 'Come up!'

'I can't. My leg. You run for it!'

He shook his head. 'No, I'm not going.' The light behind him was brighter.

'Run for it. They're here. Run for it.'

'No.'

I shouted and pleaded. 'Get away! Get away! If you don't they'll kill you, don't you understand?'

He started crying.

'Get away. Get away. Please, I beg of you. Get away . . . And don't stop. Don't ever stop. Ever . . . Hide!' I fell down on the ground.

'I can't do it,' he said. 'I'm scared.'

'No, you're not scared. You're not scared. There's nothing to be scared of. Hide.'

He nodded and disappeared.

From the ground I started trying to find the rope in the dark. I touched it, but lost it. I tried again, but it was too high up. Through the hole I saw Papa. In one hand he had a pistol, in the other a torch.

He had lost.

As usual.

The light blinded me. I closed my eyes.

'Papa, it's me, Miche . . .'

Then came the white.

I OPENED MY EYES.

My leg hurt. Not the leg that had been hurting before. The other one. The pain was a climbing plant. A piece of barbed wire twisting round my guts. Something overwhelming. Red.

I touched my leg. Something thick and warm was smeared all over me. I don't want to die. I don't want to.

I opened my eyes. I was in a whirl of straw and lights. There was a helicopter. And there was Papa. He was holding me in his arms. He was speaking to me but I couldn't hear. His hair shone, waving in the wind.

Lights blinded me. From the darkness black creatures and dogs appeared. They were coming towards us. Papa, they're coming. Run for it. Run for it.

Beneath the roar my heart was marching in my stomach.

I vomited.

I opened my eyes again. Papa was crying. He was stroking me. His hands red. A dark figure approached. Papa looked at him. Papa, you must run for it.

In the roar Papa said: 'I didn't recognise him. Help me, please, he's my son. He's wounded. I didn't . . .'

Now it was dark again.

And there was Papa.

And there was me.

NICCOLÒ AMMANITI

Considering the success of *I'm Not Scared*, which has already been translated from its original Italian into more than twenty languages and has sold more than 300,000 copies, it is ironic that the story very nearly did not become a book at all. 'At first I imagined the story in terms of pictures', explains Ammaniti, 'because I was thinking of a film. Then, as I wrote, the other part came together: the child's-eye viewpoint, Michele's fears—all the things I hadn't considered when I was writing a screenplay.' The story's cinematic origins explain the many striking images contained in the book, such as the hot, empty wheatfields of southern Italy. 'The story came to me as I was driving through the area between Campania and Puglia where the book is set. It was during a hot spell and the landscape was much as I describe it: just fields of wheat. There are no trees, few houses, nothing. I was really struck by it.' It was this harsh, oppressive setting that in turn inspired the book's storyline. 'Seeing these things I said to myself: what would kids do in a place like this? They would be alone during the day because of the heat. Then I got to thinking about a kidnapping.'

With *I'm Not Scared* Ammaniti has broken into the English language market for the first time. In many ways it's a very natural step for an author who admires English and American writers and who counts Stephen King and James Ellroy among his favourites. King's novella *The Body*, on which the film *Stand By Me* was based, contains many elements in common with *I'm Not Scared*: both are about a gang of boys and both feature the discovery of a body. 'Among contemporary writers Stephen King is one of the best at capturing a child's point of view,' Ammaniti says.

He sees his own work as more minimalist and detached than King's but he, too, writes convincingly from a child's perspective. '*I'm Not Scared* explores the world of imagination and fairy tales. Above all, it looks at the fears of children, the way they are able to cannibalise reality and what happens when they come into conflict with a threat from the adult world.'

ACKNOWLEDGMENTS AND PICTURE CREDITS: *The Janson Directive*: pages 6–8: photomontage: Rick Lecoat @ Shark Attack; *Winter's End*: pages 172–174: Getty Images/Stone; photomontage: Curtis Cozier; page 303: © Roderick Field; *The House Sitter*: pages 304–306: Getty Images/The Image Bank; page 447: © Mike Eddowes; *I'm Not Scared*: pages 448–450: Getty Images/The Image Bank; page 539 © Olympia–Giovannet.

DUSTJACKET CREDITS: Spine from top: photomontage: Rick Lecoat @ Shark Attack; Getty Images/Stone; photomontage Curtis Cozier; Getty Images/The Image Bank; Getty Images/The Image Bank.

Printed by Maury Imprimeur SA, Malesherbes, France
Bound by Reliures Brun SA, Malesherbes, France